THE JORDANS AND THE SLOVERS

They had come to Indiana to start a new life. *The Jordans* were Virginia aristocrats—the best blueblood the new world had to offer.

The Slovers were as uncivilized as the wild land they had come to conquer.

It wasn't long before the womenfolk were at each other's throats.

It wasn't long before Eric Jordan was sneaking off at night with the lovely, young Slover girl.

It wasn't long before they both found themselves at the mercy of a man they despised, Caleb Lewis, "the white Indian."

THE SCARLET FEATHER

A Moving, Passionate Novel of the American Frontier

THE
SCARLET FEATHER

DALE VAN EVERY

BANTAM BOOKS
Toronto • New York • London • Sydney

THE SCARLET FEATHER

*A Bantam Book / published by arrangement with
Holt, Rinehart & Winston, Inc.*

PRINTING HISTORY

Holt edition published March 1959
2nd printing ...... March 1959
Bantam edition published April 1963
2nd printing ..... October 1969
3rd printing ..... January 1982

ISBN 0-553-20201-4

Published simultaneously in the United States and Canada

*Bantam Books are published by Bantam Books, Inc. Its trade-
mark, consisting of the words "Bantam Books" and the por-
trayal of a rooster, is Registered in U.S. Patent and Trademark
Office and in other countries. Marca Registrada. Bantam
Books, Inc., 666 Fifth Avenue, New York, New York 10103.*

PRINTED IN THE UNITED STATES OF AMERICA

12 11 10 9 8 7 6 5 4 3

THE
SCARLET FEATHER

October

Pale gleams flickered among the upper boughs of the immense overhanging trees, but none filtered down into the pool of darkness in which lay the two gently rocking barges moored side by side against the bank. The moon, continuing its slow rise from the wooded horizon, silvered an ever-increasing expanse of the river and fringed with shadowed detail the other wall of forest along the farther bank. The border of radiance rippled nearer until at length it overran the squat scow-like hulks of the moored craft and, dispelling the darkness in which they had been shrouded, accentuated the loneliness of their situation. For the Ohio, down which they had come, was a lonely river, coursing through the solitude of a wilderness that stretched away without seeming end, unmarked by human habitation nearer than the Shawnee towns half a hundred miles to the north or the Cherokee towns twice a hundred miles to the south.

Of the thirty-two people aboard the two craft only sixteen-year-old Betsey Slover was awake to note the sudden faint brightening. Shimmers of light slipped along the cracks in the deck shed in which slumbered the five other members of her family, the two Jordan cows, and their own four dogs. She twisted to peer out between the boards beside her head. Slanting across her glimpse of the shining river was the nearer end of one of the mooring lines, glistening with patches of tiny ice crystals where its wetness had frozen in the night. It seemed to end in mid-air where its glitter was cut off by the edge of the shadow cast by the dark forest on the bank. She lay back in the straw. Deliberately she touched her fingertips to her straggly hair, her thin, pinched face, her meager breasts, and then, with a sigh of satisfaction, to the gracious swelling of her distended belly. She welcomed her so early approach to woman's full estate as nothing short of a miracle sent by heaven. But instead of another of the little kicks and jerks which in recent weeks had so much delighted her there came the knife thrust of her first pain. She clutched at her mother, lying beside her in the straw. After a round of discontented grunts and snorts Polly Slover opened her eyes.

"They's started," announced Betsey eagerly.

"Yer sure?"

"Real sure."

"How fast they comin'?"

"Cain't tell yet." Betsey caught her breath, trembled, and breathed again. "Thet was another one."

"Long's thy'se not hittin' yuh no harder'n thet—'twill be a while yet."

Polly rolled over and resumed snoring. A half hour later Betsey clutched her again.

"Thet last one was right bad," she reported.

Polly thrust an exploring hand under Betsey's blanket, nodded resignedly, and reached over her to prod Betsey's younger sister, Lina.

"Light me a candle."

Lina, only half awake, obediently crawled away over the huddle of recumbent men and animals to the embers of the cooking fire on the square of sheet iron before the shed doorway. The light of the candle as she returned played over her touseled mop of flaxen hair and the mature roundness of her body under the ragged linsey-woolsey gown. She was fourteen, but despite the womanly contours of her figure, her utterly placid expression gave her more the look of an overgrown child of four. Polly peered at Betsey's pain-contorted, perspiring face.

"Fetch me thet axe handle."

Lina handed it to her. Polly began pounding on the blanketed forms about her in the straw.

"Git yerselves up and out o' here. And take yer dogs with yuh."

Her husband, Olen, gigantic, shambling, bearded, and Jarot and Jacob, nearly as big and bearded as their father, growled mild protests, gathered up their bedding, and stumbled out, dragging the whimpering dogs. Other and more vehement growls of protest arose as the aggregation pushed in under the tarpaulin stretched over the sleeping space on deck occupied by the three Lymans, the two Jordan male Negroes, and the Jordans' eight hired boatmen.

"Go to hollerin' loud's yuh feel like," Polly counseled Betsey. "Hollerin' don't make it no easier but it makes the time go faster."

Betsey essayed a tentative groan. Her breath, taking her by surprise as it was suddenly expelled by the next cramp, turned the groan into a low, animal-like howl.

In the main cabin of the other barge, Agatha Jordan lifted her head to listen. Beside her in the bunk her husband, Duncan, at once turned toward her, as though always aware of her even in his sleep.

"That Slover girl," whispered Agatha. "Her time must be on her."

She started to get up. Duncan caught hold of her.

"Childbirth's no novelty in that family. Polly claims she's had eighteen."

"I wouldn't doubt it. She likely started when she was no older than this poor little Betsey. But don't you notice how much colder it has turned?"

Duncan waited for Betsey's second cry to diminish to a moan.

"I am paying the closest attention but I seem to have been left behind somewhere."

"I only want to make sure the children are warm."

"Ah. How could I have lost sight of how inexorably with you first things come first." He was still holding to her. "But I have a better idea."

"What's that?"

"You stay here and keep a place warm for me to come back to."

She dropped back on the pillow with a secure wife's low laugh of drowsy assurance.

"Then hurry."

He thrust his feet into felt slippers, wrapped his greatcoat about him, and felt his way across the dark cabin to draw aside the blanket hanging before his mother's bunk. There could be no question that she was warm. She slept under a mountainous feather bed with her head encased in a knitted nightcap and her throat swathed in a woolen scarf. Moonlight from the porthole illuminated her angularly handsome face, which had come, as she aged, so increasingly to resemble his own. He smiled. She had been fiercely determined to accompany them on their westward journey and having had her way, had become as fiercely determined to remain as comfortable as at home.

Duncan edged open the door of the second cabin, lighted by its dim night lantern. All his children were asleep—Eric with his new long rifle under the covers with him—except eight-year-old Cam. Thryza Carter, his mother's ward, was sitting on the edge of Cam's bunk. She saw him at the door but, drawing her quilted dressing gown slightly about her, continued to give Cam her sympathetic attention.

"Then is Betsey yelling like that just to make everybody sorry for her?" Cam was asking. "How much does it hurt, Tracy?"

"I can't say, dear. I've never had a baby."

"Why not? You're old enough. You're six years older than Betsey."

"Are you forgetting that I am not married?"

"Neither is Betsey."

"You don't know that. She may have had a secret marriage back in her mountains before she left."

There came another and more strident cry from the other barge.

"But does it really hurt more than anything else in the world? Geneva says it does."

"Geneva likes to talk. If it was as bad as that wouldn't you imagine mothers would stop having babies? But they keep right on—and are happy to—just as your mother has."

Duncan advanced into the light.

"Go back to sleep, Cam," he ordered. "And stop pestering Tracy." His smile warmed as he looked down at Tracy. "How unapt that we should all have taken to calling you Tracy. We should invariably say Thryza, very distinctly."

"Why, Papa?" demanded Cam. "Why is Thryza a better name than Tracy? It's harder to say."

Duncan looked away from Tracy's dark hair which now in the night flowed over her shoulders in a curling disorder denied it by day.

"Because Thryza has a special meaning. It means 'pleasure' —and that is what she has been to us ever since she came to live with us."

Tracy looked up at him, her gray eyes under their black brows wide and calm.

"Trite as it may sound, Duncan," she said, "I have to say the pleasure has been mine."

"What's trite mean, Papa?"

"It means it's long past time for you to go back to sleep. And you, too, Tracy."

Duncan went out to the circular brick fireplace on deck, threw more wood on the coals and, after a quick, almost surreptitious, glance around, sat on a stool and took from his pocket the small leatherbound daybook he had carried during the war. Fresh paper had been inserted to provide space for a journal of his new enterprise, but it seemed to him that this expedition to found a settlement in the western wilderness was, at least for him, but a continuation of that other conflict with the past. He turned to the first page and contemplated the familiar roster of the company of which he was as much the necessarily responsible commander as during those years with his regiment.

His mother, Louisa. His wife, Agatha. His children, Eric, Ken, Cam, Chris, and Susie. His brother, Garett. Garett's wife, Olivia. Tracy, almost the same as one of the family. The four Negroes, Ned, Clem, Hebe, and Geneva—all that remained of the hundred the Jordans once had owned. Frank Lyman and his sons, Mark and Luke. The Slover family. Ten adult men. Eleven with Eric, who at fifteen was so nearly a man. Eight women. Six children. And soon now this child of Betsey's. Another name to be added to the roster. The first, God willing, of many more.

He closed the book hastily as Garett came out and held wide the blanket draped about him to warm his gaunt nightshirted figure at the fire. Duncan looked at his brother inquiringly. Garett had been a semi-invalid since a musket ball had lodged in his spine at Yorktown in what had turned out to be literally the last half hour of the war. Garett shrugged and grinned.

"Don't always be eying me as though you doubted I'd see the next dawn. No worse night than usual. Though I have to admit that caterwauling next door is no sleeping potion. Pity the damsel couldn't have held off a few more hours. How much more appropriate had she managed to celebrate your first day on the soil of your new principality with so auspicious an offering. Never mind—she's young and may be at it awhile. The worthy Slovers may yet gain their footnote in history. What was the first white child born in Virginia—Virginia Dare, wasn't it? This Slover offspring can yet be the first on the baptismal records of Reveltown, or will it be Revelburgh?"

Duncan stirred uncomfortably. "Ours is a small company. We may well welcome every addition to it."

"How true. While I—own brother of the lord proprietor—remain childless. Yet I try, and try again. A process, I may say, with its own intrinsic rewards. Speaking of children, was there some to-do in your nursery just now? Seemed to me I heard Tracy's voice.

"Only Cam. She was asking questions."

"About the biological phenomenon in the next barge, no doubt. Remarkable child. What a thirst for knowledge."

Olivia, her pale young face flushed, came darting out.

"Garry," she cried. "Come back to bed this instant. Do you want to catch your death?"

"My ever faithful mate," said Garett. "Her anxieties for my welfare know no limit. Though I must confess it something of a boon to one in my enfeebled condition to have the capacities of a Casanova perpetually attributed to him by the one in the best position to judge."

The intensity of her fury sharpened Olivia's classic, cameo-like features into ugliness.

"You can be so utterly unspeakable."

Garett flung the blanket about his shoulders with a dignity that might have attended the arrangement of a toga.

"Very well, my sweet. Your banners wave triumphant, as always. I shall return to our coach. And no more this night will I prowl."

He went in. Olivia remained by the fire, breathing hard.

"He is a sick man," said Duncan.

"It's not for you to sort out the blame. You're not the little father of the whole world. I'm sorry, Duncan. Sick or well— I love him. You must realize that. How could I stand it another minute if I didn't?"

"And he loves you."

"I do believe he does. I have to."

Olivia drew another long breath and turned wearily toward the door through which Garett had gone. But when she reached it, she straightened and her step quickened. Duncan shoveled coals from the fire into a brazier and carried it into the children's cabin. Cam was rebelliously silent but she was holding her head off the pillow in her anxiety to listen. Tracy lay beside her.

"Simplest way to keep her quiet was to move in with her," said Tracy.

"A most unjust reward for the transgressor. Clap a sack over her head, if you have to, and get some sleep."

The other children, burrowed deep in their beds, had not awakened. When he came out Agatha was at the fire, staring resentfully toward the adjoining barge. Betsey's cries had become piercing.

"Can't you have their boat moved off a ways?" she demanded.

"As a special token of our neighborly sympathy?"

"Why pretend? Listen. Sounds like a cat in a sack. No doubt the girl's in pain but I don't like all this sluttish yowling right outside the children's window."

"When you came out with me this year instead of waiting

until next—as we at first planned—you must have guessed the many realities of the natural world to which they would be subjected. And what is more natural than childbirth? For my part I think the closer they get to natural living the better it will be for them, as it will for us."

"Whenever you start talking about this settlement of yours —of ours, I suppose I should say—you don't sound like you. You sound as though you were reading something out of a book."

"Then I will say no more." He slipped an arm around her. "Except this: Mrs. Jordan, would you now do me the great honor of going to bed with me?"

Her black eyes, often so brilliant and hard, softened. "With the greatest of pleasure, Mr. Jordan."

In the cabin doorway she lifted her head from his shoulder. "My God," she whispered. "Here come all the Lymans."

She attempted to shut the door quickly but Duncan caught it, pulled away from her and returned to the fire. Frank Lyman clambered over the rail into the Jordan barge. Clutched in his arms were his blankets, his sack of personal effects, and his chest of carpenter's tools. One by one he dropped each of his several burdens to the deck at Duncan's feet. His purse-lipped scowl of indignation seemed as durable and established a part of him as his shock of bristling white hair, his square red face, his squat sturdy figure, his work-gnarled hands. His two sons, swinging over the rail after him, dropped their loads as deliberately. Mark was a head shorter, Luke a head taller, neither had white hair and their faces lacked as yet the granitic lines time had cross-hatched on their father's but their expressions of righteous disapproval quite matched his. They took their stand a half step behind him. All three eyed Duncan defiantly.

"Never," Frank pronounced, "never will we set foot in that boat again."

He stiffened, waiting for Duncan's remonstrance. Mark and Luke edged more nearly abreast of him.

"Can't say I blame you much," said Duncan. "If I'd realized how crowded we'd turn out to be I'd have hired a third boat in Pittsburgh."

"It's been a deal worse than crowded," said Frank. "It's been like bunking in a backhouse. So far we put up with spending the nights in a tangle o' niggers and water rats—and them boatmen o' yours is the dirtiest-mouthed critters I ever did have to listen to—but when the Slovers and all their dogs come crawling in on us just now——"

"Why don't you turn in here by the fire for the rest of the night? Tomorrow it'll all be over. We'll be getting off these boats."

The onward march of Frank's protest was thrown out of step by Duncan's studied failure to take offense. Mark assumed his father's pause was a signal to take his turn at pressing their grievances.

"They ain't got the first part of an idea who might have fathered that brat she's having. She herself no more than any the rest of them. From the way they all been talking among themselves—and trying to count up on their fingers—it could of been most anybody that wears pants that ever come within eight mile of their cabin."

Luke cleared his throat and spat in the fire. "That's only the outer peel off the onion. Their place was a stop-off for pack trains, so it could of been most any mule-skinning scalawag between Pittsburgh and Richmond ever to come through their valley. But if you was to ask me, I wouldn't doubt it could of been either o' them mush-headed brothers o' hers—or maybe that real no-count, her old man—the way they all hutch together at night like a litter of rabbits."

The unction with which his sons had voiced their views set Frank off again. "When you picked up them Slovers on our way over the mountains and brung them along with us it was plain they was real trash. Me and my boys—we seen that straight off. It was plain then and it's plainer now. They're lower than trash. They're out-and-out heathen. They can't read nor write. They can't get out three words without one of them being foul. Not one of them has ever once been to church. Why they ain't never in their lives even seen a church. They ain't no better than a pack of savages."

Duncan's tone remained carefully casual. "But don't you see, Frank, that is precisely why we need them. Olen Slover grew up on the frontier, as did his father and grandfather before him and his sons after him. They're genuine bush people. They're used to getting along in the woods—not only to hunting and trapping and tracking but to making do with whatever is at hand. And Olen left behind him five married sons who, if all goes well, may come out with their families next year. We need more people. Most of all, at first, this kind of people."

Frank snorted. "The only thing we need less than Slovers is more Slovers. I don't know how you feel about your family. But me, I know how I feel about mine. I brung up my two boys to fear the Lord and to never take His name in vain and to know right from wrong and to keep their backs turned to all evildoers"

"That will do, Frank. There are several subjects on which I do not need your advice. Now will you tell me what's behind all this claptrap about the Slovers? Why are you trying so hard to pick a quarrel with me? What's your real trouble?"

Frank placed his fists on his lips and began to teeter back and forth on heel and toe.

"We got more troubles than the Slovers—that's a fact. I'll tell you what's one big one. I don't like where we're going. This Revel Creek ain't a good location."

"What's wrong with it?"

"To begin with, it's too far off by itself. It's as far as you can get from the last Virginia settlements one way and the first Kentucky settlements the other."

"You knew that before you left tidewater."

"Back there I had no more idea what this country out here was going to be like than that brat o' Betsey's has about the world he's coming into. But along the way I been talking to folks—back at Wheeling and Pittsburgh—folks that know this country. Worse than being too far off by itself, your place is on the Indian bank of the Ohio."

"Where then would you prefer to go? Have you made up your mind to that, too?"

"I have. On to Kentucky where there's more people. There ain't near enough of us by ourselves to stand off the Indians was they to come at us."

Duncan clasped his hands behind him, wheeled to frown out over the moonlit river, and then wheeled back to face the Lymans.

"I could try to remind you of any number of things, Frank. That the war with England is over. That the Indians have realized there's nothing for them to do but make peace, too. That yesterday you saw with your own eyes General Washington himself surveying his land on the Kanawha no more than a day's run from our site. That if anyone knows what he's about he certainly does. That I must be sure of what I'm doing or I would not have brought my mother, my wife, and my young children out with me. But what's the use of trying to reason with you? We've been over all this before. I invited you to come out with us because I thought that since you and your sons were Continental veterans and respected citizens in your community you could take a leading part in our new one. But let's forget all that, along with the bargain we struck back in Virginia. Tomorrow we'll get to Revel Creek. As soon as we're unloaded, Bill Granger is taking his barges on downriver to winter in Louisville. I'll outfit you and you can go on to Kentucky with the barges."

"But we come out with you. We'd of stayed home if it hadn't looked like a good idea to throw in with you."

"You were either wrong then or you're wrong now. Take your pick. Anyway, I'm staying at Revel Creek."

Frank scowled at his sons as though it had been their fault that the argument had come to so unsatisfactory a culmination. They looked away. He grunted sulkily.

"You don't leave us no out. I ain't never yet gone back on a bargain. We'll have to stay, too."

"Good. Now try to get some sleep."

In the cabin Duncan wearily dropped the greatcoat, kicked off his slippers, and slid into bed.

"You handled him just right," whispered Agatha. "Still it makes me sick that you should have to spend half the night blathering with a clown like Frank Lyman. With the river so close, I kept expecting you to tell him to jump into it."

"A pleasure I could not afford. He's a carpenter. One of his boys is a mason and the other a smith. We need him."

"We don't need to cater to him as though he were governor of Virginia."

"Have you forgotten the war?"

"What about the war?"

"That we fought so that we could call men free and equal. You may not have noticed much difference in the East but in this country out here every man is fully convinced he is as good as any other."

"I can stomach Frank Lyman—just. But are you trying to say that out here there's nothing to choose between us and people like the Slovers?"

"The time can come when you'll be glad they're one of us." His lips were touching her cheek so that she could tell that he was smiling. "Maybe we should have stayed peacefully in Virginia and reconciled ourselves to staying poor."

So often they were well into a discussion before she discovered he had not been arguing with entire seriousness. The discovery was always disconcerting but she was never able to help herself. There were too many subjects which she could not even pretend to take lightly.

"No," she said. "I'd have been happy to—for us. But not for the children. There's their future to think of. They just mustn't stay poor."

"How about me? I may be getting on in years, but don't you think I've still some future?"

She laughed softly and pressed more closely into his arms. "Nobody has to think about you. You're quite able to help yourself." She drew back from his kiss and lifted her head to listen. "She's stopped screaming. Do you think it's over?"

Betsey could feel herself floating upward out of the depths. She was not climbing. It was a kind of slow swinging, like the pendulum of the Jordans' clock. The pain was gone. All was as dark as the pit into which she had slipped. She thought to lift her hand to her dry mouth. The hand did not move. She wondered if she were dead. The possibility seemed more restful than alarming. She opened her eyes. The candle had burned down to a stump. The cows were on their feet. Lina was bending over. Then she saw her mother sitting on a box. On her lap was a bundle wrapped in sacking.

"Maw," she whispered.

Her mother raised her head. She did not look excited. She just looked old and tired.

"Yuh got yerself a boy," she said. "A boy most as big as you be."

"Give him to me," said Betsey.

"You jest lay still. You've had yerself a bad time. Quick but real bad."

"Give him to me."

Betsey struggled to lift herself but still could not move. Lina pulled back a corner of the blanket and Polly laid the bundle beside her. Now she could move her hands. She plucked at the sacking. The small naked body rolled against hers.

"He's cold," she gasped.

"We're all cold," said Polly. "It's a right cold night."

Betsey could feel herself slipping back into the darkness. She was terrified. Not for herself. She no longer mattered. But for the child who needed her, who had only her. She fought to stay with him, to watch over him, to save him.

Again she was swinging slowly upward. This time the glare hurt her eyes even before she had opened them. It was broad daylight. A steady burning pain enveloped her loins. The shed was empty except for the cows. She could hear the splash of oars. The barge was moving. On deck people were shouting back and forth. All the other blankets had been heaped over her. She was warm. And he was warm. She peered under the blankets. His eyes were tightly closed but his lips were moist and quivering. One of his two tiny fists opened and clenched again. He struck out jerkily with one leg. She pressed her cheek to the soft damp top of his head. She could feel the pulse beating in it. He was alive and strong. The tide of happiness pouring into her had all the sweep of the great river. All that she had suffered through the time before he had been conceived—and since—was as nothing compared to this reward.

"Maw," she cried.

No one answered. No one came. Outside people were still shouting. She could hear her father swearing as jubilantly as the time he had run down and axed the wounded Indian. It was odd that they should find so much of interest out there when the center of so much greater interest was in here.

"Maw," she called.

Lina appeared in the doorway for a moment.

"We're a-gittin' in," she announced. "We's most there."

Until now Betsey had felt little concern about where they were going or when they might arrive. The place had no importance. No more than had had the home back in the Virginia mountains that they had left. But now this new place took on suddenly a very great importance. It was about to become his home.

"Lina," she called. "Lina."

Lina was good-natured. She might come. Finally she did.

"Help me up," commanded Betsey. "I have to see."

Pain tore at her with claws of fire. Clutching the child against her, with Lina's help she struggled to the doorway and looked out. A long murmuring grunt of appreciation escaped her. The hard frost in the night had contrived a change in the world without to match the change in her inner world. The immense and interminable forest had been transfigured, its dun grays and faded greens turned into a blaze of color—to scarlet and gold, to coral and topaz and amethyst, to orange and saffron and lemon, to unnamed and unnamable shades and hues and tints. Small white clouds scudded across a bright blue sky, arching over the wide river, which sparkled in the sun with reflected flashes of the sky's blue and white as it flowed on around islands which were like heaps of jewels and between banks that were like walls of gigantic flowers.

Ahead, the Jordan barge was turning toward a stretch of the shore on which the forest seemed even more brilliantly aflame than elsewhere. It rounded a point on which stood a single shimmering sycamore and nosed on into the estuary of a small side stream. The second barge followed. Suddenly Olen dropped his oar and came loping into the shed.

"Whereat's my rifle?" he yelled. When he was truly wrought-up the ordinarily almost limitless range of his profanity tended to become curiously diminished. "I'll be a corn-holed muskrat if'n there ain't four buffler knee-deep in thet there crik right there by the first bend."

Duncan, standing in the prow, seized Garett's arm and pointed.

"Look. There's the rock on the bank he told about."

"A most convenient site to disembark," said Garett. "Our own Plymouth Rock, as it were."

Duncan jerked away from him and leaped from the rail to the long flat rock. Behind the rock rose a low mound sparsely covered with pine and oak, and beyond the mound stretched a patch of meadow beside which an old beaver dam had widened the stream into a pool. The three Slover men plunged past him and on to the meadow. In the anxiety of each to get in the first shot all began firing without pausing to aim. The dogs at their heels began to bark. The buffalo ran into the woods across the stream. The Slovers and their dogs ran on after them. Duncan scrambled to the top of the mound and looked about him. The scene was as familiar to him as the words on the yellowed pages of Corbit Revel's twenty-year-old letter.

"Exactly as he described it," he declared. "Even to the flat rock where boats can unload. Some of these trees are bigger than he said but once we cut them the mound will make a perfect building site—just as he said it would."

He turned to see that it was Tracy, first of the others to follow him up the slope, who stood beside him. Crisply curling tendrils of her black hair danced in the breeze, there was a faint flush under the usually smooth ivory of her skin, in her gray eyes were little flecks of lights which must have been gathered in from as far away as the sunlit ripples on the stream. She was poised on tiptoe to see more widely, her tense young body vibrant with the instinct to run to meet a new experience. The pulse of vitality in her made her presence seem to him a happy complement to his own excitement. She took one swift glance around at the stream, the pool, the meadow, the circumference of iridescent forest, and looked back up at him.

"How wonderful that you should see it first in all this color," she said, "as though it had adorned itself for you."

"For all of us," he said quickly. "We're all in this together. We must never forget that." He raised his voice. "Eric, bring me my map case." He grasped her arm and pointed. "I drew a map, based on Corbit's description. There should be a falls less than a mile upstream. I must see first off if I'm right. If

so, I shall make a measured line from here to there the base
line for my survey."

"I'll get the case," she said. "Eric couldn't wait to try his
new rifle. He ran off after the Slovers."

Ken ran lightly across the meadow and into the woods. Almost at once he all but bumped into Eric. He had not intended to follow so closely since there was considerable
question about Eric's accepting his company. Ordinarily he
did not admit that the five years' difference in their ages
endowed Eric with absolute authority but this was a special
occasion. Possession of the new rifle clearly placed him for
the moment beyond challenge.

"Don't make so much noise," said Eric. "Wild animals
have ears same as we have—better ears."

Relieved that he was not sent back, Ken began to tiptoe.
Eric resumed his slow forward progress, glancing down repeatedly at the priming of his rifle before again peering ahead.

"The Slovers waded across the creek back there," Ken
whispered.

"That's the reason I didn't," said Eric. "No use looking for
game in country that four buffalo, three hunters, and a pack
of dogs just ran through. Now stop talking. Only reason I'm
letting you come along is I maybe can use your help packing
in what I shoot. But I'll never see anything to shoot if you
keep gabbling all the time. So either stay quiet or go back
right now."

"I'll stay quiet," Ken promised.

"And don't keep so close. I don't want you joggling my arm
when I have to take aim."

They left the more open forest, where often there had
been wide vistas through the serried ranks of trees which
spread their canopies of foliage high overhead, and pushed
on into an area where there was more undergrowth. Eric
paused at each bush and peeked carefully around it before
advancing again.

"Is your gun loaded?" asked Ken.

" 'Course it's loaded. And double-charged besides. 'Case we
run across a bear."

Ken plucked at Eric's sleeve and pointed. Off to the right
and beyond a fringe of shrubbery was a little forest glade.
In the glade a young doe was grazing. She lifted her head
and cocked her big ears forward. Eric's hands froze to his rifle
while the rest of his body began to shake. The doe whirled
and rose into the air in a long soaring bound. When her
hooves touched the ground she soared again as though on

wings, and, descending, dropped from view behind a laurel thicket.

Eric jerked up his rifle in the general direction of the thicket and pulled the trigger. He had failed to wait until the gun butt was well settled against his shoulder and the kick of the double charge spun him so far off balance that he lost his hat and dropped the rifle. He clutched at them and glared at Ken.

"I told you not to joggle my arm."

Beyond the laurel thicket there was a sudden spasmodic rustling and threshing. Eric all but dropped his rifle again. His transport of chagrin became a transport of triumph.

"I hit her," he cried. "I hit her."

The boys ran around the laurel. The doe was trying to pull herself along by her forelegs. Her hind quarters were dragging on the ground. Her mouth was agape, her tonge hanging out, her eyes distended.

"I broke her back," exulted Eric.

Ken came to an abrupt stop and then edged slowly nearer, his face paling as he stared.

"Look," he said. "Look at her eyes. She hurts—she's afraid —and she doesn't want to die."

"But that's what's coming to her," said Eric. "Right now."

He held the muzzle of his rifle back of the doe's ear and pulled the trigger. The lock clicked drily. He had neglected to reload. Horrified that he had committed the novice's most elementary crime he began frantically to do so. Ken was taking no notice of his brother's ignominy. All his attention was concentrated on the animal's torment.

"Don't get so close," panted Eric. "Haven't you ever heard a wounded deer is dangerous? They got hooves sharper than knives. They can cut you to pieces."

Again he lifted the rifle. This time the piece fired. The doe's forequarters collapsed, she beat her head several times against the ground, and lay still. Her eyes were still open. One of them, filled with sand, continued for a moment to twitch. Ken backed away. A sob burst from him. He turned and ran back toward the boats. Eric drew his hunting knife, knelt, and began sawing exultantly at the doe's throat.

Betsey awoke again. The child's body clasped against hers was hot and wet with sweat. She raised herself in the straw and threw off some of the blankets. There was much trampling and thumping in the other barge. But there were no nearer sounds and she was alone in the shed. Even the cows were gone. She was content to be alone. She opened her dress and pressed the child's mouth to her breast. His lips were moist and warm but he made no effort to suckle. She pinched the nipple to make it stand out. He still showed no interest. It could be too soon for him to be ready. She gave up the attempt. The effort of throwing off the blankets and lifting him up had inflamed the pains. As they slowly subsided she drowsed again.

When once more she roused, the sun was at the cracks in the other side of the shed. One bar of light fell across the child's face. It was thin and wrinkled and had a bluish cast. He was no longer sweating. He was dry and hot. His breathing was fast and had a strange rasping sound.

"Maw," she cried. "Maw."

No one answered. Hugging the child to her, she crawled to the doorway. No one was near except the boatmen. They were in the other barge which was tied up to the flat rock, heaving boxes and barrels out on the bank. They were scowling and swearing as though in a temper about something. There were many people up on top of the mound. She could see all three Jordan women. But her mother was nowhere in sight. Then she saw Lina. Lina was kneeling on the bank downstream a little way, washing her hair. She was forever washing some part or other of herself. She took a queer pleasure in it.

"Lina," called Betsey.

Lina came slowly along the bank, wringing out her hair which was so light in color that it looked almost white, even when wet, and made her big brown eyes look almost black. When she swung her bare legs over the rail the boatmen turned to look. Lina paid no attention. She paid so little attention to anything that she seldom seemed more than half awake.

"Where's Maw?" demanded Betsey.

Lina was staring at the baby. "Whut ails him?"

"Could be"—Betsey had difficulty getting out the words— "could be he's sick."

"He don't look right, fer a fact."

"Go git Maw."

"Maw's over by the pond fishin'."

"Go git her."

"She won't come. Not right straight off, fer sure. Yuh know whut Maw's like when she gits to fishin'. Well, she's never run acrost fishin' like this before. She's got more trout piled around her in the grass than yuh could git in four bushel baskets. She's a-whoopin' and hollerin' like a wild woman."

"Go git her."

Lina set out. Betsey hitched nearer the rail so that she could watch to make sure she kept on. The boatmen again straightened to stare as Lina clambered over the heaps of cargo strewn along the bank. The inert weight in Betsey's arms suddenly became rigid. She pulled the child's face back from her shoulders. The mouth was stretched in a wide, hideous grin. He began to twitch and jerk. The tremors became more rapid, more violent. A froth gathered about the unnatural grin. She gripped him against her, struggling to restrain the spasms, and rocked back and forth, moaning.

"Have you seen my father anywhere around?"

Eric was leaning over the rail almost at her shoulder but his voice seemed to come from an immense distance.

"What's the matter with your baby? What makes him act that way?"

Belatedly the meaning of the first inquiry penetrated the darkness of Betsey's terror. Eric's father was one set apart. He was the company's acknowledged head. Whatever the difficulty, everybody else always looked to him for the answer. If anyone could help her, he could.

"Go find him," she cried. "Find him quick. Tell him my baby's sick."

The convulsion passed. The little body was limp again. He still breathed for there were bubbles in the wisps of froth clinging to his lips. She could see Eric running up the slope to the top of the mound. Now he was talking to his mother. There were many other people up there. But no one came back down the slope.

"I shot a deer."

Eric had wanted news of such consequence to be reported first to his father. But he could no longer hold it back.

"How wonderful," said Agatha. "And so soon, too. Where is it?"

"It was too heavy for me to carry by myself after Ken ran off. And . . ."

Bill Granger came puffing up the slope. After an impatient glance around, he singled out Agatha as the most likely among those present to represent authority.

"My boys need help, ma'am, gittin' them boats unloaded."

"Colonel Jordan is surveying," said Agatha. "The moment he returns, I'll tell him to see you."

The bargeman stood his ground. "The deal, ma'am, was thet the boats was to be unloaded right off so's we could git us on downriver with 'em. And if you folks had good sense you'd not want to see yer stuff just dumped off on the bank.

You'd want it piled and covered with tarps—case it rained."

"Mr. Lyman," Agatha began, "would you mind . . ."

Frank was standing by waiting to speak up.

"We're helpin' your niggers set up your tent, like you asked us to. And long's there's so much work to do, what about them Slovers that's off hunting?"

Agatha saw complexities looming with which she had no wish to grapple. "Where's Garett?" she asked Olivia.

Olivia, too, was waiting.

"He's asleep down there back of that big pine. He had no sleep last night and I don't feel he should be disturbed."

Louisa rose from her camp chair and leaned on her stick. "Ned, Clem. You go with Mr. Granger and do whatever he tells you to." She bestowed upon Frank a gracious smile. "Meanwhile, Mr. Lyman, will you not as a personal favor to me finish setting up the tent without their assistance?"

"Yes, ma'am," said Frank grudgingly. "You put it that way and there ain't nothing else I can do."

Tracy released her fingers from the grip of Ken's and rounded the corner of the half-erected tent. She had not needed to watch Eric's face to realize how much he had been cast down by the failure of his triumph to attract more attention.

"Come on," she whispered. "I'll help you bring it in."

"You will?"

He brightened with incredulous delight. A chance to impress Tracy was for him only second to an opportunity to impress his father. They hurried down the slope and across the meadow.

"It's not far," said Eric. "I'd have got it in easy if that crybaby Ken had stayed to help me."

"He's not a crybaby. He just happens to be fond of animals. Don't you remember how sad he was when your father wouldn't let him bring his dog along?"

"Yes, I remember. He cried then, too. But Father was right. The wagons were so overloaded we all had to leave stuff behind. And that dog of his was really no good. He couldn't hunt. And he was most too old and fat even to walk."

"But Ken didn't cry that day at Redstone the oar mashed his finger."

"No, he didn't," admitted Eric judicially. "Ken's all right, in lots of ways." He looked thoughtfully at Tracy. "You're always standing up for one or the other of us."

"Of course. You'd all stand up for me, wouldn't you?"

"Forever and ever." Eric reddened at the boldness of his declaration and hastily changed the subject. "The deer's right over there. I've already tied the feet together and cut a pole so we can carry it in on our shoulders."

"Hunter-style," agreed Tracy.

"Yes," said Eric, his enthusiasm restored. "And maybe Father'll be back to see us come in."

Betsey still rocked back and forth. She had shaded the child's face from the sun with a corner of the sacking and was afraid to lift it to look again. She saw Cam running down the slope, her pigtails flying. Cam climbed the rail and paused only to get her breath.

"Is he worse?" she inquired.

"Go 'way," said Betsey.

"I know something's the matter with him. I was there when Lina came to tell your mother he was sick."

Betsey stiffly turned her head to see if her mother was coming.

"Your mother said she'd be along in a minute. But then she got a big fish on her line and waded right into the pond after it." Cam paused only to catch her breath again. "Then Lina saw the sun shining on Aunt Olivia's mirror hanging on a tree and went up to look in it. And your mother went on fishing. So then I went up and told my mother about you. And she told Geneva to come down and see what's wrong with your baby. Here she comes now."

Betsey's eyes narrowed as she watched the portly old Negro woman waddling deliberately along the bank. She felt a mountaineers' scorn for all Negroes. It was a prejudice returned in kind. Geneva heaved herself over the rail and squatted beside mother and child.

"Les' have us a look at him," she said, trying to speak kindly.

"No," said Betsey.

Geneva pulled Betsey's hands away, turned back the sacking and pressed a black forefinger against the child's throat.

"The Lawd be my shephud," said Geneva. "He's daid."

"No," cried Betsey.

"When they starts out thet pewky-like," said Geneva, still trying to be kind, "it's best fer 'em when they goes quick, 'stead o' hangin' on and sufferin'. Now jus' yuh let me have him and I'll wash him up and lay him out fer yuh."

"No," screamed Betsey. "No. No. No."

November

It was another mild sunny day with the smoky haze of Indian summer softening the sheen on the river and wreathing the wooded folds of the hills beyond. The first brilliance of the forest's October color had passed, but most trees were still clothed in their fading leaves. In this pleasant pause in the onward roll of the seasons the wilderness, usually so harsh with its creatures, was lavishing upon them instead a feast of fruitfulness. Walnuts, hazelnuts, chestnuts, pecans lay on the ground in windrows. Pawpaws, buffalo berries, red currants still clung to their brittle stems. There was no plant too lowly to flaunt a sliver of sun-cured stalk or wisp of ripened seeds. Thrifty squirrels and mice scurried about laying away their winter stores. Geese and swan and innumerable lesser waterfowl, winging down from the North, lingered to feed along stream and river. Turkeys became too fat to fly. Bear gorged on the dried, sugary clusters of wild grapes. Buck deer, shedding the last velvet from their new-grown antlers, leaped with the vigor of long weeks of plenty into the frays accompanying their amours. The does they sought, beginning to shun their no longer spotted fawns, were sleek and smooth and rounded. Even the wolves ceased their hungry howling in the night.

The morning air was sweet and clean and bracing whenever a stir of wind off the river carried away the odor of spoiling meat and fish from the Slover drying racks in the meadow. In their first excitement over the prevalence of game the Slovers had taken far more than could be eaten and thereafter had neglected their initially earnest project of smoking the surplus for winter use. They had presently tired of the easy hunting but the Lymans had kept on with the enthusiasm of neophytes, crashing about in the woods from dawn to dusk. Only after dwelling on the need for days had Duncan succeeded in getting work started on the erection of log cabins to replace their temporary shelters. The Jordans still occupied tents on the flat top of the mound, except for Garett whose tent, at Olivia's insistence, had been set up out on the point where his rest, either by day or night, might be less disturbed. The Lymans had shifted bales and barrels to make room for a sleeping alcove in the tarpaulin-covered heap of cargo still on the stream bank. The Slovers had thrown together a brush and pole lean-to over the opening into the cavelike hollow in the base of the huge old sycamore at the foot of the mound on the side toward the meadow, a site which on the one hand spared them the too-frequent effort of climbing the slope and on the other relieved them from some of their neighbors' critical comment on their housekeeping.

This day began as usual with Duncan's assembling everybody for what he took care to call a "town meeting." He struggled to maintain the illusion that all had an equal responsibility for arriving at decisions just as he insisted upon terming the half-constructed pair of log cabins crowning the mound "the station."

"We are all in this together," said Duncan, using the phrase with which he faced his every attempt to reason with them. "And I'm sure that by now we're all agreed that this is a satisfactory location—better even than we had hoped—in fact, a nearly ideal site. We must all realize how really fortunate we are in gaining possession of it ahead of the great rush of land-hunters bound to flock West next year. However, this but gives us the more reason to keep in mind that if we're to have roofs over our heads before winter sets in we'll need to get on faster with the job than we've been doing. So let's examine the way we've been going at it to see if perhaps our plan can be improved upon. We started in with the thought, Olen, that you and your sons would take care of felling the trees and cutting the timbers we need. That is, that two of you would take turns at that every day while the other one hunted, since we still need fresh meat. My Negroes, Clem and Ned, are standing by to drag the logs up here. That's the hardest work but they're glad to do it. You, Frank, with the help of your sons, have undertaken to do the actual building. I, for my part, am helping wherever I can be most useful—at least part of every day, for we're also agreed, I believe, that it's important for me to finish the survey so as to determine the borders of our grant. This has been our plan, but at the rate we've been going so far, we'll never have homes by Christmas. Have any of you any suggestions that might help? You, Frank?"

"Nothing wrong with the plan." Frank looked sourly across the circle at the group of Slovers. "We'll build just as fast as the stuff's brought up to us."

"And you, Olen?"

Olen's mouth widened into his habitual amiable and placating grin which was so little in keeping with the gaunt, hawk-nosed ferocity of his countenance. His answer came in a high whining voice that was even less in keeping.

"Yuh bin mighty white with us, Kunnel. We ain't fergittin' thet."

"Thank you, Olen. But what I mean is—does the work plan suit you?"

"Whutever yuh say, Kunnel—thet's good enough fer us."

Olen rolled his eyes at Agatha, pleased that he had made two complete statements untainted by any of the profanity to which she so much objected.

"Good," said Duncan. "Now then, let's see the chips fly."

The Slovers set off for the woods at an unprecedented dog-trot. Nevertheless, when Duncan came back to the station toward noon, Frank was reclining against the half-built wall of the main cabin ostentatiously taking his ease. Mark, equally idle, was seated on a stump part-way down the slope toward the array of drying racks around the Slover sycamore. Ned and Clem were lying on their backs taking turns gnawing at a cold haunch of venison. As Duncan approached, Frank rose, portentously crooked one stubby forefinger, and set off down the slope toward the woods. Duncan, wearily guessing what to expect, followed.

"You come along, Mark," said Frank. "Where's Luke?"

"He went off down toward the woods a while back," said Mark, jumping up to accompany them.

Frank kept to the track left by the Negroes' timber dragging, on into the woods toward a stand of straight young pine flanked by a clump of cedar and another of walnut, which had been selected as the most suitable nearby source of building material. Ahead there was no ring of axe or whine of saw. Frank came to a stop, stood aside so that Duncan could see past him, and with smug satisfaction watched Duncan's face.

Jacob was stretched out beside his axe, sound asleep. It was a Slover byword that there was no limit to Jacob's need for sleep. He had been known to sleep standing up in the rain or on his knees in a canoe, but it was accepted that he much preferred his present position—flat on his back in the sun with his arms flung wide. A little beyond him Jarot sat on the ground with his back against the trunk of a pine he had felled but not yet trimmed. Duncan glanced with passing interest at the curious musical instrument in his lap over which he was bent. He had heard Slover references to "Jat's mandiddle" but had never before caught a clear glimpse of the object. Jarot had contrived it by fastening together with bits of rawhide the sound box of an old violin, the neck of a cast-off mandolin, and a homemade bone bridge for the six strings of a guitar. His fingers were plucking the strings so gently that only a whisper of sound came forth and that little without recognizable key or rhythm. All the same he was sweating with the intensity of his concentration. From time to time he took a deep breath and his lips writhed as though he were resolved also to sing, but if so his ballad was entirely inaudible.

Duncan kicked the moccasined soles of Jacob's feet until Jacob stirred and disconsolately opened his eyes. When he saw who had awakened him he pushed himself painfully upward, accompanying the effort with alternate apologetic grins and patient groans, first to his knees and then to his feet, picked up his axe, and began sadly to swing it. Duncan called to Jarot but Jarot remained deaf. He was more lost to the world than had been Jacob in the depths of his slumber.

"Yippee," yelled Jacob piercingly, and followed the cry with a drawn-out imitation of an Indian war whoop.

Jarot slowly and vacantly looked up. His eyes met Duncan's but there was a distinct interval before any light of recognition dawned in them. His gradual recovery from the trance into which he had fallen was like a return to this earth from the distance of another planet. Finally he began sheepishly to blink, laid aside his mandiddle, snatched up his axe, and resumed trimming the pine. He was not afflicted with Jacob's congenital laziness. When he did work, he flew at it with furious energy.

Agatha started from her chair and looked again. Cam was inching along on knees and elbows between the drying racks until she had reached a vantage point where she could peer through a crack in the hollow sycamore into the interior of the Slover domestic establishment. Agatha's lips tightened upon sighting this most flagrant exhibition yet of Cam's perpetual curiosity. With swift silent steps she ran down the slope, caught the culprit redhanded, and snatched her away. Out of earshot up the slope she halted to indict her prisoner.

"Aren't you ashamed? The very idea—creeping up to peek into people's houses—and right in broad daylight, too."

"That's not a house. It's a hollow tree. And I only wanted to see what they were doing in it."

"Why should you need to know what they were doing?"

"Well, I saw Lina go in there and so when after a little while I saw Luke sneak in, too, I——"

"Oh," gasped Agatha. She repressed her indignation in order first to satisfy a mother's need to ascertain precisely how critical had been an eight-year-old daughter's exposure to worldly experience. "And what do you think they were doing?"

"I know what they were doing. I could see. He was trying to get his hand down into her dress or up under it."

"Which do you mean?"

"I mean both. When he reached in at the top she just laughed, but when he reached underneath she slapped him."

"Is that all you saw?"

"Yes. Because it was just then that you came and jerked me away."

Agatha concealed her relief. "You've been a bad, bad girl. Now go straight to bed and stay there until I tell you you can get up."

Cam ran to the children's tent, her eyes filling with tears of vexation at the injustice of her punishment. Ken and Chris came running from the other way to meet Agatha at the top of the slope.

"What's Cam done, Mother? What's Cam done now?"

"You two go down and play by the pond and stay there till I call you. And take Susie with you. Don't let her get in the water. Clem. Ned. If you must gnaw on that bone take it somewhere else. Geneva. You and Hebe have been wanting to look for chestnuts. Go look for some."

Agatha's pent-up indignation found release when she turned to face Duncan striding up from the wood lot.

"Something's happened, Duncan, that you'll just have to do something about. You must see that a stop is put to it immediately. I just caught Cam watching Luke Lyman carrying on with Lina down there in that Slover hovel——"

"Which am I to do something about, Cam's spying or Luke's courting?"

"It's no laughing matter. It seems to keep slipping your mind that we have young children. And that even out here in these miserable woods there are certain elementary decencies that must be remembered."

"You may have hit upon something of a social problem,

but wouldn't it seem one better dealt with by the two families involved? Luke is a grown man—not to speak of his sanctimonious father—and the Slover girl has parents. In what way is it our affair?"

Frank, followed by Mark, was coming up the slope from the wood lot.

"Then I'll speak to Frank Lyman myself," said Agatha.

"I'd prefer you did not."

Louisa straightened in her chair under the oak which had been left to shade the area between the two cabins-to-be.

"Duncan is right, Agatha," she said. "He has to keep hounding these poor clods to get any work at all out of them and it would be too bad to confuse them by his being obliged to lecture them on their morals as well. But you, too, are right, Agatha. Something must be done about it." She looked toward the approaching Frank with a smile of welcome that at once made him suspicious. "Mr. Lyman."

"Yes, ma'am," said Frank, advancing uneasily.

"Would it surprise you, Mr. Lyman, to know your son Lucas is at the moment engaged in the seduction of the younger Slover girl?"

Frank did not flinch. "It would not surprise me, ma'am. 'Cause I'd know it ain't so. Luke's been raised to stand off from dirt. He's a good clean boy, Luke is. And he's given his promise to a fine honest young woman back in Virginia, as you'll see for yourself, ma'am, when she comes out to marry him next year. And if this ain't enough to satisfy you then I'd have you remember that none of us Lymans would go nearer one of them mangy Slovers than we could reach with a ten-foot pole."

"Your fatherly trust becomes you," said Louisa. "But I gather your other son is not so certain."

Frank looked at Mark. Mark's consternation was at a peak only to be scaled by a righteous young man suddenly confronted by the full-panoplied horror of public exposure.

"You may recall, Mr. Lyman," continued Louisa inexorably, "that I suggested the enterprise was under way at this moment. To be precise, in that big hollow tree right down there."

Frank cast one agonized glance at the sycamore, succumbed to doubt, and began to run down the slope. Olivia moved forward into the circle of spectators.

"Good Lord," she murmured, "let's hope Cam was telling the truth."

"The child may have certain faults," said Louisa, "but idle gossip is not one of them."

Frank circled the drying racks, lowered his head, and charged into the brush-and-pole lean-to. An instant later there burst from the hollow tree a muffled roar of rage. He reappeared, dragging Luke by the hair which he wore clubbed at the back of his neck. Luke wrenched free, saw his retreat toward the meadow cut off, and began to run up the slope. Looking apprehensively over his shoulder to gauge his father's pursuit he did not realize until he had reached the top that he was to be here confronted by the phalanx of Jordans. He turned toward the wood lot trail, bumped into Mark, and came to a full stop. His father seized him again. Luke shook him off. His panic passed and he was possessed by a rage of his own.

"You'd never of popped in on me like you did if that driveling sneak Mark had stood watch for me like he agreed to, like I always did for him when he took his turn."

"You swivel-tongued, tittle-tattling bastard," yelled Mark.

"Mark," howled Frank. "Mark Amos Lyman." His culminating sense of outrage at the revelation his older son, too, was guilty, held him at a loss for words but not for long. "You that left a wife and two little children at home. You that's head of a family. You that's got your own name on a pew. You . . ."

But neither of his sons was listening. They had begun to fight, flailing at one another awkwardly with their fists. Duncan and Frank separated them.

"Get out o' my sight, the both o' you," roared Frank. "You're too old for me to whop. And too low for me to look at. Get out o' my sight."

Mark and Luke shambled down toward their nook in the cargo pile. Frank looked bleakly at Duncan and then at Louisa and then again at Duncan.

"You've proved me a fool," he said. "But you'd best go to thinking on what I've said right along about your taking up with riffraff. I said right from the start we'd all rue the day. But I was weak and give in to you and your smooth talk. So now retribution has come to me. As it will come also to you. As sure as God punishes sin."

He stalked off after his sons.

"I hate to echo anything Frank Lyman says," said Agatha. "But I have to, Duncan, in this instance."

"What precisely would you have me do?"

"I'd have you call in Olen and Polly and talk to them like a Dutch uncle. Tell them that so long as we all have to live together there are certain civilized rules they will have to abide by. Either that or they will have to move out. And don't smile while you're saying it."

"I'm no more amused by a whiff of the gutter," said Duncan, "than you are. But the particular situation has apparently corrected itself."

"We're going to be cooped up with them all winter," protested Agatha. "We don't intend to behave like animals, and we can't sit watching them behave that way."

She broke off as Tracy came out. Tracy looked soberly at Duncan and Agatha.

"I've been talking to Cam," she said. "She has more to tell. She's already so excited I'm wondering about making more of it. Yet it's a story which you should hear. Shall I repeat it?"

"By all means," said Duncan.

"According to Cam this incident today was only the last of a number of other meetings between Lina and either Mark or Luke. The first one Cam knows about took place the day after Betsey got up after her illness. She noticed Betsey whispering to Mark just before starting off into the woods with Lina, presumably to gather firewood, and then heard Mark tell his father he'd left his hatchet somewhere and would have to go look for it. The next day it was Luke, and from then on both went. It was always a different direction and always until today into the woods where Cam could not follow—you having forbidden her ever to wander out of sight of camp."

"Cam's hit it," exclaimed Olivia. "That Betsey. She's determined to make all the trouble she can. She's had this terrible grudge against everybody ever since her baby died."

"At any rate," finished Tracy, "Cam thinks Betsey is always present—just as she certainly was today in the hollow tree."

"How truly deplorable," observed Louisa, with a certain relish. "Supervising the corruption of her little sister. Really—such people."

"As so often before," said Duncan, taking his wife's hand, "you have me on my knees. Anybody seen anything of Olen and Polly recently?"

"Cam will know," suggested Louisa.

Tracy came back from Cam's bedside to report that Polly had been fishing above the pond, that about an hour ago Olen had appeared at the edge of the woods across the stream, had beckoned to her, and that she then had gone into the woods with him.

"First time I've ever heard of his taking any notice of her," said Olivia, "except when he gets drunk and beats her."

"A possible ray of light on the general enigma of Olen," said Duncan, "might be that only when drunk does he feel himself anything like the man he looks."

"Don't put it off another minute," urged Agatha. "Send Eric to find them. He's always looking for an excuse to track anything or anybody."

"Eric went hunting right after breakfast," said Tracy. "He said something about knowing where a bull elk had been bedding down nights."

"In any event we know how to find Eric." Duncan went into his tent and came out with a campaign relic, a Hessian silver trumpet. "He's agreed never to wander alone beyond the sound of this."

Duncan blew three sharp blasts. Scarcely had the notes ceased to echo when, to his slightly surprised satisfaction, there came an answering whistle from Eric. Three minutes later Eric burst from the edge of the woods across the stream, ran across the pine that had been felled to form a foot bridge just below the old beaver dam, and came panting up the slope.

"What do you think, Father," he gasped, more breathless from excitement than from running. "I met the most extra-ordinary man in the woods this morning. I was stalking an elk and I didn't even know he was there—I mean the man—until he was right at my elbow. His name is Caleb Lewis. Wait until you see him. We talk about woodsmen, but he's the real article. Alongside of him these Slovers look like farmers. He's camping right there in the woods just across the creek."

"Extremely interesting, Eric," said Duncan, "but——"

Eric rushed on. "Come and meet him, Father. You've never in your life seen anybody like him. He handles a rifle as if it were a part of him—his hand or his arm—not something you pick up and set down again. He doesn't keep looking all the time to see what might be around him in the woods. He doesn't have to look to know what's there, all the way to the squirrel sticking his head out of a knothole in the top of a tree forty rods off. He moves along slow and easy, almost as though he's lazy, but when he wants to he can spring like a panther. You know how wide the creek is up there just below the falls? Well, he took the pack off his squaw's back and, with that under one arm and the hind quarters of a deer he'd just shot under the other, and his rifle balanced between them, he jumped across the stream in one easy hop."

"His squaw?" said Agatha. "Is he an Indian?"

"Oh, no. He's as white as we are. He even shaves every day. He's not covered with whiskers like the Slovers. But he's

been around Indians a lot. He was taken captive by them when
he was seven."

"I can see a full tally of his virtues will take some time,"
said Duncan. "Meanwhile would you emulate your hero's
woodcraft by showing me how quickly you can find Olen and
Polly for me?"

"Oh, they're right over there where Caleb is camping.
He'll be glad to have me take them off his hands. They're all
the time talking and he doesn't like to talk much."

"If he doesn't like to talk," said Olivia, "how'd you find
out so much about him?"

"That was mostly just from watching him. Of course, Polly
kept pestering him with question. She had a stepsister who
married a Lewis who moved to the Greenbrier after the
French war. The Greenbrier was where Caleb was taken by
the Shawnee back in '62. She claims maybe he's some sort of
a relative, a third cousin by marriage or something."

"Out of all the immensity of this wilderness," said Louisa,
"our first visitor must turn out to be another Slover."

"Oh, Caleb doesn't look at all like one. He stopped answering Polly's questions, and you could tell what he thought by
the way he'd look at Olen and then at Polly. Anyway, all his
own people were killed when he was taken, and it was so
long ago he probably can't remember too much about them."

"Once and for all," said Duncan. "Will you go tell Olen
and Polly I want to see them?"

"Yes, sir. Right now."

Eric ran back down the slope and across the stream.

"Fascinating as all this is becoming," said Olivia. "I must
tear myself away and take Garry his lunch. It's so hard to get
him to eat anything and if I'm late with it he'll snatch at that
as another excuse."

In the cook-tent she prepared a tray with a square of wheat
bread, a pat of butter, a slice of baked ham, a mug of the
milk which was reserved for the children and Garett, and a
plate on which were spaced the separate and distinct tempta-
tions of a bit of comb honey, a dill pickle, a scrap of cheddar
cheese, and a spoonful of plum chutney. As a final touch she
laid a spray of golden aspen leaves alongside the dishes on
the tray. She hummed as she worked and she was still humming when she entered the tent out on the point. Garett was
lying on his back on his cot with his fingers interlaced behind
his head. He ceased staring at the canvas above him and stared
at her.

"Is that merely a buzzing in my ears, or can it be true that that cheerful sound came from you?"

"Of course from me. It's a fine day and I've brought a fine lunch. If you weren't looking so grumpy I'd finish the sentence and say to a fine husband."

"Something remarkably untoward must have happened to put you in so good a humor."

"You don't think seeing you again after all these hours away from you is enough to account for it?" She finished arranging the tray on a bench beside the cot. "Now, as we say to Chris and Susie, if you'll eat I'll tell you a story. You're quite right. Something has happened."

Garett sat up on the edge of the cot and nibbled at the piece of bread.

"You sparkle with promise. Spare no unhappy detail."

"Now that Betsey is up and around again she's taken to undermining the station's moral props. By using that really quite luscious Lina as bait she's managed the downfall of both Mark and Luke. It would not appear that they put up much resistance. Frank just now caught them, literally in the act, and he's beside himself. To cap it all it was Cam's spying that uncovered the scandal, so Agatha's in a state, too. Even the all-wise Duncan is upset."

"Have Mark and Luke been the only victims?"

"Who else could there be? Certainly not Frank or Duncan. And not Clem or Ned, I hope."

"I'm surprised you do not suspect me."

"No, Garry. Not you. That Lina may be a very tidy morsel. And so available. But that would be much too simple and direct for you. Yours is a more complicated itch."

Garett crumbled the rest of the bread into shreds. "Itch. What a word. How expressive. How inelegantly vulgar. And yet one that leaves me more than ever confused. However depraved, what hope have I ever to sin with her? She regards all Jordans as celestial beings. And why have I been only recently accused?"

"You were away at war while she was growing up. And when you came home you were not well. Then there was all that worry about the estate. You had so much on your mind."

"Chiefly you, I trust you'll admit."

"I will. But since we left we've all been thrown so much together and you've had so little to do but sit and brood."

"Still chiefly about you."

"I know that. That's what makes it so awful."

"Makes what so awful?"

"I can see the way you eye her whenever she's in sight. I

can tell when you're thinking about her—as you were when I came in—as you are right now. I know how often when you make love to me you are wondering what it would be like, if just once, you tell yourself, it could be she in my place."

Her voice failed her. She sank to her knees on the floor between his knees, threw her arms around him, and buried her face against him. He held to her tightly. She lifted her face to look up at him imploringly through her tears.

"Oh, Garry, my dearest darling."

He did not reply. Words were no longer expected of him. Already they were again in the grip of that recourse to physical deliverance which was the one proved consolation of their marriage.

Duncan was seated in a camp chair under the oak with Louisa and Agatha on either side of him. Olen and Polly were standing before this extemporized court, smirking with anxiety to accommodate themselves to its requirements but as yet unable to fathom the exact nature of the original charges.

"Them Lyman boys ain't had no women around handy fer quite a spell," said Olen. "Yuh can't hardly hold it agin 'em fer gittin' sort o' jumpy."

"Thet Lina's big fer her age," said Polly. "It's about time she fixed to git herself a man. I tuk up with Olen here when I was no older'n her. She's some purtier'n I was, too. Yuh don't have to fret none about her. She won't have to fiddle around long 'fore she'll git herself somebody."

"You keep missing the point," said Duncan. "Nobody's talking about ordinary courtship. What we are talking about is Betsey's taking men to her younger sister, superintending the business, as it were, and doing it over and over again. That's what we think you should put a stop to."

"Betsey's had her a real bad time," said Polly. "The fun o' lookin' on is about all she's up to. She ain't yet in no shape to have none by herself."

"What's the use, Duncan?" said Agatha. "These people haven't the slightest idea what we're trying to get at."

Polly was more than ever baffled by the note of disdain in Agatha's tone. Her mechanical grin became a shade less servile. "If'n yer so hog-wild to git at all the ins and outs whyn't yuh tackle Betsey and Lina theyselves?" Without waiting for their assent she raised her voice. "Betsey. Lina. Git yerselves up here."

Betsey and Lina emerged from the lean-to as promptly as though they might have been waiting and watching for the summons.

"Should Betsey really be making that climb?" inquired Louisa.

"She's real tough, Betsey is," said Polly. "She's got pains—and she don't sleep much—but when it comes to gittin' around she's most as spry as ever."

The girls reached the flat top of the mound and moved forward, staring. Betsey's pale eyes were hot with suspicion and resentment but Lina's big dark ones were placid and only mildly curious. It was she who was the center of Jordan attention but no defendant could have faced any court with the appearance of an easier conscience. Her hair was streaming down her back and she was continuing absently to run a wooden comb through it. The movement drew the front of her ragged cotton gown across the pleasant roundness of her young breasts.

"The creature's really oddly attractive," whispered Agatha. "Even clean. But so terribly young. Those ineffable Lymans."

"Don't try to distract me," said Duncan. "Judges are supposed to keep an open mind."

Betsey and Lina advanced to a stand beside their parents.

"Betsey," said Duncan, "did you bring word—not once or by accident but again and again this past week—of where your sister was waiting, or, at least, was to be found?"

"I fetched 'em to where she was. Else how was they to know whereat to look fer her?"

"Had you no idea at all that what you were doing was bad?"

"Whut's so bad about it? The way thet Mark and Luke they come a-gallopin' like dogs arter a rabbit?"

"If you didn't think it was bad," asked Agatha, "then why hide in the woods?"

" 'Cause Mark and Luke they was skeered o' gittin' caught."

"And today when you invited Luke to the hollow tree you hoped he'd be caught. Is that it?"

"Thet surely is it." Betsey hawked and spat to emphasize her ill will.

"So your main thought was to bring us down a peg or two?" asked Duncan.

"I was plenty sick o' seein' you-uns up here so gawd-almighty sure yuh was too high up fer trouble to git near."

"And you, Lina," said Duncan. "Do you, too, have no idea that what you let Mark and Luke do was bad?"

"Why?" Lina stopped the comb in mid-air while she considered the question. "All I let 'em do was fool around a mite."

"What do you mean by that?"

"Oh . . . wrassle and tickle and—and feel some.'"

"Some?"

"Thet's right. Some down there, and all they wanted up here." In her placid readiness to make herself quite clear Lina indicated first in the area of her legs from mid-thigh downward and then the inside of her gown from the waist upward.

"But why did you let them do that?"

"It never done me no hurt. And it made them feel real good."

"And that's all you let them do?"

"Yes, it was."

"And still they kept on coming, whenever Betsey let them know?"

"They kept on a-hopin', I expect."

"And you kept on disappointing them?"

"Thet Mark and Luke—I don't like 'em too much. Leastways, not thet much."

"Nonsense," said Agatha. "It's simply incredible that grown men would get so excited and then stop at that. The girl's surely lying."

At last a charge had been made which Polly could grasp. The last trace of her fawning amiability vanished. Suddenly she blazed with rebellious rage, her husband and daughters gaping at her, petrified by astonishment.

"Whutever fetched the likes o' you out to this country?" she stormed, "will yuh tell me thet? There ain't no place out here fer you. Whut do you know about whut it's like to hunt fer yer supper? Nor whut it's like to git yer guts clawed out by a b'ar? Nor be snowed in so long yuh go to eatin' yer moccasins? Nor see Injuns axin' yer young-uns in yer own dooryard? This here ain't no country fer the likes o' you. You'd best git yerselves back wherever yuh come from. You —yuh snake-tongued, whey-faced bitch. You and yer mushmouthed man."

"Duncan," said Agatha. "Are you going to just sit there and listen to her insult us?"

"Hear her out," said Duncan. "We've been free enough with our insults."

Polly, panting and gasping, took a step nearer Agatha. Her thin gray hair had fallen down over her face. The rolls of fat on her cheeks, her bosom, her hips, even her arms and legs, heaved and tossed. She was already exhausted by the violence of a passion to which she was so unused, but her eyes still glittered.

"Yer so set on stickin' yer nose 'twixt other folks' legs—

yuh might's well git yerself a real good sniff. Betsey was only usin' them dough-faced Lymans fer teasers. They wasn't who she was gunnin' fer. Lina never laid still fer neither o' them. There was only one she done thet fer. Thet was fer yer boy, Eric."

Agatha sprang up. She was livid.

"You're lying, all of you."

"We-uns got no call to lie. We got nuthin' to cover up. Lyin's fer the likes o' them thet has."

Agatha looked frantically at Lina. "Lina. Did you and Eric ———"

Lina's eyes, round and wide with childlike calm, met hers. "Yes, ma'am. Twicet."

"You're just saying that, because you want to hurt us."

"Thet was whut Betsey wanted. But thet never was why I done it."

"Then why did you do it? What made you treat him so differently from them?"

"I already said I wasn't so partial to them. But him." Lina's smile was warm and confiding. "I like him."

Eric had put his new skill in woodcraft to practical use by crawling unnoticed within earshot of the tribunal. Having heard his worst fears confirmed, he crept away again, made the edge of the woods, circled the wood lot, and plunged away into the recesses of the forest. The blasts of the Hessian trumpet, repeated at intervals as long as daylight lasted and with greater urgency after darkness had fallen brought no response.

After a sleepless night Duncan and Agatha made their way down to the hollow sycamore at dawn to negotiate peace with the Slovers. An embarrassingly repentant Polly, scrambling from her blankets to receive them, all but groveled at their feet. The Slovers, too, had known a desperate anxiety in the night as they contemplated the imminence of winter and the prospect of being cast out by their patrons. They were as ready as Duncan and Agatha to let bygones be bygones and were instantly eager to accede to Duncan's petition. In this vast wilderness an army might search for days without finding one lost boy. The one hope was that his wanderings might be tracked by experienced woodsmen. The three Slover men grabbed their rifles and set out. In late afternoon they returned but without Eric.

"His tracks they run off plain's a buffler trace," reported Olen, " 'til he come to the crik just below the falls. They wasn't no tracks across the crik nor nowhere's else arter thet. Me and my boys we circled fer most ten miles and never picked up ary other sign." He correctly interpreted the anguished, suffering glance exchanged by Duncan and Agatha and added: "We-uns shoved a pole plumb around the bottom o' thet hole below the falls. He ain't nowheres in thet."

Tracy, listening, backed away. From across the stream came the sound of chopping. With sudden decision she ran down the slope, across the pine log, and on into the woods. The sound of chopping had ceased but she soon came to the camp of Caleb Lewis. There was already a cleared area around his campfire and the first tier of logs of a small cabin stood beside the bark shelter in which his blankets were spread. He had a short length of the split half of a pine log set up on a sawhorse of crossed stakes and was squaring it with the blade of his axe. The axe was so sharp that, when he took the bit in his hands and pushed it against the wood, long even shavings started curling up as though he were using a draw knife. She ran to him.

"Mr. Lewis."

He was fair but so sunburned that at a little distance he might almost have passed for an Indian and his face was so without expression that any guess at his age might range from twenty-five to forty. When he looked around at her she could see what Eric had meant about his eyes. They were a yellowish hazel and they seemed to take in at one glance everything about her, from the pins in her hair to the shoes on her feet.

"Yes, ma'am?"

He resumed his shaping of the pine block.

"I'm Tracy Carter. I come from the station over there. We've a lost boy—a fifteen-year-old boy. He's been gone in the woods since yesterday afternoon. There have been men from the station out looking for him but they can't find him. You're so much more experienced in the woods. Won't you find him for us?"

He kept on thrusting the edge of his axe against the pine, producing the long, curling, pleasant-smelling shavings. She had spoken impetuously, emphatically, her voice tense. Yet he appeared not to have heard anything she had said. She was suddenly struck by a fear that he might already have used the only two English words that he knew, but then, made the more nervous by the discovery of her own nervousness, she recalled Eric's account of the man's talk with the Slovers.

"Won't you?" she repeated.

"I might."

"Oh, will you please?"

He kept on thrusting the edge of his axe against the pine block, producing the long, curling, pleasant-smelling shavings.

"There's only an hour or two left before it will be dark again," she urged.

"First I plan to finish this."

Now that he had brought off a sentence of several words she noted that there was an odd spacing between them, as though it might have been so long since he had spoken English that he needed to take thought in order to be certain of his use of each. Yet it was not as though he were recalling the language of his early boyhood. His accent was more English than western American. The deliberateness of his speech served also to give a decisive finality to his remark. She strove to restrain her impatience. However eccentric his behavior she dared not risk vexing him.

The Indian woman came out of the woods carrying a log on her back. It was a burden to tax a strong man but she bore it with apparent ease. She was stocky and young with a broad, good-natured, not unpleasing face. Her leather dress was smudged by earth and smoke and pine bark but her hair and skin were clean. She came to a stop and without laying down the log waited for Caleb to notice her. He went on working.

"Your wife," suggested Tracy, "seems waiting to be told what to do with that log."

After a moment he looked around and spoke in Shawnee, as impersonally as one might address a horse or a dog. The Indian woman lowered the log to the ground, took a hatchet from her belt, and began notching the ends.

"Her Shawnee name amounts in English to something like Daisy," he said to Tracy.

He spoke again to the Indian woman. She straightened and the absolute impassivity which had marked her former occasional glances at Tracy was succeeded by a sociable smile. She advanced and stretched out her hand. Tracy shook it.

"How do you do, Daisy."

Daisy and Caleb turned back to their work.

"Do you plan to spend the winter here, Mr. Lewis?"

He did not reply.

"Colonel Jordan's grant is all on the other side of the stream. I am sure he will not object."

This observation seemed to interest him as little as had the question.

"Mr. Lewis, it will so soon be dark. There is so little time to look for him before he will have to spend another night in the woods."

"I have no need to look for him. I know where he is."

"You do? Then take me to him. Take me to him at once."

He turned over the pine block and began squaring the other side.

"Then while we're waiting—I'll run to tell his parents he's safe. They've been in agony."

He spoke to Daisy, giving her certain directions which seemed to have absorbed his entire attention. A gust of near panic brushed Tracy. He seemed abundantly able to understand and to speak English and yet he was also able, whenever he chose, to withdraw behind a barrier of Indian inscrutability.

"But you said you'd find him for us."

He lifted his axe and tried the edge with his thumb. Then, as though the pause had reminded him of her presence, he spoke to her again.

"He came to my camp last night after walking in the creek all the way down from the falls so that your people could not track him. He wants me to take him to the Shawnee so that he can live with them."

"Are you out of your mind? You cannot do that to him."

Daisy had finished notching the log. Caleb laid aside the axe and moved around the fire to help her lay it in position on the wall. Tracy followed.

"He comes of a gentle family. He has brothers, sisters, parents—all of whom love him."

Caleb returned to his axe. Tracy, still following him, laid hold of the end of the handle.

"If you're like some of the others who've spent their lives in the woods, if you feel people like us don't fit in out here, then let me tell you this: We've as much right to be here as you have. More, because we'll make something of this country and your kind never will."

He had made no effort to release the axe from her grasp. For a second time he looked at her. This was a longer and more searching scrutiny and was centered on her face and more especially her eyes.

"No need for you to try to guess what I am thinking," she cried. "You have only to listen. I'm trying hard enough to tell you."

"You are too old for him."

"Don't be absurd. He is a child and I am a grown woman."

"You are not married?"

"No. But why all this talk about me? It is Eric who counts. He ran away because he did something bad and is ashamed to face his father."

"He has mentioned you more often than he has his father."

"What maggot can you have in your mind? You are possibly

so ignorant of civilized people that I cannot begin to guess. But for Eric's sake I will try to explain, little as it can concern you. I am not a Jordan, though I have been accepted by them almost as though I were one of the family. I was adopted by Eric's grandmother when I was orphaned at twelve. When they lost their property during the war and decided to come west it was only natural for me to come with them. They asked me to come and I wanted to come. There is nothing— nothing, I tell you—that I would not do for them after all they have done for me. I do not know that you can understand anything I am saying. But I have been something like a nurse to all the Jordan children. And after that a little like a governess, and finally, more like a much older sister. I am fond of Eric. I think he is of me. Now where is he?"

"Eric," called Caleb.

A hundred feet away there was a pile of brush, accumulated by Daisy in the course of felling and trimming trees. The pile shook and Eric crawled out of it. He stood up, clutching his rifle, and took a stride away.

"Come here," said Caleb.

Tracy was blinded, for a second, by rage. From the first he must have had no other intention than to deliver up the boy. He had been leading her on to continue and to embroider her fervent appeal, possibly out of simple boorish curiosity, possibly as no more than a passing diversion. But she could not now afford the luxury of anger. She must think first of Eric.

He had halted at Caleb's call but he did not look around. He still leaned toward the woods as though pausing only to draw a deep breath before resuming his flight.

"Eric, come here," called Tracy. "Please—I want to talk to you."

The sound of her voice set him off as by the pull of a trigger. He plunged into the woods, in his frenzy to escape crashing headlong into thickets and colliding with trees. Caleb looked inquiringly at Tracy.

"Would you?" she begged.

Leaning his axe against the block he started in pursuit, running so lightly and silently that only his toes appeared to touch the ground, and yet with such incredible rapidity that in an instant he had disappeared in the forest. The sounds of Eric's blundering flight ceased and presently he stumbled into view, the lifting of his feet seemed to require a separate effort at each step. Caleb strolled behind him.

Eric kept on toward her, ever more slowly, looking everywhere except at her. His face, which had been scarlet, whitened as he approached. He came to a stop before her, let his rifle slip to the ground, and clutched at the wood block for support.

"Eric," she said, "look at me."

He only hung his head the lower.

"Why are you so afraid to talk to me?"

"I know how you feel," he whispered.

"What makes you so sure of that?"

Eric's voice steadied a trifle, as though in the opportunity to dwell on his guilt there were a shadow of relief.

"I know how you feel about anything that's mean or low. Your nose always wrinkles just as if you were smelling something bad."

"Would you like to hear what I really think?"

The impulse to make another break jerked him up and around. But Caleb stood behind him. Eric leaned back, heavily, against the block.

"It would help if you would look at me," said Tracy.

He dug his chin deeper into his chest.

"I think you've been wicked. I think what you did with Lina was bad. It made you like her kind of people and you must never forget that you're not that kind. But the grief you caused your father and mother by running away was worse."

"I couldn't stay. Not after what I did."

"What you'd done was certainly shameful. Still, it was the kind of a mistake grown men sometimes make. It was the running away that was a child's mistake."

One small corner of Eric's abject misery was lifting. He squirmed unhappily.

"Betsey said it was a chance to show how much more of a man I was than Mark or Luke."

"We've all seen how hard you've been trying to be a man. But just to be any kind of man isn't enough. You must want to be the kind of a man your father is. Keep thinking of that, when you go back now and are standing there face to face with him."

"I can't do that, Tracy. I just can't."

"Of course, if you're afraid of everything that's not easy for you . . ."

He stiffened slightly. She had saved striking the right note for just the right moment.

"Do you think he'll beat me?" he asked, clutching at so simple and dramatic an expiation of his sins.

"I hope so. But I doubt it. He's been too heartbroken while he's thought you lost."

"And you don't think—I mean—you——"

He was still unable to meet her eyes. She took his face in her hands and gently forced him to look at her.

"I'll be as much your friend as I've ever been." She released him and gave him a push. "Now scamper."

Beginning to weep, he set off at a run toward the station.

"Thank you, Mr. Lewis," said Tracy coldly.

She followed Eric. Caleb stood watching her as she walked away. His lips parted in a contemplative grin which, for one instant, showed a gleam of his white teeth. Daisy, covertly watching his face, was startled, as though she saw in it a betrayal of something in him she had never before suspected. Then, chuckling, she went on with her work.

December

Indian summer's pleasant haze was abruptly dispelled by a wintry gale that tore the last leaves from the trees and left their bare branches coated with sleet. There followed day after day of gray cloud and piercing wind. The ground hardened. The pond froze over. A powdering of snow gave the meadow the sterile look of a salt marsh. Packs of wolves, howling gruesomely in the night, each night ranged nearer. The gaunt lifelessness of the denuded trees now permitted gaping glimpses into the forbidding depths of the wilderness. No longer did the circumference of forest seem a comforting wall within which nestled the station in peace and seclusion. It had become a disturbingly open door through which cold winds whined.

The sudden change in the weather was more compelling than had been Duncan's exhortations. With the immediate need of winter quarters so sternly emphasized, Jordans, Lymans, and Slovers alike, chastened by their several recent personal adversities, ignored their differences and joined forces. Duncan postponed the last lap of his surveying in order to share the labor. Garett found tasks within the reach of his strength. Even the Slovers set their axes to ringing. The Lymans were workmen who knew their trade. With ample materials at hand the walls rapidly rose and the roofs spread to cover them.

It was Duncan's intention that the two buildings erected this year were to form two of the sides of what when completed next year would become a quadrangle adaptable to defense if the need ever developed. The main structure, therefore, was ell-shaped. In the longer side the major space was devoted to a large kitchen to double as keeping room for the Jordans and common room for the station. Behind the great fireplace at one end were two small bedrooms for Duncan and Agatha and for Louisa and Tracy and behind the twin fireplace at the other end a bedroom for Garett and Olivia

41

and a spare room, termed by Duncan the office, by Agatha the sitting room, and by Garett the throne room. In the loft over the kitchen were bunks for the children. At the corner of the ell beyond the office was a storeroom, extending at right angles from which was the shorter wing of the main building with quarters in the first section for the Negroes and in the second for the Lymans which also housed their blacksmith and carpenter shop. Next to the Lyman apartment was a gap in which eventually the gate to the station would be fitted and beyond that a detached cabin for the Slovers.

The day the tents were taken down, giving him an unobstructed view of the new buildings, Duncan stood off contemplating with satisfaction the smoke curling from the several chimneys.

"Decided yet," asked Garett, "whether the seigniory is to be officially known as Revel Station, Revel Creek, or Revel Manor?"

"Corbit would have called it Revel Hundred," said Duncan.

"Not bad." Garrett appeared to give the suggestion solemn consideration. "Not too piddling. Not too pretentious. Not bad at all."

The Slovers gathered up their rifles and axes and sack of seed corn, constituting at once the hard core and the sum total of their belongings, and moved to their new cabin. The hollow sycamore and lean-to became a barn for the two cows, adjacent to the dried grass in the meadow and capable of being barred at night to keep out the wolves.

To reward the diligence with which all had labored, Duncan proclaimed a housewarming. The haunches of Eric's first buffalo were set to roasting in the two great fireplaces and a keg of whisky was broached.

"Here's to the flowing bowl," said Garett to Duncan as they looked on from a corner at the festivities. "Behold the varied gifts it bestows. It loosens my usually so taciturn tongue. It renders you even more eminently reasonable. It brings the glow of fond reminiscence into Mother's eyes. It widens Agatha's smile to include Olivia and Olivia's to include me. It wafts Tracy to a yet higher and more cerebral plane. It exalts Frank by virtue of his adamant refusal to touch it. It stirs Mark and Luke to so manly a resolution to outdo each other that they do not falter until both are sick. It satisfies Jake's deepest yearning by putting him to sleep. It draws from Jarot strains of music more ineffable than earthly ear can detect. It sharpens Betsey's malice and sweetens Lina's charity. It causes Polly to flame like a bride when she regards her shaggy mate. But consider Olen. For him it does the most of all."

Olen was emitting wolf-like howls, leaping into the air to strike his moccasined heels together, and repeatedly announcing:

"Ain't no sunnabitch here I can't stuff his elbow in his ear."

The hoarse challenge was accompanied, however, by a grin of loving kindness lavished upon whoever chanced to catch his uncertain eye.

"You, Garett," said Duncan, "are getting drunk."

"I'm trying hard," said Garett. "And 'twould do you as much good."

"Before the night's over my whoops may rival Olen's," promised Duncan. He looked toward the door. "Caleb Lewis does not even send his regrets."

"He's a stiff-legged dog. May he continue to keep his distance."

"I don't agree with you. If we are to have a near neighbor how much better to have a friendly neighbor."

"Caleb was off hunting when you sent me over there this afternoon, father," Eric put in. "Maybe Daisy didn't understand what I meant. Maybe he's back now. Want me to go see?"

"If you like."

Eric put down his tumbler of rum and water and eagerly ran out. The door of Caleb's cabin opened promptly to his knock, letting out a wave of warm air fragrant with the mingled scents of oak fire, bubbling meat, and sweet grass. Eric was startled to discover that in the evening seclusion of her home Daisy wore but a knee-length fawnskin petticoat. By smiling signs she indicated that Caleb had not yet returned. Eric ran back through the darkening forest and was again startled when he came upon Lina waiting for him in the shadow of the station gateway. There was enough twilight left for him to see the color in her red cheeks and dark eyes. She was smiling at him as warmly and sympathetically as when last they had been alone together.

"Whenever yuh happen to look my way you jump like a bee jest stung yuh," she remonstrated softly.

"I promised them," he said, edging around her.

"To keep off from me?"

"I had to."

She was not offended.

"I know about how they tuk on. But no call fer yuh to

take it so hard. I ain't a-holdin' nuthin' agin yuh. Time'll come when you'll be yer own man."

"I promised," repeated Eric desperately.

He bolted past her and on toward the clatter of voices and laughter in the kitchen. His father and Garett, their heads together, were singing Anacreon without, however, attracting any attention from anyone else in the room. His mother was leaning over Olivia, laughing at the charcoal sketch Olivia was doing of Frank's enduring scowl of universal condemnation. Tracy was kneeling beside his grandmother's chair, providing a favorite audience for Louisa's favorite recollections. None of them seemed to notice his return or Lina's placid reappearance behind him in the same doorway. Ned and Clem were removing another joint of buffalo from its spit, but the company had already done so well that there was no second rush to the carving block. At a grudging nod from Geneva they began eagerly to slice off generous portions for themselves.

Olen fell down. From Polly burst a sudden squeal that might have been either a laugh or a cry. As though this were a signal, all five of the still upright Slovers instantly flung themselves upon the prostrate Olen. Subduing the convulsive threshings of his great limbs and heeding not at all his bellows of protest, they lifted him and bore him off to their cabin. Under cover of the commotion the Lymans withdrew, Frank weighed down by his unflagging disapproval and his sons by their belated remorse. Garett lifted his glass.

"I pronounce the house warm." He drank and threw his glass into the fire. "And my bed warmer."

Olivia sprang to guide and support his slightly unsteady steps, but he waved her aside. He bent to press a good-night kiss on the top of Agatha's head and another upon his mother's but when he bowed over Tracy's he appeared to miss his aim and instead nuzzled the kiss lingeringly among the curls at the nape of her neck. He straightened, smiled benignly into his wife's whitening face, and lifted her hand to his arm.

"Now, my sweet," he said, "let us hence. All further favors are reserved for you."

Olivia jerked her hand from his grasp.

"Olivia," said Duncan, "can't you see that he is quite drunk?"

"He's never quite drunk. He's never quite anything—except unbearable." Olivia glared at Garett. "There is one favor I can do myself. That is to spend the rest of the night right here."

She crossed to a bench against the wall and planted herself

on it firmly. Cam had for the last hour kept in the background, trusting to postpone the moment she might be made to follow the two younger children to bed. But now she darted to the ladder leading to the loft.

"I'll move Susie in with me, Aunt Olivia. Then you can have her mattress."

"Thank you, Cam," said Olivia. "Eric, will you bring it down to me?"

Eric looked to his father for guidance. Garett grinned around at the others.

"Don't be misled," he advised them. "We are merely en-kindling our ardor, after the fashion of Polly and Olen."

"This constant squabbling," said Agatha, "in front of the children—of all of us, for that matter—I find very tiresome."

Olivia leaped up and sank in a deep curtsy.

"Our most humble apologies, Your Majesty."

Louisa twisted in her chair with a glance of reserve at Agatha. "I am sure we are all finding this tiresome."

"And quite unnecessary," said Duncan, also eying Agatha.

"Hark to the Arcadian echo of our amenities," said Garett.

From the Slover cabin came another bellow from Olen fol-lowed by a screech from Polly. The sounds were muffled by distance yet oddly distinct in the cold night. All had uncon-sciously turned toward the door as they listened. The door opened. Caleb stood in it. Peering over his shoulder were Indian faces. He stepped forward into the room. Five In-dians followed and ranged themselves behind him. They blinked in the candlelight but from their narrowed eyes quick sharp glances shot this way and that. They seemed to Duncan immediately to have perceived that there were no weapons in the room aside from their own. His, Eric's, and Garett's rifles were leaning in a corner of the office.

"Are they wild Indians, Papa?" whispered Cam loudly. "Are they going to scalp us?"

They did not look too wild. None had feathers in his hair, horns on his head, or paint on his face. One even wore a battered, bell-crowned hat and another a cocked hat with a remnant of lace still clinging to it. But they smelled of smoke, sunflower seed oil, the cold night air, and, damply and pungently, of the animal hides in which they were clothed. Their bulky shapeless figures wrapped in buffalo and rabbit-skin robes, their dark expressionless faces, their very silence and immobility made their sudden intrusion that of creatures altogether alien.

"Good evening, Colonel Jordan," said Caleb, speaking slowly and distinctly. "When I returned to my house tonight

Daisy told me you had asked me to visit you. Since these old friends were already visiting me I asked them to come with me."

"They are as welcome as you," said Duncan.

Caleb stood aside and indicated each of his companions in turn.

"My Shawnee friends are Stone Kettle, Beaver Tail, Night Walker, Bone Polisher, and John Turtle."

Across every Indian face spread an immediate broad grin which appeared curiously childish by contrast with their former sinister stolidity. They leaned their rifles against the wall beside the door. In grave succession they ceremoniously shook hands with Duncan. The last, John Turtle, continued, however, to beam as though this were a social occasion of particular pleasure to him and proved able to accompany his handshake with a word of greeting.

"How do, bruder," he said.

The Indians thereafter continued to shake hands, neglecting no one present, including Eric, Ken, Cam, and the four Negroes.

"My friends had a special wish," said Caleb to Duncan, "to see this place you had built on their land."

"It is now my land," said Duncan.

Caleb, seeming not to notice the amendment, glanced appraisingly about the room. "You started slowly but you have not done badly."

"I am glad you approve," said Duncan. "Geneva, see that our guests are served something to eat."

Serving was not required. At Geneva's reluctant gesture of invitation each Indian whipped out his knife and began helping himself from the joint on the block. They began to laugh and nudge one another and talk among themselves and to stuff enormous hunks of meat into their mouths. So far no one of the whites in the room had moved from the position into which he had frozen when the Indians had entered. Each watched Duncan, waiting for a cue from him.

"You have been our neighbor for some weeks," said Duncan. "I fear we have been so occupied we have been remiss about making friends. Mr. Lewis"—he began indicating the others in the room—"my mother, my wife, my brother, Garett, his wife, my sons, Eric and Ken, my daughter, Cam, and Miss Thryza Carter."

"I have met Mr. Lewis," said Tracy distantly.

Caleb had merely nodded at each presentation, though his glance at each successive member of the Jordan household had been as intent as when upon his entrance he had observed the internal structure of the building.

"Won't you sit down, Mr. Lewis," said Agatha.

Caleb sat on the end of the bench beside the long table and, appearing to have said all that was necessary to say, began to stare at the women, first at one and then, as directly and as unabashedly, at the next. Garett, moving around the table, drew Duncan aside.

"Our dusky guests' preoccupation at the trough," he murmured, "and their captain's with his appraisal of our women-folk seem to offer the chance of a moment's word with you." He glanced through the loophole at their shoulder at the dark and silent Lyman apartment and the dark but not so silent Slover abode. "Observe our fellow defenders. We could have all had our throats cut by now and they'd be none the wiser. Think we should call them over?"

"No, I don't," said Duncan. "We still may get out of this without real trouble but we most certainly won't if all of them come stumbling in."

Garett nodded his agreement and turned back toward the room.

"Ah," he said. "The fair Olivia is getting in her licks."

Olivia had placed before Caleb a plate of buffalo tongue, buttered beans, and corn cakes spread with honey. He began to eat, ingoring the silver she laid beside the plate and instead, using his hands and his own knife. Olivia sat down across from him and laced her fingers beneath her chin, watching him intently.

"We've been looking forward to meeting you, Mr. Lewis. We've been simply dying of curiosity."

He raised his head and stared at her. Her bright smile faded.

"Your husband is sick?" he asked.

"Not really. He is recovering from a war wound."

"You have no children?"

"No."

He resumed eating, appearing to have exhausted the subject. Cam leaned on the table at his elbow.

"Why didn't you bring your wife with you?"

"I have no wife."

"Your squaw, then. Why didn't you bring her?"

He looked again at Olivia while giving Cam an explicit reply.

"I will tell you about Daisy. She is an Iowa captive—a slave you Virginians might call her. The Kickapoo who took her traded her to the principal chief of the Shawnee for a barrel of whisky. Because he is my old friend, he loaned her to me to help me out this winter."

"How very convenient for you," said Louisa.

"Then you are going to stay here all winter?" Eric asked eagerly.

"Yes," said Caleb.

The Indians, having glutted even their extraordinary appetites were beginning to range about, to inspect garments, whether hanging on the wall or on people, to examine and to handle various utensils and implements. Night Walker picked up a mug in which whisky had been served, sniffed it, and looked expectantly at Duncan. Caleb rose abruptly.

"We will go now," he announced.

The Indians picked up their rifles and docilely preceded him out into the night.

"Whew," said Garett. "A most singular visitation." He grinned at Olivia. "And did you get your comeuppance."

"Duncan," said Agatha. "You must think of some way to get rid of that man. We just can't have him living so near."

"Wouldn't it appear that he might make a more comfortable friend than enemy?"

"Cold comfort," said Louisa, "in having packs of Indians trooping in and out of our house at all hours."

"Something of a dilemma," admitted Duncan. "But it's not a choice we have to make tonight."

His discreet spying at the first streak of dawn established the fact that the visiting Shawnee had already departed and that Caleb and Daisy were again at work on the enlargement of his clearing. The same next morning brought the most authoritative advice on the problem of Caleb that the entire frontier could have offered. George Rogers Clark came ashore to call at the new settlement on the north bank. The great western hero was pleased to learn the station's founder was the same Colonel Jordan who had served with him in the Virginia campaign of 1781 against Benedict Arnold. But he was in too pressing a hurry to get on upriver to attend an Indian council at Fort McIntosh to linger longer than to take a shrewd look around and pay his respects to the Jordan ladies. Duncan, off in the woods finishing his survey, very nearly missed seeing him at all. Eric tracked his father and brought him back just as the General was shoving off. The two men squatted under the sycamore on the point. A small mongrel dog on a leash in Clark's beached bateau kept barking so sharply that they had need to raise their voices.

"You've made a good enough start," said Clark. "But if it was me I wouldn't lose much more time getting a stockade up around those two open sides."

"I do not intend to. I've had a little trouble keeping my people at work."

"Best way to keep folks at work is to lock up the grub and dole it out as they earn it."

"You do not expect the peace to last?"

"You never can count on Indians—one way or t'other. Depends some on the English, too. If they go on keeping their garrison in Detroit and their stinking traders in every Indian town it might not be too long before the hard-nosed ones like the Shawnee get to forgetting they lost the war."

"But when I came through Pittsburgh I understood the Iroquois were ready to cede this whole country out here."

"That's what they did. At Fort Stanwix a month ago. But the Iroquois ain't so important as they used to be and they ain't the Indians who live out here. The Delaware and the Wyandot—who do—they're coming to Fort McIntosh this month to sign some sort of a treaty. But the Shawnee, who live the closest of all to you, are still holding off. Maybe they'll come in. Maybe they won't."

"I've a title from the Shawnee."

The dog's continued barking was making conversation more and more difficult. Clark ordered one of the boatmen to bring him ashore and tie him to a bush at a little distance. The dog ceased barking and began to howl plaintively.

"Heard him yipping on an island we were coming past yesterday evening," explained Clark. "Some no-count mover must have pitched him off there. You were saying about a Shawnee title."

"An uncle of my mother's, Corbit Revel, who was then a trader with the Ohio Indians, was granted this land by the Shawnee in 1774. He died before he could develop and bequeathed the grant to us."

"I missed knowing Corbit. He was just before my time. But I've heard some about him, mostly good. He was about the only white man honest enough to string with the Shawnee during Lord Dunmore's war."

Clark paused and looked off along the stream bank. Ken, drawn from the station by the dog's cries, had crept to the bush and was making friends with the outcast. The puppy ceased to complain and began happily to lick the boy's hands and face.

" 'Course that was quite a while ago," resumed Clark, "and

could be the Shawnee might not feel so good about seeing
you settling in here the same as they might have their old
friend Corbit."

"Nevertheless, it's a perfectly authentic grant. And it's even
within the area reserved by Virginia for Virginia veterans.
By next spring Harmar's Federal troops will be out here and
the Shawnee will have no choice but to recognize my deed."

Clark was looking off again.

"That boy and that dog surely do cotton to one another."

"Ken had to leave his dog behind him when we left home."

"This one's about as no-count as they come but a boy can
find use for most any kind of a dog. Got any objection to
my giving it to him?"

"I'd be delighted," said Duncan. "Ken, come here."

Ken approached, endeavoring politely to conceal his greater
interest in the dog's company.

"The General wants to know if you'd like him to give you
that dog."

A sun of enchanted surprise rose in Ken.

"Yes. Yes, I would." He turned to run, remembered, and
turned back. "Thank you, General Clark. Thank you—very
much."

He ran to the bush and began fumblingly to untie the dog.

"Harmar's soldiers won't be much help," said Clark.
"There won't be enough of them to do more than hole up in
a couple of forts. And they'll be less than no good here on the
north bank. Congress keeps buttering up the Indians by passing laws forbidding settlement north of the river and if
Harmar pays you any attention at all he may try to move
you out."

"Are you suggesting then that we give up this station? Is
that your advice?"

"It surely is not. Wherever our people get a settlement
started I want to see it stick. I got a place myself on the north
bank—down by Louisville. No, sir. You hang right on here.
'Case next summer things start to look bad, I'll make out to get
word to you in time."

The two men rose.

"It's been a great pleasure to see you again, General," said
Duncan, as they shook hands. "I'm eternally grateful for
your counsel. Oh, I'd almost forgot a lesser but more immediate problem. There's a squatter moved in across the creek—
there where you hear that axe. He's not on my land. But he's
a great friend of the Shawnee. He used to live with them and
he has an Indian woman living with him now. His Shawnee
friends visit him and he brings them to call on us."

"What's his name?"

"Caleb Lewis. What I'm trying to decide is whether as a neighbor he's an asset or a liability. Should I try to make friends with him or try to get rid of him?"

"I'd like to have me a look at him."

"It's too bad to take more of your time."

"I always got time to size up a white man that's partial to Indians."

"Ken," called Duncan. "Run tell Mr. Lewis that General Clark would like a word with him."

Presently the axe in the woods fell silent. Caleb appeared on the crossing log and came striding along the stream bank out to the point. Ignoring Duncan's presentation he came to a stand in front of Clark. The two men, almost the same height and build, identically clad in weathered buckskins, each leaning on his rifle, eyed one another.

"One of my boatmen's gone sick," said Clark. "Thought you might help me out."

"For how long?"

"Far's the Muskingum. You could cut off through the woods and be back here by the third day from now."

"I might spare that long."

Caleb walked off fifty yards and called out. From the woods across the stream came Daisy's reply. He addressed her briefly.

"Telling her what to do while he's away," interpreted Clark. "Cut wood days and keep her door shut nights."

"I hate to see you going to so much trouble," Duncan protested again.

"I'm doing it for me as much as you. Whenever a white man is as thick with Indians as he is I don't want to lose time getting him figgered out. I want to know if he's working for the English, the Shawnee, or nobody but himself. By this time tomorrow I ought to have seen enough of him to make me a pretty fair guess. I'll let you know what it is."

With the puppy by turns tugging at the leash and jumping to lick his hands, Ken circled the foot of the mound and kept on to the farther edge of the meadow. He required seclusion and leisure to examine his prize. The dog was mainly yellow, with black rump and ears and a grizzling of white on muzzle and belly. He was the size of a fox terrier, though with shorter legs and a shaggy coat that made him seem larger than he was. His moods alternated between the two extremes of the most aggressive belligerence and the most fawning affection. When Ken stooped to pat him he dissolved into wriggling ecstasies of response. The next second, he had spun about to face the unknown, bristling and rigid, his ears flattened, his teeth bared, his throat resonant with fury, his eyes fixed in a sidelong glance upon the threatening approach of an enemy visible only to him.

Ken's first concern was the leash. A tethered dog was not his dog. He hesitated, however, to risk untying the leather thong. The dog might not yet realize he was his dog. He might not intend to run completely away, but if he ranged far in these unfamiliar woods he might not know how to get back. While Ken grappled with this problem, the cows ceased to graze on the frozen grass of the meadow and edged nearer to make a suspicious inspection of the canine stranger. The dog sprang to the end of the leash and barked fiercely. His barks were shrill and penetrating and as loud and sharp as pistol shots. One of the cows lowered her head. He leaped back to the safety of Ken's arms.

Ken drove the cows away with clods and, suddenly inspired, took the dog into the hollow sycamore. Here, after replacing the bars, he could experiment safely. He untied the leash. The dog rolled over on his back, paws in air, and squirmed about in the most abject submission. Ken moved away. He scrambled to his feet and followed. Ken ran from side to side of the hollow tree. He kept so closely under foot that Ken fell over him. His heart beating faster, Ken lowered the bars. The dog sat, tongue out, watching him. He stepped into the open, putting all to the test. The dog was still at his feet. He ran toward the pond—the dog kept at his heels. Whichever way he turned his faithful follower was with him. He sat down and gathered the dog happily in his arms.

"Ken," called Eric from the slope of the mound.

Ken ran to meet him. The dog began to bark at Eric.

"Look at my new dog," exulted Ken.

"I see him," said Eric. He regarded the capering, yipping little animal without favor. "What's his name?"

"Rupert," said Ken.

He had not until that instant given any thought to a name.

"Rupert? That's a funny name. Why Rupert?"

"Because that's his name."

"Well, Mother said to tell you dinner's ready."

They ran up the slope, Rupert still barking. At the kitchen door Rupert darted between their legs and into the room. His earlier efforts had been but a weak preface to the clamor that burst from him upon being confronted by the number of people assembled here. He raced about the room, barking with new excitement at each new figure he encountered. His performance culminated in his appearing to recognize in Agatha a principal enemy. He planted himself before her, his barks sharpening with ever more frenzied hostility.

"Take him outside," she directed Ken. "Take him out this minute."

Rupert had not yet identified his name. He was deaf to Ken's desperate whistles and supplications. Ken was obliged to pursue him under table and benches and at length suffer the ignominy of its having been Eric who brought the chase to an end by one swooping dexterous grab. Clasping the struggling and still barking dog in his arms, Ken faced his unsympathetic audience.

"It isn't his fault. He doesn't know any of you yet."

"You heard your mother," said his father.

Sadly Ken went to the door, dropped Rupert outside, and closed it. Immediately Rupert began to scratch on the door and then mournfully to howl. His howling voice was as big as that of a hound but lacked any bell-like quality.

"It won't take him long to get used to us," argued Ken.

"There's still the question of how long it may take us to get used to him," said Garett.

"Take your plate and eat outside," said Agatha. "And do something to keep him quiet."

Ken went out, was immediately rewarded by Rupert's overwhelmingly affectionate greeting, and ran down the slope, laughing at the dog's excited leaps upward toward the plate of buffalo stew. Duncan, coming out to watch, noted the day's first signs of life around the Slover cabin. Polly was in the yard chopping wood. She had a blackened eye and a split lip but, between her grunts as she swung the axe, was humming contentedly. He strolled over to her. She wagged her head in pleasant reminiscence.

"We-uns had us a right good time to yer place last night."

"I trust all continued to go as well after you got home."

She looked up suspiciously, saw the twinkle in his eye, and grinned broadly.

"I made out," she confessed.

"And Olen?"

"He simmered down along toward daylight. He gits him a sight o' good out'n his likker, Olen does."

"After you left last night we had some Indian callers."

He made the announcement casually but expected her to be thunderstruck by the revelation. The Slovers were perpetually conscious of the Indian threat that had tormented every year of their frontier lives. But she only nodded.

"Caleb he told us he'd be a-fetchin' some around one day," she said.

"I thought all of you were so convinced that the only good Indian was a dead Indian?"

"Not these here pet Injuns o' Caleb's. They'll never do us no dirt. Not whilst Caleb's around."

Duncan tried another stab at her complacence. The Slovers were inordinately proud of the sagacity of their dogs.

"Five Indians you could smell a half mile off trailed right past your door last night and your dogs didn't so much as growl."

Polly nodded. "These here winter nights when they's in there along with us they never fool none when they's no call fer it. They got better sense than to git theyselves throwed out in the cold."

Duncan made one more try before giving up this last of his recurrent attempts to explore the Slover mentality.

"General Clark was here this morning." He paused for effect but the great name seemed to mean little to Polly. "He's not sure the peace will last."

"Caleb he ain't neither."

"General Clark thinks we need a stockade."

Again Polly nodded. "Caleb he says 'twould look some better was we-uns to have us one." She gestured toward the cabin. "Soon's they's done sleepin' it off they'll go to fetchin' yuh poles."

Rupert's afternoon was a greater social success than had been his morning. Led about on his leash and required to make the acquaintance in turn of every inhabitant, he eventually ceased barking at any of them. After a couple of exasperated nips from the Slover dogs he ceased also barking at them. Only the cows remained his enemies.

"You can see how smart he is," said Ken. "Look how fast he learns."

All that evening, his belly distended with the amount Ken had fed him, Rupert slept peacefully and silently on the hearth. But after the candles had been extinguished and all had retired, he quickly squandered the favor he had so far painfully gained. Ken's proposal that Rupert sleep with him in the loft had been vetoed. Left alone in the vast dark kitchen Rupert was stirred to excessive vigilance. The slightest whisper of wind at a loophole or the crackling of an ember in a fireplace excited in him a spasm of frenetic barking. Intervals of complete silence in the world about him were equally as suspect and demanded as resolute a challenge.

Duncan, stumbling about with a candle, found pursuit hopeless. To Rupert his nightshirted figure was obviously a specter of nightmare proportions. Ken was summoned from the loft to effect the capture. But, forcefully exiled to the yard, Rupert, as before, clawed at the door and filled the night air with his despairing howls.

"Eric," called Duncan, "go with Ken and see that that dog is tied up down in the hollow sycamore."

"But the cows are there," remonstrated Ken. "Rupert hates them. He'll just bark and bark, way down there by himself."

"Good. Maybe he'll get hoarse."

The next day, however, Rupert proved able to render his first service to the community. Jarot and Jacob had emerged and, axes on shoulder, had plodded dejectedly off to the wood lot to cut palisade poles. Betsey and Lina, too, had come out to assist their mother in cleaning the four rabbits and three partridges she had caught in the snares she kept set in the edge of the woods. But Olen clung stubbornly to his bed. He asserted he was of a mind possibly never to get up again. The smell from the cooking pot had no effect upon him. He professed not to be hungry and doubted he ever again would be. Finally even Polly's patience was exhausted. She beckoned to Ken.

"Let's have us the loan o' thet pup o' yourn."

"What for?"

"I'll show yuh."

Polly scooped up Rupert, thrust him into the Slover cabin, and shut the door. Instantly Rupert began furiously to bark. The staccato din continued, interspersed with intermittent roars of indignation from Olen. Polly nodded complacently.

"No," protested Ken. "Let Rupert out. Olen will kill him."

"Olen?" Polly shook her head. "Olen he hollers big but he wouldn't no more hit a dog'n he would a day-old baby."

The unequal contest went on and on and became the center of station attention. Olen's swearing dwindled in volume but Rupert was tireless. After half an hour Olen surrendered. He emerged, glowered at the onlookers, shouldered his rifle and set off across the meadow and into the soothing quiet of the woods.

At dusk he had not returned. An hour after dark Polly called on Daisy to make sure he was not sulking in Caleb's cabin. She came back genuinely disturbed, having for the first time learned of Caleb's absence. Two hours after dark Jarot and Jacob made a wide circle in the woods, pausing at intervals to listen for a call or shot of distress. At midnight Duncan and Garett were still sitting by the fire waiting for word.

"There's nothing we can do until daylight," said Duncan. "Jat and Jake can't see to track him until then."

"There's one thing we can do," said Garett, yawning. "We can get some sleep. Ten to one that's what Olen's doing. With his bump of caution he's not likely to have let anything happen to him."

The door flew open. Polly, disheveled and panting, stood in it.

"Injuns," she gasped.

Duncan twisted in his chair and gaped at her, unable for the moment to accept the reality of her terror.

"But I thought with Caleb here you'd stopped worrying about visiting Indians."

Polly delivered the gist of her warning while turning to bolt out again.

"Caleb ain't here. And these Injuns ain't visitin'. Olen seen 'em. We-uns ain't squattin' here right where they know where to reach for us. You-uns best clear out, too."

Duncan pursued her into the yard. The Slovers, clutching their rifles, axes and sack of seed corn, were already moving around the corner of the house, keeping close to the wall. Olen turned to shush the low whine of one of his dogs. Duncan seized his arm.

"Where you going?"

"We aim to hide out," whispered Olen hoarsely. "But ain't no use our hidin' if'n the rest of yuh fool around so long the Injuns foller yuh to whereat we be."

Duncan shook him impatiently. "Tell me," he insisted. "We'll either join you right away or not at all."

"Yuh mind thet patch o' swamp along the bank—'bout two mile upriver? We-uns is a-wadin' crost thet and holin' up in them willows on thet little island out'n the edge o' the river."

Olen pulled away from Duncan.

"I'll show 'em, Paw," said Lina.

The Slovers, except for Lina, faded off into the darkness down the slope of the mound. Duncan beat on their doors to arouse the Lymans and the Negroes and returned to the kitchen. Garett had roused the women. All of them from indoors and out, wrapped in hastily caught-up dressing gowns or oddments of bedclothing, came swarming in, betraying their instinctive alarm by the urgency of their demands to know what was causing it.

"Will everybody be silent," ordered Duncan. "I can't tell you what's happened because I'm not yet sure myself. Now,

Lina, will you tell us—and slowly, please—what exactly did your father see?"

"A pack o' Shawnee," said Lina. She was sufficiently composed to be studying the night attire of the Jordan women while she spoke. " 'Bout three mile t'other side the falls where thet old Injun trail crosses the crik. Paw he figgers they was mebbe forty—all bucks—and all painted. They come on him so sudden like Paw had no time fer nuthin but jam hisself into a hole under a log. It was fetchin' on toward dark and they camped right there by the crik. They was so close Paw he never dast crawl off till 'bout an hour ago. Paw he figgers they's fixin' to jump the station come daylight."

"You all heard her," said Duncan. "The Slovers feel they're better off hiding in the woods than waiting here. They've already gone."

He looked around at the others with the speculative eye of the beleaguered commander whose decisions must wait upon his estimate of the temper of his garrison. Frank threw back the blanket draped about him and thrust his head out of the folds like an old turtle.

"Olen can't count past ten even when he ain't scared out of his wits. But if he did see a parcel of Indians and they are coming at us we're better able to stand 'em off here behind these walls than skitterin' around through the brush."

"I'm inclined to agree with Frank," said Garett, "but I don't like this division of forces. The diffident Slovers will fight if they have to and they're better shots than any of us. I'd say catch 'em and make 'em come back to help us hold this place."

"Think of the children," begged Agatha. "We can't go creeping off into the swamps in this kind of weather."

"This would scarcely seem the moment to hold a town meeting," said Louisa. "It's for you to decide, Duncan. Whatever you say—that's what we will do."

Duncan's nostrils were pinched and the muscles of his jaw working. "There is no getting away from the facts," he said huskily. He cleared his throat and continued in a harsher voice. "It's one fact that the Slovers are fully convinced that we are about to be attacked and equally convinced they can save their lives only by running into hiding. Nothing we can say or do will persuade them to come back. It is another fact that if we are seriously attacked we cannot hold this place with six rifles and no stockade to keep the attackers from rushing us. You and Frank, Garett, have soldiered enough to know that as well as I do. But the principal fact is that in this instance the Slover judgment is better than ours.

They have been through this kind of Indian situation many times before and we never have. Polly has witnessed the murder of three of her children on her own doorstep and Olen the butchery of both his parents. They know precisely and in detail that what they have to dread is worse than the hardship of crawling through a swamp or the shame of running when threatened. These are facts we cannot sidestep. We have to run, too. Dress warmly. Everybody take a blanket."

Announcement of the decision to flee brought with it the first chilling realization of the enormity of the threat from which they were fleeing. Frank, jerking open the door, flinched and peered into the dark yard before running across to his own door. Agatha paused to listen before running to the ladder leading into the loft where her children still slept. Olivia wrapped her arms around Garett as though reaching out to welcome, in the trial that was upon them, the need to share with him her young strength. The Negroes huddled together, their eyes rolling, their lips moving in supplication.

Duncan brought from the storeroom a bale of pemmican, tore it open and dumped out on the table the five-pound elk-skin sacks of mixed corn meal and tallow. When he had procured this supply of the standard frontier emergency ration it had seemed an insurance for which there was not one chance in a thousand they would ever have need.

"Everybody take one," he directed.

He counted his reassembling company. Ken was missing.

"That miserable dog," gasped Agatha. "Ken's gone down to the hollow sycamore to get him."

Before Duncan had reached the door to start after him Ken appeared in it, towing Rupert at the end of his leash. The congregation of so many people, together with the general atmosphere of excitement, was immediately too much for Rupert. He began to bark. Ken's desperate efforts to silence him only aroused him the more.

"I've always wondered about the stories of fugitive settlers leaving their dogs shut up in their cabins behind them," remarked Garett.

"No," cried Ken. "No. No."

"He'll have to stay," ruled Duncan.

Frank snatched the leash and tied it to a table leg.

"Eric," said Agatha. "You keep hold of Ken—hang on to him every minute we're off wherever this is we're going."

"Blow out the candles," said Duncan. "I'll take the lead with Lina. The rest of you follow in single file. And keep close to whoever's in front of you. Garett, you bring up the rear."

The door was closed. In the house behind them Rupert ceased to bark and began to howl dismally. Duncan and Lina started off down the dark slope toward the path that led along the stream to the river. The others, clinging nervously to one another, groped into line to follow.

Tracy had run out into the yard before the candles were blown out. She could no longer endure the pain of watching Duncan's pain. She knew so well his every smile, his every frown. She always knew what he was thinking, more clearly, more sympathetically, more understandingly, she was sure, than Agatha could ever know. She remembered the light in his eyes that day of their arrival when they had stood side by side on this very spot where she was standing now. He had planned for so many months, had invested in the undertaking so much of what he owned and of what he was, that to be able at last to stand here and look about him had been a great experience for him, one she had been able to share. He could see spread out before him his whole future and his children's future. She alone knew how much it was costing him tonight to be giving it all up, to be running away without a battle—he, a soldier. She alone knew that.

She leaned against the great oak and, made weak by her anguish for him, sank to the ground, burying her face in her arms. The others were moving away, unaware in the darkness that she was not with them. Her heart went out to them, too. They were his people. She could even love Agatha, because he did, and because, as his wife and the mother of his children, Agatha, too, was a part of him. A frantic longing came upon her to be possessed of the power to shield them from every danger, since if they were lost then he, too, was lost. But at this moment they were creeping off away from her through this wintry darkness, pursued by unspeakable horrors, while she was too weak to do more than lie here dissolved in helpless compassion for them and for him and for herself.

Suddenly a thought struck her. She sprang up, her weakness falling away. It was not a great service but it was something tangible that she could do for them and the personal risk to her gave it meaning. She ran down to the hollow sycamore and lowered the bars. If nothing else could be saved she might still save milk for the children. The cows were reluctant to leave their warm shelter. She belabored them with a stick, drove them into the forest as far as the wood lot, and tied them to trees. There was the chance that here they would fall prey to wolves before the night was over, or that the Indians might still find them in the morning, but no such certainty of loss as had they been left in plain sight of the station.

The preoccupation with her task ended, there swooped upon her a consciousness of the darkness of the night forest and of her loneliness in it. Indians contemplating an attack at dawn might already have crept this near their goal, might already be crouched in the deeper shadows of any thicket about her. She ran along the wood lot trail, over the top of the mound, and along the path toward the point which the others had taken. The act of running away imposed its immediate penalty. She was beset by fears she had not imagined when running toward the sycamore and the wood lot. Shadowed terrors filled the darkness on every hand waiting to spring out upon her. She clenched her teeth against the hammering impulse to scream. As she neared the point, in her blind panic she strayed from the path. Suddenly her foot was seized. She fell headlong.

The metallic rasp had told her what it was that had so savagely gripped her even before she had recovered enough to run her hands down her leg to the steel jaws. She had stepped into one of the Slover wolf traps which with typical Slover heedlessness they had set so near the path. The toothed jaws had not quite cut through the stout leather of her hunting boots but were inexorably fastened upon her foot just below the ankle. The springs of the trap were too strong for her to loosen and the log to which the chain was stapled too heavy for her to drag. She was caught like any wild animal, condemned to lie here at the mercy of whatever the dangers of the night until the light of day exposed her to yet more fearful dangers.

A shadow appeared against the night sky. She tried to scream but could only whimper.

"Tracy," called the shadow, low-voiced. "Tracy."

With a sudden great throb of incredulous and shamed delight, she realized that it was Duncan, that Duncan, himself, had come back to look for her.

"Duncan," she whispered.

He could not see her on the ground in the darkness.

"Tracy," he repeated. "Tracy."

"I'm here," she gasped. "I can't get up."

He was kneeling beside her, gripping her arms, touching her face, running his hands over her to discover her affliction.

"My dear, my dear," he said. His hands found the trap. "Those Goddamned Slovers."

She had never before heard him swear. His rage seemed to make his nearness to her even more real, more personal.

"Can you stand up?"

"Yes. I'm not hurt much. Just caught."

He took her by the shoulders and lifted her to her feet. "Now hang on to me."

He held her upright against him, felt with his toes for the hinges of the trap, and, pressing against her, thrust his full weight on them. The jaws fell open. She was free.

"I'm sure nothing's broken," she said, the tumult within her making her frantically anxious to seem calm. She stood on one leg and tried the toe of her cramped foot against the ground. "I can walk."

"Nonsense," he said.

He slung the strap of his rifle over his shoulder and picked her up in his arms.

"Hang on tight," he advised her.

Her arms were wound around him to ease the labor of his carrying her and her face was pressed in the hollow of his shoulder against his neck to escape the scrape of branches. His physical presence, like his gust of rage, was real. He was sweating and he had not shaved since the day before. The masculine smell and roughness of him were real. The straining, convulsive embrace in which they were clasped was real. The excitement and terror and pain of the last hour had made her seem able to think with a sudden extraordinary clarity. He must sense the half-terrified, half-shamed, but wholly enchanted bliss that suffused her. If he had not long since, he must in this moment be guessing. He must know by the quivering of her flesh, the warmth of her body, the beating of her heart, that she loved him. But she was safe with him. Not tomorrow, or the day after, or ever, would he let her see that he knew. Tomorrow their eyes could meet as naturally and candidly as yesterday.

"When you first stepped in the trap," he said, holding her closer as he stepped over a log, "why in the world didn't you call out?"

"There was no use. I was so far behind the rest of you no one could have heard."

"Why were you so far behind?"

"I'd remembered the cows. I took them out of the hollow tree and tied them up in the woods where they'd be more out of sight."

"You didn't! What an absurdly gallant gesture. And what a damned-fool one. The next time you get any such preposterous idea as that will you tell me about it first?"

"Yes, Duncan."

There was a sudden sharp rustle in a nearby thicket. It was

no more than a wood mouse, in its frantic flight setting up a commotion out of all proportion to its size. But Tracy had raised her head from Duncan's shoulder to listen and he at the same time had turned his to peer toward the sound. Their faces came together, his mouth brushing the corner of hers. His breath caught, his lips strayed across her cheek, and returned to find hers. The sudden kiss seemed less the venture of a suitor than the unthinking impulse of a man conditioned to the habitual caresses of an affectionate family. But her surprise that it had occurred at all released the storm of her pent-up emotion. Her arms tightened about him, her moan was a welcome. In the ecstasy of her surrender it was she who prolonged the moment. And it was he who recoiled. His start of dismay filled her with a greater dismay. She could not in the darkness see his expression clearly but she could sense with what consternation he was scrambling to safety.

"I didn't mean that," he stammered. "I don't know what I could have been thinking of. Least of all at a time like this, with the chance of an Indian in the next thicket, and you scared out of your wits and not even able to walk."

"Put me down," she whispered. He let her slip from his arms. "See. I can stand alone. Quite well." Her fingers, still holding to his sleeve to steady herself, sank into his arm. "Anyway, we both know the truth—now."

"You can't realize what you're saying. This horrible night —your running around alone in the woods—getting caught in that trap—it's been like a nightmare."

"I know very well. I've known for years. But don't be too shocked. It need make no difference, to anyone."

"You poor, blessed, crazy child. What can I say that makes any real sense?"

Tracy removed her hand from his arm and stood unassisted. "I can say all that need be said. I could have been much worse off. If I'd been left behind in Virginia, for instance. What I keep remembering is that we're not just two people. You're more than the head of a family. You're like one of those patriarchs in the Bible. You're the chieftain of a clan, of a tribe, almost. And I can be glad I have a place in it. Think of me as a kind of concubine. Not one who will ever be taken into your tent, naturally. But one who is always standing ready to serve you. That's an infinitely more tolerable role than not being here at all."

Duncan laughed unsteadily. "If you're trying to tempt me with this talk of tents and all, you're certainly succeeding. Concubine, indeed. If this were sixteen years ago I'd not be long making you repent that taunt."

"But it's not. It's sixteen years too late. I know that. Better than you do. Or even than Agatha does."

"I still can't believe any of this. I've been so used to seeing you around, always so busy and serene. Of course Agatha and Olivia have had their heads together off and on. Trust wives to sniff out anything the least bit difficult about another woman. But they'd decided it was Garett."

"There's one advantage in your knowing. I won't have to be so desperately on guard, because you, too, will be on guard. Now shouldn't we be getting on? Look. I can not only stand alone. I can walk alone. See."

On the island the main party of fugitives crouched in the darkness under the willows, shivering with cold, plucking at the frost particles forming on their wet garments, and nursing their general and special anxieties. All, except Louisa and the two younger children who had been carried, had become soaked to the waist in crossing the marsh, as again and again they had broken through the thin crusting of ice over the invisible pools.

"Anyway, Duncan's moving around," said Garett. "He's keeping warmer than we are."

"Whatever can be keeping him so long?" complained Agatha. "I told him it was useless to look for her in the dark."

"Duncan has long proved able to take care of himself," said Louisa. "But what can ever have happened to that poor girl?"

"You think more of her than of your own flesh and blood," said Agatha.

"No," said Louisa quietly, "but just next after them."

Eric, keeping a grip on Ken's belt, pushed to the edge of the willows and stared into the darkness across the marsh. He felt triply deprived. The two people who meant so much to him were out there. And his father had refused to take him along in his search. Betsey crawled to his feet and wriggled upright at his elbow. She peered out over the swamp toward the woods beyond which lay the station.

"No fire yet," she said.

"What fire?"

"First off, Injuns allus burns yuh out."

Ken started with an apprehension which had not previously occurred to him.

"You can't see the station from here," said Eric. "You're just talking."

"You'd see the fire agin the sky fast enough—oncet they set her off," said Betsey.

Lina touched Eric on the other side.

"That pine stub back there," she said. "Yuh climb thet yuh could see clean to the station."

Eric went with her. The stub, towering above the matted willows, was a dead pine, drowned when the river made one of its perpetual changes of course. It was too large, however, to reach around and the lowest branch was above Eric's reach. Lina leaned against the trunk and braced herself.

"Climb up on me," she said, "and yuh kin ketch hold thet branch."

Her body which he remembered as so soft and yielding now felt remarkably hard and firm. He stepped on her arched back, balancing himself by holding to her upraised arms, stepped to her shoulders, grasped the branch, and pulled himself up. Other branches were within reach. He climbed higher and presently, over the massed shadow of the woods, made out the faint gray blob of the pond. Of the mound or station he could see nothing but he could tell by the line of the stream exactly where the station was and that there was no spark of light about it. He tried to imagine the Indians crouched in that darkness shrouding the station, waiting for the first streak of daylight to make their screeching assault. They might already have taken Tracy, his father, too. He looked at the east. It seemed already to be paling. Hastily he slid down to the low branch and swung to the ground, catching hold of Lina to regain his balance. Again she felt soft and yielding. Then he remembered Ken and let go of her. He ran back to Betsey at the edge of the marsh.

"Where's Ken?"

"He tuk off."

"Why didn't you stop him?"

"Whut fer?" Betsey laughed. "He kept a-whinin' 'bout fire and thet pup o' his'n and then he tuk off."

"Which way?"

"End o' the island where we-uns come acrost."

Eric plunged through the willows and across the marsh to the firmer ground beyond. Rounding the upthrust root spread of a fallen poplar he came upon his father. Tracy was standing beside him. It was getting enough lighter for him to see how tired his father was.

"I keep telling you I can walk perfectly well," Tracy was saying.

"Eric," said his father, swinging around.

Eric's immense relief that they were safe became mingled with the shame of the confession he must make.

"Ken got away."

"But you were told to watch him."

"Betsey started talking about the Indians burning the station. I climbed a tree to look. And Ken got to thinking about his dog in the fire. Anyway, he got away."

His father no longer looked tired.

"He must have cut across through the woods or we would have run into him."

"I'm all right," said Tracy. "I can make it the rest of the way."

"The island's right over there," said his father. "Tell them to stay there until they hear from me. You come with me, Eric."

Eric sprang forward. His father set straight off along the bank toward the point. Eric kept at his heels. So many people had come and gone this way last night that it had become a trail anybody could follow, let alone an Indian. His not hanging on to Ken was a terrible thing. But it was almost worth it to have it lead to his being allowed to accompany his father to look for him. At the point his father stopped and grasped his arm.

"There's been enough foolishness for one night. So see that you do exactly what I say. Stay a good fifty yards behind me. Keep me in sight, though. Whatever I signal you to do— do it. If anything happens, no matter what, turn and run. I'm counting on you to take word back to our people on the island. Understand?"

Eric nodded. His father set off at a trot again along the path toward Revel Rock. As he neared the foot of the mound he left the path and crawled in the shadow of the brush alongside. Eric did likewise. It was getting definitely lighter now. The bushes and trees were beginning to take shape. He speculated on how you managed to see an Indian in the woods before he first saw you. He was relieved that he was not more scared than he seemed to be. He was scared some, of course. The trigger finger of his right hand kept trembling and the back of his neck felt hot and cold by turns. But he was not scared enough to wish he were somewhere else. He was glad he was here following his father and not still squatting back there under the willows on the island. His father was creeping up the side of the mound, keeping his head up to look around, and every few feet pausing to listen. It came over Eric that this was the hour the Indians were supposed to attack. They must be all around in the woods. Betsey and Lina could remember their cabin being burned three times and one other time when they did not run off soon enough when the Indians came at them when they were still in it and they were saved only because a company of rangers out scouting just happened to be near enough to hear the hulla-baloo. Betsey said Indians when they first jumped out of the woods always whooped and yelled and made all the noise they could in order to get people so upset they had no idea what they were doing. Some such uproar as that might break out here any minute now. He controlled the impulse to run forward to join his father. If he could see him so clearly from this distance then the hidden Indians must also be able to see him. Then he saw something else. There were columns of smoke pouring from both the station's main chimneys. The fires they had left must long since have died down. Someone must have been in the kitchen to have got them going again. Suddenly his father got to his feet, ran upright to the station, and looked in at a loophole.

All Duncan could see through the loophole was the fireplace in the end of the kitchen toward the office. It had been heaped with logs and was burning with a warmth he could feel against his face at his distance. He moved to another loophole that gave him a view of the other fireplace in which also logs had been heaped. Ken was asleep on the hearth, his arms wrapped around the dog who was also asleep. In Louisa's armchair, drawn close to the fire, sat Caleb Lewis. He had removed his wet leggings and moccasins to dry them and sat with his bare legs stretched out toward the heat. Beside him on the floor was a plate with remnants of corn bread and ham he must have found in the larder. He was smoking one of Duncan's clay pipes and sipping from a bottle of Duncan's brandy. From time to time he looked about him contemplatively with the unmistakable air of a man able to take a proprietary satisfaction in his surroundings.

Duncan waved to Eric to come on and walked to the door. Caleb looked around at his entrance but did not get up.

"You appear to have got back early," said Duncan.

Caleb grinned. It was the first time Duncan had ever seen a change of expression cross his face.

"So do you."

"We've been hiding in the woods."

Caleb nodded. His grin had faded but his eyes remained amused. Duncan continued his uncomfortable explanation.

"Olen saw them—the Indians, I mean."

"So did I. About an hour before light. Just as they were breaking camp."

"What makes you so sure they weren't after us?"

"Because I know what they were after."

"Olen says they were some of your Shawnee—and painted for war."

"So they were. That was because they were on their way to
Fort McIntosh to tell the Delaware and Wyandot they are
fools to sign a treaty."

"Do I gather, then, that our only mistake was in taking
alarm too soon? That we may still expect trouble from—
your friends?"

"That is possible. But the time to hide in the woods is not
yet. Before that time comes I will be able to tell you."

Eric came in. His mouth fell open when he saw Caleb and
Ken, but when he saw the look on his father's face he instantly
and silently closed it again.

"Go tell our people on the island it was a false alarm," said
Duncan.

Eric ran out. Caleb rose and drew a folded bit of paper from
a pouch at his belt.

"A letter for you from General Clark."

Duncan took the letter and broke the seals. Caleb began to
draw on his leggings and moccasins. The letter read:

Dear Colonel Jordan:
I met Geo Morgan at the Muskingum he says the latest Word
at Pitt is that the Delaware and Wyandot are coming in Caleb
tells me the Shawnee are Divided some want war and Some want
peace I told him to tell them they can have Whichever they
want Geo Morgan knew Corbit Revel he tells me that Back about
1772 he saw Caleb Lewis in Corbit's camp on what is now your
Creek Caleb was then a boy of maybe Seventeen Corbit had
bought him off the Shawnee and later that year sent him to
New Orleans to work for a trader and learn English Caleb was
mighty close mouthed with me but he says he spent the next
eight Years at Sea neither Geo or me ever heard of his being
around this part of the Country during the War I think I
would have heard about it if he had been and had Sided with
the English or Indians I know about and Remember all of them
Rascals My opinion after Watching him for a day and a night is
that he is like a young Horse that has not yet been gentled he
could turn out to be a real Good one or a real bad one he is
still thick with the Shawnee but he has some hankering to be
a White Man he can be some Good to you this winter and
I will keep on asking about him at Pitt and Louisville and
Vincennes and wherever I am at my advice is for the Present to
keep an eye on him but to keep him around if you can put up
with him.

Y'r ob'd't servant
G. R. *Clark*

Duncan looked up from the letter. Caleb had his rifle under
his arm and was moving toward the door.

"Why haven't you told me that you knew Corbit Revel?"

"You did not ask me."

"Why should it have occurred to me to ask you? . . . I take it you on your side have had no idea I was his kinsman?"

"Yes. I knew that."

"Then when you came here you expected to find us here?"

"No. But I expected you to come sooner or later."

"Do you propose to continue to live here, on your side of the creek?"

"Yes."

"What led you to select this valley?"

"As a boy I camped here. Many times with the Shawnee and after that with Corbit. I have been many places. I like this one best."

"You speak of him as if you had been especially attached to him."

"I had reason to be."

"Aside from his ransoming you from captivity?"

"Yes. He treated me like a son."

"Yet in the one letter we ever had from him—written from Pittsburgh the year after he had sent you to New Orleans— he made no mention of you."

A shadow crossed Caleb's face.

"When a man is old and sick and alone and knows he is dying, he thinks first of his own family."

"We might as well come right out with it, Mr. Lewis. Do you feel we have usurped some claim you might have had here?"

"No. This place belonged to Corbit. The Shawnee gave it to him. He gave it to you. It now belongs to you."

"I am glad you can take so broad a view. Let us hope we may continue to prove good neighbors."

Caleb nodded, took another long look around the room, and opened the door. Duncan hesitated, smothered his irritation, and strode after him.

"Drop in on us any time you feel like it," he said, offering his hand.

Caleb's taking it was a purely formal gesture. In his eyes there was another faint glint of amusement. He nodded again and set off for his cabin. Duncan considered going to meet his returning people, realized how tired he was, and sat down on the doorstep to wait.

The others came streaming in, their return as noisy with relief as their departure had been silent with apprehension. Garett, staggering with fatigue but still grinning, patted the log wall.

"Nothing like a night in the swamps to make you realize what a palace we inhabit."

Agatha flew to Duncan. "We could imagine we were safe where we were but you never were. You were always off somewhere. Never has there been a night so long. Is Ken really quite all right?"

In the midst of the weary rejoicing, Frank remained dour. He waited until the Slovers straggled into the yard, at the end of the procession, to deliver his pronunciamento.

"The big reason you bundled them along with us," he said, pointing a stubby, accusing finger at Duncan, "was because you claimed they knowed so much about the woods and about Indians." The finger came around to stab at Olen. "What do they know? Nothin'. Last night showed that. They ain't up to telling an Indian from a tamarack. They keep Indians off our backs? They ain't men enough to scratch the lice off their own. All of 'em put together ain't half so much good to us as Ken's dog."

The Slovers listened attentively, as though they did not wish to miss one syllable of Frank's outburst. They were not offended. While he was speaking they kept nudging one another, and when he had finished they whooped with laughter. They were forever being seized by spasms of private amusement at moments suggesting to no one else anything but discomfort or dismay.

"One thing yuh'll larn, Frank," said Olen, sobering and giving Frank a kindly pat, "if'n yuh live long enough. Yuh'll larn that it's a sight smarter t'run forty time when there ain't no real reason to run than to set tight jest oncet when there be."

"All of you get some rest," said Duncan. "Because beginning this afternoon there's not going to be any rest for anybody until we've got a stockade up."

Louisa, leaning on Tracy's arm, turned in the middle of the kitchen to wait for Duncan.

"I must admit that for once I agree with Frank," she said. "The Slovers are lazy, dirty, mischievous, stupid, and cowardly. They even laugh at things only imbeciles could laugh at. They have no single redeeming feature."

That afternoon, however, the Slovers emerged from their cabin, axes in hand. They rushed to the task of cutting palisade poles with the excited urgency of farmers getting in hay when clouds threaten.

"The lesser of two evils," said Garett. "They fear Indians more than they hate work."

Duncan's satisfaction with the development was diminished by the explanation speedily volunteered by Betsey.

"Caleb he tol' em to git a-goin'. Whenever Caleb he jest gives 'em a look they jump right out'n their britches."

"Caleb is in a position to be very helpful to us," said Duncan.

"Thet's whut Paw says. Paw says it's mighty lucky fer us Caleb he come along."

"I'm sure it is—for all of us. We're all in this together."

Betsey eyed him sharply, trying to guess whether his cheerfulness was genuine or merely to cover up her success in baiting him.

"We-uns is all behind the same stockade—thet's fer sure."

The next night Caleb took advantage of Duncan's neighborly invitation to drop in. The Jordans were still at supper. He declined the suggestion that he join them at the table and took a seat beside the fireplace in the end of the kitchen toward the office. This was the hearth about which the family was accustomed to gather in the evening, leaving the other end of the room to the Negroes and their domestic duties. To all attempts to include him in the table conversation he replied with monosyllables or not at all. He seemed merely disposed to sit stolidly as an Indian in the warmth of the fire and from his post as bystander to listen intently to whatever was said and to watch even more intently the expression on the face of whoever was saying it.

"Notice his eyes," whispered Garett to Agatha. "Damme if they're not as yellow as a panther's. Fancy a panther choosing our company."

"They're more green than yellow," murmured Agatha. "But as unsociable as a cat's—you're right about that. He makes me as uncomfortable as I could wish we made him."

When the others gathered about him at the fireplace, Caleb remained as unresponsive but, at this so much closer range, continued to stare, first at one and then at another, as intently as before. His glance tended to pass over Duncan and Garett, as though he had by now come to some conclusion about them. It was the several women who absorbed him. The conversation flagged.

"Why don't you read to us, Tracy?" proposed Louisa.

This was an evening diversion to which they frequently turned. Among the few books brought with them was a volume of Shakespeare's tragedies. Tracy leaved through the pages reflectively.

"Othello," suggested Garett.

Tracy found the place and began to read. She had a clear

and spirited reading voice which, without overdramatizing, attached color and meaning to the lines. Caleb gave no indication that the words meant anything out of the ordinary to him. But during the whole of two acts he watched the play of expression over her face as she read, his eyes straying occasionally to her hair shimmering in the candlelight or to her hands as she turned a page. Then, as though some unspoken question had been answered for him, he turned his stare on Agatha and Olivia. Olivia appeared to take no notice, but Agatha frowned, fidgeted, kept changing her position, and finally rose.

"I'm sorry, Tracy. You know how much I ordinarily enjoy your reading. But tonight I'm very tired. Please keep on. Good night, Mother. Good night, all. Good night, Mr. Lewis."

She withdrew. Tracy looked around to estimate the wish of the others about her continuing to read. Caleb got up, crossed to the door to pick up his rifle leaning there against the wall, nodded an abrupt good evening to the company, and went out.

"Personally," said Garett, "I find his calls more tolerable when he brings his Indians."

Duncan joined Agatha in their room.

"I can't stand his looking at me that way," she said. "He keeps watching my face as though he was bound to know what I might be thinking. And not only that. Once in a while" —her hands fluttered in a swift protective gesture toward her bosom and thighs—"it's as though he were seeing right through my clothes."

As so often when she was serious Duncan took refuge in lightness.

"Who could blame him—with a figure like yours?"

"You're a man, Duncan—and my husband. Act like it. I am your wife, and your wife is not for him even to look at."

The next night, and the one after, Caleb returned to sit in the chimney corner, as silent and as observant as before. Each evening after an hour or so he rose and, still silent, withdrew. Tracy had not been asked to read on either of these following nights. Instead the Jordans resorted defensively to another of their evening diversions. They played cards. Caleb declined their perfunctory invitation that he take a hand or at any rate sit with them and look on. The sole purpose of his calls seemed to continue to be the opportunity to sit and study the women of the household. When the door had closed upon him the third time the Jordans laid down their cards and looked at each other.

"This just can't go on," said Olivia. "We've always had

such pleasant evenings together. He's ruined them for us."
She looked resentfully at Garett. "When he's here even Garett
—who usually welcomes anything that makes us uncomfortable—gets so annoyed he takes half a dozen extra drinks."

"Tonight only five and a half, my dear." Garett lifted his
half glass of whisky, contemplated it, and tossed it down.
"Six, only now. Seems to me I've heard something about
Indian courtships. Doesn't the brave hang around the wigwam
until the object of his affections takes some notice of him?
I believe the next step is some sort of trial involving a
blanket. Tracy?"

"If that's so," said Tracy calmly, "in this instance he will
have rather a long wait."

"Actually," said Duncan, "the man's simply devoured by
curiosity, just as the Indians were. He's never before been
around people like us and everything about us is novel to
him."

"What disturbs me more than his manners," said Tracy—"if
you and Duncan will forgive my saying so, Agatha—is the
way he has captivated Eric. Eric idolizes him because he
knows the wilderness, how to hunt and track and all about
Indians and everything else Eric is wild to know. Eric is
over there with him every day."

"I don't like that either," said Agatha, "and I think it should
be stopped. Though Duncan thinks those are things Eric
should have a chance to learn. But what I really can't stand
—and Duncan also refuses to see—is the way he's pushing in
on us, as though he owned the place. The Slovers have done
more work these last three days than the last three months.
Why? He told them to. We seem reasonably safe from
Indians. Why? He is their friend. No wonder he feels he's the
same as commander here."

Garett put down his refilled glass. His voice was suddenly
firm.

"That'll be his longest wait of all."

The brothers' eyes met with understanding. For a moment
both their faces were as cold and expressionless as Caleb's
could ever be.

"Now that we're getting down to fundamentals," said Duncan, "may I say this: Nothing's so important to me as to do
whatever we can to hold this place until we're well enough
established to be certain we can go on holding it. To do that
I'll take any kind of help from anybody."

"Agatha's talking nonsense," said Louisa. "We all know
who's in command here. And if that man has any doubts,
either Duncan or Garett will be able to put him straight fast

enough. But there *is* something, Duncan, to deal with now, before worse comes of it. He isn't sitting around here harboring some simple courting idea. Anybody can see that. He's after a woman, any woman. He has more eyes for Agatha and Olivia than he has for Tracy. He struts about like a dog in heat. That's what's got to stop without any wait whatever."

"We could most certainly do with less frequent calls," said Duncan. "I'll have a talk with him tomorrow."

The next day brought the first hard blizzard of the winter. Duncan, leaning into the blasts of driving snow, crossed the stream which, now frozen, could be crossed at any point, and struggled through the drifts toward Caleb's cabin. Taking no account of the weather, other than that the snow on the ground eased the task of dragging logs into piles for later burning, Caleb and Daisy were still at work enlarging his clearing. The howling of the wind made speech nearly impossible. Caleb led the way to his cabin.

Duncan was struck by the spare neatness and orderliness of the single room. Everything was scrubbed and scoured and in its place. Even the blankets on the pole-and-rawhide bed were stretched taut. He remembered Clark's report of the presumed years at sea. This cabin in the woods was as shipshape as one aboard a man-of-war. Caleb turned to face him and waited calmly. Duncan had been casting about for the precise words with which to make his announcement. The man's easy assurance, bordering on insolence, hardened his purpose.

"I came to say that it would seem to us more suitable if your visits were rather less frequent."

"You have some reason?"

"We have. To put it bluntly, our womenfolk have gained the uncomfortable impression that you are looking them over, as it were, to determine which one you prefer."

"That is so. It is not good for a man to live alone."

"You have a woman."

"Daisy? She is only for this winter. And she is an Indian. I plan to stay here, and next spring I will need a white woman."

"Then you will need to look more widely. The only one available in our household, Miss Carter, has taken a strong— possibly an unreasoning but nevertheless a strong—dislike to you."

"There are two others who are still young and who have learned what it is like to live with a man."

Duncan controlled his temper. In order to stress his innate superiority to this man who was so near a savage it was necessary that his own attitude remain undeviatingly civilized.

"Unhappily each is already supplied with a man."

There was again that glint of amusement in Caleb's eyes.

"You have come to a country, Colonel Jordan, where men seldom die of old age. It is a country where young women may any day become young widows."

"If you mean that as some sort of a challenge, I accept it. Meanwhile, since we must continue to be neighbors, please feel free to call at the station whenever you have business there, but let us postpone further social calls until we are better acquainted."

Caleb accepted the ruling with the same impassive formality with which he had accepted Duncan's earlier handclasp.

"It is your house," he said.

There was for a second the same faint glint in his eyes. But Duncan was no longer so sure that this indicated a kind of unaccountable amusement. He was reminded of the alien inscrutability of the Indians about whose actual state of mind, as they had lined up inside his door that night, he had been able to make no slightest guess.

The blizzard continued into the second night. The next morning Eric was the first to venture out. He came floundering back frantic with excitement.

"They've gone," he exclaimed. "Caleb and Daisy have gone. The cabin's shut up and they took everything with them. You can see their tracks. They've gone."

"Thank heaven for that," breathed Agatha.

"Take heart, my young friend," said Garett. "Your paladin has doubtless but resorted for the winter to the more congenial precincts of his Shawnee kind. Spring may return him to us —worse luck."

"No," insisted Eric. "He planned to stay here all winter. I know he did. Something's happened."

"Let's hope," murmured Louisa, "to him."

January

The first blizzard was succeeded by another and then, after a week of intermittent heavy snow, by a third. When this one ceased to howl, it left in its wake the stillness of an intense cold. The timbers of the buildings groaned. Limbs snapped from trees. The snow underfoot creaked. The pond and the stream became one solid block of ice. The Ohio itself froze over, so changing the familiar landscape that to the people of the station it seemed that morning that they had awakened to a different world. They were more relieved than oppressed by this final weight of winter. The frozen river seemed no longer an avenue of easy approach for whoever might chance to be abroad and the snowbanked forest had again become their shield against the distant and the unknown. Behind these comforting barriers they could rest for a time in seclusion and peace. Encircled by their newly finished stockade and assured by the existence in the storeroom of ample food to supply them into midsummer, they settled by their firesides for a pleasant respite which they could feel they had earned by their recent labors and anxieties.

The one interference with their ease was Duncan's insistence on a regular guard mount. Every hour of the day or night, he was determined, there must be a man on watch at the gate. It was the usually apprehensive Olen who protested the most loudly against what he maintained was an altogether unnecessary precaution. He attempted to explain the facts of wilderness winter life to Duncan.

"Whilst there's snow on the ground we-uns got no call to fret about Injuns. They never lay up nuthin' fer winter so this time o' year they's all busy scratchin' around fer somethin' to eat. More'n thet they never like to hunt fer trouble nowhere's thet's way off from where they belong account yuh can't go nowheres in the snow without leavin' tracks. It goes agin' the grain with a Injun if'n other folks kin see right off where he's

75

bin and whut he's bin up to. Injuns ain't a-goin' to bother us none till the snow goes off in the spring."

Nevertheless Duncan continued to insist and the regular guard was established. The man on the gate could always tell when his relief was due because he could hear the distant faint chime of Louisa's clock, and with four-hour watches divided among eleven men there was no great interruption of the station's indolence. But as the days crept the long hours of drowsy huddling about fires began to lose their first appeal. Minor bickerings broke out. The perpetual feud between Lymans and Slovers developed new edges. Meanwhile the continued cold had given their many fires an appetite for fuel that had much reduced the wood supply.

Appreciating the twin need for work and wood, Duncan organized a woodcutting project in which all were to participate. He had learned by now that the Slovers' congenital aversion to work was only to be counteracted by a suggestion of play. Therefore he termed the community effort a woodcutting bee. A fire was built in the wood lot. In the ashes edging the fire Geneva kept rows of sweetened corn pone toasting. Beside them simmered a kettle of pickled buffalo tongue. Another steaming pot of ginger-flavored water was laced at suitable intervals with a gurgling contribution from a demijohn of rum.

Frank had knocked together a stout sledge to haul the wood to the station. The incline to the mound was sprinkled with water which immediately froze into a smooth glaze. With the entire corps of women and children pulling on the ropes, enormous loads of wood were snaked with ease up to the growing pile in the stockade. Duncan and Luke and Ned and Clem formed teams on the two-man saws to cut the larger logs into lengths for splitting, but it was upon the Slover axemen that the chief burden fell. Laughing and yelling, they leaped to meet the challenge. With so many eyes observing their prowess they became engines of energy. Pausing only to snatch an occasional mouthful of corn pone and tongue or another dipperful of hot watered rum, they kept their axes flashing and whirling. Before the crash of a falling tree had ceased to echo, they had it trimmed and were beginning to cut it up. There was always a new load of split cordwood ready for each return of the sledge. By mid-afternoon the heap of wood in the station yard had reached the proportions of a two-month supply for all five fireplaces.

Meanwhile the team of women and children pulling the sledge under Frank's supervision had made a happy discovery. If, returning with the empty sledge, they climbed aboard at the top of the slope they were able to coast all the way back down to the wood lot. When Duncan announced a formal end to the woodcutting, the Slovers, Ned, Clem, and Luke immediately seized upon the sledge to take their turn. Their excited yells matched those the coasting had drawn from the women and children. After a second ride down this relatively modest incline the next step was a natural one. Beyond the wood lot there rose a considerable ridge. The snow was crusted hard enough and the trees sufficiently widely spaced to make this a slide with a much more interesting appeal. Here a far greater velocity was to be gained, there was the advantage that during its rapid descent the sledge must be guided in and out among the trees, and the final zest in that when at length it came hurtling out into the cleared area of the wood lot there were brush piles to be avoided and a studding of stumps bound sooner or later to overturn it. In the event so it proved. Every flight ended at some stage with the sledge's upset, throwing its passengers sprawling into snowbanks when they were lucky and into thickets or against trees when they were not. The forest rang with their whoops of delight.

At his mother's insistence that she be given another turn on the sledge now that its career had become so much more exciting, Jarot relinquished his place to her. As he stood by the fire, laughing at the next descent of the sledge, his fingers presently began to pluck at the empty air in the curve of his arm. His laugh stiffened into a grin and then into the brooding, trancelike mask that always accompanied his desperate fumbling with his mandiddle. Garett watched fascinated.

"What can he be trying to get at?" he asked Lina.

"He's jest a-hankerin'."

"Hankering for what?"

"Nobody knows fer sure. Could be he don't hisself. It's allus jest like he was a-tryin' to ketch somethin' only he never kin figger jest whut it is and so he never ketches up with it."

Mark, on duty at the gate, came out to the corner of the stockade and began calling that his time was up. Jacob, whose next watch it was, was extracted from the sledding party and dispatched to relieve him.

"Get Jat's mandiddle," said Garett, "and have Mark bring it down with him."

Jacob picked up his rifle from the stack leaning against a tree and plodded up to the gate. Mark, eager to have his turn on the sledge, came running down with the mandiddle. Garett thrust the instrument into Jarot's hands. His fingers closed upon it but, plucking now at the strings instead of empty air, plucked so gently that no more than the faintest whisper of sound was drawn forth while he seemed to sink more deeply than ever into his trance.

"I want to try something," said Garett. "Hey, you, Clem, Ned—let someone else ride in your place. You and Hebe and Geneva come over here. Now sing something—something loud and lively—and old."

There was a slight delay while Ned and Clem got their wind and the quartet conferred. Then they launched into "Clinch Mountain."

"Louder," demanded Garett.

For a time Jarot seemed unaware of the four Negroes singing lustily immediately in front of him, then suddenly he appeared to take notice of them. He cocked his head to listen, grinned, and at once began to play the air, very briskly and decisively.

"Why, he can play," exclaimed Garett.

"Fer sure he kin play," said Lina. "Now and then back home when folks craved to dance, he uster play fer 'em most the night."

During several verses Jarot appeared pleased and interested in the Negroes' vocal performance and his own share in it; then suddenly he ceased to accompany the quartet and relapsed into his strange, inward struggle.

"I believe I've got it," said Garett to Duncan. "The man's a thwarted genius. That's his trouble. He has in him strains of music which he can't quite capture. Or maybe it's lines of poetry. The birth pangs of creation—they're what he's grappling with."

"You may be right," said Duncan. "Though so far it seems an unrewarding quest. Meanwhile, it's getting late and I think Mother's beginning to get cold. We'll be moving along."

Picking up his rifle from the array against the tree, Duncan instructed the elder children to come in when they had watched one more descent of the sledge and started up toward the station with Louisa, Agatha, Tracy, Susie, and Chris. The sun was dipping behind the western woods. The short winter day was coming to an end. As the path veered past the corner of the stockage he saw that the gate was standing open. Impatient to reprimand Jacob, he strode on ahead of the others. As his view of the open gateway widened his anger mounted. Jacob was sitting in the snow banked against the Lyman cabin, his head back against the wall, his mouth hanging open. His reaction to his arduous day had been promptly to seize a first opportunity to take a nap.

Duncan was still a step away from the gateway when he

heard a call from Agatha. He turned to look back. All four
of the Slover dogs were racing up the slope. They swept on
past him, whining with vicious eagerness. Duncan leaped after
them and came to another stop in the gateway. The twilight
was rapidly darkening but there was still light enough to
reveal with terrifying clarity what was happening.

Three Indians, who must just have emerged into the yard
from the kitchen, were recoiling from the charging dogs. One
was John Turtle but both of the others were younger men
than any of that original five who had called with Caleb. John
Turtle sprang to the safety of the top of the woodpile. One
of the others kicked off the nearest dog and dove into the
Lyman cabin, slamming the door behind him. The third, now
beset by all four dogs, caught up a stick of wood with which
to ward them off and set his back against the wall of the
Negroes' cabin. The dogs were hardened killers, accustomed
to coping with wounded bears or packs of wolves and trained
especially to abominate Indians. They easily avoided the
swinging club and gathered themselves for the concerted
lunge which must bring down their prey. Duncan, still dis-
agreeably surprised by the presence of the Indians, was
nevertheless moved to run to the savages' assistance. But
John Turtle acted more quickly.

Expertly whipping arrows from the quiver on his back, he
shot four with such incredible rapidity that all seemed in
flight at once. Each transfixed one of the dogs. With his stick
of wood their intended victim began methodically to bash
in their heads as they writhed in agony about his feet. John
Turtle sprang down from the woodpile and advanced on
Duncan, grinning happily, his hand outstretched.

Jacob had been sighing and grunting as he passed through
the protracted throes that marked one of his awakenings.
His eyes opened in time to fall upon John Turtle's advance
and his hand reached out to grasp the rifle which he had left
leaning against the wall beside him when he had sat down.
It was not there. With the celerity of a jack coming out of its
box he shot upright, dove into the Lyman cabin, and slammed
the door behind him. It was the same door through which
the second Indian had darted, but after one muffled curse
from Jacob no further sound came from within.

John Turtle gripped Duncan's hand with his own right and
with his left tapped himself on the chest. "Friend," he said.
He tapped Duncan's chest. "Friend," he repeated. The other
Indian, still clutching his bloody club, moved forward to join
them.

Duncan permitted John Turtle to continue to shake his hand

and essayed an approximation of the Indian's infinitely cordial grin. He was acutely conscious of the presence of Agatha and the others, now clustered about him, staring in consternation at their unexpected guests and at the dead dogs.

"Go into the house," said Duncan quietly to Agatha. "Don't run. Just keep moving. And when you're inside bar the door. I'll keep these two talking. Everybody else will be here any minute."

In the shadows of the woods it was getting almost too dark to see, except near the fire. Cam watched the last careening descent of the sledge and its satisfying crash against a stump at the end of its run and turned back to the other tableau provided by Garett's still fascinated concentration on Jarot's creative torment. Suddenly her shrill voice rang clearly above the laughter of the sprawling tobogganers.

"Look, Uncle Garry. Look. An Indian just took all our rifles."

Everyone looked in the direction she was pointing. The Indian was no longer to be seen. But in the flickering shadows at the outer edges of the light cast by the fire the tree against which their rifles had been stacked was now bare. The response was unanimous. All began at once to run toward the station. From the woods behind them squealed three short sharp blasts of an Indian war whistle.

The fading light from without failed to penetrate the loopholes or the small windows in the wall on the side toward the yard so that it was dark as night in the kitchen. Louisa released Tracy's arm as they crossed the threshold.

"Good heavens," she sniffed. "They've been in here. A marvel that two Indians just being in a room should leave so strong a smell."

The others groped in after Louisa and Tracy and closed the door. Tracy felt her way along the table, took a candle from the basket on the shelf over the fireplace, and lighted it at one of the smoldering coals on the hearth. As she straightened she heard Agatha gasp. She spun around, holding up the candle. Ranged motionless as statues around the walls, their eyes catching and reflecting the dim glow of the candle, were the dark, bulky, fur-shrouded figures of twenty or more Indians.

In the yard Duncan could hear the pounding of feet as the party from the wood lot ran for the gate. He prolonged the ceremony of shaking hands with the second Indian. The fugitives came floundering through the gateway.

"Father," panted Eric. "An Indian stole all our rifles."

"Shut the gate," said Duncan, taking care to keep his

voice steady and calm. "We've got three of them here. We'll
hang on to them until our rifles are returned to us."

Eric swung the gate shut.

"Friend," said John Turtle. He tapped his chest and pointed
to the new arrivals. "Friend," he repeated. It was now so dark
that his face was indistinct except for the whites of his eyes
and the whiteness of his teeth as he continued to grin. From
his parted lips came then the low coo of a dove.

Every door within the stockade opened and some thirty-five
or forty Indians emerged into the yard. A half dozen of those
from the Lyman and Slover cabins carried pine-knot torches
which cast a lurid glow over the array of dark faces and dark
figures. None was painted and only three carried rifles. But
from the fact that only a few were equipped with bows and
arrows Duncan judged that most had firearms that had been
laid aside somewhere close at hand.

"Hold it," he said to his people. "Don't make a move."

He glanced around at them, apprehensive lest one of them
make some useless and merely provocative gesture of belligerence. He need not have feared. Garett, his arm around Olivia,
was, of course, as steady as a rock. Eric merely gaped, as
though at some preternaturally theatrical performance. Ken
was holding Rupert clasped in his arms, his fingers tightly
closed over his snout to keep him from barking. Cam edged
forward, trustingly, toward her father. The Lymans, as though
unable to believe what they were seeing, had been shocked into
total inertia. The Slovers, who understood all too well what
they were seeing, had become immediately as dispirited as
though already they were captives. Jacob, apparently none
the worse for his brief sojourn among the savages with whom
he had shared his refuge, stumbled from the Lyman cabin and
edged along the wall to join the group of whites.

The Indians swarmed forward but after some elbowing for
points of vantage in the front rank did not press too closely
in upon the conference between John Turtle and Duncan.

"Friend—friend—friend," John Turtle was chanting loudly
while continually pointing in vigorous and alternate succession
at various members of his company and at individuals among
the whites grouped behind Duncan.

"Friend," agreed Duncan.

John Turtle snatched a bow from a youth beside him and
extended it to Duncan. "Friend," he said, reaching for Duncan's rifle. "Swap? Swap, no?"

It was not a situation in which a single rifle was of much
use. Duncan released his to John Turtle's grasp. The bow he
received in exchange had no string. He held it up to indicate

this deficiency. John Turtle laughed merrily and discharged Duncan's rifle into the air. By cheerful gestures he indicated that they were now equally unarmed as was the only right and proper case with such good friends.

"Friend," he said, clapping Duncan heartily on the shoulder. "Eat, no?"

"We'll just have to put up with this as best we can," said Duncan to his people. "I suggest going to your houses and mixing with them as little as you can manage."

"Eat," he said, nodding to John Turtle.

Pushing through the circle of Indians he strode to the kitchen. Tracy had lighted a dozen candles, filling the room with a blaze of illumination. Garett, Olivia, Eric, Cam, and Ken were able to follow him without being deterred by the Indians.

"What are they going to do to us?" asked Louisa.

"Nothing for the moment, except probably steal us blind," said Duncan. "All of you go with Agatha to our room. That is the most out of the way. Stay there and stay together. If any of them insist upon coming in give them anything they seem to want."

Snatching one of the candles he ran through the office and unlocked the door to the storeroom. With one of the spare axes there he began to break up the three remaining kegs of spirits—two of whisky and one of brandy. The liquor gushing out of the floor sent up choking fumes. Before he had swung his axe at the brandy keg John Turtle ran in and caught his arm.

"No. No. No," he expostulated. "Friend."

He was heart stricken. He could not find gestures sufficiently eloquent to express his disappointment and surprise and dismay that Duncan had so soon betrayed the bond of good-fellowship which had been established between them. Other Indians crowded in. The sight and smell of so much good whisky wasted brought the first dark scowls to mar the pleasure all had so far taken in the occasion. Duncan cast one last look around at the well-stocked storeroom and forced a hospitable grin. He indicated for them to help themselves.

Pushing through the press of Indians crowding the doorway, he returned to the kitchen, into which more of the Indians from the yard were rushing. They were muttering excitedly but their complacency was restored by the discovery that there remained an unbroken keg of brandy. There soon developed a boisterous procession to and from the storeroom from which each emerged clutching a ham, a side of bacon, a sack of corn meal, a crock of honey, or a string of buffalo jerky. Geneva plucked at Duncan's sleeve. The four Negroes were huddled in a corner.

"They won't let us into our place," she reported.

Evidently it was there the Indians' missing rifles had been deposited.

"Then you'll just have to get along with them in here," said Duncan. "Show them how to cook whatever they want. Cook it for them if they want you to."

The Negroes nodded. Their first panic was beginning to pass. They had already sensed that the Indians recognized in them a certain kinship of color, that for them the Indian protestations of friendliness were possibly genuine. Duncan went out into the yard. Beside the doorstep an Indian was expertly cutting up the carcasses of the dogs. A large fire, fed by logs from the new woodpile, brightly lighted the whole interior of the stockade. As evidence that John Turtle, in the midst of all the wild hubbub, was still keeping some sort of order, two Indians with rifles were standing before the door of the Negroes' quarters and there were two others on guard at the gate.

Duncan gathered up an armful of wood to account for his moving across the yard toward the Slover cabin. The Indian sentries merely watched him. The Slovers had not troubled to build up their fire. They were crouched shivering on the cold floor, too dejected even to try to keep watch through their loopholes. Duncan threw a few sticks on the coals.

"I tried to spill all the hard liquor," he said. "But they got a half barrel of brandy. That's more than enough to get the whole pack of them blind drunk. If we watch our chance we may be able to make a break for the woods before the night's over."

"No use," said Olen heavily.

"We've got to do something. We can't just sit here while they work themselves up to the pitch of knocking us all in the head."

"No use to run," said Olen. "Not with the tracks we'd leave in this snow. Nuthin' they'd like better'n the fun o' runnin' us down."

Duncan rubbed the back of his neck thoughtfully as he considered the pointedness of this observation.

"Then maybe we're wrong to try to stay clear of them. Maybe we should mix with them instead. They keep claiming they're our friends. Maybe if we did they'd get to feeling that they actually are."

Olen brightened a trifle.

"I'd surely crave to git me one last dipper o' likker whilst I still got me a neck to pour it down."

"Olen," remonstrated Polly. "Mebbe yer a-goin' to die but it ain't fittin' to die dead drunk."

The Lymans refused to budge from the refuge of their cabin.

"The end which is coming to us this night," said Frank, "is the end I foretold when we came to this accursed place. But we will not forgather with the heathen. We will spend our last hours preparing ourselves by meditation and prayer."

Duncan led his own family out into the kitchen. The entrance of the Jordan and Slover women and children upon the scene of festivity stirred the Indians to new and more exuberant manifestations of friendliness. They singled out the two youngest, Chris and little Susie, for special attention, petting and patting them and forcing on them offerings of food.

"They're said to dote on children," said Garett. "Maybe they really do."

"They're obviously still trying to seem friendly," said Duncan, "in their own benighted way."

One minor incident threatened for a moment this agreeable atmosphere of tumultuous amity. An Indian who had taken it upon himself to preside over the cooking preparations sighted the fat little dog in Ken's arms and snatched it from him. Ken burst into immediate wild protest. He pursued the kidnaper, pummeling him with his fists. His counterattack attracted general Indian attention. There were roars of laughter which presently were mingled with cries of encouragement. The tide of opinion turned entirely in Ken's favor. The dog was restored to him, his assailant reproved, and, amidst many congratulations for his temerity, he was assured that his pet would not again be molested.

The interminable handshakings of which the Indians seemed never to tire went on and on. The keg of brandy, its top knocked out, had been brought out and set up on the table where it might be dipped into the more conveniently. Many of the Indians were already beginning to show the effects, though so far it was only making them more merry and more amiable. The outside kitchen door had been propped open and there was much traffic to and from the three centers of food preparation, the two kitchen fireplaces and the big fire in the yard.

"Look, Duncan," moaned Agatha. "Look. Our cows."

A number of Indians were coming through the gateway with dismembered quarters of the two milk cows. One of them was holding a set of cow's horns to his head and greatly amusing his fellows by bawling as though to call a calf. Another had wrapped himself in one of the cow's bloody hides. The advent of the butchering party was welcomed with yells of approbation by the Indians about the fire.

"Perhaps the time will come when we can even a few scores," said Duncan. "But that time is not tonight."

After her first panic had subsided, Geneva had begun to take an interest in the cooking arrangements at her fireplace. A lifetime of purveying to her masters had taught her that there was no more certain road to approval. The establishment's largest pot, which she had slung on its crane over the fire, had clearly become the one to which the Indians were looking with the greatest anticipation. Every Indian was attending to the grilling on sticks and forks and ramrods of his own selections of ordinary meat, but it was this great kettle of boiling water which it was, appropriately, her good fortune to tend, for which the most desirable delicacies were being assembled. She accepted and dumped into it with nods of slightly surprised endorsement a sack of corn meal, a sack of dried peas, a basket of pounded pecans, and a whole ham for flavoring. On her own initiative she surreptitiously added a handful of kitchen herbs and a heaping spoonful of her precious pepper. But she clung at the mantel for support, her co-operative mood totally disrupted, when she saw that the principal ingredients for this culinary masterpiece were to be the heads of the four Slover dogs and the cows' entire intestines complete with natural contents.

Betsey squatted in a corner, her arms wrapped around her knees, watching the room with bright, sharp eyes. No ill fortune she had in all her bitterness wished these people could have equaled what now had come to them. And it was getting worse by the minute. The Indians, after all their early preparations to feast upon the station's bounty, had developed a so much greater interest in drinking that they had little left in eating. They had discovered the barrel of cider in the storeroom and were using that instead of water as a thinner for the brandy. They were drinking the mixture not in sips or swallows but in gulps. She had often heard that Indians never drank to feel pleasant or to be sociable. They knew no other aim than to get drunk as fast as they could. And when they got drunk they got crazier drunk than any white man ever could. Already they were yelling, singing, dancing, pushing one another over tables and benches, pouring drinks over each other. Soon they would be quarreling and then fighting among themselves. It would not be long after they had

reached that pitch of excitement before their knives and
hatchets would be red with other blood than their own.

She took particular satisfaction in watching the pale,
strained faces of the Jordan women. They liked to keep their
house so clean. Now it was filthier than any pigsty. They liked
to stand off from common folks. Now they were jammed tight
in the middle of a pack of stinking Indians. They liked to
think nothing was good enough for them. Now they were
having it as bad as anybody on this earth could ever have it.
They were beginning to guess that what was coming to them
was just getting started. But they had not yet begun to guess
how very much worse it was going to get. So far the Indians
were still feeling playful. But even when they were just fooling
there was no telling what to expect. Their sense of humor
was tickled by things nobody else in the world would think
of laughing at. A sample of this was going on now. A fat,
middle-aged Indian, weaving with drunkenness, his face
smeared with grease from a beef rib he had been gnawing,
had pulled down his breach clout and was looking around for
a spot upon which to relieve himself. Suddenly inspired, he
made for the fire in which he produced a great hissing and
sputtering. Geneva jumped back just in time. Her scream of
horrified disbelief attracted general attention, which turned at
once into a general roar of laughter. The next minute a dozen
other Indians were imitating the first one, against table legs,
against the wall, against each other or whoever chanced to
be within reach. Betsey began to laugh hysterically. It would
not be much longer before it would take actions far more
outrageous than these to keep them entertained. She was
resigned to the certainty that she herself would not live
through the night. Meanwhile she could watch the Jordans,
as she was watching Duncan now. He was white-faced, shaking with rage.

Then, as suddenly, she sobered. There was something oddly
out of key in the performance. It was like watching somebody
gathering himself to take a jump and then seeing him slowly
sit down instead. Duncan was shepherding his women and
children toward the door beside the kitchen fireplace that led
to his and Agatha's bedroom. Instead of blocking his way the
Indians were standing aside. Now he had his family safely
through the doorway. Still the Indians had made no objection.
John Turtle was even nodding his approval. When Duncan
closed the door and set his back against it a still sober brave
took station beside him. Betsey saw then that there were six
or eight other young warriors who had not been drinking and
who were moving about quietly through the crowd. She had

heard of the Indian custom of selecting policemen whose duty
it was to stay sober during a drinking bout in order to make
sure that their drunken companions did not do one another
too much harm. Tonight they had taken the trouble to ap-
point such policemen. A drunken Indian snatched a stick
from the fire and began to run about the room waving the
blazing end. Two of the sober ones at once took it away from
him and threw it back in the fire.

Betsey looked around anxiously to locate her father, and
when she saw him her new suspicions were confirmed. He was
only pretending to drink. He was still cold sober. All his life
he had known a deathly fear of what Indians can do to a man.
Earlier in the evening he had had no other idea than to prepare for it by drinking himself into a senseless stupor. But
he knew Indians and something since then had made him
change his mind. He had decided there was a chance of living and he was staying sober to take advantage of it. Betsey
began to consider the possibilities. She had never heard of
Indians planning an attack that they had to travel through
snow to make. Yet they had planned their coming here. It had
cost them a hard two-day journey from their nearest town.
It could be then, after all, that their visit was exactly what they
had so loudly announced it to be, a sociable call on their new
neighbors. That they were so wildly wasting the station's winter food supply was nothing strange. They would have done
the same at home. Indians were always as ready to waste
whatever they happened to get their hands on when it belonged to themselves or their friends as when it belonged to
their enemies.

There crept over her a colder apprehension than when she
had taken it for granted that she was soon to die. The threat
that now appeared was more real because it was more familiar. She could not remember a winter when the Slovers had
not begun to get hungry before March. Here it would be
worse, because there were so many people in the station and
it was a harder winter than usual. The Indians might as well
have left them dead as to leave them so little that they were
bound to starve before spring. On the floor at her feet was a
half-gnawed rib with a hunk of dripping meat still clinging
to it. She picked it up, slipped it under her shawl, and sided
toward the door. The rest of the night she spent flitting like a
ghost among the stumbling and lurching Indian merrymakers
to snatch up scraps of food. These she hid in the snow on the
yard, back of the woodpile, under beds in the Slover cabin.

It was the very quantity of brandy available that provided
an antidote to the excesses it had excited. Indian after Indian

passed from the stage of falling down to the stage of being
unable to get up again. Toward morning only John Turtle
and his sharp-eyed young policemen were still up and around.
They remained as watchful as they had been throughout the
night. Shortly after dawn John Turtle blew a number of
shrill blasts on his command whistle. Most of the sprawled
and sodden sleepers rose like men from the dead. They sat
up, stared blearily, shuddered, and staggered to their feet.
The policemen roamed about, kicking those who were slow
to awaken. Those few for whom this was insufficient were
rolled in snowbanks. No one laughed or so much as grinned.
All was in grim earnest. The frivolity of the night before had
passed. In the cold light of morning the whooping, floundering
revelers of the night before had been transposed into the
silent, attentive members of a military organization. Each
knew what was expected of him. There was the orderly bustle
of imminent departure.

Duncan's satisfaction that they were clearing out so much
sooner than he had dared hope was short-lived. In the edge of
the woods across the stream appeared two Indian youths
leading a long string of pack horses. The train was brought
into the stockade where the full enormity of the Indians'
intentions was revealed. For all their gluttony and wastefulness
they had not the night before made a fatal inroad upon the
station's winter stores. The staple bulk of the food supply, the
tiers of sacked corn, peas, and beans, had scarcely been
touched. But now they were carrying out these sacks, together
with the remaining hams, sides of bacon, festoons of jerky,
and everything else that had not previously been eaten,
burned, or spoiled, and loading it all on the horses. Duncan
began violently to protest. John Turtle no longer grinned.
His eyes were like stone.

"Friend?" he asked. "Friend eat, no?"

Other Indians crowded nearer, scowling, appearing to welcome the possibility of resistance. All now carried the rifles
which formerly had been kept out of sight. Their raw temper
was a natural aftermath of their indulgence. It was a more
critical moment than any of the night before. Duncan
shrugged, acknowledging the uselessness of protest.

"At least give us back our rifles," he said. "You don't want
your good friends to starve, do you?"

John Turtle was carrying Duncan's rifle. None of the others,
either Jacob's or any of those taken from the tree in the wood
lot, was in evidence. He pretended to understand that only
Duncan's was in question.

"Friend," he said, almost genial again. He patted the rifle

and settled it the more snugly under his arm. "Friend swap, no?"

Duncan stood with Garett in the gateway watching the Indian column parade off over the now well-trampled trail through the snow.

"They planned it from start to finish," he said bitterly. "Before they left their town they knew just what they were after. One way or another they'd have got in on us, but we made it easy. I was up on the roof just now looking off at their tracks. All they had to do was nose around until they knew just where we were. Then they came up the stream side of the mound. They knew we couldn't see the gate from the wood lot. They could just walk in."

"I'd say we had good neighbor Caleb to thank," said Garett.

"That's possible, of course. John Turtle certainly got his chance to look us over the night Caleb brought him to call. Still, nobody had to give him the idea. Indians are always hungry in winter. He didn't have to be prodded to see a chance to feed his whole village at our expense. So I don't think we have to take it for granted Caleb put them up to it. I got the very strong impression that Caleb really wants to settle here, and I think there's no question he wants to stand well with white people—particularly important ones, like Clark, for example. Actually, he may still have been saving us, perhaps inadvertently. It could have been to save face with him that his Indian cronies stopped short of cutting all our throats last night."

"Instead of just leaving us to starve," said Garett.

In the kitchen Duncan found the women already engaged in a frantic assault, with shovels, brooms, mops, kettles of boiling water, and the aid of Clem, Ned, and the children, upon the indescribable mess left by their recent guests.

"We'll never get it clean again," said Agatha. "Never in this world. All we can do is keep at it until it begins to look clean."

Duncan walked on to the storeroom. Aside from a broken sack of corn and another of beans upon which an Indian had defecated, literally nothing was left. In the loft were two sacks of seed corn which had been stored separately to make more certain that the grain would not get mixed with the ordinary corn. These now constituted the bulk of the station's food stock.

He crossed the yard to the Slover cabin. There was a delay before the door was unbarred, during which he could hear much whispering and rustling within. When they did open the door they regarded him uneasily. But he had no time to speculate upon what might account for their nervousness.

"They stripped us bare," he said.

"They done thet," agreed Olen.

"Do you think your friend Caleb set them on us?"

"He could of," said Olen, nodding his head judicially. "In one way, thet is. Them Shawnee they was nuthin' they craved more'n to axe the lot of us. Could be whut saved us was Caleb his steerin' 'em to jest grabbin' all our grub—makin' out like it was a big joke. Injuns is right partial to jokes."

"They surely laughed themselves silly," said Polly. "But more'n likely they was more to it than jest a joke. Ain't no question them Shawnee they don't want us here. Like's not they figger thet now with nuthin to eat we'll be bound to take ourselves off and they'll be shet of us."

"How can we take ourselves off—with the river frozen and the snow as deep as it is and the nearest stations in either Kentucky or Virginia as far off as they are?"

"Ain't no way we kin, thet's fer sure," said Olen, again nodding his head judicially. He seemed to be taking a kind of bitter satisfaction in the inspection of each new facet of their helplessness.

"There are twenty-four of us. Twenty-four mouths to feed. From what I can see left in our house there's not enough, even with the strictest sort of rationing, to keep us more than two weeks."

"They stripped us clean's they did you," said Polly hastily. Her eyes wandered to a rafter from which hung a row of smoked venison strips. " 'Cept fer thet mite o' jerky up there."

Duncan made an impatient gesture. The Slovers were as simple-minded as children. It was a task to catch and to hold their attention.

"We have to think of more than a mouthful here and there. We have to think of the months to come. Our only hope is what we can get in the woods. That's something you understand better than I do. Just what are our chances to get game?"

Olen blinked his mild surprise at so ignorant a question being posed by a man of Duncan's intelligence.

"We-uns got us no guns, so we got us no chance a-tall."

"How about bows and arrows?"

"The Injuns they got good ones and they know how to use 'em. Most o' them got rifles besides. All the same, come a winter like this, they go so hungry a parcel o' them allus dies off."

"You keep telling me what we can't do. We have to think

of something we can do. Seems to me I've heard of hard winters when the elk collect in yards they've trampled in the snow. With the snow so deep they can't get away and people come on snowshoes and kill them with axes."

Olen chuckled. "Oncet I come on a old bull buffalo thet had his back busted when a tree hit by lightnin' had fell on him."

Polly did not grin at her husband's wit. "They's one thing fer sure I know about huntin'. When yuh take to huntin' 'cause yuh got to knock down something or yuh ain't a-goin' to eat, thet's the time yuh never have no luck."

"What about your snares?"

"A partridge or a rabbit now and then ain't goin' to count fer much. Snarin' ain't good when the snow's deep. Besides we-uns bin here long enough so's most the game—the little as well's the big—has moved off a ways."

"Fishing?"

"The crik's froze solid."

"So what it all adds up to," said Duncan, exasperated by their unshaken pessimism, "in the light of your years of experience, is that we're sure to starve."

Polly shrugged wearily. "We're sure to git so hungry we'll go to chewin' bark and old moccasins and to grubbin' down through the snow a-lookin' fer mouses' nests. But somehow or other we'll hang on till spring. We-uns allus have."

In the kitchen the wave of housecleaning had receded from one small island about a fireplace, where Garett had found refuge. Duncan came in and squatted beside him.

"There's only one answer," he said. "I'll have to get to Kentucky and get back with something to keep us the rest of the winter."

"How do you plan to manage that?"

"Somehow I can make it overland. The river's never been known to stay frozen too long. By the time I get a cargo scraped together I can bring it back by boat."

Garett nodded soberly. "It would not appear that we have much choice. If I were only the half of a man, I'd be the one to go. Then you could be the one to stay here where you're needed and where you belong."

"I can go," Duncan reminded him, "only because I can know that you will be here."

Agatha stood over them. The flush of resolution that had enlivened her scrubbing had drained away, leaving her face pale and smudged. "I could tell the minute you came in that door." She was stricken by a sudden rush of comprehension of how much was about to be demanded of her. "When are you going?"

Duncan straightened to face her. "The sooner the better. First, because it'll be too long in any event before I can get back with what we need—with what we have to have. Second, because it'll be so much easier to get across the river while the ice still holds."

"Not today. Not now. Surely not this minute."

"No," he said gently. "It's already too late in the day. The first thing in the morning."

But in the morning the ice had already started to move. Somewhere farther upstream there had been a change in the weather. The river had risen and, in rising, had burst its frozen crust. Again its flow was in the open as it swept past with its new burden of tossing, clashing, grinding cakes of ice.

"Can you build a raft strong enough to stand that kind of pounding?" Duncan asked Frank.

"Yes," said Frank. He was always confident of his ability to build anything.

"It'll only have to last long enough to get me over to the other bank."

Olen, Jarot, and Jacob, their apathy dispelled by this sudden new interest, ran to cut logs. Frank, Mark, and Luke set to work on the lee shore of the point. Experiment soon demonstrated that a raft heavy enough to withstand the bombardment of the careening ice cakes must be too large for one man to handle. A crew of at least three would be required to get Duncan across.

"We can angle with the current over to the other bank," proposed Duncan. "Soon's I've jumped off, the three men with the raft can angle back to this side and walk back up the river to the station."

There then loomed the problem of selecting the men who were to be subjected to the risk of making the double crossing. Duncan drew Garett aside.

"I'd ask for volunteers if I thought it was any use. Should we draw lots?"

"No," said Garett. "I'm being left in command here so it's something for me to decide. We can't mix Slovers and Lymans so the crew will have to be all one or all the other. Useless as they are, we can count on the Slovers to scratch around in the woods and find something now and then to piece out what we have in the station to eat. So it'll have to be the Lymans."

Frank demurred, not, it became apparent, because he and his sons dreaded the danger but because he was opposed to the Slovers being arbitrarily excused. Garett settled the issue.

"The next bite you get to eat," he said, "will be after you've put Duncan on the other side."

The next morning all assembled at the point for the raft's launching. It was a cold, blowy day with occasional flurries of snow. The floating ice in the river kept up a perpetual grinding rumble that was like the mutter of distant thunder. Duncan had paid his farewells to his family during the intimacy of their early rising. Without further ceremony he and the Lymans jumped on the raft and it was shoved from the shelf of creek ice into the swirling water of the river.

For a time, while their poles could still reach bottom, they were able to maintain some headway toward mid-river. Their progress slowed when the water got deeper and they could only shove against adjacent bobbing cakes of ice. Then they were able to reach bottom again where there was a mid-channel sandbar, and began once more to make progress toward the farther bank. The raft was lurching and tipping under the impact of caroming ice cakes but continuing to right itself and showing no visible signs of breaking up. Suddenly a snow squall dropped a curtain, cutting off completely the view of those watching from shore. No matter how desperately they strained to see, they caught no later glimpse of the raft. When the squall passed the river was empty. Garett explained hurriedly to Agatha that at the rate the raft was drifting with the current it must have been swept around the bend, only a couple of miles away, during the squall.

From noon on they began anxiously to watch for the reappearance of the Lymans as they walked back along the nearer bank. It should not have taken them more than an hour to get across and another hour to get back. The current could have carried them a number of miles downstream during the two crossings but at worst they should have been able to wade back through the snow in another two or three hours. But the afternoon wore on and night fell and still they did not appear. A great fire was built on the point to guide their approach if they came during the night.

The next morning Eric and Jarot set off downriver along the bank. They returned just before dark to report that they had found easier going than they had expected, since in many places the snow was packed so hard they had not had to flounder through it. They estimated that they had traveled at least nine or ten miles but had found no spot where the raft could have landed or its crew disembarked. Not until the next day did Eric steel himself to tell Garett alone the rest of the story. Before they had turned back they had come to a straight reach of the river where by climbing a tree they had been able to survey another six miles of the snow-covered bank beyond.

Cam knew it was useless to attempt to question Eric, Garett, or Tracy. She could not bear even to look at her mother's drawn, white face. She went to Olen.

"You think my father's drowned, don't you?" she demanded.

Olen looked down from his shaggy height to meet the child's piercing eyes.

"No," he said carefully. "Nobody yit's got ary call fer figgerin' thet."

"Then what have you got reason to think?"

"We kin be middlin' sure the raft she never got back to this side."

"Then it went down."

"She could o' fetched the t'other bank first."

"But that isn't what you really think."

"The last look we-uns got at thet raft they was a-polin' her along like they might sure enough make it," said Olen doggedly.

Cam turned and began to run. She dared lose no time finding a place where she could surely stay safely out of sight until she was able to stop crying.

February

The extreme cold passed. A fitful wind sprang up, veered to the south, and died away. For three days it snowed, gently, steadily, heavily. Layer on layer was spread over as much of the world as was visible from the station. The two slides, the blackened embers of the fire in the wood lot, the tracks of the Indians and their horses, the reddened blotches where the cows and dogs had been butchered, the filth strewn across the snow of the yard, the frantic trampling along the river bank where the raft had been built and launched—all these reminders of disaster were mercifully covered. Winter seemed to have advanced a kind of idiotic suggestion that such things could only have happened at some other place or in some other year. Not only was the past buried but there was as yet no present to succeed it. No new tracks took the place of the old. To get so far as from the door to the woodpile involved floundering through breast-high drifts. Even the creatures of the wild seemed to have lost the will to move about. No delicate tracery of mouse trails, no bolder imprint of rabbit, marten or fox, no wallowing, lunging course of deer, elk, or buffalo, was visible anywhere across the smooth white expanse of meadow and pond.

Dark days followed, with noons as dim as twilight. A freezing gray mist hung over the snow. The leaden overcast seemed, in having banished the sun and the stars, to have obscured the distinction between minutes and hours and days. The members of the Jordan household rose reluctantly, moved about slowly and stiffly, addressed one another in low voices. Only the harsh, inexorable tick of Louisa's clock was a signal that time had not lost all meaning.

Each day centered about the morning and evening meals. The necessity of formal rationing had not been openly admitted. By common consent all referred to their situation as one of waiting for Duncan's return, which could not be delayed beyond two or three more weeks at the latest. But when Geneva ladled out the thin corn gruel to which their every repast was limited, all, by the same sort of unspoken common consent, took a very little and, as they grew hungrier, each day accepted less.

The Slovers had adapted themselves to their plight by lingering longer each morning in bed until for them time stood so nearly still that their domestic routine took no account of any difference between day and night. There had been one brief flurry of activity immediately after the heavy snowfall when the entire family had collaborated in the digging of a tunnel through the enormous drift between their door and the door of their outhouse. But thereafter only Polly ever emerged in the open, on occasional dashes to the woodpile for wood or more hesitant advances to the Jordan kitchen to "trade," as she termed it, a twist of their remaining jerky for a cup of corn meal.

"Best fer folks to take it real easy," she explained, defensively, "when they ain't got enough to eat. The easier they take it the longer the little they got to eat will do 'em."

The Jordans were convinced of the existence of a secret hoard of food which the Slovers had had the primitive foresight to lay away during the earlier days of plenty but Louisa vetoed any move toward searching the Slover cabin.

"We're not yet so put to it," she said, "that we must sink to the level of squabbling with their kind of trash."

"I absolutely agree," said Garett. "Especially when I reflect that they have three very large men while we have only Eric."

Within the week two-thirds of the Jordans were as immobilized as the Slovers. An epidemic of uncommonly severe colds swept through the household. First Garett was afflicted, then the Negroes, then Eric, then the younger children.

"I've always heard people never caught colds," protested Garett, "When they're as much off by themselves as we are here."

"We weren't so much by ourselves," said Tracy, "when the Indians were here."

Louisa insisted upon all taking to their beds.

"No doctor I ever saw," she said, "could do as much for a cold as a person can do for himself by getting into a good warm bed and staying in it."

Agatha moved her two youngest down from the children's sleeping quarters in the loft and into her room.

"Mother's been crying all night," Cam explained to Tracy. "Every night. She hates herself for doing that because it's the same as admitting something's happened to Father. But she can't help it. That's why she has Chris and Susie sleeping with her. She won't dare cry with them right there beside her."

After another endless night, Agatha sank toward morning into an exhausted sleep. When she awoke, Chris and Susie were whispering. Their faces were still flushed but they looked much improved and they were playing a game which involved counting on their fingers.

"A big bowl of pea soup," said Chris, "with globs of melted butter floating on it."

"Mush with butter," said Susie. "And sugar, too."

"We've already got mush. It's all we have, every day."

"We have not. We just have corn soup. I meant fried mush, with lots of butter and sugar on it."

"All right. You can have mush. I'll have a thick slice of ham, with honey poured over it."

"Bifkits with honey."

"You always just say what I say."

"I do not. I like honey. And I like bifkits. But if you took all the honey I'll have bifkits with maple syrup."

"Biscuits."

"I said bifkits."

"Anyway, what I'll have next is a whole buffalo hump with the fat burned black and the juice running out of it."

"That's not fair. We can only wish for what Papa will bring. He's coming in a boat."

"You can shoot a buffalo from a boat."

"He hasn't got a gun."

"He'll get guns in Kentucky."

"Is he coming today?"

"Uncle Garry says maybe."

"Every day Uncle Garry says that."

"He's bound to come pretty soon."

"Then why did Eric have to go hunting with his new bow and arrow?"

"He didn't. He hasn't got it made yet."

"He has so. Cam told me. He finished it yesterday."

Agatha sprang from bed, caught up a robe, and ran to the kitchen. The Negroes, clinging to the privileges of their ills, were still in their quarters. Only Olivia was in sight. She stood by the fire stirring the boiling corn in the pot.

"Where's Eric?" demanded Agatha.

"Hunting. Trying out that bow he made. He was off at daylight."

"But he shouldn't even be out of bed. He's not well yet."

"There was no stopping him. Though he still looked weak as a cat. I told him he ought to take at least a swallow of this but he said Indian hunters always hunt hungry. Gives them luck, they think. It likely does make them more anxious to shoot something." Olivia lifted a spoonful of the gruel and eyed it resentfully. "If you don't stir it, it burns. If you do, it turns to slime. Still, I suppose we have to be thankful we've had it. But this is the last. I thought there might be less wasted if we cooked it all in one batch." She plopped the spoonful back into the pot. "Tracy went with him."

Agatha ran to the nearest loophole and drew aside the block. Through the opening came a gust of cold air. All that she could see was a narrowed glimpse of a lifeless white slope merging with a lifeless black forest under a lifeless gray sky.

"My turn to break trail," said Tracy.

Eric shook his head and continued to flounder on through the snow. Tracy caught at his belt and forced him to pause.

"You have to take care of yourself." She grinned cheerfully. "Remember, you're the tribe's only hunter."

She pulled him back to a sitting position against a drift. He resisted for a moment, then sank down. She drew off one mitten, reached into the pocket of her blanket coat, and extended her hand toward him. In the palm was a tablespoon-sized heap of pounded corn mixed with maple sugar.

"Eat it," she said. "You'll need it to keep going."

He recoiled.

"Where'd that come from?"

"Your grandmother bought a small sack of it in Pittsburgh. It's been in her trunk. She'd forgotten about it."

Eric pushed her hand away. "Save it for Susie and Chris—and Cam—and maybe Uncle Garry. He's beginning to look like a ghost."

"I have been saving it—for times we might need it most. This is one. You can't wade miles through snow on what you've been eating. I've been watching you. You eat less than anybody, even your mother."

"It chokes me. We've got so little left and I'm the one who should be getting more."

"That's why you must eat this. Else where will you get the strength to hunt. Eat it, I say."

She caught his chin in her mittened hand and clapped the bare one to his mouth. He began to chew, without relish. There were tears in his eyes. He looked disgustedly about at the wintry forest.

"Hunt? You can hardly call it hunting. We've been plowing

around for hours and so far we haven't seen so much as a single track."

"Probably it's too soon after the big snow. In another day or two it may be different."

His thin, white face set stubbornly.

"The Slovers say the game has all pulled out. They say that sometimes happens in a hard winter. But that doesn't stand to reason. Where would it go?"

"It does seem odd. But you hear all the time about whole villages of Indians starving in the winter. They're experienced hunters and still they starve."

"The Slovers just want an excuse for staying by their fire." He stared at her accusingly. "You don't think I'll be able to kill anything with this bow and arrow, do you? You just came along to look after me."

"I came along to help, if I could. I do think that before you try to hunt in snow as deep as this you should have snowshoes."

"Who knows how to make snowshoes?" He regarded his bow critically. "I had to go by guess even to make this." He got to his feet. "You're just talking so we'll rest longer."

They plowed on. He was aware that he was tiring faster than Tracy and this made him the more determined to keep going. Getting up angrily after having fallen, suddenly he stiffened and pointed.

"Tracks," he whispered. "Just the other side that log."

They floundered ahead and climbed up on the trunk of the fallen tree. On the other side were the fresh tracks of an animal heavy enough to have broken through the thin crust at every step. It had been making its way by short hops, from the tangle of dried vines about the tree's outflung upper branches to the similar tangle about its upturned roots, and then on into a copse of scrub cedar. The imprint of its belly showed between each of the hops. It had not been in a hurry. After every three or four hops it had lain down, resting at one point long enough to have left behind a thin glaze where its body heat had briefly melted a film of snow.

"A bear?" suggested Tracy.

"A bear?" Eric was dismayed by her ignorance. "Not a quarter as big as even a small bear. A lynx. See how much the tracks look like a cat's?"

"Is a lynx good to eat?"

"Indians think so. *Look*. There he is. Right over there."

The lynx had come out of the cedars, less than a hundred yards away. He came to a stop and looked at them over his shoulder. There was gray on his tufted ears and about his muzzle. He looked old and gaunt and worn. Eric whipped out one of his arrows but did not fit it to the string.

"It's too long a shot," he whispered.

They jumped from the log and plunged forward through the snow. The lynx took several unhurried hops. He appeared to regard their approach with more unsociable distaste than actual concern. No matter how desperately they struggled toward him he continued to keep his original distance. Each time they paused for breath he ceased his weary hopping and lay down. He, too, was panting.

"It's always too long a shot," complained Eric, between long shuddering breaths.

"You must hold up for just a minute," protested Tracy. "You'll kill yourself."

"But we've got to get him. He's the only game we've seen."

"We'll never get him this way." She grabbbed his belt and held him back. "Wait. You squat over there back in that thicket. I'll circle around and get on the other side of him. Maybe he'll forget about you and come back this way, close enongh for you to get a shot at him."

"Try it and see," he wheezed.

Tracy took several deep breaths and set out. Eric crawled to the shelter of the thicket, knelt, and waited. She kept on, breaking her laborious way through the crusted snow and with each step the more painfully repenting her suggestion. She was much weaker than she had thought. Each onward lunge required a renewed and separate effort. Eventually she began to realize that, in her anxiety to describe a sufficiently wide circle, she could have lost her bearings. She had long since returned to what she conceived to be the area where the lynx last had lain down, but had not sighted either the animal or its tracks. The occasion for her exhaustion began to seem as nonsensical as a child's game of make-believe. Eric's determination to hunt with his makeshift weapon was absurd and her lending herself to the farce was more absurd. The bleak sky, the somber forest, the deep snow, were so many outward reminders that her struggle was senseless. Since Duncan had gone nothing had had real meaning, no effort genuine value. She could no longer help him. Now she had set out to help his son and had managed only to get lost in the woods, leaving the boy to freeze while waiting for her.

"Eric," she called, surrendering.

Eric's reply came from no great distance. Then she saw the lynx, not twenty paces away. He was reclining in the snow, watching her with yellow, expressionless eyes. This so

much nearer view revealed how thin he was. He looked sick
as well as starved. She pushed toward him. He did not move.
She broke the tip from the dead branch and tossed it at him.
Still he did not stir. Eric was wallowing forward through an
intervening drift.

"Look out," called Tracy. "He's right here."

The lynx turned his head toward Eric, gathered his paws
under him, and began taking short hops off to the side. Eric
straightened and fitted an arrow to his bowstring. His shivering
made his movements slow and fumbling. But when at last he
bent his bow the arrow's flight was straight. Its iron-tipped
head struck the lynx in the shoulder. The beast snarled, clawed
at the arrow, and then, animated at last, began to take long
leaps, leaving the arrow behind him in the snow. His third
bound carried him out of sight in a patch of undergrowth.
Eric plunged forward, picked up his arrow, and stared at it.

"It was a beautiful shot," said Tracy. She was too weary to
put spirit into her attempt to console him. "Just back of the
shoulder."

"What difference—when you've got a bow that doesn't
shoot hard enough to knock down a fly?"

Eric broke the arrow and threw down the bow. He was as
tall as a man, which made it seem the more incongruous that
his face should be working with the rebellious anger of a child.
She tried to remember with what resolution he had sat up in
bed to work on that bow and arrow between spasms of cough-
ing.

"These days are so short," she said. "Don't you think perhaps we should be starting home?"

"Might as well," he agreed sullenly. "We're not doing any
good out here."

He set off, his angry disgust giving him for the moment the
appearance of new vigor. Tracy picked up the bow and followed. Then, as he kept steadily on, gasping, grunting, getting up each time he fell, she began to feel remorse that she
had not taken more care to conceal her own depression.

"Eric, did you notice John Turtle's bow?"

"What about it? Indians know how to make bows."

"At the hand grasp in the middle and at the two principal
curves it was bound with what looked like deer sinew. Do
you think that could have been to make it stronger?"

"Deer sinew. We might as well wish for a rifle. Where we
going to get a deer?"

"I've got a ball of very strong waxed thread."

He swung around to face her. His eyes had brightened.
He took the bow from her and bent it experimentally.

"It migh help," he said. "It certainly might."

He went on, his stride longer and firmer. They came out into Caleb's clearing. Both stopped and stared. In a dozen places about the cabin and along the edges of the woods, holes had been dug down through the snow and into the frozen earth beneath. Eric began to laugh.

"The Slovers," he exclaimed. "They must have got hungry enough to get themselves all out of bed at once. They've been digging for Caleb's caches." He chuckled at Tracy's continued mystification. "Can't you see? All of a sudden they remembered how busy Daisy was last fall. She was always gathering nuts and dried berries and smoking ducks and fish. Indians bury food for the winter. The Slovers have been trying to guess where she buried Caleb's."

"Do you think they found anything?"

"No sign of it," said Eric, after inspecting each of the holes. "Chances are Caleb and Daisy took it with them when they went back to winter with the Shawnee."

"Let's see if they broke into his cabin."

Eric hesitated, momentarily, to commit this trespass. Tracy lifted the bar and quickly pushed the door open. In the failing light the cabin looked as neat and orderly as when Caleb had occupied it.

"The most likely place would be under the floor," observed Eric, "but doesn't look like they lifted the floorboards. They're really afraid of Caleb. If only he had stayed here this winter . . . He'd have kept them out of bed."

"If only he had never come at all," said Tracy.

"He didn't steal our food."

"His Indians did."

"They're not his Indians. And you started hating him even before that."

"How can you defend him? He's the kind of man who never thinks of anyone else. No more than does an animal."

Eric nodded, casually accepting the indictment. "That's the kind of man you have to be to get along out here."

"No, Eric, no. Don't ever joke about trying to be like him."

"It's no joke. There's not much chance of my being like him, as you saw today. As everybody will see when we run out of corn meal tomorrow. We've been the same as starving but then we'll really starve—for all the good I'll be."

He stalked away from her. She followed him up the slope along the trail through the snow beaten down by the Slovers in their sudden sorties. It was dark by the time they reached the gate. Olivia met them at the kitchen door. Her voice was strained.

"Where have you been?"

"Here. There." Eric sagged against the door frame. "Making tracks in the snow. Millions of tracks in the snow."

"Wherever you made them, did you see anything of Garett?' '

"No, we didn't."

"Could he have gone over to Caleb's with the Slovers?" asked Tracy.

"I don't know where he could have gone." Olivia's tone indicated this had been another of the days she and Garett had not been speaking. "All I know is that he's not in the house now."

Eric pushed himself away from the door frame. "I'll see if the Slovers saw anything of him."

He plodded across the yard, knocked on their door, and pushed it open. The single room was hot and close, smelled of unwashed bedding and clothing and people. Polly and Lina were crouched on stools by the fire over which was slung an iron pot from which came a more agreeable smell of simmering broth. On the hearth was a wooden platter upon which rested a beef bone, with the tines of the fork with which it had evidently just been lifted from the pot still fixed in the knob of gristle adhering to one end of the bone. Polly hastily shifted her position on the stool so that the overhang of her dress shut off Eric's view of the platter. The three Slover men, looking oddly like overgrown, bearded children as they lay side by side and turned their heads in unison to stare silently at the visitor, were in one bed. Betsey, her dull eyes suddenly sharpening with interest, peered from the tangled nest of blankets in the other.

"I came over to ask," said Eric, "if you'd seen anything of Garett this afternoon."

Lina sprang up and took an eager step toward him.

"No, Eric. We never seen nuthin' of him."

"When we come in jest afore dark," said Polly, "there was smoke a-comin' from the Lyman cabin and I heared somebody bangin' on the anvil in there. Could thet o' bin him?"

"Thanks," said Eric, backing out.

He had taken no more than two or three stumbling steps away when the door opened behind him. Lina ran to him and grasped one of his hands. He felt the greasiness and the warmth before he realized that what she was pressing upon him was the beef bone.

"Fer you," she whispered. "Take yerself a chaw on thet. It ain't meat but it's bin boiled so long thet gristle is real tasty."

He jerked his hand away. The bone fell to the snow between them. She picked it up and put an arm around him to support him.

"Yuh got yerself so hungry and so tuckered thet yuh can't even hang on to it. Here, I'll hold it fer yuh."

He pushed her away.

"Gnaw on it yourself. You may not gag on it, but I would."

"We-uns never stole it," she said. "Betsey jest picked up some bones thet the Injuns throwed down." She tried again to press the bone into his hand. "Take it," she begged. "It's mine to give and whutever is mine is right fer you to have."

"Can't you get it through your head?" he gasped. "I don't want it, or anything else of yours."

He stumbled on to the door of the Lyman cabin. There were coals still glowing in the forge. Various Lyman tools, formerly hung on the wall in a neat row, were scattered about the anvil. He went on to the kitchen.

"The Slovers haven't seen him," he reported. "But someone has been working in the Lyman shop."

Cam's voice floated down from her bed in the loft.

"I know what he was working on in there. I could see from the loophole up here when he brought it to the door to look at it in the daylight. It was a fish spear."

"A fish spear," exclaimed Olivia. "The river. That's the only open water around. That's where he went. The fool. He didn't have the strength to walk across this room. He could have fallen in, or just fallen down and not been able to get up."

She ran for her cloak.

"No, not the river," said Louisa. "The edge of a river is no place to spear fish. Garett knows that. But I *can* guess where he is. When he and Duncan were boys they used to spear fish at night by torchlight. In the pool at the foot of the spillway below the mill dam. He's up at the falls."

"But he's sick," cried Olivia. "It'll be the death of him. We've got to go bring him back."

"Leave him alone," said Louisa. "I know he's sick. But he's also a man. He knows the state we're in. If we don't let him at least try to do something it *will* be the death of him."

"He's my husband," shouted Olivia. "I'm not going to let anything take him away from me. Nor any of you. Not all of you. No matter if you all die. I'm not going to let him die."

She rushed out. Agatha rose and took her cloak from its peg.

"He might have told her what he was up to. The chances are he's fallen down in the snow before he got halfway to the falls. Olivia may not be able to get him back alone."

Tracy and Eric struggled up from their chairs.

"Sit down," commanded Agatha. "Or, better yet, go to bed. You two have tried to do too much already today. Olivia and I will have trouble enough with Garett without having to carry you back, too."

She went out. It was a dark night but there was light enough reflected from the whiteness of the snow to enable her to follow Olivia's tracks down the slope toward the pond. There Olivia had come upon Garett's tracks where he had left the Slover trail to Caleb's cabin and had started up the frozen, snow-covered stream. She had begun to run. Agatha could see how often Garett, the first of the three of them to force his way through these drifts, had fallen, and with what desperate haste Olivia had struggled on to overtake him. Her own passage was easier in the trail that they had broken, but she soon began to realize how weak she had been left by her days of fasting. She kept expecting momentarily to come upon them but the tracks led on and on until she, too, in her weariness, was staggering and falling. At last she caught a glimpse of the water of the falls, gushing from its ice-capped ledge, shimmering faintly in the dying light of the pine-knot torch. Garett, the invalid, had made it all the way to his goal.

He was stretched out on the bank above the black, ice-rimmed pool, the unused fish spear beside him. He had had the resolution to strike flint and steel, light the torch, stick it up in the snow, and then, as he reached for his spear, had collapsed. His face looked like a dead man's but from his lips was coming a weakening babble of meaningless words. Olivia sat beside him, rocking back and forth, moaning, her face covered by her hands.

"He's not dead yet," gasped Agatha. "His fever's come back on him. He's out of his mind."

Olivia dropped her hands and looked at him. Her face was livid, not with grief but with rage.

"He's worse than out of his mind. He didn't know me. He kept calling me Tracy. He kept reaching for me and trying to pull me down beside him. He kept on and on calling me Tracy and mumbling about how glad he was she'd come to him."

"You can see he's delirious," said Agatha sternly. "Get up

and help me. We've got to get him back and get him warm.
He'll die here."

"Let him die. I hope he does. That miserable slut. She's as
cold as this snow. That's why she has eyes only for Duncan.
Because she knows there's no chance of her ever having him—
of her ever having to give a man anything."

Agatha bent down and slapped Olivia hard across the face.
"Get up," she commanded.

Olivia's hysteria passed. She rose remorsefully.

"Duncan has never so much as given her a second look," she
said, gripping Agatha's arm. "You know that, don't you?"

"Yes, I know that. But Garett's the one that concerns us
now. We've got to get him home."

They soon discovered that they had not between them the
strength to lift him. Their tugging at him seemed to catch,
vaguely, at his far-wandering attention. Each time he slipped
from their grasp he laughed.

"Will you shut up?" panted Olivia. "Will you, for God's
sake, shut up?"

"You, too," said Agatha. "If we can't carry him, we'll have
to pull him."

Each took hold of one of his feet and they began to drag him
through the snow. The movement served again to rouse him
slightly from the stupor into which he had been sinking. He
began to sing, feebly but with a kind of ghastly gusto, snatches
of "The Darby Ram."

"and you'll see the same as I . . .
and you'll see the same as I . . .
and when they took its measure . . .
the devil cut it off, sir . . ."

Their agonizing progress was not so much eased as confused when they reached the pond. There they encountered
Eric and Tracy, who had struggled out to look for them despite Agatha's injunction. All four were so exhausted that
they were nearly as helpless as the sick man. Somehow they
made it up the slope, through the gate, and into the kitchen.

Louisa had dragged the mattress from Garett's and Olivia's
bed out to the family fireplace and had stretched the blankets
over chair backs to warm. Wrapped in the heated blankets,
Garett drifted off into a sleep so deep that Louisa hastily thrust
her hand under his shirt.

"His heart's still beating," she reported.

The rescue party staggered to chairs and benches.

"Mother," called Cam from the loft. "Ken's gone outside.

And he took Rupert with him." There was a strange emphasis on the last phrase.

"Ken?" said Agatha. "He went outside? Whatever for?"

She gathered herself to get up from the bench at the table. The door opened. Ken came in. His face was white and tear-stained but he was calm, almost as abstracted as though he were walking in his sleep. He was holding Rupert in his arms. The dog was limp, his legs and tail dangling. Ken walked steadily to the table and laid his burden before his mother. Only then did Agatha see the knot in the leather leash. It had been drawn hard about Rupert's neck. The dog was dead.

"Indians eat dogs," said Ken, speaking in an odd singsong, as though reciting something he had learned but that had for him no meaning. "And you'll all die if you don't have something to eat."

"Ken," cried Agatha. "You couldn't have done this? You didn't do this yourself, did you? Not to Rupert."

"Yes," said Ken. "Nobody else would have. Besides, it was better for me to do it. Rupert wasn't afraid of me."

Ken made a break for the ladder and scrambled up to the refuge of his bed in the loft. Agatha spread her arms on the table and dropped her head into them. Her weeping was weak and silent and yet shook her whole body. One of her outflung hands touched one of Rupert's paws.

"Somebody," she moaned, "somebody take the poor little thing away."

"No," said Louisa. "we've got to go through with it now. After what Ken has tried to do for us we absolutely must do that much for him."

Eric struggled to get up out of his chair. Agatha rose and shoved him back. She picked up the dog's body, carried it to the chopping block before the cooking fireplace, and drew a knife from the rack beside the block. Deliberately she began to skin, clean, and dismember the carcass. Her face was ashen, her eyes glittered, but her voice was soft, musing, hardly audible to the others in the room, watching horrified.

"So much energy in so small a body. Such a bundle of wriggling, and tail wagging, and barking. You were so full of life, Rupert. Enough to divide among all of us and give each of us life for another day or two. Ken saved you from the Indians who were such beasts that they wanted you. Now he has given you instead to us. And even I myself will accept—for I must go on trying to live, for the sake of my children. We all must go on trying to live—for the sake of one another." Suddenly her voice rose to a scream. "You all know Duncan is dead. But you won't admit it—won't even mention it. For fear of robbing poor, sad, demented Agatha of the chance to keep on hoping. But I know he is dead. I know it better than any of you. Because I knew him better. If he were alive he'd have found some way to get word to us. Even if he couldn't get back himself, he would have done that. He wouldn't have let us go on grieving and suffering. Duncan is dead. We have to face it—and go on, if we can."

Tracy crept from her bed at dawn. She was stiff and sore and so weak that she was obliged to grasp at chair backs to get as far as the kitchen door. Outside she pulled herself up to the ladder to the stockade fire step. Her first impulse every morning was to climb up here where she could see downriver. But this morning, like all the others, the gray river flowed on in sullen emptiness. No distant dark dot marked the conceivable approach of canoe or bateau.

With painful care she descended, crossed the yard to the Lyman cabin, and found a shovel. Sooner or later the Slovers would become so hard pressed that they would bring themselves to invade Caleb's cabin. She proposed to be the first to explore beneath those floor boards. Plodding through the gate and down the slope along the trail broken through the snow the day before, she walked like one carrying a crushing weight, bent over, head down, her dulled attention fixed on the path immediately before her. Not until she had almost reached the cabin's doorstep did she look up. She came, then, to an abrupt stop. An Indian toboggan leaned, upended, alongside the door, and beside it a pair of snowshoes. A curl of smoke came from the chimney. The door opened and Caleb stood in it.

Her gasp of surprise became a gasp of rage as his first glance flicked from the shovel in her hands to the holes in the snow, to her suddenly flaming face.

"Of course I came to dig for whatever I could find," she declared. "Your Indians took everything we had."

"It is common for hungry people to steal," he said. "But today you do not need to steal. I will give you something to eat."

He stood aside for her to enter. She drew in her breath, casting about unsuccessfully for words to frame a sufficiently scathing retort. But she hit upon none that seemed adequate. Swinging around, still speechless, she started back toward the station. As soon as she was certain that she was out of his sight, she began to run.

But at the foot of the slope she came to a stop. Caleb Lewis had come back. What had brought him back? Was his return a threat of some new danger? How was his coming likely to affect them? She foresaw the torrent of such questions with which she would be deluged the moment she had announced her encounter with him. To be forced to admit that she had seen and spoken to the man and yet had gained no slightest idea of his attitude or intentions was too wildly and impossibly irrational. She had to go back.

Again, as she approached the cabin, the door opened and he stood in it. When she continued to approach he stood aside. She went in. As the day before when she had noted the orderliness of his cabin, she was struck by the uncomfortable suggestion that he was a man who kept even inanimate things in total subjection. She felt the start of a new surprise before she had clearly realized the occasion for it. Hastily she looked about her again. They were alone in the cabin.

"Where's Daisy?"

She instantly regretted the personal inquiry and, before he could reply, if he had intended to reply, added: "I've often heard it's a sign that Indians are bent on mischief—when they leave their women behind, I mean."

Nothing about him was more exasperating than his habit of appearing not to have heard what had been said to him. On a flat stone by the fire rested an iron skillet with pemmican warming in it. He divided the pemmican in equal portions, shoveled one to a bark tray, stuck a horn spoon in it, and handed the tray to her. He squatted and began to eat from the skillet. The rich, sweet odor of the chopped venison mixed with dried huckleberries and goose fat made Tracy faint with hunger. She set the tray down.

"Are you truly so insensible? Or are you only trying to pretend you do not know what has bene done to us? We are starving, and we are not only men but children and women —one of them a child of four and another a grandmother. And four of our men are lost, trying to go for help."

He looked up from his eating.

"How were they lost?"

"We can't even be sure. They tried to cross the river on a raft. Three of them were to come back the same day. But that was three weeks ago and we have seen or heard nothing of any of them. You will undoubtedly be glad to know that one of the three was Colonel Jordan."

He resumed eating. Yet for once he had seemed to be giving consideration to something that she had said to him. And it had made a sufficient impression presently to call forth a far longer speech than she had ever heard from him.

"For people who have come out here there is no use to cry for help. There is no use to run for help. In this country there are very many things which the people who come to it must know how to do and which nobody can do for them." He looked up at her over his last spoonful of pemmican. "You are very hungry. It is better for you to eat."

"I can see it is useless to try to talk to you. Words seem to have a different meaning for you. And words like 'good' or 'evil' no meaning at all."

He set down the skillet and rose.

"All your people are very hungry, too."

"They certainly are. We have been living on one spoonful of corn meal a day and tomorrow we will not have even that. Can you possibly be trying to indicate you are sorry?"

"Sorry. What use is sorry?"

"What use is anything? And what is the least of all is imagining that you can begin to understand the way ordinary civilized people think and feel."

Tracy had started for the door but his next words brought her up as short as though he had cast a rawhide noose over her head.

"Maybe your people are so hungry that they would be glad to have a bear to eat."

She whirled to stare at him.

"A bear? You have killed a bear? Did you run across one on your way here?"

"No. In winter bears hide and sleep."

"I know that. But do you think you know where to find such a den?"

"Yes. That is what I think."

"You do? Then by all means go for it now."

He had scarcely so much as glanced at her since she had come into the cabin. Even when he had looked up at her news of Duncan's fate it had been past her, as though out over the icebound river. But now he gave her a sudden appraising scrutiny. "Always it is more easy to say hunt than to go hunt."

"You want me to go with you? Then I will. I can't think of anything I'd rather watch. If there is a bear, I should be so relieved to see game that somebody is able to take. There is also the chance that you may get clawed and I should not want to miss that."

"First you will need to eat. There will be work for you to do."

She picked up the tray. The pemmican had chilled and the fat turned to grease, but never had she tasted anything so delicious.

He gathered up his axe and rifle and her shovel. At the door he paused to toss his snowshoes back into the cabin.

"Won't you need them?"

He paid no attention.

"Listen to me," he insisted. "If you've any idea that I'm going to break trail for you—as you'd probably make Daisy do——"

He righted the toboggan and set off into the woods, pulling it after him. The track behind the toboggan was a firm path in which she could walk with ease. Then she saw that this was so because he was taking the trail that he had made on his way toward his cabin with the toboggan loaded. It was a route that from time to time intersected the one she and Eric had taken as they had approached the clearing. She could see in the snow, now to one side, now to the other, the marks of their sprawling lunges as they had veered and wandered. Caleb, his direction chancing to correspond with theirs, must have arrived some time last night, perhaps just after she and Eric had left the clearing. His trail, however, ran straight as a line drawn between two points. This same straight course seemed to serve him as well now, as though his destination were as predetermined as it had been then.

"You are very sure about your bear," she said.

"Today you will have better luck than yesterday."

"You spied on us yesterday?"

He shrugged. "Who can walk in the snow without making tracks?"

She thought of Eric crouched shivering in the thicket, her laborious meandering circle, the sick lynx bounding away. Contrasting his assurance now with their pitiful flounderings then, her exasperation with him reached a new pitch.

He came to a stop beside the stub of a dead sycamore. She could see in the drift at its base where she and Eric had lain back briefly to rest in one of their many pauses for breath on their homeward course yesterday. Then he saw that Caleb was turning the toboggan around so that its rolled-up prow pointed back down the trail. She realized that this must be the spot that he had had in mind and regarded the sycamore stub with sudden attention.

It was twelve or fourteen feet in diameter and was presumably hollow, though its outer surface, blackened by some ancient fire, was still hard and unbroken. The stub was not much higher than it was wide, the main column of the original tree having been snapped off at some earlier time by storm or lightning bolt. A vigorous sumac vine had taken possession of the top and its overhanging mat of branches was covered by as thick a platform of snow as might be the roof of a house. She could see nothing about the snow-banked stub to

distinguish it from the next drift or the one beyond that one
or any one of a thousand others.

"You actually think there's a bear in there?" she asked,
challengingly.

He examined the priming of his rifle and handed it to her.
"Be ready to give it to me," he directed.

With the shovel he cleared the drifted snow away from one
side of the stub. Next he broke and assembled a pile of sticks
a few feet away, got out his flint and steel, and started a small
fire. She understood that this was in preparation for smoking
out the bear which he continued to assume was ensconced
somewhere in the recesses of the hollow stub.

"Tell me," she demanded. "You've just got to tell me why
you're so absolutely certain there's a bear in there."

He glanced up at the snow-covered crown of sumac
branches at the top of the stub. She looked more closely and
noticed that in one fold of the branches there was a small dark
hole in the snow. It was no larger than a teacup but, once she
began to observe it, it looked oddly unnatural and the edges of
the snow about the tiny opening drooped inward. Some slightly
warmer current of air from within the stub had, in rising and
escaping, melted the snow, and, she was forced to admit, the
most likely source of the warmer air must be the breath and
body heat of some fairly large animal.

"So you just happened to see that little hole on your way
past? Are you trying to tell me that you never go anywhere
without constantly looking up and around—in this case it
must have been up and behind, after you had passed—for
things as small as that?"

Her question drew from him the unexpected acknowledg-
ment of a brief chuckle. It was the first audible sign of amusement she had ever heard from him. He picked up the axe and
began to cut a notch in the base of the stub. The outer dried
shell of the sycamore was as hard as iron but, swinging from
his heels, he made each easy, graceful arc of the whirling
axe so swift and powerful on its downward swoop that it
ended with the blade sinking deeply into the flinty wood. The
stub shuddered. At each alternate thud a great square chip
flew away. Any lingering doubt that there might be a hiber-
nating bear inside came to an abrupt end. The bank of snow
behind the axeman began suddenly to stir and then to heave
upward. The creature had been sufficiently aroused by the
crashing axe to make unnecessary any final resort to smoke,
and the entrance to its den proved not to be by way of the

crown of sumac leaves, but at some lower point hidden by the drift, and well away from the base of the stub.

"Look out," yelled Tracy.

The upheaval in the snow became an explosion. The bear, rearing upward on his hind legs, was made to seem the more enormous by the shower of snow flying from his shaggy coat. A rumbling, infuriated roar burst from his gaping mouth and his huge forepaws reached out for the disturber of his winter peace.

Tracy sprang forward to hand Caleb his rifle. But, pivoting without stepping back, he did not so much as interrupt the swing of his axe. He merely altered its direction as he turned and, with the same force with which he had been driving it into the stub, brought the glittering blade down upon the bear's head. The monster, his skull split, dropped to all fours, lurched forward, and sagged, legs spraddled, until he was prone. Caleb, jerking the axe free, stepped lightly aside to avoid the gush of blood.

The approach of Tracy and Caleb was not observed until they had pulled the laden toboggan into the center of the station yard. Eric was just coming out of the kitchen door on his way to look for her. His wild yell was the trigger of a sensation that developed like the eruption of a succession of bombshells. Caleb's reappearance, the tobogganload of meat, Tracy's participation in the bear hunt—each phase of the miracle struck the onlookers as in itself spectacular beyond belief. In combination they were astounding beyond comprehension. Louisa, Olivia, Cam, and Ken came running out. The Negroes, their ills forgotten, bolted from their sickbeds. The Slovers could not have boiled from their cabin with more expedition had a hornet's nest been tossed in at a window.

"Mr. Lewis," said Louisa, "I could not conceivably have imagined that I should ever be glad to see you. I do not know that I am now. But I most assuredly am glad to see what you have brought with you."

Caleb did not reply. He was looking past her at Agatha, standing in the doorway. The others ceased their excited gabble and also turned to look.

"The Lord of the backwoods," she said bitterly. "He giveth —after he hath taken away."

Caleb bent, took hold of the side of the toboggan, dumped the bear's carcass out in the snow, and strode out the gate, dragging the toboggan behind him. Olivia ran to Agatha.

"Have you completely lost your wits? Why drive him away? He was helping us, and he just might have been willing to go on helping us. God knows we need help so much we can forget a little."

"He is worse than a robber," said Agatha. "He is a murderer. Are you asking me to forget that?"

Chris and Susie, still in their woolen night clothes, pushed into the doorway beside her. She dropped to her knees and with a groan drew each of them convulsively against her. The Slovers' interest had already returned to the bear. Jacob and Jarot rolled the carcass over. Olen squatted to prod it with his fingers.

"Fat," he announced. "Might run to more'n four hunert pounds."

Agatha shoved Chris and Susie back into the warmth of the house and came forward.

"Haul it into the kitchen," she directed.

"You-uns figger to take it all?" remonstrated Polly. "Don't we-uns git us no share?"

"So long as it lasts," said Agatha, "you'll eat with us. That way we'll all get our share, our exact share."

Polly, instantly intrigued by the social aspects of the proposal, began to beam her agreement. The Slover men dragged the carcass within and embarked eagerly upon its butchering. Expertly they skinned, drew, and quartered it. No portion was wasted. The entrails were emptied and laid aside, the thick sheath of fat under the skin placed in a pot for rendering. All watched the process with breathless attention. Both fires were built up. Every kettle was got ready. The children were allowed to stay up and to dress. Garett's mattress was brought out into the kitchen. He was too weak to sit up, but pillows were piled behind him so that he could watch.

"Less you-uns wants to git yerselves real sick," advised Polly, "you'll take nuthin at first but a spoonful o' soup. And arter a spell mebbe another. Hold off on yer real eatin' 'til arter yer innards has tuk to workin' agin."

The agreement to abide by this counsel was unhesitating and cheerful.

"Put the four paws in the brass kettle," directed Polly, luxuriating in the privilege of ordering the Jordan servants about. "They make the richest broth there is."

Geneva and her helpers, frantically anxious to get on with the project, took over the actual cooking operations, under Polly's increasingly relaxed supervision and with Agatha perpetually on watch to make sure no one snatched a premature morsel. Waves of warmth from the two great fireplaces rippled across the room. These pleasant currents and eddies began to convoy whiffs from the brass kettle, an aroma of simmering meat which was faint at first but soon stronger and impregnated with tantalizing promise. The children crouched on the floor almost under Geneva's feet, their eyes sharp and intent on her every move and Polly's every gesture. They kept wrinkling their noses and from time to time they wet their lips or tried to swallow. Suddenly Ken ran to his mother and buried his head in her lap.

"I didn't have to do it to him so quick," he whimpered. "I could have waited just another day—and then I wouldn't have had to do it at all."

"No, Ken," said Agatha, silently and desperately praying for guidance. "What you did was good and fine. You must never feel sorry for having done something like that."

"What was so fine about it? What good did it do? Nobody touched it. Cam told me. It's still in that pot in the back of the fireplace."

"Last night we all felt so bad we just couldn't. But we saved it, and it may still save us, just as you wanted it to." Ken was beginning to tremble and when she drew him closer he tried to pull away. "What you did wasn't wrong darling. It wasn't wasted. We'll none of us ever, ever forget what you did for us. Love is never wasted."

"Rupert's was. I wish he was alive, or I was dead. That's what I wish."

"But don't you see, Ken?" urged Agatha, suddenly inspired. "It was you and Rupert that brought us all we have today. You know how the Indians sacrifice something before they go out to hunt because that brings them luck. Eric and Tracy missed that lynx yesterday, but after what you gave us last night, today we have a bear. And it isn't only Indian magic that works that way. It's one of our beliefs, too, that the Lord helps those who help themselves."

Ken did not reply but he had ceased to tremble. Agatha breathed a sigh of thanksgiving.

"It's still a mite weak," announced Polly, dripping a spoon-ful of the bear paw broth back into the pot, "but it's best thet way, fer a starter. The more watery she is, the more apt to stay down."

The company lent itself to the ensuing ceremony with solemn fidelity. First a sip, then a wait, then half a spoonful, then a wait, then a whole spoonful, then, finally, half a cup-ful. As Polly had forecast, gradually their digestive processes began to revive and their shrunken stomachs to expand. They became more ravenously hungry than at any time during their days of starvation. Meanwhile, joints of meat had been put to turning on spits and racks of ribs set on edge to grill. The fat sputtered and crisped, the lean browned and oozed. The smells became unbearably inviting. Anticipation became an ecstasy.

"Look at that chunk," whispered Chris. "Turning black and the juice running out—just like I wished for."

"You wished for buffalo," objected Susie, "and this is bear."

"Bear's better than buffalo."

Polly looked about her, scrutinizing each face, appraising individually the degree of impatience each was betraying, savoring and prolonging her moment of dramatic decision. She nodded judiciously.

"Time's come fer takin' one solid bite," she announced.

A roast was swung to the chopping block. Polly held thumb and forefinger to illustrate the precise size. Geneva cut off a slice and then divided it into pieces half the size of a walnut. The bits of meat were arranged on a tray.

"You pass her around," said Polly, shoving the platter at Tracy. "She was partly yer bear."

Tracy passed the tray. Each took his portion in his fingers, popped it into his mouth, and rolled it blissfully over his tongue.

"Chaw her up good," advised Polly.

At intervals, each of which seemed longer than the one before it, the tray went around again with slightly larger pieces, until the morsels had reached two-bite proportions.

"Give 'em a good hunk this time," Polly instructed Geneva, when the empty tray again had come back. "Some o' them will likely still git sick by now it won't do 'em no hurt if they do."

So far the quiet and decorum which might have marked a religious rite had been maintained. The only words spoken aloud had been Polly's in the course of her officiating. People waited patiently, accepted their portions humbly, smiled faintly as they chewed, often with their eyes closed. Their entire attention was turned inward upon themselves, as though only by such self-absorption could they adequately relish the amazing new sensation of tasting and swallowing. But now the mood of solemnity began to pass. They began to look around at each other, to realize that they had companions in their good fortune. They began to talk and to laugh. The occasion was no longer a rite. It had become a feast. Even Agatha's wan face glowed as she observed her children.

"After today," she ruled, "we'll start in making what is left last. But today, just for this once, we'll eat all we want."

The warmth in her voice, even more than the welcome sentiment she had expressed, brought cries of approval from mouths not too full for response. The Slovers, the Negroes, and the children were tearing at their meat with the avidity of hungry animals. Olivia laid aside the plate from which she had been endeavoring to persuade Garett to eat.

"You wouldn't have to worry so much about how long it may last," she said, "if you weren't so set on keeping Caleb at a distance. He would bring us more."

Eric sprang up.

"He'd ought to be here eating with us," he declared. "After all, it's his bear. May I go ask him, Mother?"

"May I go with Eric?" cried Cam. "May I, Mother?"

"No," said Agatha. Her face was white again. "If you're all bound to have him here I will try to endure it. But I will not send my children to fetch him."

"A nice point," said Garett. "And one which I, for one, can understand. But the fact remains—we need the scoundrel. Tracy. It would appear you were indicated. You've had remarkable luck with him. First you made him produce the lost Eric, now this second miracle. Go summon him to our festive board."

"No," said Tracy. "Obviously we need his help. Obviously that means our trying to be civil to him. But, speaking for myself only, I'd rather starve."

"Polly," said Louisa. "Why not you? You consider him a distant relative of sorts, do you not?"

"He's my own sister's husband's third cousin's oldest boy," said Polly, "even if he don't know it. And if he was the devil's uncle I'd crawl four mile on my knees jest to pat the stock o' thet rifle o' his'n."

She wrapped her ragged blanket cloak about her, selected a rib to solace her en route, and went out. Once more silence fell upon the company. Again there was the strain of expectation, but this time it was an uneasy silence. Only Olen and Geneva were still eating. The others had discovered that, hungry as they had imagined themselves to be, they had not been able to eat a quarter of the amount they had anticipated.

"When you've gone without fer a spell," said Jacob, making one of his rare remarks, "yer gut gits so puckered up she won't hold nuthin'."

He leaned back and fell asleep. Eric got up and went to a loophole, as though to observe Polly's progress across the stream. Under cover of fumbling with the block he stole a look at Lina. She had grown thinner, as had they all, but this had in her case merely made the softly pleasing contours of her face seem more childlike, even angelic. She looked as placid as though her mind, if active at all, were chiefly

preoccupied with a kind of brooding contentment. Nothing
about her expression suggested that she might have a care in
the world. Slowly as she had turned to look at him, he was
even slower in turning away. Their eyes met. She smiled
gently.

Garett pushed against his pillows and looked scowlingly
about him with the irascibility of the invalid.

"Great God, is this a wake? Either the wretch will join us
or he won't. Anyway, for the moment our bellies are full.
Jat, where's your mandiddle?"

"I'll git it," said Lina, springing up.

Eric peered from the loophole, replaced the block, and
crossed to inspect the nearest fire.

"Need more wood," he muttered.

At the woodpile he straightened as Lina returned across
the yard. Again she looked smilingly at him. Her smile was
not reproachful or forgiving. It was pleased and friendly. He
caught her arm.

"Are you really that silly?" he demanded harshly. "I've been
mean to you. I've treated you like dirt. And all you do is
simper and grin. Does nothing make any difference to you?
What can be on your mind, or don't you think at all?"

"Yes, I think. All the time."

"What?"

"I think," she said mildly, "that most any day now you
will git to be a man."

She went on.

Jarot seized upon the mandiddle. But its introduction into
the circle promoted no lifting of the company's spirits. He
became even more absorbed in the instrument than was his
custom. He bent over it. He squirmed and writhed. At times
he surveyed each of the others in the room with bright, curiously understanding eyes. At other times his eyes were blank
or tightly closed as though he were struggling desperately to
listen. Perpetually his lips moved and his fingers plucked at
the strings. But no whisper of sound came forth.

Olivia rose and began to pace restlessly.

"He's likely already on his way back to the Shawnee. If
he had any idea of staying on here he'd have brought his Daisy
with him."

Jarot looked up. He had heard something. The door opened
and Polly came in. She was alone. There was an elkskin sack
on her shoulder. She crossed to the table, set it down, and
jerked open the mouth to show that it was filled with pecans
and hickory nuts.

"Daisy's cache was under the floor of his cabin." Polly

glared at Olen. "Jest where I tol' yuh it would be. Only ye
never had the gumption to dig it up whilst we had us the
chance." She slapped the elkskin sack. "This is the end o' whut
we'll git from Caleb this winter. He's takin' the rest with
him."

"With him?" gasped Agatha. "Back to the Shawnee?"

Polly dropped wearily into a chair.

"Nope. He's goin' a sight further'n thet. He only stopped
off here because this was on his way to the river. He's headed
fer Redstone, the tother side o' Pittsburgh."

"Surely he might spare us more than this one sack of nuts,"
said Louisa. "We would pay him well."

"Nope," said Polly. "He's real sure he needs the rest for
hisself. When a man's in a hurry and got a good way to go
and it's the dead o' winter he wants to take along enough so's
he won't have to stop off to hunt."

"What we'd really pay him well for," said Garett, "is his
rifle."

"Might's well ask him to leave us one of his legs."

"But he can't abandon us like this," said Olivia. "He just
can't."

"He's set on goin'," said Polly. "And when thet Caleb is set
on somethin' yuh got no more chance to change him than
yuh got to push yer hand through thet wall there."

"When is he going?" asked Agatha weakly.

"Soon's he gits hisself a canoe made. He's started in a-
workin' on it now."

March

The winter, which had already seemed so harsh, took yet another turn for the worse. The drift of warmer air from the south came so slowly that the change was at first barely perceptible. The gray overcast thickened and lowered, enveloping the tops of the taller trees and settling to the very roof of the station on its mound. The next day a drizzling rain set in and persisted through the night and the day after. The drifts, without changing shape, gradually and sullenly shrank in size. The air remained as raw and penetrating as before. Only in the footpaths about the station was there visible thawing. These became rivulets of slush.

During the third night the drizzle ceased. A wind began to whisper about the corners of the station, soon began to whine, and then rose to the pitch of a screaming northwest gale. The clouds were swept away. The stars became icily brilliant. Before morning the temperature had dropped below zero. The sun, so long unseen, rose to cast a blinding glare upon a land that sparkled and glittered with insensate menace. The shrunken drifts were glazed with ice, the slushy paths frozen into innumerable points of needle-like sharpness. Every step in the open became a feat. Wood was to be hacked from the dwindling woodpile only by more arduous axe work than had been required for its original cutting. Any renewed attempt to hunt or fish had become unthinkable. The outlook in every direction, into the recesses of the wood lot, across the icy meadow, pond, and stream, along the frozen edge of the forest and bank of the river, was hopelessly forbidding.

The chill without pursued the people within. No matter how closely they huddled over their fires they remained aware of that grim sheath of ice that stretched from the doorstep across the whole compass of their desolate world. For the inhabitants of the wilderness, human or animal, March was traditionally the month of starvation. This legend which they had so often heard had taken on a sudden immediate reality.

To their hunger today was added a sharper fear of a greater hunger tomorrow. They repented having feasted so heartily upon the bear. What was left but served to postpone and make more threatening the swiftly approaching day when they would again have nothing. In the earlier days of their hunger they had sought to cheer one another by pretending to ignore their plight. Now they sought as diligently to share their worst premonitions. They talked of nothing but their extremity, examined it, dissected it, magnified it. Spring, they reminded each other, was still many weeks away, and even the prospect of spring offered few new hopes. The eventual reappearance of game and migrating waterfowl signified little to people without firearms. Even the chance of catching fish in the pond, once the ice had gone out, was clouded by the likelihood that by then no one of them would have the strength left to make the effort.

The cold however, had brought them one faint consolation. The sudden freeze in the night had postponed Caleb's departure. He, too, had been taken by surprise. He had left his nearly finished canoe uncovered in the open. The fresh, unseasoned bark had split in freezing and he had been required to start over again. There was at least a grain of comfort in his continued presence. So long as he was still here there was the possibility that he might after all relent and do something more for them before he left.

For all his grim application to the task, his work on this second canoe was marked by none of the ease and celerity with which he had shaped the first. On account of the continuing cold he was unable to strip the bark directly from a standing tree. Instead he was obliged to fell the tree, to build a long fire, and to roll the trunk near the fire to thaw, in order to remove the bark in the one unbroken strip that he required. This was a slow and tedious process, involving much rotating of the log and infinite care in handling the brittle bark. Since it was taking place on the bank of the stream, his every move was watched with the closest attention from the loopholes of the station.

The cold hung on as though it were still midwinter, but by the dawn of the fifth morning the second canoe appeared so near completion that the anxious watchers realized his departure might be near. The Slovers had as usual thronged into the kitchen shortly after daylight. Agatha had cut the community meals to one in mid-morning and another in late afternoon, but the Slovers so much enjoyed company that they always turned up hours in advance. Polly joined Tracy at the loophole and squinted through it.

"Gawd pickle us all," she exclaimed, leaning her head against the wall, "he's so near done with it he could be a-pushin' off afore noon."

Tracy bent to peer over Polly's shoulder through the loophole. "Why did he need so large a canoe? Did he tell you?"

"He never tells nobody nuthin'. Mebbe he's a figgerin' on luggin' him some truck back from Pitt."

Tracy gave a start of chagrined surprise. She turned to face Agatha and Olivia. "It just this minute came back to me. When I was in his cabin that morning there were a dozen buckskin sacks standing against the wall. They were tight and round, like sacks of corn. Or maybe it was pemmican—he was eating pemmican. Anyway, it must have been some kind of food. What else could he have taken the trouble to drag through the snow all the way from the Shawnee country? So he's not only got what Daisy buried under his floor last fall but this whole toboggan load besides. That's why he's built so big a canoe. He's got all that to take away with him."

"Seed corn, most likely," said Polly.

"But why take corn to Pittsburgh? If he wants to sell any, it would be worth much more in Kentucky."

"He ain't no hand to be sellin' nuthin'. Whut he's more likely doin' is jest takin' it upriver a ways to bury out'n our reach. Then he'll dig it up agin on his way back."

"Enough to keep us all," said Agatha, "for weeks and weeks."

Louisa rose from her chair and took Polly by the arm. Motioning to the three other women to follow, she led the way to her room. When all had entered she closed the door and confronted them. There was a feverish flush of color on her wasted, pale face.

"We are five women," she said. "Five women responsible for a family of twenty. You, Polly, have children. And you, Agatha. And so have I. Olivia, you have a sick husband. Now tell me this. Are we five women going to just sit here sniffling and moaning while one ignorant, stubborn clod of a man makes off with a canoe-load of food which could keep all twenty of us alive?"

Polly blinked. "It don't stand to reason. It don't, fer a fact. But how yuh goin' to stop him?"

"I'll tell you how. You've got three men, Polly. Give them no rest. Scream until they listen. Make them see what they have to do. Clem and Ned are big and strong. They'll do what I tell them. Eric will help. That's six men. Six men to go down there and take what we have to have."

Polly continued to blink. "Six to one ain't so much, not when the one is the only one thet's got him a rifle."

"Surely six men with their wits about them could hit upon some way to get his rifle away from him."

Polly began to shake her head.

"Thet Caleb ain't so easy to sneak up on. But supposin' they managed to git his rifle away from him and his corn and whut all else he's got—all he'd do is take off back to the Shawnee. How long d'ye think it'd be afore they was on us? Me—I'd ruther have me an empty belly than no belly at all."

"I've never known people to equal you Slovers," said Louisa, "for finding so many good reasons for doing nothing."

" 'Taint so hard to find good reasons, not when they stick out at yuh plainer'n the nose on yer face."

"Suppose," said Olivia deliberately, "suppose he wasn't able to run back to the Shawnee?"

The others, startled, regarded Olivia with widening eyes. Polly, however, began to nod understandingly.

"Yuh mean if'n he got hisself knocked in the head?" She considered the possibilities and then again voted no. "Mebbe yer Niggers or yer Eric is up to tacklin' thet. But there ain't one o' my men thet's got it in him. Was they in tight enough corner thy might shoot him from in back of a tree, but they'd never go at him with no axe. Anyways, was he somehow to git done in no good'd come of it. We'd be in the same fix. Long afore spring the Shawnee'd find out. Yuh mind whut it was like when they come down on us afore. Thet time they was feelin' as friendly as they knowed how. So mebbe yuh kin fetch yuh some idee how they'd take on oncet they started in to feelin' onfriendly. 'Twould be we-uns—not the cows—that'd wind up skinned and on the fire."

"It's just not conceivable," said Louisa, sinking down on her bed, "that there actually is nothing we can do to help ourselves."

"There's one thing we can do," said Agatha, spacing her words as though each had a separate bad taste. "We can all go down there together. We can beg, implore, get down on our knees. It might be awkward for even as hardened a brute as he to refuse five despairing women."

Polly sat down beside Louisa, once again shaking her head gloomily.

"Not fer him it wouldn't. He's set on goin', and goin' quick."

"What can this business be," asked Tracy, "that's so all-important?"

"I ain't told yuh," said Polly, " 'cause I knowed 'twould only fret yuh more'n yuh bin a-frettin'. He's made up his mind he wants him a woman and he's in a tearin' hurry to git him one so's he kin git back fer his spring plantin'.' "

"But that's ridiculous," said Tracy. "I mean, ridiculous that he should go along until this late in the winter and then all of a sudden be in such a hurry."

"A man can't git in no bigger hurry. And it's worse when he's bin off by hisself in the woods fer a good long spell. I mind oncet when Olen—he was some younger then—one winter he was mindin' a trap line over on the Little Kanawha. After mebbe two months out there by hisself, all on a sudden he jumped up and run home over the mountain through snow most as deep as we've had this year. I was over to a neighbor's and they was nobody in the cabin but my Aunt Reba. She was near seventy, cross-eyed, and bent up with the rheumatiz crookeder'n a knotty rail. But Olen he was so upset when I wasn't there a-waitin' fer him thet Aunt Reba she had all she could do to fight him off."

"No doubt Mr. Lewis may be equally impulsive," said Tracy. "But if so, why didn't he keep his Daisy within reach?"

"He's aimin' to settle here like a white man, so he don't want no squaw no more."

Polly's hearers were beginning to take a slightly less hostile interest in the several aspects of Caleb's predicament.

"Has he some special woman in mind," inquired Agatha, "back there in Redstone?"

"Naw. He's headin' fer Pennsylvany 'stead o' Kentuck' 'cause the further east yuh go the more women there is to pick from."

"Wait," said Olivia. "What about your Betsey or Lina? Why wouldn't they do him as well as anybody he'd be likely to find at Pittsburgh or Redstone?"

"Nuthin'd suit me better," said Polly, "than to see either o' them git theyselves so good a man. But Betsey she's still got the miseries in her innards."

"And Lina?" asked Agatha.

"She's in a family way, so she'd be no good to him."

"When will she—when will she——?"

"Come fall, and we're all still a-livin', you'll be a grand-mother."

"Grandmother!" said Olivia, her eyes sparkling. "I must say, Agatha, you most certainly don't look it. Starving agrees with you. The thinner you get the more becoming it is. I swear you're a more fetching woman this minute than you were ten years ago."

The two women's glances locked.

"Even ten years ago, my dear, I was not so young as you are today."

Olivia laughed. "There's few signs of your great age. Certainly not one to put a man off. Take even this dolt, Caleb Lewis. Remember his sitting those nights by our fire? He couldn't take his eyes off you. You got so flustered you had to leave the room. Remember?"

"I remember that when he looked at me his face was completely blank. No wonder. I wasn't so different from what he was used to. I am nearly as dark as his Daisy. You were the novelty. You, with your yellow hair and blue eyes."

"Agatha!" said Louisa. "Olivia! Will the both of you—and at once, please—stop this unspeakably distasteful joking."

"It ain't no joke," said Polly, jumping up. "Ain't no manner o' doubt whut could come o' Caleb findin' hisself a mite o' company, off and on, down there in thet cabin o' his'n. With any kind o' luck he might put off leavin' till it was too late fer him to go at all afore plantin' time." She turned at the door. " 'Course, could be yer jest wastin' yer time squabblin' over which one o' yuh it's to be. Could be he figgers yuh ain't his kind and he don't want no part o' none o' yuh. So save yer sweatin', whilst I find out."

"Polly," commanded Louisa. "Stop. Come back here." The door slammed. "Agatha, call her back. Make her come back. Olivia. Tracy."

No one of the three seemed to hear her. Agatha and Olivia continued to stare at each other. Tracy watched them. She was as taut and strained as they.

"I am not forgetting you have children," said Olivia. "We are never allowed to forget that. But doesn't that give you all the more reason? You would not be the first mother who has ever taken to the streets to get bread for her children."

"You have a reason as strong. At least, for you it is as strong. In fact, you have two. You have a sick husband who is so weak he will be the first of us to die. The only thing you wish more than to keep him alive is to keep him miserable. See how at one happy stroke you can gain both comforts."

"The complete madonna. Always you think first of others."

"Will you both be silent," said Louisa. "I will not listen to such idiocies."

The attention of the two women remained fixed on each other.

"I don't need you to goad me," said Agatha. "But I have no wish to be doubly shamed. He is a young man. What interest could he be expected to take in a mother of five?"

"I'll tell you what interest. Your fertility. The man has a special regard for any sort of increase. The first thing he asked me was how many children I had. When I said none, he went back to his eating."

Agatha's mocking smile became more venomous. "You tremble. You breathe hard. Just talking about this excites you. Doesn't it?"

"Ask yourself that. There is not so great a distinction between our situations. You are apparently a widow and I am the same as one. A familiar picture. Both of us starved in more ways than one. Is that the notion you keep circling around?"

"Stop it, for heaven's sake, stop it," said Louisa. The new note of weary reason in her voice captured their attention. "Stop teasing each other, or yourselves, whichever you are doing. You are quite right. Somehow we have to deal with that man. If I were younger I'd go down there myself. I'd have dreaded it more then, of course. I've had to grow old to understand how strong a woman is. In so many ways she's stronger than any man. She can stand hunger, cold—any number of things—better than a man. You, Agatha, or you, Olivia, could go down to that cabin—that is, if you were able to do it without any one else knowing—and be able to come away again without having suffered anything you couldn't get over. Your reason for going would be sufficient to save you. But under our circumstances you cannot do that. You could not take ten steps down that slope, Agatha, without everyone here, down to little Susie, knowing immediately where you were going, why you were going, and, when you came back, what had happened to you. You might get over it, but your children never could. And as for you, Olivia, you know Garett would get straight up out of his sickbed and try to kill Caleb Lewis. It would be the death of him. It is impossible for either of you. You just cannot do it."

"But I can," said Tracy. "I have no children. I have no husband. I can."

"Tracy," cried Louisa. She sprang up, livid, shaking. "It's the most impossible of all for you. It is altogether impossible."

"So I would have thought until ten minutes ago. But we've all begun to realize that we have to do something. It follows just as clearly that I am the one to do it."

"I forbid it," said Louisa, her voice breaking. "Do you understand? I forbid it."

"Maybe you can tell us," said Olivia, "why you're so much more tender of her than of Agatha or me. Is her precious virginity more important to you than the honor of your own sons' wives?"

"Certainly I can tell you," said Louisa. "You're both married women. You have been for years. The animal part of a man is no mystery to you. She has no such defense. We've already agreed neither of you can go down there, so we can speak plainly. For a girl like Tracy it would be an infinitely more devastating experience than for either of you."

"A girl like Tracy," said Olivia. "She's a year older than I am. If she's been just dreaming all this time, then it's high time she waked up. It might do her a world of good—not to speak of the rest of us."

"Especially Garett, you mean," said Agatha.

"Or Duncan," said Olivia.

The door flew open. Polly, panting and even more disheveled than when she had left, staggered in and collapsed on the bed.

"Thet goddam' ice," she groaned, pulling up her dress and rubbing her knees. "I fell down so many times, could be I'll never walk again."

"Well, did you talk to him?" demanded Agatha.

"I surely done jest thet. Real plain talk. When he knowed whut I'd come fer he spoke right out."

"What did he say?" demanded Olivia.

"I'm a-comin' to it," said Polly. "Soon's I kin git my wind. First off—he don't want to go to Redstone if'n there's any way he kin git out'n it. He don't want to lose all thet time. He'd ruther stay here and git on with his clearin'."

Louisa, Agatha, and Olivia looked at one another, appalled by the sudden necessity of facing an actual decision. Only Tracy remained outwardly calm.

"That would seem to settle it," she said.

"It don't settle nuthin'," said Polly. "He said more'n thet. He said he don't want none o' yuh a-crawlin' in and outer his bed. Whut he's a-lookin' for is a woman he kin keep. One thet kin work fer him and cook fer him, as well as sleep with him. He wants him a wife."

"But that's even more impossible," gasped Louisa. "It's so impossible it's—it's ludicrous."

"He can't be serious," said Olivia.

"Yuh kin figger thet fer yerselves," said Polly. "He knows

Garett was a magistrate back in Virginny. He wants first off to stand up in front o' Garett and have Garett read the marriage lines."

Louisa moaned and sank down on the bed, covering her face with her hands.

"That would most certainly seem to settle it," said Tracy. "Neither you, Agatha, nor you, Olivia, can do that."

"No more can you," said Olivia, stiffening with sudden fury. "Garett would never marry you to Caleb Lewis—or any other man."

"No one," said Tracy, "can manage to be more mistaken more often than you can, Olivia."

"Go ask him, Olivia," said Agatha. "We must know instantly what he really does think."

Olivia's flare of anger passed. She clutched at a chair back for support.

"I couldn't," she whispered. "I just couldn't."

"Then I will," said Agatha.

"Tell him we ain't got no time to do much thinkin'," Polly called after her. "Caleb he's a-waitin' right out there at the gate. His canoe's done and if there's goin' to be any balkin' he wants to start right in gittin' her out to the river and gettin' her packed." She struggled up from the bed and looked back from the doorway. "I'll tell Caleb the answer ain't yes and it ain't no—but if'n he'll hang on to hisself fer another couple o' jerks he'll git him one or t'other."

Louisa lifted her grief-ravaged face and looked at Tracy as accusingly as though she had brought this on herself.

"He knew when he sent that absurd message by Polly," she said, "that it could only have meant you."

"So it would seem," said Tracy.

"What does every man see in you?" cried Olivia. "That's what I can't understand."

She turned and ran out, past the silent, puzzled, staring people in the kitchen and on into her room. Garett was sitting up in bed. His face was gray-white, he looked more dead than alive, but he was grinning up at Agatha.

"So Tracy's to be our Judith?" he was saying. "Or rather, to be somewhat more apt, our Delilah—since we seem to be the Philistines in the case. Who maneuvered her into the breach?"

"No one," said Agatha. "It was her own idea. She insisted on it when she realized—when we all realized—that there was no other way."

"How true. We Jordans must eat." Garett looked around

at Olivia. "Why so distressed, my sweet? I would have thought our dilemma would strike you as the fulfillment of one of your fondest dreams."

"Don't chatter," snapped Olivia. "We haven't time. Caleb Lewis is out there waiting. You have to speak right out, and right now."

"You seem to find my decision more dramatic than—than even poor Tracy's, let us say."

"It is to me."

"Then I shall make you happy. Call in the bride and groom."

Olivia's bitterness sharpened.

"Tricks won't save you. You're caught, for once. You've got to be the one to hand Tracy over to him, to take down to that cabin of his. Tracy—do you understand? *Tracy.*"

"Yes. I'm very much afraid I do." Garett was no longer grinning. "And, since it is I who must choose, my choice is a simple one. I much prefer that we all continue to live. Apparently, if we are to live we must pay the man's price. It's as simple as that. The one question, then, is who shall pay it? I likewise can think of but one answer to that. You, Agatha, and you, Olivia, are Jordans. Neither of you can be considered a candidate. Which leaves us Tracy. As fond as we all are of her, if there must be a bait thrown to the bear she would seem to be elected."

Olivia threw herself on the bed beside him and dissolved into a spasm of weeping. Garett leaned over and stroked her hair. She fumbled blindly for his hand, drew it against her face, kissed it over and over again. Agatha regarded the reconciliation impatiently.

"First off, Garett," she said, "he has to agree to move those stores of his up here. You must be sure to come to a clear understanding with him on that."

"A waste of breath, my dear," said Garett. "He appreciates our situation even more clearly than we do. Meanwhile, wouldn't you be more usefully concerned with—ah—decking out the bride, or holding her hand or something of that sort?"

"You are such a heartless dog," said Agatha. "I don't wonder Olivia is always in such a state."

She ran out and across the kitchen to Louisa's door. It was barred from within.

In the room Tracy was standing against the wall, her eyes closed. Louisa got up from the bed, crossed to her and gripped her by the shoulders.

"Now. For the last time. Will you listen to me?"

Tracy's eyes opened. They were calm and distant. She might have been miles away from the distracted old woman who was clutching at her.

"I am listening."

"Mother," prompted Louisa.

"I am listening, Mother."

"I have had five sons. Three of them were killed in the war. I have two left. I am proud that they are my sons. But I have always wanted a daughter. You have become that daughter. Does that mean nothing to you?"

"You know how much it does."

"Then how can you do this dreadful—this bestial thing?"

"How can I do anything else? All these years I have been a part of your family. Now you are in the most desperate danger and perhaps I can save you. How could I endure myself if I did not try?"

Louisa took Tracy's face in her hands. "What makes you so sure Duncan is dead?"

"I am not sure. I—I could not be."

"You are in love with him, aren't you?"

"Yes. I have always been."

"Then, when he returns how can you face him?"

"I have thought of that, too. But it has only made everything even more clear. There has never before been anything I could do for him. Now I can."

Polly began to beat on the door.

"We-uns can't wait no longer," she called. "One way or t'other—it's got to be now."

Louisa sank face downward on the bed. Tracy unbarred the door and went out into the kitchen. She was conscious of the pitch of excitement kindled by her entrance in a company which had only in the last minutes begun to realize the significance of what was transpiring. She saw the Slover men getting to their feet with foolish, elated grins, the wide-eyed, half-frightened stares of the younger children, the open-mouthed bewilderment of the Negroes, the incredulous, numbed horror on Eric's face, Agatha, bracing herself, agonized by her apprehension that even at this last moment some unforeseen complication might intervene to strike down her rising hopes. Then she saw Caleb, standing in the open doorway. He stood there, motionless, poised, waiting, as though expecting some imminent, sudden occurrence, such as a gunshot or a buck plunging from a thicket. The rifle in his hands, the powder horn, bullet pouch, tomahawk, and knife at his waist, his tightly belted buckskins, gave him the air of a man already embarked on a journey and for whom this might as well be a moment of departure as of arrival. His expression was cold, composed, yet oddly alert. His eyes met hers. That strangely direct gaze, which had disturbed her before, seemed to pierce into the secret recesses of her mind. She shuddered, gripped by a terrifying sensation that he understood her better than she understood herself and that it was the unsympathetic understanding of an antagonist.

"I am ready," she said.

Garett threw back the covers and sat on the edge of his bed. Olivia hastily draped his uniform greatcoat over his shoulders and knelt to wrap a blanket about his legs. Caleb and Tracy stood facing him, flanked on either side by Agatha and Polly. Betsey and Lina stood by the door. Betsey's grin spiteful and derisive, Lina's warm and pleased. The Slover men peered with unabashed, leering curiosity from the doorway. Eric, in a frenzy, had driven the Negroes and the children to the farther end of the kitchen.

"Unhappily, I have no prayer book at hand," said Garett, "unless we wait while ours is fetched from my mother's trunk. However, I take it that it is the basic, legal essentials with which we are primarily concerned."

"Yes," said Caleb.

"I must ask a preliminary question." He looked at Tracy. "Are you entering into this contract of your own free will?"

"I am," Tracy said distinctly.

"And you?"

"Yes," said Caleb.

"Then we will proceed. Take her hand, please."

Without looking at her, Caleb reached for Tracy's hand. His fingers closed over hers.

"Do you, Thryza Carter, take this man for your lawfully wedded husband?"

"I do," said Tracy.

"Do you, Caleb Lewis, take this woman for your lawfully wedded wife?"

"I do."

"Then, by virtue of the authority vested in me by the sovereign state of Virginia, I hereby pronounce you man and wife. God help you both—and God help us all." Garett's gray face became still grayer. He slumped sidewise against the pillows. "You must excuse me," he whispered. "I find I must rest."

Olivia lifted his legs into the bed, pulled the greatcoat away, and solicitously tucked the bedclothes about him. Caleb released Tracy's hand, stepped around her, and pushed through the doorway into the kitchen.

"Come," he directed Olen and his sons.

His gesture of command included Ned and Clem, as well. The five followed him out.

"Whatever can he be up to now?" Agatha asked anxiously of Tracy. "Where's he taking them?"

"I haven't the faintest idea," said Tracy. Spots of color had appeared on her pale cheeks. "The only words I've heard out of him since he came in have been two 'yesses' and one 'I do.'"

She went on into Louisa's room. Agatha and Polly ran to a loophole. The men following Caleb were slipping and sliding down the icy slope. They went on across the frozen stream, past the canoe, and disappeared in the woods in the direction of Caleb's cabin. Agatha and Polly were not kept long in suspense. The men reappeared, each with a sack or a basket on his shoulder. They began toiling back up the slope, scrambling to their feet when they fell, and, when they fell again, crawling eagerly upward on their knees. The two women ran to the door. Jarot was the first one in. He deposited the elkskin sack on the table. Polly tore at the leather drawstring.

"Smoked turkey," she cried. "Jam pack full o' smoked turkey."

Jacob stumbled over the threshold, dropping the basket he had balanced on his shoulder. It burst, scattering a bushel and a half of dried serviceberries across the floor.

"Pick them up," Agatha directed the children. "Every last one."

Polly kept Clem and Ned by the door to prevent their stepping on the berries but immediately inspected their loads.

"A sack o' deer jerky," she announced. "And another o' smoked catfish. Thet Daisy, she was busier'n any squirrel."

Olen, the last of the burden bearers, set his sack against the wall. Polly gave it a kick.

"Corn meal," she marveled.

Olen straightened and regarded her coldly. Ordinarily when he came into the Jordan kitchen he snatched off his moth-eaten fur cap and sidled sheepishly into a corner. But now his bearings was clothed with all of the calm authority befitting the head of a family. After one startled glance at him Polly began to bristle.

"Yuh mind them wool socks yuh got put away some-wheres," he said. "Go fetch 'em to me."

"So yer feet got cold thet quick," said Polly. "Yuh bin squattin' indoors so long it's a wonder they ain't dropped off."

"Go git me them socks," repeated Olen.

"Yuh must o' walked most a mile. Yuh jest rest yerself fer a spell and mebbe yuh'll git the strength back to go git 'em yerself."

"I'm aimin' to go a sight further'n any mile."

"Where?" scoffed Polly.

"Huntin'."

"How kin you hunt? Yuh got no rifle."

"Caleb he'll do the shootin'. We-uns,"—he nodded importantly at his sons and the Negroes—"is goin' along to pack in the meat."

"With the footin' bad's it is yuh'll never git far."

"We tie bresh to our feet, we kin make out. Now don't give me no more o' yer lip, woman. Go git me them socks."

Polly gaped at him, then, suddenly and happily submissive, she scurried out.

"Geneva," directed Agatha, "see to it that Clem and Ned are warmly dressed before they start. They're worse than children when it comes to looking after themselves."

Caleb came in. He looked about the kitchen. Agatha's glance went to the door of Louisa's room. Caleb crossed to it.

Tracy was seated on the bed, her arms about Louisa.

"It's too late now," moaned Louisa. "I realize that. We'll just have to put up with it, if we can. I know that."

Nevertheless, she sprang up in a fury when Caleb entered.

"I trust you realize," she cried, "that you are doing the same as taking her by force? Even in this benighted country violence to a woman is regarded as the most unforgiveable of all crimes."

Caleb continued to look reflectively down at Tracy. Louisa turned her back and leaned against the bedpost.

"I will be in the woods for some days," he said. "Maybe a week. There is not enough to eat to keep so many until spring. Since I must hunt I want to lay up enough meat now so that when I come back I can stay with my clearing."

"Thank you for coming to tell me," said Tracy.

He opened the game sack in his hand and displayed a dozen skeins of linen thread.

"I will need shirts for summer. When I get back you will be helping me clear. So while I am away"—he nodded toward the small loom in the corner—"you can be weaving cloth for the shirts."

Tracy rose and accepted the skeins of thread which he was extending toward her.

"Should I say, Yes, Mr. Lewis?" she inquired. "Or, Yes, Caleb? Or, perhaps, Yes, sir?"

"It does not matter what you say. Only what you do."

He turned and went out. Louisa embraced Tracy.

"How utterly amazing," she gasped, "But what a Godsend.
A reprieve, if only for a few days. And we can hope, we can
pray, that something just might happen to him before he
can get back."

"He does not permit things to happen to him," said Tracy.
"That is, not in the woods."

Agatha ran in.

"Whatever could have possessed him to take himself off
hunting?" she demanded. "This afternoon, I mean, instead of
—tomorrow morning, say. Do you think he wanted to give
you a little time to get used to the idea of being married to
him? Could he possibly have that much sense?"

"His explanation," said Tracy, "was simple enough. He
wants to get his necessary hunting over with so that he can get
at his clearing. Meanwhile he assigns me something with
which to busy myself." She indicated the skeins of thread in
her arms. "I'm to devote my time to making him shirts."

Agatha's laugh verged on hysteria.

"Maybe we've been taking all this too seriously? Maybe,
Tracy, you have merely entered into a business arrangement?"

Tracy climbed to the fire step. One way she could see
Caleb and his five followers beginning to mount the rise beyond the wood lot. The other way she could see off down the
river. Suddenly she gripped the palisade. The dark dot for
which she had so often looked in vain came into view around
the distant bend. She watched, shaking, scarcely breathing,
while the dot became larger. It became a four-oared barge,
beating steadily against the current, the first craft of any
description that had appeared on the river since Duncan's
raft had faded from view. But as it came on and on the chill
of the evening entered into her. For the barge kept to the
shadows of the farther shore and kept on past upriver and
on out of her sight. The travelers were no more than passing
strangers who had no idea that the station existed. Her
momentary excitement had but made the more crushing the
sense of desolation creeping upon her.

April

March, after having exceeded the rigors of mid-winter, came forth with other excesses before ushering in April. The third day after the hunters had left the weather turned warm. The snow began to melt so rapidly that in another three days there were widening patches of bare ground. The earth, which had been soaked by the earlier, lesser thaw, could hold no more. Water oozed from the spongy soil, trickled, collected, flowed down every slope, filled every hollow. The stream rose, bursting its shell of ice. The pond expanded and spread into the meadow. Other dark pools gleamed in every flat of the woods beyond.

"Tain't no kind o' weather fer huntin,' " pronounced Polly. "They might's well wade home and dry off."

The unseasonable mildness continued. Spring came like a wave. Buds swelled. Willows flaunted their fluffy plumes. Serviceberry bushes paled, then whitened with blossoms. Frog choruses shrilled in the night. Flights of waterfowl appeared in the southern sky, circled, wheeled, and dropped with much boisterous splashing to the meadow's placid surface. The air was vibrant with the urgent honking of wild geese, the petulant squawking of ducks, the hoarse, thundering calls of the trumpeter swan. One morning came a flock of robins, and that afternoon another of mocking birds swooped into the station yard.

Caleb had set his return at within a week at the longest, but the seventh day passed like the others.

"Could it be that he's not omnipotent after all?" said Garett. "That he could get stuck in the mud like any ordinary mortal?"

"Let's trust he stays with the mud until he gets something," said Agatha. "The cupboard is going to be bare again in another week."

Polly and Agatha began openly and anxiously to watch. Whenever either was in the yard she kept going to the gate to look toward the eastern ridge over which the hunters had disappeared. But when on the tenth day Jarot returned, he came out of the woods on the west side of the stream and no one realized he was there until his axe began to ring. He had discovered the crossing log had been carried away by the rising water, had turned back to Caleb's cabin for the axe, and was felling a greater tree on a higher point on the west bank to serve as a new crossing.

"Do you really think something could have happened to the others?" asked Louisa.

Polly dispelled her not entirely disguised hope. "Was somethin' wrong with Olen or Jake, Jat he'd never be struttin' around like a turkey cock the way he is."

The pine cracked, leaned, and crashed, stretching, when the thunder of its fall had ceased to echo, from the knoll on the other bank to the flat rock at the base of the mound. Working his way across this new bridge, his axe swinging expertly as he came, Jarot notched the trunk for firmer footing and left of some of the branches, as he lopped them off, four-foot stubs to serve as hand grips on either side. It was in every respect a great improvement upon the earlier crossing.

"The whole winter you couldn't get those Slovers so much as to sit up straight," grumbled Agatha, watching. "Now they fly around like the devil was after them."

Jarot came in, wet to the waist and caked with mud but jaunty and cheerful. The load on his back turned out to be a hundredweight of fresh buffalo meat. Polly sniffed at it judiciously.

"Ain't bin kilt but two days," said Jarot. "Took me a extry day to git here 'count I had to circle so far to git around the high water."

"Take the six o' yuh all this time to git yuh one buffler?"

"Nope. Took us no time a-tall fer thet part. Caleb he knowed right where to go. Thet next crik east o' the ridge comes out'n a marsh mebbe thirty mile upcountry. In the middle o' the marsh they's a patch o'higher ground with a salt lick and a lavish o' young sycamore. A middlin' herd o' buffler bin winterin' there, lickin' salt and livin' off'n the sycamore bark. Caleb he knocked down fifteen the fattest the first day. Reason we ain't bin back long afore now was she turned so warm the meat started to go bad. We-uns had to camp and take to smokin' it."

Jarot lingered only to snatch at the platter Polly set before him.

"Who'd ever o' thunk dried catfish'd taste better'n fresh buffler," he marveled. "But fer more'n a week I bin eatin'

all the fresh buffler I could push down." He backed toward
the door. "Caleb's makin' him a raft. He'll have her done by
the time I kin git back to camp. Then we kin float our jerky
down thet east crik no matter how high she floods. Oncet we
git her t'other side the ridge we kin pack her right in."

The next day it began to rain, and with only an occasional
brief pause it continued to rain for eleven days. The flooded
meadow became a lake which extended into the wood lot and.
finally all the way around the mound to rejoin the swollen
stream below the flat rock. The station had become an island.
Polly regarded the rain and the rising water with increasing
pessimism.

"There ain't nuthin tricker'n smokin' jerky," she observed,
" 'cept it's smokin' it in the rain. Thet buffler meat o' Caleb's
likely ain't goin' to be worth packin' nowheres."

"Let it rain," said Louisa. "I hope the flood lasts all summer. The longer it lasts the longer before that man is back."

Tracy sat at the loom. She was not accustomed to weaving.
Louisa had urged her to permit Hebe to weave the cloth, but
Tracy had kept at it until she was now on the last skein of
thread.

"You couldn't be making a sadder mistake," said Olivia.
"That was the first thing he told you to do. The time to stand
up to him was right at the start."

"You talk about Tracy's putting up with him," protested
Louisa, "as though it were something that was all settled."

"Well, isn't it?" asked Olivia.

The long rain ended. There came one hard frost and then
a week of conventional April weather. Clouds raced across
the sky, gathering, breaking, clearing, with each day's sunshine
interspersed with passing showers and occasional brief thunderstorms. The flood waters began to recede. Moss brightened
on the black trunks of trees. The new leaves began their
magic unfolding, bathing the forest in the pale green of their
wreathing mist. A flight of passenger pigeons, so immense that
the cloud of wings shadowed the sky, hovered, settled almost
to the treetops, and then flew on to the north. Polly patrolled
the edges of the stream, watching for the moment its waters
might have cleared for fishing.

"Seen me one sturgeon today," she announced. " 'Nother
week they'll be spawnin' and we kin go to spearin' 'em up by
the falls." She sat down and blinked gloomily. "Ain't no
question somethin's happened to 'em. Thet Caleb he ain't no
hand to set on his bottom a-waitin' out no weather."

But the next day there came at last a second report from
the hunters. Jarot and Caleb, himself, appeared on the west

bank of the stream. Caleb dropped his pack on the ground and at once turned back into the woods. Jarot, carrying both packs, came across and trudged into the station. He did not look so well kept and well-fed as on his first visit. His buckskins were in tatters and he was reeling with fatigue. In the two packs were two hundred and fifty pounds of buffalo jerky.

"We brung this lot in first off," he explained, " 'cause it was some the rain got at. You'd best stew her up 'fore she spoils."

This time he had brought more than news. He was able to announce instructions that directly concerned his listeners.

"We wasn't up to workin' thet raft all the way down the crik like Caleb aimed to. The flood fetched so many trees down they was a log jam every forty rod. So we got to pack in near a ton o' jerky from mebbe fifteen mile up thet east crick. Caleb he wants to git it in right quick. If'n it rains hard again and the jerky gits wet the whole mess of it will go bad. So he wants all of you able to git around to come out and help pack."

At dawn the next morning the packing party set forth. Louisa, Garett, Betsey, Lina, and the younger children were left behind, but the other six women and Eric followed Jarot's lead, taking in single file the circuitous route that Caleb had selected the day before. It was a route that meandered from one patch of higher and drier ground to the next, skirting the ponds, swamps, and bogs that dotted the still flooded wilderness, crossed back to the east side of the stream above the falls, followed the old Indian trail for two miles, then angled to the northeast to climb the ridge and drop down to the camp on the east creek at the point where transportation by raft had been finally blocked.

Here were the scaffolds upon which the jerky had been heaped and covered with hides, with low fires burning beneath the racks to prevent any accumulation of moisture. And here, too, the travelers from the station began to gain some idea of the extraordinary exertions to which the hunters had been committed. Their torn buckskins had rotted from continual wetting until they were all but naked. They were scratched, begrimed with soot, more drawn and gaunt than during their midwinter hunger.

"Ain't nobody," pronounced Polly, after a brief interrogation of Olen, "not nobody never—made theyselves jerky in such weather. Jerky don't stand wet no better'n sugar nor salt. But Caleb he made her, come hell nor high water. And when they figgered they was done with buildin' fires o' wet wood, and new racks every time they moved camp, and pushin' rafts around, and choppin' log jams, they wasn't done with nuthin'. No matter how wore out they got by day, come night he put 'em to work curin' the hides 'stead o' sleepin'. And buffler hides wasn't enough fer him. He'd brung him along a couple o' traps and he ketched hisself thirty beaver 'tween times." She wagged her head delightedly. "Thet Olen, he's done more real work this one month than all the rest of his life put together."

Caleb, in issuing instructions to his new helpers, addressed himself directly to Tracy, as though he considered her a natural extension of his authority.

"As good a day as we may get," he said, taking a last look at the scattered clouds in the sky. "Be sure that everybody takes all they can carry. But not too much. Because they'll all have to move fast with whatever they take. Once it is off these racks it must be under a roof before it rains again."

His month-old beard was red as copper, except where the ends were singed. His eyes were bloodshot; he was as ragged and worn and gaunt as the others. But his manner was as certain as when he had left the station.

"Try to take a half of it," he continued. "Then you can get the rest in one more trip. You will have everybody with you but Olen. He is going with me to raft down the last load from the lick. Tomorrow leave two of your people at the station. Have them look closely at every piece before they hang it in the storeroom. Have them hang the best and driest in the back where it will be used last. But the rest of you come back tomorrow no matter if it rains. You can wait here ready to make another run for it when the rain stops. Is everything that I have said clear to you?"

"Quite," said Tracy.

Caleb and Olen pushed off on their raft. The burden bearers began to assume their loads. In preparation for the earlier transportation by raft the long strands of dried, smoke-blackened meat had been arranged in bundles tied with buffalohide thongs. Each weighed forty to fifty pounds. The women took one, the men two. Jarot set off at a trot, the others, slipping and sliding on the muddy ground, trailing behind him. The first scramble up the ridge proved the most difficult lap of the entire race. The incline was steep and the mud was alternately like mortar and grease. When at last they reached the top, the sky was darkening. There was a rumble of thunder in the distance. Jarot lengthened his strides.

"Just like getting the hay in before a storm," gasped Agatha.

There came the first spats of rain as they crossed the stream above the falls.

"You don't have to stay in line," called out Tracy. "Everybody go as fast as he can."

Several of the men began crowding past and ran on. The intervals in the column widened until it had separated into groups, each of which was unable to hold to the pace of the one next ahead and which in turn dissolved as each individual discovered the final limit of his capacity to keep up. Jarot had reached the station while Geneva, puffing and wheezing at the end of the line, was still a mile from Caleb's cabin. After all their exertions the rain held off, and by the time the last of the procession was floundering up the slope to the gate, the sky was clearing again.

Louisa, clapping her handkerchief to her nose against the bitter, smoky smell that filled the kitchen, regarded the great bales of jerky dropped in disorderly heaps by the weary bearers.

"In this miserable country everything's absurd," she declared. "For months we have no meat at all and now enough for an army."

"This is only the half of it," said Olivia. "Tomorrow we go back for as much more." She sank to a bench. "That is—if any of us can walk."

"I think you should be the one to stay here tomorrow, Agatha," said Tracy. "You and Eric."

"Why me?" objected Eric. "Why not Olivia? I can carry two bales."

He looked around, hoping that it had not escaped general notice that he had been able to carry as heavy a load as any of the men and that only Jarot had beaten him to the station.

"Every one of these bales has to be lifted, moved to the storeroom, opened, sorted," said Tracy. "You'll be needed more here."

"And don't argue," said Olivia. "She speaks with the master's voice."

The next day at dawn, Eric, glancing from the loophole above his cot, saw the young buck nibbling at the new sprigs of green just across the pond that still stretched to the middle of the meadow. Grasping his reconstructed bow, he ran out. Circling through the muddy wood lot he crept back against the faint and fitful early morning wind. The buck's head came up as he caught the scent that he was unable for an instant to place. The bow bent. The arrow struck with an audible, vibrating thud. The gleam in Eric's eyes, as he sprang upon his prey with his knife jerking across its throat, was darker and wilder than the mere exultation of a successful hunter. He threw the carcass over his shoulder and strode up to the gate.

The day which had begun with so fortunate an omen continued to show promise. The bearers, who upon arising had groaned over their stiff points, gathered new courage from the amount of smoked turkey and dried serviceberry stew that they were able to consume at breakfast, and set off over the bridge in unforeseen good spirits. The sky was clear and the early sun warm. Garett, trying his unsteady legs, ventured out into the yard.

"The first real spring day," he said.

"The day he'll be coming back," said Louisa.

Garett eyed her reflectively.

"What do you do when you repent of a bargain? Just how do you get out of it?"

"It was no bargain of mine. I couldn't have been more against it."

"But you weren't able to prevent it."

"Everyone was terrified. We were starving."

"There's the rub. We were starving. Now he has heaped food upon us, a mountain of food. How do we tell him now that we will not pay for it?"

"I don't know. But we have to find some way."

Eric was moving the bales of jerky into the storeroom and helping Agatha sort and hang it. Ken and Cam were engaged in the cleaning and skinning of Eric's deer. Ken was biting his lips and trying not to look too closely at what he was doing.

"If you hate it so much," said Cam, "give me the knife."

"It's dead," said Ken, doggedly, "so what's the difference."

In the Slover cabin Lina was bathing. Betsey watched, her eyes smoldering with resentment as she contemplated the smoothly rounded body which was so much more pleasantly formed than her own. Lina passed her hands over her breasts and about her waist.

"Ain't no difference yit thet I kin feel," she sighed.

"Jest wait. 'Fore long yuh'll go to poddin' out like yuh'd swallered a punkin."

A pleased, faraway look came into Lina's eyes.

"D'ye see thet buck Eric got this mornin'? One shot was all it took. Jest as neat as any man could manage with a rifle."

Betsey smiled with a different kind of pleasure.

"Yuh know why he's bin workin' so hard with thet bow and arrer. Yuh know thet, don't you? Mebbe yuh ain't seen him down there in the wood lot shootin' over and over again at thet poplar stub. It's a stub 'bout the size of a man. He's got so's he kin hit the same spot every time, jest under the chin."

"Yer seein' things," said Lina. "Things thet ain't there."

"I bin seein' plenty o' things plainer'n you. He'll shoot Caleb 'fore he'll let Caleb have her. He'll drive an arrer into him jest as fur as he done into thet buck."

Lina placidly shook her head.

"Tain't only Tracy he's thinkin' about," persisted Betsey. "His father's dead. And Garett's sick. He figgers he's the man o' the family. He figgers thet whutever's got to be done he's the one thet's got to do it."

Lina, continuing to shake her head, began to draw on her clothes.

Chris and Susie were down on the flat rock, dangling one of Polly's fish lines in the water. A school of tiny perch, too small to take the hook, had congregated about the bit of red flannel. Suddenly there appeared another fish as much too large as the perch were too small. A five-foot sturgeon glided slowly in from the darker depths, rubbed against the rock, and came to rest on the bottom immeditely below the staring anglers. Chris lowered his hook and jerked it up and down before the armored snout. The sturgeon paid no heed. Chris handed the line to Susie and jumped to his feet.

"Watch him," he commanded. "Don't scare him off—just watch him."

He ran up to the shop, found Garett's fish spear, and ran back with it. The sturgeon still lay on the bottom beside the rock, his fins and gills barely moving. Chris poised the spear in both his hands. The two children were so intent that they were unaware of the barge that had turned from the river into the estuary. Chris plunged the spear downward with all of his strength. The previously somnolent fish was transposed instantly into an engine of energy. Surfacing with a tremendous splash, he circled and headed downstream, his great tail whipping a wake of froth, the spear sticking straight up out of his back like the mast of a ship. A loop of the line attached to the spearhead caught Chris' ankle and jerked him into the water.

Lina sauntered across the yard past Ken and Cam, preoccupied with their deer-skinning, smiled at Louisa and Garett on the bench beside the door, and slipped into the kitchen. She could hear Eric and Agatha in the storeroom. Eric's bow stood in a corner. She snatched it up and started back toward the door. The bow was too long to hide under her dress. Eric spoke from the office doorway.

"What are you doing with my bow?"

"I—I was only looking at it."

Eric advanced on her.

"Give it to me."

She ran behind the table to escape him. He stepped on a bench and vaulted over it. She twisted in his grasp and attempted to throw the bow into the fire. He caught her arm in time but she clung desperately to the bow. He was wrenching it from her by main force when both suddenly ceased to struggle as they heard Susie's first scream from the yard.

Susie, continuing to scream, came through the open doorway like a small cannon ball. She was in a state of excitement too intense for intelligible expression. "Oh—oh—oh," she kept crying. She cast one wild look around the kitchen and ran toward the storeroom. As she neared her mother her screams at last began to gain coherence.

"Mama—Papa's back. Mama—Papa's back. Mama—Papa's back."

Agatha dropped an armful of jerky and leaned weakly against the wall beside the nearest loophole. In the narrow opening to the outer world the incredible vision seemed to leap upon her. Duncan was at the top of the slope, scarcely a dozen feet away. He was wearing a new, snuff-colored serge suit and a new, ruffled shirt, but no hat. He looked strong and well. He was carrying Chris on his shoulder and both of them were laughing. Everything about the moment seemed to her incredible, including particularly the final circumstance that both Duncan and Chris were streaming wet and Duncan's free hand was dragging an enormous fish. Her knees buckled and she sank, fainting, to the floor.

Duncan came into the kitchen, still carrying Chris and dragging the sturgeon. Garett, Louisa, Ken, and Cam, exclaiming and gesticulating, trailed after him like a comet's tail. Lina stared and laid the bow in her hand carefully on the table. Eric came through the office doorway carrying his mother's limp body in his arms. Duncan put Chris down, let go of the fish, and took Agatha from Eric. Eric ran before him to open the door to their room. Duncan placed Agatha on their bed and knelt beside her.

"Duncan," she began to whisper. "Duncan."

Eric softly closed the door and turned to face the others.

"Let them alone for a minute," he advised earnestly, including Louisa and Garett in his admonition as though they were as much in need of it as the hysterical younger children.

The second day's packing party wound out of the woods into Caleb's clearing. The main procession kept on toward the bridge. Caleb and Tracy, whose loads were composed of the buffalo hides and beaver pelts, turned off to deposit these

at his cabin. Betsey sprang up from the stump where she had
been waiting and ran to intercept them at the door.

"The Kunnel's back," she announced.

Her sharp eyes studied their faces. But her planned sensation seemed a sad misfire. Each was motionless for a second,
as though listening to something in the distance. That was
all.

"He got in mebbe two hours ago," persisted Betsey. "He
came up from Louisville. Bill Granger fetched him in one o'
his barges. He brung hams and bacons and more'n a hunert
sacks o' corn. They got plenty to eat now up at the station
without yer jerky."

Caleb swung his huge bundle to the ground and, loosening
Tracy's shoulder straps, tossed her pack of beaver pelts to the
doorstep.

"He's alive," whispered Tracy, closing her eyes. "I was sure
of it. No, I wasn't—quite."

"You had best go up and see him," said Caleb.

Tracy's eyes opened.

"You are giving me your permission to see him? Is that
it?"

"No. I am telling you to see him. So that you can tell him
that if you are not back here by dark I will be coming up to get
you."

Betsey brightened.

"He brung new rifles fer everybody," she said. " 'Course
Paw and Jat and Jake they'll stand off out'n yer way and the
Lymans ain't with him. So you'll jest have the Jordans to han-
dle. But all the same, Caleb, you'd best watch whut yer about.
They don't aim to let yuh have her. Before his paw got back,
Eric, he was figgerin' to shoot you with his bow and arrer.
Now all three o' them got rifles and the Kunnel he's got him
a new brace o' pistols."

Tracy's face was drawn but she was meeting Caleb's eyes
steadily. "What I decide to do," she said, "will not depend on
anything Colonel Jordan says or does, and even less on what
you say or do. And when I have made up my mind I will
come back to tell you what I have decided."

"You have had a month to make up your mind."

Caleb had spoken so quietly that Betsey's hopes sank again.
She edged around until she could look up at Tracy.

"What he wants yuh fer is to work fer him like Daisy done,"
she said. "Thet's whut Maw says. Maw says was pleasure
whut he had most on his mind he'd o' picked Agatha. He was
most took with her. He liked Olivia next 'count o' her yaller
hair. But when he thunk it over some he figgered thet he

better have him a woman he could keep around all summer
to help him with his clearin' and plantin'.''

Caleb looked down at Betsey. She flinched, backed reluctantly away, and ran to overtake the others.

"There would be some relief," said Tracy, "if I could be
certain that what she said was true."

"What is true," said Caleb, "is that I want a wife. And if
you are lying about coming back, then I will still come up
to look for you."

"I will come," said Tracy. "Because we are agreed on one
thing. We are agreed that we will settle this between ourselves.
We are, aren't we?"

"If," said Caleb, "no one stands in our way."

Tracy walked off toward the bridge, one second almost
running, the next coming almost to a stop. At the top of the
slope she found Garett sittting on a bench at the corner of the
stockade.

"I am here soaking up this blessed sun," he said. "I am also
here waiting to give you the gist of the news. Everyone inside
is still too delirious to get out a single connected sentence on
any subject, while you will be obliged to grasp our situation
clearly—and quickly."

"How true," said Tracy, sitting beside him. "Is he—well?"

"Very. Overflowing with more energy than ever. His ad-
ventures were harrowing but simple. He got safely off the raft
on the south bank. He could not see in the squall but he took
it for granted the Lymans had succeeded in returning here.
After two days of wallowing through the snow he saw a
fire. Unfortunately it turned out to be a camp of snowbound
Cherokee on their way south after paying a visit to their
Shawnee cousins. They took him captive, estimating him to
be worth a good solid ransom. But after they'd got him to
their town down on the Tennessee he ran across Old Tassel,
an elderly chief who used to be more friendly to whites than
Indians are able to be in these land-grabbing days. Old Tassel
happened once to have known Corbit Revel, and Duncan
made such a play on being Corbit's kinsman that finally the
Cherokee let him go on his promise to forward his ransom
when and as he was able. He got back to Kentucky none the
worse except for the delay of two months. There he learned
that after he had left the raft, the estimable Lymans had
floated on downriver to Louisville rather than returning to
the station to share our poor fortunes. He had realized all
along the desperate straits to which we must have been reduced and was every day in a greater frenzy to get back to
us. He had little money and less credit, but Duncan can

talk most anybody into most anything. With some help from
Clark he got together a boatload of supplies and persuaded
Bill Granger to ferry him up and here he is—late but, thank
God, nevertheless here. So, all's well that end's well—so far, at
least. Now, if you've got your breath and collected your wits,
go in and face the music."

Tracy paused in the kitchen doorway. Across the kitchen
and through the open door of his and Agatha's room she could
see Duncan. He was wearing a dressing gown and sitting on
their bed. Agatha was beside him with her head on his shoulder. His other arm was around Cam on the other side of him,
and Susie was in his lap. Ken and Chris were at his knees
and Eric stood over the family group like a guardian angel.
She started across the kitchen to greet him but her feet, as
though obeying a will of their own, took her instead through
the door of her own room. She leaned back against it, eyes
closed, hands clenched, thinking that the last moment in which
there would be time to think was upon her. She must be sure
that she was recognizing what might lie in wait ahead—for
her and for Duncan and for everybody, even Caleb Lewis.
While assuring herself that she was still thinking, she began
to pack.

Louisa opened the door. She was weak with happiness and
grasped at a chair back as she moved unsteadily toward the
bed. "What a miracle! I'll never miss saying my prayers again.
I thought I saw you come in. You haven't even seen him yet,
have you? He's been asking for you." She was letting herself
down on the bed when she saw the array of Tracy's things
spread out upon it. She straightened to stare incredulously at
them and then at Tracy. "What's the matter? Whatever are you
doing? Packing! You're not. Have you lost your wits, child?
Don't you realize? Duncan's back. We're saved. You most
of all."

Panic seized her as she peered at Tracy's pale, set face. She
groped behind her for the door and, turning, ran to break in
upon the family reunion.

"Duncan," she cried, beckoning wildly to him from the
doorway. "Tracy. Come. You must stop her."

"My God," murmured Agatha, raising her head.

"Tracy," said Duncan. "Where is she? I haven't even seen
her yet. What's come over all of you? Why do you look so
odd?"

"She's actually going," said Louisa. "You have to stop her."

Agatha pulled Susie from Duncan's lap into her own.
Duncan looked with a mingling of bewilderment and impa-

tience from his mother to Agatha and then to Eric. It was Cam who spoke up.

"Tracy married Caleb. She's going to live with him."

Duncan sprang up.

"She's what?"

"Caleb wouldn't give us anything to eat unless she married him. So she did."

"But this is incredible. What could the lot of you have been thinking of?"

"We had no choice," said Agatha. "We were starving."

"Uncle Garry married them," said Cam. "After the wedding Caleb went hunting and he just got back."

"And this very minute she's packing to go down to that cabin of his," said Louisa. "That's what you must stop."

"Garett?" said Duncan. "Even Garett lent himself to it? All of you. All of you taking advantage of that girl's loyalty to us."

His accusing stare came around to Agatha. Her lips tightened.

"We thought you were dead and we knew we soon would be. No one urged her to do it. It was her own idea."

Duncan gathered his dressing gown about him and strode out. He burst into Tracy's room with outstretched arms.

"Tracy! They just this moment told me what had happened. Thank God, I got back in time."

Tracy straightened slowly and turned to look at him. He stopped in mid-stride, his arms dropping to his sides. Her glance lingered on his disheveled hair and the dressing gown. A half smile twisted her lips.

"I remember when that gown was new," she said. "You wore it the night Chris was born. You could be home that night because you were on your way from the north with your regiment to join General Greene in Carolina. Seeing it on you when you came in made it seem for a moment almost as if we were back in Virginia and everything was still like it was then."

Duncan took another slower step toward her.

"Everything still is. And you are just as safe. That's what I came to tell you the moment they let me know. You don't have to go through with it. I will take every responsibility for that. You're not listening to me. I'm here. I'm right beside you. Can't you realize that?"

"Yes. I realize it. I'm trying to find words to say what I meant to say first—or try to say. Something, at least, about how happy I am that you are back, and safe and well. No one

could ever be missed as they have missed you. No one could
ever be as important as you are to them."

"Or they to me. And you, too. You are the same as one of
us. You must never forget that. We never can. And you must
also realize that I could have no more intention of letting
that man have you than letting him have Agatha or Olivia."

"I am married to him. Didn't they tell you that?"

He dismissed the fact with a gesture of impatience.

"No contract is valid when threats are involved. If you
are concerned about mere legality we can easily have it
annulled. But the devil with all that. What counts is that I
am here in time and that now you are safe. That man can go
back to his wigwam."

"But he will not do that. He is as set on keeping that place
of his as you are this one of yours. You are neighbors and
you will go on being neighbors. As much as though he were
the owner of an adjoining plantation in Virginia. You would
not consider that so poor a match, would you?"

"Match? You can call it a match?"

"What else is it? You should be able to guess that it is not
a matter of sentiment. It is a practical arrangement, serving
his convenience, and mine."

"But it is very much a matter of sentiment with you, and a
most misguided sentiment. The convenience of which you
are thinking is our convenience. You conceive that you are
doing us a great service. But you are not. You could be doing
us no greater disservice. Your dishonor is our grosser dishonor. I tell you I shall never permit it."

"It is too late to ask for your approval. And we are not
concerned with dishonor. You keep forgetting that I am married to him."

"You are merely talking wildly. It's no wonder. If we continue to discuss it I'll be talking wildly myself. But we've no
need to continue. If you will compose yourself enough to listen I'll tell you why. Added to everything else that makes him
impossible is a final abomination. He's worse than the ignorant
offscouring of an Indian camp. He's an outright Tory. Clark
has been able to learn why he wasn't known on this frontier
during the war. He wasn't here. He was serving in the
English navy."

He waited for her shocked revulsion. Instead she looked
past him, her attention appearing momentarily to wander.

"But that only makes it even stranger," she said. "The
way he speaks, I mean. His accent is a little more English
than American but it is not at all the sort of English he might
have learned below decks on a man-of-war. He picks each

word with so much care, as though not only the meaning but
the sound was important to him. Could he be so set on being
his own man now that he's that anxious to let nothing remind
him of having been an Indian or an English seaman or
whatever else he may have been?"

"What the devil difference how he talks? How can you go
on chattering about his confounded accent when I've just
got through telling you he's a traitor? An enemy."

She remained calm.

"The war is over. It is no longer a crime to be an English-
man. For a man living this near the Shawnee it is even an
advantage."

"Have you been bewitched? What can have come over
you? You've always been so lucid, reasonable, intelligent.
Are you trying to make me believe that you no longer have
even any regard for your country? I can't make sense of anything that you have been saying. Surely you don't want to go
to him?"

"No. But that is what I am going to do."

Olivia came running to Garett on his bench at the corner
of the stockade.

"Garry. You've got to come. Duncan can't do anything
with her. Maybe she'll listen to you. She always does."

"What can I say that the eloquent Duncan has not already
said far better?"

"She's not listening to him. She's too full of the idea that
it is for him that she's doing it. But somebody's got to make
her listen. And, if anyone can, you can."

"Why are you in such a twitter? It wasn't so long ago that
you were hounding her to the altar."

"I know. We had to then. But we don't have to any more.
We have food and guns and everything. We just can't all sit
back up here and let her go off to live in a hut with a man
like that."

"A man like that." Garett pointed with his pipe. "Look at
him down there now. He isn't waving his arms and running
around in circles. He isn't bothering about why we are, or
what may come of it. He's grabbing his chance to ship his
hides and furs off to market by Bill Granger. He never misses
a trick."

"Are you trying to tell me that Tracy's that calculating?
That she's thinking about him as a girl back home might
think of a suitor who had money?"

"Far from it. I'm merely suggesting that she's clear-sighted
enough to put her finger on a few of the facts in the case. And
that we might as well be, too. Tick some of them off for

yourself. He has saved us and is waiting for his reward. He lives on our doorstep. He has the Slovers and the Indians in his pocket. He has the conscience of a savage. He is in a position to build us up or cut us down. Duncan's coming back hasn't altered a one of them. And it has added a new one of which Tracy could be the most sensible of all. Her secret is no longer a secret. We all know now that she is in love with Duncan. If she permitted his return to persuade her to stay, she would have Agatha after her with a sharper knife than yours has ever been. We would all be driven to taking sides. To Tracy, with her regard for the children as well as Duncan, the situation would be intolerable. So what else can she do? Think it over for yourself. If she can't stay here, where else can she go?"

Olivia sprang up from the bench, her face sharpening with fury.

"How could I have been so slow? It's just beginning to come over me. Of course, that's just what you want. She's been a brassbound virgin. You've never been able to get near her. But after she's a married woman, and restless and lonesome and unhappy down in that cabin, then everything might be different. That's what you're counting on, isn't it?"

"My darling," said Garett wearily, "if only this world were as simple as it appears to you, how much simpler all would be for the rest of us."

Tracy walked steadily across the bridge. Hebe followed a step behind, carrying her small cedar chest. At the edge of Caleb's clearing Tracy paused and took the chest.

"You can go back now," she said.

"Yes, ma'am," said Hebe.

She stammered, striving for some word of comfort or farewell, but then, her frightened stare going past Tracy to the cabin, she turned and ran. Tracy went on. The sun had set but the red glow of the sky shimmered through the forest's young green leaves. There was a curl of smoke from the chimney and the cabin door was open. She stopped at the threshold.

Caleb, stripped to the waist, was standing beside a basket of water before the fire, drying himself with a rabbitskin blanket. His back was to her, though she knew him too well to imagine that he was unaware of her approach. His damp skin, away from the line of tan on his neck and wrists, was a glistening white. His entire back, from his shoulders to his belt, was barred with a fearful pattern of welts and scars. At some time, whether in the course of Indian torment or shipboard discipline, he had been mercilessly flogged. Tracy shivered. This testimony that he himself had suffered violence and pain, perhaps degradation, made his lack of ordinary human feelings seem so much more an ingrained and essential part of him. He turned to glance at her in the doorway but waited to speak until he had drawn on a new buckskin shirt.

"You can put your chest on that shelf."

Tracy stepped into the cabin, placed the chest on the shelf, and turned again to face him. He still stood by the fire, surveying her.

"So he did not keep you from coming."

"He tried. They all did."

He continued to regard her thoughtfully.

"Still you came."

"I made a bargain. I am keeping it."

"Then there is the cooking place. There is the axe and the hoe. And there is the bed."

May

The weather, so long a bitter enemy, had become an indulgent friend. Each day, whether sunny or rainy, was pleasantly warm. The forest, once more a luxuriantly solid green, again seemed an encircling and protecting wall. Nature, released from the restraints of winter, was absorbed in the urgency of her annual increase. Redbud ornamented the river bank, azalea flamed on the ridge, strawberries and wild currants ripened, mulberries darkened, crabapple blossoms faded and dropped to make way for the fruit to come. Buffalo were calving, deer watching their still-hidden fawns. Birds, furiously concerned with their nesting, quarreled, mated, built, and sang with equal abandon. Waterfowl, littered marshy shores with eggs in such numbers that Polly, returning from her fishing, was able without straying from her path to gather an apronful.

In turning favorable the weather had lost significance. It was no longer the tyrant. The people of the station were able each day to awaken to the assurance that nothing beyond their control was to interfere with that day's labors. These were violent and demanding. The lengthening days remained still too short for half of what there was to do. May was first of all the planting month. The whole meadow, at last dry again, was dug up and checkerboarded with the traditional pattern of corn hills. The Slovers devoted themselves to the corn planting with unexpected diligence. Their lifelong acquaintance with hunger inclined them to take the same active interest in the brief, arduous labor of planting that they might take in the running down of a wounded buck. But they were not so inclined toward the next and more protracted task of enlarging the area of arable land. For them the process of cutting brush, grubbing roots, felling, piling, and burning trees was uninspired drudgery. Duncan, however, was insistent. There was better land for future crops to be had by attacking the forest margins of the meadow but he was determined first to clear the area between the station and the river.

"We have to get this patch of trees down," he explained, "so that movers coming down the river can see the station. Unless they can see it before they've drifted on past, not a one will ever stop to find out we've got good extra land. We've got to have more families. The Indians may not let us alone indefinitely and we can't hold this place without more people."

Olen was as always mildly anxious to please but not deeply impressed either with the reasoning or the need for new inhabitants.

"We got us no call to fret about Injuns," he said, "long's Caleb's here. And if'n he shoves off, we-uns can't hang on here nohow."

"But we can't fool along forever, depending on Caleb," said Duncan. "The place is ours, not his. We've got to get to the point where we can take care of ourselves."

Agatha brought their lunch to the woods where the men were working. It had been established that were the Slovers to go home for their midday meal it took most of the afternoon to get them back to work again. They accepted their portion with sheepish grins and mutterings and, made uneasy by Agatha's presence, withdrew out of earshot to eat. Clem and Ned followed them. Eric took his corn bread and ham and moved the other way to the bank of the stream. He worked as hard and long as any of the men, yet seized upon any moment's respite during the day to run back to the building of his bark canoe. Duncan sat down against a stump, rubbing his cramped hands over his knees. He had lost pounds, and the formerly faint frown line between his brows had become a permanent and deepening crease.

"You're working much too hard," complained Agatha.

"There's so much that has to be done. And to get anything at all out of Olen and his boys you have to work right along with them."

"If you make yourself sick, then everything will really go to pot. And Eric's as bad. Look at him. Instead of taking a few minutes' rest when he can, there he is sweating over that miserable canoe. Caleb can make a canoe, so he's bound to. Anything Caleb can do he has to prove he can, too."

"I'd gathered that most of the hero worship had soured. I don't think he's been near Caleb since Tracy moved over there."

"He hasn't. He's moped and snapped and been impossible to live with. Cam says he even grits his teeth when he's asleep. He'd put each of them on a pedestal—a different kind of pedestal, of course—and he can't forgive either of them for falling off. I'm not really sure which one he thinks has fallen the farthest. Don't smile. You're as bad as Eric. Tracy's going to live in that cabin has done something to you, too. You can't stand the idea that she did it because she thought we needed help. You're beside yourself with anxiety to prove you're a better man than Caleb Lewis."

Duncan's smile broadened. "But you don't think I am?"

"I know you are. A thousand times better. And in a thousand ways. But we're talking about getting along out here in this stupid wilderness. Take this matter of clearing. You've had six men working with you. And you haven't opened up as much land as he has working alone. He works hard, too, but he doesn't break his back doing everything the hardest way. He just girdled the trees before they budded, let them die, let the sun in, and planted his corn."

Duncan swung around to look across the stream. In the encircling wall of green forests there was one break. Opposite the station some hundreds of trees had become gaunt and lifeless skeletons. Through the bare trunks Caleb's cabin and the clearing immediately around it were now visible from the Jordan side.

"And what a wretched sight," said Duncan. "Like an abscess."

"True. It's a slovenly Indian trick. But he'll have a corn crop this year."

Duncan transferred his regard from the dead trees to her flushed face. "You seem to be inviting the case for the defense. The principal part of it is floating past." He rose to his knees and looked out over the river. "Not a boat in sight, as luck would have it. But during this one morning there have been seven. And they've been eight or ten every day this week. Four or five times as many this spring as ever before." He became suddenly earnest. "That's what counts. The number of people beginning to come to this country. That's what will go on counting and go on being the only thing that counts. Growth. This country's going to grow. And the people who will be most advantaged by it will be the people who are ready to grow with it. Compare us to the Slovers if you like. Five years from now they'll be just what they are now. Or to Caleb. No matter how he works on his place it'll still be just a one-man farm. They can't plan past tomorrow and he can't see beyond his girdled trees. Now consider our outlook. In five years we'll have twenty or thirty families. We'll have a mill and a store and a school and a church. We'll be a town.

That's the difference between our kind of people and the Slovers and Calebs. We're ready to grow with the country. Can't you grasp the significance of what I'm saying?"

"I do love to listen," said Agatha, "to anything you say."

The burst of activity to which spring had committed the people of the station knew one exception. The day after Tracy had left, Louisa had not risen until noon. The next day and every day thereafter she had remained in her bed. She declared she was not ill, but she had little appetite and grew more and more listless. Her one interest was in demanding of whoever came near her what they could tell her, however slight, about Tracy.

"Olivia and I saw her again today," said Agatha. "We took her a pan of Geneva's gingerbread. She was glad to get it. You know she was never much of a cook."

"How did she look?"

"Black as an Indian," said Olivia. "She works out in the sun all day. Caleb had brought seeds with him from the Shawnee and she's put in a big kitchen garden—pumpkins, squash, beans, melons—I don't know what all. Besides that she has to get wood and water and help him drag logs around and—well, everything that Daisy had to do."

"How does he treat her?"

"You mean besides working her like a slave? I don't think he beats her. Anyway, there're no marks on her."

"But how does he look at her?"

"He never does. At least not while we're there. He's too busy ever to look up or to say anything. She scarcely takes time to talk to us herself."

"Why hasn't she come to visit us?"

"She keeps saying that she will," said Agatha. "But she's got so much to do all day, and at night she's so worn out, that she keeps putting it off. That's her excuse."

"If you want to know what I think," said Olivia. "He won't let her come. He undoubtedly thinks if she started in running up here she'd get harder to handle."

Ken was the most frequent visitor at Caleb's cabin, but his reports were more enthusiastic than enlightening.

"Caleb's caught a pair of buffalo calves," he told Louisa. "They're not black like big buffalo. They're almost red. They play around just like our kind of calves, and butt and kick up their heels and suck your fingers. He's got them in a log pen so's the wolves can't get at them at night. And he's got another pen of baby turkey chicks. Fourteen of them, only so big. But they're growing fast. And he's got a pet coon that got tangled in one of his rabbit snares and didn't choke to death because he worked his fingers under the noose. It's already over being wild. It's just as tame. I call him Spec. He runs to meet me 'cause I always catch a frog for him on my way over there."

Cam's observations were more practiced and detailed, but even they failed either to relieve or confirm Louisa's fears.

"There's not much to see," she said. "They're just working all the time."

"How does she look, when she looks at him?"

"You mean, does she look as if she hates him? I don't know. She never looks at him, not while I'm there."

"And does he never look at her?"

"Oh, yes. Once in a while. But he doesn't take any notice. It's just like she was a stump, or maybe not there at all."

"Doesn't he ever speak to her?"

"Oh, yes. When he wants something. Like, 'Bring me the whetstone.' "

"Does she always obey?"

"Well, she doesn't jump as though she were afraid of him. But she does what he says."

"What does she say to him when she brings him the—what was it?—the whetstone?"

"She doesn't say anything. She just hands it to him."

"Haven't you ever heard her speak to him?"

"Only once. They didn't know that I was around. It was just getting dark."

"Really, Cam. I'm glad you visit them so often, but you shouldn't spy on them."

"I wasn't spying. I had a needle for her. She'd broken hers. But I didn't get a chance to give it to her. She was feeding corn mash to the buffalo calves. Caleb had just finished washing himself after he'd quit work. He walked over to the pen and said something to her but not very loud and I was too far away to hear it. That's when she spoke to him. I heard only the last word. That was 'animal.' He laughed. It's the only time I've ever heard him laugh. Then he went into the cabin and she followed him and they shut the door."

Louisa suppressed a moan and spoke hastily. "She was probably talking about one of the calves."

"That's what I decided. Because if she'd been calling him an animal, he wouldn't have thought it was so funny, would he?"

Duncan and Eric were of no use to Louisa. Duncan, whose judgment she valued above all others, was as tight-lipped on the subject as Eric. Garett had likewise remained aloof from the newlyweds but he was ready enough with his opinion of their situation.

"It's not too hard to guess why she doesn't visit you. She's ashamed. She's brooding over her social descent. She shrinks from facing us and our questions and our pity, particularly Duncan's."

"You don't think Caleb Lewis has forbidden her to visit us?"

"I'm sure he'd be glad to see her completely weaned from us. But I think what sticks most in his craw is plain resentment. No man is so callous he isn't griped by a woman's conviction she has debased herself by putting up with him. Marriage is no joke for the best of us and they're likely having a time with theirs. But I don't see what good could come of our trying to interfere. It's something they have to work out for themselves. Maybe she'll civilize him. Maybe she'll knife him in the night. Maybe she'll just decide she can't stand it and come back. She's made her big move, like Ken did when he strangled his dog, and there's nothing we can do now but wait and see what comes of it."

Louisa shivered and drew the covers around her. "All these years I've thought we Jordans were something a little bit special. But look what we have come to."

Duncan became increasingly concerned about his mother's decline.

"You must realize she's getting old," said Agatha, unpacking his lunch. "Tomorrow will be her sixtieth birthday."

Susie, who had come to the clearing with her, jumped up, instantly excited.

"It is?" she exclaimed. "Are we going to have a birthday party?"

Duncan and Agatha exchanged glances .

"Not a bad idea," said Duncan. "It might cheer her up. We'll take a day off. It'll do us all good."

"It'll only make her feel worse, if Tracy doesn't come."

"Tracy will feel bound to come. That's another advantage. It'll break the ice, get things on a more normal footing. Go ask her."

"I'm not at all sure that she'll feel bound to come, or that Caleb will permit it. But I'll try."

"Wait. We'll get three birds with our stone. Eric's the one to go. He needs some of the nonsense jolted out of him."

Eric came over from his canoe.

"The bark split again," he said. "That's the third time."

"Maybe you need Caleb to show you how to do it. You

can mention it to him now because we want you to go over there. Tomorrow's your grandmother's birthday. We're going to celebrate it. Run over and ask Caleb and Tracy to join us."

Eric paled and stiffened.

"No, Father. I—I can't do that."

"Why not? Caleb used to be your model."

"It's not Caleb. It's Tracy. She—she—I can't."

"She's not got leprosy, you know. All she's done is get married, which she was bound to do sooner or later."

"But not the way she did it. She didn't have to go through with it, not after you came back. I—I can't."

Eric backed off and ran to his canoe.

"Why, the sanctimonious young puppy," said Duncan.

"He's always looked up to her as a creature a cut above an angel and he can't get used to the idea she's mortal. But you should talk. You haven't been near them either."

"That's so. And not because I feel Tracy has fallen from grace. It's just that I can't stand the man. But, very well. I'll take my medicine. I'll go myself."

Duncan, crossing the bridge, saw Tracy on her knees in her garden among her sprouting vegetables. He veered off toward the sound of Caleb's axe in the edge of the woods. Caleb looked around from the log he was hewing. A dozen other squared timbers were piled nearby.

"A new cabin?" inquired Duncan.

"Barn for the stock," said Caleb.

"We're having a barbecue tomorrow. It's my mother's birthday. Will you and Tracy come?"

Caleb began whetting his axe blade with the stone.

"I have work."

"My mother is particularly fond of Tracy. She has been missing her."

"She has work, too."

"Does that mean that she has not visited us because you have forbidden it?"

"No."

"Then you mean she has not wanted to come?"

"I do not know. I have not asked her."

"Have you any objection to my asking her?"

Caleb tried the edge of the blade with his thumb and looked at Duncan.

"I agree with you. She is a fool. But she will be there tomorrow."

"Are you trying to tell me that she will not pay a visit to her own people unless you order her to?"

"Which way do you want it? Do you want her to come? Or not to come?"

"Of course I want her to come. My mother needs to see her."

"Then she will be there."

Duncan was still fuming when he rejoined Agatha.

"Things have got to such a pass that we can't observe my mother's birthday without getting that man's sanction."

"He must be pretty sure of himself to want her to start seeing us again."

"He's more sure of what he doesn't want. He doesn't want to admit that his wife has any reason to feel she's been degraded by marrying him. Now when she turns up tomorrow, I don't want you and Olivia to make it all worse by badgering her with questions. Just let her tell what she feels like telling."

"We'll do our best to remember our company manners," said Agatha tartly.

The next day Eric, bent on devoting the holiday's leisure to his canoe, was up as early as any working day. The family had not finished breakfast when he came running back from the point.

"There's a big boat turning into the stream," he announced.

Duncan and Garett ran out to the gate and around the corner of the stockade. Moored beside the lone sycamore was a huge, square, floating platform on which were three sheds, two wagons, a number of horses and cattle, and twenty-five or thirty people. Duncan grasped Garett's arm.

"Look," he exclaimed. "That must be one of the new kind of boats they were talking about in Pittsburgh last year. A flatboat. The first on the river. See what it can carry, so long as it has only to drift downriver with the current. A mover can bring along everything he owns."

Eric was already halfway back to the point. Duncan ran after him. Garett, following at his slower pace, was soon passed by the children. Olen, Jarot, and Jacob, stimulated by the prospect of the day's festivities, had also risen early to dig a barbecue pit. They dropped their shovels and joined the procession to the point. In the kitchen the women peered from loopholes. People were disembarking from the strange craft that looked so much like a floating barnyard and turning their stock out to graze on the new grass along the shore. Duncan and then Garett were shaking hands with the visitors. The Slovers had joined the assemblage. Everyone was talking and gesticulating. Cam was the first one of the welcoming delegation to return with a report. She burst in out of breath.

"A flatboat," she said. "A two-family flatboat. People by the name of Baxter. On their way to Kentucky. And who do you think's with them? Ida Lyman, Mark Lyman's wife. And her two children. One's four, the other only two. And Maggie Cobb. She's the girl they were always talking about who was waiting to marry Luke Lyman. That's why the Baxters stopped their boat here. To leave Ida and Maggie off with the Lymans. They though were still here. Ida is crying, but Maggie looks as though she might be able to wait till they get to Kentucky. Anyway, Grandma, they'll all be here for your birthday party. Father invited them."

"Thirty extra people," exclaimed Agatha.

"Be enough meat," said Geneva placidly. "Thet buffalo Jat shot, she's gonna be roasted whole over thet pit they dug. They'll be a plenty to go round."

Garett returned with the next report.

"Baxter and his brother have fourteen offspring," he said. "Six of them boys old enough to work. Then there are three unattached white men and five Negroes—making a total of sixteen men and four women, counting the desolate Lyman ladies, and ten children, besides six horses and eight cows. A veritable colony. Duncan is talking Baxter's arm off, enlarging upon the many advantages of our situation here. He wants you all to do what you can to make them feel at home. Naturally, it would enormously improve our position if they could be persuaded to settle here."

The Baxter party, staring all about them in eager, open-mouthed curiosity, were shepherded into the stockade. Hiram Baxter, a sturdy, graying fifty with a perpetual civil smile, had little to say but was giving encouragingly close attention to all of Duncan's observations. The Baxter women were ill at ease at first, especially when they were presented to Louisa, Agatha, and Olivia, but soon gained more aplomb and began to chatter about their experiences aboard the flatboat. Ida Lyman, small and dark and agitated, alternately sniffled dutifully over her great disappointment and scolded the two children clinging to her skirts. Maggie Cobb, big and fair and calm, surveyed the buildings, equipment, and people of the stockade with a regard almost as intent as had been Caleb's appraisal on the occasion of his first visit. She paused with heightened interest when she noticed Jarot and Jacob preparing the buffalo carcass for its suspension on a hickory pole over the fire pit. Jarot, exercising the prerogative of the hunter who had performed the actual killing, shoved Jacob aside so that he might be the sole object of her inspection.

"You the one that shot it?" she asked.

"Last evenin'," he said, swallowing hard but getting out the words. "Jest afore dark."

"Far off?"

"Up on the ridge."

Maggie surveyed the carcass again. "Most as heavy as a good two-year-old steer. How'd you get it in all in one piece?"

"Trimmed like she is—with the feet, head, and hide off and the guts out—she don't weigh more'n four hunnert pounds. Me and Jake we just tied her to a pole and lugged her in."

"Lavish o' buffalo in these parts?"

"Middlin' lavish. They come and go."

"Sounds most as good as havin' your own herd o' cattle."

"We-uns don't lack fer meat, not twixt spring and fall, leastwise."

Jarot, having completed the arrangement of the carcass on the spit that transfixed it, lifted one end of the pole to the notched upright in which it was to turn. Before he could get around the fire pit to lift the other end into position, Maggie had picked it up, given it a practiced jerk and a swing, and had fitted it into the notch of the opposite upright. Jarot permitted himself a direct look at her. She was tall enough to come to his shoulder and probably weighed a hundred and fifty or sixty pounds. But there was no fat on her. She was plump only where it was natural for a woman to be. The hand she raised to tuck back a lock of her straw-colored hair was calloused by years of hard work. Her blue eyes, looking right back at him, were as honest and matter-of-fact as a child's.

"Yer right strong, fer a gal."

"That one end wasn't no heavier'n a good-sized hog. Since Pa died I been doin' all the butcherin' back on our farm."

"Sell off yer farm?"

"Ma, she married agin. I'd heard some about this new country out here so I took a notion to come along out with Ida."

Jarot had finished binding a crossbar to the end of the pole. He grasped the bar, gave the carcass a quarter turn, and tied it with another leather thong in its new position. He glanced under his arm at Maggie's face as he spoke again.

"Luke Lymán, he ain't here no more."

"Ain't so many folks in Kentucky, Ida and me won't run across the Lymans somewheres down there." Maggie contemplated the gigantic roast on the spit. Its under side was beginning to sizzle. "I got me a Continental musket Pa brung back from the war. Reckon it would hit hard enough to knock down a buffalo that size?"

"It might, was yuh to stick it in his ear."

"What with did you shoot this one?"

"A Lancaster rifle. Want to see it?"

"Yes, I would."

They walked off together toward the Slover cabin.

"Take grateful notice," Garett said to Duncan. "You could be drawing most unexpected support from a most unexpected quarter."

The company was too numerous for the kitchen and in any event the roasting buffalo was becoming the center of attention. Louisa's chair was moved to the yard where she held impromptu court. The general excitement had restored some of her vitality. She seemed more her old self and betrayed her continuing inner anxiety only by the frequency with which her glance returned to the gate. But Tracy's appearance was delayed by another unusual event. After a month during which so many scores of craft had sailed unconcernedly past, on this one notable day a second boat had swung out of the river and poled into the stream.

"We've become a bustling port," said Garett.

Bill Granger, on his way from Louisville to Pittsburgh, tied his barge at the flat rock. He welcomed Duncan's suggestion that he and his four boatmen attend the barbecue and even volunteered to bring along a small keg of whisky. Duncan drew aside to read the letter from Clark which Granger had brought him.

"Good or bad?" asked Garett, watching his face.

"Both. Clark says the peace is already showing cracks. The Miami have started raiding outlying stations in Kentucky and the English have sent all the tribes new supplies of gunpowder from Detroit. He thinks the Wyandot and Delaware will stay quiet this summer but he's not so sure about the Shawnee. He's still after them to come in to talk treaty but they keep on putting it off."

"What's the good part?"

"Caleb. It's wonderful that we should be able to take comfort in being reassured our only neighbor is a Tory. Clark's found out a little more about him. When Caleb came back after the war, he went first to Detroit where he worked for a year in the English fur trade. Clark thinks it's safe to assume he's hand in glove with English Indian agents and traders like Alexander McKee and Matthew Elliot. At any rate, Clark promised to warn us if he considered the time had come for us to pull out and he doesn't think it has—yet. It's his judgment that if we can keep on good terms with Caleb we may feel reasonably safe here, at least through this summer."

"Which gives us some three months to recruit enough new settlers to hold the station with or without Caleb."

"Exactly."

The barbecue festivities, which had been given so much impetus by the arrival of so many unexpected guests from the outer world, were presently electrified by two more sensations. The first was Jarot emerging from the Slover cabin to saunter across the yard loudly strumming his mandiddle. He was drawing from it an inspiriting and provocative dance tune, but what brought the universal gasp of amazement from all who knew him was the circumstance that he had shaved off his beard. The band of dark tan across his nose and eyes, contrasting with the strange white of his lower face, gave him the rakish and somewhat piratical aspect of one wearing a mask. The second, immediately following sensation was Tracy's appearance in the gateway. She was smiling, her hair was carefully dressed in a high-piled, formal arrangement set off by an ivory ornament, and she was wearing her best blue silk gown. But what was far more astounding even than Jarot's beardlessness had been, was the final touch to her toilet. Her nostrils were transfixed, Indian fashion, by a single, small, vividly scarlet feather.

Louisa had taken advantage of the attention attracted by Jarot's music to have her chair moved to the corner of the shop where she would be nearer the gateway. Agatha and Olivia had scarcely got her settled when Tracy appeared in it. They sprang up, gasping and staring, but she bent swiftly past them to kiss Louisa. She straightened, laughed lightly, and touched a rueful fingertip to the quill piercing the delicate edge of the dividing membrane in her nose.

"I'm so sorry about this," she apologized. "But once I'd got it in I didn't dare take it out again."

"Why," asked Louisa faintly, "did he make you wear that ghastly thing?"

"He didn't. Far from it. It was my own last-minute inspiration. I was sure he'd object to my coming up here flaunting this squaw's gewgaw. But he fooled me, as usual. He took no more notice of it than he did of my dress or the way I'd done my hair."

"Is it as hard as that to find something about you to which he objects?" asked Olivia.

"Oh, no. He objects to practically everything about me. But he regards his opinion of me as of no more importance than my opinion of him."

Louisa looked helplessly from Agatha to Olivia.

"Is the man made of stone?" exclaimed Agatha.

"Granite," said Tracy. "A granite, white Indian. That's my lord and master."

"There must be some way to get back at him," said Olivia.

"So I would have thought. I still keep losing my temper and trying something new, however absurd, like this thing in my nose, in the hope of disturbing him. But it's no use. He simply takes no interest."

"You could stop working so hard," said Agatha. "That should catch his interest."

"It would trouble me more than it might him."

"When he comes up here today," said Louisa, breathing deeply, "I shall have a talk with him."

"He's not coming. He's too busy making more stock pens. Bill Granger brought some of the things from Louisville Caleb asked for in exchange for his hides and furs. They included a crate of young chickens, a pair of pigs, and a bull calf to grow up with his buffalo heifers."

Louisa reached out a suddenly trembling hand to grasp one of Tracy's.

"How, my dear, how, really, are you getting along?"

"I keep too busy to wonder. We both work, as you must have noticed, every hour of every day, from dawn to dark. That's a blessing in its own way. It helps to make it all seem more like the strictly business arrangement you, Agatha, said it might turn out to be."

"That only accounts for the days," murmured Olivia.

"At night," said Tracy, as calmly as she had explained the scarlet squill, "we sleep together, of course. I have no real basis for judgment but I should guess he is somewhat nearer an ordinary man in the dark than he is in the daylight."

"However can you stand it?" moaned Louisa.

"That I admit surprised me, too, at first. But I suppose it is something the average woman can stand more easily than she can any number of other trials. That must be so if you remember how many resigned wives you have known."

Duncan came striding, hands outstretched from the shop through which he had been showing Hiram Baxter.

"Tracy, I thought I heard your voice. I'm so glad you got here——"

He broke off to stare, dumfounded, at the scarlet quill.

"It wasn't Caleb's doing," said Agatha, coming quickly

to his rescue. "Tracy did it herself, trusting to aggravate him. But he took no notice of it. Like all husbands, he's blind at the oddest moments."

Duncan, recovering, took Tracy's hand, bent over it, and drew back to survey her.

"An Indian princess in a ball gown. Even that feather is bewitching. Bear with me for a second." He turned, lowering his voice, to Agatha and Olivia. "Talk to Ida Lyman and Maggie Cobb. If we could persuade them to stay it might help decide the Baxters to stay. Explain to them that they may have trouble locating the Lymans in Kentucky. Clark had them run out of Louisville when he heard how they had deserted us, and there's no guessing where they may have drifted by now. Tell the women, as if you were thinking only of their relief, that if they do stay here, we can send word to Kentucky and have the Lymans, when they can be found, come here to join them."

"You would really take the Lymans back," exclaimed Agatha, "after the way they have acted?"

"Why not? They're good workmen. We need them as much as we did before. We need anybody we can get."

Agatha and Olivia moved away slowly, reluctant to miss any further exchanges between Duncan and Tracy. He turned back to her.

"Forgive the attention to business, even in this first moment of your first visit. But these are days we can't neglect a single item."

"I'm very aware of that. We keep busy on our side of the stream, too."

"It seems to agree with you. You look positively blooming."

"Thank you. Though it's not equally flattering that you should seem so surprised. After all I am not quite a fugitive from captivity. I have been working like a slave, that's true. But then, so have you." Tracy's color had heightened but she was addressing Duncan with the same artificial ease with which she had the others. "And there's one compensation which you foresaw even before we left Virginia. That's a satisfaction in seeing things grow and other things take shape where there was nothing before. That's what we all came to this country for, isn't it? To make it over, to make something of what was nothing. It isn't easy. We didn't expect it to be. But in just the doing there is a reward of a sort."

"Courage," marveled Duncan. "The most remarkable courage."

"If you are intimating that I must be unhappy, of course I am. I am living with a man who's as much a stranger as when I first came to his door. But we've got thirty acres in corn and three pens of livestock and by this time next year all this will be doubled. That's why we came here, isn't it? To build, and keep on building. That's what you've always said, isn't it?"

"Yes," said Duncan quietly. "That's what I've always said."

The first tentative stampings and caperings of the dance were getting under way on the hard-packed earth of the yard as the persistent, shrill, thumping rhythm of Jarot's mandiddle became increasingly irresistible, even to the most diffident. Olen and Polly, whooping to signalize each change in the movement, broke the ice and were soon joined by Bill Granger with the younger Mrs. Baxter. Jarot sat on a bench, his great, sinewy fingers darting and thrusting among the strings with inventive abandon. He did not once look toward Maggie seated beside him on the bench, but the raptness of his gaze fixed on the air before him betrayed his consciousness of her nearness. Each moment his music vibrated with a wilder exuberance.

The oldest Baxter boy ran to drag Maggie from the bench and into the dance. She remained in demand, as the boatmen and the other Baxter youths sought their turns as her partner. Jarot continued to play with the same strident vivacity, but it was as though his hands were moving over the strings of their own quite independent volition. His whole attention was on Maggie, his burning eyes following her every movement, gesture, change of expression. Bill Granger, dancing with her, embarked upon an elaborate cakewalk which, on one of its strutting parades, carried them as far as the gate and beyond Jarot's range of vision. He continued to play, but as she went out of his sight he became rigid and his white face turned a brick red. They were back in a moment or two and prancing once more among the other dancers, but the cloud over Jarot did not lift. Duncan, having danced once with Ida Lyman, threaded his way among the weaving couples to do his duty as host by Maggie in her turn. She released herself from Granger's grasp but backed away from Duncan as well, and, evading the pursuit of other admirers, ran back, flushed and smiling, to sit once more on the bench beside Jarot.

His playing stopped in the middle of a bar and he turned to look at her, awed by the miracle of her return to him. His lips began to move, silently, and his fingers to pluck, soundlessly. Beads of sweat burst out on his forehead. He writhed and trembled. He was a man in torment. She stared at him, fascinated by his mysterious struggle.

Garett clutched Duncan's arm. "Look. Again the birth pangs of genius, by far the most painful seizure yet."

No longer marked by his beard, Jarot's face revealed nakedly the intensity of his emotion. It was an emotion too deep for expression but which yet struggled despairingly for the release of expression. The dancers, left stranded by the silence, turned to stare. Maggie leaned nearer to him, looking with helpless, puzzled sympathy into his haunted eyes.

Garett clung to Duncan. "Don't miss a second of this. I swear, I've the strongest premonition this time he's about to be delivered."

Jarot's fingers suddenly swept across the strings, bringing forth a single, harsh, triumphant chord. In the silence that followed the breathing of the crowd was audible. No one spoke or laughed. The silence continued. Jarot turned slowly from Maggie and bent over his instrument. Again his fingers began to move. At first there was no more than the faintest whisper of sound but it persisted and gradually gained form and body and rhythm and became a wailing, minor-key lament with a short staccato movement of eerie melancholy endlessly reiterated. His eyes brightened. His struggle was all but won. The last height was before him. He was finding words to go with the melody. As suddenly as when he had struck the initial chord he raised his voice in a husky, plaintive baritone:

> "If'n I could sing
>   Ain't no words I'd find
>   'Cept them thet's about
>   When I seen yuh last."

He struck several minor chords and, brightening again, embarked upon a second stanza:

> "If'n I could talk
>   Ain't nuthin I'd say
>   'Cept how long it's bin
>   Since I seen yuh last."

This time the succeeding chords were more confident. He was no longer so astonished by his achievement. He was able to recognize his aptitude and to welcome his own delight in it. With more and more assurance he kept on:

> "If'n I could write
>   Ain't nuthin I'd spell

> *'Cept how good I felt*
> *When I seen yuh last.*

> *"If'n I could fly*
> *Ain't no place I'd fly*
> *'Cept straight to the place*
> *Where I seen yuh last."*

He paused momentarily, frowning, then, beginning again to beam, embraced the blessed release of one final burst of improvisation:

> *"If'n I could pray*
> *Ain't nuthin I'd ask*
> *'Cept to find yuh agin*
> *Where I seen yuh last."*

His hearers, not realizing the phenomenon was consummated, waited appreciatively for more. Jarot, the excitement of his inspiration waning, was gripped by the significance of what he had done. He was afraid to look at Maggie even though her low, throaty chuckle indicated she might not have been displeased by his offering. Sudden panic seized him.

"Hey," he yelled, springing up, "thet buffler must be most done."

Tracy, sitting on a stool beside Louisa's chair, laughed and applauded along with the rest.

"That was really wonderful," she said. "Jarot's tried so long and so desperately and now he's finally brought something off. Maybe there's hope for all of us."

"There's none for you, child. Not while you're so bitter."

"It's good to be bitter." Tracy rose. "You need to be to keep on."

"You're not going? You haven't eaten. You scarcely got here."

"I've made you all sufficiently uncomfortable for one day. And I must get back to my chickens. They'll become another of my little chores. I'll send you the first egg."

"You mustn't blame Duncan. He has so many responsibilities."

"Of course I don't blame Duncan. Nor Caleb, either. I don't even blame myself. It's been one of those irrational accidents that you could see coming but couldn't escape, like a falling tree or an overturning canoe."

"That—that frightful object in your nose. That wasn't to annoy Caleb. You wore it to punish Duncan."

"No. No, that's not true. I'm sure it isn't." Tracy gave further consideration to the charge and again shook her head. "I'm very sure it's not. Duncan was always at a great distance. And now he's at an infinite distance. Caleb's the one who is near, the one I have to deal with." She bent to kiss Louisa. "You mustn't take it so hard. I'm tough and, as you say, I'm bitter. I'll manage."

Duncan found Garett in the gateway, watching Tracy crossing the bridge on her way back to her cabin.

"That defiant little feather," mused Garett. "And such a red one. No trace of white feather about that girl." He turned to look into Duncan's face. "So. The verdict, eh?"

"Baxter looked and listened with the most amiable attention but his mind had been made up before he landed. He likes everything about our location except the several disadvantages that it's on the north bank, it's too near the Indians, it's too isolated, and it's on land where Congress has forbidden settlement. He was on his way to Kentucky and he still is."

"And the two homeless young ladies?"

"They're no use to us without the Baxters. In any event, they're going along to keep on looking for the Lymans until they find them."

"Perhaps we should borrow Caleb's canoe and spend our days out in mid-river, hailing movers' boats. You know, like pitchmen at a carnival. We might steer an occasional unwary yokel into our tent."

"I've a better idea. Bill Granger's on his way to Pittsburgh. The corn's all in and the clearing can go on, at least after a fashion. So I'm going with him. By the time movers are this far downriver they have it long since settled in their minds that they're on their way to Kentucky. But if I can talk to a few of them before they've even got their boats loaded I might get them to thinking about heading for our place."

"Not bad," agreed Garett. "Not bad at all. It's about the last shot in our locker—so ram it home."

Duncan's announcement that he was again leaving the station drew from his mother none of the anxious protests he had expected.

"A wonderful idea," she said. "You can take Tracy with you."

"Stop and think. You have always had such good judgment."

"I still have. And it is for you to stop and think. This is a heaven-sent opportunity for her to get away. You can send her on to Virginia. Anywhere would do, anywhere that she was beyond the reach of that brute."

"It's out of the question."

"You've been working too hard, Duncan. You've got so wound up in your plans and anxieties. Haven't you seen how really wretched she is, what a truly dreadful time she's having? Have you so soon forgotten that she's doing it all for us? Perhaps we couldn't save her before. But we can now. And we must."

"So we do, as soon as ever we can. But that time is not now. Suppose she was wild to go and was here begging me to take her. . . . I would have to give her the same reply I am giving you. For a very simple reason. I cannot go at all if I must take her with me. I could not leave unless I were sure Caleb Lewis was here and still posing as the station's protector."

"But that day you came back from Kentucky—then you tried your hardest to keep her from going down there at all. You were not so afraid then of what Caleb Lewis might do."

"True. Because then I was staying here myself. Now we are talking about my leaving. And I can't if the station is falling apart. The Slovers, for instance, would clear out overnight if they weren't counting on Caleb."

"The station. Always the station. If only the Indians had taken it when they first came. And us, too. We'd have been more able to hold up our heads."

"That's ridiculous. Of what should we be so ashamed? You've been brooding too long. Tracy is not a child. She did what she did with her eyes open. We must help her as we can. But breaking up her marriage to Caleb does not come first. This land, this place, our home, and future—that comes first. Forgive me if I harp on what must be so self-evident."

"What you can't forgive is her going to him after you had tried to stop her. You're jealous."

Duncan laughed. "Thank God, you've not lost your sense of humor. Along with every year getting more and more set on your own way. Now chirk up. We're not so badly off. We'll get everything worked out and back in the place it belongs. Including Tracy. Just have a little patience."

The Baxters were trailing along the path to the point and their flatboat. At the end of the procession, Maggie and Jarot walked side by side, neither looking at the other, neither speaking. At the sycamore they came to a stop. Jarot thrust his rifle at her.

"Here," he said.

"You're givin' it to me?"

"Yes."

"What for?"

" 'Cause I want yuh to have it."

"Is that all you got to say to me?"

"Whut else kin I say to yuh?"

"You might ask what I might think o' stayin' on here."

"I might."

"Would you like to know?"

"I might."

"Then why don't you ask me?"

Jarot gulped, wet his lips, and shuffled his weight from one foot to the other.

"First you say, Maggie," she prompted.

"Maggie."

"Yes? Well . . . go on."

"Maggie . . . j'ever figger none on how yuh might make out was yuh to stay on here?"

"That ain't no way to say it."

"How'd yuh want me to say it?"

"Ask me straight out."

"Maggie, will yuh stay on here?"

"Yes, I will."

June

Summer had had the effect of seeming to tame and temper the wilderness. Every stir of air from the forest brought with it the pleasantly soothing aroma of pine needles, sun-soaked bark, moist leafage, resinous earth. Wild animals, apparently more attracted by the clearing's expanse of green corn than repelled by the nearness of people, returned again and again, sniffing and snorting with curiosity, to the edges of the woods. Deer, always the most stubbornly venturesome, began feeding in the corn at night. They had changed to their reddish summer coats, and the does were accompanied everywhere by their fawns. Everything living was responding to the increase in the warmth and length of the days. Serviceberries and purple raspberries had ripened, providing clusters of fruit which bears avidly stripped from the vines with simian dexterity. In lagoons along the river and pools at bends in the stream, wood duck cruised with their attendant fleets of ducklings. The first fireflies twinkled in the dusk. The corn had suddenly started to grow so fast that the taller stalks were six feet high. Tracy's garden had flourished and become an irresistible attraction to rabbits, woodchucks, and field mice.

She lay awake that morning in the first faint gray of dawn, listening to the birds' preliminary twitters and chirps which would soon burst into full-throated chorus as the light brightened. The night had in the last hour turned slightly cooler and she would have reached down to draw up the blanket had she not been aware that Caleb, beside her, had also awakened. She waited tensely for his first move which was usually, though not invariably, to spring silently from the bed to get at that day's work. There came a sudden snort of panic from one of the pigs. Caleb was in the middle of the floor, rifle in hand, in one leap so swift and lithe that the bed had scarcely quivered. For a second she could make out his pale, taut silhouette in the open doorway and then, his bare feet noiseless, he had slipped sidewise into the darkness along the outer

172

wall. The morning before there had been the tracks of a
panther at the edge of the clearing. The beast had evidently
returned to make a closer inspection of the pigpen.

Caleb's shot came from the corner of the cabin. The
panther's scream of pain and rage was repeated once from
a greater distance, testimony that in the half-light even
Caleb's marksmanship had managed only a hit, not a kill. He
was in the room again, feeling for shot pouch and powder
horn. Leaning the reloaded rifle against the wall, he returned to the doorway and stood there, half-turned, listening.
The growing light accentuated the lean flat muscles of his
shoulders and thighs and picked out the ladder of ridged
scars on his back. He took a step over the threshold and
again paused, strangely irresolute. She knew he was resisting
his impulse to return to the bed. But she knew him too little
to be sure whether he was resisting because he regarded the
recurrence of his physical need for her as an admission of
weakness or because he felt a preliminary delay added to
his eventual enjoyment. He slipped from view and next she
could hear him splashing in the stone-lined pool he had dug
by the spring. His summer custom of taking night and morning baths in it was one of his least objectionable Indian
habits. He was in the room again, reaching for his hunting
shirt. Then he had dropped it and was coming back to her.

His second rising was only slightly more deliberate than
had been his first. Her passing moment of victory in their
constant duel was already ended. He dressed in silence, his
selection of leather shirt instead of cotton indicating that this
was one of the mornings he proposed to hunt. Even his silence
was more aggressive than the most loudly proclaimed purposes of other men. He stuffed a handful of pounded corn
and jerky into his pocket, picked up his rifle and strode out.
The wounded panther would have left a trail of blood
splotches. She knew he would not be back until he had completed his kill.

She dressed slowly and lingered over a breakfast of raspberries, followed by one of the trout Polly had brought the
night before. Still unhurried, she set about feeding the stock,
the coon playing about her feet and tugging at her skirt. She
gave an extra portion of marsh hay to the calves, of acorns
to the pigs, and of corn to the turkeys and chickens, and returned to sit on the doorstep. For once she felt less urge to
fill every waking hour with the forgetfulness of constant activity. The rows of corn immediately before the cabin had
grown so high that she could no longer see the station, shielding her from the perpetual reminder of the stark differences

between her present and former existences. After the cool of
the earlier morning it was pleasant in the sun. She leaned
her head against the doorframe and all but dozed.

The green wall of drooping corn fronds rippled and parted.
Eric stood before her. Taking care not to meet her eyes, he
set down the heavy burden under which he had been staggering. It was a stone mortar, encrusted with earth and yellowed by age, of the sort Indians used for grinding corn.
From his belt he took the stone pestle and carefully laid it
in the mortar.

"Jat and I found it just now when we were grubbing out a
stump," he said, still without looking at her. "It must have
been buried by some flood. Maybe once there was an Indian
town out there by the point. Olen thinks so because we keep
coming on arrowheads and beads and broken pieces of clay
pots." He kept on talking rapidly, as though he were crouched
within the refuge of the continuing sound of his own voice.
"You remember we've got an iron hand mill for grinding
our corn. But I've noticed you have to pound yours in a
wooden bowl. So I brought you this. You can make corn
meal faster in it, and more at a time. Now I have to be getting
back. I could see the Slovers sitting down even before I was
out of sight."

Tracy tried helpfully to treat Eric's peace offering as an
occasion of no special moment.

"Thank you, Eric. It will be a big help. But you've got so
hot lugging the great thing. Let me get you a drink of water
before you go."

She came out of the cabin with a buffalo horn of water.
Eric drank it all, started again to go, and then seemed to
have become deeply interested in the primitive design en-
graved on the horn.

"It appears to be an Indian attempt to represent a buffalo
hunt," she volunteered. "Odd little figures, aren't they?"

"I only used the mortar as an excuse," said Eric, turning the
horn over and over in his hands. "I was going to come over
anyway. Since Father's been away I've been trying to think
about—about things. I've had to. Uncle Garry can't do much
and I've had to—sort of—feel responsible. About keeping
up the place, I mean."

"Your mother says you've been working like a man."

"That part's easy. I'm talking about trying to think. I've
been trying to look at things a little more like—well, maybe
the way father would."

"That's not a bad rule."

"What I'm trying to say is I'm beginning to see what you've done couldn't have been so wrong."

"What makes you think that?"

"Because when you really stop to think you have to realize there couldn't be anything about whatever you did that could be anything but right."

Eric thrust the horn at her and bolted back into the corn. Tracy sat down on the doorstep and burst into tears. When she looked up, Caleb stood there, the carcass of the panther hanging over his shoulder. As always, to be suddenly made aware of his physical nearness, as when awakening beside him in the night or catching sight of him unexpectedly, stirred in her an instant throb of excitement as intense as a sudden realization of the presence of an enemy. This unwelcome and painful spasm of response was the more bewildering because she had schooled herself so resolutely no longer to fear or hate him. He, she had reasoned patiently, was in his way as innocent a victim of their predicament as was she. The sense of her own fairness made her the more determined to conceal from him this repeated inner tumult since it would be even more unfair to permit him to discover he was capable of arousing in her any sort of emotion. The instinctive defence at which she clutched whenever he approached her was to conjure up the image of Duncan to stand protectively between them. This figure of a man so different and about whom she felt so differently was a reassuring reminder that she herself could not have changed no matter how much her situation had changed. Caleb was for once giving her a second and more attentive look. He had never before seen her weep.

"You are maybe going to have a baby?" he inquired.

She sprang up. "I am what? My God, I trust not. I'm sure not. I don't see how a woman who felt as—as sterile as I do—could—could possibly."

He turned away and hung the panther by its heels to the rack on which he dressed his game.

"Bring me the basswood bowl," he directed.

She brought it to him. Cutting the panther's throat, he caught the blood in the bowl and, taking it with him, sprinkled the blood upon the earth around all the outer margins of the vegetable garden. He returned to the rack, ripped off the hide, and carved the flesh of the carcass into pieces the size of his fist, tossing the fragments into the hide spread out on the ground. Next he disjointed the bones and added them to the pile. Then, bundling up the hide with its contents, he walked to the back of the clearing and began dropping a fragment of flesh or bone at every step or two along the edge of the woods. He was soon out of sight behind the corn but when he came into view again from the other side it was obvious that he had continued the process around the whole outer circumference of the planted area. When he had used up the last of the pieces, he cut the hide into strips and tied them at intervals to the branches of trees. He washed at the pool and returned to the doorstep, shaking his hands to dry them in the sun.

"Were you performing some sort of Indian magic?"

"No. Just spreading panther smell."

"It certainly will smell. In this heat the place will soon stink to heaven."

"That is what will keep the deer away."

"Not for long. Animals, wood rats, ants, and bugs will eat up those scraps of meat in a day or two."

He was generally careful to enlighten specific instances of her ignorance.

"Still the smell of panther will hang on. Enough to keep deer out of the corn for maybe three or four weeks."

He went into the cabin, spooned powder from the keg into his powder horn, added a handful of bullets to his shot pouch, and filled his game sack with sugared corn. She realized that something had happened which he had not foreseen and that he was preparing to set out on a longer journey than one of his occasional early morning or late evening hunts. He came out again and glanced at the sky, the corn, and the stock pens.

"General Clark is here," he said. "At the bridge just now I talked to him."

He paused, still not looking at her. She sat down again on the doorstep and began deliberately taking the pins out of her hair.

"He wants me to go with him to the Shawnee," he continued. "I will be gone maybe four days. Maybe ten. I do not know how long he will want to talk to them or they will want to talk to him."

She rose, went into the cabin and returned to the doorway, a dab of soft soap on a chip in her hand, on her way to the pool to wash her hair. Several times since he had returned with the panther he had stepped around the mortar resting on the ground beside the doorstep without appearing to see it. Now he prodded it with one moccasined toe and looked at her inquiringly.

"Eric brought it," she said. "He'd noticed I needed one."

"Tell Eric I do not want him to come here when I am not here."

"So now you are afraid your wife might prefer a boy? Colonel Jordan is hundreds of miles away. So far he has been the one of whom you were the most afraid."

"And not only Eric," persisted Caleb calmly. "Garett, too. He never comes when I am here. Be sure he also stays away when I am not."

He turned to go but she set down the chip of soap and, her loosened hair shaking down as she sprang forward, overtook him before he had moved into the corn.

"Do you actually think that I have you that much?"

"I think you do not care what you do."

"Otherwise I would not have come here in the first place—is that it?"

"No. You came to serve them. You still serve them. That, too, is what I think."

"What right have you to think anything, about people like us, about the rules they live by?"

"I can see what they are like." He glanced toward the station. He was tall enough to see over the corn. There came into his eyes that occasional glint of amusement that offended her more than anything else about him. "They talk much. But they must have other people do for them."

"You are so sure you are better than they are?"

"Even they can see that."

"Then why take my feeling for them as some sort of a reflection on you?"

"Because it shows I have picked a fool for a wife."

"You'd have done much better to stay with your Indians."

"I was born a white man."

"So I was born one of the Jordans' kind of people."

He looked at her. It was an impersonal appraisal that seemed to take no account of the pleasant disorder of her dark hair curling about her shoulders, the flush that had reddened her cheeks, or the flame of resentment in her gray eyes. His slow nod was grudging and fair.

"You have worked in my field. You have warmed my bed. You have tried to do some of your part."

"What is this other part you want of me?"

"I want you to remember that I am not a fool."

Clark, standing in the station gateway with Garett and Stephen Lockard, shook hands with them when he saw Caleb crossing the bridge. He joined Caleb at the foot of the slope and the two set off at a woodsman's trot up the trail along the stream toward the falls.

"George is a truly stubborn man," said Lockard, looking after them regretfully. "For me to pay a visit of several days to a comparatively unspoiled Indian town would have been the capstone of my western trip. But his first answer was no and so was his last. A recognized Indian trait is a high regard for the sanctity of ambassadors. I can't believe there'll be any serious danger." He took off his broadbrimmed hat, pulled a handkerchief from his pocket, and mopped his neatly trimmed, graying beard, his smoothly broad brow, and his closely cropped, silvering hair. He looked his age, which was approaching fifty, but there still was in his manner the eagerness of the young student just beginning to glimpse something of the extent of the horizons of learning. "I'm desolate to have missed finding Duncan here. Still, George and I will likely meet him on our way on upriver and, if not, I'll be able to look for him in Pittsburgh. But what about Thryza Carter? I haven't seen her since she was twelve, before the so untimely death of her father. Didn't I hear someone say something when we first got in this morning about her having recently got married? Where is she? And who is the fortunate young man?"

"She married Caleb Lewis."

"No. Not that stone-faced son of the forest George met down there when we first arrived? Not the mysterious friend of the Shawnee who has so engaged official curiosity that General Clark himself has come this far to confer with him?"

"You can see the roof of their cabin," said Garett dryly, "there over the top of the corn."

"I must see her."

"Want me to take you over?"

"Don't trouble. My sudden appearance will give her a pleasant surprise. And it happens that I have what may be a rather significant message for her."

Lockard crossed the bridge, pushed his way through the stand of corn, and came out into the narrow open space before the cabin. Tracy was seated on the doorstep, bent over so that her damp hair hung over her face, while she ruffled it with her fingers to speed its drying in the sun.

"It is not often that a naturalist has the extreme good fortune," said Lockard, "of coming upon a wood nymph engaged in her toilet."

Tracy, startled, tossed back her hair and looked up. She sprang to her feet.

"Stephen Lockard," she exclaimed incredulously.

"Have I aged so much that you have any doubt of it?"

"Of course not. But the last I heard, before we left Virginia, you were still in Paris with Dr. Franklin."

"So I was. For seven long years. But now I am again in

Amérique Septentrionale, making a long-anticipated inspection of this extraordinary western wilderness." He stepped back to survey her with the candid gallantry permitted an older man who had been a friend of the family when she was a child. "Not the least one of which I have just come upon. When last I saw you, you were a little girl in pigtails and starched muslin. Behold how you've grown up, and into how remarkably beautiful a woman."

"In a cotton shift and with her hair down," said Tracy. "Won't you come in? A backwoods cabin is one of the more special features of this wilderness you have come so far to inspect."

He followed her in. She stepped to her tiny mirror and began doing up her hair. He looked around at the plain, bare interior.

"Obviously the woman's touch," he remarked. "Neat as the captain's quarters on a well-run ship."

"Actually my husband's touch. I am an indifferent housekeeper. But he has the soul of a sailor, if he has a soul."

He did not miss her bitterness but he continued to smile.

"It could be that I have news for you about his onetime seafaring. Though that, of course, is none too likely, since he must have told you more than he has others."

"If you're talking about his past, he has told me nothing."

"Then I do have news for you, very welcome news. Presumably it has been resentment of the assumption that he was an English sympathizer that has led him to refuse any explanation. But his connection with the Shawnee makes his case so important that General Clark has gone to some trouble to look up his history. His serving the English during the war was not by his own choice. It appears that the first year of the Revolution he shipped from New Orleans aboard an American marchantman. The ship was captured and he was impressed into the English navy. Instead of accepting his lot he served the English so badly that he was repeatedly punished with all the severity for which that harshly disciplined service is noted. In the West Indies—during the engagement between Rodney and de Grasse, to be exact—he finally managed to escape. These personal difficulties with the English have led Clark to suspect that Mr. Lewis might after all be more inclined to lean toward our side than that of our late enemy. At any rate, he has sought him out on the chance that he will help persuade the Shawnee to listen to our government's peace proposals."

"I'm glad you've told me this," said Tracy. "It helps explain a number of things. But I somehow doubt Caleb's wartime experiences have inclined him to any side other than his own."

Lockard's exceptionally intelligent eyes, perpetually alive with curiosity, crossed her face as she spoke and roved on to the drinking horn lying on the table.

"I gather that in your case marriage, as in so many others, has not resulted in an immediate, miraculous relaxation of every tension." He leaned forward to pick up the buffalo horn. "This, by the way, is not of Shawnee manufacture. It is a product of the culture of the so little known Indians of the far western plains. I saw one very much like it in a collection in Paris sent by a French trader from the banks of the Missouri. Notice the design, crude and misshapen, yet vigorous. Since you are a married woman it is permissible to point out the extravagant glorification of the buffalo bull's maleness. In every quarter of the world of which I have heard any report, savage magic is more preoccupied with the encouragement of procreation than with any other aspiration."

His head turned instantly as a low bird note drifted in from without through the open doorway. He tiptoed to the threshold and waited until a repetition of the call enabled him to locate the bird perched in the top of one of the taller cornstalks. "Clearly a representative of the grosbeak family but with a color configuration never before described." He whipped his notebook from his pocket. "You will pardon my taking a couple of notes? This will make the thirty-seventh new species I have identified since I left Pittsburgh. I visited the great Linnaeus while I was in Europe, by the way. You will be interested to know that he showed me a letter he had received from your father the year before he died. It contained a list of Virginia toadstools." The bird flew away as he edged nearer. He put the notebook back in his pocket and turned to Tracy. "May I be so bold as to ask, what is that peculiar odor?"

She explained the use Caleb had made of the panther's remains. Lockard laughed.

"A fascinatingly practical evolution of an almost universal primitive rite. Most savage peoples are convinced that blood will promote the growth of their crops. In some instances, unhappily, they require maidens' blood. In others it is considered sufficient if young women spend a night reclining in the newly sown fields. I trust I'm not boring you with my display of erudition?"

"Indeed no. We've been looking at the wilderness as just trees through which to chase game or to be cut down to make room for corn. It's a wonderful relief to be reminded people can actually have wider interests. Are you on your way to Kentucky?"

"Alas, no. I've already been there and my too brief tour is almost over. So soon as General Clark returns from his embassy we will continue on upriver and at Pittsburgh I shall set out for Philadelphia."

"Then you must have already seen a great deal of this western country. Really seen it, I mean, with eyes able to see more than trees and soil and game. What did you see that interested you most?"

"Aside from the present moment," said Lockard, bowing, "I was most captivated by a deposit of enormous bones I came upon around a salt spring in Kentucky. Evidently at some earlier period numbers of much larger animals than any now living roamed this immense valley, including one much on the order of an elephant, though considerably exceeding in size any we now know in India or Africa."

"Surely you're joking?"

"Very much to the contrary. I have the proof in General Clark's canoe. I am taking back with me to present to my old friend Tom Jefferson a thighbone somewhat taller than a man and a tusk more than ten feet long."

"Oh, I'd like to see them."

"Then most certainly, my dear, you shall. This very minute."

They pushed through the corn to the stream bank. On the bridge Lockard paused and indicated the station cornfield.

"The Jordan meadow has been returned to its original role. Once it was an Indian cornfield. Most such small, apparently natural open areas in this wooded country are to be accounted for in that manner. You realize, of course, the origin of this knoll in which the stockade was built. It, too, was made by man. There are scores of such mounds up and down the Ohio, many of them much larger than this one. Who built them? We do not know. Surely not the Ten Lost Tribes or the legendary Welsh, as some claim." They walked on along the path downstream. "But their numbers must have exceeded by many hundredfold the present number of Indians. They flourished and then they disappeared, leaving no trace but these mounds, not even a legend."

Clark's two canoemen, leathery veterans of his Revolutionary army, had established their camp under the sycamore on the point and gone to sleep in the shade. Aroused by the approaching murmur of Lockard's voice, they grunted wearily when they had awakened enough to identify the source and rolled over to go back to sleep. Then one of them caught a glimpse of Tracy and they sat up to watch her. Lockard went to the canoe drawn up on the beach and lifted from it two long, heavy objects wrapped in deerskin. He untied the lashing and revealed the monstrous bones.

"This is a tusk," he said, "and that one is as clearly a legbone. Most of those smaller ones are teeth. You can imagine the proportions of the catlike animal which would have canines the size of those. The ground about the salt spring is a bog. Animals of our time still come to lick the salt. But these great earlier animals were so ponderous they sank in the mud and were trapped. The salt in the mud no doubt helped to preserve their skeletons. There are acres of such bones. We can see them, we can feel of them, we can know such animals once existed. But that is all we can know. The range for speculation is unlimited. Could the mound-builders have lived at the same time as these giant animals? Could they, too, perhaps, have been giants? Can you not begin to imagine the questions for which we as yet have no anwers? You must forgive me for rushing on like this. I have been talking steadily—it could have been for hours. I get carried away when I reflect on such matters. I assure you it is occasionally possible for me to stop talking, and I can prove it by doing so."

"Only don't prove it now," begged Tracy. "You can't guess what a comfort you are to me. Please keep on, and on, and on. Don't stop talking to me as long as you are here."

Stephen Lockard's visit was also an event in the Jordan household. Each evening they sat late with him, plying him with questions about mutual friends in Virginia, listening to accounts of his long journey which, beginning in Paris, had taken him to London, Boston, New York, Philadelphia, Richmond, and Louisville, before bringing him here, and relishing particularly the light thrown on what had been going on in the outer world by his anecdotes of recent contacts with figures such as Franklin, Washington, and Jefferson. But presently they became even more interested in the preoccupation to which he devoted his days. Each morning he rose early and, armed with his notebooks and collector's kit, set out upon an enthusiastic investigation of the flora and fauna of the region. Upon each of these scientific excursions, which lasted as long as there was light to see, he was accompanied by Tracy in the role of guide, assistant, and disciple.

"A real change for Tracy," said Agatha. "She may have been going days at a time without hearing a word spoken but she's making up for that now. If she remembers a tenth of

what Stephen says she'll have enough talk to think about to
do her for the next ten years."

"Stephen must be fifty," mused Olivia, "but he's always
so bubbling over with ideas. Would you guess all of their
talk is strictly scientific?"

"He was a great friend of her father's," said Louisa re-
provingly. "They went to King's College together. And then
they both taught at Mr. McDonald's school. That was before
Stephen went to Philadelphia to write for Dr. Franklin's
paper."

"Olen's gone out with them twice," said Eric, bringing up
another defense. "And I went yesterday. Mr. Lockard doesn't
shoot too well. When there's a bird he wants to add to his
collection we shoot it for him with that little fowling piece of
his. Once in a while there's a larger animal which we bring
down with a rifle so that he can examine the markings. I
shot a long-tailed fox yesterday which he was sure had never
been listed before. I skinned it for him so that he could take
the hide with him."

"Sounds scientific as all get out," said Garett.

"Oh, I don't doubt he's adding this and that to his collection," said Olivia. "But I keep thinking about that particular
idol of his, Dr. Franklin. He must be all of eighty, but I seem
to have heard he still has quite a taking way with him."

"What Olivia's getting at," said Garett, "in the light of her
inimitable confidence in humanity, is that were Caleb to turn
up suddenly, all might not appear so Arcadian. Maybe we'd
better consult the oracle. Cam, come here."

"I was with them all yesterday afternoon," said Cam, "after
they had come back with Eric's fox. They had specimens
spread out all over the cabin floor—butterflies, and flowers,
and bugs, and dead birds, and even two snails. I was helping
them sort them. He was teaching Tracy the Latin names for
everything. It was just like school. Only they laughed so
much."

The report Cam brought back the next evening produced a
ripple of deeper concern in the family council. It had been
an excessively hot day and her face was red from the heat as
well as from excitement over what she had to tell.

"I saw them up by the falls just a little while ago," she
began, developing her narrative with careful regard both for
exact accuracy and maximum suspense. "Oh, it was all right
for me to go that far. Polly was going up there to fish and I
went along with her. Only it was so hot that Polly sat down
before we got there and went to sleep under a bush. I was

just going to come back when I heard Tracy laugh. I left
Polly and went on. Then when I saw what they were doing
I squatted down quick so that they didn't see me. So you've
all got to promise me you'll never tell Tracy I told you."

"I promise," said Garett, "on condition this proves a revelation proper to unveil in the presence of your grandmother."

"Oh, they weren't doing anything bad. Only sort of funny.
You know that pool just below the falls? They were taking
a bath in it."

"What's funny about that? Nothing could have been more
sensible on a day as hot as this. I took a swim myself this
afternoon, right down here in the pond."

"Only you wore your pants. And they didn't have any
clothes on."

The three women looked at one another. Garett continued
to smile.

"The Arcadian idyll," he murmured, "would seem to have
taken on idyllic proportions."

Cam sighed, content with the effect she had created.

"Of course, they couldn't see each other. You know that
big rock that sticks out in the pool. They were on each side
of that. And when they got out to dress, the rock was still
between them. Then, when they got out, I didn't stay any
longer. I ran back here."

"You're so hot, dear" said Agatha. "Why don't you go
wash your face and put on a fresh dress?"

Her voice was gentle and yet Cam withdrew hastily.

"My inimitable confidence in humanity," Olivia taunted
Garett.

"What they were doing was foolish," said Agatha, "but for
all we know just as innocent as it was foolish."

"Stephen Lockard is a gentleman and our guest," said
Louisa, coming firmly and directly to the point. "I trust
Tracy as I would myself. There's no occasion for us to take
any position. For us to let them guess that we feel the slightest
anxiety would be insulting to them as well as excessively bad
taste on our part."

"I agree we could easily make things worse," said Garett.
"It's their affair, not ours. I even confess to a crass hope that
they're enjoying it. But when Caleb gets back it can become
very much our affair."

"We should insist on Tracy staying up here while he's
away," said Louisa. "It's not right for her to be alone down
there in that cabin in the woods, especially at night."

"I asked her to come up here," said Agatha. "I told you
then I'd asked her. The day he left. But she said she had too

much to do, too many things to look after. I got the distinct impression that no matter how bad a time she's been having she feels more comfortable down there than to be seeing too much of us."

"That's absurd," said Louisa. "I still can't believe she stays away from us for any other reason than that he insists upon it."

"Besides, she's not been too lonely," said Olivia.

"For Olivia all roads lead to the same Rome," said Garett. "Anyway, Mother, nothing's to be gained by bringing her up here, even if she would come. Caleb's a man who knows his own mind. If he'd wanted her up here he'd have sent her up before he left. And you must remember our foremost problem is to smooth his feathers, not to ruffle them. I assured Duncan that while he was away I'd keep the peace with the man. It would seem to follow, Eric, that some reliance on your woodsman's craft is indicated. You probably could use a relief from your clearing labors. Why don't you start in tomorrow morning keeping an eye on the old Indian trail above the falls? Caleb's due back most any day now. We don't want him walking in on some chance tableau involving his wife with a stranger which any husband might misinterpret. A few minutes' warning of his approach might be a salvation—ours as well as Tracy's and Stephen's."

Eric returned late in the afternoon of his first day's trail-watching with an immediate report on results.

"I ran into John Turtle. He was coming this way." Eric grinned sheepishly. "For the best part of an hour we stayed behind trees, each of us making signs for the other to come out first. But finally we met and shook hands. I'm glad I didn't try to shoot him. He had a letter from General Clark. Then we sat down and had quite a long talk."

"Talk?" said Agatha. "Has he learned so much English? The last we saw of him the only words he knew were 'friend' and 'broder' and 'swap.'"

"They're still the only words he knows. But Indians are wonderful at making signs. If you pay attention and watch closely and make them do it over and over again, you can catch on after a while to almost anything they want to tell you."

"Why was he so anxious to talk to you?" asked Garett.

"He kept making a great show of being our best friend, just as he did when he took all our food. He was pretending to be just passing the time of day, but what he was really trying to do was give us a scare by proving how much the Shawnee knew about us. He knew that Father had gone. He knew about Jat's new wife. He knew about Mr. Lockard being here. He knew how much clearing we've done."

"Caleb could have told him all that," said Garett.

"That wasn't the way he told it. He kept grinning all the time. And he knew things Caleb couldn't have told him, like Mr. Lockard's and Tracy's collecting. But what hit me hardest was that he referred to Caleb by the same slighting, sarcastic sign for 'big white man' that he made for General Clark. And when he referred to Mr. Lockard and Tracy in the pool he laughed as though that were a good joke on Caleb. I don't think the Shawnee feel as close to Caleb as they did before he sent Daisy home and took Tracy in her place. And I don't think there's a possible shadow of doubt that they've been watching everything we were doing every day since the snow went off."

"Eric," exclaimed Louisa, "you can't mean that all this time they've been hanging right around the edge of the woods, that they have been able to see us while we couldn't see them? Really, Garett, the longer I'm here the less certain I am that this is quite the most suitable place we could have chosen for a home."

"I wish Duncan would get back," said Agatha.

"I can even wish Caleb would," said Olivia.

"Where's the letter?" asked Garett.

"It was for Mr. Lockard. I gave it to him when I ran into him and Tracy down along the stream. They were turning over rocks looking for salamanders. He'll be along in a minute."

Lockard came in. His bows of greeting were hurried and unaccompanied by his usual flurry of urbane remarks. He sat down gravely and ran his eye again over the opened letter in his hand.

"George is not coming back here," he said. "He wants to talk to two other Shawnee chiefs who are off in a hunting camp somewhere in the forest to the east. He instructs me to take his canoe on upriver and wait for him at the mouth of the Muskingum. He says the Shawnee listened to him politely for five days but have given him no answer. He also says Caleb Lewis will be back here some time tomorrow." He refolded the letter and put it in his pocket. "Eric, would you be good enough to tell General Clark's canoemen that we will be embarking this evening? Explain to them that the General advises our traveling at night until he is able to rejoin us." He watched Eric go out and then, his gravity deepening, turned to survey the three Jordan women and Garett. "I am not one, as you may have noticed, who is ordinarily at a loss for words. But I find myself very much in that condition now.

As a preface to what I am about to say, may I remind you that Edmund Carter was my dearest friend. He was an unworldly man but equipped with a singularly fine mind. These qualities his daughter has inherited. I was fond of her when she was a child and I find my regard for her reinforced now. It is a pity her father did not live to enjoy the fulness of her development into womanhood. The bright, warm-hearted child he and I once knew has become one of the most intelligent, sensitive, truly fastidious women it has ever been my good fortune to encounter."

"You don't have to praise Tracy to us," said Louisa. "We know her."

"Then how could you have permitted her subjection to this totally odious marriage? Or, if that originally was in the nature of an abduction, which I can only assume it must have been, why do you not save her from it now?"

"Please, Garett—wait," said Louisa. "Mr. Lockard, do you consider yourself her faithful friend?"

"I do. And I think she accepts me as such. With one reservation. She positively refuses to consider her personal situation any concern of mine."

"Then make it yours. Before you leave, go down there. Plead with her. Make her come back to us."

"I'm surprised at you, Mother," said Garett. "It's not usually your way to sidle off from the truth. You know your challenge is foolish. You know she won't come. No, Stephen, the truth is as plain as it is simple. You have eyes and the brain to use them. You can see it, too. The truth is that this hole in the woods which we inhabit is too narrow for civilized niceties. The truth is that he is stronger than we are. He knows it. We know it. And she knows it. There you have it. If you can see a way out, I'd be happy to hear of it."

"I do not," said Lockard. "But there must be. There has to be."

Lockard stood at the edge of the corn in the deepening twilight, watching the swift graceful movements of Tracy's shadowy figure as she fed the stock. Not until she had returned to the cabin doorway did he step out to confront her with a gesture that was as abrupt as a decision suddenly reached. Her face was only a pale blur in the darkness except when the brief flash of a firefly lighted for an instant her wide eyes.

"I've been thinking over that letter from General Clark," he said, "and I've decided I'd better leave tonight."

Silently she slipped past him into the cabin. From the

doorway he saw the first faint gleam as she lighted the candle
from a coal on the hearth. The glow lighted her face as had
the firefly. But this time the revelation endured. The golden
brown of her skin in the sun seemed now an ivory pallor. She
rose and placed the candle on the table. He entered. They
faced each other across the table.

"I knew all along how short the time would be," she said.
"And now it is over."

"It does not need to be over. He is returning tomorrow. But
I am leaving tonight. Come with me."

Her face paled, her eyes closed, she took a long shuddering
breath. When she did not reply he plunged on with more and
more urgency.

"By this time tomorrow you will be beyond his reach. He
cannot blame the Jordans. He can only blame me, a stranger,
and I, too, will be beyond his reach. You cannot fear his
pursuit, for we shall, by the day after tomorrow, have joined
General Clark under whose wing you will be completely
safe. At Pittsburgh we can consult with Duncan. You must
know how heartily he will approve of what you have done.
Then I will take you on to Virginia. But we do not need to
plan so far now. All we need to consider now is what you
do tonight. And to face what will happen to you if you do
not seize this opportunity, the like of which may never
come again."

She opened her eyes. Whatever the inner turmoil with
which she may have coped during his plea, she was calmer
now.

"Please sit down," she said.

"Why?" he demanded. "Why do you hesitate?"

She took the other stool across from him and leaned toward
him, spreading her hands beseechingly out on the table top.

"I want to tell you. I want to, desperately. I have had
nobody to talk to. When I am alone, no matter how hard I
try to think, I become confused."

She paused. He tried to help her.

"You conceive you must stay to guard the Jordans."

"That is true. But it is not so true as it was at first. He
wants to stay here, and he cannot if he ruins them."

"Then from what do you shrink?"

"I will try to tell you, if you will only listen. I will try to
confess to you as honestly as though you were a priest."

"Shall we say, rather, your physician?" He smiled. "I would
not want to be set apart from other men except by the warmth
of my regard for you."

"What most sets you apart for me is that you are able to

think. That is more good to me at the moment than your sympathy. If I stay here instead of going with you it will be because I have begun to feel, just these past few days while he has been away, that I might after all be of some use here. I'm trying to get at something that's still so unclear to me that I don't seem to hit upon words that say what I think I mean."

"Keep trying. When you do find words they will tell you as much as you are trying to tell me."

"Perhaps what it comes down to is that I committed myself to this marriage as cold-bloodedly as he did. I have been punished for that. And the damage that has been done to me has already been done. Nothing worse can happen to me. But there is possibly a slight hope for him. He is struggling, however awkwardly, however blindly, to better himself. There may be something in him worth saving if it can be saved. No other possible good can ever come out of any of this. Should I throw that away, too?"

"So what it really comes down to is the perpetual feminine illusion that any man, even this one, can be domesticated."

"Don't goad me. I don't want to improve his manners. I don't want to make a husband of him. What I think I do feel is a kind of sense of justice. Perhaps if I stay I can manage to help him, if only a little. If there *is* a chance for him, even though I have none, shouldn't he have it?"

"What chance, as you call it, is there for him?"

"Maybe there is none. Those scars on his back are more than skin deep. The one spark of warmth in his life was his regard for Corbit Revel and that ended in a terrible disappointment. Everything that has ever happened to him has inclined him the more to put his trust in nothing but his own strength and cunning. Yet this is the only spot where he had ever even caught a glimpse of something that appealed to him, and all these years afterward he has come back to it."

"You argue his case with great spirit. Are you absolutely certain that this sense of justice is tempered by no trace of any more personal impulse? Do not answer unless you choose."

She laughed harshly. Her reply came with a rush, as though it were one she had been eager to proclaim.

"Why shouldn't I choose? Of course, I am certain."

Lockard stroked his beard. "I can see that while you have had a difficult time, his has not been an easy one. But I can also see that there is hope for neither of you. Get away, my dear. Get away while you can. Get away now, tonight." He rose, came around the table and placed a hand on her shoul-

der. "You are endowed with so much that can still make
your life a full one. You have so much to look forward to.
So very much. Come with me and begin."

She laid her hand over his. "You've been a Godsend,
Stephen, at a time I needed it most."

Lockard, looking up past her, snatched his hand from her
clasp. She turned. Caleb stood in the doorway.

He set his rifle against the wall beside the door, unslung his
game sack and dropped it to the floor, hooked his thumbs into
his belt and regarded them thoughtfully. The lacings of his
leggings were filled with shreds of leaves and bits of bark, his
moccasins were frayed, there were wrinkles of weariness about
his mouth and eyes, and his face was smudged with a two-day
beard. He must have made the long journey from the Shawnee
town in one headlong plunge through the forest. His unnatural calm clothed his presence with a kind of total menace.
Nothing about him forecast the possible range of his intentions. Tracy could hear Lockard's breathing behind her.
She started up from her stool into a position between Caleb
and her guest. But Caleb did not move from his place in the
doorway.

"This is Mr. Stephen Lockard," she said. "He was an old
friend of my father's, and of mine, when I was little. He
came here with General Clark, as you probably know."

"How do you do, Mr. Lewis," said Lockard. "I am delighted by the opportunity to meet you before leaving." The
conventional words echoed meaninglessly across the cabin's
silence. "General Clark wrote me to meet him at the Muskingum and I came over to say good-by to Mrs. Lewis."

"Mr. Lockard is a naturalist," said Tracy. "That was also
one of my father's interests. I have been able to help him with
his collecting while he was here."

"As I've already remarked, Mr. Lewis," said Lockard, "it's
been a great privilege to meet you." He edged forward and
picked up his hat from the table. "But I shall have to be
going now." He was speaking carefully as though to one slow
of understanding. "General Clark suggested we travel at night
and I shall have to be off."

He took a tentative step around the table. Caleb did not
move from the doorway. Lockard glanced helplessly at Tracy.
There were beads of perspiration on his broad brow. Caleb
continued to regard them silently and thoughtfully, his stare
transferring from his wife to her caller and then back to her.

"How do you like my place, Mr. Lockard?" he asked.

"Your place? Ah . . . very much. What you have done
with it in one season is remarkable."

"And my wife. You find her remarkable, too?"

"Why—why, yes—of course. But she has always been that. You see I have known her since she was a little girl."

"Look at her." Lockard's gaze remained fixed on Caleb's expressionless face. "Do not look at me. That is not what a cabin at night is for. Look at her." Lockard looked desperately at Tracy. "She is not so little any more." Lockard wet his lips. "Is she?"

"Don't answer him, Stephen," said Tracy. "You don't have to, any more than I do."

Lockard maintained his outward urbanity. "A husband has certain inquisitorial rights, recognized in even the simplest societies." He looked back at Caleb with a smile. "No, Mr. Lewis. No, of course not. She has quite grown up since last I saw her."

"But to you she is still like a child."

"Caleb," said Tracy. "Must you try so hard to be disgusting? Because there is no need to try, not for you."

Caleb stepped forward to the table.

"I swear, Mr. Lewis," said Lockard, "since you seem to feel so strongly the need to be reassured, you have been in no way wronged. There has been nothing between us. Not so much as a gesture; not even a thought."

"Stop it, Stephen, stop it," cried Tracy. "Can't you see what he's doing? He's making you grovel just to prove something to me. All he's really proving is his resentment of anything he can't understand."

Her blazing eyes came around to Caleb. He was grinning.

"I'll tell you why Stephen is here," she said. "He came tonight because I asked him. I have been begging him to take me back to Virginia with him. You are able to understand so little. But maybe you can understand that."

"You will be in his canoe and in his camp many nights on your way to Virginia. But when he thinks of that he thinks only of telling you about frogs or reading to you out of a book. Is that what you want me to understand?"

"All I want you to understand is that I'll be glad to be in his camp, or anywhere but in this cabin."

Caleb seized her arm and jerked her around until her back was to Lockard. Deliberately he raised his open hand and slapped her. It was not a hard blow but he repeated it with the back of his hand from the other side. She screamed with rage. Lockard sprang forward in protest. Caleb released her and looked at him. Lockard's shoulders sagged. He picked up his hat and walked on around the table. In the doorway he turned.

"You may have proved that I am weak. But have you proved that you are strong enough to hold her?" He looked bleakly at Tracy. "It is just possible that you have."

He went out.

"Your father's friend," said Caleb. He stood aside, opening her way to the door if she were disposed to take it. "If you do not hurry he will be in Virginia before you."

She darted to the fireplace, snatched up a stick of wood and struck at him with all her might. He caught the descending blow with one hand and, continuing to laugh, twisted the stick from her grasp. She lifted the brass kettle and swung it at him. He inclined his head no single fraction of an inch more than was necessary to evade its swing. The kettle flew from her fingers, hit the wall behind him, and rebounded to his feet. He stuck his toe against it before it came to rest and accelerated its roll back toward her. She looked about wildly for another weapon. His mocking glance went to the hatchet leaning beside the fireplace. She came at him with it. He held her against him, her arms pinioned to her sides, until she dropped the hatchet. He was still laughing. His physical superiority fired her fury to a final pitch of infantile frenzy. She writhed in his grasp and bent, striving to sink her teeth into one of his restraining hands. He was still laughing, more amused than ever. He shoved her away and stood watching her, his thumbs again hooked in his belt. She overturned the table, extinguishing the candle, and ran out the door.

She paused in the corn, panting, listening for his pursuit. But the empty doorway behind her remained empty. He righted the table, relighted the candle, and sat down on the edge of the bed. He was still chuckling.

She worked her way through the corn with infinite care to make no rustle. Once across the bridge she began to run along the path down the stream. The canoe camp on the point was deserted. Not too far out on the dark river there was the faint glint of what might have been the splash of a paddle.

"Stephen," she called. "Stephen."

There was no reply. She sank to her knees and waited for Caleb to find her. But he did not come. At length she stumbled slowly back along the path. When she reached the rock she kept on up the slope. Reaching the shadow of the palisade she kept close to it and edged around the corner toward the gateway. She had no way of knowing whose turn it might be to be standing guard on the fire step above.

"This is Tracy," she called softly.

"Tracy. Good God, what's the matter?"

She gasped with relief upon recognizing Garett's voice. "Not so loud, Garett. Don't wake up everybody. I just ant to talk to you."

The gate swung open. Garett drew her in and dropped the aken bar back into place.

"I thought you people ought to know straight off," she hispered. "I've no idea what Caleb may try to do. Because ve left him."

Garett gave a low whistle. "And high time, too. But why hisper it? Shout it from the housetops. Come along. Let's oll out the family and drink to such news."

"No, Garett. No. I can't stay here. This will be the first lace he will look for me."

"He can't look till he gets back."

"He's already back."

"Oh. So that was the last straw."

"Stephen was going to take me to Virginia. But Caleb ightened him so that he left without me."

"That Caleb has a genius for detecting clay feet." Garett t go of her arm and stroked his chin reflectively. In the arkness she could not see his face but she could imagine his uizzical grin. "Have you then some idea of where you will o, where he will not as promptly know where to look for ou?"

"No. I haven't thought. Anywhere. Anywhere but here." he need to find some more sensible reply to his question rced her to begin to think more connectedly. "Yes, I mean. do have a very clear idea. Give me a paddle, a sack of mething to eat, and a rifle. I'll take Eric's canoe. Going wnstream with the current I can easily get to Kentucky in few days. And if I travel only at night he can never catch e before I get there."

"So you're really through with him?"

"Yes," said Tracy fiercely.

"What a good thing."

Garett leaned past her and struck the barrel of his rifle arply against the iron triangle suspended by a rope beside e gate. The clang of the warning gong echoed across the ent yard. He seized Tracy's wrist and began towing her by ain force toward the kitchen door.

"No, Garett," protested Tracy. "No."

"Yes, Tracy," Garett mimicked her. "Yes."

"Garett," called Olivia from the doorway. "What is it?"

"She never goes to bed before I do," murmured Garett.

"Even when I'm doing my turn on night watch. Astoundin
woman, really." He called ahead to her. "Light a candle."

He dragged Tracy after him into the kitchen. A glow sprea
from Olivia's candle. She turned, holding it up.

"Tracy," she exclaimed. "What's wrong?"

"Nothing," said Garett. "Quite the contrary." He thrus
Tracy into a chair and stood over her. "Sit there. And b
quiet. All I want from you for the next ten minutes is tha
you spend them keeping in mind that I'm commander here.

Eric slid down the ladder from the loft, the childre
scrambling down after him. Agatha and Louisa, strugglin
into dressing gowns, came out of their rooms. All stare
astounded, at Garett and Tracy. Louisa ran to Tracy's chai
but Garett held her away.

"Sit down—all of you," he directed. "And be quiet."

Polly, her bare feet sticking out below the blanket wrappe
around her, came to a stop in the doorway, her blinking eye
searching the gathering anxiously for a first inkling of th
cause for the alarm. When she saw Tracy she grunted wi
relief and turned to call out into the darkness toward the fi
step of the stockade.

"Olen. Jat. Jake. You-uns kin come down. 'Tain't Injuns

"Call them in," said Garett.

The Negroes from their cabin and the rest of the Slove
thronged in and ranged along the wall. They stared at Trac
and Garett, sudden acute curiosity replacing their earli
alarm.

"Light more candles." said Garett. "I want to be able
see everybody's face. Besides, it's an occasion for illumin
tion. We're about to be able to look one another in the ey
for a change."

While more candles were being lighted, he went to th
mantel, took a pistol from its case, charged it, and thrust
in his belt.

"Something has come up that's better settled now," he sai
"than to let it wait until morning. Eric, go over to Caleb
cabin and tell him that Tracy is here."

Louisa sprang past Garett and sank to her knees besi
Tracy, wrapping her arms around her. Eric darted out th
door.

"Now," said Garett, "we're about to hold what Dunca
liked to call a town meeting." He surveyed the compan
"Everybody will have to make up his mind which way l
wants to jump." He swung around to Tracy. "When Cale
comes up to get you, will you want to go back to him?"

"No," said Tracy. "And I will not. But I don't want to sta

here, either. I never intended that. You dragged me in. The last thing I want is to make trouble for all of you."

"That's for us to decide. We're very good at deciding how much trouble we can tolerate." He surveyed the company again. "Well?"

"What else can we do?" said Olivia. "Of course she can stay here."

"Did you expect we'd say turn her out in the woods?" said Agatha. "Or over to him?"

Louisa tightened her clasp about Tracy. "We'll never let her go again. Never."

Garett, still impassive, looked across at the Slovers. The men were exchanging uneasy glances. Maggie nudged Jarot, seemed about to speak up herself, and then waited, watching Polly. Polly selected a chair and worked her blanketed bulk comfortably into it.

"When a man and the woman he's wedded with takes to fightin' twixt theyselves, thet ain't no time fer other folks to take sides. 'Specially when both man and wife is young. Fore long they'll go to noticin' how cold the bed's turned. Let 'em alone fer a spell and they'll figger out some way to git it warm agin."

The Slover men nodded and grinned, pleased by the ease of Polly's solution.

"But we still have to decide," said Garett, "what we'll do if he comes up here and tries to take her back whether she wants to go or not."

Polly chuckled. " 'Tain't never easy to take no woman thet way. Not when she fer sure don't want to be tuk. And me I wouldn't never hold with nuthin like thet. But it ain't nuthin fer none o' you menfolks to fret about. Ain't no call fer nobody to take to wavin' guns nor axes. One broomstick will do. Yer women and Maggie and me—all we got to do is stand in the doorway and he kin never come near her till she says she wants him to."

"The judgment of Solomon," said Garett.

Eric stood in the doorway, breathing hard from running.

"Did you tell him?" demanded Louisa.

Eric nodded. He squirmed unhappily, as though he were the bearer of peculiarly difficult tidings.

"I had to wake him up. He was asleep—or acting like he was."

"But did you tell him that Tracy was here? And that she was going to stay here?"

"Yes, I told him that. He just turned over and went back to sleep."

July

The procreant heat of summer settled upon the little valley. Occasional evening thunderstorms kept the earth moist. The corn shot upward, the faint whispering rustle of its growing now and then audible on a still night. In the meadow it stood nine and ten feet high and on the virgin soil of Caleb's bank it was twelve. The green jungle of towering stalks was so dense and luxuriant as to seem an added defense, a kind of moat interposed between the station and the shadowed edges of the forest. On the open side toward the river, where the clearing was under way, smoke from the burning piles of logs and brush wreathed and drifted lazily. The great river, now widely visible, was no longer lonely. More than a thousand boats had passed so far this one season. Beyond the smoke and the corn and the river, the wilderness was intent upon its own increase. All manner of fruits and nuts and roots and seeds were ripening. Bear and buffalo were mating. Their roars and bellows rumbled through the hot afternoons and in the warm darkness of the nights.

The dismal wail of a wolf, complaining of a poor night's hunting, roused Garett just before dawn. As he listened he heard the nearer scratch of Ned's bare feet on the doorstep and then the faint creak of the opening kitchen door. Ned, having stood watch the second half of the night, was coming to announce the night was ending. His palms patted on the bedroom door. Olivia, still half asleep, clung instinctively to Garett to keep him beside her. He caught her hands, kissed them, the curve of her shoulder, the tip of one ear, and got up.

"Worst thing about summer," murmured Olivia drowsily.

"Is what?"

"The nights are so short."

"Don't tell me you've so soon forgotten how long ago we went to bed?"

"No." She stretched and smiled, her eyes still closed. "Of course I haven't. How could I?"

He completed his hasty dressing, kissed her again, picked up his rifle, and went out. The sky in the east was beginning to pale. He drew a deep breath. In the summer's warmth more of his strength had returned to him than he had enjoyed since Yorktown. He beat on the door of the Slover cabin. The steady drone of snoring within broke into a confused chorus of grunts and wheezes. Since Eric's encounter with John Turtle, Garett had insisted on an inspection of all the nearer edges of the woods every day at the first streak of daylight. The Slovers had not protested so violently as he had expected; the early morning search for Indian sign served to postpone by a couple of hours other tasks to which they objected more, such as hoeing corn or clearing land. He knocked next on the door of the shop. The summons, as usual, brought a low laugh from Maggie and an immediate howl of anguish from Jarot. Jarot was a slow awakener and it was one of Maggie's delights to expedite the process by tickling him while he was still somnolently defenseless. His spasm of resistance and her vigorous persistence all but shook the cabin. Much of their marital love-making verged on physical contests that amounted to feats of strength.

Ned had roused the sleepers in the Negroes' cabin. Geneva waddled out, yawning, and went into the kitchen to kindle the breakfast fire. Hebe gathered an armful of wood and followed her. Clem went to the grindstone and began sharpening his axe. Olen, Jacob, and Jarot let themselves out the gate and separated to make their respective circles through the nearby forest. Garett climbed to the fire step over the gate to listen and watch in the growing light. Polly, rifle in hand, climbed to the fire step on the opposite side of the stockade. There was nothing out of the ordinary to be heard or seen except the flicker of a campfire on a small island half a mile up the river.

"Jest movers," called Polly. "Yuh kin see the nose o' their boat a-stickin' out behind thet willer."

Garett's survey of the encompassing walls of green came around to the tremendous stand of corn on Caleb's side of the stream. A wisp of smoke rising into the still air behind the tasseled crestline of the corn was the one sign of the existence of his cabin or his presence in it. He was their only neighbor and the center of their perpetual interest, but his every activity down to his simplest daily tasks took place behind that masking green barrier. For all that could be seen of him from the station, he might as well have lived a hundred miles off.

Eric came out, chewing on a great hunk of cold roast venison, and climbed up beside Garett. He, too, looked across the stream.

"Smoke," said Garett. "He's still there."

"Oh's he's going to stay," said Eric. "When he came he came to stay; and that's what he's going to do. He's still working just as hard as last month or last fall. He's clearing another strip back of his cabin and he's filling his barn with hay from the marsh. I went hunting with him last evening."

"What did he have to say about Tracy, or about us?"

"He didn't have anything to say about anything. When you hunt with Caleb you hunt. You don't talk. He only spoke once. A mile or so downriver on a burnt-over slope there's a patch of the biggest and sweetest blackberries you ever saw. He shot a bear that was feeding on them. Then he ate four or five handfuls of the berries. That's when he finally said something. He said 'Good.' "

"He said a little more than that two weeks ago when you went down to his cabin to get Tracy's things. I never got quite the straight of it."

"He had her stuff all packed in her chest and didn't say anything at first. Then when I started to walk off with it he called me back and handed me his second rifle, a light one he'd taught her to use. He said to tell her not to wander outside the stockade without keeping it always with her. I told him she had said she didn't want anything of his. He said this was hers. When I told her that, she didn't say anything but she took the rifle."

"Better not tell her about the blackberries. She'll be right out after them."

"She'd spotted them a week ago. She's going after them today."

"She's been working harder than she ever did for Caleb. From daylight to dark she's off dragging in something to eat or grabbing something you or Olen have shot so that she can pickle it or smoke it or salt it away. She's been after me to have a cellar dug under the storeroom, so there'll be a place to lay away more. I suppose you can't blame her. After what our getting hungry last winter cost her, she wants to make sure we never get hungry again."

Eric had grown in more than stature. There was a new air of maturity about him and his most common expression was the wrinkled brow of concentrated thoughtfulness.

"I wonder. She's always looking for berries or wild celery or something on his side of the stream. It's almost as though she wanted to keep going where he might catch sight of her every now and then."

"You could be right. But, if so, hers would seem a fairly dim hope. The man's about as impressionable as this gun barrel. I thought you'd given him up for good and all. Are you taking up with him again?"

Eric squirmed uncomfortably. "He's a lot different from us. But the ways that make him different aren't all bad. I like to hunt with him. Every time I'm with him in the woods I learn something new. Look—Jat's come out into the clearing. Clem and I can get going."

Eric jumped to the ground, slung his rifle over his shoulder, gathered up axe and saw, and set out for the clearing with Clem. Olivia came from the kitchen with a plate on which were a square of hot corn bread spread with goose liver, a mound of stewed serviceberries stiffened with pine-nut meal, and the half of a cold roast duck. Garett took a last look around, saw that Polly was still at her post, and dropped to the ground beside Olivia.

"Maggie's door is open," she whispered.

"It is? Then by all means let's stroll out where she can see us."

Garett seized the duck, began eating it and, with Olivia beside him carrying the plate, sauntered around the corner of the shop. Through the open door they could see Maggie making the bed. Toward the back of the former Lyman quarters still stood the forge, anvil, workbench, and rack of tools. The forward half of the cabin had become Jarot's and Maggie's home where were ranged their bed, table, and cooking place. Garett and Olivia, looking at each other, walked slowly past.

"Surely is a nice day," remarked Garett.

"Couldn't be nicer," agreed Olivia, slightly louder.

Maggie looked up from her bedmaking.

"Come right in," she said, cheerfully.

"We were just out enjoying the beautiful morning," said Olivia.

"We don't want to trouble you so early," said Garett.

"No trouble at all," said Maggie. "Come on in and get at your rat-catchin'. Never no tellin' when Jat'll get back and whenever he does his grub is waitin' for him. I already got your fire started."

Garett and Olivia, murmuring apologetically, hurried past her to the back of the shop. He started to put the half-eaten duck down on the plate, but Olivia pushed it back at him.

"Finish your breakfast first," she insisted. "Once you get started you'll forget all about it."

Garett took two or three more hasty bites of the duck,

crammed some of the corn bread into his mouth, and turned
to poke at the charcoal in the forge. Olivia set down the plate,
picked up the hand bellows, and began blowing on the fire.
He thrust a wedge-shaped piece of iron into the coals.

"When you get time," said Maggie, regarding them from
the doorway, "Jat and me we need a new skillet the worst
way. Our old one that Polly give us has got a hole burned
through the bottom of it."

"The very next thing we do," said Garett, "will be to make
you one. Soon's we've finished this pair of hinges for Geneva's
cupboard."

Maggie went out and presently Tracy took her place in the
doorway. Her rifle was slung to her shoulder and she carried
a basket in either hand. Garett and Olivia were by now
completely absorbed in what they were doing. He was taking
up the glowing iron with tongs and transferring it from the
forge to the anvil. She dropped the bellows and handed him
a hammer, with which he began to give the iron carefully
measured strokes. Without looking around he handed the first
hammer back to her and she instantly handed him a second
lighter hammer with which he continued his shaping of the
metal. They were bent intently and together over their work.

"Vulcan himself," said Tracy.

"Not to speak of Aphrodite," said Garett, grinning at
Olivia. He glanced up at Tracy's baskets. "You better hold
up your berrying for the moment. Our spies aren't back yet.
But it ought not to be long before Jat shows up. Jake must
always take a nap while he's out and Olen see a turkey or
something to stalk. But Jat likes to get back to his Maggie."

Tracy stepped aside so that they could see past her into
the yard. Maggie was crouched over her array of bark boxes
ranged along the palisade opposite the buildings. She had
brought with her from the east a packet of assorted fruit-tree
seeds—apple, pear, peach, cherry. These she had planted in
boxes and already the seedlings had sprouted. But this morning she was moving the boxes and arranging them on the
ground in a rectangle that suggested the outlines of a cabin.
She stood back, studied the effect, and moved three so as
slightly to enlarge the smaller of the two rooms.

"It won't do Jat much good to hurry back to his Maggie,"
said Tracy, "if he puts off much longer building her a cabin
of their own. You can hardly blame her for getting tired of
living in a factory."

Garett laughed sheepishly and poked the wedge of iron
back into the charcoal. Olivia began at once operating the
bellows.

"I can't imagine getting to my age," he said, "before discovering it was so much fun to make things with your hands. And what a blessing Olivia takes to it, too."

"What a blessing that Olivia is so easy to manage," said Olivia.

"What makes that so simple is that no more is required than to encourage her to get her finger, her nose, or her elbow into everything."

"Not everything," amended Olivia placidly. "Only into everything that's yours."

"Polly's getting down," said Tracy, "so evidently all's judged still well. Cam wants to go with me. Is that all right?"

"It is if she stays with you."

Garett and Olivia became again engrossed in their project. Tracy and Cam let themselves out the gate. Hebe, with her two buckets suspended from a shoulder yoke, accompanied them as far as the bridge on the first of her many trips to the stream each day to keep the station suppied with water. In the kitchen Agatha had spread out on the table a softly tanned deerskin from which the hair had been scraped, and with a bit of charcoal was marking it with the outlines of a garment. Polly, summoned by Chris, came in to advise her.

"All the children's clothes seem to have fallen to pieces at once," said Agatha. "I can't see anything for it but to start dressing them in buckskin."

"Ain't nuthin' in this world so oncomfortable as buckskin," said Polly. "A buckskin shirt is hot when it's hot, and cold when it's cold, and wet when it's wet. And buckskin pants is worse. But one thing is sure. Buckskin wears a sight better'n cotton."

Cam came running in.

"Polly," she exclaimed, "Tracy and I just saw a really big catfish. He's lying on the bottom right alongside the bank. Tracy thought you might want to come down and spear it."

"Whereat?"

"Just a little below the bridge on Caleb's side of the creek."

Cam began to speak with more care as she came to the more significant part of her report. "We had to take the path on that side in order to get around to the blackberry patch down on the river that Eric was talking about. When you go down that path a little ways you get to a place where you can see past the edge of Caleb's corn into his barnyard. Caleb was working with his calves, trying to break them to wearing a yoke. The bull calf from Kentucky was behaving but the two buffalo heifers were kicking and jumping and trying to fight off the harness. Ken was over there watching. When we got to where we could see, Tracy pretended her shoe was untied and stopped so she could watch, too. That's when I saw the catfish and then she told me she'd wait there and for me to run get Polly."

Polly, accompanied by Cam carrying the fish spear and followed by Lina at a more leisurely pace, joined Tracy on the stream bank.

"He's still right there," said Tracy. "He hasn't moved."

Polly gripped the spear. Her bulk seemed to drop away from her. For the next few seconds she moved with the quick lightness of her long-lost youth. Leaping through the fringe of reeds lining the stream bank, she struck downward mightily with the spear. The immediately ensuing upheaval cast a shower of water over the onlookers. Polly, drenched and whooping in triumph, took a turn of the line about her ample hips and leaned her weight into the pull. Tracy seized hold of the line to help. The threshing monster was dragged up on the bank. Polly drew her knife and, watching for her chance among its convulsive contortions, drove the blade to the hilt between the eyes. The great fish lay still. Polly regarded it complacently.

"Must weigh more'n a hunert pounds." She knelt, withdrew the knife, and began to disembowel the fish. "Weather like this it's best to clean 'em straight off."

Cam, her interest in the episode satisfied, strolled off around the end of Caleb's cornfield to indulge her greater interest in a closer inspection of his calf-breaking. Lina wandered on lazily along the path, looking for an inviting place to sit down. She had grown very large about the waist these past few weeks but she carried herself with the serene grace of a ship gliding over a calm sea.

"When is she due?" asked Tracy.

"Some time next month. She's gittin' along real good. She won't have her no trouble." Polly glanced across the estuary at Eric and Clem still working alone at their clearing. "Olen and Jat and Jake—they kin surely figger ways to spend time with their pokin' around through the bresh these mornings. But they don't feel so foolish doin' it as they done at first. Not since they found out Caleb he was out lookin' around every mornin', too."

"He is? Does he think then there's any real danger?"

"Not yet, he don't. But he don't like the idee o' even one Injun snoopin' around. Not without his knowin' about it."

Lina had found a spot that suited her and had settled down against the moss-covered trunk of a fallen tree. She appeared to be dozing in the sun. On the path across the stream Betsey came into view from the direction of the marsh. She was carrying a string of half a dozen ducks.

"She nets 'em in the marsh over around thet island we snuk to thet night," said Polly. "Nuthin Betsey craves so much as smoked duck. They's about the only thing she ever gits hungry fer. She's kept arter 'em 'till she's got most four dozen strung to the rafters."

"She looks so much better lately and seems to be in so much better spirits."

"Thet's a fact. I figgered out why quite a spell back but she only tol' me herself jest last night. She's on her way to havin' her another young-un."

"What! Who?"

"Nobody here. But yuh mind thet day o' Louisa's birthday shindig when Bill Granger's boat stopped off and he brung up thet keg o' whisky?"

"Surely not Bill Granger?"

"Betsey ain't sure whether 'twas him or which one o' them no-count boatmen o' hisn. Anyhow, arter they all got theyselves good and drunk and arter it got dark she was down there on thet boat with 'em most o' the night."

"But—but I thought she wasn't well. Even if she had drunk too much too, how could she stand it?"

"She never tuk a drop. She knowed whut she was doin'. I reckon she figgered it was a case fer kill or cure. Anyhow, she come through it. She tuk to her bed fer mebbe a week but when she got up she stayed up and tuk to eatin' more and stopped actin' so mean. Soon's we can't keep it from 'em no longer, Louisa and Agatha and Olivia they'll most likely go to lookin' down their noses agin, but me I ain't yellin'. Betsey she can't abide it not havin' a brat of her and when a body wants somethin' thet bad it's no more'n right fer 'em to have it." Polly wiped the blade of her knife on a clump of grass, struggled upright, and poked at the fish with one bare foot. "It's too heavy fer me to lug up the hill. When Olen turns up I'll send him down to fetch it." She looked off toward the continuing commotion in Caleb's barnyard. "I misdoubt me some Caleb he's ever goin' to git them buffler to pull even in the traces. But Caleb he ain't no hand ever to give up easy. Thet's one thing yuh might's well git straight in yer head. He ain't bin actin' much like it but he wants yuh same's he done from the start. It was you, then, and nobody else. He fooled me some then, but he ain't foolin' me no more."

"You have to admit he has a marvelous way of showing whatever it is he feels, if he feels anything."

"A man like him's got a right to expect his woman to be the first to give in."

Wagging her head, Polly trudged away toward the bridge. There came a splintering sound from the direction of the barnyard but Tracy took care not to look again. Hastily picking up her baskets, she hurried on along the path past the drowsing Lina toward the river bank. When she had pushed through the willows to the beach to turn downriver toward the berry patch, she saw a barge anchored a hundred yards out and a man rowing a skiff from it into the mouth of the creek. He twisted at his oars to see where he was going and, catching sight of Tracy on the bank, swung the prow of his skiff toward her. Twisting again, he called out:

"This Revel Creek?"

"Yes, it is," said Tracy.

He pulled again on his oars, drove the bow of his skiff into the bank, and began fumbling in his shirt.

"I got a letter for Garett Jordan," he said. He stretched from the seat to hand it to her. "I told his brother in Pittsburgh I'd drop it off here."

The moment Tracy had hold of the letter he picked up his oars and, obviously relieved his mission had cost him so little time, began vigorously to row back to his barge. Tracy ran all the way to the station. The gate was open now that the scouts had at last returned from their morning patrol, but they had not yet left to join Eric in the clearing. Olen, Jarot, and Jacob, all brandishing shovels, were circling about the center of the yard, studying the ground and striking at it with shovel points to illustrate their varying views on some debate that absorbed them. Polly and Maggie, equally interested, were taking an earnest part in the discussion. Garett and Olivia were watching from the doorway of the shop. Tracy ran to Garett.

"A letter from Duncan," she announced.

Garett tore it open. In it were two folded sheets of paper, one of them sealed. Olivia, pressing against him the better to see, snatched the sealed one.

"It's for Agatha," she said. "I'll take it to her. She won't want to wait an extra second for it."

Olivia ran to the kitchen with Agatha's letter. Garett smoothed his and began at once to read it aloud to Tracy.

> *"Dear Garett:*
> From all I have been able to learn since reaching Pittsburgh the general situation in this western country has changed materially since we came through here last fall and, I am sorry to say, the

chance has been very much for the worse. I have been able to talk to men as well-informed as John Neville, John Heckewelder, and George Morgan. All agree that conditions in the west, particularly north of the Ohio, are drifting toward a possible crisis. The man who has agreed to deliver this letter on his way to Limestone is in a hurry to be off and so I will try to say what I have to say in a few plain words. The principal event which has so much changed every prospect has been England's persistence in maintaining her garrisons at Detroit and Niagara, which forts formerly under the peace treaty, they had agreed to turn over to our country. This enables English traders to continue to move freely among the Ohio Indians to furnish them with guns, gunpowder, and whatever else they desire. This in turn has encouraged the Indians to renew their objections to American settlements north of the Ohio. They are said to be even now holding councils in which they are shaping their demands that the Ohio be recognized as the permanent boundary between our country and their tribal lands. Congress has become so aware of the threat that it in turn has renewed its prohibition of any settlement whatever across the Ohio. General Harmar arrived here last winter with his detachment of federal troops but his soldiers are too few to offer more protection to the frontier than the garrisoning of one or two log forts. So far Harmar's best thought on the most likely way to prevent a new Indian war is to discourage white settlement on the Indian side of the Ohio. In a number of recent instances he has even ordered his soldiers to burn cabins found on that side in order to require the settlers to withdraw. In spite of all the talk about the Indians renewing the war, which from their point of view was not actually ended by the peace treaty between the United States and England with regard to which they were not consulted, it does not appear that important hostilities are likely this summer. They are still occupied with their many conferences in which they are endeavoring to work each other up to united action while Joseph Brant, the Mohawk king, is said to be planning to go presently to London in the hope of enlisting further English aid. Before making any general move they will undoubtedly wait to know the result of his embassy. What we do have to be prepared for, however, is the possibility of nuisance raids this year and the probability of more general attacks next summer. In the meantime be constantly on your guard. I shall return within the month and have every hope of bringing with me a sufficient number of new families to make our position more secure. Until then be sure to keep on the best of terms you can with Caleb. I have written this so hastily that I have scarcely had time to read what I have written. Do not let it give you the impression that I am discouraged, for I am not, as I know you are not. We have seen our country come through many severe trials before and it will continue to do so. As will we.

Yr' aff't bro,

Duncan

"Well, well," said Garett. "Looks like Duncan's finally beginning to get his eyes open."

"He's not been so blind," protested Tracy. "Last year when he made all his plans for us to settle here he had no reason to expect anything like this. Nobody foresaw then the English would hang on to their lake posts. That's what's made all the difference."

"Admitting Duncan can do no wrong, suppose we turn to a safer subject. During your singular sojourn with Caleb, did you get no inkling from him of this apparent change in the Indians' temper?"

"None. Though that doesn't signify. He might not have told me if he knew."

"At any rate he seemed to feel no growing need to be watchful himself. He didn't hesitate, for example, to leave you alone when he went off hunting."

"I'm sure he is still quite certain that neither he nor his property is in the slightest danger."

"And it didn't bother him that the Shawnee were creeping up to spy on the station?"

"He might not have known that. There were no Indians ever hanging around on his side of the stream, you may be sure, and you must remember he never hunts on this side. He could have learned for the first time about a number of things like that when he went to the Shawnee town with General Clark. Naturally, I know nothing about him since he got back. I do know that he made the two-day journey in one, whether or not his hurry to get back meant anything. And Polly tells me that now he looks around the woods every morning just as you make the Slovers do."

"It's obvious that something has come over him. For one example, can you guess what the Slovers are doing out there now?"

Garett nodded toward the activities in the yard. Jarot and Jacob had begun to dig a hole over which Olen and Maggie were erecting a scaffolding.

"Surely not another barbecue pit?"

"No. A well. That crossbar will be to support the rope and pulley to hoist buckets of earth. When Olen met Caleb in the woods this morning Caleb asked him why we didn't have a well in the stockade. The slightest suggestion from Caleb is to the Slovers the equal of a royal command. It's a fact that if we ever were besieged it'd be a big help not to have to depend on carrying water up from the stream."

Tracy's eyes became increasingly thoughtful as she contemplated the diggers. "On this mound they'll have to dig a ways to strike water. You or Duncan could never have got them to work that hard. It had to take a hint from Caleb. It's the first real sign of his taking our side."

"Don't go too fast. It may not be a free choice for him. In Clark's letter to Stephen he remarked on the existence among the Shawnee of a peace party and a war party. He said Caleb seemed to have as many old friends in the one lot as the other but some of the more ardent leaders of the war party were beginning to cool off on him. What I'm getting at is that if he's bound to keep his place here he may sooner or later be obliged to take our side."

Tracy appeared not to be listening. "In planting the idea of the well on Olen he could only have meant to help us. Now that he's made this overture, isn't it up to us to make some gesture in return?"

"Such as your going back to him?" The smile on his lips was mocking but his eyes were troubled and thoughtful.

"No," declared Tracy with instant violence.

"Then you haven't, as Polly put it so much more neatly, as yet begun to miss him?"

"Don't be absurd. All the same, there's still this one thing about him we have to face. He is sacrificing something on account of us. If we weren't here he could have that place of his to the end of his days and the Shawnee would have no slightest objection. It may cost him a great deal to befriend us and we do have to try to meet him at least part way. I haven't spoken to him since that night I left. But I'm beginning to wonder if I shouldn't try to have a talk with him. An intelligent talk, I mean, just for once."

"No harm in trying. I've one suggestion. While you're at it try also to remember that intelligence has a way of coming down as the temper goes up."

"I'll do my best. But none of you up here can have any idea how really infuriating he can be."

"I have some idea. And I think Duncan assembled a very good one."

"No wonder. Two men could not be more different."

"I know. Duncan's everything that's wise and reasonable and noble."

"No. Those aren't the ways they're the most different. Caleb isn't stupid, or irrational, or ignoble, at least in the kind of world he knows."

"That's the right frame of mind. Give him the benefit of every doubt. Just hang to that thought and go down there and see if you can't find out just where we stand with him."

Tracy met Cam and Ken on the bridge.

"He put the calves back in their pen," said Cam. "They
broke the yoke and he's gone to the woods to find a piece of
ash to make a new one. Are you still going berrying? Where'd
you leave your baskets? Don't you want Ken and me to go
with you?"

"Your mother just got a letter from your father," said
Tracy. "You'll want to hear what he said, won't you?"

"Oh, yes," said Cam.

She and Ken went flying up the hill. Tracy kept on
wedging her way among the tremendous stalks of corn, until
she came out into the narrow dooryard before the cabin. The
coon came scuttling from under the doorstep to clutch at
her skirt and make murmuring little squeaks of greeting. The
door stood open and she saw that the interior of the cabin
was as neat as ever. Caleb was nowhere in sight. She walked
on toward the barn and stockpens. Her garden was doing
well and had been kept carefully weeded. The calves were
crusted with dried sweat and still rolling nervously bloodshot
eyes, but appeared otherwise well-kept and flourishing. Two
of the hens that had been setting when she left were stalking
importantly about their pen followed by trails of cheeping
chicks. The sow had not yet farrowed but, sprawled contentedly in the sun, was of a size to promise an imminent
and significant increase in the pig census. The young turkeys
were two-thirds grown and Caleb had been obliged to con-
trive a latticed roof of saplings to keep them from flying out
of their pen. She walked back to the cabin door and sat on
the step.

Caleb's return was so noiseless that she was aware first of
his shadow before looking up to see him. He stood before her,
axe in hand, his rifle slung to one shoulder, and a roughly
squared section of ash log balanced on the other. He eased
the log to the ground, set the axe against the wall, and leaned
on his rifle, looking down at her. The Indian impassivity of
his gaze kindled in her the familiar flare of resentment. She
drew in her feet with the immediate impulse to rise and walk
away from him.

"You have come back?"

He must have intended his words to convey as much un-
concern as did his manner. But he hurried them ever so
slightly. She settled back on the doorstep.

"No. I have come to talk."

"What is there to say?"

"Some of the things we should have said before I came
back that first time."

"I am listening."

"You have been helping us."

"When you say us, do you mean us? Or them?"

"I mean everybody at the station. I think we, at least I, we you something in return. So I want to help you."

"How will you do that?"

"I will come down every morning and every evening—all lay, if necessary—and do all the work I did when I was living ere."

"What good is that?"

"You have much more to do here than one man can do."

"I do not need help." He nodded in the direction of the tation. "That is what they need."

"Everybody needs help."

"I do not think I do but I know I do not want it."

"What is it that you do want?"

"The same as in the beginning. I want a wife."

"Do you still want me?"

"Yes."

"Why? You have never been satisfied with anything about e." He did not answer. "Have you?"

"You might learn."

"So might you. Though we do not seem so ready to learn, ither of us." She rose to face him. "It will do no good for me come back and I will not. But there is something else we an try. I have come down here to talk to you. Why, tomor-w or the next day, do you not come up to the station to talk me? Any white man would do that if he wanted to per-ade his wife to come back to him. You are not obliged for-ver to act like an Indian. Come as often as you like. You ill be welcome. I'm not promising anything. I'm only saying at there is no slightest hope whatever for what you say you ant so long as we go on feeling as we do about the other's ind of people."

He had listened attentively and appeared to give her appeal me consideration. But after a moment he shook his nose.

"No. If here you feel always the feather in the nose, then ere is not the place for you."

"That is how you have made me feel."

"Then it is better you do not come back." She turned to . "But you are here already." The words burst from him. Why do you not stay here?"

"Feather and all?" she taunted him.

He did not reply. She started away and he made no move stop her.

Lina squirmed into a more comfortable position against e log and opened sleepy eyes. Across the stream, nearly a

hundred yards wide here where its estuary broadened before
curving against the sandy point to empty into the river, Eric
was swinging his axe against the base of the last tree standing
between the station and the Ohio. She watched him contentedly for a while and then dozed again. A rustle in the undergrowth caught her attention. She opened her eyes. A great
six-foot rattlesnake was slowly worming his torpid length
from the stretch of sun-baked open along the path into the
comparative shade and seclusion of a tangle of juniper brush.
She watched idly. Then, struck by a sudden thought, she
sprang up and broke a long dead branch from the fallen
tree. With its forked end she began teasing the snake, pre-
venting its escape into the shrubbery and forcing it to retreat
toward the more open bank of the stream. She worked with
the huge reptile coolly and smilingly. When she had maneuvered it to the location she had selected, she struck it
several harder taps. It coiled to strike, its fangs gleaming, its
rattle buzzing fiercely.

"Eric!" she screamed. "Eric! Help!"

Eric dropped his axe, snatched up his rifle, and ran to the
stream bank. He paused there, half-crouched, the rifle ready,
his glaring eyes frantically searching the woods behind her
for evidence of the danger threatening her.

"A snake," she cried. "A big rattler. He's after me."

Eric instantly threw down his rifle, stripped off his powder
horn, and plunged into the stream. His flailing arms whipped
the water of the estuary into a froth in the desperate urgency
of his swim across. He scrambled, dripping and gasping, up
on the bank beside her. She had already found a weapon for
him. It was a long heavy pole of water-soaked driftwood.
He grasped it.

"He's right there," she said, pointing.

The rattlesnake had been neglected while Lina had become
belatedly concerned over how well Eric could swim. While
she watched his crossing the creature had started to move
off. But upon Eric's leap toward him he coiled once more,
lifted his great triangular head, and resumed his lethal buzz.

"Watch out," said Lina. "He's so big he kin strike a good
ways."

Eric shook off her clutch and sprang on to the attack. He
swung the heavy pole and continued to hammer wildly until
he had beaten the reptile into a pulp. He dropped the pole
and straightened, breathing deeply and swaying with a momentary faintness mingled with his relief.

"He surely was a big one," he whispered. "Never saw a
bigger one."

"You come very quick," she murmured. "I only had to yell oncet and there yuh was a-churnin' crost the crik."

"Of course," he said.

He looked around at her. In the brillance of the sunlight his vision of her was breathtakingly near and clear. He looked at the flaxen brightness of her hair curling about her shoulders, at the startling glow of her dark eyes against the whiteness of her skin, at the moist red curve of her lips, at the satiny sheen of her throat, at the pleasant lift of her bosom. But then his glance reached the swelling bulge at her waist and he looked abruptly and painfully away.

"I ain't never bin skeered o' snakes," she was saying. "I can't figger whut got me in sech a fret all on a sudden over this one. Must o' bin 'cause o' the time thet's on me."

He looked helplessly at her again. Usually she seemed so calm and peaceful, almost sleepy. But now she seemed vibrantly alive. Her eyes were shining, her lips parted, her breast rising and falling. She seemed on tiptoe to accept and to welcome something extraordinary, something mysterious. She lifted her hands and pressed them against that portion of her that seemed thrust out toward him, that he was struggling so desperately not to notice. Hastily, he looked away again.

"He's gittin' thet spry, and strong, too," she went on. "Sometimes he gits to jerkin' around like a frog in a teacup. Look—he's right here. Most as close to yuh as I be. Yuh don't have to be a-feared to look." She took one of his hands and held it against her. "Here, yuh kin feel, too. Whut's in there is jest as much yers as mine."

He jerked his hand away.

"I don't want to feel. I don't want to look. I don't even want to think about it."

He plunged into the stream and swam back to the security of the other side as furiously as when he had rushed to the rescue. Lina looked after him, smiling sorrowfully and forgivingly.

Through all the next week the station was in a continual tumult of activity. The well-digging progressed earnestly and succeeded beyond every expectation. Long before the shaft had been sunk to the level of the stream, water gushed into it and rose slowly in the well, cool and black and glistening, to within ten feet of the surface. Olen was astonished to the point of alarm by this apparent violation of natural law and was only partially reassured by Garett's suggestion that there must be some subterranean channel leading from the heights of the adjacent ridge which their digging had chanced to

intersect. With the well achieved so much more easily than
had been anticipated, the Slover men were encouraged to
undertake the construction of a cabin for Jarot and Maggie.
Eric, Ned, and Clem, the major clearing completed for the
moment, began the excavation of Tracy's proposed cellar under the storeroom.

There was but one untoward incident to disturb this pro-
ductive week. In the course of one morning's patrol Olen
sighted a bull elk with a broken arrow protruding from his
shoulder. He whistled for Jarot and Jacob to join him and
the three set out to back-track the elk in order to determine
how near the station the Indian had shot him. They advanced
with extreme caution at first but then went on more boldly as
they observed that the elk's gait had been normal during the
hour before Olen had sighted him and that there were no
splatters of blood marking his course. Crossing the old
Indian trail above the falls they came upon clinching evidence. Here they found where the elk had bedded down for
the night and where upon getting up he had lingered to
browse. It was clear that the Indian hunter's range had been
at a considerable distance and that his unsuccessful arrow
had been launched days before. But in setting out to return
to the station they came upon another kind of Indian sign
that gave them new pause. Near the stream crossing, a tree
beside the trail had recently had a strip of bark peeled from
it. On the gleaming fresh surface of the scar had been painted
a number of the odd, sticklike designs of Indian picture
writing.

"Injuns—mostly Shawnee, I reckon—bin using thet trail
off'n on," said Olen in reporting the discovery to Garett.
"But ain't bin no Injuns foolin' around in the woods this side
the trail. Not since we-uns bin goin' out every mornin'. Thet
I kin swear to."

"But the picture writing must mean something," said
Garett. "Could it have been meant for Caleb?"

"Nope. We-uns tol' him about it 'fore we come back up
here. When we tol' him whut it was like he knowed whut it
meant without goin' to look at it fer hisself. 'Twasn't war
sign. 'Twas woman sign." Olen chuckled. "Some Injun'd lost
track o' his woman and he painted the tree there so's any
other Injun comin' along who happened to run crost his
woman would tell her he was a-lookin' fer her."

"Admirable device," agreed Garett. "Good's a notice in one
of our newspapers."

During the week the moon waxed until there came the

night it became a <u>perfect</u> great ball of copper rising above the wooded hills across the Ohio into an evening sky still faintly blue. In the kitchen the first candle had not yet been lighted. Tracy came upon Agatha leaning her head against the wall beside a loophole, gazing out at the moon over the river. In its pale reflected light her face looked even paler, her eyes large with yearning, her lips trembling like a child's. When she was thus off guard, she looked as lost as any child could ever look. She was but half a woman when Duncan was away from her. For all the devotion she lavished upon her children, she lived only for the moment of his return. Tracy shuddered, brooding over her own loneliness which was so much greater because for it there could never be hope of relief, and went out into the dusk of the yard.

The shadow of the palisade darkened the area of the half-finished new cabin, the well, and the woodpile, but the other half of the enclosure was bathed in the glow from the rising moon. Garett stood guard over the gate with Olivia leaning beside him on the fire step. She said something and he drew her closer to him. Jarot and Maggie sat on the shop doorstep. He was softly strumming his mandiddle and her low laughter was even softer. The Slovers had retired except for Lina who sat on a bench before their door. She was idly combing her hair, humming as she inclined her head first one way and then the other. Eric was crouched in the shadow behind the woodpile, watching her. His figure, barely distinguishable in the darkness, was as rigid as though chained to the ground. From some distant, undoubtedly likewise moonlit recesses of the forest drifted the faintly echoing rumble of a bull buffalo's longing. That tremor in the warm air seemed to Tracy to merge with Jarot's strumming, with Maggie's soft laughter, with Olivia's whisper and Garett's murmured response, with Lina's humming, with Eric's anguished tension, and to share with the moon's radiance in the universal invitation of the midsummer night. She turned abruptly back into the dark house.

Louisa, her arms clasped about her knees, was sitting up in bed, staring at the loophole in the wall before her. The shaft of moonlight that came through it fell upon her calm face, etching more deeply and yet making more beautiful the lines of age upon it. Tracy came in.

"Shame on you," she chided. "You should be asleep."

"I can remember when I couldn't sleep on a night like this," said Louisa. "And when I get to remembering, I still can't."

Tracy sank down on the edge of the bed, keeping her face turned away from the shaft of moonlight. Louisa reached out, touched her, and then withdrew her hand.

"Caleb says I'm a fool," said Tracy, suddenly giving way. "He could not be more right. There could never have been a more utter fool."

Louisa touched her again and waited.

"It is worse this time than when last he went away. Even then when I thought he might be dead. *So* much worse. That day his letters came. While Garett was reading his to me, all I could think about was what he must have said to Agatha in the one to her. When he is here I can stand it. I know I have to. But when he is away I sometimes don't see how I can."

Louisa cleared her throat before replying with unsympathetic calm.

"So you've made up your mind that living for a while with another man, even Caleb, has made you want Duncan more than ever."

"It's dreadful to admit it. But it must be so. Only you can hardly call it making up my mind. I scarcely seem to have a mind."

"Mind or no, you've surely been in a state ever since you came back. You've been tearing around as though you didn't dare ever stop for a minute."

"So I have. And for the same reason. When I was down there I worked as hard as I could from morning till dark because I couldn't endure thinking. I still can't endure it."

"For fear you may decide which man you most want not to think about?"

Tracy started up with a cry of protest and sank slowly down again. "How can you say such a terrible thing?"

"I didn't say anything. I only asked a question. And if I were a girl as mixed up as you are I wouldn't rest till I'd found the answer. You'll only feel worse the longer you put it off."

Tracy's shoulders sagged, her head bowed, her hands were twisting a corner of the bedspring into a knot.

"I'm worse than mixed up. I really must be losing my mind. Even my dreams are crazy. I've often dreamed of Duncan. Last night I did again, after I'd finally got to sleep, and then I woke up grabbing at you to make sure I really was here with you. For right in the middle of the dream it came over me that it wasn't Duncan any longer I was dreaming about. It was Caleb. Yet in the dream I'd gone on feeling just as if— as if—oh, I don't believe it. I can't believe it. I can't." She clutched at Louisa. "It's all very well for you to sit there mumbling as though the answer were easy."

"It's never easy for one who's been raised as you have," said Louisa, her pitiless calm unshaken. "Least of all for one who's so sure she has to think before she can tell what she feels. But the answer's as simple as bringing an iron near to a magnet. You've been away from the both of them for a while. Being near either of them again now will tell you fast enough whether it's he or the other. You can't go to Duncan to find out. He's hundreds of miles away. But Caleb's right down there in his cabin."

"You can't be suggesting I go back to him!"

"You left him once. You can leave him again."

"You're more mixed up than I am. No one's been so set against him as you've always been."

"As I still am." There was no emotion in Louisa's voice, only an immense weariness. "But I am also an old woman. One of the few advantages of age is that you begin to see how little use there is in trying to make anything go away just by going on saying it isn't so. You've already been hurt all you could be. You can't be hurt any more. And this time you'll finally know. Or is knowing what you are the most afraid of?"

Tracy stood up.

"No. I'm not afraid of knowing. I—I want to know. I have to."

She moved from the doorstep along the shadow of the wall to the ladder in the corner of the palisade behind the kitchen. The yard was deserted except for Garett and Olivia over the gate and all of their attention was alternately on the forest beyond and on each other. She climbed to the fire step, swung over the parapet, and dropped to the ground outside. On the bridge she began to run, but at the edge of the corn she paused. To force her way through it would set up an unavoidable rustling. She shrank from giving Caleb so premature an advertisement of her approach. Circling carefully around the cornfield she crept past his pool. At the corner of the cabin she came to a sudden halt, frozen. From within came the murmur of Caleb's voice and Daisy's giggling reply.

She crept away as silently as she had approached. The storms of rage which had so often protected her from him before failed her now. The one sensation that overwhelmed and possessed her was of her own terrifying inadequacy. She seemed to be falling and continuing endlessly to fall in sickening helplessness into bottomless depths of shame from which there could be no faintest hope she might ever escape.

August

It had not rained in more than two weeks. Day after day the sun blazed from a cloudless sky and each day the heat became more oppressive. The ground inside the station baked hard, pitch oozed from the logs of the palisades, springs dried up, the stream shallowed, the broad leaves of the corn yellowed, the forest turned tinder dry. Only the new well resisted the dryness and the heat. Every morning Olen peered down it, grunting with satisfaction upon being again assured that the water level had not fallen by so much as an inch. By now he had taken all credit for having personally selected the precise spot beneath which had so long lain hidden so manifest a miracle.

The third week the inevitable forest fire cast its towering black and yellow shroud across the sky. Later in the year there were often such fires, set by Indians in the course of their immemorial fall game drives. But in weather as dry as this one was bound, sooner or later, to be set going by chance —by burning grains of powder from a careless hunter's primer pan, by a mover's abandoned river-bank campfire, by a bolt of lightning from one of the distant thunderstorms murmuring along the horizon. Once started, such a fire spread endlessly across the limitless expanse of woodland, devouring in a day years and centuries of patient growth, in a pitiless devastation that would rage on unchecked until finally subdued by the next heavy rain. This fire was an immense conflagration, though happily on the other side of the Ohio. It burned over the southern hills for days, at times seeming to smolder, at others casting huge billows of flame from treetop to treetop. A strange traffic coursed to and fro upon the river. At each flare-up the water was dotted with the heads of swimming wild animals—bear, wolves, panthers, rabbits, herds of deer and elk and buffalo. The majority were seeking desperately to flee the flames, but almost as many, deranged by their terror, were struggling as desperately toward

216

them. The night sky was as fiery as the open door of some monstrous furnace. By day, if the wind veered to the south, choking clouds of smoke rolled across the river to curl about the station.

Yet this season of heat and drought and fire offered certain redeeming compensations. The corn had matured until every morning there were new young roasting ears turned tender enough to eat, and the blueberries in the marsh had suddenly ripened in incredible profusion. The people of the station, long since wearied of their principal diet of fresh meat, drank deeply from their enchanted well and gorged blissfully on green corn and blueberries. At last there came a night when a prolonged thunderstorm quenched the great fire and left damp cool air after its passing.

"Them blueberries," said Polly next morning, "they's right at their best. But they'll go bad fast arter the soakin' they got last night."

A berrying bee was organized to gather a major supply to be dried and stored away for the winter. Maggie, Betsey, Cam, Ken, Geneva, and Hebe assembled to accompany Polly. Tracy, who had seemed so much more affected than anyone else by the heat that during the whole three weeks she had seldom ventured from her room, bestirred herself and joined the group. Garett called Eric.

"So many people will keep up a chatter loud enough to carry for miles. Take Jat and cut over the ridge to East Creek. Look particularly to see if there've been any Indians back around that Shawnee hunting camp Jat spotted over there last week. Then work your way to the river and down to the marsh."

Eric nodded.

"I saw Caleb again last evening just before the rain," he said. "My trigger spring was broken and I asked him to show me how to put in a new one. That seemed as good an excuse as any. I like to drop in on him now and then."

"And a good idea, too. What did you decide?"

"You can't tell. He acts just the same. And he's working just as hard. With Daisy to help he's been able to get more done, in spite of the heat. He's cleared another couple of acres back of his stockpens. His corn's not as yellowed as ours. It'll be a week or two later than ours getting ready to harvest. And he'll have more. He's been able to keep the deer out of it better than we have."

"He didn't have any sage remarks to make about Indians?"

"No. But while she was away Daisy learned a little English from some trader she worked for in the Shawnee town and she likes to show it off. With the help of a few signs she was telling me that John Turtle paid Caleb a visit night before last. He talked with Caleb a while out in the yard and then went off again without even waiting to have anything to eat. When I asked her if they'd had some sort of an argument she wouldn't talk about it any more."

"On the other hand, it could as well mean some sort of a reconciliation with the Shawnee—signalized by Daisy's return."

"It could. But I hardly think so."

"You think she just came running of her own accord when she heard about that picture writing up on the trail."

"I think Caleb put that there himself, all right, to save him the time and trouble of going after her. But I don't think the sign meant any more than that he'd simply decided he needed her again. There's no use John Turtle or anybody else trying to argue with him. He doesn't listen; he just keeps on going his own way, whatever that is."

Eric and Jarot set out. The rain had obliterated the earlier sign of Indian hunters in the valley of East Creek. After they had made sure there had been no new tracks since, they zigzagged down the valley and climbed the lower slopes of the nose of the ridge thrust out into the main river bottom. They could see the berry-pickers scattered through the marsh below but were immediately gripped by a much greater interest in what they could see in the estuary of their own creek beyond. There was a sizable flotilla of boats drawn up on the shore of the point from which upwards of half a hundred men were disembarking. The figures were too far away to identify but the craft were trading bateaus, not Indian canoes. The berry-pickers were unaware of this fleet's arrival, since in the marsh any view of the open river was cut off by the offshore island and of the estuary by the fringe of brush along the nearer side of the point. Eric and Jarot, keeping to the more open higher ground, ran around the marsh and on to the point. In another quarter of an hour they were running back to the marsh, Jarot making for Maggie and Eric for Tracy. The berry-pickers straightened in surprise to greet the messengers. One after another, as they heard the news, they snatched up their half-filled baskets and began to run toward the point. Tracy was the farthest away and the last to hear.

"Father's back," Eric announced. "And General Clark's with him along with a dozen boatloads of soldiers."

The vanguard of berry-pickers, too excited to go around by the path, burst through the shrubbery out to the point

nd there paused to stare. The newcomers did not look much
ke soldiers, for instead of wearing uniforms they were
ressed in odds and ends of buckskin and linsey-woolsey, and
nost of them were as ragged and shoeless as the poorest
nover. But there was a small brass cannon in one of the
eached bateaus; a flag on a staff thrust upright in the sand;
eside the staff two neat, pyramidal stacks of muskets, to
ne of which a drum was hanging; one of the ragged men
vas pacing solemnly back and forth along the path with a
ayoneted musket on his shoulder, and most of the others
vere engaged in spreading their rain-soaked blankets to dry
n meticulously straight lines on the ground under the direc-
ion of a fiercely mustached, older, and stouter man who had
he frayed stub of a plume in his battered, three-cornered
at. At Polly's puffing approach the sentinel ceased his meas-
red tramp and confronted her with musket at port.

"Be yuh sure enough soljers?" she inquired.

"Company C, First American," said the sentry stiffly.

Captain Valentine Telford, stripped to the waist, was shav-
ng at a little mirror hung on the trunk of the sycamore. He
vas young for his rank but bore himself with a cultivated and
nmistakable air of command. Without looking around and
vithout raising his voice, he spoke distinctly and coldly.

"Sergeant, a sentinel on post does not carry on a conver-
ation with bystanders."

"Yes, sir," said the mustached man. "Jenkins—look alive."

The sentry hastily resumed his pacing back and forth. Cap-
ain Telford slowly turned, razor in hand, to survey the group
f gaping onlookers which by now included Jarot, Maggie,
Betsey, Cam, Ken, Geneva, and Hebe.

"Sergeant, could you postpone the entertainment of visitors
ll you've got camp established?"

"Yes, sir. Most certainly, sir."

Sergeant Redfern advanced scowling on the berry-pickers.
They backed away, continuing, however, to stare with un-
atisfied curiosity at the cannon, the flag, the stacked muskets,
ne Sergeant's hat, and the eagle tattooed on the Captain's
ack. Cam and Ken were torn between their interest in the
ovelty of this military spectacle and their desire to waste
o more time before seeing their father. After a brief struggle
ey scampered off toward the station. The others lingered.

Captain Telford resumed shaving. Tracy, running along the
ath from the marsh, rounded the spreading hazel bush
where the path took its turn, and all but plunged into him.

was his turn to gape, open-mouthed, at this flushed and
artlingly vivid face that had sprung so suddenly and at

such close quarters upon his view. He had paid scant hee
to the other intruders but this new invasion struck him instan
ly as a different case. With one hand he had been stretchin
his lower lip in order to get at it with the razor and she wa
so near that for a second he could feel her hastened breat
on that raised bare forearm. He peered over it at her. I
began to come over him how very much different, in truth
was this one from the others. His military aplomb topple
His blush was not so apparent on his tanned and still half
lathered face but it spread like a crimson tide across th
whiteness of his naked torso.

"Oh, I beg your pardon," said Tracy. "I had no idea th
path ran right into your camp."

She stepped around him and ran on, the grinning Eric a
her heels. The Captain, for the moment forgetting his soldierl
dignity, craned to look after her. His expression did no
escape Betsey's sharp eyes. Taking advantage of Sergean
Redfern's pause to tug on at his mustaches while taking
second and less passing look at Maggie, she circled him an
sauntered toward the sycamore. The Captain peremptoril
gestured her nearer. As she advanced her scrutiny was ope
and direct, but he had regained his usual color and seeme
undisturbed by her contemplation. He inclined his head i
the direction of Tracy's receding form.

"Who was she?"

"Tracy Lewis."

Betsey waited. He concentrated on the next two strokes o
his razor before making another equally casual remark.

"Bit awkward for a soldier to be taken quite so completel
by surprise."

"Eh?"

"Never mind. But when you see her next time will yo
convey my apologies? Tell her I do hope she wasn't to
upset?"

" 'Tain't likely." Betsey ran another appraising glance ove
his muscular arms and chest. "She's bin married long enoug
to git her eyes open."

"Oh?"

" 'Course she's a widder now—sort of. She lives up at th
station."

"Oh."

The young Captain appeared capable of making quick de
cisions.

"Sergeant Redfern, will you please be good enough, an
without further delay, please, to clear the camp of visitors
Also to have my locker brought ashore and my tent set up?

He waited with increasing impatience for these instructions to be carried out, ducked into his tent, threw open his locker, and set about arraying himself in his new dress uniform.

Cam came running from the kitchen door to meet Tracy and Eric in the yard.

"General Clark's on his way back to Louisville to build a fort. We're going with him. We're going to give up the station and move to Kentucky."

Eric bolted past her and on into the house. He came to as sudden a stop, astounded. The whole atmosphere was one of excitement and jubilation, his mother tearful with happiness, Garett's quizzical grin more overt than usual, Louisa and Olivia laughing, the children whooping, the Negroes chattering.

"Cam says—Cam says—" Eric could not get the words out.

"It's all true," said Agatha. "Isn't it wonderful!" She saw his expression and slipped an arm comfortingly about his shoulders. "Your father'll tell you all about it in a minute. But first he wants to talk to Tracy."

She glanced past him at Tracy and nodded toward the office. Tracy went in and closed the door. Duncan had his little brass strongbox open on his desk and was sorting papers in and out of it. He whirled to face her. He looked as buoyant as the day of their arrival when they had stood together on the top of the mound.

"You can't begin to guess what a relief it was," he exclaimed. "To learn you'd left him, I mean. You represented the one complication that made me hesitate for a second about this move to Kentucky. But now there can be no question of your going along with us. Can there?"

"None. So you really are giving up this place."

"I'm giving up nothing. This land's still ours. It will always be. And in time we'll be back on it and have everything here we ever counted on. Can't you grasp what it really means? This isn't a retreat. It's a seven-league-boots advance. The opportunity opened up suddenly through some men from the East I met in Pittsburgh. I've got hold of pre-emption rights on a fifteen-thousand-acre tract on Green River. Actually by way of an option on shares in a land company. You can hardly call that a disaster. I'm attached to this place, too. But by the time we get the Green River tract developed the Indian situation will have improved enough so that we can come back here and build this one up next."

"Then all you've lost is just the year we've spent here?"

"I wonder you're not even more bitter. I'm not forgetting what this year has cost you. We can never forget what you did for us. Never. And we'll never stop trying to make it up to you. If there's anything on this earth anybody can ever be sure of, you can be sure of that."

"I'm sure you—all of you—will want to. But if I seem bitter it's not because of that. What I keep thinking about is that the year was a sort of test of his kind of people and our kind. It was almost a personal duel between you and him as well as between me and him. And look how it's coming out.'

"That's nonsense, and you know it. The way it's coming out is that we'll have holdings so broad there'll be proper places, besides mine, for Garett and Eric, and Cam when she marries, and the others, and you, too, you may be sure. While he'll have just a cabin in a clearing, if the Indians let him keep that. My view hasn't narrowed. It has widened, vastly. Can't you see that?"

"Dimly. I can see what you see."

"Good. I've so much more to tell you the moment I can. But so much to do that has to be done this instant." He paused on his way to the door to give her one more earnestly beseeching look. "I can't tell you how happy I am that you're back with us. You belong with us. You're one of us."

He went out. Eric was waiting for him. After one glance at his son's face he smiled understandingly and placed a hand on his shoulder.

"I don't wonder you're taken aback. I was myself, at first. I couldn't stop thinking of all our work and all our hopes. Any more than I can stop thinking now of the way you've taken hold while I was away. Later I'll go more fully with you into my reasons for the move. But what it amounts to is that we have little choice. With the turn the Indian attitude has taken it had become clear we couldn't get settlers to join us here. Even if we were able to hang on here alone—for years to come that's all we'd be doing, just hanging on. While down there where we're going we'll have a thirty-family town established before snow flies."

"But do we have to depend on what other people do? Why isn't it what we do that counts?"

Duncan removed his hand from Eric's shoulder. "You'll just have to trust my judgment. We haven't time now to debate how I arrived at it. Naturally, if we're going to move, the sooner the better. And if it's to be soon, it must be at once, in order to take advantage of Captain Telford's military escort. River travel is becoming as dangerous again as it was during the war. Two flatboats were taken not thirty iles from here just this week."

Eric's face was getting whiter. "That only makes it seem
ven more like—like running away."

Duncan stiffened. "You have become a man in size. I must
sk you to act like one. You will take Clem and Ned and
egin at once moving our stores down to the rock. That's an
rder."

"Yes, Father."

Duncan turned to address the others in the room.

"Will each of you start picking out what he wants most to
ake. Space is limited, so we can't take everything. There will
e room, however, for everything we really value."

He went out into the yard. The Slovers were gathered,
ilent and staring, about the well. He walked over to them.

"We have to leave today," he explained, "so that we can
ravel with the soldiers. So better start right in getting to-
;ether what you want to take."

" 'Twon't take us no time to pick up whutever we own,
Kunnel," said Olen.

Polly jerked her head toward the open gateway and the
ornfield beyond. " 'Twon't be more'n two-three weeks till
het corn she'll be eared out good."

"We can't wait for it," said Duncan shortly. "And we won't
tarve without it, you may be sure."

Clark and Captain Telford came through the gate. The
General's faded buckskins were made to seem the more dingy
y contrast to the Captain's resplendence in his blue broad-
loth uniform, pipe-clayed white crossbelts, dangling dress
word, and high, plumed shako. The young Captain veered
ff to take up a strategic position where, while waiting polite-
y for the General, he could see, without seeming to peer,
hrough the open door into the kitchen where the women
f the household were dashing about. Clark came over to
Duncan.

"I'm shoving off now," he said. "I have to get on to Louis-
ille at the earliest. But I've advised Captain Telford to wait
or you."

"He won't have to wait long," said Duncan. "We'll be
oaded before dark. I know you're anxious to get your fort
tarted."

"Good. I just had a talk with Caleb Lewis. He didn't tell
ie too much, but what he did say fits everything else I've
een able to pick up. The Shawnee haven't threatened him
irectly. But what friends he's still got among 'em keep on
udging him to get out soon's he harvests his corn. They say
f he stays here he's bound to get mixed up in the trouble

that's coming at any white holding on this Indian side o
the river."

"When is he getting out?"

"He says he's not. I made him a proposition to throw i
with me when he pulled out here this fall. I've got a propert
across from Louisville that I never find enough time to wor
on myself."

"You trust him that much?"

"Well, the Indians are near enough through with him so
he's stuck with staying a white man, and I'd trust him to loo
out for anything he figgered was his."

"Still, he turned you down. You'd have thought he'd hav
jumped at the chance."

"He said he liked it here."

"Maybe then I could ask him to keep an eye on my plac
for the next three or four weeks. We're going to have t
leave some things behind I'd like to be able to send bac
for, and there's that corn crop which would be worth some
thing at Louisville prices."

"No harm in asking him."

"And not much use, either, I'd say, on second though
Chances are the main reason he's staying on here is he'll b
able to consider the whole place his from now on."

"He'll earn it if he does. Beyond about next spring whoeve
tries to hold this station will have to hold to it hard. Wel
I'm off. The turn things are taking, I think you're making
very sensible move, as I told you when you first mentione
it back in Pitt. This country north of the Ohio—I doubt it
going to be quite the place to raise a family for the nex
five-ten years."

Clark waved to Captain Telford, who came to attentio
with a smart salute, and strode out the gate. The Captai
made instantly for Duncan.

Tracy was helping Geneva sort and pack her kitchen ute
sils. There was a smudge of soot on her nose, and she wa
wrapped in one of Geneva's voluminous aprons with th
strings tied around her under her arms. She looked up t
see Duncan with the now so brilliantly caparisoned Captai
bowing at his elbow.

"Tracy, may I present Captain Telford," said Duncan, hi
eyes twinkling. "For the past week my very good friend an
for the week to come our providential protector. Val—Mr
Lewis. Before we get to Louisville let us hope you are privi
leged, like us, to address her by the much more agreeab
name of Tracy."

The Captain bent low over her hand, which was at the moment slightly grimy.

"We can pray for the future," he said, "but for the moment, Mrs. Lewis, my most earnest wish is to strive to correct the sad impression made by our first encounter."

"Which leaves us the new problem," said Tracy, making a civil effort to match their masculine humor, "of how next to correct the impression I must now be making." She glanced from her soot-streaked apron to the Captain's immaculate attire. "Best take flight while you may, Captain Telford. We are all so busy that if you linger here you may become inveigled into some most unsuitable task."

"I shudder but I do not flee. I am completely at your mercy, whether that mean scouring pots or—name what you will."

"You are too kind, Captain Telford, and we shall be sure to take the most ruthless advantage of you." She smiled brightly at him and, continuing to smile as brightly, turned to Duncan. "Your every move today is so breath-takingly swift. Even to starting so soon making everything up to me."

Duncan laughed and took her hand. "That's because I'm so happy you're back with us." He glanced at the Captain who, continuing to grin, was listening politely to their banter. "This may not be too poor a start, but it is only a start. I hope to do better." His glance came back to Tracy. "But why do you look at me so strangely? Just as when last I returned, you keep studying me as though you were having difficulty convincing yourself that I was really here."

"I'm sorry, Duncan. So much has been happening that I must be in a kind of daze. I assure you that I could not be more convinced that you are here." She stood on tiptoe and lightly kissed his cheek. "And I couldn't be more happy that you are. So many things are getting straightened out today."

She drew back and looked up at him, her smile broadening at his bewilderment. Suddenly the hand in his clasp went limp. She was no longer looking at him but past him. He wheeled. Caleb stood in the doorway.

Duncan immediately started toward him. The two confronted one another at a corner of the table. Caleb hitched the strap of his rifle over his shoulder, reached under his leather shirt, and pulled out a belt in which there were a number of pouches. He dropped the belt on the table. It fell with a solid clunk. The two men were the same height and their eyes on a level. Their glances were equally direct and challenging.

"You are leaving," said Caleb.

"Yes."

"I am staying."

"So I understand."

"I have come to buy your place."

Duncan continued coldly to study his adversary. Everyone in the room had ceased what they were doing to watch and listen. Tracy had backed against the fireplace. Her eyes were burning.

"I can understand," said Duncan, "with some difficulty, that is, your wish to buy. But there would seem to be a greater difficulty. You cannot afford it. I admit the buildings and the corn are not worth much, thanks to your Indian friends. But the land will still be here for years to come."

"I came to buy everything. Take with you what you can. Whatever you leave will be mine. For it—along with buildings, corn, and land—I will pay you now fifty guineas and I will give you a note promising to pay you in three years from today whatever more either General Clark or George Morgan say the land then is worth."

"Guineas, did you say? Do you know what guineas are?"

Caleb undid one of the pouches in the belt and shook five gold pieces from it. Duncan contemplated him with new antagonism and yet with a kind of grudging wonder.

"That was quite a risk you ran, working in the English fur trade the very year you deserted from the English navy; but it would appear to have been a profitable one."

"I have come to buy," said Caleb. "Do you want to sell?"

"I do. You have made, under the circumstances, a very reasonable offer. I may say that I should prefer to see the property come into the possession of almost anyone else. But these are not times we can pick and choose." Caleb was opening more of the pouches and shaking the heavy yellow coins out on the table. "I further feel, Mr. Lewis, that I should caution you. In this country now, gold pieces are so scarce as to be literally unheard of. They are worth many times more than their face value. I assume you are aware of that."

"I have already said that I have come to buy."

"And I have said that I will sell. I will make you out a bill of sale."

"I do not want that. I want Corbit Revel's title."

"So you would. A final righting of the injustice over which you have brooded so long. Very well, come with me to my office and I will sign his original grant over to you."

"And I will sign the note saying what more I will pay."

He followed Duncan into the office. Garett picked up one of

the gold coins, tossed it in his hand, and dropped it, ringing, back on the table top. He crossed to Tracy.

"That Duncan," he marveled. "He's lighted on his feet again. He'd sunk our last penny in this place. Then, before he'd hardly started to face up to the fact it was a dead loss, a land company angles to get him as western manager and throws in as bait a larger tract in a safer region. On top of that comes this offer out of the blue of enough to give his new development a running start. Just to be privileged to finger one of these solid gold guineas, people in Kentucky will rush to build him three such stations as this."

Tracy did not reply. His roving glance, passing over the meat block upon which had been piled the contents of Geneva's cupboard in preparation for packing, settled on the protruding neck of a brandy bottle. He snatched at it.

"Glasses, Geneva. Glasses for everybody. A libation is in order."

Bottle in hand, he followed Geneva about the room, forcing glasses on everyone and spilling a dash of brandy into each. Duncan and Caleb came out of the office.

"A toast," cried Garett, lifting his glass. "A salute to the new lord, and lady, of the manor. May their tribe increase."

Caleb's glance passed over Tracy as calmly as it did the others. He kept on out the door and through the gate. At the bridge she overtook him.

"There's one thing I want to know," she said. "That I have to know."

"There could be more than one," he said. "But who could tell you?"

"Last winter," she accused him, "when the Shawnee took all our food—it really was you who put them up to it—you who sent them—you who told them exactly what to do and how to do it. Wasn't it?"

He regarded her thoughtfully. "What do you do when you want something so much you are sure you must have it? Do you wait? Do you pray? Do you hope for someone to give it to you? Do you just sit and shiver? Or do you reach for it?"

"Reach for it? Is that what you call what you did? You plotted and schemed. You took advantages any savage would scorn to take. You sat over here like a great spider. From the moment you came you began to plan to get our place away from us. And the awful part is that you have. You have wound up getting exactly what you wanted."

"No." He glanced up toward the station and then up the stream along the border of the cornfield toward the falls. "I was ready to be a neighbor. It was not Colonel Jordan's land that I wanted. That was Corbit's to give and he did not give it to me. It is mine now but it is mine because I have paid for it."

She stared at him wildly. "Then why did you do it? Could you have been so out of your mind that you could put us through all that just to get you a white wife?"

"No. I was for a little while so out of my mind that I was sure there was just one white wife I had to have."

Her laugh was harsh with venom. "Then there is still one slight consolation. That was one game you lost. You no longer have her. After all your reaching you've come out with just what you had when you started. Daisy."

"That is so. It is also so that I am no longer out of my mind." He glanced up toward the station where Captain Telford had appeared at the corner of the stockade. "The young soldier is waiting for you. Do not keep him waiting. He could be your Daisy. He is another of your kind of people."

Caleb walked on across the bridge and into his cornfield. Tracy's clenching of her hands made her aware that she still was swathed in Geneva's apron. She tore it off and wadded it under one arm. Slowly she began to climb the slope. Captain Telford watched her, frowning, one hand on the hilt of his sword. But when she joined him he was surprised to see that she seemed quite casually calm.

"Was he annoying you?" he demanded, still frowning.

"I was just saying good-by," she told him cheerfully. "After all, we were married, for a while."

"I watched him while he was talking to Colonel Jordan. I have never seen a man to whom I took a more instant dislike. It is perhaps as well that I will not be here long enough to be obliged to meet him. Colonel Jordan's brother just now gave me a brief account of the circumstances of your marriage. If you will forgive my saying so, I have never heard of a more heroic sacrifice."

"You are very kind. But do not make it worse than it was. He did not mistreat me. It was just one of those instances of a leap in haste followed by repentance as hasty."

"You must believe me," said the young Captain, "when I say that I deeply sympathize. And that any service I can render you—here, en route, after we reach Louisville—will gratify me as deeply."

"You can be of service to me this minute, as a matter of fact." Tracy's hand fluttered to the tightly buttoned neck of her gray homespun gown. "I lost a locket in the marsh this morning. I'm sure I know just where it must have fallen. But everybody's so busy packing and we women and children are not supposed to wander off from the station alone. Would you mind walking over there with me?"

"Would I mind!" The Captain offered his arm with a flourish. "I warn you, madam. Do not mock me. I am a very forthright fellow. Do not be misled by my outwardly sunny nature."

She tossed the apron against the foot of the palisade and laid her fingers on his arm. They descended the slope and set out along the path toward the point. She glanced up at him.

"You do look the part."

"Of being a very forthright fellow?"

"No. Of being a soldier. A born soldier."

"Does that so astonish you?"

"Yes. Since the war all anybody's been thinking about is how to make money. Especially out here where everybody's rushing around so wildly looking for land. Even Colonel Jordan. Why are you so different?"

He replied with sudden sincerity. "Very simple. I love my country. It's young and helpless and needs defenders more than ever. I am honored to be one of the few it has. Nothing else would do me."

"I'm glad I asked," said Tracy, the tips of her fingers pressing his arm ever so slightly.

They had reached the edge of the camp on the point. The sentry presented arms. The lounging men sprang to attention.

"At ease," said Captain Telford. "Sergeant Redfern, send Corporal Rhodes with twenty men to report to Colonel Jordan at the station. They are to assist in any way they can in moving his cargo from the stockade down to the bank. Send Corporal Heston with the boats to that flat rock you can see from here to begin loading. Heston is boatman enough to see that the loads are divided equally. Remind him to make sure no boat is overloaded."

"Yes, sir," said the Sergeant.

Tracy and the Captain walked on. At the turn in the path by the hazel bush she looked back toward the station, her eyes darkening. He was watching her, noting her every change of expression.

"A great pity, really," he said, "to have to give up the place after you'd all worked so hard, and Colonel Jordan had made such a promising start with it."

"I know. But I know, too, it's all for the best. He'll have so much better chance where we're going. We'll all be much better off."

They walked on. The path was narrower now. To avoid the

shrubbery on either side she leaned closer to him. A projecting root tripped her and she clutched at him to regain her balance.

"Mrs. Lewis, you weren't hurt?" He covered the hand on his arm with one of his own and gazed down into her face beseechingly. "Do I have to call you Mrs. Lewis?"

"I don't like the name much myself. But, after all, I'm no longer Miss Carter."

"It's a dilemma easily avoided. I don't deserve it yet. But may I call you Tracy?"

She dropped her eyes. "Yes, Captain Telford."

"Thank you, Tracy."

She gently withdrew the hand under his. "The path is so narrow. Perhaps I'd better walk ahead."

She went on. He followed, giving himself over to the luxury of contemplating uninterruptedly this one aspect of her at least. After several excursions among the folds and contours of the gray gown his attention centered on the gleam of bare skin visible between its collar and the curls at the nape of her neck. Since she could not see it, there was no need to conceal his smile. It was a smile that suggested he was passing rapidly from the stage of dawning hope to that of eager anticipation. She paused in the shadow of a low spreading dogwood to look ahead into the open marsh.

"I'm trying to remember just where it was," she explained. "There was a little pool. I was in such a hurry I jumped across instead of going around. That's where it must have fallen."

He bent to look into her averted face.

"The locket must have meant a great deal to you. You seem so disturbed."

"I'm just being foolish," she said quickly. "I don't know why, but all of a sudden I was thinking again of our leaving. And then of all the other people this year who've had to give up places on the north bank. I've heard that many of them were so bound to hang on that the Army actually had to burn their cabins to make them move."

The Captain's smile vanished. He drew himself up as though throwing the mantle of authority about his broad shoulders.

"That was across the river along the stretch between Pittsburgh and Wheeling." He nodded judicially. "I burned out a dozen or so of them myself. But don't waste your sympathy. Most of them were scum. Bush rats, runaways, troublemakers. But no matter what they were, they'd been repeatedly warned, repeatedly ordered to leave. Congress had prohibited settlement on that side. Laws are meant to be obeyed and it's the Army's duty to see that they are."

"Then our settlement here couldn't have been legal, either?"

"Strictly speaking, it wasn't. But it represents a rather different case. Up there the squatters were just across the river from our older settlements. They stirred up the Indians and constituted a threat to the law-abiding people on the Pennsylvania and Virginia side. Here there are no settlements on the other side and the station's been in the hands of superior and reputable people. When General Harmar heard about it he agreed with General Clark that it was actually an advantage to have a station on this stretch of the river."

"Then the Army just chose to make an exception in our case?"

"It amounted to that. Though not an official one, of course. We've merely looked the other way, as it were."

"Well, I suppose you need to worry even less about it now. It certainly should make no trouble with the Indians now that Caleb owns it. He's almost a Shawnee himself. He grew up among them."

"He did?"

"They still accept him as one of them. So there's not much chance they'll object to his keeping the place. He has friends among the English, too. People like Alexander McKee and Matthew Elliot. And he was in the English navy during the war."

"But didn't I hear Colonel Jordan say something about his having deserted?"

"Oh yes. But that was after the war. He was too anxious to get back to Detroit to wait for a discharge. As you just saw, he knew he could make money in the fur trade."

All preoccupation with gallantry had been swept from the Captain's candid young countenance. His thoughtful frown was stiffly official.

"His having the station begins to sound like making the Indians a present of a fortified post right smack on the Ohio. Does General Clark know him?"

"He doesn't know about his buying the place. But he's met him several times. He thinks he knows him quite well. He thinks he's changed. He trusts him."

"You should have reason to know him better. What do you think? Do you trust him?"

"What does it matter what I think? It's General Clark's judgment that counts."

"Not with me, it doesn't. George Rogers Clark is a great patriot and an extraordinary man. He's also one of our Indian commissioners and I've been instructed to build a fort to cover his negotiations with them. But he's no more a general than you are. He has never been a line officer. He served only with the Virginia militia during the war and he's been just a civilian since it ended. He can't speak for the Army of the United States, while I must. I have my orders and the duty of carrying them out is my personal responsibility."

"Then I should think you'd feel like talking to Caleb yourself and then making up your own mind about your duty. Oh, look."

She ran swiftly away from him along the path and knelt among some low bushes with her back to him. By the time he had recovered from his astonishment and had overtaken her she was rising and wheeling triumphantly to face him. From her fingers dangled the locket at one end of its chain.

"Isn't that wonderful," she exclaimed. "I just happened to catch sight of something glittering in the sun. And there it was. Right there beside the path." She bent to examine the locket. "Look, you can see where this link was soldered to the locket. That was where it broke. That must have been how I lost it."

The Captain nodded absently. His face was stern.

"Remarkably fortunate, your finding your lost locket so promptly. But that it gave you an opportunity to tell me what you just have is far more fortunate."

He stood aside. She walked on before him. At the camp he spoke to Sergeant Redfern with crisp decision.

"Detail another twenty men to help move Colonel Jordan's goods down to the landing place. And I want ten more, in your personal charge, to come with me. Have them fall in with muskets and bayonets fixed."

The slope between the station and the flat rock was crawling like an ant heap as men scrambled back and forth, laden with sacks, bales, bundles, boxes, and articles of furniture. Captain Telford, preceded by Tracy, and trailed by his column of reinforcements, encountered Duncan at the landing place.

"I'm giving you another twenty men, Colonel Jordan," he said, "in the hope that the loading may be further expedited. Sergeant Redfern, will you post your guard at the bridge? Instruct them that no one is to cross, either way, except by my personal permission. Then come with me."

The ten with bayoneted muskets took up their station. Captain Telford, followed by the Sergeant, strode across the bridge and on into the corn. Duncan watched in growing astonishment. He turned to Tracy.

"What's come over the man?"

"A certain act of Congress prohibiting settlement on this side of the river. I gather he's remembered that he's a federal officer and that it's his duty to enforce it."

Duncan stared at her incredulously.

"This is your doing. Why? Can you tell me why?"

"Very easily. I just couldn't stand the idea of Caleb's taking over this place. We've put too much of ourselves into it for him to have it."

"You mean what you can't stand is Daisy's moving in."

"No. Daisy counts for nothing. It's Caleb's having it. After the way he's treated us. That's what I couldn't stand."

Captain Telford stepped out of the corn and looked about him at the cabin, the barn, and the stockpens. There was no one in sight. He glanced into the cabin, made sure that it was empty, and went on around the corner. There he came to another pause. Daisy was on her knees in the garden, digging onions. She looked up, grinned shyly, and got to her feet. The day was warm. Her plump body glistened with sweat. Her working costume consisted of a bark apron about her hips. She stared with mounting admiration at the Captain's military finery, then, recalling her manners, bent to pick from the ground a sleeveless, vestlike garment of ragged doeskin. This she slipped on, giggling, and looked up to give the Captain another less shy and more sociable grin.

"Who are you?" he asked.

Daisy struggled with her recently acquired stock of English phrases and came out with:

"Caleb's woman."

Captain Telford looked around to share his disgust with Sergeant Redfern and became aware that Caleb stood leaning on his rifle three paces behind the Sergeant.

"I see," said the Captain. "There seems to be a new Mrs. Lewis."

Caleb's glance took in Daisy and came back to his visitor. "Have you come because you want this one, too?"

Captain Telford took a long breath and counted ten. "No. I have come to announce what I had conceived to be a somewhat disagreeable duty. I find, instead, that it is one in which I can take considerable satisfaction. I must remind you that settlement on this side of the river is contrary to law. I am an officer sworn to uphold the law. I am here, therefore, to inform you that I shall be obliged to burn your station."

Sergeant Redfern's hand crept to the butt of his pistol. But Caleb neither replied, nor moved, nor changed expression.

"If you wish to come with me to my camp I can show you a copy of the order which directs me to take such action in every such case, without exception."

"I do not need to see it. I am sure that you can read."

Captain Telford took another long breath. "It is the stockade that chiefly concerns me. I do not propose to permit a man of your stripe to maintain what amounts to a fortified post right on the Ohio. If you accept the situation quietly I will leave you the corn and this cabin. But I must warn you that if you attempt to create any sort of disturbance I will leave you nothing."

Again Caleb made no reply. The Captain strode off toward the corn. Sergeant Redfern fell in step at his heels, giving the impression of a man laboring to look back over his shoulder while continuing to stare straight ahead. Caleb started to walk after them. Captain Telford swung around.

"You will not be permitted to cross the bridge."

"I do not want to cross the bridge. But you have said you will burn my place. Do you also forbid me to watch you do it?"

The Captain went on. Duncan was waiting for him beyond the guard posted along the bank at the other end of the bridge.

"Are you actually going to burn him out?" he demanded.

"Yes. Will you let me know, please, when you have removed as many of your effects as we have space to transport?"

"But, Captain Telford, I really must lodge a most vigorous protest against this action."

"One does not protest the law, Colonel Jordan. One merely obeys."

"But we've always had tacit permission for this location. And I've sold the station to him in good faith. You're placing me in an impossible position."

"As I understood the transaction, he purchased from you whatever you were unable to carry away. However, that's a matter for you to settle with him."

Duncan glanced across the stream. Caleb sat on the other bank, his forearms on his knees, his rifle lying on the ground beside him. He appeared to be taking a merely sardonic interest in the activity on the station side. Behind him, Daisy crouched, peering impassively from the first row of corn.

"May I cross to talk to him?"

"Certainly, if you wish."

As Duncan approached, Caleb got up and waited for him

o speak with the same composure with which he had been
vatching the loading of the boats.

"I wanted you to understand, Mr. Lewis, that I had nothing
o do with this. I protested as strongly as I could. But Captain
Telford considers his duty clear."

Caleb nodded. "Under that foolish uniform the young man
s a soldier."

"One thing I can do. Since I am unable to hand over all
hat you paid for, I am ready to make an adjustment on the
price you paid."

"Nobody else will blame you. Why should I? It is not
your stockade that he will burn. It is mine."

"I must insist that you say what you consider the buildings
worth so that I can return that portion of your purchase
price."

"I would not have paid a shilling for them. This land. This
stream. This valley. This place that Corbit picked. That is
what I bought. I can build another stockade."

"Why try so hard to pretend? You've no need to grope
for excuses. For what could one man, even one as headstrong
as you, do against soldiers and bayonets and cannon? Actually
nothing would have pleased you more than to have been able
to sit in that house and remember that we built it for you."

"It is always easier to forget than to remember. When
you first came you were able to see a little of what Corbit
saw here. Like a tanager flying into a bush. For a moment
you saw a streak of light. Then it was gone. Now you have
forgotten even that."

"You are a childish fool."

"The young man is calling you. Your people are ready to
go. They are leaving from the same rock on which you
landed."

The line of loaded bateaus rocked in the shallows at the
point, their prows grounded on the sandy beach. Most of
the soldiers and passengers had already taken their assigned
places in them. Duncan stood on the shore waiting for the
arrival of Captain Telford and his guard detachment. From
the station on its mound flames leaped into the air.

In one of the boats Eric lay prone, his face buried in his
mother's lap. Her hands crept caressingly through his hair,
over his neck and shoulders. She tugged gently to make him
look up but he stiffened against her touch.

"It wasn't your father's fault," she murmured. "He did all

he could to stop it. He tried to give Caleb some of his money back. What more could he do?"

In another boat Tracy sat between Garett and Olivia. She stared not at the smoke rising in the sky but out over the river into the distance. Olivia had an arm around her. Garett was holding one of her hands.

"There's one consolation, my dear," he said. "It was a close, hard game, with neither of you ever giving an inch. But you would certainly seem to have taken the last trick.

"I can still see him sitting there by the fire those first nights," said Olivia. "That awful unblinking stare of his. There he sat, sizing us up. It was our being Corbit Revel' people that meant the most to him. He was beginning to think he wanted to be like us, to have one of our women, to live in our house, to belong to us."

"No, that wasn't what he was beginning to think," said Tracy, spacing the words as though each were being forced from her. "What he wanted, even from the first, was that we should belong to him. We weren't punishing him when we pushed him away, and took back our woman, and took even the house away from him. Because long before he'd made up his mind that we weren't up to being counted Corbit Revel's people."

Captain Telford came along the path at the head of his final file of soldiers. Duncan went to meet him.

"Where are the Slovers? When they didn't show up here I assumed they were helping you."

"And I thought they were with you." The Captain scowled. His temper had been deteriorating steadily this last hour. "Everybody was instructed to assemble here."

Duncan strode on and came to a stop upon seeing Olen shambling along the path toward him. He was alone.

"Go get your family," directed Duncan impatiently. His temper too, had frayed. "And be quick about it. If you're not here in five minutes we'll go without you."

Olen shifted his weight uneasily. It always pained him to deliver unwelcome news. He gulped, clawed at his beard and stared past Duncan at the sycamore.

"We-uns ain't a-goin', Kunnel," he said. "We-uns reckon we'll jest stay on here and string along with Caleb."

September

The setting sun appeared to be sinking into the farther end of the long westward reach of the river. The twin channels on either side of the island were transfigured into mirrored paths of crimson and gold. A flukey breeze, riffling the water, brought from the unbroken walls of forest on either hand puffs of air which smelled alternately of the heat of the day and the first cool of the evening. On wide mud flats along the shrunken edges of the Ohio, cranes and herons stalked stiffly or stood on one leg, blinking into the sunset. Fleets of ducks drifted with the current, quacking conversationally, from time to time a tail rearing abruptly upright as its owner dove expertly for some morsel on the bottom. Thrushes and catbirds and mocking birds raised their defiantly cheerful evening chorus in one last spasm of thanksgiving before yielding to the silence imposed by the night.

A herd of buffalo trailed single file from the north bank woods, drank noisily, and then, following the old cow who was their leader, waded on out through the river's late summer shallows. The half-grown calves, now as black as their elders, shouldered, splashed, and butted one another. As the herd neared the island the old cow's head came up. She sniffed suspiciously. After one warning grunt, she veered away from the island. The herd, bunching together in her wake, trotted behind her through the midstream shoal, swam briefly through the slightly deeper southern channel, and galloped into the woods.

The twilit loneliness of the river was suddenly relieved by the appearance of a solitary boat, wallowing around the bend above the island. The flat-bottomed scow, of a draft so shallow as to enable it to negotiate the seasonal low water which for weeks had denied the river to heavier craft, was poled by a man whose mien suggested he bitterly regretted having clung this late in the year to his determination to get on to

237

Kentucky. With his ragged family of a wife and a half dozen small children clustered about him, he was driving his pole wearily against the muddy bottom while peering ahead nervously for a safe haven in which to camp for the night. Perceiving the island, he poled his scow toward it and ran aground on the shoal that stretched upstream from its point. Cuffing first his whimpering children and then his scolding wife, he got out in the water, shoved his ungainly craft free, climbed aboard again, and drifted disgustedly on past in the deeper channel, unaware of the coldly narrowed eyes watching him from the shadowed island.

Stretched on the ground in the shrubbery at the water's edge were a dozen Indians, observing expressionlessly the mover's progress. Their oiled dark bodies remained so entirely without any twitch of movement that they had the appearance more of animals than of men. Beside them were two bark canoes as carefully hidden as they from anyone passing in the open river. One of the Indians looked at the sky and grunted. All sat up, reached into their game pouches, and began to eat a handful of pounded corn and jerky.

Fifty yards away, in the center of the little island, Tracy sat against a tree, watching the slowly darkening sky. The days since she had been taken had fallen into a routine so unvarying that she knew each hour of the twenty-four what next to expect. Her every daylight hour had been spent in the heart of such a thicket as this. It was always on an island in mid-river. Always at dark her captors reassembled and got back into their two canoes. Always she was prodded into the prow of the first. The other trailed a quarter of a mile back. The Indians paddled hard all night on upriver. They hid on another island at dawn and waited through the daylight for the return of darkness. There had been eight such days and nights since the night she had been snatched from her bed in a house on the very outskirts of Louisville. The memory of that outrageous moment was so vivid that she was still moved more by chagrin than dismay each time she reflected upon the savage cunning with which they had managed to carry her off while there were a hundred people within call.

There was a faint rustle in the shrubbery in the direction of the Indian bivouac. She looked across at the gnarled and wrinkled squaw, squatting five feet away, watching her, who had been her constant companion since her abductors had returned to their waiting canoes hiddden in the Louisville marshes. The old crone's eyes were steadily upon her, day and night, for she seemed never to sleep. It was only at this moment that her attention ever wavered for a second. She too, had heard the rustle and her glance always flickered toward it. It was the moment before another departure when one of the braves brought a strip of jerky or a dab of pemmican for the women to share. Tracy waited, with a kind of perverse satisfaction in the predictabilty of the gesture, for her keeper to snatch at the food. But the old woman instead gave a slight start. Tracy, too, looked around and was herself immediately overwhelmed by astonishment. The figure outlined against the pale sky was not one of the Indians. She scrambled up to her knees.

"Eric," she gasped.

He knelt beside her, grasping her arm reassuringly.

"I hope you haven't been having too bad a time," he said.

"I didn't hear anything. Where'd the Indians go? How'd you find me?"

It was getting too dark to see his face clearly but she could sense the forced cheerfulness of his grin.

"You're not saved, worse luck. I'm their prisoner, too. Have been since the night they took you. Only they've kept me in the second canoe and would never let me come near you."

"Then why are they letting you talk to me now?"

"I suppose they've got so far away they're beginning to feel safe."

"But how'd they take you?"

"My own fault. They may not give us much time to talk, so let's compare what we know as fast as we can. You remember that had been the day of the election. I marched that night in the torchlight procession. I was pretty set up that Father'd only been in Louisville two weeks before they'd picked him to be a delegate to the state convention. But when everybody got out to Major Belden's and they'd started that dance— well, I didn't feel like dancing. I took a walk, off where it was quieter. I don't know just where I went, through some woods and down along the Beargrass. Anyway, when I got back it must have been nearly midnight but the dance was still going on. At the edge of the woods there were maybe a dozen Indians lying on their bellies back of a rail fence, looking toward Major Belden's house and the barn where the dance was. I'd gone off by myself to try to think. Anyway, I wasn't paying any attention. I stepped right on one of them before I knew they were there. They grabbed me. It was that easy. They made me lie down with my face against the ground. Then after about an hour they made me run with them through the woods down to the river. I hadn't heard any noise around the Belden place or sounds of alarm or any

shooting, so I decided they'd given up trying to do anything
there. How'd they get you?"

"I didn't feel like dancing either. I told Mrs. Belden I had
a headache. She took me to a back bedroom. I lay down
on a bed. I must have dozed. There was an open window just
beside the bed. The next I knew the quilt on which I was
lying was jerked over my head and I was bundled in it so
tightly I couldn't make a sound. Then I realized I was being
carried out the window but there wasn't a thing I could do
to help myself. This same quilt." She plucked resentfully at
the quilt on which she was kneeling. "It's all so fantastically
irrational. We'd spent a year wandering about the woods on
the Indian bank and now the both of us are taken right in
sight of Louisville."

"When small Indian parties get among the settlements they
don't pick and choose. They just hide and watch and wait for
a chance to steal a horse or burn a cabin or axe somebody or
do anything else miserable they think they can do and still
get away. It just happened that night to be our bad luck."

"I can understand the bad luck part. I'd heard everybody
talking about the danger from Miamis, and how they'd been
getting bolder every week this whole summer. So being captured wasn't so outlandish. But what I can't understand is why
they're taking us this far upriver."

"They're just on their way home. That's the big reason
Indians like to take prisoners. So they can show them off to
their home folks."

"But the Miami towns are up in the Wabash country.
That's off the other way altogether."

"These Indians aren't Miamis. They're Wyandots. Their
towns are up by Lake Erie. So they are on their way home.
They're probably planning to head north up the Scioto or
the Muskingum."

"But what were Wyandots doing as far away as Louisville?"

"That bothered me, too, at first. But Indians travel a lot
more than most people think. They're always visiting each
other, like Cherokee wandering around up here or Northern
Indians seeing the sights clear down to Florida. These Wyandot could have been visiting the Chickasaw, or the Osage,
or the Missouri. Then on their way home it probably just
struck them as a good idea to take along a Kentucky captive
or two."

"What do you think they intend to do with us?"

"I don't think we're in too much real danger. The Wyandot
aren't supposed to be at war with us, not yet anyway. We'l

be able to get in touch with some English trader and get talk about ransom started."

It was too dark now to see his face at all but in his tone there was the continuing earnest effort to reassure her.

"The wonderful part about being taken by Indians," she said, "is that there's some comfort to be had in any prospect short of burning."

"They haven't burned anybody," said Eric hastily, "not in more than two years."

There came the brief harsh squawk of a disturbed wood duck that was the usual signal for a new start. The old woman instantly grasped Tracy's arm and turned her toward the beach. Eric slipped off into the shadows. Tracy took her accustomed place in the prow and the first canoe shoved off. The six Indians of its crew settled to the tireless, night-long rhythm of their paddling. Tracy squirmed until she had arranged the folds of the quilt under her knees. For the first time she was permitting herself to realize the extent of her weariness. During the whole interminable stretch of eight days and nights, she had remained so determined to keep always on the alert for the faintest opportunity to escape that she had dozed only in snatches. But there had been an immense relief in discovering Eric was near, even if only as a companion in misfortune. She was no longer alone. If there was anything to be done he would know when and what. For this once she might rest. She pushed the old woman away to make more room, curled up on the quilt in the bottom of the canoe, and let herself drift into the deepest of sleeps.

Hours later she realized dimly that they must be camping again. The canoe was being dragged up on another beach and she was being lifted from it. She was more weary than ever and bitterly resentful of being disturbed. It was so much more inviting to drop back in the refuge of sleep.

When finally she began at last to awaken of her own accord, ever so slowly and still reluctantly, it was to the smell of broiling trout. Not once during all that driving dash up the Ohio had the Indians built a fire. It crossed her mind vaguely that they must have turned off the main river into the Scioto. The persisting smell of the grilling trout began to make her aware that she was hungry and she began tentatively to stir. Her limbs were sore and cramped from those nights in the canoe, but the long sleep had left her rested. Though she had not opened her eyes she could tell that it was daylight. A deeper mystery began to pluck at her attention. She was

not on the hard ground but on a surface comfortably soft,
and there was a clean blanket over her in the place of the
quilt which had come to smell so strongly of Indian grease
and pitch from the canoe and river mud. Slowly, only idly
curious as yet, she opened her eyes. Instantly she was in the
grip of a fantasy far wilder than the desperate sensation of
being carried off by Indians. She had awakened in Caleb's
cabin in the very bed which once she had shared with him.

Driven by an immediate spasmodic impulse to protest, she
cast aside the blanket and swung from the bed. Daisy, squatted
on the hearth, glanced over her shoulder and grinned amiably.
Tracy sank back on the edge of the bed. Daisy swiftly transferred two of the smoking trout from the skillet to a bark
tray, added a square of hot corn bread, and advanced, her
offering extended. Her grin was broader than ever. Her attitude was unmistakably, and therefore the more grotesquely,
hospitable, even welcoming. Tracy sprang past her to the
doorway.

Caleb was working in his cornfield, engaged with furious
energy in the harvest of his corn. He moved steadily along
the row, bending down the tremendous stalks, his knife flashing, ears of corn flying over his shoulder into little heaps on
the ground behind him. He had thrown aside his shirt and
the muscles of his arms and shoulders and the scars on his
back stood out in the sun. The summer had tanned him nearly
as dark as an Indian. She clung to the door frame, suddenly
and irrelevantly aware of her hair hanging in a tangle about
her shoulders and of the torn and bedraggled blue silk dress
which had suffered so rudely since she had been taken in it.
She sank down on the doorstep and covered her face with
her hands. When she looked up again he was standing before
her, buttoning one of the white linen shirts that she once had
so rebelliously made for him.

"It's no use your trying to make me believe you somehow
saved me from those Indians," she said.

His eyes were grave and intent with something of that
look of concentrating all his faculties that was in them when
he lifted his rifle to take aim. Then his lips parted slightly
in what for him was almost the equivalent of a smile.

"I have counted on my fingers all the different things you
might think," he said. "But that you might think I would try
to fool you never came into my mind."

"Then you admit that you had this done to me because of
what I had done to you when I burned your stockade."

"Yes. So soon as the Slovers told me that it was you who
burned it I knew what I had to do. When you left me the
night your father's friend was here, I waited. When you did

not come back I decided you knew what you wanted. You had been here long enough to know and there is no use having a wife unless she does know. Then the burning was like finding a trail that I had lost. It came over me that I had not after all made a mistake in the beginning. A woman who can get that mad at me is the one I must have."

She stared at him.

"And now that you've had your Indians dump me back in your cabin, how long will it take you to discover you are still making mistakes?"

"Not long. In a month if you want still to go back to Louisville I will take you back."

"You will not have a month. I have friends. Colonel Jordan; Captain Telford; General Clark. They will come for me."

"It is true that they will be looking for you. But they will not know where to look. They will think first of the Miami. Before anybody comes here we will already know what we will do."

"If you wanted me to believe any of this, why didn't you come to Louisville to talk to me?"

"You would not have listened to me in Louisville. It was only here that there could be another chance for us."

"Along with all the other chances of what might happen to me while I was being bundled through woods and in and out of canoes by a pack of wild Indians?"

"You were never out of my sight from that first minute I wrapped you in the quilt."

"So you were right there in the second canoe. I half guessed it. But you never came near me. Why? I was as helpless there as I am here."

"There was no use to talk to you until you were ready to listen."

"And a week of believing I was a captive of the Wyandot might make me more ready to listen?"

"Yes. That is a part of what I counted on."

"Well, I am listening. You're so quick with all your answers. Have you thought up an excuse for carrying off Eric, too?"

"I did not plan that. Once we had hold of him I could not let him go to tell your people too soon where you were."

"During this month you expect me to try again to get used to you, am I supposed also to get used to Daisy?"

"You make too much of Daisy. You have not once had reason to think about her since that day I first saw you. But if the sight of her bothers you I will send her back to the

Shawnee." The hint of a smile was again around the corners of his mouth. "That will make Jake very sad. He had been sidling around her. To have a wife as willing to work as she is would be for him a very good catch."

She dropped that topic and clutched at another.

"Did you give Eric to your Wyandot?"

"No. He is here. Up there with the others."

"He is?"

She started up, desperate to escape his steady gaze, to delay, until she could breathe again, his detection of her surrender.

She ran through the corn but came to a stop on the bridge. All of the meadow corn had been cut. But this monument to the Slovers' month-long surge of industry was as nothing to the tribute presented by the spectacle of the rebuilt stockade. A wall of palisade poles once more ringed the crown of the mound. The vision burst upon her like the sudden unfurling of a banner in the sun. That which she had herself destroyed seemed miraculously to have been restored to her. Elation possessed her. She ran on up to the open gateway and again paused, hungrily, to stare.

An immense crib of leather-bound saplings, already half filled with corn from the meadow and with storage space waiting for Caleb's, stretched along the back wall of the stockade. In the center of the yard were great piles of logs, some of which had already been notched and squared, though actual construction of new housing had not yet commenced. The inhabitants still occupied brush shelters set up against the wall beyond the site of the one-time Slover cabin. Olen and Jacob were at work with axes, squaring more of the timbers. Jarot and Maggie were carrying logs already shaped to other piles nearer the spots where they would be used. Polly and Betsey were raking and sifting the ashes of the former buildings to recover nails, locks, hinges, and other items of ironwork. Eric was on his knees, bent over a strip of birch bark kept flat on the ground by stones at its corners, drawing lines upon it with a charred stick. When he saw her in the gateway he sprang up, leaned down again to pick up the strip of bark, and ran to her, brandishing it exultantly.

"Look. I can remember all the dimensions of father's plan for the first buildings so that we can put them up again just like they were before. We won't have to guess where doors and windows come or stop to saw holes after the walls are up. We can cut every timber the right length to fit and get everything up in half the time."

"Eric," said Tracy.

Her voice broke. For a second he misinterpreted her emotion.

"You're wondering why I didn't tell you, last night when we were talking, that it was Caleb himself who had taken us?" He laughed. "That's easy. He told me not to. And I had to do whatever he wanted. Because I had to make sure he'd let me stay here."

"Stay here? Eric! Is that what you really want to do?"

"It is. It certainly is." He saw that she wanted to believe and sought eagerly to convince her. "That night I was walking around in the woods, I'd kept on thinking about everything until I'd decided to run away and come back here. So it was the greatest luck in the world when I was taken. That'll make everything so much easier for Father and Mother to understand. There just couldn't have been better luck. I still can hardly believe it."

He seized her hand and ran, pulling her after him, to the nearest brush hut. Lina sat on a stool nursing twin babies. When she saw them coming she bent unhurriedly to slide the two small bundles into a cradle and rose to face them. She gave Tracy a quick welcoming smile but her entire interest was in Eric. She stared at him in hungering happiness, still unable fully to grasp the good fortune of his return to her, her fingers meanwhile fumbling slowly to draw the front of her cotton dress over her plump white breasts with the moist glowing nipples.

"See," said Eric, pulling Tracy down over the bright new cradle which smelled of fresh basswood and Indian sweet grass. "Two of 'em. Two boys. Two more rifles."

"Maw said I was a size to have me four," said Lina, "but they was only the two. Look—yuh kin see how much they take arter Eric."

"They're beautiful babies," murmured Tracy.

The young parents had already turned away from the cradle. They had eyes only for each other. Lina's fingers at the buttons of her dress were trembling. Eric, leaning closer to help her, was trembling, too. Tracy walked back toward the gate.

The Slovers had straighted from their labors to watch and now surged forward to greet her. But Polly, so smeared with ashes as to look even more disreputable than usual, peremptorily waved them back and came on alone. She took Tracy by the arm, led her aside in the gateway, and looked sharply into her face.

"Of course I'm going to stay," said Tracy. "You do want me to, don't you?"

"It ain't fer we-uns to pull on thet string one way nor t'other. Long's Caleb wants yuh, then sure's Christ's good we-uns do, too. We ain't total foolish. But if'n thet's whut yer aimin' to do they's something I figgered I'd best tell yuh straight off. Me and Olen we-uns had us a mess o'brats 'fore them yuh see here. Nine o' them's still livin', five boys and three gals, all married. Week 'fore last we got us a chance to send word back to 'em by a mover who'd changed his mind about Kaintuck and was headin' east. Come spring they'll all be out here."

"How wonderful for you," said Tracy, "to have all your family together again. And if there is another Indian war, with nine more men there'll be so much better chance to hold the stockade."

"Caleb figgers on holdin' the stockade. Make no mistake about thet. But there's something more yuh got to figger on yerself. Them young Slover sprouts and the men the gals married up with, they had theyselves thirty-some young-uns when we left and they's likely had half a dozen more by now. Thet's a slather o' folks to find room in one stockade no bigger'n this. Come real Injun trouble yuh and Caleb won't be able to stay quiet-like down in that cozy little cabin o' his'n. Yuh'll have to shove right in amongst us. Thet's whut I figgered yuh better know about so's it wouldn't come at yuh one day like something jumpin' out'n the bushes."

"Thank you, Polly. I'm sure we'll manage. But there's an equally friendly warning I might give you, about another kind of family problem that may prove harder to handle. As soon as Colonel Jordan finds out Eric is here, he's going to try to take him away. Eric's his oldest son and he's made many hopeful plans for him."

"Soon's a boy's growed enough to make him boys of his own," said Polly, "he ain't a boy no more. He's a man. And it's a man's place to make up his mind fer his ownself about whereat he belongs." The calm with which she had begun her reply gave way as she continued to consider the question. Suddenly she became as livid with rage as when she had defended Lina's choice before the Jordan tribunal. "Whut kind o' talk is thet? Whut kin the likes o' them Jordans say thet makes any sense about whut's good fer Eric? Eric's a good boy and he's on his way to bein' a good man. But he ain't never goin' to be up to whut's come to him. Thet gal is thet ready to give, and she's got thet much to

give, and she's bound to give all of it only to him and never to
nobody else. Most men never gits theyselves even a sniff o'
luck like thet." She paused for breath and began as suddenly
to glare at Tracy. "And as fer you. Yuh know right well how
bad yuh wanted to stay with Caleb. Right from the start.
Only yuh wouldn't never let on. Mebbe even to yerself. Yuh
kept tellin' yerself he wasn't good enough fer yuh. Why yuh
ain't bin woman enough to be let wash his pants. Like's not
yer squawkin' now about his comin' arter yuh with Injuns.
Yuh ain't got the wit to notice thet only goes to show one
time more the size man he is. He traded with them Wyandot
no more'n one month all of three years back but they remember him so well they come runnin' like dogs when yuh whistle
the minute he let 'em know they was a way they might help
him a little. And thet's something else thet could stick in
yer craw. Whut the Injuns think about him is a-goin' to cost
us all plenty 'fore we're through. Oncet the war gits started
up next summer every no-good buck Injun north o' the Ohio
is a-goin' to figger they ain't no better way to make a big
name fer hisself than to try to take this place away from
Caleb Lewis. Goddam' if I kin figger whut a man like him
wants with you."

Polly grunted, spat, and swung around to stalk back to her
ash-shifting. Tracy sprang in front of her.

"Look at me," she demanded. "Maybe you can tell something by that."

Polly stared, gulped and gathered her to her ample, soot-
streaked bosom.

"Do yuh some good," she declared, "to take a stick to me,
I'll find yuh a big one right quick. I git so used to takin' the
hide off thet no-count Olen and them turnip-headed boys o'
mine thet I'm allus a-blattin' out nine times more'n I mean."

Tracy clung to her. "If I can't even find words to tell you,
whatever can I say to him? After all we've done to each other,
how can I make him understand?"

"Will yuh fer Gawd's sake leave off talkin'," cried Polly.
She gave Tracy a push and watched, beginning to sniffle
and to dab at her eyes, as Tracy walked slowly down to the
bridge.

Daisy was sitting on the edge of the flat rock, dangling her
feet in the water. Beside her on the rock was a basket con-
taining her few personal belongings. Covertly she watched
Tracy's approach. It was apparent that she was waiting, with
philosophic docility, for some indication of the next move
that might be expected of her. Tracy met her glance, gave
her an impersonally friendly smile, and kept on across the

bridge. Daisy scrambled to her feet, snatched up her basket and ran eagerly up the slope to the stockade gateway.

Tracy could hear the rustling of the bending cornstalks and the rasp of the knife. Caleb was at work directly between her and the cabin. The sounds ceased. Breathing faster, she kept on through the corn and pushed between the last two stalks separating them. Once more they were face to face. He looked at her gravely and turned toward the cabin. She followed. At the doorstep he faced her again. He was still grave.

"I knew you would need another dress," he said. "But there was no chance in Louisville for me to buy you one. So I told Daisy to make you something to wear out of that cloth you wove. It might not look just the way you like but it will be better than nothing."

He went back to his harvesting. She went into the cabin. Spread out on the bed was the dress. She held it up. It hung from her hands in the straight lines of one of Daisy's own deerskin garments, but its stark white simplicity was relieved by touches of neat red and green embroidering at the hem of the skirt and about the neck. On the hearth was a kettle of warm water and on the stool beside it a strip of clean blanketing to serve as a towel. She striped off her bedraggled clothing and devoted a luxurious and leisurely hour to bathing, combing her hair, and, at last, to arraying herself in the new white dress. White, she reflected with a forced smile, was traditionally a bride's color.

She paused in the doorway. Caleb was at the end of a row at the farther edge of the clearing. He was working away as steadily as ever. She wondered if beneath his outward calm he could be in anything like such a state as she. Her heart began to beat so hard she choked. She slipped around the corner of the cabin and, cravenly temporizing, pretended to make an interested inspection of the stockpens. The young chickens and turkeys were almost grown, the calves had put on weight, there were nineteen pigs; but all of these familiar images were blurred. Then she heard Spec's squeaking whimper. He had been tied by a leather thong just inside the barn door. She released him and he cavorted about her feet as, at last, she walked steadily toward Caleb. He stopped work and watched her as she slowly approached, but she was unable to look up at him.

"I had to tie up the coon," he said, "else he would never have let you sleep last night. Then I forgot to untie him."

She regarded the windrows of corn on the ground.

"Shouldn't I get a basket and start picking them up?" she proposed.

He placed his hands on her shoulders but still she could not look up at him.

"You have made up your mind?"

"Yes," she whispered.

"I am not much for talk."

"Yes, I know." She was trying to smile. "According to you it's only what people do that counts."

"But I have something to say and I am going to try to say it. You have to believe I want you. Twice I have proved that by taking you when you did not want to be taken. But that is not what I am trying to say. There is something more that you have to believe."

She pushed his extended arms aside, threw herself against him, and wrapped her own arms about him.

"There's only one thing I have to believe," she declared, "that it had to be like this—that it could never have been any other way."

GREAT HISTORICAL SAGAS OF AMERICA'S FIRST FRONTIERS

The Producer of the KENT FAMILY CHRONICLES now brings you the WAGONS WEST and COLONIZATION OF AMERICA series. These books are full of the spectacular adventure and romance that followed America's first settlers as they struggled in a new land.

The highly acclaimed WAGONS WEST series by Dana Fuller Ross:

☐	20419	**INDEPENDENCE!**	$3.25
☐	20417	**NEBRASKA!**	$3.25
☐	20420	**WYOMING!**	$3.25
☐	20421	**OREGON!**	$3.25
☐	20422	**TEXAS!**	$3.25
☐	14260	**CALIFORNIA!**	$2.95
☐	14717	**COLORADO**	$3.25

The thrilling COLONIZATION OF AMERICA series by Donald Clayton Porter:

☐	20349	**WHITE INDIAN**	$3.25
☐	20362	**THE RENEGADE**	$3.25
☐	20579	**WAR CHIEF**	$3.25
☐	20361	**THE SACHEM**	$3.25

The new SAGA OF THE SOUTHWEST series by Leigh Franklin Jones:

☐	20096	**REVENGE OF THE HAWK**	$3.25
☐	20556	**HAWK OF THE DOVE**	$3.25
☐	20635	**WINGS OF THE HAWK**	$3.25

★★★★★★★★★★★★★★★★★★★★

Buy them at your local bookstore or use this handy coupon:

Bantam Books, Inc., Dept. LE, 414 East Golf Road, Des Plaines, Ill. 60016

Please send me the books I have checked above. I am enclosing $_____
(please add $1.00 to cover postage and handling). Send check or money order
—no cash or C.O.D.'s please.

Mr/Mrs/Miss _____

Address _____

City _____ State/Zip _____

LE—12/81(A)

Please allow four to six weeks for delivery. This offer expires 5/82.

"WHY HAS THE GIRL BEEN BROUGHT HERE?" CROAKED THE WITCH.

The saya bowed low before the witch and gestured toward the princess. "It is claimed she bears the Mark of the Expected One."

Shrill laughter filled the gloomy night, making flesh crawl. "We shall decide that," said the witch. "Leave us."

The saya departed, leaving a frightened and naked Princess Sharon under the scrutiny of the witch and her two ugly sisters. They cackled and whispered together, then beckoned her forward to a bubbling caldron.

The witch held up a hazelwood ladle bearing a foul-smelling brew. "From the mysteries of the seven planets and the sun which revolves around them, so has this potion been culled.

"Drink, Sharon, Princess of Samarkand. Drink and share all we offer."

SAMARKAND
GRAHAM DIAMOND

PLAYBOY PRESS
PAPERBACKS

FOR THE REAL PRINCESS AND THE SAYA

COME, O WEARIED TRAVELER,
SIT BESIDE ME, LISTEN TO
THE TALES I HAVE TO TELL,

OF THAT SPLENDORED CITY
OF LONG AGO, WHERE RICHES AND
GLORIES REIGNED UNSURPASSED
IN THE PLACE WHERE WEST MEETS
EAST AT THE VERY CROSSROAD
OF THE WORLD,

AND HEAR THEN THESE FABLES
FOR TOO LONG UNRECOUNTED,
OF THE GOLDEN DAYS OF

SAMARKAND.

The ebbing fire crackled in the windless chill of a winter night, the dark-haired youth hunched slightly forward in his place, rubbing his hands slowly above the small, leaping flames. Dark shadows cascaded across his chiseled features, adding a harsh pall over his deep-set black eyes. They were large eyes, thoughtful, piercing to gaze upon, carved into a face far more sensitive than might seem at first glance.

At the hoot of a midnight owl the youth lifted his head and gazed first at the starry velvet sky, then at the perfect half-moon, and finally upon the thick trees sweeping down the side of the mountain. He stared at the indistinguishable boughs wrenched into hideous forms, shapes so often spoken of in Kazir folklore—demons and devils and all manner of hushed *night-things* that the village wives would whisper about during the long, cold months. Then he grinned, reminding himself that such demons did not really exist. They were for children; he was almost a man.

"Can you see the lights now?" came the husky voice of Shoaib, the youth's father.

Tariq turned toward the old man and somberly nodded. Yes, he could see the lights, could see it all from his lofty vantage point. First there was the vast sweep of the plain, with its fields of wheat and grain for as far as the eye could see, then, beyond, was the dim outline of the city wall, huge, massive, slabs of quarried stone, centuries old, piled higher and higher atop each other until the wall almost reached the heavens themselves, and behind that were the great teardrop towers, enormous domes glittering in silver moonlight, minarets and temples, with great balconies from which the mullahs, the holy men, would call the people to prayer. This was his first glimpse of the sacred city, the now hated city, and he gazed transfixed with a mixture of fear and awe.

Shoaib the goatherd stood; with hands on hips, his thick, silvered brush mustache hiding his scowl, he also gazed down below at what was once the Kazirs' home. A slight breeze brought a chill to his flesh, and he pulled the fur collar of his bearskin jacket above his ears. Then he spat into the fire, watching as a flame hissed and danced brightly.

"You must never forget this night, Tariq," he told his son softly. "Set your eyes upon Samarkand, and always remember that you have seen her. You, a son of the Kazirs, the people forever forbidden to enter inside her gates until our time has come."

Tariq nodded, peering up at the aging man with eyes that vowed to keep this promise. "I will not forget, my father. I swear to you: Tonight shall be burned into both my heart and my memory."

Shoaib smiled. "Good. Then all is as it should be, my son. And also remember that I myself was brought here to this very place upon reaching your own age. It was the first time I set eyes upon Samarkand as well, and never has the memory deserted me."

Shoaib shut his eyes in recollection. Tariq observed him respectfully but sadly as he noted the arching lines and creases marring the pockmarked face, the deep folds along the sides of his father's mouth and underneath the eyes that seemed so much more exaggerated in the darkness. Truly his father had passed many years, many seasons of a Kazir's grief; few more would be left.

As if reading Tariq's thoughts, Shoaib looked down at his son and suddenly said, "My days are numbered. For me it is not possible to live and see our ancient city given back; but for you, Tariq, it shall be different.

You are young, strong, healthy, even as a Kazir, a child of the Steppes, must be to ensure his survival. You are a leader, Tariq." He sighed again and turned away from the youth, gazing down at the harsh, lifeless soil at his feet. "I bless the name of the Prophet that you are here to take my place when the time at last comes."

"Father, please!" cried Tariq. He was pained to hear this strong and cunning Kazir elder speak now in such a fatalistic fashion, even if he knew that much of what Shoaib said was the truth.

His father took a single pace toward the fire, stooped, and placed his hand upon his son's shoulder. "Listen to me, child," he said, speaking in a tone barely louder than a whisper. "Since three generations before the days of my grandfather have the Kazirs been driven into exile from our sacred lands. Were we meant to be step-children of the forests and the Steppes?" He shook his head, narrow eyes squinting. "No, Tariq. We left Samarkand because we had no choice, because our homes were usurped by those who would deny our rightful place. Samarkand belongs to the Kazirs, no matter who now sits upon her ebony throne. One day, one day soon, we shall return. Every Kazir has vowed it in blood. And we *will* have back what is ours."

Tariq listened silently, knowing of these things as though they were a part of his very being. Every Kazir youth is told of how it had been in the old days, when his people freely governed their own lands and lives and were rulers instead of outcasts in Samarkand. He knew of the injustices and rebellions, the terrible conflict in which the Kazirs were once and for all hurled from their homes, their culture uprooted and thrown to the winds like autumn leaves. The proud and noble people fled the fertile plains, the river lands and valleys, the city itself. In shame and grief they led their camels, goats, swine, and sheep, headed far from the empire to the Steppes and to the forests, resetting their tents and sowing seeds upon hard soil, eating bitter herbs in memory of their loss.

Nearly a century had passed since then, and now the Kazirs, well adapted to their new life, had come to hate Samarkand—for what it had become, for those who governed in splendor and wasted it away—yet they still loved the city; to them it was sacred, the place where the Prophet's word had first come after sweeping out of the Arabian deserts, the place where West met East at the crossroad of civilization. Samarkand was the center of the world, the city through which all caravans must pass, home of a thousand trade routes from Damascus in the west to Cathay in the east. The Kazirs *were* Samarkand, and Samarkand was them—even in the depths of their exile.

From high atop the tallest walls a pale orange glow glimmered, teardrop towers, reflecting moonlight, cast a softened outline against blue stars. Tariq gazed at them for a long time, wondering what manner of men now dwelled inside; for those lofty towers were part of the palace, the most splendid palace of the most splendid city, stolen these many years.

After a while the youth turned back to his father and asked, "Shall the Legend truly come to pass in my lifetime, Father?"

The goatherd stared into the embers, a finger rubbing along his mustache. "I do not know," he replied at length, thinking it wiser to always remain honest. "But how long can our people be expected to wait? Have the Kazirs not suffered enough? Is not the mere sight of our beloved city, now forbidden to look upon, too painful to bear?" He shook his head slowly, wearily. "One day, and soon, we must decide whether to wait for the Prophesy or to raise our banners anew, come down from the Steppes, and fight. Mullahs cannot govern our lives forever."

Tariq noticed the hint of contempt in old Shoaib's voice when he spoke of the priests. Among the religious

Kazirs, the holy men always held a special place of reverence and honor; but even a boy could see that they promised rewards only of a later life, rarely giving hope for a better life now. Yet, they *did* speak of the Legend. . . .

"The century is not yet done, Father; there is still time." Shoaib nodded slowly, spitting once more into the fire. The mullahs had predicted a Hundred Year Solitude to befall the Kazirs before these ancient wrongs might be righted. Now that time was nearly passed.

"Allah asks much of us, Tariq" was all he said. "Mortal men grow impatient, even Kazirs"—he smiled grimly—"but what you say cannot be denied. In the years to come, when you are a full man and a leader and I am turned to dust, then we shall know if the mullahs have given us reason to match our limited patience."

Tariq wrapped his blanket more tightly around his thin but broad shoulders and leaned back, resting his head against his rough leather saddle. It was nearly time to sleep; by dawn they must be far gone from this hill lest a patrol of Samarkand's soldiers catch them.

Shoaib was yawning, making a more comfortable place for himself at the edge of the fire's glow; Tariq did the same, but positioned himself so that as he rested he could still look out at the distant walls and towers. There was a total stillness in the air, a quiet that he found he could almost listen to—windless voices, soundless, yet compelling. *Samarkand,* they whispered. *Samarkand* : . .

And he thought upon the Legend once more, the Legend so many of his people clung to: a vague promise of returning home; veiled visions recounted by the mullahs, speaking as though drugged, of things that young Tariq, son of Shoaib the goatherd, could hardly understand; a prophesy of One who would arise and lead the Kazirs from exile, a leader who, enigma of enigmas, would come neither from the Steppes nor from the forest but from the hated palace of Samarkand itself.

Weary after such an eventful day, Tariq tried to sleep, but sleep eluded him. He stirred restlessly, growing uneasy at the thought of the Legend and how it was to come to pass in but a few short years.

"Father, are you asleep?"

"No, my son. What disturbs you?"

"If the mullahs are wrong, Father, if there is no new leader for us, no one to bear the Gift to retake our home, what will happen?"

Shoaib knit his thick, bushy brows and frowned, mulling over the question slowly. Tariq was already a man in so many ways, he knew; yet he was also a child, far away from bearing the duties that would be imposed upon him. There was so much for him to learn and so little time to teach. Shoaib grew angry at himself, silently cursing for having a son so late in life.

"Tariq," he replied at length, "the moment you speak of has not yet arrived. When it does, it will be in your own time, not mine. Thus, you must ask this question again; but only you can provide the answer."

The handsome peasant youth stared up at the stars and, smiling inwardly, made the promise: *So I shall, Father. When the time does come, I surely shall.*

Part One:

AT THE CLOSE OF THE HUNDRED YEAR SOLITUDE

Along the narrow ledge the Persian cat moved slowly, poking his head at the twisting vines curving over the yellow stone; he paused in his tracks at the sight of a nesting hummingbird perched on the bough of a hickory in the garden, then picked up his ears and turned his head at the sound of sandaled footsteps on the veranda behind.

The girl stopped, head slightly tilted, and smiled when she saw him. The cat's tail curled and he retracted his claws as she swept him up, holding him at half-arm's length, sweetly laughing. "You devil, Majesty!" she cried, feigning anger. Then she cradled him in her arms, running her fingers through the perfect white coat, tickling at the magnificent ruff around his neck. Majesty slit his green eyes, growled, then squirmed and slithered out of her grip, landing feet first on the stone. He shook his thick coat and pranced off toward the garden.

Sharon watched for a moment, still smiling, as he wound his way among the rosebushes, instinctively dodging the thorns.

"One day, Majesty," she admonished, waving a warning finger, "the gardeners are going to catch you, and I'm not going to be around to get you out of trouble."

A warm summer breeze swept across the veranda and the multileveled gardens. Broad leaves rustled; grass gently swayed. Overhead a small flock of sparrows dramatically switched their path of flight and now soared east, in the direction of the old city. Sharon pushed away a loose tendril of hair from her eyes and strode from the portico to the garden.

17

She was a tall girl, straight-shouldered, well proportioned. She had the richly textured chestnut hair of her mother and large, expressive brown eyes. Her nose was almost classic, perhaps a throwback to unknown Greek ancestors first come to Persia and then to Samarkand during the days of Alexander. Uniquely Arabic, however, were her high cheekbones and full mouth. Her paternal grandmother had been a full-blooded Bedouin, daughter of a sheikh, married off to the brother of Samarkand's then reigning king, Prince Fahlad, her grandfather. Thus was she somewhat apart from other young women of the court, whose heritage remained unmistakably Persian.

Beyond the winding path to the fountain stood a carved stone bench. Sharon pressed out the creases in her *khafti* and sat, letting the hem of her long, colorful robe swirl with a sudden gust. She amused herself by tossing off her sandals, leaning back, and watching the cat run circles around the trunks of trees. Majesty had been a special gift for her, how long ago now? Ah, yes; he'd been brought from the Persian court by her father five years before, a present for her fourteenth birthday. And since that time the cat had been an almost constant companion. At night he would slip into her rooms, cleverly avoiding the palace guards and servants, jump onto her bed, and curl himself into a ball at her feet, protectively alert at the slightest sound, staying until well past dawn.

For many—chambermaids, guards, and the like—the cat was just a nuisance, a palace pest given free reign of the grounds by the young princess. But, for Sharon, he represented something much more. There was an understanding between her and this Persian feline, a mutual bond that somehow said, "You take care of me, and I'll take care of you." Fanciful? Perhaps. But Sharon enjoyed believing that this unspoken bond uniquely existed between them.

It was early afternoon; much of the household was

now closed away behind doors, resting or sleeping during the hottest hours, a custom of these climes as ancient as the city itself. So, Majesty ran about freely, without worry of being chased away. He darted happily among the trees, cutting spryly across the narrow path leading down from the garden and out toward the rows of willows lined behind the carefully pruned hedges.

Sharon called for him to come back, but the cat clearly had a mind of his own; he was out to explore, and nothing was going to stop him. She slipped back into her sandals and got up hurriedly. This time she'd have to keep him leashed, she knew. As much as she hated to do it, it was for his own good. Majesty was heading away from the garden grounds and out in the direction of the greenhouse—her father's special pride.

For many years her father had been the emir's special ambassador, traveling to the courts of a dozen and more distant lands. Well regarded and respected, and always well received, her father had never failed in opening new avenues of trade for Samarkand that spanned the world. His love for botany followed him everywhere, and ever mindful of adapting rare flora and fauna to Samarkand's climate, he had brought back some of the world's most exotic plants to be studied: thus the well-tended greenhouse. If the cat ever got inside, Sharon knew there would be hell to pay.

The thin glass walls of the structure showed themselves to be blurred by moisture. Coming closer, she could almost feel the stifling damp heat from within, almost make out the shapes of the fleshy flowers with brilliant leaves, the twisting tendrils of climbers and creepers hanging down from the ceiling and wildly splashing out across the walls, each one of a kind; there were no others like them anywhere within a thousand kilometers of Samarkand.

Sharon suddenly stopped in her tracks, put her hand to her mouth, and gasped. The greenhouse door was open; she could discern the blurry, dark figures of two men walking slowly among the rows of shelved pots as they talked. The taller of the two was her father, the other as yet indistinguishable. And beside the door, ears pointed straight up, nose sniffing away at the aromas, was Majesty.

She took a brave step forward, wondering how she was going to explain any of this should the cat be noticed. Dashing from the hedges, she beckoned to her pet, vainly trying to get his attention. Majesty, whether he had seen her or not, seemed far more interested in examining the strange things inside the peculiar house. He slinked his body through the slightly ajar door and went inside. Sharon held her breath, expecting to see the cat come racing out any moment, her angry father on his heels, cursing, shaking a fist.

To her surprise—and momentary relief—that didn't happen. Instead, her father and his companion came out alone, eyes downcast, faces serious. And the man she'd assumed to be the gardener in charge of the greenhouse was none other than Hezekiah, Hebrew court minister, right hand of the emir, one of the most powerful figures in all of the empire. A black-speckled silver beard framed his square jaw handsomely; his small eyes were steely gray, intelligent and cunning; and he walked with a proud gait, a swagger, that had always impressed Sharon as much as it left her in awe. Certainly it seemed strange to find him here with her father like this, the two of them alone, speaking in whispers and in secret.

She momentarily forgot about the straying cat and focused her attention on them instead. Along the narrow dirt path through the junipers they walked, slowly, faces long and worried, her father nervously toying with the tiny earring in his left ear as he listened. Sharon, keeping out of sight, skirted the path and stayed close to the thick trunks and branches. At five paces behind, she could hear almost everything.

". . . And the caravan arriving from Tabla last night has confirmed it," the somber Hebrew was saying.

"Their tents were in sight until the caravan reached the river itself."

Amrath nodded darkly; such news, disturbing as it was, had not been totally unexpected. Less than three weeks before, a dispatch from the border garrison had been received saying much the same: Huns from the north had been sighted massing along Samarkand's outermost borders. Fierce nomadic tribesmen from beyond the Steppes in endless numbers were moving like locusts with their cattle and their women from the barren regions toward the fertile plateau of empire territory.

The implication was clear: If the Huns dared cross the great river, Samarkand would be compelled to force them back; it would be a costly war, with no guarantee that even if defeated, the Huns would not return.

"The emir has called upon General Le-Dan to take up the offensive," Hezekiah went on. "Already our army from the west prepares to march."

Amrath's brows rose in speculation. "Is that wise? Le-Dan is needed where he is; the Kazir rebellion grows worse."

"We are taxed to the limit," agreed the minister. He stopped beneath a bough and pulled a leaf from a twig; holding it in the palm of his hand, he stared at it briefly before crushing it and throwing it to the ground. "But there was no choice: It was either Le-Dan or dispatching troops from the city."

Amrath sighed heavily. The petty rebellions at home were costly and dangerous enough; they ripped apart the very fabric of Samarkand's peaceful empire. Beset by religious fanatics across the Steppes and in the forests, rebellious Hameliks in the southern regions, and a broadly based unrest within the city itself, inspired without question by the new and unknown Kazir leader, it was all Samarkand could do to hold its own; if not squashing these revolutions completely, at least quell them. But now, if all these reports flooding into the palace were true, and the Huns were indeed intent on crossing the ancient borders in search of new lands for their unlimited number, the empire would find itself fighting on every front, beleaguered, without the resources to endlessly carry on the battle. Cracks had appeared in Samarkand's fiber long ago, and now those cracks had deepened, turned into fissures that perhaps could never be repaired.

"And the emir?" asked Amrath.

Hezekiah frowned. It was no secret that Amrath's cousin was weak and ineffectual. Doting upon his games and his women, he had never given the growing difficulties the attention they deserved. Dissatisfaction within the palace was rife; once even Le-Dan himself, the empire's finest soldier, had sworn to resign his post and return to his ancestral home in the east unless matters were put into his own hands. The emir had had little option but to comply, and the general had moved Samarkand's best-trained and -equipped army to the Steppes, to fight an ongoing battle against bandit phantoms, who claimed not only autonomy for their own lands but also the right to rule over Samarkand itself. Kazirs they were, whose sense of righteousness turned them into fanatics believing that their holy cause could not fail; and, though steeped in superstition and magic, they had time and again proved formidable opponents for Le-Dan, a rag-tag, ill-trained, and ill-armed bunch holding the might of Samarkand to a standstill.

Now Le-Dan was being recalled from the Steppes to face an even greater threat. The Huns were a dreaded race, burning everything in their wake, leaving behind pestilence wherever their armies had marched. Clearly they must not be allowed to cross the river.

Amrath shook his head slowly from side to side, feeling the growing sense of helplessness that had overtaken him these past few years. Like a dam ready to burst, Samarkand struggled to hold back the waters of destruction for just a while longer, at times having to resort to packing its armies with foreign mercenaries, despised men of the Asian central plain, whose very presence often only made matters worse than they already were. It seemed a no-win situation, with the city itself sitting upon a smoldering fire ready to explode. The Huns might be all it took to light the match.

"There was a near riot outside the dome temple this morning," Hezekiah continued.

Sharon's father snapped from his thoughts. "Was there much . . . bloodshed?"

"Fortunately, no. Our mounted legion held them in check. But the people are worried, Amrath. The mullahs have been openly speaking treason against the emir. They say he must be driven from the throne if our empire is to survive."

Sharon held her breath and stifled a gasp.

"The emir will not stand for such open displays against the throne," Amrath countered.

"Action is already contemplated. That's why it was so imperative that I speak with you. He plans to imprison the *ayatollah* as a symbolic gesture of his resolution. If the leader of holy men is chained and treated as a common criminal, all the mullahs shall publicly decry the emir's weakness. They shall claim that Allah has turned His face from Samarkand, that our city and our empire are disgraced, and that the emir must be removed—by force, if necessary."

Amrath was both pained and shocked. It was true that his cousin had not proved an able leader, but such open rebellion by the people of Samarkand could prove the last straw. He put his hand on the Hebrew's stout shoulder and looked him squarely in the eye. "You must speak with the *ayatollah*," he implored, "make him stop these statements, at least in public."

Hezekiah scowled. "I am a nonbeliever," he reminded his friend. "The mullahs treat me with suspicion. But, in any case, matters have gone too far for that. What the *ayatollah* says is of little consequence." His eyes darkened and he furrowed his brows. "It is the emir himself who must be dealt with; there is no other way, unless you care not that the people turn against the palace and destroy what it has taken a thousand years for Samarkand to build."

Amrath listened intently, knowing what the minister said to be true. He sighed deeply, biting his lip and shivering at the thought of facing the outraged monarch. "What is it you want me to do?" he asked at last.

"Speak with the emir—today. There is no time to lose. You must make him realize the risk of inflaming the people further. They bear the burden of our taxes, send their sons to fight his battles and die, permit his whims to divest the city of its wealth. Shall we forget that Samarkand is no stronger than these very souls we abuse? If our emir does arrest the holiest of holy men, there will not be enough soldiers in all our provinces to contain the wrath of the people. Disaster surely must follow—for them as well as for us."

The meaning of Hezekiah's words was not lost upon the graying cousin of Samarkand's monarch. The emir for too long had lived in a world of dreams; the reality today was far different from what it had been in times past. And now, Amrath realized sadly, all these portents of doom seemed to be converging at the same moment.

The Legend, he thought suddenly, remembering Kazir folklore, the Hundred Year Solitude . . . How did it go? *And from that day shall come a time, a day of reckoning when mighty Samarkand shall fall, and fall again, yet be regained in the name of those who loved her most. . . .*

A strange legend of a stranger people. Amrath sighed. Of all the empire's enemies, it was the Kazirs he feared the most. A tribe of seminomadic, semibarbarians, whose inner strength and will had not been defeated in almost a full century of conflict. Amrath wondered which side God was truly on.

"Will you speak with the emir?" came Hezekiah's strong voice.

Amrath nodded dourly; he put a gentle hand on his friend's shoulder and nodded. "Yes, I'll speak with him, but will he listen?"

Both men stood silently for a moment, listening to the songs of tiny birds in the trees but hearing only their own thoughts, their own doubts.

At length Amrath hunched his shoulders and cast his gaze away from the scarlet-robed minister. "Ah, what has happened to our dreams of youth, old friend? Where have we gone wrong?" And there was such sadness in his eyes that Hezekiah was deeply moved. But there were few words of solace to be shared, only the mutual and certain knowledge that if Samarkand did not act—and swiftly—all that they and their forefathers had built would crumble to dust.

Shadows were lengthening; the two men turned around first in the direction of the greenhouse, then abruptly crossed the path to the wide walkway and made their way toward the standing guard at the arched palace entrance.

For what seemed a long time Sharon stayed where she was, hardly daring to breathe. She shuddered with the realization that these whispered words were not meant for her ears; indeed, if her father even suspected her of eavesdropping, both his anger and his punishment would be monumental. And in that moment she felt her whole world go insane around her. It was impossible, a jest of some kind; such terrible events could not be!

Within the dusty city of Samarkand, and even within the palace walls, talk of coming wars and strife was common. Among superstitious peoples, there are always portents to be feared, legends both real and imaginary spoken upon the lips of would-be prophets. But this was different, Sharon knew. Hezekiah was not a man to spread rumor; his title and duties made him one of the most respected, if not feared, men in all the city. And the look of despair upon her father's face, that too assured her that what she'd overheard was no mere gossip, no chatter of washerwomen or senile old men.

The fears were as real as Samarkand itself, and the knowledge of it gnawed at her stomach. She must speak of what she'd heard, find out if these dire forebodings were as terrifying as they seemed. Yet to whom could she repeat them? Whom could she trust?

Sharon breathed hard to catch her breath. Then, needing to run from the garden as fast as she could, she scooped up the straying cat and rushed back to her private chambers.

Thin wisps of pale-blue moonlight slanted through the double windows and past the curtains, burning away the pleasant darkness of Sharon's bedroom. Pensive and sleepless, the young princess rubbed at the goose bumps crawling up her arms and pulled her Persian quilt more tightly around her. Majesty, huddled snugly between the folds in the blanket and the satin sheets, stirred slightly at her restlessness.

Sharon stared wide-eyed at the star-filled night, letting her eyes wander randomly across the roofs of the distant domes and steeples shadowed in a hazy half-glow of light. How peaceful the city seemed at this hour, she mused, how content, how right, as if nothing at all were wrong in the world. She pulled down her blanket, shivered at the nip in the air, slipped into her slippers and pulled on her robe. Chestnut hair tossing like a horse's mane as she shook her head, she walked quietly to the curtains and opened them wide. Then she strolled onto the small stone balcony beyond the chamber—a veranda especially built at her request nearly three years before.

The view from her rooms in the high palace tower was nothing short of spectacular. From this vantage point she could clearly see it all: the sweep of the city, the ancient walls beyond, the rich, fertile plains beyond that for as far as the eye could see. The slightest turn of the head afforded more of this panoramic vista. To the south she could see the river, and past it, arcing to the west, the dark patch of giant trees and dense shrub known to all as Grim Forest.

The wood was aptly named, she thought, shivering with a small smile. How the very mention of that place used to scare her. The superstitious servants used to claim that in parts the forest was so dense, so dark, even the sun could not penetrate between its thick leaves and misshapen branches. Only fools and fanatics dared to step within those strange boundaries. Gypsies and Kazirs were said to dwell there, but few others.

And tales abounded of weird and uncanny doings late at night among the forest's inhabitants, especially the Three Hooded Witches, aged hags as old as creation who one night each month burned the fire of their infamous cauldron, conjuring up all manner of evil portents. But whether all this was real or imaginary, Sharon honestly could not say. No sane person ever had reason to go even in daylight, much less after dark. Still, Samarkand's more superstitious, hillfolk and the like, swore to this very day that all this was so.

When Sharon was a little girl, a trader from Damascus came with the first spring caravan to the palace. Displaying his wares of silk and perfumes and exotic spices from the west, he quickly gathered an audience of chambermaids and other servants and, after selling his goods, went on to recount firsthand tales of these very matters, his own experiences while traveling alone through Grim Forest. Sharon, although it was well past her bedtime, sneaked from her room down to the kitchens to listen. It was a grisly story he told—of devils whisked from graves, and ghouls and skeletons come to life at a single calling of the three hags. The servants shuddered and gasped, believing it all, and Sharon was so frightened that she fled back to her rooms and stayed awake all night. The next day, still upset, she refused to leave her bed, and it took her patient father almost until suppertime to convince her that what she'd heard was nothing more than a traveler's way of passing a long night and nothing more. That episode was long past in her life, yet she'd never quite forgotten it.

As she stood musing, staring out at her beloved city and wrestling with the troubling matters she had overheard this afternoon, her attention was abruptly turned to a tiny reddish glow fanning out against the night sky. Curious, she leaned forward, slim hands clutching at the low balcony wall. The hue spread bit by bit, and as it did, there came a low din of distant noise.

Horses? Troops on midnight maneuver? Sharon was puzzled; but then the noise grew in intensity, and she could almost make out the muted cries.

She peered at the glowing color again and gasped. *Fire!*

Within minutes a terrible roar filled her ears; flames leaped and popped higher and higher into the velvet night. Colors began to swirl before her startled eyes: glowing orange tipped with crimson and fading to a bluish pall at the fringes. And the mighty silos at the edge of the walled city burst into flame, one after the other, until half the sky was immersed in a rainbow of flashing heat.

There were screams now as citizens poured from their quiet mud brick homes into the streets and plazas and emptied bazaars. Horns blasted, and troops poured from the multitude of barracks located outside the palace grounds. Messengers on horseback came galloping through the gates, shouting the news through soot-blackened faces. The eastern quarter of the city was burning out of control. There was panic in the streets, and the soldiers were helpless to stem the tide of the mobs rampaging to reach safer parts.

Sharon watched and listened in horror. Below, in the vast square just outside the palace walls, angry hordes of peasants were gathering. Palace soldiers, rushing from the opened gates with drawn swords, came swarming at them, trying to stem the panic and turn the mindless mob about. Among their number, in the forefront of the surging crowd, came a dozen screaming mullahs. Exhorting the people to break through the gates and inflaming them with rhetoric, they chanted for death to the emir.

At first the guards were hard-pressed to keep them back; but suddenly, behind the blare of a trumpet, charged a hundred horsemen. With reckless abandon they broke into the crowd, gleaming swords swinging above their heads, and fiercely cut down any and all who got in their way. Screaming rose to a deafening pitch; the mob fled helter-skelter down the many byways and narrow streets. Women knelt beside the bodies of slain loved ones, weeping and wailing, calling to Allah and tearfully pleading for the carnage to stop. Those mullahs who had survived the onslaught were quickly cornered and arrested, dragged away in the direction of the old stone prison and its deep dungeons.

Sharon was visibly shaking; she spun from the awful sight of the fires and the bloody massacre and strode through her bedroom and out into the hall. The braziers in the tiled corridor burned dimly at this late hour. Twisting shadows danced across the concave ceiling and along the walls like grisly images of *nightthings.*

The two guards on duty looked with surprise at the young princess standing before them.

"My lady?" said the first.

"What is happening?" she flared.

Mutely the guards exchanged quick glances. "Not to worry, my lady."

She glared at the black-cloaked soldiers, noticing their expressionless features, their calm and steady demeanor while the city went mad around them.

"Not to worry?" she panted, gesturing beyond the open door of her room to the scarlet-glowing sky. "Haven't you seen? Haven't you heard the screams, the fighting?"

"Everything is under control," assured the taller of the two. "The situation is being well taken care of; there is no need for alarm."

Sharon was frantic. "Are you insane? People are being slaughtered in the square!"

Both men stared blankly.

"Look for yourselves!" she cried. "Samarkand is
aflame!"

"Everything is well under control," repeated the first
soldier, and, as if giving emphasis to his words, his large
hand gripped strongly the hilt of his scimitar.

"Take me to my father," Sharon demanded. "I want
to speak with him now." These soldiers were treating
her like a stupid child; she could see things were *not*
under control. But as she spoke, the screams outside
had all but ended, replaced by the harsh clatter of hoofbeats against flagstone as more cavalry charged across
the square and through the main thoroughfares, routing
the mobs as they found them.

"Your father is not to be disturbed, my lady. He is
with the emir, discussing the situation. Please, go back
to your rooms and try to sleep."

She let out her frustration with an angry toss of her
head. "Then take me to Hezekiah."

The guard shook his head slowly, face bathed in soft
shadows. "The minister is also occupied, my lady.
There are serious affairs of state to be discussed."

In disgust, Sharon pushed him aside and started down
the long corridor. The second soldier hesitantly began
to pull his sword from its sheath. "Forgive me, my lady,
but you must return to your quarters."

Sharon spun around hotly, the hem of her robe swirling. Her cold glare made him uneasily return the scimitar
to its place.

"Amrath's orders," said the soldier evenly. "We were
instructed to make certain that you are safe." And he
bowed his head, his hands folded into a pyramid, fingertips touching his forehead.

"I don't want to stay alone. Take me to Zadek."

"Zadek, my lady?"

She spoke of the mystical mullah sequestered within

his rooms in the highest tower—a strange man, with few friends, now an outcast from the religious sect to which he had sworn to devote his life. Once he was said to have had the emir's ear and favor; now, though, through circumstances never fully explained, he lived the life of a virtual recluse, seeing only a select few inside those rooms and spending his days and nights alone with his enigmatic writings. Many considered him mad, a raving lunatic; to others he was merely a fool, little more than a court jester, allowed these bizarre freedoms because of some whim of the emir's. To Sharon, however, he was neither. Once a friend of her father, as well as her tutor, only Zadek might provide some of the answers she needed, especially now.

"I'm sorry, my lady," said the first soldier, "but you'll have to go back——"

"And if I refuse?"

"It would be better that you didn't."

His warning was not enough for the strong-willed young princess; she tightened the belt of her robe and stepped past both guards, taking long strides as she crossed the corridor. When she reached the wide vestibule, she came upon the narrow winding stairway leading up to the mystic's private chambers and started the long climb. At the slit window on the first landing, she paused and looked out. The sky had begun to darken again, light from the fire steadily dimming. A few flames still leaped across distant steeples, and billows of heavy smoke were rising across the face of the moon. A dull orange glow shimmered over the thousands of tiled roofs spread out from one end of the city walls to the other. The fire was ebbing, no longer out of control, and the streets, even in these brief moments, had all but returned to an eerie quiet.

She climbed higher, shivering a bit at the currents of icy air flowing through cracks in the stone, passing through what seemed like endless darkness until at last, out of breath, she reached the top—the highest point in all of Samarkand.

Sharon smoothed her robe and tried to brush her hair back into place with her hand; then she entered the low-ceilinged hallway. The smooth walls were patterned with ever-shifting shadows cast by thin night candles struck into rusted iron frames at random places along the dank corridor. The hall was desolate and forbidding, but at the far end a tiny flame of butter-yellow light flickered outside twin, massive arched doors. Sharon hurried her steps and crossed the threshold to the light, hesitating at the doorstep of Zadek's strange domain and, wondering if perhaps she had not made a mistake coming here like this.

Her hand took hold of the black-iron knocker and she tapped it once against the thick oak door. The sound echoed hollowly all the way back to the stairs. To her surprise, Zadek did not come to the door and inquire who was there; rather, his gravelly voice, unperturbed by an unexpected midnight visitor, bade her enter.

She pushed the door open slightly and stepped slowly inside. The air was heavy with incense burning from a single brazier placed near the center of the room. A waning candle flickered from a holder, almost extinguishing when a rush of wind followed behind her from the opened door.

Sharon stood still, breathing heavily. Her brocaded robe gleamed dully in the dim light, barely concealing the smooth roundness of her breasts. Against the pallor of her troubled face, only her mouth provided a touch of color. She let her gaze wander round the room; it was oval and claustrophobic, exactly the way she remembered it, filled with worn tapestries and paintings depicting grim night scenes of forests inhabited by strange flying beasts of mythology and unknown birds with plumes of gold, hissing fire. On a near wall hung the mural of a map, a sweeping map of the known world, showing every land and city from Damascus in the west to the vast regions of Cathay in the east. In the north were the barbaric lands of Rus, with its pine forests and frozen lakes, bleak ranges of mountains, sheets of snow and ice that never melted; in the southwest, Arabia, its endless deserts and caravan routes to the holy city of Mecca; and much farther east, beyond the empires of Persia and Samarkand, the huge subcontinent of India.

Zadek's sparse furniture was dusty and worn. Apart from a few handcrafted vases and sculptures set on pedestals, there was only a chair and a huge table. The table was cluttered with mounds of papers and scrolls, all writings from which the renegade mullah would translate and study. Among them were some Sharon knew to be ancient Egyptian hieroglyphics; others were sacred tablets written by the mysterious monks of Lhasa, that hidden city high in the heavenly like mountains of faraway Tibet. Also among the papers could be found transcripts of the Koran, the Moslem bible, in its original Arabic, dating from the time of Muhammad himself, and biblical texts in Hebrew, Persian, and even Urdu. It was said that Zadek read, wrote, and spoke in no less than eleven languages and was basically familiar with seven or eight more.

There was no sign of the mullah as she pensively searched the chamber; but then came his voice, seemingly distant, calling to her by name.

Startled, she crossed from his workroom and pushed aside the thick velvet curtains. Then she saw him, his silhouette stark against the night sky, standing with his back to her at the edge of his balcony. He wore a purple *aba*, hood flung back. His hands were clenched firmly behind his back, feet slightly apart, body straight and rigid. He too had been watching the fire and the mobs below.

"How . . . how did you know it was I who came, teacher?" she asked tensely.

Slowly Zadek turned around and smiled, providing

no answer. She stared into his extraordinarily deep-set eyes, black as coals, and felt a flush of anxiety. Zadek was never one to make her feel comfortable—not with his uncanny sense of presence, his strange ability to look into her eyes and somehow read her innermost thoughts.

"Forgive me for intruding," she apologized.

Zadek fingered his gold necklace, heavy links polished to a reflective shine, fastened to a huge emerald that dangled just below his breast. "You are troubled and you wished to speak with me," he told her in a low tone.

Sharon nodded. "Yes, teacher, but if I have disturbed you . . ."

The gray-haired priest of Islam flared the nostrils of his hooked nose and shook his head once. He was not a tall man, but his stout build and carriage always made him appear far larger than he actually was. His face was long, pockmarked, ears slightly too large for his head, with a thin mouth, almost feminine. A pointed goatee protruded from a square-set jaw, making his profile seem devillike when observed in shadows.

He held his place for a time, studying the girl, thinking how long it had been since she had been here last. He twirled the pearl ring on the middle finger of his left hand and beckoned for her to join him on the balcony. She did so hesitantly.

"These are evil days upon Samarkand," Zadek whispered. Sharon stood at his elbow while his gaze swept the horizon, his pronounced frown betraying his own anguish.

"Can you tell me what is happening?" she asked.

The mullah fixed his eyes on the far-distant mountains and heaved a deep sigh. "We are in the last days of glory, young princess. Look upon the face of Samarkand and weep."

She had come to Zadek seeking comfort and assurance; instead, his strange words were frightening her even more, and she trembled. "I'm frightened, teacher.

Tonight, don't speak to me in riddles. Too much is happening, things I don't understand."

Zadek nodded somberly, knowingly. "What is it you want to know?"

She tugged at his sleeve, forcing him to look at her. "I overheard something today, teacher, something . . . I should not even repeat." There were tears in her eyes and she bit her lip. "I saw my father and Hezekiah in the garden today, speaking in whispers so no one might hear."

"Of war?" His eyes burned into hers. "Of the menace of the Huns who gather across the river?"

Sharon swallowed and nodded, a suggestion of red from the sky's glow crossing her features. "How did you know?"

Zadek smiled again, only this time more deeply. " 'Tis no secret, Sharon. Reports of their movements have been pouring into Samarkand from every caravan."

"Will"—her voice was slow and deliberate—"will this be the crusade you once told me of?"

He looked down gently at the young girl beside him, seeing her not as the full-grown woman she was, but rather the child he'd known since her birth, the daughter he had predicted for Amrath in the days when they were still friends. "No, child, the events of which you ask shall come later, in another time and age. But know that these Huns, this terrible scourge upon the face of the earth, shall cost us greatly. A time of mourning is at hand."

Sharon put the back of her hand to her trembling mouth. "And will Samarkand fall?"

Zadek thought for a long while before answering. Then he said, "There is rot within far worse than any enemy without. To be saved, we must look to ourselves, to our own peoples. United, there is no foe that cannot be beaten, but divided . . ." And he ended his sentence with a sad shake of the head.

The princess pressed him further. "But we *are* divided, Zadek! See below—women crying in the streets, the fires . . ."

The cunning, mad mullah grimaced. "Brother against brother, father turned against son." He spread out his hands as if to encompass the entire city below. "We are our own greatest enemy, Sharon. Have we both not seen it every day of our lives? Or are you and I as blind as the rest? A house divided cannot stand, must one day fall." He sighed wistfully. "If only the emir had listened . . ."

Sharon's eyes dramatically narrowed and she looked at her companion with growing trepidation. "Speak the truth to me, teacher," she implored. "Hide not what you have learned. What was the reason for these fires, for the people to turn upon the palace and the palace to turn against its people?"

Zadek was emotionless when he said, "The *ayatollah* has been arrested, dragged from the Great Mosque and taken to the dungeons."

Her heart beat like a drum; she felt the blood rushing to her head. "But that's impossible! I heard my father say he would speak personally with the emir, stop such folly from occurring——"

"The emir's mind was set, child; he would not listen. The *ayatollah* gave no fight, no struggle; he submitted himself to Samarkand's law without questions. And now the people are enraged. The damage has been done, and there is no man who can undo it." He put his arm around her as she choked back a tear, and led her back inside. She sat upon a scarlet-laced cushion, eyes filled with tears, and held her hand out numbly when he handed her a stemmed goblet filled with honeyed wine. Lifting the brew to her lips, she took a sip, closed her eyes.

"I don't understand any of these things, teacher. What is happening to our world?"

"It is changing," replied the mystical priest. "Like the seasons, there is a time for everything. Every flower, no matter how beautiful, must sooner or later wilt and die.

It is sad to see, yet"—here he paused—"yet from its roots another flower shall grow to replace it, perhaps one even more lovely than the last."

"What are you saying?" cried Sharon, looking up at him sharply, denying everything he was telling her. "Samarkand has stood for a thousand years!"

"And is a city or even an empire so different from a single man, Allah's greatest creation? I think not. Each of us is allotted his time, his moments of glory, and each of us must face the inevitable reality that he is mortal. We live; we die—so it has always been, Sharon. Think of the invincible Alexander; shall it be otherwise for Samarkand than for him?"

There was a deep, prolonged silence between them after Zadek had finished. Sharon found herself alone with her thoughts, listening to the sounds of night. The breeze was blowing gently past the curtains, causing the candle's flame to flicker and shadows to jump. She heard the last clatter of distant hoofbeats in the again quiet city and knew that an uneasy peace had been restored, but restored by the sword, and she shuddered to imagine the terrible toll it would have taken.

She drank the last of her wine with a single swallow, refusing Zadek's offer to refill the goblet. Then she stood and aimlessly paced back and forth beside the doors to the balcony. Things were happening so fast, she could no longer think straight. She felt troubled, tired, bone-weary, and sick at heart. In the space of a single day she had seen her safe, secure world turn upside down, cruelly crumbling before her very eyes while she stood helplessly by. She was now in a world she hardly recognized, a world facing destruction, and there was no one who had either the skill or the courage to avert it.

"What is to be, Zadek?" she asked sullenly.

"In the new Samarkand? Who can say?" He ran a forefinger across his chin, drawing the outline of his beard.

She tapped her foot impatiently. "Are we doomed, then? Is there no hope?"

The mad mullah crossed the room and withdrew a tiny leather pouch hidden behind one of the larger stone icons in the corner of the room. Then he sat cross-legged upon the floor, untied the cord, and poured the contents into an open palm. Four colorful tiny stones trickled down, one as white as ivory, one as blue as the sea, one ebony black, and the last fiery red.

Zadek closed his hand around them tightly, shook his fist in the manner of a soldier casting dice, then hurled them to the floor at his feet. Sharon watched with wonder as the stones seemed to quiver and slowly began to glow, first dully, then more brightly, until the light they cast shone over his face and flowing robe. The mystic shut his eyes and spread his hands above the stones, lost in deep concentration.

Sharon had seen the gems before; the Glowing Rocks of Babylon, they were called, said to have been stolen from the Persian emperor Darius upon his death at the hands of conquering Alexander so many centuries before. What roads these fabled stones had traveled through the ages, Sharon had no idea, only that somehow the strange defrocked mullah, Zadek, now had them in his possession.

"What do you see, teacher?" she asked.

Zadek opened his eyes and bowed his head, his gaze intent upon the gems as they glittered, their light dancing like snakes. He held his breath and bit hard at his lips, his features distorted as though suddenly he were in torment.

She repeated the question, no longer afraid.

"I see," he rasped, speaking as if no one were there, "death and pestilence, frightful events that are cloudy yet clear to me. The chasm among us grows wider, and the day of reckoning grows perilously close. I see fires, huge, billowing fires across the land, from the mountains to the southern deserts. I see a scroll, a holy scroll of Islam burned and trampled underfoot, while a nation in chains weeps for a cause lost." He stopped briefly, catching his breath, then quietly went on: "Rubble and ashes from which a tree shall grow . . . and upon a pale horse there comes a rider—faceless, hooded—and the rider gathers together the remnants of all that has been lost and brings them together to reclaim what has unjustly been stolen. And the grim faces of my forefathers smile, for through their struggle, one has come to bring the Gift."

Sharon peered at him strangely, recalling other inferences long forgotten about such a person— a Prophet, a new savior, to rid the land of evil and restore justice. It was an ancient belief, she knew, passed on from generation to generation—but not one of Samarkand.

Tears had begun to fall down Zadek's bumpy cheeks. He cleared a thick throat and said, "At last . . . at last the time has come. Praise be to Allah that I should live to see the day my people come home at last."

Sharon drew back a step, stifling a gasp. The glowing stones had cast an eerie light across the oval chamber, dancing prisms of blending amber and indigo seeping through her as if alive, making her flesh crawl. And as Zadek spoke of these things, of forefathers and prophets, she *knew*. The whispered rumors rife throughout the palace were true: Whether meaning to or not, Zadek had betrayed himself.

She took a step closer to the humbled figure and glared down at him. "Tell me, teacher, and speak from your heart: You welcome the incursion of the Huns, don't you? You want to see our city crumble."

The mullah looked up at her with sad, furtive eyes. "Only that it may be reclaimed."

Her heart skipped a beat. "You're a Kazir, aren't you?"

Zadek nodded, locking his eyes with hers. The glow of the stones started to fade. "My mother was a Kazir, yes, and from her I learned the promises made by God to restore our tribe to its rightful place."

A Kazir! A traitor!

Sharon would never have believed it, never have listened to the malicious gossip, but now the priest had confirmed it with his own tongue. And the very thought that this man, this holy teacher whom she respected and loved more than anyone except her father, should be a traitor to the city and the emir he served sent her reeling.

"Listen to me, child," he said as she stood before him, pale and trembling. "Much has been misunderstood. The Kazirs and the people of Samarkand share the same ancestry; like separate branches of the same tree, we have a common root. You need not fear me because of what you have learned."

Her mouth turned down mockingly. "I'll not betray you, Zadek," she flared. "You need have no fear; I'll keep your secret. I owe you that much."

Zadek winced at the sting of her words, hurt as though struck by an arrow. He loved the young princess as though she were his own, and the thought that now she would inwardly turn against him was too much to bear.

"Temper your hatred," he pleaded. "You begged me to speak to you of what I saw. Now I have, and you are pained by it. Hatred is an evil thing, young princess; it consumes until nothing is left. I have hidden the truth from you for too long, shamed the memory of my mother and my forefathers. Now I must pay the price."

Sharon felt confused; by all rights she should call out Zadek immediately for what he was. A Kazir was her enemy, the enemy of all she stood for. This man who had spent his life within the palace as a virtual spy should be punished for his crimes.

Knowing her thoughts, Zadek said, "Never once have I been disloyal to Samarkand. I have lived among you for too long, come to accept your customs and ways"—

he sighed sorrowfully—"come to love you. My mother's people know me not; to them I am as hated as the royal family itself."

She drew a deep breath and turned away from him. Tears were ready to burst from her reddened eyes. "Oh, Zadek," she said, clutching her arms tightly, "I don't know what to do. Whom can I turn to now?"

He stood, a hand outstretched toward her. "I am still your friend, Sharon; that much has not changed."

But she shook her head and moved away. From now on, there was no one she could trust.

Samarkand, city of myth and fable, bustled with frantic activity on the morning that announced the beginning of the sacred holiday period of Ramadan. The seven black gates of the city were opened wide to allow the steady stream of travelers to enter. They came in caravans and wagons, by mule and by camel, but most of all they came on foot, thousands upon thousands of weary pilgrims, here today on their pilgrimage to the Great Mosque.

Amid snorting camels and road-blocking donkeys they packed the streets and plazas, jammed the parks and avenues, crowded outside the Square of the Prophet and stared up at the lofty minarets, waiting for the priests to appear upon the balconies and issue the first call to prayer.

On a day such as this there was little distinction between the classes. Peasants, dressed in simple cotton *lungis* draped over their bodies, stood beside merchants and farmers, craftsmen and money changers, all patiently looking to the moment the arched temple doors would swing open and allow them to enter. Women carried infants and hushed them as they cried, while pilgrims fell to their knees, facing west to Mecca, and loudly prayed. Among the throngs the hucksters roamed, pickpockets and thieves, prostitutes and solicitors; beggars by the score, many deformed, crippled, or blind, lined the streets with open palms and pleaded with passersby for a few paltry alms with which to sustain their miserable lives for yet another day.

Along the paved streets of the Lower City, with its

odors and clamor, jasmine gardens and houses with high barred windows, the festive atmosphere rang. Torpid flies buzzed in and around the canopied street stalls, the smell of dung and spices thick in the air. From fortune-tellers to fire eaters they came, mobbing every byway and alley, jovial and carefree, babbling in all the varied tongues of Samarkand's empire as they strolled among the sights of the city that was the crossroad of the world. By carriage to the Square of the Prophet came noblemen and their women, the ladies of the court stunning in their *ghararas,* flowing gowns of exquisite color, gold dust liberally sprinkled on their eyelashes and over their pinned hair. Others came finely garbed in draped robes of wool and soft linen, embroidered with gold spangles, needle-weaved to perfection. All wore the traditional silk veil pulled high over their faces, leaving only their dark, mysterious eyes exposed.

By midmorning the sun was blazing down on what would prove to be a merciless day of heat. Across the high parapets, where stern-faced palace soldiers stood solemn guard, cottonlike clouds scudded, giving momentary relief from the sun's increasing glare. The wild flowers across the endless fields beyond the walls glistened dryly in the light, the looming foothills behind sweeping away as they climbed to higher elevations along the edges of the arid Steppes. The procession to the city seemed never-ending, the fertile plains teeming with life, all manner of traveler marching now upon the dusty roads, peacefully come to celebrate the holy month.

But, among this procession were other travelers— travelers with thoughts bent on malice. Mingling among the crowds, they knew they would not be recognized— at least until their grim work was done, and it then would be too late.

The Great Mosque, ribbed amber dome glistening in sunlight, stood like a mighty monument at the extreme southern end of the Gate of the Prophet; the sandstone palace walls, watchtowers rising high above all, stood opposite at the north, near the fringes of what was called the Old City. From the voluted parapets carved in relief with intricately designed motifs, palace officers and court administrators peered down with curiosity upon the surging crowd. Among them, draped in his finest robe of silk, dazzling crown upon his head, stood the emir of Samarkand—a slight, frail man, well into his middle years, who nervously twitched at the sight of the huge gathering. Although noisy, the rabble, behind their barricades, remained peaceful, and the emir allowed himself a satisfied smile.

Since the arrest of the *ayatollah* eleven days before, and the subsequent fires and mullah-inspired riots, there had been a total calm within the city—in fact, everywhere—a strange quiet that was inexplicable, considering the precarious state of affairs. The daily reports from distant garrisons told of a sudden cessation of all hostilities, even among the bandit Kazirs, constant troublemakers throughout the Steppes. There seemed to be no activity whatsoever across any of Samarkand's long borders, most curiously in the western province where the hordes of idol-worshiping Huns massed.

No one in the empire was enjoying this respite more than the emir himself, who had come to believe that the holy man's imprisonment had once and for all put an end to such petty and costly rebellions. Yet, there were those who counseled caution, advisors within the palace who held other opinions. They saw these tranquil conditions quite differently; to them, this was the calm before the storm.

Sharon, accompanied by other members of the royal household, also came to pray. She followed at the end of the procession into the mosque as the great doors at last opened. Her carefully coiffed hair came loose in the slight breeze, small curls dangling across her forehead. Her face covered by a silk veil, she crossed the walk, head bowed in humility. She wore the traditional *quamez,* a long-sleeved tunic loosely belted by a silver sash, as well as the eastern *shalwar,* pendulous women's pants, well suited for Samarkand's climate.

A mighty roar rose from the crowd at the sight of a mullah come upon the balcony of the minaret. The darkly garbed priest called out in prayer, and the crowds fell to their knees. Many lay prostrate, arms outstretched, others bent low with foreheads touching the ground. And when he was done, the soldiers stepped aside, permitting the pilgrims to pour inside, hundreds more forced to stay across the steps when the mosque's courtyard was filled to capacity and the great gates shut.

On this festive day, there was a gay mood throughout the city; it seemed as though all strife were forgotten. Once the prayers were done and the crowds emptied from the huge temple, Samarkand came to life anew. The markets of the Lower City reopened, visitors jamming the bazaars where exotic foods were openly cooked and sold, the air heavy with the smell of meats and heady wines. There was singing and dancing and displays of acrobatics and dramatics representative of almost every culture within the far-flung empire.

The festivities would continue well into the night, a carnival that came but one day each year, always to be enjoyed but today especially savored, for the troubled city would, for a time at least, ring with laughter and music and gaiety.

An Indian fakir sat cross-legged and shirtless, playing a low melodious tune on his pipe as he coaxed a coiled snake to weave its body up from the woven basket. Sharon watched and smiled, always intrigued by the abilities of these strange snake charmers, and mingled with the crowd as the serpent swayed its scaly body in time with the music. When the song was done and the snake returned to the unlidded basket, content to rest until it was called again, the gathering applauded and threw a scattering of copper coins at the fakir's feet.

The Indian bowed before them, then hastily scooped up the coins before a beggar or a thief had the chance to steal away from within his grasp.

"We must return to the palace, my lady," said Hezekiah, gently nudging Sharon's elbow. "I gave your father my word that you would be back well before dusk."

Sharon glanced up at the bright afternoon sun, wincing as its light reflected off the low tiled roofs of the enormous bazaar and hurt her eyes. "But it's early," she protested. "The sun won't set yet for hours."

The Hebrew scowled. Amrath had put the girl under Hezekiah's protection for the day, sternly commanding that Sharon not be allowed the normal freedoms she might expect. Ordinarily, his daughter, as well as many of the palace court, would think nothing of mingling with the people during this special day, even sharing the revelry well into the night. But today was different from those in years past, Hezekiah knew: Danger was unquestionably brewing—no matter what the emir might think—and a cursory glance across the markets, showing the host of soldiers on duty along the roofs and in the courtyards, only confirmed his belief.

A group of merrymakers jostled the young princess; Sharon laughed, but sour Hezekiah pulled her away quickly.

"They meant no harm," said Sharon, looking on as the merrymakers danced from one side of the busy street to the other. At the far end of the constricted avenue, where it broadly opened into a spacious plaza lined with trees and fountains, a large stage had been set upon a platform, actors at the center busily giving a comical performance. Peals of laughter resounded from the jovial and agreeable crowd. Sharon's attention was caught briefly by the scene, the caricatures of noblemen and -women, and she looked on with amusement. "All right, minister," she said at last, returning her attention to the man beside her. "I suppose you're right. We can leave now."

Hezekiah nodded, thankful that the teeming masses seemed so preoccupied and that the day had passed without incident. Along the street they walked, heading toward the plaza, ever aware of the pungent smells of sizzling foods wafting in the air. Ignoring beggars, they wove their way between canopied stalls where a vast array of merchandise was displayed and offered for barter. At the edge of the crowd, Hezekiah took Sharon by the arm and steered her across the dusty square in the direction of the nearby Square of the Prophet and the safety of the palace walls.

"I think your fears were unfounded, minister," she chided him as they passed a stern-faced patrol of royal troops, who smartly saluted the minister and the young princess. She glanced around, feeling that her own suspicions, although unspoken, had been equally unfounded.

"Perhaps so," Hezekiah observed. "But the day is not yet done."

Before the last word had rolled off his tongue, there came screaming from behind. Hezekiah spun around, instinctively shielding the girl from possible harm.

A potbellied merchant, red-faced and profusely sweating, was shouting at the top of his lungs for soldiers to come at once. "Catch the thief!" he bellowed from behind his stall of spices and rare foods. But there were so many people around that it was virtually impossible to tell whom he meant. Suddenly, though, there was the fleeting shadow of someone pushing mindlessly through the throng. A veiled woman was knocked down, and her cries brought passersby running to grab the commonly garbed offender.

"He's the one!" thundered the merchant. "That's him! Catch him! Don't let him get away!"

The accused thief was hemmed in by outraged citizens on all sides. He darted to break free, knocking over several other fat merchants with a single shove, wrestling another to the ground, and leaped like a cat over

the nearest stall, kicking over roll upon roll of expensive
fabric, linen and silk tumbling into the street.

Soldiers with drawn swords came racing from their
posts. At sight of the glistening scimitars, shoppers,
pilgrims, and passersby ducked and scrambled in every
direction, causing still further pandemonium. The thief,
aware of the life-and-death chase, bolted down the
clearest avenue of escape—the almost cleared path of
the road to the Square of the Prophet.

"Seize him!" cried the captain of the soldiers, panting to reach the criminal before he had a chance to dis-
appear among the crowds, and from another direction
rushed more of the emir's black-cloaked guards.

The thief stopped abruptly, a soldier wielding his
sword before him. The thief was fast, Sharon saw—
young, clever, as quick on his feet as any. He sidestepped the thrust of the soldier's blade, flung himself
forward just enough to topple his adversary, then,
springing back onto his feet, charged ahead. But the
guards were everywhere, pressing, forming a wide circle
from which the thief could find no route to freedom.

The youth froze in his tracks, eyes darting to and fro,
crouching defensively as he pondered his next move.
There were few he could make. The troops had
cleverly cordoned off this entire section of the street
and wedged him in solidly, so solidly that no matter
where he looked, he was confronted with glittering,
finely honed steel.

"Grab him!" commanded the captain of the guard.
His front line drew in close for the kill. The thief pulled
a small dagger from within the folds of his dirty robe
and brandished it threateningly.

"Better for you to drop the weapon," hissed the captain. Three brutish guards held their scimitars at arm's
length, points aimed for the young man's heart.

The potbellied merchant came bounding through the
phalanx, panting and cursing. "He's the one, m'lord!
I saw him take the food myself!"

The youth dropped the knife, letting it fall at his feet, where the blade clanged against the stone. "He lies! I stole no food from him or from anyone else!"

The merchant sputtered. "Are you going to take the word of a beggar? Sirs, I beg you! Arrest him at once! Is there no justice left in Samarkand?"

The captain of the guard, a sadist, rubbed a finger at his brush mustache and smiled thinly. "What do you say, beggar?"

Sharon saw that the young man was frightened and yet, despite his accuser and the host of troops ready to slay him should they be given the order, he held his ground firmly. "I am innocent," he repeated, fires burning in his eyes, a dark flush spreading across his cheeks. "This man has wrongly accused me. I am no thief, nor am I a beggar. I have come this day to Samarkand to celebrate at the mosque like all other pilgrims."

The captain raised his brow mockingly. "Oh? You are a pilgrim, then? A mullah perhaps?" His men began to chuckle.

Undaunted, the youth shook his head. "No, not a holy man, merely a traveler here to pay homage."

The captain's mouth turned down at the corners and he pushed past his aides and stood face to face with the youthful stranger. "Where are you from?" he demanded.

"The hill country, captain."

The soldier scrutinized him closely. You had to be careful with these beggars, he knew; half of them would sell their own mothers if it served their purpose. Scum, vermin, a plague upon Samarkand they were. It was a shame he couldn't deal with them all. Food for the rats in the dungeons was more than they were worth.

"The hill country, eh? Are you a herder, then . . . of camels, perhaps?"

The youth remained brazen and defiant. "A herder of goats, captain, as my father was before me and his before him."

There were snickers; the captain held his nose and

spit at the beggar's sandaled feet. "I thought the smell seemed familiar." His men laughed loudly.

The youth tensed; veins bulged in his neck as though he was struggling within himself to stay his temper. Tall and as scrawny as a will-o'-the-wisp, he was nevertheless muscular, Sharon saw—a lean frame ruggedly formed, very much the product of hillmen whose sparse existences left little room for fat.

The captain stepped back a pace, his eyes never leaving the eyes of the peculiarly bold stranger before him. "Theft is a serious crime in Samarkand, *hillman*"—he said the last word bitingly, sarcastically—"punishable by death."

"I did not steal."

The soldier snapped his fingers. Without turning around, he said to the perspiring merchant still standing out of breath behind him, "Do you still say that this *hillman* robbed your stall?"

The merchant stood firm: "I do."

The youth shot him an angry glance. "Liar!"

The captain gritted his teeth and snarled, *"Haram'-zada!"* ("Son of a bastard!") He drew back his arm, letting his balled fist lash out powerfully, catching the unaware hillman squarely in the solar plexus. The youth doubled over in pain and coughed for breath, tears streaming down his eyes.

"Off with his head!" rasped the captain. "Hold him down! We'll teach this scum a thing or two!"

Sharon, shocked to see this brutality, tugged at Hezekiah's sleeve. "Minister, please," she pleaded. "You're not going to let them do this, are you?"

The Hebrew shrugged. He was a worldly man, had seen this and far worse than this many times during his long years of service to the emir and the empire. Although it might seem unjust, he also knew that Samarkand must never bend its laws, rigid though they might be. The hillman had been accused of a crime, and as a criminal he must be punished. "There is nothing I can do, Sharon," he said, shaking his head with a single, sorrowful gesture. He took her arm again. "Come, let us leave. An execution such as this is not meant for such eyes as yours. Let the guilty pay for their deeds."

She looked up at him, revolted. "But how do you even know he's guilty? How can you be sure?"

"The merchant has sworn——"

With a grimace of disgust, she pulled away and marched forward. The youth had already been brought to his knees, hands bound behind his back. A butcher's block of wood had been brought and placed before him, that the executioner might more easily sever his head from his body. The merchant stood by gloating, while other observers numbly pressed closer to get a better view. Pickpockets, whores, thieves, and criminals themselves, they all seemed nevertheless eager to watch a fellow criminal spill his blood.

"Are you ready?" said the captain to his executioner. A huge soldier with the neck of a bull nodded slowly. The captain's thick lips spread in a grin. "Pray, hillman. You don't have much time to let Allah hear your sins."

To the shock of everyone, the youth, although trembling as two other soldiers held him fast, peered up at the captain of the guard and spit in his face. The enraged soldier turned crimson. "I can make you sorry for that," he promised. "Cut off his fingers one by one, then his ears, then his manhood. Let him watch while he dies. I want him to enjoy it."

A cruel smile crossed the executioner's face as he put down the scimitar and drew from a scabbard at his side a razor-sharp double-edged knife—a far better tool for such delicate work. He wiped the side of the blade several times on his tunic, admiring the weapon as he turned it over in his hand. Then he kneeled beside the prisoner and yanked his head back by the hair. The youth grimaced and pressed his lips tightly together as the executioner lifted the blade to the side of his ear.

"Stop this at once!"

Her shrill scream left them all startled. The executioner stared up; the captain of the guard put his hands to his hips and watched disbelievingly as the young princess pushed her way inside the circle and purposefully strode to the center. "Release him!"

The captain was astounded. "My lady?"

"You heard me: Release him. Untie his hands and let him stand on his feet."

That the woman who confronted him was the princess Sharon, daughter of Lord Amrath, the perplexed soldier knew full well. As a member of the royal family she must be obeyed at once, her word unquestioned. Yet, she was demanding something far from her own realm, well removed from a woman's understanding.

He made the respectful pyramid with his hands, bowing so that his fingertips touched his forehead. "Forgive me, mistress," he said haltingly, "but this man . . . this man is a thief and must be punished. You heard for yourself——"

Sharon turned from him and confronted the merchant: "You, are you certain that this is the man who stole from you?"

The merchant bowed as well, more deeply, his palms spread before her as he said, "That is the one, my princess, I swear it. May Allah strike me if——"

She moved slightly toward him, her stare making him uncomfortable. "And how can you be so positive?"

"The thief wore exactly the very clothes this man wears now."

Sharon smiled slyly. "What clothes, merchant—a filthy *lungi?*" Then she laughed, looking past the sullen soldiers to the crowds behind. "See there, merchant, how many others are garbed in identical garments? And could you single out one from the next?"

The merchant mopped his brow and bit tensely at his lip. Among the onlookers, there were at least twenty men dressed no different from the prisoner.

"And did you see the face of the man who stole from your stall?" Sharon asked.

"No, mistress, only a fleeting shadow behind the hood."

Sharon scoffed. "Then how are we to know that this hillman here has committed the crime?"

While the merchant sputtered, unable to answer, the captain of the guard glared at the girl angrily. "Would you mock our justice, my princess, and allow this rabble to run wild through our streets without fear of punishment? Free this man and word will spread of it. There will be no controlling the beggars and thieves——"

Sharon waved an imperious hand, her eyes narrowing as she boldly met the soldier's angered stare. "Samarkand is a land of laws and justice, captain, and justice is all I seek. Prove the hillman to be guilty and I shall applaud his beheading; otherwise, free him." It was a demand, not a request. The captain clenched his teeth and turned to Hezekiah.

"I beg you, minister, don't interfere with our duties, don't allow the rabble to have a free hand. The man is guilty. Look at him." The youth, although still on his knees, glared at the captain and those around him with contempt, displaying a cocky defiance that almost dared them to mete out the punishment. "Give me a moment more and I'll make him talk," added the soldier. "He'll admit his crime, all right, even if I have to break each of his bones one by one."

Hezekiah said nothing; Sharon stepped forward and confronted the youth herself. "Did you commit the crime?" she asked tersely.

The young hillman shook his head, his gaze fixed on hers. Cunning eyes, Sharon thought as she looked at him—devious, calculating. "No, mistress, it was another. It was my misfortune to be nearby when the merchant sought out the real thief."

"He lies," growled the captain. "Every word out of his mouth is a lie. I know these hillmen well enough, having served along the Steppes for years before gaining service within the palace."

"What do you say to that, stranger?" said Sharon.

The youth let out a deep breath, shaking his head again. "I am innocent. By the Prophet, I give my word of honor."

The captain of the guard snickered. "The word of a hillman is the word of a thief—worthless. From which part of the Steppes do you hail, beggar?" he asked. "Speak quickly!"

"I am not of the Steppes."

"Oh, no?" The soldier, unconvinced, drew closer to the youth, kneeling, so that his breath was hot on his face. "I wonder. You have that look about you . . . that look I've seen before."

"I don't know what you're talking about."

The soldier stood, a triumphant smile parting his lips. "This man is not a hillman," he announced. "I stake my life on it. Everything he's said here is a treacherous lie. Let me take him to the dungeons for further questioning."

Hezekiah spoke for the first time: "What are you saying, soldier?"

The captain pointed a long finger at the man on his knees. "This one is a Kazir; I'm sure of it."

There were gasps from the crowd. A Kazir loose in Samarkand!

Sharon looked over at the Hebrew. "Is this possible?"

The tall minister shook his head doubtfully. "I . . . I cannot say. The Kazirs are a strange people, vowing never to cross inside the city's gates until this prophesy of theirs has been fulfilled."

"Talk for fools," shot back the captain. "Kazir spies have been causing us trouble for years. And this man is one."

The young man peered up at Sharon with plaintive eyes. "I did not steal from the merchant," he repeated. "I am blameless."

"Well, someone must pay for my goods," growled the rotund owner of the stall. He turned to Hezekiah: "I am a poor man, my lord, with many mouths to feed."

Sharon frowned; she snapped her fingers and pointed to the merchant. "Pay him, minister."

At that, Hezekiah reached inside his belted pouch and threw to the waiting merchant three small pieces of silver. They clattered at his feet, and he swept them up, tucked them safely away, and bowed deeply before the lady of the court. "May the Prophet's blessings be upon you, mistress. May this kindness be repaid by Allah a thousandfold and more."

"You may return to your stall now," she said curtly in dismissal, not watching as he back-stepped slowly, humbly repeating his blessing again and again. Then she turned to face the captain of the guard. "Payment for the stolen merchandise has been made. Are there further charges against this hillman, or can he be released?"

The soldier squinted; his dark brows furrowed downward at a slant. His contempt for the young princess was plain, even if unspoken. "You care not, then, that this man may be a Kazir?"

"A tortured man will admit to many things," she observed. "Rack me in your dungeons and I too shall freely swear to being a Kazir—aye, and a Hun as well."

"You mock me, my lady."

Sharon waved her hand expressively. "No, captain, I told you before: I wished only to see justice served, and now I have. Get about with your work. Enough time has been wasted on this matter."

The soldier bowed politely, her arrogance sticking in his throat like a pointed bone. "Untie the hillman," he commanded.

Without a moment's hesitation, several of his men slit the heavy cord and freed the youth of his bonds. The young man raised himself and rubbed at the rope burns on his wrists as he followed Sharon's movements with slowly shifting intense eyes. To his surprise, the royal princess held out a hand to help him back onto his feet. He reached for it, then winced when he saw the open palm, its deep lines crisscrossing from her fingers to her wrist. Momentarily he drew back, reluctant to take her hand, but then he reached for it thankfully, and for the second time during this encounter their eyes met.

"I owe you my life," he told her emotionlessly.

Sharon's face remained cold and impassive. She felt strangely drawn to this dirty-robed youth, although she couldn't say why. Something about him, though, intrigued her, something she couldn't quite explain.

"You owe me nothing, hillman," she replied. "I believed in your innocence, nothing more. But heed my warning: Tarry not too long in Samarkand lest the same fate befall you twice. This time you may not be as fortunate as the last."

The young hillman nodded, the fires in his dark eyes burning as strongly as before; he dusted off his *lungi* and stood his place, studying the girl far too boldly for a man of such low rank, and even Hezekiah's glare at his insolence did not deter him.

The crowd had all but dispersed, the holy men come again to the balconies of the minarets to issue the call for evening prayer. Hezekiah drew close to Sharon and took her by the arm. "The hour is late, my princess."

She nodded, her eyes still locked with those of the stranger. "What is your name?" she asked.

"My father called me Tariq."

"Death to the emir!"

The cry resounded everywhere. Sharon spun to see an ox of a man come leaping down from a nearby roof. Bounding from the tiles, the hooded assassin pulled a long curved dagger. Screaming, his eyes wild and ablaze, his mouth frothing with dark spittle, he spread his arms as if trying to fly and, with his loose robes flapping madly behind, lunged for the Hebrew minister.

Sharon stood-frozen; citizens were fleeing amid screams and wails and the dreaded cry of "Assassin! Assassin!"

The knife glinted in the sunlight; Hezekiah, caught off balance, tumbled to the ground as the weight of his attacker smashed solidly.

"Death to all traitors!" wailed the mullah-garbed crazed murderer.

Hezekiah rolled as the blade slashed down; the tip of the knife cut deeply into his shoulder, causing a smear of crimson to spread across the collar of his robe. Straddling the minister, the assassin pulled back his weapon and made to lunge again. Three snub-nosed arrows *twanged,* archers on nearby roofs taking dead aim; they hit with terrible impact, catching the attacker squarely in the small of the back. His curved blade tumbled from his hand; his eyes rolled in their sockets, scarlet and glassy from the effects of hashish. A low gurgle emitted from his throat as he made to choke the minister, thick hands almost closing around his neck.

The last arrow sailed a straight course and pierced through the assassin's throat. He reeled backward and sprawled dead across the ground, pools of blood oozing from the open wounds.

With the speed of lightning, palace guards were clambering all over, forming ranks three deep and scurrying from one end of the square to the other. Sharon knelt down beside the stricken Hebrew and stared at his ashen face. He was not dead—at least not yet—but in his shock he could not recognize her or anyone else.

"Seal the area!" barked a soldier. "Post more men at the gates! We don't know how many more assassins are loose!"

Trumpets were blasting in every direction, mounted palace soldiers thundering into the open, swords in their hands, horses rearing, while thousands of pilgrims and citizens began to run, insanely, mindlessly, unaware of what had happened or what was yet to come.

"Protect the princess!" someone was shouting, although Sharon could not tell who. In the blur of events, all she knew was that soldiers were suddenly all over her, shielding her from harm and protecting her person with their own lives to ensure her safe return to the palace.

She stood slowly, looking down at the blood on her hands and not realizing it had splattered across her *quamez*. Dizzily she watched as Hezekiah was tended to and carefully lifted.

"Sharon! Sharon, are you all right?"

Frantically Amrath was pushing his way forward, disregarding the efforts of his own bodyguards. She saw him and flew into his arms, sobbing. "Father, it was terrible. It was——" He hushed her and tried to lead her away. "It's over," he said. "Everything is going to be all right."

"My lord." A green-tunicked officer nearby beckoned to Amrath. "This man, this assassin . . ." Other soldiers were kneeling beside the corpse of the killer, an awesome figure even in death.

"I don't understand it," mumbled the shaken Amrath, joining them. "This man was a mullah; look at his robes. But why would a holy man have done such a thing?" Such a brutal killing defied comprehension.

"But he's *not* a holy man, my lord. Look." And the officer ordered his men to throw off the dark hood. The head was shaven, face dark and swarthy, a small jade earring protruded from the lobe of his left ear.

Amrath gasped. "A Hun!"

"Aye, lord," said the officer darkly. "A Hun spy, disguised as a holy man to deceive us."

The implication was too clear for any of them to ignore. Sharon looked at her father with the growing realization that the worst was true. Zadek had been right: Samarkand would have to fight her battles not only upon the field but also right here, against an enemy that was unseen yet everywhere—perhaps even observing them right now.

The thought made her shudder and she glanced painfully around the square as if seeking someone or something out.

"What is it, Sharon?" asked Amrath with concern. "Is anything wrong?"

She shook her head, using a bloodied hand to push her unkempt hair away from her eyes, and said nothing; but in her mind she could think only of the strange youth whose life she had saved moments before. Could he too have been a part of this plot? she wondered. Had he been the one to somehow signal the assassin while he hid from view? And was she herself partly to blame for all these events by freeing him?

She would never know for certain. One thing was sure, however: The young man who called himself Tariq was gone, nowhere to be found. He had disappeared into Samarkand's back alleys as quickly and mysteriously as he had come.

Over the darkened hills rode the messengers, a midnight ride that had begun a hundred leagues away at the border of the river. For two full days and nights the riders had made their journey, braving both elements and dangers, pushing their fine stallions to the very limit of their endurance along the gullies and ravines, across treacherous desert sands, and through the parched hills of the Steppes, where their movements were monitored continuously by bold Kazir tribesmen jealously guarding their mountain passes. Nothing must stop them; no one must deter them from reaching the city of Samarkand with the greatest speed.

Straight through Grim Forest itself they galloped, oblivious of the secret eyes that observed them closely as they passed, giving no thought to the dire warning that never must the unholy wood be crossed by night, for their message was too important. There was no time to travel the safe roads or even to pass the word along by caravan; they must reach the city sparing no haste. There was no time for meals or for sleep or for any of the luxuries men take for granted. These were dark times—as murky as the overcast skies that had followed them every step of the way—beclouded by bleak events and altramentous prediction of worse yet to come. But these noble soldiers of Samarkand gave no consideration to what had been or might yet be; they knew only that they had a duty to perform, an obligation to meet.

61

The emir must be reached no later than this very night, or truly all might well be lost.

Swiftly through the high East Gate they passed, while sentries on duty in the high towers watched, torchlight illuminating their somber faces. The clatter of iron-shod hooves was harsh against the flagstone streets as they rode past the central markets and down the tree-lined boulevards that led to the Square of the Prophet and the sacred temple. The palace walls loomed grimly ahead, ill-lit by the setting moon and the small handful of silver stars piercing through the thin layer of clouds.

In the still of the night, many a lamp was lighted. Curious citizens, wakened by the sound of trotting horses, sleepily peered out in growing trepidation. The midnight ride of soldiers from the frontier could only be an ill omen, and with wildly beating hearts they held their breath, wondering what grave news was about to be delivered.

The emir of Samárkand, aroused from a fretful sleep, walked from his private chambers and down the long palace corridors until he reached the spacious throne room. There he took his place upon the resplendent throne and tensely waited. His fierce eyes were dimmed; lines of age and worry threaded across his drawn face. His forehead was tinged with tiny beads of perspiration that glistened in the dim candlelight. Around his throat dangled a thick gold chain fastened securely in the front with a multicolored gemstone handed down by his fore-fathers, a stone like no other, symbol of both rank and title. His hands, usually powerful and steady, now trembled slightly as he clasped the armrests of his seat; his breathing had slowed and become laborious, and he looked up slowly as Amrath, also rudely awakened by the guards, came cautiously into the room. The noble took his place silently at the right of the throne, and the emir sighed deeply, painfully aware of the absence of his trusted minister and advisor, Hezekiah, who now lay close to death.

The riders strode into the room proudly, uniforms soiled and sweaty, giving somber testimony to their arduous ordeal of the past few days. They bowed low before the emir, hands in the traditional pyramid, fingers touching their foreheads. The emir stretched out his hand and bade them stand. A servant quickly offered them each a goblet filled with sweet juice which they gratefully drank before relating their news.

"I bear a message from General Le-Dan," said the first, refreshed from his drink and refusing the servant's offer of another. He placed the silver goblet back on the tray and looked at his liege squarely, his eyes tired and bloodshot. "Our forces have been defeated at the river," he began. "Le-Dan has been forced to retreat."

Amrath stared at the emir with shock. The king of Samarkand shifted his weight uneasily and beckoned the soldier to come closer. "Is that all?" he asked.

The messenger shied his eyes from the stare. A long shadow from the throne crossed over him as the emir leaned forward.

"No, my lord. The Huns have crossed into empire lands by the thousands—tens of thousands. They have pillaged every village in their path and burned every field. Many people have been butchered under the direction of this Hun king"—his mouth turned down contemptuously—"and those unable to reach the safety of the mountains have been captured and made slaves, the men to work as beasts of burden, the women to become camp followers and whores to serve the Hun army."

"And Le-Dan?" asked Amrath. "What of the general?"

"Safe for now, but our forces have yet been unable to regroup. A counterattack has still to be planned, but it is the general's hope to at least slow down the enemy advance and give you time——"

"Time?" The emir knit his bushy brows and looked at the messenger uncomprehendingly. "Time for what?"

The soldier fidgeted. He had already grieved and incurred the wrath of his liege and was reluctant to aggravate him further, but his orders had been implicit, given by Le-Dan himself: He must not hold back anything, no matter how painful it might be. "The general believes that the Huns will not be content to merely hold the lands they have taken. He expects a direct assault to be mounted immediately."

"An assault upon closer provinces?" said Amrath.

The messenger let his eyes drift to the aggrieved ambassador. "An attack upon the city itself."

The emir was aghast; it was difficult for him to control his shaking hands. "These Huns would never dare!" he seethed. "Our garrisons will be alerted across every shire and province; we'll mount a display of force that will send this barbarian army fleeing back across the river at the very sight of us!"

The look the soldier gave Amrath convinced him that the emir's hopes were at best far-fetched, at worse, the utterings of a man demented.

"At what strength has Le-Dan estimated their army to be?" asked Amrath.

The young man shuddered; he had been there at the battle, in the thick of combat, and stood his ground as bravely as any other soldier when the Huns had overrun them completely. Eight thousand men had fought the scourge, holding the heights while the Huns crossed the river in their boats and then mounted their horses. Eight thousand had been there to block the endless thrust. Now fully six thousand lay dead across the dark fields, the rest running away like cowards as the advance of the enemy only increased as the day wore thin and the long night began.

"Such numbers as I have never seen," said the soldier at last to his listeners. "They come with ten thousand

beasts and as many horses. Lumbering machines of war
follow closely behind—massive structures as high as
Samarkand's walls themselves, each with towers jammed
with dozens of archers. Their infantry has no end; thousands fell beneath Samarkand arrows, but for each who
died, there were two to take his place."

"And cavalry?"

"Wild barbarians who ride like the wind, devils on
horseback who heave glittering swords from their saddles and never once break stride."

Amrath nodded; he had been carefully following the
reports since the day the Huns were first sighted. He
knew that this brave youth had neither exaggerated nor
sought to defend Samarkand's loss with lame excuses.

The emir frowned. "You may leave," he told the
messengers. "Billet yourselves in the kitchens and be on
call. I may require that Le-Dan be given a message of
our own."

The soldiers bowed low; then, tossing their cloaks behind, they pivoted with smart military about-face and
marched from the throne room, leaving the emir and his
advisor alone in the chilled night.

There were tears welling in the emir's eyes as he
faced his longtime friend and advisor. Fear welled in his
gut and it was all he could do to stop the terrible shaking. "Amrath, what are we to do? Is all lost to us now?"

His weakness was all too apparent to Amrath; the
emir was incapable of facing the situation, at least
rationally. For almost a lifetime he had ignored the
strife and dangers that had steadily been growing like
weeds throughout the garden of the empire. Now those
weeds were about to lay fallow the land, and the emir
did not understand why. But whose fault was this?
Amrath painfully asked himself. While the emir bandied
about with his horses and his games, his toy soldiers
and his concubines, what had others done to fill the gap?

The answer was obvious and filled with regret: nothing. Like the emir, they too had soaked the kingdom, alienating Samarkand's peoples while living in a dream world of ages past, when the empire truly had been invincible. Like gluttons they had feasted—all of them—sheltering themselves within the palace walls, pretending that the world around them remained unchanged. No, casting blame upon the emir now was pointless.

The emir stood up shakily, his face as white as a sheet. He put his hands to his temples and massaged them slowly. "I . . . I must think," he mumbled. "I need time. . . . Perhaps by morning we can speak of these matters again."

"Forgive me, my lord," said Amrath, stepping in front of him, "but these matters cannot wait. Urgency demands we take positive action at once."

The emir waved his hand wearily. "No, no, not now. Send for the commander of our southern forces, if you will. Call council for noon tomorrow. But don't wake me too early; I am tired."

"But, my lord!"

Amrath's plea was ignored. The emir stepped down from his throne and shuffled from the chamber. "The Huns will never dare lay siege to Samarkand," he muttered. "The messengers were wrong. Le-Dan is wrong. He must be replaced. Yes, yes, that's it. We'll find a new general to lead our armies, and I shall be there to watch his glorious victory. Upon my boldest steed I will ride, at the very head of our forces. The banners will flutter in the wind and our people shall cheer as we pass." He turned around and looked at the mute advisor, his eyes glazed. "Alert the stableboys to have my white stallion ready in the morning. Instruct the servants to search my harem for a new woman; I'm cold tonight and have need of warmth."

And then he was gone, his muffled footsteps slow upon the stones. Amrath stood as he was and put his head in his hands. The news of the disaster had been the final breaking point. The emir had lost his mind; he was as deranged as the maddest monk, useless to both himself and the people he served.

The glory of Samarkand had come to an end.

The machines and armies of war rumbled throughout the land. With each passing day the menace of the Huns came ever closer, sweeping to the south and the west, steadily heading in the direction of the once all-powerful beleaguered city.

Panic invaded even the peaceful, serene countryside. Farmers gathered their families and their cattle and fled over every road while the Huns pushed on behind, cutting a wide swathe of terror, their advance troops ravaging all that stood in their way. Entire villages were burned and elders put to the sword, drawn and quartered, castrated before the horrified eyes of their families, bodies left to rot in dry ditches and gullies. And amid the raging, uncontrollable fires the Huns marched on, easily defeating each pocket of resistance, subjugating the pitiful survivors and claiming them as chattel in the name of their dreaded khan, Kabul the Hun, scourge of the East, a cold-blooded heathen who, in the name of his dark god Ulat, massacred the innocent by the tens of thousands.

For almost thirty years Kabul had been the bane of northern Rus, sending those tribes into bitter exile far from home while his masses carved a new empire atop the ashes of the dead left behind. Ten sons did the Hun king sire, each in the image of his hated father, each now in command of one of Kabul's ten armies. As brutal as the man whose seed flowed through their veins, they led their legions across windswept lands, pushing ever south to warmer climes, depending on force and fear to instill loyalty among the many tribes they had conquered. And this number had no end: Harmaneks and Fuliwas in the north, the brave Sunnis of the mountains of the Indian subcontinent, Luwais in the south, Devishers in the east, Ashanites as well as Mongols and the Rus themselves—all these and more, in a new empire never dreamed of that one day would stretch from the heartland of Europe to the Great Wall of Cathay. Now these armies marched upon Samarkand, crossroad of the world, city of cities, from where the evil Hun intended to rule his empire forever.

Sharon cradled the Persian cat and watched from her rooms while the city struggled to protect herself. For weeks, now, a constant stream of frightened and exhausted peasants had swelled the population of the walled city. By the thousands they had come, some from as far away as the river lands, traveling on foot in sheer desperation to keep but a single pace in front of the advancing Huns. The city was in a state of constant turmoil. With the emir locked in his private quarters and refusing to see anyone, Amrath and a few others of the Imperial Council had been forced to take matters into their own hands. The results were both harsh and unpopular, but there had been no other way. Samarkand could no longer take inside her walls all those who came seeking refuge. There was a shortage of food, of shelter, of fresh water. Cleverly, the Huns, as they pressed from strategic point to strategic point, poisoned the wells and the streams, insuring that the city was daily cut off from new supplies. Already the storehouses were half emptied and severe rationing had been imposed. Among the squalid sections of the city, where refugees squatted helplessly in the open streets, there had been reports of starvation and disase. Fanatical mullahs now openly called for insurrection and stirred much of the populace into a frenzy while the Singers of Doom proclaimed Judgment Day.

Majesty arched his back, retracted his claws, and

sprang lithely from Sharon's arms to the sun-baked stone of the balcony floor. The princess paid no heed as he hissed at a potted plant; she leaned forward, hands firm at the rounded guard rail, and peered below.

The sullen crowd outside the palace gates had turned ugly. A doom-singing mullah stood upon a flat roof, his arms raised to the heavens as he cried for the palace gates to be opened. A cohort of silent guards manning the turrets and long outer wall observed him coldly and carefully, ignoring his pleas and holding their places bastionlike to keep the crowd from pressing in closer.

The palace had become a fortress, Sharon knew, as much beset by enemies within as the city was by her enemies without, and each day saw matters grow only worse.

The shadow of a man crossed over the wall, and Sharon turned to see the silent figure of Zadek approach. The mad priest flexed his jaw at the calls of the Singer of Doom, then, toying with a silver pomander secured to the belt of his robe by a thin cord chain, greeted the young princess with the traditional bow.

It was the first time she had seen him since the night of his admitted secret. These past weeks Zadek had not left the sanctuary of his rooms once. Now he stood before her hesitantly, unsure of his welcome. Sharon could bear no hatred, though, and she smiled as she rose. "I have missed you, teacher."

Together they surveyed the city below, neither speaking, feeling the shimmering heat that rose from the pavements. A hot, sultry wind was blowing, carrying with it the dust of the distant desert, which settled thinly across the length and breadth of Samarkand. A bad omen, thought Sharon.

Zadek, in his strange way, lifted his eyes skyward and stared at the perfect quarter moon hanging like a dagger sheath above the tallest of the steeples. Beyond the city walls a great caravan had assembled and begun to move, south and eastward toward the closest frontier.

The foreign merchants had gathered their goods and wares, burdened their beasts until they almost staggered under the weight, and led them over the rugged terrain. Slowly the camels marched, trekking in a single line for as far as the eye could see.

"The rats are already deserting," observed the princess with open bitterness. Unescorted, vulnerable to both sandstorm and attack, the merchants had decided to flee rather than stay and wait.

" 'Tis better they go," replied the mullah. "Samarkand has no place for those who would not stay and defend her."

She turned to Zadek, her luminous eyes wet. "And you, teacher? Why do you stay? Surely you could find refuge among the Kazirs."

He shook his head strongly, sighing and closing his eyes. "My place is here, Sharon, as much as your own."

She drew close to him, took his callused hand, and squeezed it. "Forgive me for hating you, teacher. I was wrong—wrong about so many things."

Zadek squelched the lump in his throat. For himself there was no fear; he had already lived a long and full life. Only Allah could call him away now, and when that time came, he would be ready. But for Sharon he grieved, grieved more than he could tell her; her life had yet to begin.

Night closed in swiftly; in the distance, merely the faintest glow across the horizon, he could see the dull glow of red—the night fires of the Huns, the vanguard of Kabul's armies, now less than three days' march from Samarkand. The battle was about to begin.

For long, tense days the Hun army gathered strength, spreading its array of forces in every direction until Samarkand was completely surrounded. By the thousands the tents were set, less than two leagues from the great walls themselves. The siege was on. Maneuver followed countermaneuver. Amrath set the city's forces on full alert; towers were fortified and archers manned every meter of space across the long crenellated walls. Pitch, bail, boiling water, and other defensive weapons against the onslaught were daily carried to the highest points in the watchtowers, while the Huns slowly brought their offensive strength into full play. From one end of the vast open plain before the city to the other, the terrible machines of war rumbled into position, massive wheels groaning beneath incredible weight, causing the soil below to tremble as they rolled.

Huge towers had been constructed and fortified with sheets of iron, each tower carrying a half-dozen platforms of solid oak, connected with ladders and jammed with soldiers. One by one the towers were rolled closer, steadily moving a cautious path closer to the main gates, while the archers of Samarkand raised their bows and waited.

Then came the engines: awesome machines well tested previously in the storming of cities, such as ballistas of such sturdy framework as to support javelins three meters in length. Behind the framework were mounted flexible strips of timber light enough to be hauled back by a windlass and then released with such force as to drive the missile forward with impact enough to smash a wall a meter thick. Iron-tipped spears were hauled in wagons so heavy that entire teams of mules had to struggle merely to reach the machines.

Mangonels rumbled forward, wooden arms with spoon-shaped ends well mounted and solidly braced. The base of each arm was lashed to a crossbeam, the lashing springing the arm's action. Over the crossbars the arm would fling, catapulting forward hulking rocks of dead weight from a far distance. One direct hit would be more than enough to shatter even the most fortified turret and send it crumbling to the ground.

Flanking these weapons of destruction, the infantry marched; garbed in skins and the rough-hewn cloths of the north, they trampled forward, shields and spears in their hands, swords and throwing axes dangling from their waists. Behind them, three, four, and five ranks deep, stood the archers, each one a veteran of many long years of battle and conquest, now eyeing the fabulous city of Samarkand with growing lust. From the nearby heights, where the main camp of Kabul's army waited, the mounted troops of his legions soothed their restless steeds. Shaven-headed, ears and fingers bejeweled with riches stolen from a dozen different raped kingdoms, they too bided their time, awaiting the signal for the charge, the moment they had waited for since crossing the river so many weeks before. The prize of prizes was within their grasp: the city renowned for its wealth and power, its fame and glory, as much as for its beautiful women—Samarkand, now weakened and divided, as ripe for the taking as a pearl from an oyster. The mighty khan of Huns knew that everything he had ever desired was within his grasp. He would not surround the city; he would storm it, and issue such destruction and bloodshed that the world would shudder and remember for a thousand years to come. His troops would revel for weeks amid the spoils that waited. The people of the city would provide an army of slaves such as other kings could only dream of, while he, Kabul, would forge his dynasty. Nothing could stop him now.

Part Two:

THE SANDS OF THE PROPHECY

Dawn came pale from the eastern horizon. As the light grew brighter, it filtered softly between the yellow and still budding leaves of the thick forests circumventing the city. It was the warm sun of a late spring day that was shining; flocks of tiny birds soared high amid the soft clouds wisping by; the grasses of the fields swayed deeply with the tender breeze blowing down from the faraway mountains. This was a perfect morning, a day for strolling lovers, for ballad singers and poets to gain inspiration for their verse, for young children to romp playfully among the flocks and herds of the countryside. But this day saw none of these things. Instead, there was only the grim shadow of war spreading across the land like a blanket, the groan of machines swinging into place, the anxious blare of bugles signaling the commencement of attack.

No later than the crack of dawn had the drums begun to pound a steady beat—*boom-boom, boom-boom*—a slow, irritating cadence to which the fearsome Hun army moved. Trampling the grass, uttering fierce and frenzied war cries, they came, wave after wave of untold numbers swarming like locusts until they obliterated all. Hun commanders, shirtless, long-haired and bearded, rode their horses expertly to and fro among the ranks, swords gleaming in the sunlight as they barked directives and deployed their armies to full advantage.

The sound of trumpets blasted throughout Samarkand, heralding the moment of combat. By the hundreds her soldiers mustered from their barracks and drill fields, clambering with all haste up the stone steps to the turrets and the towers and the crenellated walls. They took to their positions, scarlet and silver cloaks rustling, bronze breastplates rattling, plumes of their helmets blowing with the wind, and gazed down in awe and respect at the full magnitude of the enemy they faced. From hill to hill and field to field they came, these tens of thousands of battle-hardened barbarians, black banners of Kabul clinging to spears and spikes alike, raised proudly in the glimmering light, tilted toward the walls of the once feared city. The host moved in steady rhythm, paving way for no man or beast as they lifted their shields from the glare and readied to block the downpour of arrows already being mounted against them.

And on came the mighty war machines; siege towers rolled across the flat, sun-baked soil, pulled by teams of rugged oxen eighty and one hundred strong. Taskmasters took to the whips, urging the oxen forward as they slashed their straps through the hot air. The beasts grunted and pressed on, cajoled and spurred by the sweaty skinners. Ballistas and mangonels were set in rows, dozens of them strategically placed before the gates and towers, missiles stockpiled beside them endlessly, grim operators ready to load and let loose the flying torrent.

From the walls, the captains of Samarkand issued terse commands to their anxious troops. With the sun in their eyes, they looked on and waited, listening with concern as the war cries grew louder and the enemy prepared to rush. From the low, grassy hills in the east the cavalry charged, three thousand horsemen tearing onto the plain, horses kicking up dirt behind, sending up swirling clouds of thick dust that all but covered their advance.

Surrounded by key aides and commanders, Amrath stood stoically at his place in the highest watchtower, peering down at the moving forces as though they were an army of ants. He looked impressive in his emblazoned robe of amber, scarlet sash around his waist, from which a small curved dagger hung loosely in its metal sheath.

Glumly the aide closest to him pressed his elbow and said, "My lord, we are ready for your signal."

Amrath nodded somberly. For a moment he toyed with the notion of sending for the emir—after all, the liege of Samarkand had both the duty and the right to be here now—but then the graying noble shook his head. The emir cringed in his rooms, kept company only by his toys and his favorite whores. Even as the empire faced final disaster he would not leave, would not face the reality before them. Bitterly Amrath clenched his teeth and said, "I'm ready, Commander. Give the signal now."

The burly soldier bowed and turned. Cupping his hands around his bearded mouth, he called to the battlements below. The cry was repeated by lower ranked officers, and within moments the trumpets were blaring once more, this time issuing the call for the defense to begin.

Thousands of long-shafted arrows sailed high over the walls, whistling down in a steady rain as they fell upon the first charging ranks of the Huns. There were screams as the barbarians fell, dozens of them at a time, quickly trampled underfoot by comrades behind. Shrieking at the top of their lungs, brandishing weapons and calling the name of their foul god Ulat, they pressed on, oblivious to anything in their way. The cavalry came roaring over the plain, thundering in splendid array, just as the deadly engines sprang into action.

Weighted javelins sang from the ballistas, surging forth like great, terrible rockets. One after another slammed against the walls high and low, many falling well behind into the city proper, where they crashed into homes and pavilions, causing widespread damage. Panic-stricken citizens foolishly bolted from the safety of their homes and ran amok, wildly screaming and wringing their hands while the battle raged all around.

Javelins ripped into towers, shredding hastily built barricades along the walls and setting ablaze wooden fortifications. Then, with even more tremendous impact, sailed the boulders, the rocks clumsily released by the spoonlike arms of the mangonels. Again and again they struck, wreaking devastation across the length of the city's defenses. Mammoth boulders smashed and crumbled masonry that had withstood the elements for centuries.

A fearful direct hit tore asunder the highest fortified tower set at the edge of the western wall, almost directly above the main gate. While hundreds of Huns came groaning forward with weighty battering rams, a flying debris of thousands of pieces of the shattered tower rained through the air, mangled men caught by surprise, with no chance even to scream as they were literally catapulted from their positions and sent hurtling like rag dolls in every direction.

"To the gate!" cried Amrath, shaken at the ferocity of the fight and the speed with which the Huns had come so far so fast.

The commanders concentrated their firepower, directing a barrage against the battering rams, while others set flame to the vats of pitch. Over the side the liquid was poured, black and fiery, spilling below like a mountainous wave. Those beneath the downpour looked up in terror. Throwing down weapons and shields, they ran like madmen to elude the burning tar. For many, though, flight was too little too late; with furs and protective armor blazing, they staggered and fell blindly, tumbling on top of one another in grisly acrobatics, wailing and moaning as flesh burned, turning their bodies into human torches.

The earth itself smoldered, then caught. Fanned by the wind, it was not long before the flames had carried to the fields and tinder-dry grasses of the plain. The cavalry was forced to turn and charge back for the hills, while all around, horses reared and whinnied in fear, incredible billows of thick, black, nauseating smoke from the pitch lifting high into the sky in terrible fumes.

But there was little cause to cheer among the defenders of Samarkand. Amrath left his post and ran down the parapet at the frantic request of one of his most trusted aides.

"My lord, look!" cried the soldier, his twisted face blackened by smoke.

It was a sight no man would ever forget. Even amid the rage of heightened battle, the siege towers still rumbled forward, inching forward in a straight line one by one, fresh archers and swordsmen boldly standing upon the wide platforms, eagerly waiting to reach the walls and rush over into the fray.

Amrath mopped a worried brow. "They must be stopped!"

Ranks of city archers were called from other posts and formed into two lines along the broadest of the walls. There they lit their own arrows and, on command of their captains, strung a line of flying fire against the approaching towers. Many were set ablaze. Huns scrambled down, climbing as fast as their hands and feet could carry them; others, balls of flame dizzily dancing about them, chose to jump instead. As they did, other archers aimed at the human targets, catching many midflight, causing them to parody new dances in the air as their limbs gushed forth blood, splattering the earth before they hit.

The war cries were growing louder, more intense. Although hundreds upon hundreds of Kabul's finest troops lay lifelessly scattered everywhere before the walls, there were still more charging barbarians than could possibly be counted. The blazing pitch had not deterred them, nor had the raging fires or even the unrelenting rain of arrows that pounded in wave after wave in never-ending succession.

The soldiers of Samarkand released their own catapults. Rocks tumbled through the air speedily, landing below with mighty thuds, breaking the backs of scores of attackers at a time. As the cries of the dying and wounded rose to a deafening pitch, the first of the battering rams reached the gate. Back it swung, then forward, slamming against the solid oak and iron braces, chains lumbering, carriers falling left and right as more pitch and boiling water was thrown from the heights. Scalded, flesh turned purple and black, many staggered and dropped, only to be replaced by more and more scrambling men seemingly coming from nowhere.

"The south gate has been breached!" came an anxious call from behind. Amrath, his eyes smarting from the smoke, turned to find a panting runner sweeping before him. "Sire, we need reinforcements," the youth pleaded. "The enemy has broken our first line; the wall has been smashed. We were forced to retreat."

Amrath swung around and arched as far over the parapet as he could. Directly below, the assault on the main gate was continuing as before, but well beyond it, near the curve of the city wall, he could plainly see cohorts of barbarians swarming through a gaping hole that had once been the city's second most important entrance. Soldiers, tunics bloodied, lay piled in heaps where they fell in stout but futile defense. And the Huns, taking full advantage of their one major breakthrough, were diverting more forces from behind to swell the ranks of those already broken through.

Missiles whistled centimeters from Amrath's head; he bravely faced them and made a quick count. By his estimation, enemy forces were entering inside the city at the rate of no less than one hundred a minute. Given just a little more time and free rein, this breach would signal the doom they had all feared, long before this morning was out.

"Every other man to the breach!" he barked.

His generals complied, but the unmasked worry in their eyes told him of the desperation of the situation. Each defender taken from his post meant that much less defense of other, still well-fortified positions.

While the battle to block the advance through the broken gate continued with renewed fury, the first of the siege towers reached the wall. Shouts of victory poured from the throaty barbarians. They swung out from the platforms, many falling at the initial barrage of arrows, and pressed along the walls in hand-to-hand combat. Burly Huns, curved swords held high, moved a wheel of death, pushing back the weary defenders, slashing out viciously and toppling them from the walls. Samarkand's troops held ground as best they could; but no sooner had they managed to somehow halt one thrust than from behind came another. More and more towers, some badly burning, were rolled into position against the walls. The Huns clambered over comrades and enemies alike, boots squeaking in pools of dark blood that stained the entire length of the walls.

Iron balls slammed helter-skelter, poking more and more holes in the defensive structure. Fire arrows darted into the thick of sweaty bodies. Hun archers kneeled in lines, shooting freely, not caring that they were now hitting as many of their own men as the enemy. Another catapult sounded; this time a major tower beside the main gate was squarely hit. Its masonry erupted outward with tremendous force, those within sent reeling backward, smashed against solid rock. The air howled with the sounds of the javelins and boulders and iron balls. Direct hits upon the populated centers of the city sent women screaming through the streets, sheltering their infants as roofs collapsed on top of them, walls crumbled, and raging fires consumed house after house, streets and markets and mosques.

Sensing quicker victory than they had expected, the sons of Kabul came riding through the breach, sword arms held forward, blades pointed in one direction only —the palace itself.

Wounded soldiers were trampled underfoot by the bold steeds as they vainly tried to stop the charge, but it was a useless gesture; the cavalry, rerouted well away from the burning fields, had circumvented the strongest positions entirely and come surging through the open gaps. Citizens recoiled in horror at the sight, dashing for some unknown protection as the Huns recklessly cut them down, giving no thought to the innocent.

Against his will, Amrath was dragged from the fiery watchtower and, surrounded by aides, pulled away from the wall to the last bastion of Samarkand's strength. Down to the inner wall they escaped, barbarian axes flying all about. There a pitiful remnant of the proud army stood fending off wave after wave of rushing Huns. The main gate gave, its doors sent hurtling off their hinges. Like the wind came a thousand Huns, bloodstained and grimy, eyes crazed, minds bent on plunder and rape.

"The palace," rasped Amrath, yanking the sleeve of the nearest commander, "we must defend the palace."

The soldier grimaced with the pain of his wounds and looked at the brave noble evenly. "We cannot, my lord. Even were we to try and force our way——"

In his anguish and frustration, Amrath pulled away from the wounded commander and jumped to the steps of the battle-scarred parapet, pulling out his dagger. In his mind he had one thought and one thought only: to somehow make his way to the palace and save his daughter.

With a wild scream, cleaving an ax, a broad-shouldered, hirsute barbarian tore down from the top of the wall. Amrath dodged his flying blade barely in time; the tip of the ax grazed his ribs. Paying no heed to the deep crimson stain spreading over his garments, he plunged his dagger with an upward thrust into the attacker's heart. As the Hun pirouetted and doubled over, the valiant lord bolted down the bloodstained slippery steps and made his way to the open street.

Everywhere was mayhem as he fought a path to reach the smoke-filled Square of the Prophet. Hun cavalry came charging by, mindless of his presence. Thin white billows were rising from the temple dome, and he realized that the enemy had already taken the square as a first position in storming the palace. With a sinking heart filled with grief, he knew that the assault upon the solid walls of Samarkand's heart would begin any moment. There was so little time for him to get there first. . . .

He whisked around, falling flat to his stomach as a sword-wielding horseman cut a low swathe with his blade, missing him by inches. Amrath rose slowly to his knees, then to his feet. Screams were filling his ears as he dumbly pressed forward, vowing that while a single breath yet remained in his pain-wracked body he would continue on, face whatever was necessary to reach Sharon and save her.

Corpses of women lay coiled at his feet, butchered after they had been raped. Through the smoke and haze he could see crying children bending over their mothers' remains, and old men, noncombatants but useless to the Huns, lying spread-eagle on the cobblestones, faces twisted in gruesome death masks, hatchets and snubbed arrows protruding from their backs. Bloodied and ragged citizens ran amok mindlessly, calling out pitifully as they dashed between the flames and advancing troops. It was an awful sight, the worst Amrath had ever seen. With a sigh of despair he blotted all these atrocities from conscious thought as he stumbled forward, the pain in his side growing worse.

A handful of slain palace soldiers lay before him; he gagged at the sight of their slit bellies and decapitated heads. One he recognized, a youth conscripted into service by Hezekiah, the son of a longtime court ally and friend. Amrath wept openly, wondering why God had decided to take such terrible revenge upon Samarkand. What sins had been so shamefully committed that the once glorious empire should be reduced to such waste and rubble?

From a distant roof, a hidden Hun archer raised his bow and fired. When the arrow hit its mark, Amrath froze. A burning sensation crawled from the back of his neck and down to his legs. He could not move; paralyzed he stood, hands feebly reaching to pull out the dart embedded in his spinal cord. The dagger dropped from his grasp and tumbled hollowly to the ground. He still did not seem to know what had happened; he tried to move forward but found the world spinning dizzily around him. His eyes frantically searched for the dome, the golden dome of the magnificent temple that rivaled the holy one of Mecca. Double images danced before him as he slid to the ground.

"Sharon," he mumbled. "Forgive me. I did . . . my best. . . ." And then he felt nothing, not even the searing heat of the fire as it encompassed and consumed him.

The roars of the invaders continued. Resistance at the broken walls had all but ended, the last gatherings of defenders being systematically isolated and killed. Then, as the afternoon sun blazed at its height, through the smashed and twisted main gate came the king of the Huns himself: the mighty khan, Kabul, stoic and fearsome in his horned helmet, powerful arms tanned and golden, red beard flowing halfway down his swollen chest. He rode upon a fine white Arabian stallion proudly, reining in the snorting horse as he crossed over the smoldering piles of rubble and ash.

His followers wildly cheered his presence, inspired by their lightning victory. They raised their blood-soaked weapons and shouted his name over and over again. Kabul smiled grimly; he lifted his own brilliantly shining scimitar and howled like a jackal the name of

Ulat, dark god who had delivered unto his tribe this glorious day.

Charred and limbless bodies were trampled underfoot by the khan and his flanking sons. They laughed lustily, clasping one another in gleeful embrace, victoriously marching through the smoke-filled streets where humbled citizens of the world's most fabulous city stood in chains.

Kabul halted, looked about at the carnage, then fixed his stony glare to the front. Behind him the machines of destruction were being rolled inside the gates. "To the palace!" he cried. "And let no one survive!"

The attack on the palace had so far lasted well into the early hours of morning, the palace guard doggedly giving the invading hordes the fiercest resistance they had yet encountered. Red-hot light from the flaring flames slashed against the high, gray, thick walls, pushing back the glowing night. Fiery javelins still sailed overhead, grim, death-stalking missiles tearing across the sky until they hit their mark. The teardrop towers were a shambles, loose stone crashing down as though from a volcanic eruption; steeples and domes were bathed in leaping flames, each shooting higher than the one before it, sending servants, slaves, and wounded soldiers scurrying from one end of the enormous compound to the other in a frantic effort to save their lives.

Shivering with terror, Sharon clutched her arms and stared as the familiar walls, so safe, so protective, now gave way under the blows of iron balls and boulders. A hail of arrows crashed into the double windows, sending slivers of glass flying through the air. Around her, troops hit the floor while servants huddled tightly together, weeping, as the carnage came ever closer. To the tallest spire she and other members of the royal family had been led in the search for safety; but now even this last stronghold was about to be overrun. Outnumbered and exhausted, the last of the palace guard had made a strong stand along the throne and chamber rooms, manning the walls and guard posts up to the lofty tower zenith. From here any who dared look could see the immensity of the wreckage and the slaughter.

She pressed herself tightly against the wall as another arrow slammed past the torn curtains and hit against a tapestry, sending it askew. The floor was littered with fragments of glass, smashed vases, crumbled stone.

"We've got to find other shelter," the wounded captain of the soldiers told them.

Sharon dared a quick peek from the open window, shuddering at the sight of a cohort of barbarians clambering over the walls of the garden below—her garden, now a blood-soaked battlefield where scores of defenders lay scattered and unmoving. The brave soldiers had taken their positions stoutly, a desperate last attempt to at least keep the inner chambers free; but it was as futile a task as trying to hold back the tide of the ocean. The Huns had already domineered their way into every building of the compound save this one, and it was only a matter of time until they captured it as well.

A last defender cried out from the garden; Sharon saw the hatchets bury into his chest, saw him cartwheel backward and sprawl across the rosebushes.

The ceiling shook; thunder like an iron ball crashed into the chambers directly above. Panicked, Sharon spun and dived for the balcony just as the upper floor gave way and crashed down on them all. The defenders and huddling servants were instantly buried beneath mounds of rubble, many instantly killed, some writhing to free themselves, softly moaning.

Sharon crawled on her knees. She put her hand to the side of her face and felt something warm; blood was trickling from the corner of her eye. She stood up shakily and picked her way across the room. A hand stuck out from the piles of stone, fingers beckoning. By the time she was able to reach the injured soldier and clear away the debris, he breathed his last breath. Tears filled her swollen eyes. There was nothing she could do—not for him, not for any of the others, not even for herself. Crying, she stood up again.

There was moaning from somewhere behind her, and she turned to see a hand emerge slowly from the smashed brick, fingers crooked and bleeding. She ran toward it and frantically worked to clear away the fallen wreckage. At the sight of the bloodied face she gasped. The old servant recognized her and tried to speak, but she hushed him and helped him to stand. Noises were coming from the balcony. A barbarian had climbed up from the garden and was hunkered atop the wall, peering into the destroyed chamber. He saw her and grinned.

The old servant blindly stood in front in an effort to protect her. "No!" she cried. In the blink of an eye the Hun drew back his arm and flung his ax. The blade wheeled and ripped through the servant's neck, sending him spinning.

Sharon screamed; her attacker laughed with the fire of lust raging in his dark eyes. He came forward, drawing a knife from his belt. Sharon turned and ran, not daring to look behind. The folds of her draped dress encumbered her as she struggled over the rubble, lungs choked with dust. She broke past the shattered doorway and came panting out into the open corridor. It was deserted and silent, an eerie ghost of its former self. Doric columns stood cracked and groaning, the walls and ceiling slowly caving in; the tiled floor was cracked, and braziers lay where they were knocked over by servants in flight, causing tiny fires to smolder in every direction.

Down the grand, opulent hallway she raced as fast as she could, knowing her pursuer to be close behind. Heart thumping savagely, she dashed dumbly to the darkened hall at the left, close to the imperial chambers of the emir. At the recess of an arched entrance she stopped to catch her breath, not looking back but hearing the heavy trampling of boots. Behind a torn curtain she took refuge, sweat glistening over her golden skin, and bit her lip hard to squelch a scream.

The Hun paused in his search. Through the shadows she could see his silhouette dimly. He toyed with the knife, squinting as he examined the corridor in an effort to discern which way she had come. He started one way, then inexplicably turned, heading closer to her. Sharon shut her eyes and prayed: *Merciful Allah, don't let him find me!*

Lizardlike, from a black chamber across the hall, a hiding servant scrambled. The Hun saw her and gave chase. The woman tripped over a smoking brazier and begged for mercy. The Hun laughed loudly, threw her to her knees as she tried to stand, and then pushed her far into the shadows so that no one could see.

Sharon's flooded eyes could not bear to look. While the frightened servant girl moaned and pleaded, Sharon discarded all thoughts of somehow trying to save her and, ignoring the tightening knots in her stomach, bolted from the curtains, following a twisting stairwell to a low level of the imperial chambers.

A single torch burned in its sconce. These rooms were as silent and foreboding as those above, only here the maimed corpses of several palace soldiers blocking the way gave grim testimony to the fight that must have taken place only moments before.

Sharon swallowed hard and fought down her terror. The Huns were already loose, probably combing the palace chamber by chamber. She knew she had to find someplace to hide.

A weapon, she thought; *I need a weapon.*

But there was nothing. A fallen soldier still held his bloody sword; Sharon lifted it and groaned with the weight. Too heavy; she could never use it. She brushed aside loose hair wildly falling in front of her eyes and felt the pin that clipped her hair at the nape. She pulled it loose slowly and sighed. The gold pin glimmered in the darkness, its tip as sharp as a razor. It wasn't much, but at least it was something. She grasped it tightly in her right hand and started to move forward again, cautiously stepping into the shadows.

She was more afraid than she had ever been in her life, only this time there was no one to call to help. She was alone—totally alone in a world gone insane. Where was her father? she wondered. Still upon the battlements, struggling to keep the city alive? Or had he been captured, perhaps at this very moment facing a torture worse than death? *Death*—the word made her shudder. Was Amrath already dead? She shook her head and pushed down the thought. No, he was alive, probably looking for her at this moment, coming to rescue her and whisk her away. Deep in her heart she knew this wasn't so, knew it to be only a frightened girl's prayer; yet it was something to cling to, a ray of hope in an abyss of darkness. Only that thought kept her going.

Long minutes passed in total silence. Nowhere was safe—nowhere. She had to keep moving. . . . She reeled around at a peal of sudden laughter. Then she froze, her eyes adjusted to the dim light. At the very end of the hall a door stood slightly ajar, needle-thin streams of light spilling out into the corridor. She drew a deep breath and took a single, agonizing step closer. The laughter came again, shallow, strange.

Huns? Or something else?

One part of her told her to run, to flee from here as quickly as her legs would carry her. But something else gnawed, an instinct assuring her that this was not the enemy; there was no need to panic.

The door was only paces away. Crying was mixed with the peculiar laugh now—deep sobs, a voice curiously familiar. Drawing courage, Sharon went to the entrance and kicked the heavy door open wide. Brightness flooded her eyes and she shaded them with her hand; then she looked inside—and gasped.

The room seemingly had not been disturbed. On the thickly piled rug sat a man cross-legged, back arched forward, face grinning like a court jester's; if he saw her, he paid no attention. In his hands were several gaily painted toy soldiers, one holding a sword, the other a chain and spiked ball. The man played with the toys in mock combat, hitting first one, then the other, and making low sounds of make-believe battle. When the head of one toy was lopped off clumsily, the man roared, then began to cry.

Filled with despair, Sharon stepped farther inside the chamber, stopping beside a brightly burning brazier. "My lord!" she cried.

The emir of Samarkand turned around slowly, lifting his chin and staring at her coldly. "Who are you?" he demanded. "Who brought you here?"

Sharon gulped and curtsied respectfully. "My . . . my lord," she stammered. "Don't you recognize me? Sharon, my lord. Daughter of your cousin, Amrath . . ."

The emir twitched his nose. "Amrath? Amrath? Oh, yes—our ambassador. How is he? Does the Persian court delight him as I suspect it does?"

Taking another step, she gazed into the emir's eyes, noticing that they were glassy and reddened. "My father has not been in the Persian court for more than three years, sire. You recalled him yourself. Don't you remember?"

The emir frowned and sighed. He waved a hand in the air imperiously. "Detail, detail; why must I always be bothered with such trivial matters? And what are you doing here, anyway?" His gaze became more quizzical, more strained.

"The fighting, sire. Surely you know——"

"Fighting? Yes . . ." His mouth turned down distastefully. "Leave," he commanded in a regal tone. Sharon backstepped. "Go on!" he shouted. "Get out! Get out!"

"But, my lord, you are not safe here. The enemy has

invaded the palace; your guard is no longer here to protect you."

Her words must have triggered something within his fever-racked brain, for the emir of Samarkand suddenly covered his face with his hands and began to weep openly, unashamedly, deep, unbridled sobs. He looked at Sharon between his fingers and asked, childlike, "How did this happen, Princess? What is going to become of us?" And as he moaned in his agony, his head bobbed up and down uncontrollably, like an apple in a barrel of water.

Sharon lowered her gaze respectfully, pained to see the once mighty emir appear before her like this, an empty shell of a man. "We must flee at once, my lord—seek some hidden shelter where we won't be found. Come with me, sire. Perhaps together——"

He shook his head sorrowfully, resplendent crown askew. "It . . . it's too late for that," he sniveled, trembling.

"But there's no other choice, lord. Please . . ." She held out her hand for him to take and he stood slowly. His shoulders sagged; the torture in his face was pitiful for the girl to look upon. "Then all is lost," he said, sighing. Lifting his face to the ceiling as though to the sky, he said, "Am I to be found and captured by the barbarians, dragged before this king of Huns like a dog in chains?"

There was noise from outside; Sharon could hear muffled calls of enemy troops as they raced the length of the labyrinth of hallways. Every minute was precious, she knew—every second. To delay was to be found for certain. "We must leave, sire—*now*. Follow me out."

"No!" the emir said, stamping his feet, his voice echoing across the chamber. "I shall not run away!" He spread out his arms grandly. "This is my empire! I am the emir!"

"There is no empire!" flared the young princess.

"Look about you, sire. Are you blinded to the truth? Samarkand has been taken; we are a people defeated."

"Liar!" She jumped back as he pounded a fist into an open palm. The madness had overcome him again; he was no longer rational. "Never will I leave!" he raged, spittle sputtering from his lips. "Do you hear? Never! Speak to me not of it!"

She lowered her head. "No, my lord, I shan't." Her voice was a whisper. The trampling of boots was getting closer. She could help him no more.

The demented liege of the all-powerful city grinned broadly; he bent down and picked up his toy soldiers and played with them as before, acting as though nothing had happened, as though she were not even there.

Anger surged through Sharon, uncontrollable and instant. She wanted to grab him, shake him, beat him, throw him out of his world of make-believe and force him to see the shambles that remained. While he had played games, the city had burned, had been overrun and destroyed. Didn't the fool understand? The empire was smashed. His life had become as meaningless as her own. They were both trapped, trapped like drowning rats on a sinking ship.

Her mouth was dry, her hands wet with perspiration. She shut her eyes to clear her confusion and felt her body shake. Then she turned and walked back to the bleak corridor, suddenly no longer enraged, not even caring if she was found and captured.

"I no longer hold you responsible, sire," she said. "The guilt belongs to us all."

The emir was smiling, lost in his crazed thoughts. "Send in the servants," he commanded to no one. "Hurry; I think I shall bathe before I take my ride."

Sharon kicked aside a velvet cushion blocking her path and stared into the gaping blackness of the corridor. Which way? she asked herself. Which way——

The shove sent her sprawling. As she lifted her head,

she gasped; she was looking directly into the face of the Hun. It was the cruelest face she had ever seen: grim, pockmarked and scarred. Thick brows of devilish scarlet slanted over mean, desperate eyes—intelligent, filled with animal cunning. The man wore a breastplate dented from the tips of Samarkand arrows. His frame was awesomely powerful; he seemed as big as a tree and strong enough to yank one out of the ground by its roots. A nerve twitched malevolently in his cheek as he laughed loudly, taking his hand from the hilt of his bejeweled dagger sheath and running it along the side of his red brush mustache.

He glanced briefly at the emir, then faced the girl again. Sharon felt his eyes pour over her; a purple tongue ran over cracked lips while he admired the suppleness of her exposed thighs. She pulled the hem of her *khafti* down to cover her legs, and the Hun laughed once more.

"Who . . . who are you?" stammered the emir.

A golden tooth glinted as the barbarian sneered. Moments later another Hun stood behind him, this one as large, only older, with a flowing crimson beard.

"See what I have found, my liege," bellowed the first intruder, gesturing toward both captives.

Unspeaking, the second Hun strode boldly inside, his eyes reflecting the dim light like hot fires in a pool of black. He pulled off his leather horned helmet and dropped it to the floor. "You have done well, my son, very well indeed. I shall have to reward you most grandly. Name your prize."

The younger man grinned and bowed. "I shall find something worthy, Father," he replied, his gaze still upon Sharon. She turned away and cringed.

"Be gone!" cried the emir. "I did not send for you! I don't even know you! Are you from Le-Dan's army?"

At the question, the two Huns roared. The older man pressed his face close to Samarkand's liege. "I have waited a long time for this moment, *Emir.*" He said the title with open contempt. "For years I have dreamed of it."

The emir frowned at the stench of his breath. "Go away," he said, fondling his toys. "I have no need for you. Find quarters in the barracks."

Kabul, khan of the Huns, looked at his eldest son and winked. "But, sire," he mimicked, mockingly bowing low before the liege, "I have traveled so long to meet with you, to give you my gift . . ."

The emir's eyes widened; he stared at the fearsome barbarian like a small child. "A gift?"

"Yes, sire, something for you to play with, to keep and appreciate."

"What is it?" The emir seemed no longer frightened, only curious.

Kabul lifted a jeweled dagger from his belt. The gems sparkled in the light, sending cascading starlike images across the wall. The emir opened his mouth and gasped. "The blade is for me?"

Kabul nodded gravely. "Aye, sire, for you and you only." And he lifted it for the emir to see.

"No!" screamed Sharon. "Don't do it!"

But her words fell upon unhearing ears. As the emir of Samarkand opened his palm to receive the gift, the king of the Huns swung back his arm and brought it up sharply, the blade tearing through flesh, ripping straight through to the emir's lungs. Kabul pulled the blade out with a single stroke; the emir gurgled, stared. He stood frozen in his place, blood dripping from the side of his mouth. Kabul pushed him lightly and sent him tumbling backward, where he fell dead across a pair of twin black-laced pillows. Then the king of the Huns spat on his corpse.

Sharon, hands to her mouth, whirled and started to run. Kabul's son put out an arm, blocked her passage through the door, and sent her reeling against the wall.

Kabul laughed. He wiped the blood from his blade onto the emir's fine robe and sheathed it, then looked over at the girl; she was trembling from head to foot.

"What shall I do with this one, Father?" His own knife glinted unevenly. Sharon huddled in the corner, eyes wild with fright. Mutely she waited for the king's answer.

"A woman should never be bruised," Kabul chastised. He lifted the collar of Sharon's *khafti,* exposing a purple welt from where his son had hit her. His eyes examined her like so much horseflesh. "Do you like her, my son?"

The mustachioed barbarian frowned. "Too delicate, Father. See, her skin is white as milk beneath her robe. Her back will be weak, no good for working the fields."

Kabul's mirth grew. "You have no refinement, Osklath. This woman is of the court, a lady of quality. She must be treated as gently as a flower, otherwise she may wilt." And they both chuckled.

Sharon squirmed, sickened by the feel of his dirty fingers pressing up and down the nape of her neck. She flinched when his hand slid lower, glancing over the firm skin of her breasts. Kabul's mouth curved upward with desire. Osklath, watching intently, slitted his eyes. "Perhaps you were right," he growled. "Give the woman to me."

"Not so fast," rejoined the khan.

Sharon drew back, feeling her terror increase like a sharp weight in the pit of her stomach. She had the sensation that none of this was really happening to her, that it was all a nightmare, a terrible nightmare from which she could not force herself awake; but it was real, all too sickeningly real.

Kabul yanked her forcefully by her hair. "My son has taken a liking to you," he hissed. "Would you prefer him first—or me?"

"I'd rather be *dead!*"

He pulled her to her feet, ripping the fabric of her *khafti,* and propelled her forward, thrusting her into the now open arms of Osklath, whereupon the barbarian began to maul her. Sharon wrested to break free, but it was no use. Osklath held her in his viselike grip, his head lowered, his thick lips wetly kissing her neck. She pounded at him with her fists and kicked wildly. Osklath howled as the toe of her shoe bruised his shin. "You Arabic vixen!"

The back of his hand slammed across her mouth; she moaned and staggered backward, blood trickling onto her laced dress.

The chisel-featured king put his massive hands on his hips and guffawed with delight. "A wildcat, this one. Be careful, my clever son. Are you certain you want her? A woman like this will take a firm hand to train."

The younger man seethed with anger, outraged and humiliated by this palace bitch, made to look the fool in front of his father. His lips pursed with froth and he glared at the shivering girl with clear hatred. As she gasped, he made to draw his knife. "I'll teach you manners, Samarkand whore," he vowed, stepping toward her.

Sharon pulled away, desperately searching for someplace to run. There was a small doorway at the far end of the room, behind the thick curtains. If only there was some way to reach it; but Kabul stood in the way, unyielding.

Osklath juggled his knife from hand to hand, pacing her slowly, faking stabs and cruelly laughing when she whirled backward. The blade lashed out, missing her face by mere inches.

"Don't scar her!" bellowed the khan. "Do you want to see her ruined? Then she's no good to anyone."

"But she insulted me!"

"Bah!" The king spat at his son's boots. "I trained you well to be a warrior, to kill men; taught you to hunt, to fear no man and no beast, but I regret never having taught you more about women. You disappoint me, Osklath."

The younger man reddened at the rebuke. "One day, old man," he hissed, and the venom in his eyes was unmistakable. The rivalry between the khan and his eldest son grew more intense with each passing season.

Kabul swelled his chest in a stance that dared Osklath to turn the knife on him. "Issue your challenge, *boy* . . . if you think the time has come."

Their eyes locked, neither man flinching. Slowly, though, Osklath began to waver. Kabul towered over him, twice his age but still with the strength of a mountain bear. The younger man sheathed his weapon with a scowl.

More noise came from the corridor, first the running steps of Huns, then a few low, distant screams. Sharon knew that other palace guards or servants had been found and put to death.

"Leave us," rasped Kabul. "Go; find your brothers, secure the palace. I want no man left alive by dawn. Take the women, bring them to the courtyard, and divide them equally."

Osklath looked suspiciously at his father. "And this one?" His eyes darted to Sharon. "You intend to keep her for yourself?"

The king made no reply; a severe warning crossed his features, one that told his eldest son not to press him further.

Osklath hesitated, then crossed his hands over his chest as he bowed. Then he turned around and strode in a huff from the room. The moment they were alone, Kabul faced Sharon again. His tongue ran lightly over dry lips and he snapped his fingers. "Come here."

The girl did not move.

Kabul looked at her sharply, forcing her eyes to stay fixed with his. She was terrified of this man, frightened as she had never known fear before; but, at the same time, she found herself almost hypnotized by his cold, piercing eyes, transfixed, unable to turn away no matter how much she tried.

The khan sensed her inner turmoil and, seeing it as a passive surrender, grinned with pleasure. He put out his hand, fingers tightening as he grasped her bare shoulder. The fabric of her *khafti* hung limply over her supple breasts.

Somewhere in the recesses of her mind, she knew that this was his way of deliberately taunting her, proving his prowess and her own weakness to stop him. She heard herself stammer, "If you touch me, I'll kill you."

Kabul tilted his head, amused greatly by her boldness. "I enjoy a woman who fights," he whispered. Then he chuckled. "Perhaps the emir"—he glanced at the corpse, so frail, so effeminate—"was more to your liking? Half a man instead of a whole one?"

"Haram'zada!" she spit at him. Son of a bastard!

He grabbed her by both arms, pulling her fiercely toward him. His eyes were burning into hers now, callously, like black fires, but his voice remained even, almost soft. "I can do with you what I want, Samarkand tramp—make you my concubine or my slave, give you to my sons, let them share you with the captains, even throw you with the other women, the whores who service the lowest of my soldiers. Is that what you want?"

Sharon pulled to break free, tears streaming down her cheeks, hair wildly tossing as she struggled. Kabul, his desire risen to its most heightened pitch, ignored her whimpering pleas for him to stop and forced her closer, his hands sliding down her arms, clamping them at her side. Then up against his firm body she was taken, stifled and suffocated by his smell, his brute weight, the feel of his mouth harsh upon her own. She compressed her lips, shaking her head. His hand squeezed at the sides of her mouth, forcing it open so that his tongue could ravish it. With all her effort she fought to push him off, but he remained as solid as a rock, unyielding, hard, mocking.

He threw her to the floor roughly, peeling off his armor before she could regain a single breath. Off came his furs, his belt, tossed haphazardly to the side. Slightly slitted Mongol eyes glared at her appreciatively. His breathing was heavy and laborious, the bulge of his manhood thick against the cloth of his breeches.

Then he was on top of her, immobilizing her with his weight, laughing while she cried out when his foul hands caressed her, insolently squeezing her breasts, his mouth closing over her nipples, teeth hurtfully sinking into tender flesh. His legs pushed hers open; he pressed all the harder as she squirmed and sobbed, crying with her shame, her fear, her loathing of both him and herself. She clawed at him with her fingernails, causing long, needle-thin cuts to crisscross his back. But Kabul was by now too immersed in his lust to pay any attention to her writhings.

She screamed loudly, a shriek that echoed from the chamber and down the dark hallway. He had penetrated her, robbed her of all virtue, disgraced and shamed her forever. His body heaved, lunged, attacked. She shut her eyes and moaned. The pain was excruciating, like a terrible fire racing through her loins into her belly and through her entire system, and anguished wails issued from her throat. Still he showed her no mercy, no pity. His thrusts became faster, sweat gleaming over his hairy body. His heartbeat pounded against her own, two wild drums, one in the throes of ecstasy, the other in abject horror.

"I'll kill you!" she cried. But the khan of the Huns paid no attention. She was helpless against him, a lamb against a wolf. Sharon clutched her hands together, feeling suddenly numb. A sharp pain dug into her palm and she winced. The hairpin! She still had her weapon!

Kabul's shoulders began to shake with fury. A low, gurgled sigh came from his throat, and he swelled in the joy of his savage pleasure. Deeper he thrust, but only momentarily; then he sagged, fulfilled and spent.

In that split instant between ecstasy and reality, Sharon was able to wrench herself almost free. As the khan rolled his head to the side, away from her, Sharon brought her arm up high, holding the golden needle like a dagger. With all her strength and courage she thrust it deeply into his right eye, pushing it clear through the pupil and past the optic nerve. The eye instantly contracted into a bloodied mass, spouting crimson, oozing from the socket like a river and staining his chest, her *khafti,* and the floor.

He screamed an unearthly scream, a terrible wail of excruciating agony. Dazed, wild with the convulsive lancination, he tried to scramble to his knees, his hands to his face. The pin was deeply embedded, stuck right through the soft matter inside his skull, and he couldn't pluck it out no matter how much he tried. He rolled about insanely, flailing his arms and moaning in unmitigated misery.

"My eye is blind!" he howled like an animal. *"I can't see!"*

Sharon hoisted to her feet, shocked by what she had done. The mighty king of the dreaded Huns groveled at her feet like a dog, aimlessly tossing to and fro. On the floor, blood spread in small pools and streams, racing through the cracks in the tiles. Kabul groped to grab her, cursing, frothing at the mouth. He cried for his sons, then for his generals and captains, finally for anyone, anyone at all, to come and release him from his agony.

There was clamoring outside; his men had heard the pitiful moans but had yet to find from which of the hundreds of chambers they came. Numbed, Sharon watched him suffer; but the clatter of boots growing louder snapped her back to reality. And the knowledge of what she had done hit home. If she were caught, if Kabul was to name her as the one . . . The consequences were too real to contemplate. She shuddered at the thought of the tortures she would have to suffer.

The hidden secret chamber behind the curtains!

She had to get out, and get out fast. She bolted over the motionless body of the slain emir and across the chamber. Kabul's shrieks rang in her ears, his wails becoming louder. Past the drapes she pushed, reaching wildly for the brass catch, turning it and flinging the door open.

She found herself in another hallway, this one also dark and extremely narrow: the emir's secret chambers —a labyrinth of dim corridors and rooms that led deep down beneath the palace to the drainage system and catacombs. As fast as she could she ran, her own pain intensifying. Confused and exhausted, she passed the hall, dived into a tiny closet of a room, and paused breathlessly. She could still hear Kabul's cries. He had already been attended; the shouts of stunned barbarians calling out to one another assured her of that. She clutched at the terrible soreness between her legs, wincing at the smears of blood staining her dress. He had hurt her, more than she realized; she could barely stand, much less walk or run, but what choice was there? She must not be caught—at least alive.

She filled her aching lungs with the dusty air and darted back to the hall. It angled downward, first gently, then sharply. Silent and dim, these chambers made her more afraid than ever. She pictured herself being cornered, trapped by surging Huns running wild after her, and a low scream escaped from her throat. Shaking, she took hold of the rusting handgrips embedded in the cracked walls of stone and pushed herself forward, ever forward, hoping to find some invisible corner where she might rest and tend her wounds.

Advancing Huns had already found the hidden doorway and were now leaping and bounding through the corridor, darting into every room, every recess, every archway in their effort to seek her out. And each and every one vowed an oath to find this girl, find her and bring her back, for she had done to their khan what no man on the face of the earth could have succeeded in doing.

Sharon followed the course, her eyes barely adjusting to the light. It was cold, strong drafts of wind pushing down at her from ancient air vents somewhere above. She wrapped her arms over her breasts and continued on. Shouts behind were growing louder, the march of boots closer. Ahead, the passage divided. Without thinking, she ran to the right, not knowing which level of the subterranean chambers she was on. After a few moments she was forced to stop again; once more the hallway divided, this time into three more passages, one darker and more dismal than the other. She chose the darkest, thinking it the safest. Footsteps raced off to the other side; she knew that the Huns were continually being forced to follow in smaller numbers as they searched every one of the entrances.

I'm going to make it, she assured herself. *They'll never catch me here. I'm safe. I'm going to be safe.*

Strong hands grabbed her from behind and pushed her down. She started to scream, but her attacker blunted the sound by thrusting his fingers into her mouth. Sharon bit hard, trying to force him to free her. He didn't, though; instead, he wrenched her head backward and spun her around, his frame pinning her against the wall. Sharon sobbed; she had been caught! After getting so close, she had been taken!

The man's breathing was loud; he held her pinned, not speaking as she lowered her head and sobbed. It seemed like forever until she stopped crying, although it had been only a few moments. Then she lifted her face and dared to look at her captor. His own eyes gazed deeply into hers and she gasped. She knew that look; she knew those eyes, brooding, dark, tranquil.

Sharon put the back of her hand to her mouth and whispered the name, "Zadek."

The mad mullah stood silently, observing the girl with startled eyes. He stared at the stains and rips in her soiled *khafti,* grimacing at the thought of what must have happened. Sharon felt uncomfortable under his knowing gaze; she leaned back against the wall, inhaling deeply until her breathing flowed smoothly.

Zadek put his hands on her shoulders and smiled. "Allah be praised! I never thought to see you alive again, child. How did you manage to escape?"

Her eyes flickered wetly and her voice started to crack at the memory of the brutal scene. She went into as little detail as possible, but the mullah gasped loudly with unbridled shock when she related what she had done to the king of the Huns. He slapped his hand at the side of his face, brows lifting almost to his scalp.

The young princess, shamed and fraught with despair, nodded gravely. "It's true, teacher. I had to do it; there was no other way."

She was crying again, and Zadek took her into his arms. "Hush, child. It was Allah's will that you escape from this brute. You did only what fate had long ago ordained."

"But when they catch me, Zadek——"

"They'll not catch you, Sharon. They'll not find either of us." He peered darkly over his shoulder. Down the bleak passage came the soft dripping of water into pools. They were well below the last palace level, on the edge of the dark catacombs—secret chambers long in disuse, constructed centuries ago by men whose names and faces had long been forgotten.

"I know these tunnels," said Zadek somberly. "There is a way out of the palace, leading beyond the walls and into the city streets. Your forefathers used them long ago to slip away unknown, and for us they shall provide our best escape from the city."

Sharon looked up at her companion with disbelief. "But the Huns have captured everything. The city is burning, people are running wildly to flee from the waiting chains——"

"All the better to give us cover. But come; we must be gone from here swiftly, before dawn, before we are missed." He took her hand and urged her away. Sharon hobbled with pain as he led her quickly along the slanting corridor and deeper inside the chilly shaft.

The tunnel reeked with the foul smell of palace sewerage seeping slowly into the drainage channels at the nearby shallow river. As they ran, the heavy resentment of her bitterness gnawed at her; the thought of Kabul's evil seed implanted in her womb sickened her. She was unclean, forever unclean, and no bath, no soap, no warmth or love would ever wash it away. She was scarred by the king of the Huns every bit as much as he had been scarred by her. And in that strange way, their two lives would somehow always be entwined—a deep and acrid hatred that would follow them both till their dying day.

A hawkish wind was cruelly blowing from above, catching in the shafts and whipping to a frenzy. Zadek removed his cloak and put it round the shivering girl. Wordlessly, eyes grimly studying the black world of the catacombs, he brought her from one shaft to the next, crossing places where no footsteps had passed in generations. Rats squealed and fled between their legs as they hurriedly ran; finely spun cobwebs tickled at their faces; hideous water bugs, all but unseen in the shadows, scurried over muck and slime-infested walls of damp rock. And all the while it became harder and harder to breathe.

How long they had been running, Sharon could not tell. All sense of time had been lost within the confines of these foul catacombs; but the echoes of chasing soldiers rushing through the tunnels had long since ceased. She well knew the veritable maze they were in, one from which there might be no escape at all if Zadek chose for them the wrong passage even once. More than one hapless soul had been lost here and doomed to death in these gloomy quarters, as the crumbling skeletons about gave grim and positive proof.

Zadek, though, seemed to be as sure-footed as he was swift, never once faltering or even hesitating no matter how dim the passageway. He had been this way before, Sharon knew. He was familiar with each and every turn and twist, every nook, every cranny, every cesspool. But for what purposes the mad monk had been here before, she could not say, nor did she dare to as much as hazard a guess.

Down, down, downward they ran, on and on without a stop. Breathless and aching, at the next turn she tugged at his sleeve. The mullah looked over his shoulder at the girl. Her eyes begged him to pause, to let her rest her wounds if only for a moment, but Zadek would have no pity; he roughly grabbed her and forced her on until she kept up with him by sheer will alone. Of strength, there was none left.

Ever farther, ever deeper, ever colder; soon the last glimmer of light was completely gone and they found themselves thrust into a world of absolute blackness. Clinging to Zadek's tunic, Sharon held her breath while the monk stretched his arms out stiffly before him and, with groping fingers, felt his way inch by agonizing inch, groping for hidden obstructions. The wind was still whistling, the kind of sound that had always aroused fear in the superstitious servants. For a long while she wondered if Zadek had lost his way, as his somber face turned only more dour with the passing minutes and no evidence of light ahead.

His voice was a thin whisper, like that of a ghost or *nightthing*, when he turned to her at length and said, "Walk softly, girl; we're almost there."

Her hands and feet were numb with the terrible cold; she nodded at his words, all the while blowing hot air from her mouth across her fingers. She looked about slowly, carefully. Zadek took a single step in front of her and stopped. "This way . . ."

"How do you know, teacher? I can see nothing."

She could make out his sly smile, the glow of his strange eyes. "Nor I . . . but listen carefully."

She strained her ears; no sound came. She was ready to question him again when the first distant noise shattered the eerie silence of the labyrinth. An animal in pain? The cry was ghastly to hear. Or perhaps some demon from the bowels of Grim Forest? At this point Sharon was about to believe anything. But no, the sound was all too human; it was the cry of men—tortured men in pain, dying upon the rack slowly while their backs broke and limbs were crushed.

Zadek put a finger to his lips and bade her follow carefully. Soon the screams were closer and now too the shouts of crowds. Sharon listened with anxious trepidation. She could imagine the mobs of panic-stricken citizens rushing helter-skelter through the streets above in a desperate attempt not to be caught, not to be rounded up and herded like cattle by the rampaging, slave-taking Huns.

Zadek took her to the end of the tunnel, where the concave ceiling lowered dramatically and a new shaft to the side slanted sharply upward. The monk raised his head to peer into the darkness above. "There is an open sewer beyond," he told her. "It leads past the Square of the Prophet, beyond the temple. With luck and darkness on our side, we might yet break free of the palace compound and reach the Lower City streets."

Sharon bit tensely at her lips. Breaking out from these tunnels would be a welcome relief, she realized, but to what end? Every alley of the Lower City by now was crawling with looting Huns bent on taking as many slaves as possible. No one could hope to be safe in the open streets, and she told him as much.

Again the mullah gave her one of his mysterious smiles. Saying nothing in reply, he took her hand—more gently this time—and led her up. Suddenly the air was becoming thick; they both began to cough loudly. Wisps of heavy smoke had filtered between the slats of the grating and were lowering to the tunnels. A red glow brightened the passage, and Sharon saw that Zadek was leading her into an open inferno of hell itself, where blazing whirlpools of fire were whipping through the once beautiful Lower City.

Covering their faces with open hands, they stopped at the wide grating roughly dug into the earth and peered up toward the street. Huge tongues of flame seared above. Nearby, there was screaming and pleas for mercy as trapped residents of the quarter cowered from the heat that was about to envelop them.

"We can't go out there!" cried Sharon.

"We must wait," answered the mystic. "In minutes the fires shall pass; only rubble and charred ashes will remain. Then we can make our escape."

Sharon found herself shivering with chills despite the wash of perspiration broken out over her abused body. The nightmare was still far from over; in many ways she fully understood that it was just beginning. But Zadek had been correct again, though. The flames of the flash fires were sweeping above in a frenzy, now fueled by sultry gusts of wind, whirling down the war-torn streets with dizzying speed and color, orange and yellow changing to amber then crimson as they whipped along the byways and crossroads, searing the magnificent edifices of stone, statues of marble, and cobblestone pavements, only to die among the valleys in deep shades of indigo and dancing purple. Within the space of a few heartbeats the once busy street was still and empty—empty save for the heaps of smoldering bones and the blackened walls of the temple.

Zadek wrung his hands in rage and extended his arms upward. His neck popped with blue veins as he heaved at the well-fitted grating, grappling with all his strength to loosen it from its place. The iron grille, slightly bent out of shape, was scalding hot from the heat of the fire. Zadek's eyes slitted catlike, and he groaned softly as he pushed and pushed again. Sweat poured down his bony face; Sharon could almost feel his pain as the heat burned his ill-protected hands. With all his effort he pushed again and this time the grill gave way, leaving a space barely wide enough for a man to crawl through.

"Quick! To the street!"

Fixed in her crouched position, Sharon stared at his hands; they were badly blistered, the flesh raw and bleeding between his fingers.

"I'm all right." Zadek grimaced.

"No, you're not! Your hands——"

The mad mullah's mouth turned down distastefully. There was no time for the niceties of tending to wounds, only the dire urgency to get out of the tunnel and out of the city—fast. "My hurt can wait, girl," he snapped, openly angry. "Now, do what I tell you!"

Sharon gulped. "Yes, teacher."

"Wait for me." And with agility that astounded her, the gray-haired priest of Islam pulled himself up and out, leaping to his feet as easily as Majesty had ever done. His swollen hand reached down into the space as he bent toward her. "Take it! Hurry!"

She did as he asked, not daring to question. It was a struggle; the hem of her dress caught on the twisted grill, the fabric singing and smoking as she yanked herself up. Zadek pushed her to the ground and doused the small flames; then he pulled her beside him, and the two lonely escapees from the palace looked about in awe. Their faces were cast in scarlet shadows spreading from the nearby raging fires across the Square of the Prophet. Everywhere they looked, charred corpses, faces in the shuddering death-mask smile of the dead, greeted them. Sharon drew back, frightened. Zadek put his pain-wracked hand on her shoulder, urging her away. "Come," he said softly. "Do not look too long at the carnage."

She shied her gaze from the awful sight, nodding, her nostrils filled with the burning stink of death. "What now, teacher?"

He grasped her hand fiercely. "Come."

Over grisly remains of fallen citizens and enemy soldiers they bolted, picking a path between the rubble and hulking forms of dead and dying mules and horses, riderless, sprawled hither and yon, flesh aflame and foul. As the stricken animals writhed and moaned, the predators had already begun to circle above. Sharon looked up at the sky; tens of dozens of large vultures glided, waiting for the opportune time to descend. The carrion were illuminated in their flight, not by the glow of stars or moon, but by the reflection of the fires, the terrible licking tongues of flame that had encompassed the famed teardrop towers and steeples.

They scrambled away from the broad bypass, beneath the desolate series of arches that led to the public plaza. Beyond the smashed and twisted gate stood the high wall of the temple. A hundred and more palace guards lay dead across the length of the parapet, and a handful of laughing, looting Huns were already busy robbing the corpses of whatever struck their fancy. They wrenched rings from fingers and displayed the plumed helmets of Samarkand's crack guard proudly, tossing them about like toys, hurling bodies over the wall and roaring with glee as the mangled corpses smashed onto the stone streets below.

A few stray dogs barked and scurried out of sight witlessly. From the distance sang the trumpets of the enemy, announcing to all their forces that the day had been won. Zadek paused in his tracks momentarily and pulled Sharon behind the largest of the crumbling arches. They cowered in the shadows.

"What is it, teacher?"

His hand roughly fell over her mouth. As the sound of trumpets grew louder, her eyes widened. Up the street, passing right before them, came a cohort of mounted Huns. Stern-faced, bloodied, but riding proudly, they heralded the advance guard.

Zadek lifted his gaze toward the heavens and sighed deeply. Tears rapidly fell from his tired eyes and rolled down his cheeks, washing away some of the grime. "The war is done," he mumbled sadly. "There is no more resistance. Kabul reigns."

His words weighed heavily on Sharon. For all she had seen this bitter day, no matter what the event or what she had been eyewitness to or partaken in, it was still too incredible, too unreal to believe. But in her heart she knew it was true: Samarkand, her beloved home, home to her family and ancestors, was no more. In its place stood little but hollow ruins of the world's most beautiful city, ruins of what had been the center of a mighty empire. But from these ashes and corpses, she knew, another Samarkand would arise, alien and barbaric, the new capital fortress of Kabul and his hordes, from where he would govern his blood-soaked domain.

The hoofbeats of horses clattered slowly, echoing as they passed through the line of arches. Behind them, bound with rope and chain, staggered a hundred or more captives—women mostly, faces ashen and blank, eyes swollen from crying but crying no more, now fixed straight ahead and staring into empty space. Sharon gasped at the sight, feeling overwhelming pity and grief for these young girls and mothers who had already been brutally beaten and raped, had watched helplessly while their husbands and parents were put to the sword, and now were forced to face a life of misery as slaves to the conquering army. Slowly the gang of prisoners passed, urged to move faster beneath the taskmaster's whip.

"Is there nothing we can do to help them?" she asked as they disappeared into the shadows.

Zadek shook his head, and Sharon said no more.

Dawn was getting nearer, and the mullah knew they must make their move before first light. He half dragged the frightened girl away from their hiding place and they dashed as fast as they could to the battle-scarred wide boulevard. From here, with luck, they could reach the old bazaar, a tangled cluster of houses and twisting alleys from where they might be able to elude the Huns a while longer. Twice more as they ran they were forced to seek shelter, fleeing more soldiers, these on foot as they crossed the avenue in search of spoils. Some held high the black banner of Kabul, others long spears, the heads of slain Samarkand soldiers firmly affixed to the tips.

The roving bands were rampaging at random, barging into every home, looting and pillaging, drunkenly sacking everything in sight, putting to the torch the small houses when they were done. Sharon and Zadek watched as a young girl was found hiding in a basement, dragged into the street kicking and screaming, raped, and then butchered. Sharon could no longer look; with trembling lips she buried her face and wept, Zadek unable to comfort her.

At length the avenue was clear again, and while the Huns moved on, laughing and shouting, Zadek pulled her to a nearby alley. It was pitch black, the high walls on either side well protecting it from the light of the fires. Blindly they rushed to the rear, hoping to find a low wall they might scale. Suddenly Sharon stumbled; at her feet lay the body of a young child, a girl not more than eight or nine, in a pool of blood.

A figure jumped from behind; Zadek spun, drawing his curved dagger. The silhouette made to run, and the

mullah tackled him from behind, pinned him to the
ground, and brought up his dagger.

"Please, no!"

Wide, frightened eyes stared up at him—the eyes of
a boy. He was shivering under Zadek's weight, his arms
and legs thrashing in an effort to break free.

"Please don't kill me!" he cried. "Spare my life! Take
me prisoner!"

Sharon shared a quick glance with Zadek, and the
mullah relaxed his hold, putting away his knife.

The boy was surprised. "You'll . . . you'll let me go?"

Zadek grimaced. "We're not Huns, boy. No harm will
come to you. But who are you? What are you doing
here? Speak quickly!"

The boy lifted himself slowly, eyes darting back and
forth between the priestly-garbed man and the tattered
girl. "My name is Asif," he said, wiping dirt off his
hands onto his ragged shirt. "And I was hiding here all
day with my sister."

Sharon turned to the lifeless girl. "Was she your
sister?"

Asif nodded. "Yes, my lady. We fled our home after
the Huns breached the walls, and came here before
darkness fell, hoping that the enemy soldiers would not
pass this way."

With a frown, Zadek said, "But they did?"

The boy hung his head on his chest. It was then that
Sharon noticed that his black, curly hair was matted
with dried blood from an oozing wound across his scalp.
"They found Iona first," Asif said quietly. "Two roam-
ing barbarians, drunk with honeyed wine. Iona tried to
run, but it was too late. Before I could protect her,
they . . ." He did not finish the thought; the frail body
gave evidence of the Huns' brutality. Then Asif smiled.
"But they paid for their crime, I promise you," he told
Sharon. He pointed to a dark doorway near the edge
of the alley; inside lay two bodies, each with its throat
slit from ear to ear, one straddling the other.

Zadek's heart grieved deeply for the boy, and he put his hand gently on Asif's shoulder. "It was a brave act, boy. Your father would be proud of you if he knew."

"But he will never know, will he?" And Asif began to weep.

"Where is your father?" questioned Sharon. "Your mother?"

Asif looked up at her, his urchin's face marred by the scars of this bitter day. He was no more than eleven or twelve, Sharon saw—an age when he should be learning a trade, playing games with other boys his own age. Instead, the youth had seen his home destroyed and his sister ravaged and had killed two men to save his own life—a heavy burden for one so young.

"My father is dead," he said softly. "I don't know what happened to my mother—perhaps dead also, perhaps taken prisoner. There was no way for my sister and me to reach her when the fires began."

"I understand," said the princess. She held out her hand for him to take, and Asif did so reluctantly. Then he pressed himself against her and sobbed. She kept him close, his face buried against her breasts, and ran her fingers through his hair. "We have much in common, Asif," she whispered. "You and I have both lost everything we had this day. We are both orphans."

Zadek turned to Sharon, his nervousness increased by the sound of running boots and raucous laughter from down the street. "We must not tarry, Princess. Time is precious."

Sharon nodded; she took the boy stoutly by the shoulders and forced him to look at her. "Listen to me, Asif. You cannot give up hope. My companion and I escaped the palace just as you escaped your home. Stay low; keep hidden as long as you can. Maybe Allah will smile upon us both."

Asif nodded with understanding of what she was telling him; then, as they turned to leave, he blurted, "Can't you take me with you?"

Sharon turned her eyes to Zadek, but the dour mullah seemed reluctant. "Having the boy with us shall make our efforts all the harder," he said. "Alone we could travel more swiftly——"

"And leave him here to his fate? No, teacher. Let him come. Perhaps together we can find a way out of Samarkand."

There was a pleading in her eyes that Zadek could not deny. He glared sternly at the hopeful boy. "You will do everything we tell you?"

With a single bob of his head, Asif agreed that he would.

The mullah smiled. "Very well, then. Come, we're going to try and slip past the enemy troops in the bazaar."

"You must not go that way!" cried the boy. "The area is being used as a gathering place for the slaves."

Sharon grew tense. "Are you certain of this, Asif?"

"I am, my lady. I saw it with my own eyes."

Zadek sighed; he folded his arms and gritted his teeth in despair. "Then we are lost. The bazaar affords the best way to the city gates. Without it we have no chance."

Here Asif smiled a knowing smile, one that told his companions it was wise of them to let him come along. "I know another way out," he said boldly.

Zadek's brows turned downward with skepticism. "What way?"

"From the eastern market."

"We'd never make it," scoffed the mullah. "From my tower room I saw the market aflame. It will burn for days."

"Perhaps," agreed Asif. "But what if we were able to *ride* our way through it? The eastern gate will take us to the dunes, a place where the Huns could never hope to catch us."

"He's right," said Sharon. "The desert gives us our best chance."

A sour grin parted Zadek's cracked lips. "A good thought, my friends, and I agree completely. But, to pass the fires, we shall need the best horses we can find, and where are we to get them?" He put his hand on his hips and sighed, looking at his companions like a teacher chastising well-meaning pupils. "We can never make it."

"*I* can find us horses," announced Asif.

A huge fireball ripped across the sky, sending off shooting stars to light up the night. Beneath the roar, Zadek said, "You? But how?"

Like a thief adept at his trade, Asif bounded from his place, leaping high enough to grasp the slanted roof of the nearest building. Then, pulling himself up, he crawled to the top, positioning his legs firmly against the tiles. "Come and see for yourselves," he called back; and he laughed while the monk and the girl hoisted themselves up and slowly worked their way to his side.

From this height they had a panoramic view of all that was happening in the Lower City. To the east, as Zadek had said, fires were raging; but off to the north, where the palace walls converged with those of the square, the Hun army had begun to gather its weary horses, hundreds of them, all corralled in makeshift stables, ill-guarded by only a handful of grumbling troops eager to leave their posts and join in the pillaging of their compatriots.

"What do you say?" said the youth with a wink. "Stun a few of those guards and we can take our pick of their calvary."

Zadek leaned forward, shakily balancing himself against the crumbling tiles. It would not be as easy as the boy made it seem, he knew. They would not only have to ride safely away, but also have to elude the rear guard of soldiers billeted on all sides of the eastern quarter. Dodging Hun arrows would be only half the task, for then they would have to ride straight through those flames, ride like demons before they were en-gulfed. Still, Asif's idea afforded a chance for breaking out of the walls—a slim one to be sure, but the only chance they had. Staying put was even worse. By day, the starkness of light would make their escape impos-sible. If they were to risk it, they would have to do so now—ask no questions, shut their eyes, and ride like the wind.

He looked back over his shoulder at the pensive girl straddling the slanted tiles. "What do you think?"

To his surprise, Sharon showed no fear. With a tiny smile, the first he had seen, she said, "Let's go."

Sharon's whole body ached as she stood hidden beside a gutted doorway, waiting for Zadek to give the signal. Smoke, as it had been all night, was rising into the night sky in thick columns. Before her, mere shadows themselves in the darkness, tired horses shook their manes and wheezed. Only a few soldiers could be seen guarding them. As the Huns had little to fear, there was no need to station more than a few; besides, with the sacking of the city still under way and far from complete, there were not many men to spare for such mundane work.

Zadek crawled on his elbows around the shed, lifting himself inch by inch. His eyes at the level of the low wall, he gazed from one end of the closed-in compound to the other. It was quieter than he'd expected. A few of the soldiers were already in a drunken stupor, snoring on their bellies, fallen to the ground right at their posts. As for the others, they marched back and forth dutifully, hands at the hilts of their swords, tiredly watching the silent streets. Occasional laughter or the ruckus of a brawl was the only sound to break the monotony, and they itched for the moment they would be relieved.

The sentry closest heard faint sounds when Zadek dashed to the far end of the wall. His slightly slanted eyes narrowed in speculation, and then he smiled when a stray dog appeared from a nearby alley and barked at him. What he did not know was that Asif had positioned himself upon the roof, and when he came leaping down, his bloodied knife in his hand, the unaware Hun did not

121

even have time to whirl around and face his attacker. The blade glinted in the pale light as it cut downward through shirtless flesh. The sentry grunted and fell clumsily to the ground. Asif deftly withdrew the blade and, to make sure his prey was dead, slit his throat in the same manner he had the two who ravished his sister.

Like the crack of thunder Zadek bolted up over the wall and charged behind another watchful sentry. The shuffle of the monk's boots made him turn, and he lowered his hand to his sheath. The blade never made it out. Zadek, with a single motion, jumped to the side off balance, arched his back, and threw his dagger in an underhand motion. The blade *thrushed* through the air, right on the mark. Startled, the Hun careened and staggered where Asif was already waiting to do the rest. The orphan dragged the body from the path, grinning.

When Zadek whistled softly in the call of a nightingale, Sharon came running from the doorway. She pushed the gate open wide, grabbed the bridle of the closest horse, and expertly mounted the saddleless steed. The mullah had taken a gray gelding and was leading him to the gate. Asif chose a spotted mare. Then, urging the horses on with quick heel jabs to the flanks, the three fugitives stormed past the gate, releasing all the other horses.

From every direction, stunned by the breach, guards came running, swarming like ants from their posts. Arrows and axes sailed and quivers were emptied; but, by the time the riders had reached the end of the street, it was too late to stop them. The horses thundered over cobblestone toward the markets and the fires, zigzagging, bounding across mounds of rubble and smashed wagons, dodging the whistling shafts that darted by their heads and slammed fiercely into the stone walls behind.

A frantic call to arms was issued; responding to the blare of bugles, drunken and dazed Huns mustered to give chase; but their horses were running wildly and freely by now, bounding along the empty streets in every which way.

Toward the billowing clouds the fugitives rode, right through the searing flames, leaping over burned barricades, charging with heads low in the direction of the eastern gate and the dunes beyond.

Amid the havoc the panicked horses tried to break free; only the sure and steady hands of the riders kept them from rearing or bolting, even as the heat intensified and the animals could barely breathe.

Asif led the way, his mare pushing on wildly while licking fingers of flame tore at her flanks. Only paces behind came Sharon, the young princess whipping her stallion with the reins. Last came Zadek. The priest kicked out and sent a charging Hun tumbling over, his face crashing onto the rough cobblestone. A line of Hun archers were kneeling ahead taking aim. Behind an overturned wagon, they held their bows taut. Just as Asif's horse scaled the wagon, their arrows sang through the air. Sharon plummeted ahead, bravely facing the onslaught. She could see nothing before her save the shifting flames dancing over the roofs. Hoofbeats clattered in her ears; she was dimly aware of shouting as enemy soldiers turned to run and give chase.

Then through the wreckage of the gate Asif passed, beneath the ornate arch and out beyond the thick city wall. Sand swirled everywhere, blinding him as, glancing backward, he tried to see if the others had made it as well. A terrible commotion arose from behind; Huns upon the parapet of the crumbling wall let loose a torrent of snubbed darts. Hundreds littered the sky at once, all sinking deep into desert sands well away from their mark. The sky was growing clearer; Asif could see the stars. The fires were more distant now. He slowed his exhausted horse to a canter, and when he looked around again, he smiled: Two more horses were tearing across the dunes, passing the smoldering hulks of burnt and smashed war machines, catapults forbiddingly still with throwing arms still in place, the cool night sands running red with blood from fallen barbarians scattered everywhere. The two black silhouettes rose and fell with the mounds as the riders evaded arrows flying from the walls, and soon they were out of range, like Asif, well away from the terror that was Samarkand, with nothing but open desert before them for as far as they could see.

A shade of blue dawn greeted them by the time they reached the waiting Asif, and with not a word passed between them they pressed on, Zadek in the lead, horse tracks quickly disappearing as the wind of the desert blew.

They followed the old caravan route for a time; then, as the sun rose high and the heat of day began, they shifted their course to the north. From the heights of the dunes they could look back and see the city hazily in the distance. A thin pall of dark smoke cast an ugly shadow across the perfect blue sky; the shattered walls and towers stood like skeletons against the horizon, and Sharon bit her lip to stifle more tears at the sight of her home—the home to which she could never return.

The riders paused along the ridge of the tallest dune, each staring glumly at the city, each lost within his own thoughts and memories. Still no one spoke; there was no need for words. Into a long and bitter exile they had been thrown, with no shelter or safe destination. For a hundred leagues in every direction the Huns would claim the land, and the fugitives knew full well that Kabul would never rest until the princess who had maimed him was caught. They must flee and hide, seeking refuge wherever it might be found, always with uneasy minds and eyes forced forever to look behind.

Ahead stretched nothing but desert, majestic in its quiet beauty of ever-shifting golden sand. Far off to the west, they could almost make out the line of the smoky hills and the vast shadow of the feared Grim Forest.

Sharon sighed. She shifted her gaze from the city of Samarkand for what she believed to be the final time and bravely turned to the thoughtful mullah sitting silently upon his weary horse. "Where are we to go from here, teacher?" she asked softly.

Zadek lifted the hood of his *aba* over his head and shaded his eyes from the glare of the sun. Northward, sweeping away across the length of the horizon, stood the range of low mountains, red in the morning light— rugged, harsh lands, but the only territory of the conquered empire still free of barbarian rule. His eyes were glassy as he stared long and hard at the range. It would be a long and most difficult journey to reach it, he knew. They would have to cross many leagues of parched, waterless lands, carrying no food or water save for the small waterskin, half empty, that dangled from his belt, and with no guarantee that even should they cross the desert successfully, they would find the shelter they sought. Quite the contrary was true. Still, there was nowhere else to go.

"We must travel to the north," he said at length.

Sharon's brows rose. "To the Steppes?"

"Aye," replied Zadek with a somber nod. "It is the only place we can go, the only chance we have of never being found—north to the Steppes, to the home of my mother's people, to the mountain fortress of the Kazirs."

Above the rise they could see the vultures, hundreds of them, circling high over the sand dunes, squawking, diving below to feed.

The riders stopped their horses and stared. It was a grim sight. The birds, the terrible stench of death carried on the wind—both contributed to the uneasiness of the fugitives. Zadek dismounted and handed the reins of his steed to Asif. With the back of his hand he wiped away a thin layer of sand from his mouth and, exhausted, began to climb to the zenith of the rise to peer down below. "Wait for me," he told his companions. Then he walked off slowly, stumbling at times, until he became a tiny figure at the top of the mound. He stood there for a long time, and Sharon shared an anxious glance with Asif.

"I'm going, too," she said, and before the youth could reply or try to stop her, she had eased herself off her horse and begun the uphill trek. Knee-deep in sand, she negotiated the hill and came silently to the mullah's side. Together they stared below. Sharon stifled a gasp: Hundreds of bodies—men, animals— lay littered in a gully, grisly vultures feeding on the carcasses.

"The merchant caravan," mumbled Zadek with a scowl.

Sharon recalled it well, thinking of that day, just before the battle, when the foreign merchants had fled Samarkand in hopes of reaching Persian territory before the Huns came. Their corpses proved that they never made it.

126

Zadek glanced from one end of the gully to the other. Tents, torn and shredded, flapped noisily in the wind. There were campfires scattered about, dried camel dung heaped in piles within them. Servants and masters lay side by side; hundreds of barbarian arrows stuck out of the ground in every direction.

"The Huns must have attacked by night," said Zadek with a frown. "See; the caravan was bedded down."

"They never had a chance," whispered the girl, as she pictured what must have happened—the cooking fires barely lit when, like locusts, the barbarians came sweeping over the dunes. No one, nothing was left to live to tell the tale, only the despised carrion joyously feeding from the massacre, and now them—three forlorn fugitives desperately trying to cross the desert, who had come upon this foul battlefield by accident.

"I'm going down there," said Zadek. "Perhaps we'll find something, something we can use."

The people of Samarkand were a superstitious folk, and Sharon was shocked to hear the mullah so dryly speak of walking among the dead. Many would have called it desecration, the work of *nightthings* or heathens. Yet, she also knew he was right. Perhaps there was something of value to them—food, water, weapons —something that could aid them in their dangerous journey. It was taking from the dead so that they might live. And so it was much to Zadek's surprise that the princess said, "I'm coming with you."

The vultures flapped their wings and soared into the sky at the sight of the intruders, leaving the desolate merchant camp once again in total silence. The wind seemed to whistle like a demon as they crossed the camp, handkerchiefs held over their faces to blot out the stench, and slowly began to rummage through the scattered litter.

Most waterskins had been pierced by arrows or ripped by knives, their precious liquid long since evaporated into the sand, but Zadek did find a small one hidden beneath a fallen beast of burden. He took it in his hands and sighingly thanked Allah for at least this much. He almost didn't hear when Sharon shouted to him from the opposite end of the site.

"Teacher, look!" she was calling, almost gleefully.

Zadek, hurrying to her side, almost had to laugh when he saw the two camels feeding from debris behind a dune that had kept them out of sight. They chewed slowly at their meal, hardly blinking as the mad monk grabbed their bridles and pulled them back to the gully. "We have been blessed," he said to Sharon with true humility. "With these desert creatures to carry us, our journey shall be completed."

The saddlebags on the beasts were packed with food, blankets, and a handful of small tools. The waterskin one carried was nearly full, in itself almost enough for the entire trek to the Steppes. The mullah lifted his gaze to the heavens and said a silent prayer. Fate had played a strange trick, he realized; it was more than mere chance that had brought them here this day. Their safety had been all but ensured by divine will; that there was no other explanation he was certain, only why he and Sharon had been bestowed with these gifts, he was unsure. But there *was* a purpose, even if he did not know it—a reason why they alone were spared and all others had perished.

They gathered together all they could find and, leaving the exhausted horses behind, left the camp and continued on, Zadek and Asif upon one camel, Sharon upon the other. When they were well away, and the bitter-cold desert night had finally replaced the day, they finally stopped, for the first time in nearly two days. Beneath the panorama of ten thousand glittering stars in the velvet sky they ate and rested, talking sparingly, contemplating what the future might hold.

And then they fell into a restless sleep, mindful of the hardships that still waited.

The sun was scorching, the heat intolerable. Faces covered, they pressed on, and with each passing hour the stark red mountains of the feared Steppes came that much closer. The camels worked their way up and down the difficult terrain, taking them unhaltingly over routes rarely traveled. They crossed wide open valleys where the land beneath their feet was rocky and parched, land where rain was seen less than a handful of days every year. During the afternoon hours, when the sun was at its hottest, they rested again, rubbing at aching muscles, napping, making themselves comfortable as best they could. Then, as the day began to wane, they started the journey once again, traveling in the cooler hours of evening and long past sunset. During the entire time, they had not once caught sight of a Hun patrol—good news, perhaps, but they held no illusions that Kabul's men were far behind. It was Zadek's only hope that they could reach the Stronghold of the Kazirs before the enemy did.

It was well before noon of the next day that Asif first noticed the peculiar darkness obliterating the sky—not clouds, he soon saw, but dust, thick, swirling, carried by forceful gusts of sultry wind. A desert storm was heading straight in their direction. Within minutes the wind was scourging like rain, lashing at them like whips, blinding them, drenching them with billions upon billions of tiny particles of powdery, rough-grained sand. The dark fury of the storm grew only more fierce; they could see nothing at all of the terrain that surrounded them. Going on was futile; they knew they must stop. Quickly they dismounted, holding the reins of their camels firmly, huddling together between the lumbering beasts as best they could. The sky above became lost, and by dusk they could see neither the moon nor a single star. Shouting above the din of the wind, Zadek called for them to stay perfectly still, knowing that to step merely a pace away from one another could separate them forever.

It seemed like an eternity until the standstorm passed over. The howl of the wind was terrific, a gruesome screeching like the cry of the damned, and Sharon shuddered with the frightening premonition of evil. Slowly, though, the wind abated, gusting frenziedly across the dunes, carrying the storm out of sight. The fugitives lifted themselves from their places and peered about.

The scape of the desert had radically altered; new mountains stood in silver moonlight where before there had been ruts and valleys, and at the places where there had been only flat tablelands now stood dunes. The map of their desert world had been totally changed; only the menacing peaks of the Steppes remained in place as before—huge monstrosities, unbending against time and elements, a stark reality that not everything was different.

"We must not lose more time," said Zadek, ignoring the painful itch of his flesh caused by the pounding sand.

Sharon nodded knowingly; she pushed back wildly tousled hair and took the reins of her wheezing camel. The dromedary dropped to its knees and let her mount; then, with the others behind, she moved on, awed by the silver glow of the modified landscape. And this time they rode straight through the night, cold as it was, not once pausing to rest until well after the crack of dawn and the new sun hung like a ball of flame in the east.

Days passed painfully slowly, as though they had embarked upon a cruel and never-ending odyssey. The red-hued mountains of the Steppes were well-defined shapes by now but always teasingly out of reach, no matter how far or fast they traveled. Late that evening the riders came to an oasis. The swaying palms seemed more a mirage in the crimson shadows of the setting sun, but the oasis proved no illusion, and, thankfully, they reached it just as the chill of night began. In the morning, they washed themselves of sand in the placid, clear water of the pond, stuffed their saddlebags with fresh dates, replenished their waterskins, and rested beneath the leafy branches of the palms. Then they moved on again, refreshed, with renewed zeal and hope.

By the fifth day of the arduous trek the sands of the desert had started to recede, bit by bit but surely. Scattered signs of weeds and other vegetation had here and there begun to poke out from the rocky, hard soil. Soon they were climbing in elevation, along hills barren and difficult, passing trees with trunks long since dead and withered, now bent grotesquely out of shape by both weather and time. A little more than a day later, Sharon excitedly pointed and laughed; rabbits appeared from a hole and scampered across a field of pale, yellowed grass. And beyond the field, there were real trees, alive and healthy, full-budded leaves dangling and swaying from thickly barked branches.

Zadek dismounted and looked about. Up in the crevices, feeding from weed at the heights of nearby hillocks, stood wild mountain goats, animals that had long ago adapted themselves to this land of outcasts. For the first time since their ordeal began, the mullah permitted himself to smile.

He glanced over his shoulder, gazing at the extensive dunes, alluvial plains and depressions, and heaved a sigh of relief. The saline soil at his feet told them that they still had a long way to go, but at last they had crossed the desert and stood upon the threshold of the Steppes.

Turning back to the bare hills, his eyes intently followed the winding course of a wadi. "Beyond these scrublands we should reach the first Kazir village," he told his companions knowingly. "Best we make all haste. Kazirs look doubtfully upon strangers who enter their lands after darkness has fallen. It is one of their customs: A welcome visitor arrives only in the brightness of day."

Sharon felt her brief moment of elation suddenly vanish. So painful had been her ordeal in escaping from Samarkand that she had given scant consideration to what might happen at journey's end. Now, as she looked at the Steppes before them, betoum and jujube trees lining the crests of the red hills like silent sentries, she was thrown back into unwanted reality.

Kazirs, she thought with a small shudder; the very name still roused fear inside her. This was the traditional enemy she had been taught both to loathe and to respect. In Samarkand, death was the immediate sentence for any trespasser caught inside the city walls; she wondered now if perhaps the Kazirs had a similar law for her.

The gravelly voice of Zadek broke through her troubled thoughts. "There is no need to be frightened," he assured her, as if reading her mind. He climbed back into the saddle, his camel chewing on a saltbush. "We have much to barter with the tribesmen; our knowledge of the Huns and their khan in exchange for Kazir hospitality."

"I hope you're right," mumbled Asif.

Kazirs, it was said, were renowned for their gracious cordiality to friendly strangers—surpassed only by their cunning and wrathful treatment of those considered to be enemies. Zadek pondered these two extremes; then he scowled, dug his boot deeply into his dromedary's flank, and urged the beast forward.

The bottom of the brilliant crimson disk that was the setting sun barely touched the peak of the highest scrub hill. Sharon leaned forward in her saddle, hand tightly clutching at the leather horn. Along the crevices of the rocky hills at either side, a handful of stray sheep were feeding. At sight of the strangers, the sheep scrambled away, prancing over the heights and behind

the trees. She pulled in gently at the reins, and the
camel's bridle jangled. Then she stood in the stirrups
and peered around slowly, thinking it certainly curious
that these sheep had run freely, with no shepherd or
sheep dog to keep them close to the herd.

"How far to the village, teacher?" she asked.

Zadek shared her open uneasiness. He indicated beyond the next hill. Without another word, they started
up again, trudging toward the crest. As they went over
the rise, the fugitives were greeted by a small, fertile
valley nestled tightly between lumbering hills, flaming
scarlet in the evening light. Past clusters of fruit trees
and furrowed fields they could see the village, a horse-
shoe arrangement of stone houses with thatched roofs,
guarded by a low wall on one side and the face of the
rocky hill on the other.

The mullah searched the terrain slowly, doubtfully.
The air was as still and quiet as in the moments before
a storm. Nothing seemed to move, not a blade of grass,
not a leaf.

"Where is everyone?" said Sharon. She too was
disturbed by the unsettling calm. Surely at sundown,
the time for supper, there would be some signs of
activity: farmers returning from the fields, women
drawing water from the stream or wells, smoke rising
from the chimneys. From here, the village looked deserted.

Zadek led them down the dusty path. A few chickens
gobbled from a broken coop set beside a tiny, window-
less house.

"We're alone," said Asif anxiously.

Zadek peered about darkly. The light of day was
growing dimmer, and he had to strain his eyes to see.

"What do you think it is?" said the princess.

The priest of Islam halted his camel. Looming
shadows danced down from the ledges of the hills,
casting strange shapes over the road and leaving them in
darkness.

"There are two possibilities," he answered sourly. "First, that Kazir lookouts saw us coming and evacuated the village. They are peculiar folk, wary of any stranger. Although we may not see them, you can be certain that even at this moment they are watching us."

Sharon arched herself to peer up at the crevices. It would be easy for armed men to be observing them now, hiding behind the boulders with taut bows ready to loose.

"And the other possibility?" she asked.

"That we were not the first to arrive." His eyes slitted and he hissed to himself. "Kabul's armies could have passed this way days ago."

They rode on, reaching the village just as the last glimmer of sunlight faded and the azure sky began to sparkle with a plethora of stars.

"Teacher, look there."

As Zadek yanked the reins and swung his camel round to see, Asif clutched his arms around the mullah's waist more tightly. A long, feathered spear had been implanted in the ground near the stream. Zadek dismounted and walked cautiously to the water. He kneeled, put his hand into the stream, and tasted a finger with his tongue. Then he spat. "Poisoned; the stream's been poisoned."

The spear, in the shadows of twilight, seemed to be piercing through a rock. Zadek came closer to inspect it. He stared at the shaft and grimaced; it was no rock that the tip had been dug into but a skull—a human skull.

"Huns?" gasped Sharon.

Zadek nodded. "We had better move on."

"But to where?" cried the anguished girl. "The khan's soldiers by now must have taken everything. The Steppes no longer offer us refuge, teacher. You were wrong. We shall have to flee to other lands."

He shook his head severely as he looked toward the mountains in the distance, ragged peaks jutting past the moon, groping at the clouds and stars. "No, Sharon, I am not wrong."

"But here is the proof!" she protested, and her arm swept grandly in an arc encompassing the silent village. "If our city fell to the barbarians," she said, "then what chance had these simple villagers against their hordes? It defies common sense, teacher. Surely the armies of Samarkand could do more than common hillmen."

The mullah smiled an enigmatic smile, his eyes still focused upon the heartland of the Steppes, and replied, "There are things in this world that you do not yet understand, child. My mother's people have not been taken—although I admit that their struggle could have been costly. But the Kazirs live free, I promise you."

Sharon scoffed; a defiant glare smoldering in her eyes told him that her Samarkand ways and beliefs would not so easily change.

He overlooked the slight. "We must ride deeper— into the mountains, where the Stronghold lies."

She was yet unconvinced. Looking at him evenly, she said, "And how are we to find this 'Stronghold'? How are we to find these bold fighters?"

Zadek smiled again, answering simply, "We won't have to; the Kazirs shall find us."

Part Three:

SHE WHO BEARS THE MARK

A sand runner poked its head up slowly from behind the fallen tree and peered out cautiously, its bug eyes darting in different directions. Across the low mound a family of beetles crawled along the rim of a damp rock. The sharp-eyed lizard stood alert and ready, its head held high, the front part of its scaly body raised on the forelimbs so that its webbed fingers cleared the hot sand. Then like hellfire it bolted, scurrying toward the insects, lashing out its tongue and scooping them up to digest.

Sharon watched the curious episode with interest, amused as the lizard, finished with its prey, burrowed like a rabbit deeper into the earth to await its next meal. How strange this whole new world was to her, this world of desert and Steppes, where the sun beat down mercilessly by day upon a parched earth, and nights were as cold and bitter as any she had ever known. There was little vegetation; not very much, save the most stubborn of weeds, would grow here in this nearly waterless land. Yet the desert teemed with life, dozens of species, all sharing what little there was. Very strange.

One learns to adapt, she mused. *Given time and circumstance, you can get used to anything.*

She flipped the pebbles she had been toying with into the sandy pool—fresh water, unspoiled. It had been three long, dreary days since they had left the deserted village, pressing north as Zadek had insisted, ever gaining in elevation until now, from the rocky ledges, they could peer down at will at the vast sweep of desert behind. Until today, there had been no repeat of the carefully nurtured valley they had passed—no more villages, no sign of farms. Still, as they climbed into the mountains, there was a change in the air. No longer stale; everything seemed somehow fresh, exhilarating, clean. Yes, that was it, Sharon told herself; the Steppes were clean, unspoiled by either man or beast. From the lofty heights of the peaks, it made no difference what man or tribe ruled the world below; here you were free, wild, untamed—closer to God.

She sighed. No wonder the Kazirs had chosen the Steppes for their exile; you could hide here for a lifetime and never once be seen.

Time drifted past slowly. Zadek had rested himself comfortably beneath the shade of a palm, Asif close by, lost in a deep sleep after the long morning's ride. It was pointless going on in the midday sun; and Zadek had been most astute in his sense of direction, finding this grassy oasis just when it was needed most.

Sharon pressed a clean, damp compress over her swollen body. The wounds were beginning to itch—a good sign; her sun-bronzed flesh was healing. Lazily she watched the last of her pebbles sink to the shallow bottom, then continued braiding her hair. She frowned at the tears in her soiled *khafti,* wishing she had a change of clothes. She dreamed of silk, the soft Persian silk of *ghararas,* their gentle touch against her skin. She would probably never see a *gharara* again, much less own one, she knew. Only the rough-sewn cloth of the desert for her wardrobe now; wild flowers in place of exotic perfume; sand instead of soap.

She was drifting through a peaceful daydream, half asleep, when a series of sharp grating sounds interrupted her fantasy. She listened for a moment, vaguely puzzled by what seemed a scraping against rock. It wasn't the camels; they stood tethered beside the trees, chomping scud. A wild animal, perhaps? A wolf or mountain cat creeping up along the cliffs? She tensed and sat up straighter. Her gaze spanned the crest of the hillock. Green grass, deep and rich, swayed slightly in the mild breeze. Behind, where the grass receded and the arid soil of the Steppes returned, she could see nothing but the sharply jutting ledges in the rock wall that rose well above the oasis.

The sound stopped; she stood up. Long shadows were working their way down from the heights, lengthening as the afternoon sun tiptoed its way to the western horizon. She shaded her eyes and squinted, looking almost straight up at the cliffs. They were as empty as before, encrusted mica in the rock reflecting the light blindingly.

I must be imagining things.

Then there it was, a hulking shadow looming above her, and at the top of the heights stood the silhouette of a man. Sharon put her hand to her mouth and gasped.

The intruder put his hands to his hips, massive hands at the end of massive arms bulging with muscles, and stared down at the trio of strangers. If he seemed frightened or upset by their presence, he did not show it. He arched his head over, looking first at the mute girl, then at her sleeping companions. Sharon got her first good glimpse of him as he took a step forward. He was tall and broad, his head shaven completely except for a single thick lock of hair at the center of his crown, knotted, which fell down the back of his neck like a ponytail. His neck was like a bull's, his fists powerful and awesome. He wore a peasant tunic under a fur vest; his boots were made of fur as well, but ruggedly sewn and almost reaching his knees. Sharon had never seen boots like that before.

The intruder studied her intently, and she shivered when he put a hand to his fiercely clipped dark beard and scratched at his chin. A long double-edged dagger hung in a sheath from his burly waist, glinting in sunlight. But he made no move to draw the blade.

Sharon stepped lightly toward Zadek, nudging him with the toe of her shoe. "Teacher . . . teacher . . ."

The mullah stirred with a yawn. He looked up at the startled girl, perplexed, then bounded to his feet at sight of the moving shadow cast down from the cliff.

"Say nothing and don't move," rasped Zadek. "Don't even breathe too quickly!"

Sharon gulped, her heart pounding in her chest. She wasn't breathing at all.

The mullah pushed off the hood of his robe and extended both his arms skyward, showing the intruder that he held no weapon. That they were confronted by no mere hillman, the priest of Islam was certain; nor was he a Hun, by his dress. That left only one possibility.

"We are not enemies," he called. "See; we bear no arms." He unstrapped his dagger slowly and openly, letting it fall to the ground. Unimpressed by this display, the intruder made no move or reply.

"Take us to your village," Zadek went on. "We have come from the sacred city"—at this the watchful bear of a man flinched—"and wish to convey to your elders dire news."

The intruder lifted his right arm and made a secret gesture with his hand. To Sharon's amazement, other men suddenly appeared from behind nearby trees. They had been here for some time, she realized, hiding and watching, never once betraying themselves.

Zadek turned to greet them; he bowed, hands in a pyramid, then opened them, palms forward. "We are friends."

"Take them!" called the man on the cliff.

His companions drew razor-sharp knives and wielded them before the princess and the mullah. A few drew cord and blindfolds from their tunics, and before the priest of Islam could protest, they had pulled Asif to his feet and begun to tie all three at the wrists and ankles.

"What are you doing?" cried Zadek. "We are not your enemies———"

A blade at his throat warned him to be silent. And while the three of them stood mute and shivering, the blindfolds were tightened over their eyes and the bonds knotted and expertly secured. They were led slowly to the camels and lifted into the saddles.

"Signal the camp," Sharon heard someone mutter. The sound of running steps followed; she was sure she heard the galloping of a horse beyond the rise.

Then, bumpily, the camels trod from the smooth oasis grass onto the rocks, first upward, then sharply down. Their captors never spoke, not even among themselves, and it was only the cold bite of the wind hours later that told Sharon that day was done and the long night started. Wherever they were being taken, it was far from where they were—a new journey, perhaps the most hazardous they would take; and what waited at its completion they were too frightened even to guess.

It was a flat, almost perfectly circular patch of land that they had been brought to—striped like the scales of a snake, unbroken except for a dark scattering of rock. The circle was totally surrounded by high granite cliffs, sharp and jagged, with a series of ledges layered right to the top.

Sharon, Zadek behind her, and Asif behind him had been taken off their camels long before and forced to walk through a tunnel. It seemed a long time until they reached the open, and it was there that their blindfolds were at last removed and the bonds untied.

Sharon's eyes teared from the light as she scanned the unfamiliar surroundings slowly, seeing the enclosed circular patch almost as a prison. High above, along the heights of the chalky cliffs, unknown jailers stood mutely, peering down at the prisoners. She stood tensely, not daring to move. Off toward the west a red ember of dying sun burned, turning the waters of a nearby pool almost the color of blood. Overhead a gray lid of clouds was rapidly blotting out the last light of day.

Zadek rubbed at the rope burns on his wrists and also looked about at the enclosure. Along the cliffs above, at least twenty hillmen gazed down at them, while at the mouth of the low tunnel entrance another group had gathered. Only the lumbering giant of a man who wore the scalp lock was familiar. The rest, four similarly dressed men and one woman, watched. The men were dressed in the simple garb of the Steppes: light-colored tunics covered by rough-hewn robes, and

144

sandals made of hide; but they stood tall and they stood proud, bowing to no man. *Free Men of the Steppes,* Sharon thought, recalling to mind the Kazirs' own description.

Their captor with the scalp lock suddenly moved toward them from the shadows. It seemed to Sharon that there was a mocking laugh in his eyes he he paced before them. He folded his arms, muscles bulging beneath his shirt, grinning when the terrified Asif shied away from his stare. Zadek, though, remained defiant; he held no fear of this barbarian brute or of his companions. He met the angry glare evenly.

Sharon could not be as brave as her teacher. She could feel her flesh beginning to crawl the moment the steely eyes turned her way. The hairs along the back of her neck started to prickle, and she involuntarily flinched, wondering if the same foul thoughts now ran through his mind as they had Kabul's.

"Where did you find them?" The voice was that of the woman beside the tunnel entrance.

The scalp-locked barbarian turned to her. "At the Green Pool, saya. They were resting themselves and their beasts, likely as not waiting for the blanket of darkness to cover their movements before continuing their journey."

The woman nodded; she dug the heel of her sandal into the gravelly dirt, squashing an insect. Then she too stepped out of the shadows. She was quite young, Sharon saw, little more than her own age, slender and not very tall; but she carried herself with poise and dignity. She seemed very different from other hillwomen Sharon had seen, women whose backs had been bent and whose breasts sagged like those of old hags from long years of tilling and harvesting the brittle soil.

A mass of brown hair—short, recently clipped at the nape of her slim neck—curtained the saya's features as she studied the faces of the prisoners. Her almond eyes were a similar color, deep and brooding, her mouth small, her cheekbones high. Her skin was well darkened by desert sun, a testimony to her life of the Steppes. Of her simple dress there was nothing of note, only the leather necklace that hung from her neck and below her breasts. Dangling from it was a small piece of what looked like antelope horn. Although to Sharon it seemed no more than common adornment, she noticed that Zadek seemed most interested by it.

"And why did you bring the infidels here?" the saya asked abruptly of the brute with the scalp lock.

The broad man pursed his lips. "To answer your questions, sava." He replied in a thick accent.

At that the woman smiled, though only briefly, as if openly doing so was something she was not used to. "You did the right thing, Roskovitch," she answered at length. Then, as the burly man stepped aside, she turned her eyes again to the outsiders, openly displaying mistrust and hostility, the same that all hillfolk reserve for those they know have come from the city and its decadent ways.

To Asif she said nothing, not giving the boy a second glance, but of the mullah she asked, "You wear the robe of a holy man; are you one?"

Zadek nodded somberly. "A humble follower of the Prophet and his word, saya."

A small smile parted her lips. "Then why are you not at your mosque at prayer?" Someone snickered from behind.

"The sacred house of worship has been destroyed," he replied truthfully, adding, "as has the city, as have much of your own lands." Then he peered glumly skyward, glancing once more at the listening but unseen men atop the cliffs, knowing that his voice had carried to every ear.

The saya seemed to grow tense; she fondled the horn on her necklace and pressed her thin lips tightly. "What have you seen, holy man?"

Zadek bowed his head respectfully. "Only little,

saya, but enough—too much, perhaps. After crossing
the desert, we came upon Kazir lands and the village
that guards the border—a peaceful village, saya, deserted save for a few stray sheep."

"So?" Her tone was guarded.

Zadek said simply, "A Kazir would never let a single
sheep remain unguarded . . . unless he were dead."

From the side, Roskovitch became visibly angered
at the brazen way in which the outsider from the
city spoke to his saya. His hand slid down toward the
hilt of his dagger, and Sharon was positive that this
time he would have lifted it had not the level-headed
woman stopped him before steel greeted daylight.

"Who are you, holy man?" she snapped. "What is
your name?"

Zadek's hands formed a pyramid as they touched
his lowered forehead. Then he gave his name, boldly
and proudly, so that everyone could hear and there
would be no mistake or reason to repeat it.

The saya glanced uneasily at Roskovitch. "I am
familiar with your name," she admitted, assessing him
carefully. "Can you prove who you are?"

"I can . . . if called upon to do so."

"They say you are a renegade, a madman and
worse."

Zadek smiled mysteriously. Roskovitch grunted, saying, "The hated palace priest of Samarkand, is that not
so?" He spit out the words contemptuously.

The saya threw back her head and glared, her face
bathed in darkening shadows of approaching night.
"What do you say to that, holy man?"

"That a man serves those he must in this life of
pain." Then: "But blood runs thickly, saya, as a Kazir
woman must know." He glanced sharply at Roskovitch.
"Even an outcast from the bitter land of Rus would
understand, especially when he also once came to the
Kazirs for protection."

The saya looked at Zadek straightforwardly, not so

much as flinching at his correct guess. Roskovitch, though, let his jaw hang with surprise. "How did you know that, holy man?" snapped the saya. Speak—now!" It was a command, the threat behind it barely veiled.

"There is much I know of the Kazirs," the mullah told her. "I am not the outsider you have thought me to be."

"Liar!" The voice shot like an arrow, echoing over the chalky walls, and another man stepped forward from the tunnel. Tall, sinewy, but not as large as Roskovitch, he had beady, intense eyes, black as coals, and a thin scar that ran from his temple almost down to his scowling mouth. "This man is not to be trusted," he said through clenched teeth. "How dare he even speak like this?"

Zadek remained calm and steady. "From the blood of my mother," he whispered, "blood that flows through my veins that even you cannot deny."

The woman was astonished. "You claim to be of the Blood?"

"I do. The Kazirs are my people as well as your own. Let no man try to deny it."

The outraged man spat at his feet. "I should flay the skin off your bones for this blasphemy, holy man," he seethed, pulling out a tiny dagger from the collar of his tunic, behind his neck. The finely honed blade glimmered in the dimming light.

Zadek stiffened but made no move to thwart any sudden thrust.

His adversary grinned. "If you won't fight, then die as you deserve—like a dog!"

"Sheathe your blade, Yasir!"

Yasir spun, dagger in hand. He peered into the blackness of the tunnel entrance. The hatred in his eyes intensified when he saw who had spoken. While Sharon held her breath, another man stepped into the open, although not close enough for her to catch a glimpse of his face.

A grim frown made Yasir's features all the harsher. The two men faced off, glaring at each other for a long moment, tension thick and mounting between them. Anyone could tell that neither bore love for the other; they were obviously rivals, each holding the other in disdain.

The saya stepped between them, pushing them apart. "Enough of this," she warned sternly. Then, to Yasir: "Do as my brother said; put your knife away. There is no need for it here."

Yasir hesitated, but he knew that the demand of the saya could not be disobeyed—at least not here, within the confines of the Stronghold. Outside it, though, this little matter would have been resolved differently.

The saya looked again at the mullah. "So you say you are of the Blood?"

There was no emotion in Zadek's lined face as he replied, "I do, as much as any man. Chapter and verse I know the Laws, exactly as every child is taught by his mother while his father serves as Guardian to the land."

Sharon was perplexed by his answer, but she could tell that the saya had been impressed.

"If all this is so, holy man, then why do you come to us now?"

The mad mullah's response was typically cryptic: "Because I now know that I had been charged to wait."

The saya's eyes narrowed; she asked, "What is it that you have so patiently waited for, holy man?"

"To bring to you one who can help."

"Can help?" A sudden incomprehension showed in the saya's brooding eyes, and she stared hard at the graying man of the Book.

"It is true," said Zadek, "although I would not be truthful to claim I have always known it. Indeed, I was not certain until only days ago—on the black day in which sacred Samarkand fell to the heathens."

"The holy man speaks to us in a priest's riddles,"

declared Yasir. "Are we, Free Men of the Steppes, to be so deceived by these twisting words?"

"What exactly are you telling us, holy man?" said the saya.

Zadek grimly let his eyes drift to Sharon, who remained silent at his side. "This child," he rasped; "I have brought her to you to serve the Kazirs' purpose."

"What purpose?"

"Can you not guess?" He glanced around slowly at the puzzled faces. "Oh, Kazirs, has the time not come? Is not the Hundred Year Solitude at an end? And are we not ready to begin what must be begun? What has been laid down in the Laws for us to obey?"

"You say many things, holy man. Speak plainly; do not tire our patience."

Zadek's eyes smiled kindly at Sharon, who stood there quivering, not comprehending anything he had been saying. "I say to you all," he went on, "under the open sky, under the shadows cast by the moon, that this child of Samarkand is the One, the One for which we have all reason to hope. With her there shall be a new glory. Without her there is only the darkness we have known—with the Huns at our backs and throats."

They listened in total silence, astounded, disbelieving their own ears. At length the saya turned to her brother, the young man washed in shadows that deepened as the last rays of sunlight faded and the sky turned purple. "What do you say?" she asked, shaken.

Before he could reply, Yasir boldly stepped forward, enraged. "This holy man seeks to make fools of us all!" he cried loudly. "Are we to take his word like children, that a—" he leered at Sharon—"bitch of Samarkand is called out as the One?"

At the insult, Zadek flushed; a man of peace, he nevertheless lifted his hand as if to strike. "Dare not speak so, defiler!" he boomed, so fiercely that his voice reverberated off the rock walls.

But, where another might tremble at the mullah's wrath, the cunning Yasir only laughed and taunted him further.

"Let the judges decide," called out the saya's brother. He tilted his head and let his eyes search the stony silhouettes of the men on the cliffs. Then, raising his arms wide and high, his desert robe swirling gently behind in the sudden breeze, he told them, "You have all observed and listened, and you have heard what the holy man claims as truth——"

"You believe him, then?" snickered Yasir.

The saya's brother shot around. "I did not say that. But only fools and hags laugh at things they do not understand." Again he addressed the judges. "Before the holy man is called out as an impostor, let him prove his claim."

"And I say the holy man lies!" called Yasir. He came close to Sharon, sneering; then he glared at Zadek. "Tell us, holy man, who is this woman? Does she too claim to be of the Blood?"

Zadek shook his head, sadly admitting that she was not.

"Then *who,* holy man? Tell us who she is!"

It was the saya's brother who spoke, coming out of the shadows for the first time. "She is the daughter of Amrath, lord of Samarkand, niece to the emir."

Gasps filled the air; the judges peered down at the frightened girl in shock. Even Yasir was taken aback. "How do you know this?" he sputtered.

The young man smiled slyly and stood before the girl. Shivers ran over her body and she felt goose bumps rise on her flesh. She stared at the man confronting her, not daring to believe her eyes, yet she knew it was true.

"Do you know me?" he asked.

She nodded slowly, swallowing hard. He seemed somehow different now—older, more a man—but he was the same; the stare of his eyes into her own assured her of that. "You are the one whose life I saved . . . that day before Ramadan, during the festival."

"And you gave me your hand to lift me from the dirt."

"Tariq. You are Tariq."

He smiled once more. She could feel all eyes turning to her suddenly, gazing down from above with an understanding of things she did not share. Even Zadek seemed somehow different. Was he the same kind, wise teacher who had always comforted her and been her friend, or was he someone else—a Kazir, back among his own strange people, standing now in the fading light and speaking of things she could never explain? She wanted desperately to pull away from Tariq's piercing look, but she forced herself to meet it.

"Give me your hand again," he said, and dumbly she complied. Tariq opened her palm and searched it slowly, noting the deep lines crisscrossing one another, the deeper lifeline that cut from her middle finger almost to her wrist. Tariq nodded several times, then released her and turned to Zadek. "I believe you, holy man. Once I too doubted, even though I saw with my eyes, but now I doubt no longer; she bears the Mark."

"Impossible!" bellowed Yasir.

Tariq boldly confronted him: "Then look for yourself."

"Never!" He pointed a bony finger at the girl. "She is the living embodiment of our enemies, the blood of the Samarkand kings!"

"Samarkand has no more kings," observed Zadek. "She must be taken in by the Laws and accepted as one of your own."

Tariq glanced at his sister. "The holy man speaks the truth," he said. "Let the Laws decide. What say you, Carolyn?"

Carolyn tightly gripped the antelope horn on her

necklace, her face etched with questions. "You know that we must put her to the test."

Her brother nodded. "I would ask of the judges nothing more."

Yasir spun toward the younger. "I shall *never* accept such blasphemy! The holy man is a dreamer, a fool at best, or a clever spy sent to bring this girl among us to create disunity."

"Think of me what you will," said Zadek. "My life is of little consequence. But the Mark she bears is there for all to see, and not even you can deny it."

Yasir hotly spurned the offer. "You are all fools, then. I shall listen no more. I vote no! The girl is an impostor." And he turned to leave, heading back toward the tunnel, the judges of his own clan making ready to leave with him.

"Go now and the bonds that hold our clans shall be broken," warned Tariq. "Will you not stay and reconsider?"

The fiery rival made no reply. Tariq reached out and grabbed his arm. "Care you so little for justice and truth?"

Their eyes met like thrown daggers. "You are the biggest fool of all, Tariq," growled his adversary. "Tears would fill old Shoaib's eyes if he could see you now, whimpering like a toothless hound at the feet of a Samarkand bitch!"

In a fit of fury, Tariq drew back his fist and hit Yasir, sending him sprawling into the dirt. The older man wiped his mouth with the back of his hand and spit blood. He looked up, not at his rival, but at the stunned saya, standing mute in the shadows. "Your brother shall pay for this," he snarled. Rising slowly to his feet; he lifted his arm and pointed to Tariq.

"Tariq, son of Shoaib, before all judges, before the saya of the Stronghold, I call you out, man to man, as a Kazir calls upon another! Shall you meet me now in the circle? Or do you claim the right to sanctuary—

while your sister lends her protection?" The air ran cold as he spoke, and his sneer seemed as loud as a clap of summer thunder.

A small pulse throbbed in Tariq's throat. Yasir had been spoiling for this moment for years, he knew—ever since Shoaib, on his deathbed, proclaimed his son successor. There was no room for two to claim leadership of the clans; Yasir knew this well and so did he. Sooner or later the bad blood between them was sure to surface, as it must when a nation is divided. His judgment told him to avoid the confrontation—it was what Carolyn silently begged with her eyes, what Shoaib would say were he here—but Yasir's affront had been total. Kazir law demanded Tariq reply honorably and fight to the death, if need be, against the man who publicly derided him.

Tariq knew that the eyes of the judges would be upon him now, assessing him as his father's son, watchfully anticipating his response. The Stronghold was neutral ground for all the clans; he need not answer to the call, need not face Yasir within the confines of the circle. There would be no shame. Yet Tariq was proud and vain, as were all Kazirs, and to let his rival shame him thusly would only make things worse later.

No, thought Tariq, as he glared at his adversary; let it be done now, once and for all. Only one of them would walk away from the match this night, and that one would lead the tribe to its destiny. Let Allah's will be done.

"I accept your challenge," he replied softly, keeping his gaze steady.

Yasir's smile broadened. He was bigger than Tariq, older, more experienced. Five others had been slain at his hand in the circle, he proudly recalled, and his reputation with the curved dagger was unmatched. Without a word, he stripped off his robe and raised his weaponless hands to the sky. Tariq, five paces opposite, did the same.

Carolyn looked briefly at her brother, suppressing a sigh. She knew from the start that Tariq would meet the dare. How could it be any other way? Solemnly she called upon the judges to remain at their places and make certain that both combatants fought fairly, with neither seeking advantage over the other.

A torch was brought and the oil-soaked rags lit by a single spark of her flint. At once shadows pranced, dodging the brightness and seeking refuge behind the ledges. Carolyn handed to Roskovitch a piece of shale, and the barbarian from Rus proceeded to draw a circle in the ground roughly seven meters in diameter.

Zadek pulled Sharon and Asif back, nudging them closer to the smooth rock walls.

"What is going to happen, teacher?" she asked, breathless and shaken.

"A time-honored custom that cannot be broken," replied the mullah with a frown. "A test of leadership, as ancient as the Kazirs themselves."

Sharon's heart was beating wildly, her mouth parched and tongue swollen, as both combatants were stripped of all weapons and, wearing only tunics, brought by Carolyn into the center of the circle. Roskovitch held the torch while another man brought forth a long piece of hemp, tying one end to Yasir's left wrist and the other to Tariq's. At his signal, they both pulled it taut, making certain the hemp was well secured. Carolyn snapped her fingers, and another Kazir brought forth a wrapped cloth of silk, which he opened beside the light of Roskovitch's torch: Two curved daggers gleamed, and he displayed them high for all the watching judges to see.

Carolyn turned to her brother. Tariq stiffened, his focus on the man he would face. "You have been challenged," said the saya, "so the choice of blades is yours."

Tariq nodded stoically. It seemed to Sharon that the younger man was clearly at a disadvantage. The broader, well-seasoned Yasir kept a mocking look upon his face, seeming almost eager as he picked up his dagger and fondled it slowly, assessing its balance, its weight. He was no stranger to such weapons, it was plain. He wiped the flat edge of the blade over his tunic, grinning as metal reflected golden flames from the torch; then he stepped back lithely, like a preying panther, yanking gently at the hemp, making slashes into the air.

For Tariq, the matter at hand remained more somber. It was not that he had not killed men before; he had, many, all enemies of his people. But, unlike his opponent, he had yet to spill the blood of a Kazir, a kinsman, and Yasir was such a kinsman, cousin of his cousin; despite mutual hatred, they shared the same bloodline.

The saya sighed deeply, looking first to one, then to the other. "No man may cross beyond the line," she said, indicating the marks Roskovitch had made. "And neither shall keep the blade in other than his right hand."

Tariq nodded; Yasir scowled. They both knew the rules of the match well enough: one against one in a vendetta duel that every Kazir boy is taught about by the time he reaches the age of nine. Yet they understood that it was the saya's solemn obligation to repeat it for them now, before all, so that no doubt or question concerning the fairness of the circle's rules could ever be raised, or its outcome be suspect. Once the challenge had been met and the fight done, it was forever finished. There would be honor in defeat as well as in victory, neither shame nor blame, the integrity of the saya unblemished, for the slightest infraction of the strict rules meant instant death to the offender.

From a goblet filled to the brim with sweet water, each of the fighters drank a long draught. Then to their opposite corners they silently marched, awaiting the signal. When Roskovitch held the torch above his head, Sharon flinched. Flames leaped when he swung it down, and, like tigers, the two ready combatants moved toward the center, pacing each other, stalking, tugging lightly at the hemp.

Yasir feinted a lunge, and Tariq deftly back-stepped. Yasir knew his ploy had worked; he pulled hard at the cord, forcing Tariq toward him, and while the youth plunged forward, dragging his heels to regain his balance, Yasir struck. The curved desert dagger whistled by Tariq's scalp, slashing downward and tearing through the rough fabric of his tunic. Tariq twisted away smartly, the way Roskovitch had taught him, parried, and forced Yasir to resume his guard, but not before a thin crimson line spread slowly along his left arm.

Carolyn winced with the blow, not daring to breathe until it was certain that no serious damage had been done. As saya, it was her sworn duty to be certain the match was fair; she must not show the slightest favoritism. This she would surely do, for she also lived by the harsh code of the Steppes. Still, seeing her brother's plight had taken its toll, it was all she could do to mask her growing worry.

"Yasir will kill him," whispered Sharon as the two men continued to thrust and parry, aghast at how easily the larger man held Tariq at bay.

Zadek frowned characteristically, saying in a low voice, "Sometimes the wolf must play the bear's game. But the match is not yet done."

While the gloom of night thickened, Yasir lashed out again and again, forcing Tariq to turn with a spin, ducking swiftly from the glimmering blade. The outer rim of the circle stood only inches from his feet; he must not cross it, he knew, but must keep as close to the center as he could, for just one step outside the arena would give his foe the right to claim victory.

The hemp tightened; Tariq gripped it fiercely with his left hand, managing to counter the quick succession of blows intended to stun. Then up went Yasir's arm, just as Tariq had regained a measure of free movement. A powerful uppercut of steel thrusted toward the younger man's jugular. Sharon contained a squeal of horror as Tariq stumbled, knees almost buckling with the strain as he caught Yasir's knife hand by the wrist and the two men grappled like wrestlers. With sandaled feet scratching against gravel, Tariq yanked the hemp with all his strength. Yasir, caught off guard, was momentarily dragged forward and toppled over. Sharon was amazed and thankful when the smaller man's knife slashed furiously. The sound of ripping fabric was coarse in the still night air. Yasir pulled back, grunting; a stream of dark blood ran along his shoulder. Leaping to his feet like a wounded animal, he let loose a wild torrent of harmless slashes in the air that kept Tariq from further advance.

Tariq crouched; Yasir jabbed. They paced each other for long moments. Each had underrated the other, it was now clear, and there was no more room for mistakes. When Yasir feinted, Tariq's knife chopped, his arm fully extended. The tip of his dagger played at the hairs of Yasir's exposed belly, and the larger man once more was forced to back-step, for the first time finding himself now pushed toward the line of the circle.

Roskovitch could not contain a small smile. Unlike the saya, he was not sworn to impartiality, and his grin only broadened when Yasir, now panting, successfully dodged the whistling lashes.

A flash of blows and counterblows ensued, so fast that it was impossible to count them. Yasir used his greater weight to full advantage, constantly pressing, leading Tariq in a backward dance. But the youth was aware of such tricks, and with one of his own he struck a piercing blow, the tip of his blade only at the last instant blocked from driving into Yasir's heart. The larger man cursed, beads of sweat glistening on his darkened face. The hemp twisted when Yasir pulled it taut, and he quickly loosened it. Sharon gasped: Tariq had begun to stumble again, his foot twisting over a rock. A laugh of triumph bit through the air. Yasir's

knife came down for what he was sure was the death
blow; but as his arm swung down, Tariq's own came up,
like a hammer, splitting through flesh and ribs, the cold
steel probing deeper and deeper. Yasir stood unmoving, his eyes wide, staring in disbelief at the semi-fallen
younger man, his own knife forgotten. Then he grimaced, gurgled, dropped his blade and clutched instead
at the knife stuck straight through his gut. Blood pulsed
over his fingers and hands, and he fell to the ground,
groaning.

"The death blow, lad!" cried Roskovitch, his anxious
features hardened in the shadows.

Tariq stood over the writhing body; he bent over,
pulled out the bloodied blade, and lifted it high, ready
to plunge into Yasir's heart. The beaten foe stiffened;
through glassy eyes he looked up at Tariq, showing no
fear. But the awaited blow to end his life did not come.
Tariq wavered, then dropped his knife arm to his side.
Sweaty, out of breath, he grimaced with pain and rubbed
at his left arm, the wound beginning to throb.

Yasir cleared his throat. "Well?" he grunted. "Do it!
You've won. Do what you must!"

The saya watched pensively; the judges above, satisfied that the match had been fair, tensely waited for the
son of Shoaib to take the life of his hated rival. Still
Tariq made no move.

"You must do it," whispered Carolyn.

Her brother looked at her harshly. "No!" he said.
And, to the shock of the judges and the saya, he threw
the knife down, the handle of the blade wobbling as the
shaft struck upright in the dirt. "I shall not kill you,"
he told Yasir. "You are a good fighter, too badly needed
to have your life wasted like this."

Yasir was stunned. Holding his wound tightly, he
rose to his knees and gazed up at the man before him.
Tariq's eyes were cold and impassive. "Had it been
you upon the earth, I would not have hesitated," he
rasped through his pain.

Tariq nodded. "I know. Perhaps that is the difference between us, then. But my decision is made. Leave the Stronghold, Yasir. Return in peace to your clan. No man shall harm you, I promise it. Nor do I ask favors of you in exchange, only that your life be spared in return for the girl." His gaze rested on Sharon, who was standing breathlessly beside the rock wall.

Yasir looked to her as well and nodded darkly. "I accept your bargain."

Only Zadek smiled when Tariq said, "Then go. Allah's will has been done. She has been given sanctuary among us. Let those wiser than you or I decide if truly she bears the Mark."

Glumly the Persian physician stood up, candlelight flickering from the table beside the huge bed. Scar-faced armed men guarded the door of the once opulent chamber, their hands firmly at the hilts of gleaming scimitars poking through their belts.

The physician ignored them, directing his attention instead to the mute slave girl standing meekly at the foot of the bed. "Open the curtains," he directed, and the girl nodded and complied. A wash of brilliant sunlight swept through the room, bathing the gloom with a golden glow. The physician rubbed the aching muscles in his shoulders, sighed, and let his gaze linger upon the cloudless blue sky outside. The shattered public buildings of the city stared back, broken and scarred, blackened by smoke, twisted and misshapen by flame.

A hand, large and powerful, touched the physician's arm. He turned and looked evenly into the eyes of the sinewy man at his side, then he shook his head.

Osklath slitted his eyes; his lower lip twitched. "Your procedures have failed?" he asked.

Upon the bed, the sleeping man stirred briefly. The physician kept his voice low so as not to wake him. "There was little I could do," he admitted with a shrug. "I told you before: The eye is beyond repair; he will never see from it again."

Osklath grimaced. This butcher of Persia was playing games with him—not to be trusted, like all the others. "And the pin?"

Again the long-faced physician sighed. He was weary, more weary than he had ever been before. For eighteen hours he had worked on the eye of the khan, his instrument tray soaked with blood—grim proof of his efforts —but what had been asked of him was impossible.

"No man of medicine could remove the golden pin," he said truthfully to Kabul's aggrieved son. "It is too deeply embedded. It would damage the brain, perhaps causing hemorrhage, perhaps even killing your father."

Osklath looked away. He could have this Persian racked for his failure, make him squirm like a worm as every centimeter of flesh was torn from his bones, but what good would it do? It still would not make him cure the khan.

"Listen to me," said the physician. "The worst of the torment is over. The optic nerve has been shattered, deadened. The terrible pain shall diminish, to recur only upon occasion. Already the eyelid has been sewn over the inflicted eye. A patch will cover the disfiguration."

Kabul turned from his side to his back. The slave girl immediately brought another goblet of strong wine to his lips, hoping it would put him back into his fitful sleep. For weeks the khan had been in indescribable agony, out of his mind with suffering. Many physicians captured in Samarkand as well as India, had tended him, but not one had been able to do anything. This Persian, famous throughout the East for his skills, was the last hope. And now he too had been unable to put Kabul out of his anguish.

The khan gulped down the wine greedily, the only pain-killer he had found. The slave made to fill the goblet again, but the physician stopped her. "More is useless," he said. "Let him be." Then he bent over the agonized body, his hand forcing the khan's head back on the pillow. One eye stared back blankly, the other, pus-laden and badly swollen beneath the stitched lid, a hideous sore like a festering cancer.

"Your fever has broken, great khan," said the physician.

Kabul's single eye cleared; he studied the face of the

man hovering over him, noting the bloodied surgical robe. "Who . . . who are you?" he asked weakly.

The man of medicine bowed. "Your servant, my lord, brought to Samarkand only a day ago to tend your ailment."

Kabul listened, only half aware of what was going on around him. His good eye looked to the solemn guards, then to his son. Osklath showed no emotion.

"Have you much pain," asked the physician.

Kabul shook his head slowly.

"Good. I have done all I can. Now I shall return home."

The khan glanced at his son; Osklath nodded. "He is not a slave, Father. I paid him in gold to come to Samarkand. He is free."

Kabul's fierce eye dimmed from the effects of the heavy doses of wine forced into his body. Deep lines threaded his tired face. His forehead was bathed in sweat, and the slave girl, at the physician's command, wiped it away with a silk cloth. With great effort he lifted his head. He gripped the physician's collar tightly, froth from his twisted mouth dripping over his matted beard. "Where is she?" he hissed.

"My lord?" The physician seemed perplexed.

"She is gone, Father," said Osklath.

The khan's features changed dramatically, becoming cruel, as he peered venomously at his son, his swaggering son, who he knew must have relished this moment.

"We searched the city for fully a week, Father," Osklath continued. "Every alley was combed, every street and every byway. Our soldiers went through the palace in full force, seeking her down in the cellars and catacombs——"

"And?"

Osklath paused before answering. Was there a hidden smile behind those impassive eyes? Kabul wondered as his son gazed down at him plaintively. "And the woman you seek has escaped."

Kabul balled his hands into fists; he tried to rise. Veins were bulging from his thick throat and forehead. "I want her!" he boomed, the strength in his weakened body coming only from sheer hatred. "Do you hear me? I want her found!"

Osklath folded his arms across his vest and lowered his head respectfully. "We are trying, my lord. Already troops have been dispatched into this accursed country-side. Some days ago word reached me of three fugitives who fled Samarkand—two men and a woman, I was told." He shrugged. "Perhaps the woman is she, but we are not yet certain."

Dark spittle was flying from the khan's purpled lips. The Persian physician tried to calm the agitated man, but Kabul brusquely pushed him away. He lifted his hand and pointed a bejeweled finger that shook with rage toward his son. "I warn you, Osklath," he sputtered, "fail me not in this matter. Find her—and find her now!"

"I shall, great khan, I give you my word. I shall bring you her head."

Kabul pounded a fist at his side. "No!" he bellowed, not her head! Alive! I want her alive, do you understand? She must be brought here to me so that I can——" He was making to get off the bed as he spoke, but suddenly, inexplicably, he was thrown back and his body began to quiver. Osklath looked questioningly at the silent physician.

The khan put both his hands to his swollen sewn eye and started to scream, loudly, frightfully. It seemed his lungs would burst from the pressure. Then his pain-racked body convulsed uncontrollably and he swayed back and forth, twisting and rocking, howling and screeching in his agony.

"You assured me that the pain would leave!" barked Osklath to the man of medicine at his side.

The physician grimaced. "Yes, my lord, and so it

shall, but always it may return, at least in brief spasms. There is nothing anyone can do."

And as Osklath and the physician looked on helplessly, the rages of Kabul's tremendous torment heightened, a ghastly sight to see. The great khan of the Huns was now a man demented by his terrible pain; he would be so until the last day of his life. The Persian stepped back and shuddered. He wondered about this Samarkand girl, who she was and what the khan must have done to her to make her seek such a horrible revenge. And it frightened him to think about what Kabul would do if he ever succeeded in finding her.

What bothered Sharon the most was that no one had told her just where they were going. Led away from the Stronghold in blindfolds, she and her uneasy companions had waited nearly nine days before the saya came to their tent and announced that on the morrow they would be taken on a journey. When questioned, Carolyn had said nothing, only that Sharon and Zadek had better prepare, for it would be a long ride before they reached their destination. The boy, Asif, was given into Roskovitch's hands for training, that he might be a Kazir warrior.

And so it was already late afternoon of the tenth day that they left their guarded tent high upon a windy ridge, received fresh horses, and were brought by Roskovitch to the nearby open uplands. Alone in the field, sitting expertly upon an unsaddled fine stallion, the saya waited. The gray sky for days had been forever threatening, though the rain had yet to begin. The horses lined up, Carolyn in the lead, then Sharon, then Zadek, the rear brought up by the ever-dour Roskovitch, with the awestruck Asif sitting behind him. The Rus had taken a liking to the boy instantly.

"We shall have to travel fast," the saya told them all mysteriously. "But word has come that we are expected." And without further explanation, she kicked her heels sharply into the stallion's flanks, and the bold steed raced off over the rocky terrain.

Below lay a vast plain, stretching hazily into the distance, dry but scattered with patches of grazing land, laced with wadis, whose banks swelled only during the brief rainy season that was almost upon them. Winding streams, shallow and dark, merged and crossed the sweep in a crescent, running beside lakes of sand, hilly mounds, poking out of the endless flatlike islands. Behind stood the cliffs and rock walls of the Stronghold; high above, both the savanna and the grassy hills where they had found the oasis known as the Green Pool. But of sight of the Stronghold fortress itself, there was none; it was completely hidden by the natural surroundings, so much so that an entire army could pass it and miss it entirely without anyone even suspecting it was there.

No wonder Le-Dan could never find these Kazirs, Sharon thought as they passed from the rocky heights and onto the plain. And she could only admire these strange hillmen for their hard-learned desert abilities. Very much like the old city saying:

> *Blink an eye and a Kazir stands before you;*
> *Blink again and he has gone.*

Once on open ground, they heard the first malevolent rumbles of thunder in the distance, and within moments a harsh rain was pouring down upon them. Before long the soil had muddied, hooves clomping through thick, wet sand. Carolyn led the way; she pulled the hood of her *aba* over her head, not pausing or breaking stride as her companions tried to keep pace. Here and there huge trees grew rigidly out of the ground, tall as steeples, with thin branches that all too easily bent with the furious gusts of wind. The trail led them constantly west, and it was not long before the first line of faraway mountains and forest appeared on the horizon. They rode on in single file over narrow defiles, in some places slippery and dangerous. And through it all, right up till the descent of night, there was no talk or communication of any kind between them. The few times Sharon had purposely slowed her horse to allow Zadek to catch up, she found the mullah now seeming as secre-

tive and silent as her other companions. Of the saya and
Roskovitch, the sturdy, trustful watchguard for the
journey, she could properly understand it, but not of
her teacher. Had he changed so much these past days?
Or was it her? All she knew was that the gloomy and
stoic lifelong friend would not reply to any of the questions she posed, as if he also understood far more than
she about where they were going and for reasons unknown was unwilling to share it.

It was well into night before the rain slackened, and
after Roskovitch had carefully scouted ahead for a
time and returned, Carolyn called for camp to be set.
They ate meagerly, without a fire, and Roskovitch stood
guard while Sharon slept. She was awakened, just before another gray dawn cracked, by the saya gruffly
shaking her by the shoulders and telling her to prepare
to ride. A few cold biscuits served as breakfast, and
Sharon, cold and scared, forced them down miserably
to help ease the rising tension in her belly. Again she
asked the saya where they were going; again Carolyn
ignored the question. And minutes after the pallid dawn
had begun to light up the sky, they were on their way
once more.

By midafternoon the outline of the horizon had become more pronounced and definable. Thick forests of
trees rose in the distance like the billowing sail of a
ship against the sky. They were headed toward Grim
Forest—she needed no one to tell her that—but for
what purpose she still had no inkling.

Without explanation, Roskovitch was suddenly riding beside her. Although he didn't speak, she saw him
make the sign of the horns with his hand, warding off
bad luck and evil. Superstition ran deep in the hearts
and minds of hillmen; but the barbarian from Rus was
a man who didn't seem afraid of anything. Thus, the
realization that even he feared the spells and enchant-
ments made her shiver, for soon they would all be entering the place where no man ever goes.

Night was pressing in once more, shadows looming over the muddy trail from the branches of the great clustered trees. Over roots gnarled and twisted they slowly made their way, deeply into strange bogs and mires, where the wind whistled strangely through the leaves and reeds and the slow but constant drip-drip of water off the leaves sounded like the soft tread of tiny footsteps. Not a bird sang from the trees; not a bullfrog croaked from the ponds. There was only the occasional hoot of owls high in the branches, whose eyes seemed to follow them every step of the way.

Sharon closed the *aba* she had been given more tightly about her and bit her lips to stop them from trembling.

"We stop here," Carolyn said unexpectedly, swinging her stallion around and dismounting. She tethered the reins beneath a huge moss-filled rock and waited while the others did the same. Sharon could see little in the darkness, only that ahead there was the reflection of water—a lake, sunken in a bowllike descent, surrounded heavily by bush and tree, tall grass, and undergrowth.

While Zadek and Sharon stayed behind, the saya moved down to the lake's edge, pulling off her hood. With hands on hips, she seemed to study the place; then, satisfied that all was well, she cupped her hands around her mouth and uttered a low, discordant cry that carried across the water, like the call of some waterfowl, only somehow more forbidding and lonely.

Zadek's calloused hand closed over Sharon's. She looked at him and was relieved to see that his eyes were kind and loving again. Reassuringly he said, "Bear yourself well, young princess; there is naught but your own fear to be afraid of."

The horses stopped feeding; they picked up their ears sharply and began to stamp their feet restlessly. Sharon squinted hard and gazed over the lake. A dark shape— a log, it seemed at first—had begun to float over from the other side. The moon peeked out from the overcast for barely a moment, but in that time Sharon could see that it was a boat coming their way, rowed in long sweeps over the silver water by a single silhouetted figure.

It took a very long time for the boat to reach the jetty, and when the oars were pulled in, they could see the rower stand and beckon to them. Face covered in shadows except for his eyes, the rower wore a long, heavy robe that covered all but his hands.

Carolyn pulled her necklace from within her tunic and displayed the antelope horn. "I am the saya," she said. The stranger looked at the charm briefly and nodded; then he gestured for them all to climb into the boat. There were two slat benches spread across the middle; Roskovitch, Asif, and the saya sat together on one, while Sharon huddled closely to Zadek on the other. The oarsmen returned to his own place and dipped his oars below the waterline. The first long stroke pulled them cleanly away from the jetty, and in a few moments they were far from land.

The opposite bank lay some three hundred or so meters ahead, Sharon reckoned, but it seemed a long way indeed as the tiny boat inched its way forward. Sharon dipped her fingers into the water, pulling them out as fast as she could; it was frigid, cold as ice, and her gloom only intensified.

A greenish slime dripped from the oars, breaking across the ripples around the prow. Sharon looked ahead, trembling. The dark water stretched on and on, and even bleaker was the stark outline of shore, a tall hillock cutting high into the black sky. As they drew close to the mossy banks, they saw a dim glow of light, a small torch, its orange flame casting lumbering hideous shadows. Who or what was holding the torch, she could not see.

Panic was closing in upon the young Samarkand princess, as if the realization of where she was was finally beginning to dawn. It was all she could do to stop her hands from shaking, while the silence covered the boat like a black cloak.

The oars splashed more loudly, the torch now more defined. A hooded figure was holding it as a beacon, guiding the boat to the small jetty—a figure almost identical to the oarsman. And at last the journey was reaching its climax. The boat hit against land and came to a bobbing halt. The figure with the torch pushed the light toward them. Sharon could see no face within the hood, only two beady eyes studying her and her companions.

Carolyn was the first to stand up and reach land. "I am here," she announced enigmatically. The hooded figure greeted her with a hand placed on her shoulder.

The saya glanced behind as she started to walk the weedy path away from the lake. "Follow me," she said sharply. "The boy stays behind." Asif turned back and went to sit in the boat.

The torch guided the way as they tramped over soft tuft, upward along the tall hillock Sharon had noticed during the journey. They negotiated the way between the trees and shrubs over a comfortable bed of dampened earth until the summit was in sight. As Sharon gazed skyward, she saw another glow, this one a soft hue of amber that ran from one end of the crest to the other, even shooting faintly upward above the gently swaying tops of the trees. There was also an odor in the air; she wrinkled her nose, trying to identify it: something sweet yet also sour, pleasant but also foul. It made no sense at all.

With eyes glued to the trodden path before them, Carolyn urged them on with swift motions of her hand. Zadek was puffing from the long climb, Sharon exhausted, but at last they reached the top and, side by side, stared out at the weird sight.

There was a large clearing ahead, surrounded in part by the densest forest they had yet encountered, partly by a dark palisade. Undefined trees, large and bent, hovered over the grassy open land like apparitions, and when an owl hooted from somewhere near, Sharon nearly jumped out of her skin. In the center of the clearing was a patch of soft, weedless soil, and upon it, slightly elevated, was something dark and sinister, a vat or a great cooking bowl; Sharon could not tell which. Made of iron, set on stubby legs, the cauldron had been placed over a small fire, which popped and crackled loudly, sending fiery shoots of embers high into the air. And there was the low sound of something bubbling—Percolating, boiling liquid that sent off the peculiar odor she had been smelling. Another hooded figure, the third so far this night, stood in shadows above the black vat, stirring its strange contents with a thick ladle larger than a shovel.

Carolyn prodded Sharon forward. The princess took a deep breath and then froze. "No," she said. "No! I'm not going!" Petrified, she pulled away as Zadek tried to calm her, and raced away into darkness, hoping to get back down the hillock and far away from this gruesome place.

A fallen oak, massive and blackened, uprooted by a strike of lightning during a storm long before, blocked her path. She tried to run around it but drew back in fear as a dark form appeared before her. The torch pushed its flame toward her face and Sharon gasped; it was the same hooded figure who had led them from the boat. Licking shadows caressed her; before she could turn to run again, another hand had reached out and grabbed her shoulder, the hand of the oarsman, a hand softer than she would have imagined.

"Come," said the soft, barely audible voice of the oarsman. "There is nothing for you to be afraid of."

Sharon shook her head vehemently, her amber hair flying in front of her panicked eyes. "Never!" she cried. "You can't have me! You can't——"

It was Zadek's hand now that took hold of her. He

pressed the terrified girl closer to him and forced her
to gaze into his lined, haggard face. Looking into his
eyes, black as coals, black as the night, she found herself again transfixed by him, by this pervasive power
the mad mullah held over her. Without uttering a word,
he gently nudged her forward, his strength assuring her
that everything was going to be all right.

"Do you know where you are, child?" asked the
hooded figure carrying the torch.

Sharon was still shaking. She moved her head slowly
from side to side.

The figure turned in the direction of the bubbling
vat, a hand sweeping across the clearing. "It is called
the Place Beyond the Northwest Wind, the Shelter of
Fire and Oak."

Sharon gulped. She had heard of it, at least references to it, but long ago, very long ago; she could not
recall where or when.

"Why . . . why have I been brought here?" she asked
weakly. The hooded figure gave no response; it was
Carolyn who said, "To learn if you truly bear the
Mark"—she glanced at Zadek with open skepticism—
"as this holy man claims."

Sharon frowned. "I have no such Mark," she insisted.
"I don't understand . . ."

The saya smiled cryptically. "We shall see, Samarkand princess; we shall see."

A muggy drizzle had begun, with a thin fog swiftly
descending. All traces of sky were soon blotted from
her vision, and Sharon felt her heart pound quicker and
quicker as the torch-carrying figure put a clammy hand
upon her arm and led her slowly toward the cauldron.
Dancing apparitions bounded along the trunks of the
trees, awesome shadows leaping across her path. The
ground beneath her feet was soft and murky, and she
imagined it to be a quagmire sucking her down, down,
down into the hellish bowels of the earth.

At the foot of the mound she was ordered to stop.

One by one the dark-robed oarsman and the torch-bearer joined their companion at the cauldron. A hue of purple glowed about them as they stood together, sparks from the fire still shooting up from behind, and Sharon gasped as she remembered the forgotten words, taught her long ago by the palace servants:

> *In the Place of Oak and the Place of Fire,*
> *Hidden in the Shelter from the Northwest Wind,*
> *Lies the coven where the hearts of men cry in*
>   *anguish,*
> *And the laughter of Three Hooded Witches*
>   *rob their souls.*

This secret clearing in the forest—it made sense to her now! Unbelievable, insane, yet all too true. The legends were real; what better proof could there be than her own eyes? Sharon had come face to face with the witches of Grim Forest!

"Why has the girl been brought here?" the croaking voice of the witch with the ladle asked.

Carolyn crossed her arms and bowed her head low before the inquisitor. "So that the claims of the holy man may be proved or disproved."

The witch looked sideways to one sister, then to the other. They all nodded in agreement. Then the one in the middle, the eldest, shot a glance toward Zadek. For the first time in her life, Sharon saw her teacher behave as though he were truly frightened. His knees were wobbling when the eldest asked, "And what is your claim?"

He cleared his throat and forced himself to look squarely into the witches' penetrating eyes. He gestured toward Sharon. "That the girl bears the Mark of the expected One."

Shrill laughter filled the gloomy night—fearful, malevolent laughter that made Sharon's flesh crawl.

But Zadek held his ground. "It is no jest. She *is* the One."

The eldest witch glowered at the tall monk of Islam. "*We* shall decide that, holy man," she said, sneering. A long, bony hand lifted from her sleeve. "Go!" she commanded the mullah and the barbarian from Rus. "The eyes of men are unwanted here. Cloak your faces and return to the lake. The girl shall be brought to you when we are done."

Roskovitch, sworn to the protection of the saya, looked hesitantly at Carolyn. Carolyn nodded, assuring him she would be safe; no harm would come to either her or the young princess. Zadek bowed deeply and turned to leave of his own accord. As Roskovitch followed on his heels, Sharon tensed. When they had vanished into the shadows, and she felt herself alone with these three dreaded conjurers of *nightthings,* she trembled and hung her head, not daring to look up.

The eldest witch grinned toothlessly. "So," she whispered, a whisper that brought chills to Sharon's soul, "you would claim to be the One."

Sharon shook her head. "I claim nothing," she replied, the words forced from her throat.

"Remove your robe."

The princess complied, too frightened to do otherwise. She untied the loose belt around her waist and let the dyed woolen garment fall to the ground at her feet. The witches stared and mumbled among themselves. "And now your tunic," uttered the eldest.

Fear flickered in Sharon's eyes; she looked briefly, quizzically, at the somber face of the saya. Carolyn nodded.

Sharon pulled the cotton blouse over her head and dropped it. Naked and ashamed she stood before them all, shivering in the cold and the steady drizzle, her supple young skin strangely colored by the dim reflection of the cauldron's fire.

The eyes of the witches poured over her, a syrup descending thickly along every inch of her body, every curve and fold of her flesh, seeping into the very pores of her skin, and all the while they cackled and whispered to one another, speaking in a tongue so ancient and forgotten that no other person alive could have identified or understood it. Sharon felt unclean, humiliated.

The eldest dipped the ladle into the bubbling brew, and the old hag Sharon had known as the oarsman took a sip. Next it was passed to the one who bore the torch. She also drank from the foul-smelling brew, her gnarled hands rubbing together while she smacked her lips in delight.

The eldest dipped her spoon again and, carefully holding it out, bade Sharon come forward. The princess did as asked, too petrified not to obey. The hazelwood ladle was put to her mouth.

"From the mysteries of the Seven Planets and the Sun that revolves around them," chanted the eldest, "so has this potion been culled. Drink, Sharon, princess of Samarkand. Drink and share all we offer."

For the first time, the other witches spoke. "Snake and frog, frog and snake," incanted one. "Bat's blood pure and pig's blood vile; goat's milk soured and calf's milk spoiled . . ."

"The figs of life and the mushrooms of death . . ." The third finished the verse without a pause from where her sister had stopped: "Thy enemies are caused to fear thee, as a king rides a wolf, as the Lords of Old charge their powers into thee. Drink, Sharon, princess of Samarkand. Drink so that we may see you all the more clearly."

Mesmerized, Sharon looked deeply into the eyes of the eldest and put her mouth around the lip of the ladle. The strange liquid burned as she swallowed, sweetly pungent, racing through her veins and hotly spreading over her nude body. The light rain was like a wet blanket serving to cool the sudden fire that was raging within her.

"Drink once more, princess of Samarkand," came a

voice, but whose it was she could no longer tell. Again she felt the brew swill in her mouth, thinly trickle into her belly, and surge forth through her limbs.

It seemed that a drum had begun to play, a low, lyrical beating—*doom-doom, doom-doom*—and a soft, ethereal flute started to weave a doleful tune. But where were the players? Sharon glanced around in growing trepidation. She could see nothing but the trunks of the gnarled trees, the white bog lifting and swirling from the sodden earth. The Three Hooded Witches laughed.

"Sharon of Samarkand," they seemed to whisper, "Sharon of Samarkand," again and again, as if in song, perfectly matched with the drum and the flute.

Sharon felt her head begin to spin; the world was growing dimmer around her, and she could not distinguish the swaying forms. Hands were touching her, lightly, softly, fingers with sharpened nails probing the recesses of her young, perfect body, cupping her breasts, feeling their way down her back and up her spine, over and between her legs, across her face and lips, examining every centimeter of flesh, while she helplessly reached out, dizzily groping to stop the world in its spin.

On and on the examination went; but how much time had elapsed, she could not tell. Time had lost all meaning, just as the world had seemed to lose its own. She could distinctly hear her name being chanted, yet somehow it was someone else they were calling. She was someone—or something—else, lifted from her former self and somehow set free to drift out of her body, to roam and drift, to soar above the treetops like a bird, to burrow deeply into the earth like a worm, to spread herself out limitlessly like the notes of the strange flute music that now filled her ears.

Sharon of Samarkand . . . Sharon of Samarkand . . .
Who was she now; what was she now? It did not seem to matter. The potion had changed her, its magic turning her into a new form, a new being. She was flying with gilded wings, racing toward a huge, blazing sun

set in a perfect sky, glowing in warmth, basking in the sun's purity, encompassed forever. She was a drop of water in the ocean, feeling the spray of crashing surf, surrounded in a world ultramarine, so peaceful, so tranquil, as though she had always been there and would never want to leave.

Her hands . . . Her hands were being held out before her. The witches were staring at them, running their fingers along the lines etched into her palms. And they were still chanting, not her name but something else, something she could not understand. But it did not matter; nothing mattered. She was the master of the world, mistress of the sky, goddess of the sea. They and she were one, and she wished for the hallucination never to end.

For the first time she could see the faces of her examiners. Within the shadowed curtains of their hoods, all became clearer to her. They were ugly, dreadfully ugly—stringy black hair, matted, filthy, hanging loosely over pockmarked faces filled with warts and moles. Their cheeks were sunken, white as clouds, noses crooked and broken over twisted and misshapen harelips. Aged they were, ancient, as old as creation, their eyes slitted like cats', cunning, intelligent, seeing straight through her, examining her soul as their hands continued to probe her flesh. Yet . . . Yet they were beautiful—maidens from fairy tales, cream-skinned goddesses whose perfect forms had mingled together and blended into her own, hair as rich and pure as morning sunlight, splashing freely over faces filled with love and warmth, breasts firm, hips rounded, skin young and tanned beneath colorful dresses of the finest silks. It was a dream world, Sharon knew, a fantastic, incredible dream world into which she had been whisked.

She was floating again, feeling their touch, writhing with pleasure while her flesh shimmered with beads of perspiration. A lotion was being spread over her, and she sighed.

Abruptly she came crashing down. Her eyes had begun to focus, and she found herself lying upon the wet dirt, the drizzle pattering around her. The palm of the eldest witch was upon her belly, pressing forcefully until it hurt.

"She carries the seed of the impure!" cried the witch. "She is blemished!"

Her sisters drew back, bony hands retreating into the sleeves of their robes. "Unclean! The girl is unclean! She has been *touched* by the Vileness!"

Sharon was sobbing now; she could not control it, could not control her body from shivering or her tears from flowing. "No!" she wailed, tossing wildly upon the earth. "It's a lie! It's a lie!"

But the witches hovered over her, this time like vultures, poking her, prodding her, fingers digging cruelly and savagely. "She must be cleansed!" they chanted in unison. "She must have the evil seed removed!"

Sharon put her hands to her ears to blot out their laughter. The seed of Kabul was in her belly, its terrible legacy there someday for all to see. The witches could not be fooled, no, not these wizened hags whose magic had permeated Grim Forest since time immemorial. They knew; they knew it all—her shame, her anger, her pain, and her hatred, the terrible abuses that had been inflicted upon her, so that her purity was forever gone, stolen from her by a black thief in the night. They could feel it, live it as surely as she had been forced to, and now force her to live it again.

In her state of illusion she was once more in the palace, beside the pitiful, demented emir. And then came Kabul, the great khan swaggering as though drunk with triumph, banishing his vile son from the chamber, once more touching her, forcing his will upon her while she struggled to break loose. And then his scream, his ghastly, shrill scream as she plunged the needle deeply, as deeply as she could, reliving every split second of that moment of horror.

Sharon was screaming and rolling on the ground, the hands of the witches now changed to Kabul's hands, the drizzle turned to his dark blood pulsing from his infested eye, pouring over her, drowning her in it, choking her so that she could not breathe. She gasped for air, her hands shooting out before her like arrows.

"Don't touch me!" she yelled at the top of her lungs. "Don't touch me!"

But the Three Hooded Witches did touch her, again probing her womanhood, learning all her secrets and drawing them into their own minds and experience. Another fluid was being spilled from a vial over her. It stung, stung like ten thousand bees buzzing about her head, injecting their poison into her skin, draining her blood.

"Cleansed!" chanted the witches as the drumbeat became a frenzied blur. *"Cleansed, cleansed . . ."*

Through her agony, Sharon could feel her head being lifted and a goblet put to her lips.

"Worms and lizards, lizards and worms! Weed and slime, slime and weed! Take the poison from her belly, scatter it forever to the winds!"

What they had just done, Sharon could not tell. All she knew was that suddenly there was an awful pain deep inside her stomach, growing swiftly until it had spread through every limb. She was paralyzed by it, numbed beyond her senses. "No, no!" she raved. *"Nooooo!"*

Leering, hissing, mumbling incantations, the witches did what had to be done. Her torment reached unimaginable heights, and she could feel the weight of her burdens squashing life itself from her.

"She must be freed, she must be freed!" rasped the witches. "Skin and bone, oil and fat! Lard and grease and the head of a snake!" And something foul and sickening was jammed into her mouth, stuffed in gruffly and pushed down her throat before she could vomit it out.

She grabbed her stomach, doubling over, intense pain

swelling. Softly she moaned, not caring what would happen next. Amid her shame and pain she wanted only to die, to sleep forever in a peaceful sleep, to never have to open her eyes and face the world again.

The cauldron was spitting fire, shooting off wild embers of shattering light that blinded her, hot ash searing her already agonized flesh. Through it all, dimly, Sharon was sure she could hear the witches laugh, cackling among themselves, pointing at her broken form as it lay huddled and defenseless in the rain-soaked dirt.

As Sharon tried to get up and face the hags, she felt the world beginning to spin again, trees and forest zooming past her eyes at breathtaking speeds, so fast that watching was making her sick again. She shut her tear-filled eyes tightly and wrapped her arms around herself. Then suddenly she could feel nothing, and she smiled: The pain was gone, and the suffering and hatred as well. Once more she was at peace, as before, when she had soared to the sun. And at last she was able to fall into the restful slumber she had been praying for—the first sleep since fleeing the city that was not filled with terrible nightmares and memories.

With large, amazed eyes the saya peered down at the stilled child of Samarkand and felt herself shudder. She glanced at the witches, all three mute before the cauldron, then turned back to the girl. She herself had seen or experienced nothing of what Sharon had been through—and neither had anyone else. Ever since the girl had drunk from the ladle, no one had so much as touched her once. The witches had asked questions only, and Sharon, drugged by the brew, had been compelled to answer and relive everything they had wanted to know.

"You may bring her back now," said one of the hags suddenly.

Carolyn's eyes darted to the eldest witch. "She is . . . all right?"

The Three Hooded Witches nodded as one. "The

potion has done its intended work; the poisons have left her body. She is free."

"And what of the Gift? Did the holy man lie? What shall I tell the Judges? Does she truly bear the Mark?"

"The holy man spoke the truth," said the eldest gravely as she replied from the shadows. "The girl has the Gift; she must learn how to use it. You saya, must teach her. It was her suffering that gave us the true answers; this khan of the Huns has created his own downfall. The girl shall lead the Kazirs well. The Prophesy is fulfilled. Sharon *is* the One."

The horses clomped slowly in the fading darkness as they followed the deep ruts and scars of the wadi, winding their way to higher terrain. Paled slivers of gray were eagerly pushing up along the rim of the horizon, heralding the coming of a new dawn like an advance guard. Through long shadows they crossed, moving out of the dark and into light, the shades retreating from the brightness. The last vestiges of forest were already well out of sight, and the riders pressed the road in search of the hidden trail back to the Stronghold, where Tariq would anxiously be awaiting their arrival.

The golden sandy majesty of the Steppes lay before them, an endless desert jewel tucked at the foot of the sweeping mountains to the north. Sharon sat tall and still in her saddle, grasping loosely at the reins of her horse, trying to piece together the puzzle of the journey. Her companions, as always, remained outwardly gloomy and close-mouthed. But it seemed to the princess that now when they looked at her, either purposely or by accident, there was a glimmer of awe in their eyes, a new respect that she somehow commanded, which she did not yet understand. Even Zadek seemed singularly different, as though the hours she'd spent with the strange witches had cast some unknown mark or pall upon her, a mark that left her no longer—in his eyes, anyway—the young girl who had been his pupil.

Events of the night before last were sketchy to her at best. It was easy enough for her to recall the overwhelming fear that had taken hold during her time at the clearing, even the hypnotic stare of the witches' eyes as she was handed the ladle and made to drink, but everything that transpired afterward was still mostly a blur, like a bad dream that was all too vivid and yet, when she tried to recall it, slipped elusively away—forever out of reach no matter how hard she tried to pull it back.

When she had awakened yesterday morning, it was in a dew-wet dawn. Someone—who? the saya?—had dressed her and covered her with blankets, and she was surprised to find herself well away from the clearing, taken back across the lake and to the very spot Carolyn had led them just before the pilgrimage in the forest began. Roskovitch, Asif as his shadow, had been silently squatting over the small morning campfire and had handed her a cup of steaming broth to take away the nip in the air. Save for a few brief words about preparations for the ride back to the Kazir Stronghold, nothing else had been said, neither by the saya, who always seemed to remain quiet and introspective, nor by Zadek.

The only communication seemed to come from Carolyn's ever-searching eyes, at times making Sharon most uncomfortable. What was it that the saya was thinking? Did she still see Sharon as an intruder or, worse, an impostor, as Yasir had claimed? Or was it something else again, something that an outsider among the Kazirs could never hope to understand? Whatever, Carolyn seemed as mistrustful of her as she had that night before the judges, and Sharon wondered if she were not waiting for something, biding time until she too could make her own claim against her.

Carolyn's antelope horn bobbed loosely from her necklace as her horse trotted from the bank of the wadi onto the flat terrain of the plain. Far in front, glistening in all the colors of the spectrum, glimmered the high rock walls of the Stronghold. A small pleased smile worked its way over Carolyn's otherwise drawn face. Roskovitch reined in behind her, grinning from ear to ear, and then he whooped joyously, gave spur to his horse, and, with his scalp lock flying wildly in the breeze, galloped toward the hidden fortress.

A heady wind had started to blow as the last leg of the journey neared completion. Dark thunderclouds were rolling in rapidly from the west, which was already black in midafternoon. The riders, exhausted and eager to reach shelter from the approaching storm, picked up speed. They crossed the yellow grass of the plain swiftly, splashing over a shallow, muddy creek and cutting a dusty trail between the water-starved trees of the Steppes.

"Behold the Stronghold of the Kazirs," rasped Zadek to Sharon as they approached the perimeter. She looked up at the massive walls, secret recesses along the ledges, and rocky heights hiding a dozen watchful sentries, and it occurred to her that she was seeing the secret entrance, something that no outsider had ever done before —or at least had ever lived to tell about.

Beside a solitary oak sapling, there stood an enormous red-trunked tree rooted to the earth like a great statue—thick, straight as an arrow. She stared at it in wonder, judging it to be perhaps fifty or more meters high—higher by far than the tallest steeple in Samarkand—and with a breadth of at least nine at the base. No branches spread from the scarlet trunk for at least a third of its height, and those that did seemed to poke out abruptly, almost artificially. There were no leaves, though; the branches were totally bare, but the bark near the root was rich and healthy, assuring her that the tree was not dead.

As the saya led her companions toward the sheer, smooth wall, Roskovitch halted beneath the shadows of the tree. His horse reared on its hind legs, and the barbarian from Rus cupped a hand around his mouth, issuing a shrill call, the cry of a loon.

In response came another cry, almost identical, from high, high up in the tree's topmost reaches, carrying down upon the increasing wind.

"The signal," said Carolyn matter-of-factly to the startled girl and the mullah. She laughed as Sharon gasped when the face of the mountain before her started to rumble.

The princess stared in disbelief; the rumble turned slowly into a grind, the sound of rock sliding over rock, and right before her eyes the smooth wall split into two, one face pulling to the left, the other to the right. A black canyon opened before them, deep as an abyss and as dark and foreboding.

"Praise be the Prophet!" wheezed Zadek, his body shaking with the resonant roll of the massive slabs receding into unseen recesses. And as he spoke, lightning struck and the world was bathed in pale blue light, briefly giving the Samarkand fugitives their first glimpse into the fortified Stronghold.

"A city!" gasped Sharon, leaning forward in her saddle and staring in shock. And so it was—a Kazir city, as unlike Samarkand as the desert was to the sea, yet a city nevertheless, made up of hundreds upon hundreds of tents and structures built of the mountain's stone, climbing up the rocky heights. It was a veritable beehive, clusters atop one another in seemingly never-ending succession. And so vast, so incredibly vast, was the Stronghold that there were fields of green behind the city; furrowed land, well watered and tended, where harvests were already being sown.

"Allah's mercy," Zadek was heard to mumble as the saya led the way between the opened walls.

"There is much more to be seen," said Carolyn with an air of obvious pride. She gestured grandly all around, waving on occasion to one or two watchful guards posted atop the inner parapets, their curved Kazir daggers clinging to their waists. Within deep clefts, a host of others watched while the band of four gained entry. Sharon was about to ask the first of a thousand and one questions when the noise from behind caused her to spin around; the smooth walls were closing behind her tightly, shutting with a hollow clang as each side slid perfectly back into place.

The sky was suddenly black above, the storm almost directly overhead. Zadek squinted into the distance; he rubbed his eyes, not daring to believe what he was seeing—a deep, fertile valley, with brown fields and herds of grazing sheep bunched randomly along the gentle slopes, a Garden of Eden amid the dry and arid Steppes. Shirtless men were tilling the fields, wielding rakes and hoes, and as the first rain pelted the soil, they ran and sought shelter inside the many whitewashed sheds that dotted the land.

Carolyn wiped water from her eyes and pulled the hood of her *aba* closely over her head. A stableboy came running; he bowed respectfully before the saya, then took her horse when she dismounted. "Where is Tariq?" she asked.

The boy pointed past the tents. "At the Greeting Place, saya, awaiting your arrival."

Zadek lumbered off his own animal. Roskovitch swung Asif down first, then he gave Sharon his arm, and the Samarkand princess followed as he showed them the way.

They scurried down a street, the only main thoroughfare by the looks of it, Sharon thought, and quickly they were ushered inside a stone edifice with a thatched roof far larger than any of the others around it.

Tariq loped like a young panther on the prowl the moment the canvas flap swung wide. His dark eyes glowed with joy at the sight of his sister, and he threw his arms around her.

"Did it go well?" he asked at length, holding Carolyn by the shoulders at half-arm's distance.

The saya smiled one of her mysterious smiles, glancing back at the priest and the girl who stood meekly at the door's entrance, rain dripping from the eaves onto their wet robes. "The holy man did not lie" was all she

said. And Tariq, looking handsome and powerful in his
colorful Kazir robe, laughed.

"Come inside," he said to his hesitant guests. "We
have been expecting you."

The hearth crackled with fresh logs of dried wood;
the strangers stepped closer to the flames, holding up
their palms to greet the warmth. A tall window at her
back let in the only outside light, Sharon saw. A few
scattered candles, unlit, protruded from ornate silver
candlesticks atop the hand-woven rugs. The walls were
bare save for a magnificent Persian tapestry above the
fireplace. Worn leather cushions, set around the center
legless table, provided the only seats. A scroll and piece
of parchment covered the polished tabletop.

Tariq left the saya's side and stood before his uneasy
guests. Politely he greeted them in traditional fashion,
fingertips brushing his forehead, head lowered with his
chin on his chest. "Welcome, holy man," he said. "Welcome, Sharon, princess of Samarkand."

They returned his hospitality with time-honored bows
of their own, and took places on the cushions when he
gestured for them to sit. "You must all be tired and
hungry," he told them, clapping his hand for a servant.

Carolyn unclasped her *aba* and laid it down carefully; then she sighed and nodded. "Feed her well,
brother," she admonished, looking down at the frail,
slim girl. "She will have need of strength."

Sharon shifted uneasily, calmed when the reassuring
hand of the mullah closed around her own. She began
to say something, but the saya stopped her abruptly.
"There will be time for questions later," she said.
"Right now you must eat, then rest. Your own quarters
shall be provided."

Sharon looked briefly at Zadek, then turned back to
the somber saya. Her new life was still a confusion;
none of it made any sense. Why had she been brought
here? What was expected of her?

Carolyn folded her arms over her breasts and gazed

at the troubled girl with an emotionless expression. "Soon you shall know all you need to know," she assured, as if already knowing what was on Sharon's mind. "For now let it suffice that you are here to be *taught*." She smiled secretively again. "And *I* will be your teacher."

"A Kazir must learn to fight," said Carolyn, with enough dramatic effect to drive the point home. "From the prairie village to the tents of the Steppes, a Kazir learns at the earliest age possible how to protect both home and family."

In the open yard, Sharon looked on with wonder as small children, both boys and girls, had been coupled and shown how to protect themselves against a Kazir's many enemies. Across dusty earth the paired combatants fought with wooden knives, parrying, thrusting, feigning blows, while several adults instructed them. Sharon watched with fascination, thinking now of the night Tariq had fought Yasir in the same kind of combat, only they had used blades of flashing steel, not blunted wooden toys.

The place was hot beneath an unrelenting sun, shadeless, and swirling dust, kicked high into the air by the ever-shifting mock combatants, filled their lungs. Kazir parents showed no pity for their young, Sharon realized; they forced them to learn in the worst, most brutal conditions possible. "A necessity," Carolyn had said. "Our enemies show no mercy; we must teach the children accordingly."

Harsh but true; yet there was a rough desert wisdom to all this. These children would grow up strong, unafraid of any man or beast, and fully adapted to a way of life born out of desperation—just as it had been for Tariq a decade before and for Shoaib before him.

The saya brushing dust from her blue-dyed tunic, nudged Sharon's elbow, and the two of them walked openly among the children practicing their lesson. All were too busy fending off opponents to pay any attention to either the saya or the "stranger," as Sharon had come to be called during these first weeks in the Stronghold.

In front of them, Asif had been paired with a hefty youth of about eleven, with curly black hair and olive skin. He caught his opponent off balance and wrenched him to the ground. The other child jerked away and, leaping like a mountain cat, pounced on Asif and pinned him by the shoulders. Then he struck with the wooden weapon at Asif's belly.

"Strike for the heart!" Carolyn reprimanded. "Your enemy would do no less. The heart, boy, the heart!"

The boy stood up and bowed to the saya apologetically for his error. Sharon shuddered at Carolyn's lack of mercy; it seemed to her that, after all, the contest was only for sport, not to be taken so seriously.

There was something of a sneer on the saya's lips when she turned to her companion. "You think me cruel, don't you?"

"Not cruel, but bitter, like all Kazirs—hateful of anyone and anything that doesn't conform to your desert ways."

If eyes could kill, then surely Carolyn's glare would have taken life from the princess. "When I was seven," she said coldly, as if giving a lesson, "I saw my village ravaged by soldiers—Samarkand soldiers. Every able-bodied man was butchered, and the women led off like chattel to serve as slaves in your city. My own mother took her life rather than face what lay before her. Can you understand that, outsider? Our duty here is to see that it cannot happen again."

Sharon bit her lip and mutely let the confrontation pass without further quarrel. She knew that there was nothing she could say that might even remotely begin to change a lifetime of bitterness.

They walked from this yard out toward a field where

the same sort of intense instruction was being given, only this time to youths slightly older than the last group. A few of the pupils seemed almost to be men, and their weapons were given accordingly. They fought with long, curved scimitars, glistening in the sunlight, and small, rounded desert shields—the weapons of Kazir cavalry.

"What else do Kazir children learn?" Sharon asked, shading her eyes from the intense brightness.

The saya looked at her curiously, as though she did not understand the question. "Everything that needs to be taught," she replied cryptically. "To care for the land, to tend the flocks, to recite scriptures from the Book." She looked at Sharon, smiling thinly. "And you? What is a princess taught?"

Sharon mused thoughtfully before answering. There had been so many things: art, music, poetry and philosophy, the history of her empire, as well as that of Persia and Islam. She'd been indulged by some of the best tutors in the world, pampered and spoiled, shown nothing but luxury, taught subjects and feminine skills a Kazir could never dream of. Yet, it had been her world that now lay destroyed, not the saya's. Carolyn had made her point very well indeed. Samarkand's children were dead, while the Kazirs continued on as they always had.

"How am I to help you, then?" she asked in open frustration.

The saya's answer was unexpected but straightforward. "Today you cannot, but soon you shall. You bear the Mark. Zadek has said it; the witches have agreed. You are the One chosen, the One to regain for us all we have lost."

Sharon shook her head slowly and sadly. Chestnut hair fell in front of her eyes and she pushed it back with a single stroke. "I am no use to you," she admitted, feeling a sensation of helplessness sweep over her. "If the truth were to be told, had it not been for Zadek, I doubt I could have fled my way out of Samarkand."

"That no longer matters. You are here now, among us, one of us——"

The girl laughed bitterly. "Look at me, saya. How can I lead you? I know nothing of this way of life." She tilted her head and stared behind at the children in their war games. "Even they understand more."

Carolyn agreed. "Perhaps; but you can be taught."

"Then teach me." Her eyes were sincere.

The saya turned about, the hem of her robe swaying with the breeze. She looked slowly at the city fortress, pride still in her eyes, but with the certain knowledge that even this way of life was nearing its conclusion. For a century her people had endured their solitude; now the time was close for it to end. How could she explain to this girl of Samarkand how much they needed her, needed not what she was at this moment, but rather what she was destined to be—a force that would wrench them from this existence and bring them back out into the light?

"A flower cannot grow without sunlight and water," she said after a time, knowing that her companion would not yet understand. "Without these, a garden cannot bloom."

The children, their lesson finally done, began to laugh and frolic, the way children the world over always do. Sharon's attention was caught by their laughter, by the joy in their eyes and the warmth of their smiles. She'd been brought up to believe them her mortal enemies, just as Carolyn had been taught to think of her. That had changed now, though, at least on her part. If there was any way to be of service to these rough but gentle people, she would gladly render it.

She put a hand on the saya's shoulder; Carolyn momentarily flinched. They had led such disparate lives, Sharon knew; it would be difficult for them to become friends. Still, there was little reason for them to remain enemies—not now, not while a much worse and deadly foe threatened them all. "Show me what I need to know, saya," she said, an honest humility in her voice that could not be missed. "And if I can help you, I shall."

Carolyn sighed deeply, her eyes on a bird flying overhead, a sparrow, young from the nest, finding its first wings. "It will not be easy for you," she warned, returning her gaze to Sharon.

"I don't want it to be."

"Then you think you are ready?"

Sharon looked up at the tiny winged creature now. *You and I have much in common,* she thought. *We must both learn to fly. But first I think I had better learn to walk.*

Carolyn, her clipped hair severely pulled behind a tight kerchief, edged in from her place upon the dusty soil, the wooden knife's blade horizontal with her eyes. Sharon self-consciously backpedaled, unsure of her footing. The saya came at her quick as lightning, sinuous as a desert snake. She slashed upward. Sharon's arm lifted to parry, but by the time her knife hand came down, the saya was no longer there; from somewhere came a small, exuberant cry, and Sharon turned to find Carolyn right behind her. The wooden knife poked deeply into her ribs, and as Sharon wheezed with the sting, the fast-moving saya tripped her and sent her sprawling.

Sharon lifted herself up slowly from the dirt, spitting dust, flexing a painful jaw. Her eyes cleared to see a handful of Kazir children formed nearby in a cluster, silently watching her as she staggered to her feet, their eyes filled with amusement at the clumsy stranger. It was rare for a Kazir child to see an adult who could not protect himself in combat, and Sharon could feel them laughing at her.

"Again," said the saya suddenly.

Before Sharon could respond, Carolyn was circling her once more, pressing in close, while the wooden blade cut lightly into the hot, stagnant air. With slow and uncertain movements, the Samarkand princess kept her opponent in full view, determined not to fall for the same trick twice. Yet, no sooner had Carolyn lunged than Sharon's vision lost track of the target and the next thing she knew, she was on the ground again, eating dust. This time the children were laughing openly.

The saya stood over her triumphantly, her antelope horn catching sunlight and shining. This time a hand was offered to Sharon, a rough hand that gruffly yanked her upright and left her standing dumbly in the open space of the bare yard.

"Want to try me again?"

Sharon slitted her eyes. The saya was taunting her purposely, she knew, realizing that the match was less than equal. Still, there was the same stubborn pride in the princess as within the fierce and wild Kazir saya. Without replying, she began to circle, remembering to use the same motions Carolyn had been using. The saya was well aware of this; she smiled and compensated for it by shifting her own stance, forcing Sharon to come at her with the sun in her eyes.

The wooden blade smacked into Sharon's soft belly. Air rushed out of her lungs, and she tottered, her own weapon slipping from her grasp when the saya tripped her for the second time.

She spit the dust out of her mouth with a scowl. Carolyn threw back her head and roared with laughter. Hands on hips, she said, "You have spunk, sister—at least for a city woman." Her tanned skin crinkled with her mirth. "Come on, then, one more time."

Sharon grudgingly got up, scooping up her weapon. Her ribs ached; her legs felt like lead. The taste in her mouth was foul, and her lungs were clogged with the ever-present desert dust that swirled over the high walls of the Stronghold. Her heart was pumping madly; she could feel humiliation rise with temper as the sure-footed saya danced circles around her.

This time Sharon feinted a few thrusts of her own. Most fell wide off the mark, but one, the last, saw the edge of her knife whistle inches by Carolyn's face. The saya pulled back, looking startled; then she grinned. She crouched, hunching her shoulders, her brown eyes sparkling with tiny fires. A cry of lusty jubilation roared from deep in her throat. All Sharon knew next was that her well-held weapon had skitted from her grasp, and she grunted, head ringing with bells, as her shoulder hit the earth forcefully beside the sober-faced children.

Someone handed her a cup of water; Sharon took it gratefully, gulping it down in great swallows, unaware —and not caring—of who had brought it for her. When she caught her breath, and her eyes stopped stinging, she peered up to see a tall, dark figure over her, blocking out the noon sunlight.

It was Tariq, the grin on his face stretched from ear to ear, tanned features shaded by his turban. He gave her his hand and eased her up slowly.

Sharon pouted. "It isn't funny," she said.

Tariq nodded. "No one said it would be——"

"She'll learn," said the saya, purposely stepping between her brother and the panting princess. There seemed a glow of satisfaction in her eyes when she spoke, and Sharon resented it—hated her for it. And all she could think of was somehow turning the tables on her smug and complacent instructor, finding some way, some trick, to make her be the one to eat dust next time.

"Let her rest for a while," said Tariq to his sister.

Sharon stiffened and shook her head. "No. I'm ready now," she blurted, regaining some of her strength.

Carolyn looked at her with some surprise, measuring her anew and, if nothing else, giving her credit for her dogged determination.

Tariq, though, frowned. He called to the waiting Roskovitch, and the barbarian from Rus grinned as he walked from the picket fence, where he had been quietly observing, and strode to the center of the yard. There he took the wooden knife that Tariq held out and smiled at the Samarkand fugitive.

"Watch us well," Tariq advised Sharon. "We're going to demonstrate how it's done."

Roskovitch stamped his feet and curled his body,

shoulders swinging at a low angle while Tariq, playing
the part the saya had, came at him. When Tariq's blade
sliced close, Roskovitch danced lithely away, bouncing
back upright in a single fluid motion. Then, with a
quick series of lashes, he not only forced Tariq to retreat, but sent him reeling off balance as well.

"Did you see that?" Tariq panted.

Sharon nodded slowly.

"Watch again."

The trick was repeated, this time with variation. The
fighters moved faster, becoming blurs, but when they
were done, the barbarian from Rus had left his attacker
lying prostrate upon the ground. Tariq laughed and
leaped to his feet like a cat. "There's a trick to knowing
how to fall as well," he said, and he lunged for Roskovitch, agilely balancing as he kicked, twisting his opponent's legs and causing him to fall. Roskovitch, taken
by surprise, thudded on his rump loudly.

Sharon laughed. Childlike, the barbarian shared her
mirth. Then he sprang up and the procedure was reen-
acted, this time, though, with Roskovitch ready for the
blow, fending it off successfully and, in one wrenching
movement, twisting Tariq by the arm and hurtling him
to the ground.

"Think you're ready to try it?" Tariq asked, accepting Roskovitch's extended hand and pulling himself up.

The Samarkand princess held out her hand, balling
her fist around the sweaty wooden hilt. She faced the
saya boldly, saying, "Come at me again."

Carolyn complied, weaving a slow pattern around
her. "Not like that," said Sharon, "the way you did
before."

The saya glanced at her brother; Tariq nodded, and
with a broad smile Carolyn came at her. She feinted,
then lunged. Sharon was ready. Exactly as she had seen
Roskovitch do, she moved into a crouch, back-stepping
momentarily until she was sure of her footing, then
came forward, her knife cutting through the air. The

saya's hand closed on her wrist; they grappled, and Sharon could feel the weight of Carolyn's lithe body press against her as she tried to sweep her legs up from under her. Sharon successfully pushed her away and, losing no time, went back on the offensive.

Her right ankle shot with pain, tears rolling down her dirt-streaked cheeks, she forced the breath into and out of her labored lungs and kept the swiftly dodging saya at bay. The children were no longer looking at Sharon mockingly; mutely they kept their places, moving slightly only whenever the combatants came too close. They knew that the stranger could never hope to defeat the skillful saya, yet no one could deny Sharon's courage or will. She fought with zeal and renewed energy where there should have been none, taking her blows without complaint beneath the torture of the unrelenting midday sun and hiding her hurts as a Kazir would do, never letting the enemy know the full extent of the damage.

"Well done!" cried Roskovitch as Sharon parried and blocked a new and furious attack. And when Carolyn, chagrined, grew impatient with the wearisome length of the match, Sharon allowed herself the small luxury of a smile.

She had not beaten the saya, she realized, and with her exhaustion only rising, she knew that Carolyn would soon regain the upper hand. Yet, there had been victory in this moment, sweet victory born of the knowledge that the next time would see her do better still.

Everything ached. The wool blanket felt rough and heavy against her bruised flesh, and Sharon pushed it aside. She couldn't remember when she had fallen asleep, only that the brief walk to her tent had seemed endless. She had reached her bed in a state of near collapse and could not recall if she had had supper last night.

She groaned as she propped herself up, eyes blinking from the streams of brilliant sunlight pouring past the partially opened flap. The sounds of morning were in the air—barking dogs, herders leading sheep to pasture, cowbells clanging—and the smell of cooking fires long since lighted. For an instant she forgot where she was, recalling instead pleasant childhood memories of the countryside in summer, where her father had taken her to spend happy weeks away from the shimmering heat of the city.

"Are you awake?" It was the saya's voice. Carolyn stepped inside; she stood with her hands on her hips, bare, well-tanned arms jangling with bracelets. She breathed deeply of the early-morning air and peered down questioningly at the stiff form of the girl on the bed. "Where does it hurt?" she asked.

Sharon gritted her teeth. "Everywhere. When I——" She lifted herself and moaned, falling back against the pillow, her forehead beading with perspiration. She sucked in air and let it out slowly, angered to have the saya here, seeing her like this so she could gloat over her.

Carolyn sat at the edge of the blankets, pushed Sharon slightly, and with strong, knowing hands massaged her shoulders and neck. "You did well yesterday," she told her. "Tariq was very pleased, and so was I."

It took all the effort Sharon could muster to turn and face her. Carolyn's face glowed with the sunshine. There was no hostility, no hint of suspicion, in her eyes. "Zadek says that you're a fighter. I didn't believe it."

"And now?"

The saya looked through the flap to the cotton clouds rolling swiftly above. She shrugged. "We'll see." She stood, reached inside her colorful tunic, and handed Sharon a tiny vial of palm oil. "Rub this in," she advised; "it will make you feel better. You can have breakfast if you like, but I'd advise you to eat sparingly. It's difficult to keep food down."

Sharon stared at her uncomprehendingly.

Carolyn laughed lightly. "I'll be waiting in the yard in one hour. Be there." Then she spryly breezed from the tent, walking out into the sunlight. Sharon felt her face flush crimson with rising anger; she yanked the pillow from the bed and threw it toward the open flap, her mouth tightly pressed in consternation.

Bitch! she cursed after the saya. *Someday I'm going to pay you back for all of this!* She swung herself off the bed and grabbed the vial of palm oil. She loped to the flap and pulled it shut, pounding a fist into her thigh in frustration. Then she rubbed herself down, grudgingly conceding that the palm oil worked, put on her desert tunic, and made ready to face the arrogant saya again.

She spit out the dust, lifting her head slowly, noticing that a trace of blood was mixed with the spittle. She had been doing well this morning, she knew, better than expected; that's why this time Carolyn had hit her. They had been grappling, each trying to wrench the wooden knife from the other, when unexpectedly Carolyn had drawn back a fist and hit her squarely in the face. Sharon had toppled, hitting the ground heavily, dizzily seeing a night sky of stars swim before her blurred vision.

She rose to her feet to find Carolyn defiantly glaring at her with her balled fists set upon her rounded hips.

"You cheated!" snapped Sharon. "That wasn't part of this lesson!"

The saya sneered, wiping perspiration from her brow. "Tell that to an enemy," she flared back, eyes slitted in the bright light. "Or would you expect a rampaging Hun to obey the rules and fight you fairly?"

The point was well taken, Sharon knew. Still, the saya was continuing to treat her with disdain, and Sharon knew that she wasn't going to take it much longer.

Pursing her lips, she came on again when Carolyn beckoned. They fought each other well, going over the motions step by step, scuffling at times, stalking at others. When the saya lunged, Sharon parried; when she stabbed, she sidestepped away, careful not to allow herself to be caught with the sun in her eyes. All morning they fought and well into the afternoon, observed at times by not only the children but many of the adults as well, come to see this stranger with the Mark stand up against the fiercest woman in the Stronghold.

"Enough for now," said Carolyn as the sun had begun to descend in the west. She dropped her knife to her side, panting, her body greased with perspiration and dust. Sharon proudly ambled to her side. The two women faced each other evenly, and Sharon casually handed over her wooden weapon. As Carolyn took it unsuspectingly, Sharon drew back her right hand and let loose a powerful fist, hitting the startled saya forcefully. Carolyn tumbled backward, falling against the low stone wall. She recovered quickly but, stunned, returned gracelessly to her former stance, her eyes widened with anger.

Sharon looked at the thin stream of blood curdling down from her nose and over her mouth and grinned openly. "Everything's fair in war, right?"

The saya, flustered, looked about with embarrassment. Off to the side, standing in the lengthening afternoon shadows, Tariq smiled. Sharon glowed with her own special pride and pleasure as she handed Carolyn her handkerchief, saying, "You're still bleeding." A large black-and-blue bruise swelled on her lip when she wiped the blood away.

Sharon waited until the soiled piece of cloth was given back, poised for a counterblow that was sure to come; it didn't, though. The saya pulled off her sweatband and let it fall to the ground. "You're learning" was all she said.

The night sky was perfect, the constellations trailing away across the horizon while a hazy blue moon hung low, a crescent above the silver cliffs of the enclosed Stronghold. Supper fires were gaily flickering, the sweet smell of skewered lamb filtering slowly through the air. The people sat around the fires waiting in anticipation of the celebration to begin, while beyond the field, high along the parapets of the ledges and the chalky cliffs, somber guards stood watch.

A cool summer breeze softly sifted through the trees, carrying away the dank, arid air of the day. Shadows cast by the flames climbed high above the tents and stone structures, shifting along the rock walls, covering the massive Stronghold like a protective blanket, keeping its presence well sheltered from unwanted eyes.

Sharon and Zadek took their places beside the fire, greeting in traditional Kazir manner those already seated. The flames licked hungrily into the night, the turning slab of shank dripping its juices, causing the fire to hiss and burn more brightly. Sharon glanced about at the faces of the young couples gathered round her; a few she recognized, most she didn't. Some would be guests to the Stronghold this night, she knew, recently arrived from other far and distant clans across the Steppes and the deepest reaches of the forests. But Roskovitch was there, with young Asif by his side.

It was the Third Eve of the Ewe, Zadek had explained, a time-honored and traditional night for rejoicing, dating back countless ages to the Kazirs' earliest foundings. Sharon had listened intently, learning more and more every day about the strange environment of which she had now become a part. In recent days the mullah had taken great pains to begin to teach her the many and often contradictory Laws upon which the Kazirs based their lives. They called them simply the Word of the Book, taken exactly as the Prophet himself had spoken them centuries before, only now molded to blend with the harsh existence of the Steppes and the deserts. And in this short time, Sharon had found herself beginning to understand a little better the deep emotions that bound these diverse tribes together: It was the land, the love of the desert, the love of the endless plain, even as they recalled the love of Samarkand, the city they had founded long, long before her own ancestors had taken it and claimed it for themselves.

And so on this sacred night, here within the confines of the secret gathering place called the Stronghold, the Kazirs came, putting aside the many small rivalries and feuds that plagued them, united in both religion and common history, together forging the beginnings of a new dynasty that she would somehow be a part of.

"Welcome, Sharon," said Tariq. Dressed in his finest robes, his head wrapped in a white turban, making his features seem all the more golden, he bowed and greeted her. "Welcome, Zadek."

The mullah folded his hands and bent his forehead against his outstretched fingertips. Then, one by one, the others around this fire were introduced, everyone interested in meeting the stranger, the outsider who claimed to bear the Mark. To Tariq's side came a tall, stocky young man, broad-shouldered, with a patrician face and classical features that indicated to Sharon a Greek bloodline. Ami, he was called, and she quickly learned that his own clan, the Fuliwas, were the closest by blood to Tariq's.

Close by, Kazir musicians had started to play— strange, wild desert music, rooted not here among the Steppes of Asia but south, in the Indian subcontinent.

They sat cross-legged upon skins of tigers, dressed in simple cloth robes, adorned with arm bracelets, bronzed images of coiled snakes that shimmered and danced almost with a life of their own as they reflected the firelight.

The *tablas,* mellow hand-held drums set between their knees, began to beat a slow, driving rhythm, while the strings of the *sarod* plucked ethereal nótes that echoed across the sheer walls of rock. Added to these came the whining drone of the *tamboura,* its bagpipelike coarse sound almost a plaintive cry, a strongly accented undertone that set the mood.

The Kazirs were a somber and serious people, even when festive, and the slow movements of their dancers writhing before the flames only increased the sense of severity. Conversation remained proper but informal as they waited for the lambs to be readied. Hot loaves of pita bread, circular and hollowed, were passed around and dipped into dishes filled with spicy *houmous*. When the hissing fires indicated that all was ready, the saya stood and, against the backdrop of stars, recited the traditional prayer. All heads bowed in humility, for this night was perhaps even more important than the occasion in years past. And although Sharon did not yet fully grasp its meaning, the momentousness of the evening was not lost on her. The air had begun to crackle with excitement, the gathered leaders of the clans leaning forward expectantly.

Sharon leaned over, dipping her greasy fingers into a water bowl and wiping them clean on waiting towels. "Why is this night so special, Zadek?" she asked.

The mullah greeted her with one of his mysterious smiles. He placed a betel nut in the palm of his hand, folded a small betel leaf around it in quarters, then placed both leaf and nut between his gum and cheek, enjoying the satisfying taste. He did not have a chance to answer. Ami, chieftain of the Fuliwas, his veiled and beautiful wife Sara beside him, stared at the Samarkand fugitives. He opened the cap of the goatskin vessel and filled the clay goblets placed beside each guest. Opposite him, sullen and silent, sat Yasir, his wounds fully healed but his scars remaining.

"Does she have a Name yet?" Ami asked of Tariq as he filled his cup to the brim.

Tariq's features were all but lost in the shadows; he swallowed the well-chewed piece of meat and shook his head. "No, cousin, not yet."

Ami seemed surprised. He sat back, listening to the sounds of the dancer's finger bells as the veiled *askrat* twirled before him, her perfect body swaying seductively with the music.

"She is not ready," broke in the saya.

Sharon felt her discomfort rise; it dawned on her that it was herself they were discussing. Eyes downcast, she picked a piece of lamb from her bowl and put it into her mouth, chewing the sweet meat gingerly as Ami said, "She *must* be ready; the hour is close at hand."

To this Tariq nodded. He looked at Sharon. "I know," he whispered faintly. A silence ensued between them.

Around the other fires, though, the mood of the night had become more joyous, the atmosphere heady. Downing their wine in drinking bouts, some of the men had risen to join the *askrat* in her dance, snapping their fingers and clapping their hands, spinning while their desert robes flowed behind, voices lifted in song with the music—happy folk tunes rarely sung these bitter days—while tambourines kept time with the steadily increasing beat of the *tablas*.

Ami downed his wine and gently placed the empty goblet at his side, refusing Sara's offer to refill the cup. His dark eyes flickering as the flames licked before his face, he glanced first at his friend Tariq, then at the saya, and at length at the others seated comfortably around the small fire. The pungent smell of meat was thick in the air still, skewered kabob being passed around. "She must be given her Name," he insisted, looking now at Sharon directly.

She shifted uncomfortably. They were talking about her as though she were no more than chattel, she thought, as a herder might speak of a prize sheep or goat, or a trader discuss the price of a young foal.

Tariq made a quick, impatient movement, then, clasping his hands around his knees, leaned back against the jut of a great rock. "Her strength has not been put to the test," he pointed out.

"Then why are you waiting?"

"The clans are growing restless," interjected Sara.

"Aye," agreed Roskovitch. The burly man from Rus tore off a piece of meat from a leg of lamb and tossed the bone into the fire. The flames crackled. "The Huns are on the march."

Sharon tensed; her eyes grew wide and frightened at the mention of her sworn enemies. They were coming after her. Kabul would make good his vow. . . .

Carolyn toyed with her antelope horn, her face growing dark. "What have you seen, Ami?" she asked.

"Huddled like sheep, a column of the khan's cavalry has moved west from the city. They skirted the edge of the forest, burning everything in their wake. I gave the order for fields to be destroyed before we evacuated." Here he bit at his lip, intense eyes betraying his concern. "They are moving toward the Steppes."

"So it has begun," Tariq murmured under his breath.

Yasir glared meanly at the young son of Shoaib. "And where is your promise they would never attack our lands?" He spat into the fire. "Our forces should have moved weeks ago—aye, upon the very day these outsiders were found."

Tariq minced no words: "We are not ready yet," he insisted. "We must have more time." Then, to Ami: "Can you buy us some?"

The chieftain folded his arms and sighed. "A little, perhaps, but not much. Forays are already spreading across the desert, near the perimeters of my land. I cannot keep my men in check for long. They wish to fight."

"I understand," said Tariq. "But our heads must remain cool. A direct confrontation now could spell disaster."

Yasir sneered. He cracked the thick, meaty bone in his hands and threw it toward the resting dogs, which yapped and raced for it. "I say we muster at once, send the signals to every clan, have our forces prepared to ride with a day's notice."

"You are impulsive," said the saya. "My brother is right. Our strategy must be to wear the enemy down—badger him, strike lightly at his flanks, his patrols, run him dizzy until his army is in disarray. Once they are helpless within our territory . . ." She smiled grimly, letting there be no mistake about her intent.

Yasir gruffly wiped his mouth with the back of his hand. Grease covered his fingers and he wiped them into the soil. "Talk, talk; talk is easy. We need action —now! And this one"—he turned to Sharon—"this one you claim bears the Mark, she does not yet even have a Name!"

Anger etched into Tariq's rugged features. "She will earn one," he said quietly, "I promise you."

The wail of a horn blared through the night, above the music and the singing, catching everyone by surprise. Suddenly the music stopped and the dancers froze in their places. The lonely wail was heard again, urgency in its shrill blast. All at once soldiers of the Stronghold leaped to their feet, Tariq in the forefront.

A terrible rumble, like thunder close by, came from behind. Sharon turned, and in the distance she could see the high walls, black in the shadows, begin to move, groaning as they split, and two riders gallop through the entrance of the Stronghold. They rode low on their saddles, not pausing before the sentries, racing through the city of tents, along the edges of the looming walls of rock, past the guarded ledges and cavernous recesses without breaking stride, reining in fiercely when they reached the brightly burning fires.

The first rider expertly jumped from his saddle, sweeping grandly and low before the waiting saya and her brother. "My lords, the enemy advances," he announced, wiping grime from his beard. "Advance units have been sighted as close as the approaches to the Green Pool."

At the mention of the oasis, Tariq looked darkly at his sister; her own brow was knit in apprehension.

"Are you certain of this, man?" cried Roskovitch. "What is their number? Which direction do they ride? Speak!"

The rider rose from his position, still panting to catch his breath, while his steed nervously whinnied behind. His arm shot out toward the south. "Only a small advance guard has reached the oasis," he told them, hastily adding, "but you can see the glow of campfires lit across the desert. Their number I cannot say, my lords, only that surely a large force will soon follow."

"By the Prophet's beard!" grunted the barbarian from Rus.

"You see?" chimed Yasir, a finger pointed at Tariq accusingly. "While we sit idly and spill words, our enemies have begun to mount their attack." He glared at the younger man standing in dancing patterns of shadows. "Will you take action now, or must we wait until they bang upon our doors?"

Tariq ignored his rashness, knowing this was the time for calm heads and sensible decisions, his eyes fixed on the fire. A knot in the dry wood exploded with a loud crack, and the leaping yellow-blue flames danced higher and higher, wisps of smoke rising into the crisp night above their heads. Beside Tariq, Kazir warriors, hands within, clutching at the hilts of their swords and scimitars, waited for his response.

"Well?" growled Yasir, ready to jump into a leadership role the moment it seemed Tariq might falter.

But Tariq didn't falter; he cast his gaze upon the scalp-locked barbarian. "Roskovitch, prepare to ride!"

The burly man's eyes squinted; he grinned sourly, spinning on his heels and seeking out his bold Arabian steed, Asif trailing him.

"And you, Ami, as well," the young chieftain said. His hand darted out. "And you, and you, and you . . ."

One by one the chosen Kazirs bolted for the stables. Whooping, shouting war cries, the Kazirs mounted, ready to ride and to fight. Desert horsemen all, they calmed their anxious animals, stroking the flowing manes, easing onto the saddleless backs.

"We go," said Tariq, satisfied. The eyes of the saya caught his attention.

"She must earn her Name, brother. Take the outsider with you; let her fight."

Hand to his bearded chin, the handsome Kazir paused to consider. His horse was swiftly brought, and he mounted the mare with a single movement of his body. Then, peering down as he took the reins, he said, "Is she ready?"

Carolyn's smile surfaced slowly, enigmatically. "Every wolf must test his teeth," she observed, and then she unstrapped her curved dagger from her waist and handed it to Sharon.

Zadek gasped; protective of the Samarkand princess, he stepped between the two women. "No!" he cried. "She is not ready."

The saya sneered as if she expected this response, but Sharon reached out, took the extended blade, sheath first, and, opening her robe, tied it securely around her slim waist, not looking up to gaze into Zadek's disbelieving eyes.

"Are . . . are you certain?" he stammered.

She lifted her head, pushed back her hair, and smiled. "I am, teacher," she assured him.

Zadek, pained to see her depart like this, so untested, took her firmly by the shoulders. "Tonight shall be no mere game, child," he warned. "The blade you carry is made of steel, not wood. And if you err, there shall be no second chances."

Sharon nodded; she understood—perhaps too well. But, if indeed her destiny was what the holy man had claimed, what Tariq had put both his life and reputation on the line for, then she must prove it, one way or the other. "The saya is right," she said, glancing Carolyn's way. "It's been long enough. Let tonight be my test."

"Then find your horse," called Tariq roughly, hiding a pleased smile at her response. "And perhaps this very night you shall earn your Name."

With the speed of thieves and outlaws, the small band of Kazirs rode between the mighty opened walls, guided toward the oasis by the stars in the same manner that mariners are guided upon the sea. Across these waters of sand they raced, swirls of dust clouding behind them, Tariq and Roskovitch in the lead, the bold barbarian heaving his scimitar above his shaven head as he sang the songs of war. Even Asif was there, astride a pony, small dagger at his side. They hurtled through barriers of dune and rock, scrambling down into the folds of darkened wadis, then up and out again, regaining footing upon the endless flat of the plain. In the distance behind, the walls of the Stronghold disappeared, the light of the fires within no longer a telltale giveaway to prying eyes searching the sky. Like the wings of a condor they spread out over the parched earth, hooves clattering thunderlike over rock-strewn terrain, tramping weed underfoot, gaining slow progress against the grim vastness ahead.

Sharon could feel the rush of wind whistling past her face; she pressed herself forward on the horse, both hands grasping the loose-fitting bridle, her veiled face feeling the relentless beat of desert-blown sand. She kept steady pace with them all, boots digging into the stallion's flanks, reining the animal in, then kicking again to make him leap gracefully and high over the narrow winding stream before her, like the wind itself, leaving those behind her to splash in the muddied, dark waters.

The Green Pool was dim and still when the riders silently approached. Tariq and Roskovitch dismounted. Together they peered into the distance. There were no fires lit, no sounds of drinking soldiers to be heard—only faint rushes of a breeze pushing through the leaves of the palms and the restless patter of horses tethered beyond the trees, where a sole sentry sleepily stood midnight-to-dawn watch.

Tariq signaled for his men to fan out; they all dismounted and took well-concealed positions along the heights of the dunes. Ami led one group of men off to the left, Tariq another to the right. Roskovitch, Sharon at his side, held the center group in place. Silhouettes of slow-moving horses stood out against the sky; once into position, both groups mounted again and awaited the signal for the charge. Asif was ordered not to take part but to hang back. If anything went wrong, he was to return to the Stronghold with the news.

Roskovitch spat into the wind. He peered down at Sharon in a kindly way, the first time she had ever seen the gruff barbarian treat her with deference. Disturbed and fretful, he instructed her in a low voice to stay close come what might.

"You needn't worry," she replied. Sliding the dagger from its sheath, she felt its weight, admiring the steel's glow in the moonlight. She collected her thoughts slowly, trying to recall every moment of training she'd been given these past weeks, remembering the saya's words and seeming cruelty.

A terrible cry resounded through the chilled air, the cry she'd heard Samarkand soldiers try to describe after

they had come into combat with the desert Kazirs—a
war cry like no other, they had said, and as Sharon
listened to it now, piercing the night and sending shivers
along her spine, she at last knew what they had meant.

Rising from heavy sleep as though in drunken stup-
ors, the small group of Huns jumped up in disarray.
From both sides charged the Kazir horsemen, hollering
and whooping, brandishing curved swords high over
their heads, spinning them round like tops, and the
closer they came, the more furiously pitched were their
cries.

Roskovitch blew his horn, calling for the attack from
the front. Her own cry lost amid the screams and terrible moans from the beset Huns, Sharon charged into
the frey; each man she saw took on the hated countenance of Kabul, him and his sneering son Osklath.
The Huns raised their rounded leather shields in
self-protection. They staggered and fell under the blows
of fast-moving stallions and swinging blades. Reeling,
falling to their knees, they tried to scramble and dodge
the onslaught, but, shrieking the name of the Prophet,
the Kazirs cut them down, lopping off limbs, kicking
spinning bodies into the deep waters of the pool, tearing
apart the camp completely.

Lost in the melee, no longer aware of who she was
or why she was here, Sharon fought as well as a Kazir
woman had ever done, fending off attackers on both
sides, slashing her knife through soft fur vests and
leather armor.

"For God!" cried the Kazirs, the shout above the
awful din. "For freedom! *For Samarkand!*"

Fire raged through the Green Pool, the tents of the
enemy ablaze, dark smoke billowing. The last mournful
cry faded into nothingness, and the Kazirs regrouped
slowly, leading their horses to safer ground. Sharon
peered back in a daze at the carnage she had helped
create, shaking her head at the numbing sight, not able
to control her shaking. She had killed this night, taken

human lives. Faceless men they had been to her, without identity, but the image of Kabul had burned in her vision, and when she had plunged her dagger into their flesh, it had been his flesh, not another's.

At the edge of the swaying grass, she paused, wiping blood from both her knife and her hands by sifting them through the cool sand. She was not aware of the figure behind her. It was Tariq, his face dirtied with smoke and blood, his fine robe splattered like that of a butcher—and twenty-three slain Huns gave testimony to the slaughterhouse the oasis had become.

He put a gentle hand upon her shoulder and felt it tremble beneath her robe. "You needn't be frightened," he told her softly. "It's done; we can go home now."

Sharon raised her head, her eyes red and blank. "I'm not frightened," she answered truthfully.

Tariq nodded and sighed. "But it's still not easy killing a man, is it—even an enemy."

Her eyes suddenly became alive. She sheathed her dagger with a single stroke, the way Carolyn had taught her. "No," she said in agreement, "it wasn't easy, but I'll do it again and again—until I slay the khan."

Tariq drew back. The vengeance in her blood had not been sated, her deep hatred barely touched by this brief encounter. Little more than months ago he had first seen her in the marketplace of Samarkand; it seemed more like years. Sharon was hardly the same girl he remembered. She had changed much over these weeks, perhaps more than anyone, including Zadek, had realized. She was no longer a frightened child gazing out into a world she could not understand. Now she was . . . what? He shook his head, not knowing what to think.

Roskovitch wiped the edge of his scimitar on the sandy earth and kneeled beside the outsider with open pride.

"Did she fight well, Bear?" asked Tariq, using the barbarian's bestowed name.

The man from the cold lands of Rus looked up at his chieftain, wise eyes that had seen much slitted like a snake's. "She fought like a panther, this one," he said. "The holy man did not lie; she is a leader, all right. Mark or no, I for one would follow her anywhere."

Tariq cocked a brow. "Even into hell?" he queried of the Christian.

Roskovitch grunted. "Aye, Tariq, even into hell." He looked once more at Sharon. "She has earned her Name among us."

The young chieftain listened and nodded slowly. Silver light gleamed down and cast the three of them in tinted shadows. "And so you have named her," he told the barbarian. "The panther."

Sharon began to wake from her foggy haze of hatred and murder. She was grieved for the first time at what she had done—grieved but not sorry. If need arose, she would do it again.

"Return first and give word to the saya," Tariq commanded one of his men. "Tell her that the Samarkand princess is dead and in her stead we return with her successor, the One who bears the Mark: the Panther of the Steppes."

Part Four:

CLAWS OF THE PANTHER

It was twilight; winter's sudden onset was in the air, fields withering across the hills, leaves turned to brown, crimson, and gold as they tumbled from the branches and scattered to the dark soil below. A gusty wind whipped through the empty streets of Samarkand, causing shutters, tightly bolted, to clatter and dust to swirl high above the rooftops, while stray cats and dogs hunted for shelter among the dark alleys and crumbled bricks of once grand homes. Through breaks in the cloud cover, evening stars glimmered down bleaky upon the nearly deserted ominously silent city.

In a mood as bleak as the sky, Kabul, great khan of the Huns, peered past the thick drapes of his opulent throne room, scowling as his gaze fixed below across the unbroken view of his domain.

" 'Tis time, sire," said the Chinese physician.

Kabul turned to face the little man with slanted eyes and a perpetual smile that played across his yellow face. The physician bent over in a deep, respectful bow, then gestured toward the velvet divan. Kabul took his place, not bothering to give a second look at the dozen hair-thin needles laid side by side upon a tray. Shirtless, although it was cold, he sat silent and sullen, letting the physician poke his needles through his flesh while he stared grimly at the dancing flames in the fireplace opposite.

With delicate, almost feminine hands, the physician took the longest needle, twirled it lightly, then plunged it through Kabul's bulging bicep. The khan winced.

"Did you feel pain, my lord?" questioned the well-trained physician from Cathay.

Kabul shook his head. No, it didn't hurt, it never did. He'd been receiving these strange Oriental treatments for months now, his last hope of diminishing the terrible pain that came almost daily in spasms. Acupuncture, the Chinese called it, or so he was told—needles stuck through various vital points of his body at weekly intervals, poking unseen holes all over his body, hardly drawing blood, in an effort to release him from his torment. Grudgingly he had to admit that sometimes these treatments worked; at least his suffering was less. But he never had trusted these strange Orientals, always smiling, always so polite, even when they invaded your body with their instruments, making you feel more like a pincushion than a man.

The second needle went into his leg, the third into his belly. The physician wiped perspiration from his forehead, then proceeded to stick in the fourth and fifth. For almost an hour Kabul sat like this, still and unspeaking, while the diminutive man played games up and down his flesh.

"How do you feel, my lord?" asked the Oriental after the last sharp needle had been sunk.

Kabul grunted in response. His eye was burning again, a sure sign that a spasm was close. He put his hand to the heavy eye patch, fingertips needing to yank off the fabric and scratch at his sewn lid, satisfying the terrible urge; but slowly the burning sensation dissipated. The needles were working, as the physician had assured. The spasm had been controlled, and for that Kabul was more than grateful. The Oriental was worth twice his fee, twice his weight in gold for the service he rendered. With him here to cure the ailment, Kabul could feel almost like a man again, the ruler of his empire, and not a howling animal forced, as in times past, to writhe upon the floor insanely, unable to think, unable to see, unable even to rise to his knees and beg.

The needles were removed with as much care as they had been put in. Thin bloodstains spread over the white towel on the tray. "Rest now, my lord," said the physician, cleaning his hands and bowing. "Your affliction shall not disturb your thoughts tonight."

The khan rested back on the divan, rubbing his biceps. Across the stone ceiling danced patterns cast by the flames. A night without misery; perhaps two, or even three or four . . . His dark god had indeed blessed him with the coming of the Oriental. He thought back to the butcher of a Persian who had operated on his eye, and felt his temper rise. He had actually let the swine leave Samarkand freely, as Osklath had promised, before changing his mind. And he did not regret having had him dragged back, racked and scalded with boiling water, allowed to die slowly and miserably for failing in his task. It was just punishment for the Persian. How much Kabul had enjoyed watching as the dog's own eyes were blinded, driven through with pins, so that the butcher could at least feel what the mighty khan was forced to suffer.

"Rest well, Chinaman," said Kabul as the physician withdrew. Then he sighed, stretched out on the divan, and pulled a blanket over his body. He fell asleep swiftly this night, his dream a sweet nightmare in which he finally caught the girl who did this to him and paid the bitch back in kind. How she would scream when he repaid her! How she would beg and moan and squirm and plead . . .

And how he would enjoy seeing her die with the tortures that a thousand demons in hell itself could not inflict.

The freshly driven snow was knee-deep, and Sharon and the saya led their horses slowly through it, stepping carefully along the rutted and white-blanketed folds in the land, making their way among the limbs of thickly crusted trees that dripped icicles knifelike from overhead boughs and pushing deeper into the forest. The lake was frozen solid. Over the ice, dismounted, they continued on, tightening their cloaks about them while a nasty wind sliced across the lake and cut to the bone. The ice glimmered pale blue in the last vestiges of dusk, and as night took over, they reached the other side and started the long ascent up the dark hill, burrowing a path through the snow until they reached the crest and the clearing where the Three Hooded Witches waited.

Flame and smoke from the fire beneath the cauldron seemed to hang motionless in the frigid air of Grim Forest. Catching her breath and pausing, Sharon unconsciously brushed wet flakes from her heavy fur collar and passively stood while the hags upon the mound, behind the vat, cackled among themselves, the liquid of the cauldron ceaselessly bubbling.

"She comes, she comes, *hee-hee*," gloated the tallest, the one in the middle, as she fixed her glowing eyes upon the cold, tense strangers.

Her sisters bobbed their heads in agreement. Bundled tightly in their robes, faces hidden within their cowls, so that only their glowering eyes could be seen, they beckoned for their guests to step closer.

Carolyn tethered the horses, fixing the reins firmly beneath a large rock, and while the mares restlessly snorted and stamped, the two women made tracks toward the mound. The night sky was flawless, a pure velvet backdrop against which ten thousand stars twinkled. A loon cried from a distant tree as Sharon and the saya stopped at the foot of the mound, hands folded before them, heads respectfully lowered. Sharon's chestnut hair glimmered red in the glow of the firelight as she pulled down her hood. Chin raised, eyes fixed straight ahead, body poised, she seemed a different person from the frightened girl they had seen only months before.

"They say she has earned her name, *hee-hee*," chortled the second grim sister.

"Aye," chuckled the third, glancing quickly at her hunched siblings. "So she has, so she has."

"And she has gained pride," interjected the first, nodding with approval. "Vanity, vanity; she is no longer afraid."

They laughed again in their strange way, but this time Sharon did not draw back. They were right, she knew. She *did* have pride now; a belief in herself that had not been there before. Zadek had instilled it, the saya had stubbornly forced it out, and Tariq's trust had reinforced it.

The witch in the middle leaned over the boiling vat, unperturbed by the hot steam rising. "Is this so, Samarkand princess? Have you earned that which you were intended to earn?"

There was a brief broken silence, when Carolyn said, "She has, old hags. The name belongs to her; no other may claim the right to take it away."

The witches nodded with satisfaction. Snow, gusted by a sudden wind, began to swirl all around. The middle sister rubbed her bony hands one over the other, warming them in the lifting steam.

"They call her 'Panther,'" said the second sister with glee, "'Little Panther of the Night.' They claim she has shown great courage, *hee-hee,* as befits she who bears the Mark."

"And she has spilled their blood, *hee-hee,*" cackled the third. "Vile blood, they say; the blood of her enemies, they say." All three exulted with chuckles.

Sharon rubbed at her arms, still cold despite the flames that hissed and popped before her. Both she and the saya had been summoned here this night, commanded to ride alone to the forest, with only the cold winter's wind as escort; but for what purpose, the saya had not told her, merely that the hour had come and Sharon was now ready to stand before them again. She had been bewildered by this, thinking she'd seen the last of these hags, having successfully passed their tests the last time. Now, though, it seemed there would be more.

"No Kazir shall ever again call her 'outsider,'" Carolyn said. "She has earned her due among us."

The lessons had been well learned, Sharon knew, as the witches listened gravely to the low voice of the saya. Since the night at Green Pool oasis when she had taken her first life, all had changed. Now she had been accepted, trained as one of the Kazirs' own, and sworn to the defeat of their common enemy. Roskovitch the Bear, the scalp-locked barbarian from Rus, had spoken before Tariq and the Stronghold elders in her favor; he, the man who had frightened her so that first day. The judges had listened in stony silence to his testimony and to Zadek's as well. She who bore the strange Mark that still she had yet to fully comprehend had been bestowed with her name among them, and Tariq had been the first to proclaim it. Even the saya had been forced to acknowledge her right to use it, and now she wore it like a badge, sworn to these Kazirs out of desperation, sharing with them the common hatred of the conquerors of Samarkand, determined not to let the usurpers gain their footing on the Steppes, the last bastion of freedom against the invading hordes.

"Rats' claws and the teats of a goat," rasped the witches in unison. "Spine of a monkey and testes of a lizard!" The witch in the center peered closely at Sharon. "Do you know why you have been brought here tonight?"

Sharon shook her head. "Only that the saya said it was your command."

The hag sprinkled a vial of colored powder into the cauldron, and the boiling liquid hissed and burst into fire, ocher fingers of flames raiding the sky. Protectively Sharon put a hand against her face, pulling back at the sight. The witches laughed loudly and mockingly. Images, mere shadows to Sharon and the saya, appeared within the swelling fire. All three hags stared into it deeply, lifting their arms, wrinkled flesh clinging to bone. The wind around them picked up violently, almost lifting Sharon and Carolyn off their feet. And the witches chanted together, clouded by smoke and fire that writhed like serpents from the black iron cauldron. Faces gaunt, lips devoid of color, Sharon and Carolyn looked on in amazement. What their hosts were seeing within the fire was clearly not meant for their own eyes, eyes of mortals, but whatever it was, it was a dark vision indeed, for even the three hags seemed visibly shaken by the unfolding predictions. The flames grew so intense, so enormous, that the two women were forced to step back and shy away their eyes.

When at last the fire had dimmed, Sharon looked up; she was trembling, gaping at the wet pools of melted snow almost covering the entire clearing. Her heart was banging like a drum up into her throat, and her feet felt rooted to the earth when the witches beckoned her alone to come forward.

Sharon took a few uneasy steps and then kneeled, head lowered.

"Evil times are upon the Steppes," whispered the witches throatily. "The shadows of death grow long and deep; a turbulent ocean of blood pours from the sky, seeping poisonously into the soil and spoiling it forever." Silence, all-pervasive, ensued, then: "Lift your head, daughter of Samarkand, so that you may see."

Bravely Sharon tilted her face to peer into the bubbling cauldron. She blinked her eyes, denying her own vision, but there it was, so lifelike before her that she could almost reach out and touch it: the shaded image of a face, twisted, vile, hideously ugly, with a black gaping hole where once an eye had rested.

"The khan!" she gasped breathlessly.

"Aye, 'tis Kabul, the mortal enemy of your peoples, whose insane hatred cannot be quenched without the blood of the Kazirs."

Sharon was shaking all over; her eyes were glued to the dark image that crept closer with the blowing smoke. The one-eyed barbarian stared back at her, seeming to recognize her, and she stifled a scream.

"Yes, he can see you," sang the witches. "He has been called from the depths of his fitful sleep, his mind burning with the memory of the thing you have done to him. And his armies march, daily gathering in strength, a vise upon the Steppes and the desert, slowly closing in until all he seeks is within his grasp."

Sharon was sweating; she shook her head violently. "No! Never! He'll be stopped! He *must* be stopped!"

The laughter of the witches was a terrible bell in her ears, drowning out sanity. "The Kazirs are doomed," they chanted. "The world to the west is doomed——"

Sharon arched herself backward, hands to her ears, still denying the truth of the vision. "No! No! It must not be! It must not be!" But, before her widened eyes, she saw the lands burning with fires greater than those that had swept Samarkand. There was the screaming of children, the anguished cries of their mothers unheeded as they were butchered like sheep while she helplessly looked on.

"Who is to stop them?" sang the witches. "Who is to stop them?"

Sharon was moaning upon the ground. "The Kazirs will stop them! Tariq will stop them!"

This time the laughter was painful, a spiteful wail just like the cry of the loon, like the call of *nightthings,* squeezing her mind until she could no longer think.

"Who will stop them?" sang the witches anew. "Who? Who?"

"I . . . I don't know."

The laughter became even louder, a vicious roar penetrating her soul. She thrust her hands forward, palms up. "Stop! *Stop!*"

Cackle followed malevolent cackle. "Summer and winter, winter and summer! She bears the Mark and has earned her name! You must fight the fight," came the rasping voices in unison. "You must win the battle."

Pleading, crying, shaking her head, refusing to hear what they were telling her, Sharon called, "How? How can *I* be the one? How can *I* stop the destruction?"

The tallest of the witches rose to her full height, no longer bent and twisted. A thin hand shot out from her sleeve, fingertips throwing what looked and felt like a bolt of lightning. The flash scorched the earth at Sharon's bended knees. Charred, damp soil smoldering around her, she cried out with the sudden burning that filled her body. Again the lightning struck, hot, white, singing at the hem of her *aba.*

"The Gift," hissed the witches, "she must have the Gift!" Their hands lifted in the frosty air, drawing strange and incomprehensible designs.

"Like the plague they have come, and so they have taken root. . . ." A bolt of blazing green fire whipped past Sharon's head and smashed into a tree behind. Bark ignited like tinder, and billows of porous black smoke swirled in the wind. "And they must be plucked from the very earth!"

The ground began to shake, and Sharon fell forward, her hands digging into the dirt. The stricken tree seemed to dance, its branches alight, twisting and reeling, its trunk swaying this way and that while the eerie fires dizzily spun, finger flames groping for the stars.

"On the wings of a bat, so shall she come!" sang the hags. "Locusts to darken the sky, plagues to counter plagues!"

"Come, princess of Samarkand," demanded the eldest, "come and receive what is rightfully yours."

It was all Sharon could do to lift herself and dare approach the hissing cauldron. From the corner of her eye, she could see Carolyn behind her recoiling in terror. The green fire was crackling everywhere around the saya, burning to cinders everything in its wake, yet not touching her, leaving her alone, a prisoner inside the walls of flame.

The third sister put her hand directly into the boiling liquid. Unscathed, she brought out a dazzling blue-hot knife. The blade glowed in the light, its razor-sharp edges glimmering hotly. "Kneel!" cried the hag, and Sharon, shuddering, complied.

Hands yanked at her long, flowing hair, jerking her head back so that her tear-filled eyes were forced to stare up toward the stars. She felt the heat of the blade drawing close, smoking, hissing, felt the edge slice through her hair. The smell of burning hair filled her nostrils; chestnut locks, fanned by the wind, blew high above her head, sizzling as they swam upon the breeze, flaring like small torches until they burned out and disappeared.

Sharon screamed out as the edge of the knife lightly pressed against the back of her neck, its searing heat scalding her flesh. "The Gift!" cooed the witches. "She has received the Gift!"

The ground was quivering once more, an earthquake rocking the clearing in the forest with unleashed fury.

Sharon no longer could tell what was going on around
her; she fell upon the earth and in a mixture of shame
and fear hid her face, not daring to glance up while the
three sisters exultantly began to dance in a circle around
her. They were whirling now, chanting, eyes staring but
unseeing, feet hardly touching the ground but pattering
softly as they weaved in and out, hands beating a slow,
forceful rhythm.

Sharon let air trickle out of her strained lungs. There
was a terrible tightness around her head. She touched
her scalp and abruptly pulled her fingertips away from
the heat, feeling as though her whole head was afire.

Then it stopped, suddenly and inexplicably; the pain
was gone, the ground no longer shook, the green flames,
only moments ago swirling about her like the fires of
hell, vanished totally. Stars brightly flickered once
again, and the rustling of wind among the branches remained the only sound.

"It is done," said the eldest witch hoarsely. "Cover
her."

The saya, breathless and still afraid, ran forward
and kneeled beside the panting princess. She drew a
dark scarf from her robe and wrapped it about Sharon's
head, pinning the two loose ends at the nape of her
neck.

"Go," hissed the witches. "Go and do what must be
done."

Sharon struggled to regain her feet as fiercely as she
was struggling to regain her senses. Was it all over, truly
all finished? The hags had bestowed upon her the Gift,
whatever it was; yet she didn't feel any different, could
not explain the meaning of any of the things they had
done to her.

Filling her lungs with frigid air, she blew a steady
stream of white smoke between her lips as she exhaled.
The three sisters, standing behind their cauldron once
again, glared at her with cats' eyes, faces impossible to
distinguish behind the shadows of their cowls.

"We have helped you all we can," said one tersely.

"And the Gift?" whispered the shaken saya.

A hand pointed to the scorched black earth at their feet: The burning knife was still there, only now it had changed form; in its stead, clinging to the sodden soil, lay a coiled, snakelike hulk of metal. Sharon bent down and picked it up; it felt heavy, weighted, dead. She stared at it, seeing that its head, when held away from the shadows, seemed to resemble that of a cobra. Two small holes for eyes had been burned into it, and a slit across the bottom seemed to hide the tip of a pitchforked tongue. Yellow scales ran its length to the pointed tip of its tail.

"Take it; carry it always," rasped the eldest. "But, be warned: Only the one who bears the Mark may use it, and then only for a single time."

"How . . . how will I know when that time has come?" asked Sharon.

The witch grinned toothlessly. "Only you may decide, Little Panther, only you may decide." She lifted her gaze toward the velvet sky. "When the hour of need arrives, call upon its power, and the secrets of this forest shall do your bidding."

"I shall not misuse it, old hag," Sharon promised, tucking it safely away beneath her belt.

The witches nodded. "Return to your Stronghold, Samarkand princess. The son of Shoaib has need of you; the Kazirs have need of you."

Sharon turned to the saya, looking at Carolyn with humility. "The Hundred Years of Solitude are done," she said, holding her ground firmly in an open display of her courage before them all. "I shall not turn away from the people of the Steppes, from those who have taken me in, given me both shelter and home. Their enemies are my enemies. Let the khan send whatever armies he will, my vow shall be kept." She clasped Carolyn's shoulder and gazed deeply into the saya's haunting eyes. "Samarkand is fallen, but, while breath remains in my body, the Steppes and the Kazirs shall remain free. From this day forward let the word be spread"—and here she lowered her hand and clenched the coiled metal snake—"that one day we will regain *all* that has been lost."

The dancer appeared from behind the swaying curtains, illuminated by the soft glow from the ebbing brazier. She was a perfect specimen of Asian beauty, olive-skinned, coal-black hair long and flowing, a fitting crown to complete her exquisite body. Both sensuality and passion flittered across her delicate face, slanted eyes flashing with amusement, heaving breasts straining against the thin veil of silk that covered her flesh. Kabul, one arm fondling the hips of the Persian slave beside him on the divan, smacked his lips hungrily and stared with lust while the dancer drew closer.

The music began, and the dancer moved tauntingly nearer, arms lightly hanging at her side while her fingertips caressed the firm curve of her belly. She was young, the great khan realized—fifteen, sixteen, no more—and her bold, provocative movements stirred his blood and quickened his heartbeat. He forgot about the woman at his side as he reached for the goblet of wine, spilling some over his beard and chest while he gulped it down, never once letting his eyes stray from the exotic girl.

A mild spring breeze was pushing through the opened windows, setting the curtains to swaying in perfect time, it seemed, with the music. The drum quickened its beat, the dancer cavorting more wildly, more seductively. Kabul wiped his mouth with his hand, then reached out to grab the girl. The dancer laughed and slowly spun away, just out of reach. The khan would have scowled had she not held his attention so completely. As the flute's notes picked up in savage stac-

232

cato, the slave girl raised her hands, and unpinned the small clasp at the back of her neck. The scanty dress tumbled to her feet, exposing her naked form, glistening with beads of perspiration, thighs rounded and firm, hips and belly swaying to the drums while the bells on her toes and fingers jangled lustily.

Kabul pushed away the Persian, who, falling to the carpeted floor, scooped up her own garments and scurried from the chamber, an unconcealed jealousy burning in her violet eyes. The young slave girl was aware of this; she laughed at the sight and flung her full attention back to the waiting khan. Kabul felt his body tense with desire and expectation when the dancer cupped her breasts, teasingly offering them, nipples ripe and red, mere inches from his face. The great khan of the Huns chuckled greedily, thinking of the long hours of the night ahead and how much this dancing virgin was going to please him. Then, as the music reached its crescendo, she floated lithely about him, like a summer flower, wild and free, innocently displaying her charms, not daring to conceal the full extent of her shapely form.

She flung a kerchief at him; Kabul reached out and grabbed it, his mirth rising. Whoever had chosen this girl for him tonight had done a good job of it. Whichever son, he must be well rewarded for finding one so delicate yet so provocative here in this infernal dusty city of Samarkand.

The drone of the music ended abruptly; the dancer knelt at his sandaled feet, head bowed, mouth panting, hair tossed wildly over and below her breasts. Her hands touched the golden inseam of his dark robe, awaiting his pleasure. Kabul leaned forward and tilted her face toward him. She stared up into his scarred face, not even wincing at the ugly folds of deadened skin around his eye patch.

"What is your name, girl?" he asked, voice low and shaking, giving away his urgent desire to possess her.

A gong sounded from the outer chamber before she could reply. Kabul shot his gaze in the direction of the bronzed door, angrily sitting up and wondering who would dare to disturb him now, at this moment of pleasure.

Osklath and his youngest brother, Frizul, a near duplicate of the eldest son, stepped smartly into the room and bowed. Both were dressed in battle armor, ringlets in their chain mail jingling, knives and swords dangling from their belted waists.

"Forgive us, great khan," muttered Frizul, glancing at the naked girl and then at his father.

A vein throbbed in Kabul's thick neck; he toyed with the gold bracelet around his bicep. "I left orders not to be disturbed," he hissed at them both. "Get out, both of you! See me in the morning!"

Frizul nodded, half turning to leave, but his brother stopped him. A slight smile broke across Osklath's desert-tanned features. "We have news, sire," he said, "that perhaps will make your displeasure at least understanding of why we came so hastily."

Kabul cast his treacherous son a baleful eye. "Well? Speak, then—and get out when you're done."

Osklath lowered his head. "We have received word from the Steppes, sire—word, possibly, about this renegade, this Kazir woman who has rallied her people against us."

The khan took another draught of wine and then spit on the floor. When he snapped his fingers, the slave girl scooped up her garment and hurried from sight behind a screen, and the musicians quickly left the chamber.

The khan was sick to death of the tales of this unknown woman. All through the winter she and her band of ragged hillmen had one way or another thwarted every thrust upon the Steppes his armies had tried. Like demons these hillmen came, it was said, sweeping out of the night, from the edges of the forests, and pouring down upon his men like swarms of locusts.

They struck swiftly, horses tearing down upon his unsuspecting legions, then disappeared back into the desert and the darkness, unscathed by his best troops. He had begun to suspect the worthiness of his own sons; after all, they were in charge of his armies now, and if they were stupid enough to fall prey to this . . . this *woman,* how could he blame the hapless soldiers who had failed to find her and her thieves?

"What is it this time?" he asked gruffly. "Are you here to report another failure?"

Osklath and his brother seemed embarrassed.

The khan sighed. "I thought as much." He shut his good eye and leaned back, crossing his legs casually, ignoring the sting in his arteries where the Chinese physician had stuck his needles.

"You do not understand," said Frizul haltingly. "These hillmen fight like no others we have ever encountered. They say that their leader, this Panther, has been given special powers by witches and that——"

"Enough!" boomed the khan, his deep voice echoing down the palace corridors. He wiped sweat from his brow and peered meanly at his youngest son. "Did I sire a fisher woman?" he barked. "You call yourselves commanders of my men? *Ha!* I could do better with a host of jabbering Mongols to lead my forces!"

"But, my lord," stammered Frizul, "the tales are true!"

Kabul pulled at Osklath's hair as he removed his helmet. "First you told me that our last expeditionary force was halted by a plague of frogs—a plague of *frogs!*"

"That was true sire," panted Osklath. "They were set upon our forces at night while our men rested in their tents. Thousands of them came over us, frightening the horses, kicking over the campfires——"

"Until you were in such a bloody panic that you couldn't even *see* the hillmen until it was too late and their horses came charging over the dunes!" The khan was livid as he finished the story. "Am I right?"

Frizul gulped and nodded.

Kabul spat again. "Frogs! Five hundred men turned back by frogs! And now what? Again these lame excuses about witches in the forest, spells and demons, ghosts and a woman who calls herself the Panther and cannot be caught by my ablest soldiers?" He leaned forward and pounded a fist into an open palm. "I'll not have any more of this, do you hear? My own sons, no less! I'm told that the troops laugh at me, treat my name without the fear and respect it took half a lifetime to command!"

Osklath stuck out an arm. "Not true, great khan. Everyone knows that these matters are out of your control."

"Nothing is out of my control, boy," seethed Kabul, flexing his jaw, "*nothing*. Now, give me your news and get out. I don't want to see either of you again tonight!"

Both sons bowed deeply, and when they rose, it was Osklath who spoke: "As you know, since the onset of spring, five of our caravans to the east have been attacked, their goods stolen, slaves freed—"

"Yes, yes, I know all that. My coffers are the poorer for it; you needn't remind me. What else?"

And, at your instruction, we sent a small, light force to trail behind another caravan, hoping that it would be attacked and our men could confront the Kazirs by daylight."

"And?" growled the khan.

"And we were right. The caravan *was* attacked, as it reached the edge of this Grim Forest. The hillmen led a daring charge across the slopes of the dunes and overwhelmed our forces. We lost all our goods and a hundred slaves in the bargain, although many, we are sure, shall surely die as they try to make their way across the desert on foot."

The sixth caravan! Kabul felt his face flush with

anger. When would it all stop? He, the greatest con-
querer the world had ever seen, was being pricked to
death by a handful of pesky mosquitoes. Wild men
from the Steppes, who by all rights should have been
wiped out days after Samarkand had been taken, had
instead hampered his movements, successfully hid from
his legions, been the worst thorn in his side he had ever
known, and all because of the woman they called Panther.

"Is that all?" he asked wearily at last.

Osklath smiled enigmatically. "Not quite, sire. You
see, although our escort troops were beaten back, this
time they successfully took a prisoner—a hillman, but
a man he hardly is, merely a boy, my lord, though several of our best warriors swear he fights more like a
demon."

Kabul's brow rose in speculation. "And you bother
me now with *this?*" he snorted. "The capture of a wild
child of the hills? Do what you must, Osklath. Drag
him below to the dungeons; rack him, scald him, flay
his flesh layer by layer. Exact any and all information
you can and then be done with it. Of what interest is it
to me that you have caught him?"

Now it was Frizul's turn to smile, and he did so wry-
ly, his thick lips turning sharply upward, reminiscent of
the khan's own smile. He rubbed at the edge of his
thrice-broken nose in a nervous habit and said, "We
have already done all you say, Father. He has talked,
although at times we thought he never would. Indeed,
he's been near death on several occasions these past
hours, but our torturers are highly skilled, my lord, and
were each time able to revive him. Hide as thick as
leather, but in the end he saw things our way. He
pleaded for his death, begged. Of course, we have denied it—at least until we are finished. A curious matter,
though . . ."

"How so?" The khan's curiosity was roused now,

and he regarded the unwelcome visit of his sons in a new light.

"It seems, great khan," said Osklath, "that this ragged urchin is not of the Steppes at all."

Kabul stood, roughly reached out, and grabbed Osklath by the collar of his tunic. The younger man did not flinch. "What does that mean?" growled the khan with agitation.

"It means, sire, that the boy was a fugitive—a fugitive from Samarkand itself—the day the city was taken by our forces. And"—at this point his eyes danced with amusement as he stared into his father's puzzled face—"he is known to this woman they call the Panther of the Steppes, as she is known to him."

Kabul let loose his grasp, and sank back onto the velvet divan again. His burly hand grabbed a bunch of purple grapes in a bowl, and he stuffed several into his mouth, spitting the pits on the floor. "Are you certain of all this?" he asked.

"Quite so, my lord," responded the eldest son. "Believe me, it took breaking nearly every rotten bone in his fragile body to uncover what we did."

"Well, rack him again!" barked Kabul, outraged that his son should be here before him now with but half the story to be told. "By the living gods, here is our chance to find out who she is, from where she gains her authority, and why these hillmen fight at her side the way they do!"

Osklath, his leather helmet safely tucked between his armpit and elbow, sauntered slowly over to the bowl of grapes, plopped one between his molars, and chomped down slowly, savoring its sweetness. "We have done all this, my lord, I assure you. Have no fear on that account. But, alas"—and here he sighed, wiping his soiled fingers on his cloak—"the boy will not divulge more than he already has. We tried, sire; believe me, we tried. At this very moment he lies unconscious, incoherent, on the verge of death. It is far too perilous to question him further; I fear the pain may have caused him to lose his mind."

Kabul frowned. "And so you have turned him into a babbling idiot, I suppose?"

Osklath stiffened. "The youth Asif has served his purpose, great khan; have no fear of that much."

Kabul swung around, biting at his lower lip, glad at least to have learned something of this insufferable woman who had caused so much misery. "Then what have you to tell me?"

The slave girl poked her head out from behind the screen. Osklath hesitated, but his father's wave of the hand told him to proceed; she could be trusted.

"The Kazir main force, sire," Osklath went on quickly, "lies hidden in some unknown compound they call the 'Stronghold.' Though we cannot yet be sure of its exact location, from the pieces we have put together, we have an idea where it may lie. It might still take some time—these Kazirs must be dealt with slowly— but I give my oath before you now that it will be sought out and found and razed to the earth when it is. Without this Stronghold, Kazir power shall diminish; their source of strength will be gone, and the wild clans shall be far easier to deal with."

Frizul chuckled softly. "Tell him the rest," he whispered.

Kabul peered questioningly at both his sons. "Well? What more? Speak, damn you both!"

"Only a small matter, my lord, but one that we, er, knew should be brought to your attention without delay. It is true that we do not yet know the true name or identity of this so-called Panther, but we have learned far more than we hoped." He paused, letting his father's curiosity boil with his rising anger at the slowness of his response. "It appears, great khan, that this very woman who leads the Kazirs against us and vanishes like the wind is someone you yourself are personally acquainted with."

"I?" Kabul was more than puzzled. "How in the name of hell's demons would I know her?"

Osklath was abrupt in his reply. "Because, sire, she is the one who stole your eye."

The khan stopped chewing his grapes and rose once again, looking at his sons with disbelief. The silence that followed was frightening, and Frizul shuddered. "You are making a poor jest, Osklath," Kabul sputtered.

"I do not joke, Father." Osklath's face was drawn as tight as a drum as he spoke, and Kabul searched his eyes and his soul. "She *is* the one. The boy has sworn it, sworn it by his Prophet."

In that moment the great khan forgot all about the pleasures that awaited, forgot about his son's too-plain gloating, forgot everything in his empire save his relentless hatred and desire for revenge. Could it really be so? he wondered. Could she actually be one and the same? Or was this some clever Kazir trick, a ploy to arouse his anger and have him send off his armies in a futile chase across the desert, while the Kazir tribal elders plotted some ingenious plan to regain their lands? Still, how could he let this moment slip by? What if she *was* the one?

"Find her," he rasped, veins popping from his forehead and neck, his mouth twisted almost as hideously as his sightless socket. "Find her for me and bring her back, and I give my word, before all our gods, before all I hold dear and sacred, that if you do, I shall reward you beyond your wildest yearnings."

The glitter of half an empire and more ran through the minds of both sons. What wonders they might do with it, what new and even greater empires they might carve. Kabul was getting old; his judgment was clouded by his hatred. Satisfy the venom and he would only be weakened further still.

Osklath believed this; so did Frizul. Silently they plotted against both the khan and each other, thinking also of ways to mollify or be rid of the eight other brothers who would demand their share of the booty.

"Your will be done," answered Frizul, bowing deeply to his shaking father. "Tomorrow I lead my own army of Immortals to the Steppes to route these hillmen once and for all and to bring you the prize you desire most."

Kabul nodded his approval, his one eye suspiciously cast at the mute Osklath, who was obviously biding his time for a more opportune moment.

He put his hand on Frizul's shoulder, smiling as the youngest of his brood beamed. "Trust me, Father; I won't fail you this time."

"I know you won't. Go. Bring her quickly. I have waited too long for this debt to be repaid."

It had been easy—too easy, perhaps. The silent battlefield was putrid with the stink of death. Overhead the carrion cackled, black wings fluttering in the first rays of dawn's light as they circled in broad sweeps, patiently waiting for their time to feed off the remains.

Torches were still ablaze, flames fanning wildly as the desert winds blew cold. Standards and banners of gold and crimson, proud flags of the invincible Immortals, stood stuck in the dirt, broken and bloodied, scattered along the full length and breadth of the shallow wadi. Across the towering dunes the red sand barely hid the pools of blood that spilled down over the rocky crevices and cracks in the arid earth, seeping slowly beneath the surface of the dry riverbed, turning the top layers of sand into mud. There were mules, horses, and camels on their sides, gasping for air, their bellies riddled with snubbed arrows shot by keen-eyed Kazir marksmen. All along the sandy terrain lay the still, grim corpses of hundreds upon hundreds of Kabul's staunchest warriors, smashed and twisted, all having well paid the price in full for Tariq's carefully laid ambush.

For days the khan's army had ridden and marched, through blistering heat by day and frigid cold by night, drawn unknowingly deeper into this hostile country where only a special few had ever survived. Kazir scouts had done their duties well, spying from safe distances, giving Frizul's forces encouragement with false luring hints of quick victory, all the while leading them on, forcing their lines to run thin, their supplies to be too swiftly drawn upon. And they, when the time was right, they struck as they always did—silently, swiftly—severing the army in two, catching half defenseless in the wadi, the other half stretched out along the hills and dunes. They had had no chance this night against the swift Kazir horsemen, as any observer to the grisly scene would quickly testify.

Tariq, flanked by the Bear, Roskovitch, on one side and the Panther on the other, walked a long walk through the human debris. Helmeted corpses stared glassy-eyed everywhere, their cloaks aflutter in the breeze. There were no survivors of this short, bitter campaign—no survivors save one, who, bloodied and out of his mind with shame and disgrace, now waited with his head hung low on his chest while desert riders held his arms outstretched behind him.

Tariq approached slowly and cautiously. One of the men pulled the Hun by his hair and forced him to look up. Through swollen eyes that trickled with blood, he stared at the rugged face of the Kazir chieftain, having no idea who he was. His burnouse covering most of his features, Tariq studied the man intently, as a good leader always will do with his captured enemy.

"Well," gasped the Hun, his lungs filled with desert dust, "what are you waiting for? Kill me!"

Tariq turned away; Roskovitch shook his head. The soldiers holding the prisoner threw him to the ground, drawing scimitars and nudging the tips of their blades against his throat. Frizul gurgled.

Another figure, dark in the graying shadows, came forward and stood over the postrate Hun. Frizul strained to clear his vision, to get a glimpse of the Kazir leader in flowing robes, bloodied dagger firmly sheathed inside a loosely linked belt. The face was veiled, but he could see the eyes narrowed and smoldering—a woman's eyes.

Sharon put her hands to her hips, contempt clear in her gaze. The youngest son of Kabul fidgeted beneath the stare, for the first time feeling afraid. He did not have to ask who she was.

A pulsing smear of brilliant red crossed from the eastern horizon and spread upward in the sky. All at once the blue shadows of night faded, leaving the stark sands of the wadi and the dunes almost blinding in the early-morning sun. The woman arched her face upward in greeting of the day. Under her veil of silk, Frizul could see her smile.

"Your army is defeated," she announced, looking down at the warrior-clad man at her feet. Frizul made no reply; seldom had he heard a woman speak with such authority in her voice, as though she were a queen and this terrible desert her domain.

Frizul's eyes watered from the brilliant light. "What . . . what do you want of me?" he croaked. The peal of laughter from her surrounding companions made him cringe. "Is it ransom?" he cried. "Spare me and my father shall pay you well for my return," he promised.

Sharon unclasped her veil and peered down at him scornfully. "We seek no payment, son of Kabul."

"Then . . . then what?"

"Where is the lad?" It was the gravelly voice of Roskovitch that spoke, the barbarian from Rus personally prepared to tear the heathen apart limb by limb, if need be, to regain the youth he had grown so fond of. He kneeled beside the Hun and forcefully grabbed his leather collar, his breath hot upon Frizul's anxious face, hissing, "Asif, where is he? What have you done with him?"

A knot tightened in the pit of Frizul's belly; he dared not tell them. "I . . . I don't know what you're talking about," he stammered.

"Bah!" The Bear of the desert pushed him gruffly and spit into his eye. "Take him back with us, Little Panther," he urged. "He'll make us all good sport."

"Aye," chimed the mad mullah, suddenly at Roskovitch's side. "Perhaps there can be an exchange——"

Sharon looked at her companions sharply. "Ten of *him* won't replace Asif," she flared. "No, we won't take • him back. No prisoners, remember? That is the code of the Kazirs."

Roskovitch's dagger glinted as he pulled it from its sheath. "Then there is no more time to be wasted. Leave him to me."

Frizul squirmed, petrified of the wild barbarian. He would have bolted from the ground, preferring the shafts of Kazir arrows to being left alone with the scalp-locked warrior from Rus, but the tips of the scimitars pressing at his jugular kept him firmly in place.

Sharon pondered for a brief moment, then shook her head. Her short-clipped hair caught sunlight as she threw off the hood of her *aba*. "No," she said. Then, to Frizul's guards: "Let him up; release him."

"You cannot be serious." Roskovitch was aghast with bewilderment. "Why would you do this?"

Ignoring her friend's protest for the moment, Sharon snapped her fingers, and the sturdy soldiers hovering like leopards over the confused Hun stepped back, scimitars still in hand but no longer threatening. The Samarkand fugitive beckoned him to rise, and Frizul, disbelieving his own eyes, did as commanded, climbing dumbly first to his knees and then to his feet. He rubbed at his aching and swollen wounds, standing wobbly and suspicious before her. The two enemies locked eyes in mutual distrust.

"Then what is it you intend to do with me?" Frizul asked at last.

Sharon did not conceal her smile. "Allow you to return to Samarkand," she answered simply.

If her companions were surprised, Frizul was stunned. His brows furrowed in the same manner Sharon recalled in his father, and he gasped, "Do you mean what you say? I am . . . *free*?"

She toyed with the tassel dangling loosely from her

desert headdress, her tanned face impassive, her eyes cold and unmoving. "No Hun can ever consider himself to be free while our lands lay beneath your father's yoke," she told him acidly. "But yes; I do give you the freedom to return to your khan, so that you may tell him what happened here this night—and all you have encountered. Go."

Frizul looked about, started to move toward the bank of the wadi, then stopped. A thin, almost wry smile broke over his cracked lips, and he stared grimly across the burning sands. "Ah, I see," he mumbled. "So you condemn me to death not by your hand but by the desert itself." He gestured grandly, almost arrogantly, about him. "It is some fifty leagues to Samarkand," he remarked bitterly. "Alone like this I'd never survive the journey."

Sharon cocked her head sideways, eyes squinted tightly against the sun. "My offer was genuine," she insisted. Then, to her lieutenants: "Fetch the Hun a waterskin filled to the cap, and a swift horse as well. I want him to reach his destination quickly, before his presence fouls the desert."

Frizul watched tensely as both provisions were brought to his side. He uncapped the waterskin and took a long draught, swilling the water around in his mouth and spitting it out. "You really do mean to let me go, don't you?"

The desert woman nodded. "I gave my word. No one shall follow; no arrows shall sail at your back. As you said, you're free."

Frizul bowed his head, an expansive, mocking grin written into his dour features. He took the waiting reins in hand, limped to the saddle, and mounted. Leaning forward, he peered down at the strange leader of the Kazirs. "Perhaps we shall meet again, Desert Panther."

Sharon grasped the neck of her cobra, the metal coiled around her belt. "Perhaps we shall, Hun. Remember, though, this meeting, and serve Kabul my warning: He must not dare to set foot upon the Steppes again. These are our lands and ours alone."

The ungrateful Hun sneered at the group of Kazirs staring at him; he kicked sharply at the horse's flank and broke quickly onto the open sand, swirls of dust clouding behind. The Panther, he knew, made few mistakes; letting him live had been one.

In the silence of the tent, Zadek, sitting cross-legged with eyelids tightly drawn, spread his palms slowly across the burning colored stones. The Glowing Rocks of Babylon shimmered, strange light intensifying, sending a rainbow of hues rippling across his features. Opposite, also in the same stony silence, sat Sharon, Tariq, and the saya upon cushions.

Zadek bent forward and began to sway, back and forth, back and forth, while his lips soundlessly mouthed the secret words to call upon the stones' power. A strong desert wind brewed outside, reaching over the high Stronghold walls, whipping down below in furious frenzy. The sandstorm had lasted for three days now, with no sign of abating. A bad omen, Carolyn had said, tight-lipped, gripping her antelope horn —a foreboding of the struggle that lay dangerously before the Kazirs. And when she had spoken, no one had scoffed, for the saya knew better than any who had come before her the lore and legends of the Steppes.

The mad mullah's face broke out in glistening sweat; his lip curled; his nostrils flared. Sharon stared at his haggard, anguished face, noting the ever-deepening lines. Age had sapped his vitality more quickly in these climes, she knew, and although he would never speak openly of it, she was fully aware of the lung sickness that steadily worsened.

Zadek cried out suddenly, a short, muffled cry. His shoulders shook mightily; then his whole frame dramatically sagged. Tariq made to rise, but Sharon's quick hand stopped him, her eyes urging that he return to his place and remain as still and silent as before.

A patchwork quilt of color bounded across the walls of the tent, first darkening it, then lighting it briefly. The stones seemed more alive than Sharon had ever seen them as they danced upon the mat, tints unevenly blended. She gazed into the shadows with widened eyes. Inexplicably, it looked to her as though the reflections of the stones were battling one another, each hue at war with the next, and the harmony they had always projected before was missing. Her heart began to beat savagely; something was wrong—very wrong!

Zadek put his hands to his heart and grabbed fiercely at his tunic. His body shook, he groaned, and then he slumped forward. The glow of the pebbles vanished as suddenly as it had come. The sounds of wind once more rushed to their ears, and all was now the same as before this séance had started.

Tariq bolted from his place and tended to the mulluh. Zadek's lips parted to take the sip of wine and he coughed strongly, regaining his senses.

"What's happened?" cried Sharon, her brooding eyes large with worry.

Zadek lifted himself slowly, a hand to his throbbing temple. He shook his head as if to clear foggy thoughts, then said, "He is dead."

His companions stared at him in total shock and grief. "Are you certain?" demanded the saya. "Did your vision actually *see* him?"

Taking a deep breath to fill his aching lungs, Zadek hung his head low on his chest, sadly, like the man who learns that his favorite son has been lost in a war. "No, saya," he whispered, "I did not see him, but the stones never lie, never deceive." He shuddered. "They spoke of death, of a great loss to us all." And with great effort, more than his companions could ever know, he forced himself to look at them. "Asif is gone. His earthly form could take no more of Kabul's torture."

Hand to her mouth, Sharon gasped. Tariq winced, sucking in dusty air.

"Would that I were wrong," continued the mullah, himself close to tears. His eyes lifted to the ceiling of the tent, but he was staring far past it, far past the sandstorm that raged above; he was looking to the sky, to the heavens themselves. "Praise be the name of the Prophet," he mumbled. "Asif has no more pain. He rests easily, in the arms of God."

Tariq's shoulders sagged; he leaned forward and put a hand on Zadek's arm. "Then he is at peace, holy man; for that much we must be glad."

"Aye," agreed the mullah. "The khan can hurt him no more. He has fallen a hero of the Kazirs——"

"And a hero of Samarkand," added Sharon quickly. She looked away so as to hide her welling tears. She did not want Tariq to see this sign of woman's weakness.

"The Kazirs have lost a friend," said Carolyn, hands folded in her lap. She smoothed the folds of her *aba* and closed her eyes in a brief prayer, then said, "He shall not be forgotten."

Sharon glanced up sharply. "No, never forgotten. To me he was like a brother."

"And to me as well," admitted Tariq. He smiled warmly at the teary-eyed princess, hoping to give comfort and assurance; but then his features darkened as he thought of his friend Roskovitch and how much the Bear had come to love the boy. To him, Asif was like a son, and now that son was dead. Telling him what had happened would be the hardest thing he'd ever had to do. The barbarian from Rus would be wild in his grief.

"Who . . . who bears direct responsibility for his death?" Sharon said, catching the others by surprise.

"All our enemies," replied the saya glumly.

Sharon's expression was hard and cold. "No," she said simply, "I want the name of the man whose hand did this. One man, Zadek, only one. Which?" Her gaze was as piercing as it was frightening.

The mullah swallowed. "It was . . . it was Osklath. I saw him in my vision."

Osklath!

The Samarkand princess glowered with hatred. *Osklath*—she despised the very name. How well she recalled him, his swagger and his arrogance, how well she remembered his own lust when Kabul sent him from the emir's chamber. *Osklath*—she would never forget. Next to Kabul himself, there was no man, no Hun in all their armies, she craved revenge against more.

"The eldest son will pay for his crime," she vowed. "Asif's blood shall not go unpaid."

Tariq cast a worried look at her. "I feel as you," he told her, "but we must move with caution. Haste will not serve our cause—or Asif's either."

Sharon folded her arms around her knees, turning her gaze away from Tariq's. If Asif was dead, she thought, it was because of her; under her banner he had so bravely fought; shielding her name, he had withstood the terrible injuries Osklath had inflicted. She shut her eyes and pictured the lad, the enormity of his loss heavy upon her shoulders. "You are right, Tariq," she whispered. "Personal grief must not color my actions." She shivered and started to cry. "But leave me now, all of you. I need to be alone."

She woke to the sound of wind pushing at the flaps of her tent, woke from a formless dream filled with dire forebodings she could not remember. She lay still for some time, knowing by the silence that the hour was late; it was nearly dawn. The fury of the sandstorm seemed to have passed at last, and now the wind, although strong, was no more than common for a summer's night.

The wax candle flickered; Sharon threw off her heavy wool blanket, leaned over, and made to blow it out. It was then that she heard the wail; animallike, deep and mournful, it sounded as though some gravely wounded beast was on the prowl. Unconsciously she reached for her dagger; the eyes of the cobra glowed in the light. She lifted herself up and listened again. The painful cry was as loud as before, this time in human voice lifted to the gods. Sharon moved to the flap and pushed it aside just enough to peek through.

Amid swirling gusts and thickly rising dust, she saw the burly figure of Roskovitch, the scalp-locked barbarian on his knees, balled fists pounding the ground. He was drunk, drunk out of his wits with the pain of Asif's death. She saw the sinewy warrior raise an arm and curse to the heavens, asking why the youth instead of he had been the one to be taken that day. Then he fell to sobbing again, oblivious of the silent world around him, caring not for anything in this life to relieve his torment.

Sharon veiled her face from the onslaught of wind and forced her way out of the tent. She wanted to comfort him if she could, perhaps let his grief somehow be added to her own, but what could she say? What could she do?

"Leave him alone" came a voice from behind.

She turned, startled, to see another figure lonely in the night, a silhouette against the shadowed backdrop. "Tariq!" she exclaimed. "Why . . . why are you here?"

The young chieftain met her questioning gaze. "I could not sleep," he told her truthfully.

"Nor I," she admitted. Then she looked again toward the giant of a man humbled like a dog upon the earth, biting her lip to stifle sobs of her own.

"He took the news very badly," said Tariq, drawing to her side. His face seemed haggard; there were dark rings beneath his eyes. It was as if he too had aged far too much in the past year. "For a time I feared I could not constrain him."

"He'll be all right," said the Panther. "He needs time, that's all."

"You do not know him as well as I, Sharon. The Bear is too proud, too stubborn."

Through her tears, Sharon somehow was able to smile. She reached out and brushed her fingertips against Tariq's cheek. *Proud and stubborn*—how very much the same Tariq had been that day long ago when they first met.

"It is better to leave him," Tariq said, not realizing her thoughts. "Go back to your tent, Little Panther. Time enough to console the Bear tomorrow."

Sharon nodded; there was nothing she could do to ease Roskovitch's grief. Turning to leave, she suddenly shuddered.

"Is anything the matter?" asked Tariq. "Are you ill?"

She shook her head. "No, not ill, only frightened." A hound barked and she jumped. Tariq took her arm and turned her to face him. "Are you sure?"

Her large eyes were filled with tears now. Tariq pulled back the flap of her tent for her to enter. It was with total surprise that she looked up at him and said, "Don't leave me yet; I'm afraid of being alone."

He followed her inside, eyes picking out the sparse furnishings. Sharon could have commanded much of the booty stolen from the Hun caravans, he knew—enough in gold or silver or precious stones to one day make her a woman of wealth again—but the princess had chosen to take nothing. She seemed more than content to live with the most basic necessities—the old way, the way of the Kazirs.

She sat down near the banked fire, still shivering.

"Perhaps you have fever," said Tariq, concerned. He could not recall having seen her behave this way before. "I can send for Zadek. He has many medicines——"

Sharon stopped him with a shake of her hand. "No, nothing. I'll be all right. This will pass."

Moonlight slanted through the tent flaps, silver rays casting down over her cheek, sliding from her shoulder to the soft mounds of her breasts beneath her tunic. Her skin seemed strangely tinted now, fair, almost milk-white instead of desert tanned—the way it had been when she was brought as an outsider to the Stronghold.

Tariq felt a stirring from deep inside. He wanted to reach out and touch her, hold her in his arms. Oh, this feeling for her was not new; he thought he might have felt it even that day he first laid eyes upon her, and again when he'd stood before the judges and elders, ready to kill Yasir, if need be, to save her life. He was in love with her, had been all this time, though until this very moment he had not let himself admit it.

A strong gust of wind pushed its way inside the tent, causing the curtains to dance and the candle flame to blow out. Tariq made to relight it.

"No, don't." Her voice was a whisper.

In the darkness he looked down at her, heart throbbing so loudly he was sure she could hear it.

She lifted her arm, extending her hand to him. He took it slowly, closing his fingers around hers, feeling the sweat of her palms. She gave no resistance as he pulled her down beside him; not touching save for their hands tightly held, they gazed deeply into each other's eyes. Then he let his fingers gently explore the side of her face, pausing in their search to wipe away a fallen tear. "You know how I feel about you," he whispered. Her own fingertips rested on the shallow curve of his neck. "Shhh . . . you needn't say it. And need I tell you that I feel the same?"

Tariq smiled as he pulled her to him, and their lips met softly in a lingering kiss, a lover's kiss, stolen now in the few moments they had found to be together. Sharon settled her head against his chest, awash in the glow of feeling his strength around her. It almost made her able to forget, to forget it all, the suffering and pain, the torment, the fear. . . .

As his lips caressed the side of her neck, she pulled away, panting. "No, Tariq, don't," she pleaded, out of breath and suddenly snapped back to reality. "You mustn't ever do that again." Her eyes were aflame, narrowed and burning. "Promise me; promise!"

"But why, girl? I love you, and you just told me you feel the same."

She looked away, ashamed, unable to greet his forlorn gaze. "It . . . it can never be, Tariq. You of all people should understand."

His voice was a growl. "I *don't* understand—any of this." She tried to tear away when he grabbed her by the shoulders, and sobs rose as she fiercely shook her head, denying not only him but everything she had dreamed of and yearned for as well.

"Don't you see?" she cried. "It can never be! Not you and I, never you and I!" Her hands beat at him, and he pulled her closer again, letting her weep into his shirt. Soothingly he stroked her hair and kissed the top of her head. This time when she looked at him her eyes were dry, although puffy and red. She sucked in a long breath and held it. "How can I explain to you?" she said softly. "It's not that I don't care, because I do; you *know* I do."

"Then what?" He was as perplexed as ever.

Her face darkened and she shut her eyes, wishing she were dead. "I am unclean," she stated flatly, emotionlessly. "I can never love honestly, not after"—and here she faltered—"not after what they did to me."

Tariq forcefully made her look at him. His face was warm, loving, his eyes kind and devoted. "It makes no matter, Sharon. To me you are the same as when I first saw you."

Her smile was bitter. "That girl is dead, Tariq, murdered by the same dogs who slaughtered my people and my family. Like Asif, she fought them, struggled to the best of her ability . . ." The words were painful for her. "God, how I tried to stop him, but he wouldn't; he *wouldn't!*" She was crying again, her hands to her ears desperately trying to drown out the echo of Kabul's laugh, the laugh that still haunted her dreams. And in her shame she buried herself against Tariq, seeking the peace and forgetfulness she'd not yet found.

"I do understand, Little Panther," he comforted. "Cry; it's good for you, good for all of us. I know and I understand how you feel."

"Then you must also know that our love is forbidden. Kazir law would never allow a chieftain to wed a woman once violated by the heathens."

Tariq stopped stroking her hair. Sharon was right in this much, he realized: Such a love was strictly against custom and law. The saya would be the first to tell him as much. "But you are one of us now," he protested, "the One foretold by the Prophesy. Our clans ride beside you, follow you blindly, even into the face of death. Surely, then, you and I can——"

A finger to his lips hushed him. "I may well be bearer of the Gift," she acknowledged sadly. "Even your sister cannot deny me that. But *marriage,* Tariq?" Her sigh was wistful. "How can it be? An outsider from Samarkand, who once carried the seed of the king of the Huns . . ."

The young chieftain shifted his gaze from hers, sadly realizing that what she said was true. It could cause great divisions among the clans; many would demand his removal, saying that Shoaib's son was no longer fit for the title he bore. Perhaps at some future time, when the Steppes were free again, the Prophesy fulfilled and Samarkand returned to the Kazirs, he and Sharon might yet find a way to share their secret love; but not now, not while the khan pressed so closely, not while some of the elders still harbored suspicions about the girl he held in his arms.

"We *shall* find a way, Sharon," he said at last. "No matter what anyone says . . ."

She reached up and kissed him lightly, fleetingly. A smile worked its way around her mouth, but it was not a happy one. "Someday, yes," she told him, not believing a word of it although her heart wished for nothing more. "But until that time, my love, no one must ever know. No one must even *suspect*."

Again she was right; there was no denying it. Their secret must be kept, through trials and separation, though their hearts might break for merely a glimpse of each other. Anything less could tear asunder all they had worked so hard to begin.

Frizul, disgraced, slunk away from his father's wrath like a mangy hound. The khan, a scowl of contempt burned into his face, watched his useless son slither from the throne room. Failure again; it was too much to bear. And this time it had been a force of his best warriors, the undefeatable Immortals, men who had boldly scaled these very walls of Samarkand with impunity, taken the city and the palace, defying everything that the enemy could throw at them. Now, before some ragged band of thieves and shepherds led by a whore of a Samarkand bitch, they had been destroyed completely, and he, Kabul, khan of khans, ruler of an empire such as Asia had never seen, was forced into abject humiliation. At this very moment other kings in far-away places, such as Persia and Cathay, would be laughing at him, secretly jeering and snickering, saying that a mere woman, ill-armed and desert-trained, had successfully cut off his balls.

Kabul pounded a fist upon the ornate ivory arm of his throne. Had Frizul not already disappeared from the chamber, tail between his legs, the khan would have killed him with his bare hands.

"She makes me a laughingstock!" he boomed.

His many aides, advisors, and ministers shied their eyes, looking disconsolately at the marble floor. A slave appeared from behind an arabesque screen to offer the agitated khan a goblet of honeyed wine. Kabul knocked the silver tray out of his hands, and as it clanged against the floor, he kicked the servant in the belly, sending him sprawling at the feet of his courtesans.

"I'll make eunuchs of you all!" he blustered to them. "Spineless dimwits! Scum of the earth!"

"But, sire," protested one, a hawk-nosed soldier who had served his master well these many years during every campaign, "how can we fight those we cannot find? Show me this desert Stronghold . . . aye, give me its location and five thousand men, and I'll wipe this scourge from your memory forever! But"—he frowned deeply with his own displeasure—"how may we—any of us—fight an army that remains as elusive as the wind?"

"The wind? Bah!" Elbow on the rest, chin upon the back of his fist, Kabul looked away with disgust. "If I had both my eyes," he seethed, "if only I had both my eyes . . ."

"You would still be blind."

The words shocked every man in the chamber. Who in his right senses would dare to speak to the mighty khan thusly, especially at a moment like this, when his rage was so great?

"Is that you, my son?" said Kabul, not even bothering to look up.

Osklath stepped over the shivering slave on the floor and smartly marched to the velvet rug before the throne. There, helmet tucked in his arm, he bowed respectfully. "Yes, my lord, it is I."

"*You*," muttered the khan, spittle flying, "I should think you would be halfway across the city by now, beside that asinine younger brother of yours."

Osklath smiled, unperturbed by this fit of temper. "Ah, Father, you do me an injustice. Certainly Frizul failed you, even with his legion of Immortals. They were bound to fail; anyone could have told you that."

Kabul peered up through his good eye, hating the very sight of his arrogant, cocksure eldest son. "If that is so," he rasped, "then why didn't you tell me?"

Osklath's grin remained. "You didn't ask."

Fuming, veins popping, the khan began to rise from

his cushioned chair. Osklath had gone too far this time, many were thinking. He'd taunted his father for the final time. Kabul's fit of anger would surely cost Osklath his life, and good riddance, or so thought many, including his brothers.

Indeed, for a moment it seemed as if the mighty khan was about to strike his son the blow of death; but, as his hand clasped the hilt of his scimitar, he started to laugh, loudly and boisterously, like a man deranged. His belly was shaking and tears rolled down from his one eye. Then he plopped back into his seat and sighed.

"Have I underestimated you again, my son?" he asked.

Osklath shrugged; it would not be the first time.

Kabul reached for an apple and took a large bite, the juice dripping down his chin and onto his flowing beard. Then he said, "Tell me, boy, if you were me now, what would you do? How would you handle this matter?"

Osklath rubbed at his own beard, rocking from toe to heel as he pondered. "If I may say, sire," he answered at length, "our armies can never defeat the Kazirs upon the Steppes."

A sudden rush of whispering ensued. Once more Osklath was playing this dangerous game of cat and mouse with his father, toying, perhaps, with his very own life. The khan ran a sleeve threaded with gold over his mouth; he narrowed his good eye, nostrils beginning to flare, a sure sign that he was nearing the end of his patience. "*What* did you say?" he hissed.

The chamber hushed at his words, silently crackling with expectation as all waited for Osklath's reply.

"That the Steppes cannot be taken," said the eldest son boldly, hastily adding before Kabul could draw another breath, "The desert has been both home and mother to these thieves and rogues for more than a century, as I understand matters. Forced into exile by the rulers of Samarkand themselves, they have had to adopt the ways of the desert as their own. They cling to the dunes like lizards, camouflaged by the very sands, unseen yet observing all, defiantly proclaiming their domination . . ."

Kabul listened with a scowl. "Excuses," he muttered.

"It is so, Father. Our armies are lost upon these lands, marching across the infernal Steppes like sightless children, unaware of these silent Kazirs who prey upon us like carrion, attacking our lines in quick forays, then disappearing into the sands themselves."

There were murmurs of agreement from across the hall, but Kabul faced off opposite his son, feet wide apart, legs like massive columns, thick arms bulging as he stood with fists upon his hips. "Dare you tell me that all our forces are useless against these . . . these Kazirs? That we have been defeated by a bunch of scoundrels and mindless savages? Sons of pigs and whores, they are!" His eye blazed with madness. "I still command ten armies, Osklath," he warned, arm shooting out, index finger shaking at his son, "and each of them shall be committed to ridding my empire of these pests! The time of excuses is past, do you hear?" For effect, he peered slowly about the room, looking from general to general, while they lowered their gazes in fear. "I want the Steppes rid of this woman and her vermin! Bring me the heads of the Kazir chieftains—or I shall claim your own!"

The courtesans shivered with the knowledge that Kabul boasted no empty threat. He would tolerate no more failure, they knew. Only Osklath remained defiant, undaunted by his father's tirade, and while the khan rattled on, reminding all that his dungeons yet had plenty of room for them, the eldest son folded his arms and met his father's burning leer evenly.

"The Kazir Stronghold cannot be reached by crossing the desert," he told the khan brazenly, "no matter how many armies you intend to commit."

The mighty Kabul turned crimson.

"But"—and Osklath smiled—"perhaps there is yet a way."

Kabul came closer to his son, his breath hot on Osklath's face. "How?" he rasped.

"These Kazirs are a strange folk, sire—superstitious and steeped in their religion. They revere the place known as Grim Forest."

Members of the court began to whisper among themselves, as surprised as the khan to hear him speak of it.

"A place of bogs and mires," called a soldier from the back.

"Aye, and of witches and ghosts as well!" said another.

Osklath laughed, noting the fear in their sweaty faces. "The finest soldiers in the world," he mimicked scornfully, "shaking at the very mention of it! Do you see, my father? Are *these* the men you would entrust your armies to? Cowards!" Then he spat on the floor.

A dozen hands lowered to the hilts of their swords. Kabul bade them hold their anger and turned back to his son: "You know as well as I that this accursed forest is unapproachable. Each time our patrols have entered, they have never come out."

"So, even you, my father, have fallen victim to these tales of washerwomen?" He gazed out past the veranda to the distant landscape shimmering at the edge of the horizon. "Our great empire is sent reeling in the face of the threat of witches and goblins."

"And you, Osklath," said the khan, screwing his eye tightly, "you do not fear any of these things, even though my finest generals swear to their truth?"

Osklath replied with a contemptuous sneer.

"I lost three hundred men in that dark forest," shouted one of the generals in the forefront, "a cohort of our finest troops—brave, fearless men, O great khan. But that night we camped near the bogs"—and here the soldier's body began to shake with the awful memory—

"I could hear the cries, the screams of pain, as they were set upon by demons."

Many heads nodded in agreement, but still Osklath sneered. He turned to the agitated soldier. "And did you see these 'demons' yourself?" he demanded.

The soldier sadly shook his head. "It was not possible. A dense fog had settled no sooner had the sun set. A man could see no farther than the tip of his nose. Like a blanket we were covered by the haze, setting our horses to panic and our stoutest men to shiver. But those poor souls who had billeted out of sight with the advance guard, their screams were not shrouded by the mists, I tell you—nor the cries of the demons as they set upon our men. It was terrible, my lord khan, the worst thing I have ever heard. And I and my own men, camped near the forest's edge, were unable to help them in any way."

"Evil gods must dwell in that dark place," attested another of Kabul's fiercest warriors, and he quickly went on to recount his own brush with the devils.

The court listened in horrified silence, and when he was done, Kabul turned again to Osklath: "Well? What do you say to that?"

The eldest son frowned. "I say that we have been duped. I say that the effects of wind howling through the trees and animals crying out in the night have played a part in tricking our minds. Aye, and the Kazirs have, because of it, been given many a victory. They have played to our own superstitions. It was they who attacked our forces, they and they alone, cleverly using both the fog and our own active imaginations to rout us. And like children we fled, daring not to enter the wood again, believing the folktales of Samarkand as much as the hillmen do themselves."

"And what of the tales of the witches?" asked the general. "With my own eyes I have seen the glow of their burning cauldron. Above the treetops, aye, and over the sky itself the shadows of their flames dance.

Will you tell me I am mad, Osklath? Was this nothing more than a vision implanted in my mind?"

"I saw the glow as well!" called another in the chamber.

Osklath shook his head. "I know nothing of witches or of cauldrons; nor do I fear them," he chastised. "A hag's blood runs as red as your own." He looked again at the khan, letting out a long, angry breath. "Cannot you see that the Kazirs play us for fools? They keep us well away from the forest for their own shrewd purpose. They concoct their wizardry to hold us at bay, my lord; that is all, no more. There are no demons."

Kabul chewed tensely at his lip. Tales of Grim Forest were rampant throughout Samarkand, and he was most disturbed at his officers' reluctance to sweep the wood once and for all. Yet, superstitious as they might be, he also knew his generals to be no cowards. If they fled the forest, it was with good reason. And he, like they, had begun to curse the day they had taken the ancient empire of Samarkand.

"Of what importance is all this to you, Osklath? Why do you stress the forest so? Up till now we have done well to ignore it. There is little value in it one way or the other. If it be true that demons dwell there, so be it; we need not arouse them. And if as you claim, all this is but a ruse, what care I? Leave the forest be, Osklath, and let us return to the matter of finding this Kazir Stronghold."

His son's lips curved in a small, tight smile. "Exactly, lord khan . . . exactly."

Kabul's face soured. "You puzzle me, Osklath. Speak your thoughts."

Osklath bowed, then flung his cloak behind him. "Before the boy Asif died, he spoke loudly in his delirium. I listened carefully to all he said, lord, and this much I learned: that the Stronghold lies less than a day's hard ride from the forest. Its approaches can be

found by an old trail, a wadi, that crosses the land at
the forest's edge."

The chamber fell to its former silence. Kabul ran a
finger over his fat lip, listening, occasionally nodding.
"Go on," he said.

Osklath grinned from ear to ear. "The forest is the
Kazirs' weakness; pass through it and we can reach the
Stronghold in full force. Bypass the desert entirely and
catch their fortress unaware, smashing them once and
for all."

"How can you be certain of all this?" questioned
Kabul most cautiously. "The boy was delirious, as you
said."

"But cunning like a fox," Osklath went on. He
grinned often as he recounted the rest of the story.
"Late that night, as he lay delirious, I slipped beside
him. Asif's eyes opened wide, although his fevered brain
did not let him recognize me. 'Tariq,' he said, 'is that
you?' 'Yes,' I replied. 'Yes, Asif, it is I.' Then he leaned
back and sighed, telling me he was glad I was there.
'What have you told the enemy?' I asked. 'Nothing,' he
replied. 'Not even how the Huns may reach the Stronghold?' 'Not even that, Tariq, not a word about the
forest.' It was then, Father, that I realized I was on to
something. Bit by bit I coaxed him and urged him to
speak, and bit by bit he told me these things. Putting
together the pieces was easy, my lord. He died in my
arms, thinking me to be his friend Tariq right until the
last moment."

Kabul listened with awe, knowing now that he had
severely underestimated his treacherous son. Osklath
had deviously gleaned more secrets about this enemy
than could ever have been hoped.

"Exactly what is your proposal, Osklath?"

He bowed sweepingly. "That we waste no more time,
great khan. Send out your best army immediately. *I*
shall be the one to lead them through this Grim Forest
of theirs, through its very heart, and burn everything in

my wake. Ashes shall be my legacy, that and the bones of those who dare oppose us. Then I will seek out and take the Kazir Stronghold."

The kahn thought quickly. "And what reward do you seek?"

The reply was curt but honest: "Half, my father, half of everything . . . for now."

"This is foolish talk, my lord!" cried the general, with open hostility toward the crafty Osklath. "Your son speaks of committing all our forces to deal with a minor threat. Listen to me, sire, forget this forest and the Kazirs; aye, and forget the desert as well! What are they to us? Pests, thorns in our sides, nothing more. At this very moment our legions await the march west. The Turks already have put up defensive forts all along their border—yes, and the savage Christians as well. If we are to gain all of Europe, we must strike now, not stand idly by, wasting our time with a gang of pitiful hillmen."

This was a strong argument, Kabul saw. It was true: His best legions were daily growing more restless, awaiting the long march toward the rich city of Constantinople, where half the world's gold lay ripe for the taking. These Kazirs at best ranked far too low in priority to be dealt with in such a strong fashion.

Kabul turned to his son with a sigh. "Time presses me, Osklath. I have not enough years left to me that more urgent matters cannot be given their due."

A small sneer broke across Osklath's features. "And what matter could be more urgent than the woman who stole your eye?"

Kabul gulped, the mention of the Samarkand princess sending his brain into a fever.

"Forget this woman," pleaded the general. "The Turks——"

The khan silenced him abruptly with a wave of his hand. Then, to his son: "You really believe you can find her, bring her back to me . . . alive?"

Osklath met his father's stare evenly, his own features alight with the promise of it. "Aye, great khan, into your hands shall I personally deliver the woman, to await your pleasure."

The thought of having the palace bitch within his grasp once more made Kabul oblivious to everything around him. Though his officers protested greatly this costly campaign, he heard them not. For him, there was nothing that could mean more than finding *her*. Though he be claimed king of the world itself, it was her and not the crown that he lusted after more—her and only her.

"This opportunity I offer should not be missed, Father," grunted Osklath, baiting him further, gleefully observing his madness. "We can make the Kazirs pay dearly for what they have done. Never again shall you be scorned by other kings. You shall make examples of all these rebels, for every kingdom to see, so that all may shudder at your might. What say you, sire? Shall I gather your armies and march?"

This would be the decisive battle, Kabul knew. One way or another the Steppes would be rid of this scourge. Frizul had been a boastful fool, he and his Immortals. Ah, but the clever Osklath was another matter entirely. If any of his sons could take this Stronghold, it would be he. Let the boy succeed and his own thirst for revenge could at last be quenched. But . . . what if even Osklath should fail? Kabul laughed deeply to himself; then his eldest son would no longer be the threat he had become. The Kazirs, an unwitting ally, would rid him of this danger once and for all. How ironic, mused Kabul, seeing that either way he could not lose.

He clasped Osklath by the shoulders with both hands. "Take as many of my armies as you think you need, my son. Go, burn away this accursed forest we dread, raze every village of these hillmen, crucify their menfolk upon every hill from here to the Persian frontier. Leave no survivors to relate the tale but let the corpses speak for themselves."

Osklath smiled broadly, thinking of the hero he would be when all this was finished. Kabul's other sons and generals would scorn the great khan, without question pledge allegiance to Osklath. Half an empire indeed! Give him victory over the Kazirs and Osklath knew he could have it all—everything.

"I give you my solemn word, Father: When I am done, the entire world shall cringe at the very mention of the name of the king of the Huns."

The Fuliwa had ridden hard to reach the Stronghold, storming past the massive red-trunked giant of a tree, through the sliding walls of rock as the horn signal was given, and to the waiting group gathered at the edge of the fortress. His chieftain, Ami, had instructed him to lose no time in reaching the Stronghold; with no explanation other than that there was a matter of dire urgency, he was to beseech Tariq and the Panther to go to Ami at once. It was a strange request, for Fuliwa land was far from the safety of the Kazir fortress, well across the blazing Steppes, almost at the foothills of Grim Forest itself. Tariq had looked at his friends with trepidation. "Ami would not send for us like this," he said, "unless the matter was one of the utmost importance."

And knowing this, neither he nor Sharon could refuse. Swiftly their horses were brought to them, and following the messenger's lead, in the small hours after midnight they set off on the journey, companionless save for the Bear, brought as watchful escort. Over the rutted hills and gullies they made haste, until at length the land flattened and only the distant haze of the faraway northern mountains stood starkly before them. Here they broke stride, negotiating the red sands slowly, aware that hidden behind the bluffs, already watching them, were Fuliwa scouts, signaling their arrival.

"Meet me at the Mound of Meditation," Ami had asked, referring to a singularly jagged hill that poked its way above the plain like a citadel and from whose heights the Fuliwas for a century had guarded their own mountain passes from the north.

It was a dark and silent moment when the small band tiredly arrived after sunset, the only stirrings that of wind-driven sand pelting them from the direction of the forest. The Fuliwa messenger, a stout and tight-lipped fellow, spoke not a word as he climbed from his saddle and approached the hill. He hooted softly, like an owl, and while Tariq peered into the night, that hoot was repeated from somewhere up above.

There was the scent of woodsmoke in the air, from a fire doused no later than the last flicker of sunlight. The messenger, as unseeing as the rest, ushered them upward along a narrow defile between the rocks, hands thrust forward as he felt his way. Sharon stayed close behind him, first among her companions to reach the top. There in the shadows, the white of his eyes keenly showing from the recesses of his hood, stood Ami, alone, in the middle of a cleared dirt circle. He waited for all his visitors to reach the top, and when Roskovitch, the last, came panting into the open, he gestured for them to sit.

"Were you followed?" he asked, once they had gathered together in a tight circle and the Fuliwa messenger had gone to stand guard in the darkness.

Tariq shook his head in reply. It was unusual for his friend to greet him in this manner, and it only added to his concern about why they had been called here like this.

Ami wasted no time. "The Huns are on the march," he told them soberly. "They are burning everything before them. Women and children have been put to death by the score, country villages abandoned, fields set ablaze." Protected from the ravages of flying sand by the sheltering rocks all about, he pulled off his hood. It was then that Sharon saw his face: eyes puffy and red, jowls sunken with fatigue and smeared with grime. He pulled the cap from a goatskin and offered the clear mountain water to his guests. Tariq downed a swallow thirstily, handing it to Roskovitch after Sharon had refused.

"We have faced their armies before," said the Bear, returning the skin to its owner and waiting while Ami took a long draught himself.

"Not like this one we haven't," snapped the Fuliwa coldly. "Column after column of horsemen, the khan's finest cavalry, followed by thousands of foot soldiers fanning out like ants across the hills, marching with all speed. My spies have seen them; they left Samarkand in the dead of night five days ago, turning east——"

"East?" Sharon seemed surprised.

"We shall muster our forces along the Steppes," said Tariq with the authority vested in him. "My men shall join your own as soon as we can——"

"There isn't enough time for that," Ami broke in, rudely cutting off his friend. "The Huns are not headed for the Steppes"—he stared at his guests one by one—"they move toward the forest."

The shocked silence lasted for only a second. "Impossible!" cried Roskovitch. "Why would they even consider such a thing? The wood would only slow them down, encumber them, make them ripe marks for our own forces."

"Why indeed," agreed Tariq, "unless . . ." He glanced sharply at the Fuliwa chieftain.

"Unless they *know*," he answered.

Sharon gasped. "Are you saying they've discovered the secret route to the Stronghold?"

Ami's dark gaze needed no words to reply.

"I cannot believe it," said Tariq. "No man knows the secret save our tribesmen, and no Kazir would ever tell."

"Yet the Huns *do* know," insisted Ami, leaning forward and placing a steady hand upon Tariq's shoulder.

"How can you be so positive?" Sharon said, her eyes

glaring darkly at her host. "Did your spies hear of it from the khan himself? Whose lips claim this thing?"

As she spoke, Ami looked at her with a growing sadness that was unmistakable. "The lips of one even you would believe," he answered after a time. And then he stood, calling softly into the darkness. Tariq and the Panther exchanged puzzled expressions as a tall, lumbering figure appeared out of the black—a pained and deathly ill figure of a man who stumbled upon shattered limbs, a stout crutch supporting his weight. The man wore a simple white robe with the stitching not of Kazir women but of those of Samarkand; Sharon recognized the weave instantly. Hollow, vacant eyes stared at her; she was appalled at his drawn features, sorrowful and haggard, like those of a man risen from the very brink of death itself. Around his neck was a deep red line, the scar from where a slave ring had been fixed. The man hunkered over her, eyes pleading for recognition. Sharon stared at him blindly, thinking only of how the poor creature must have suffered, what terrible torments he must have endured.

"Don't . . . don't you know me?" he croaked in a thick, breaking voice.

Sharon shook her head. "Have we met before, stranger?"

The man sunk his head, openly weeping, hands covering his heavily lined face. Ami went to his side, gently led him over to the Bear, and helped him sit. There the stranger dried his eyes and, accepting a sip of water, forced himself to look at the woman again. "You have changed much, Princess," he said, gazing at her face.

Sharon stirred uncomfortably. "I had thought you dead," he went on, "and mourned you as much as I loved you . . . yes, even as I loved Amrath."

Goose bumps crawled over her flesh, and Sharon's eyes widened. Could it be so? Could it really be . . .

She rose slowly, walked to him, and knelt at his feet, tears now streaming down her desert-tanned cheeks.

Then she took his trembling hands, encasing them firmly in her own. "Hezekiah," she whispered. "Praise be to merciful God, you're alive!"

The Hebrew minister, once so strong and tall, now little more than a heap of bone held together by rotting flesh, gravely nodded. "Aye, princess, brought back from the world of the near dead."

"My scouts found him alone near the edge of the desert," said Ami. "He was in a daze, closer to death than even now, a wounded horse at his side."

"But . . . but how?" stammered the girl, more perplexed than ever. "You were in the palace when the city was taken; no one could have escaped!"

Hezekiah ran his hand through her clipped hair, remembering the long girlish locks he was so fond of, the chestnut color turned to fire in the sunlight. "I did not escape," he said. "As I lay in my bed, resting from the assassin's attack, they broke into my quarters like savages, killing my guards and servants. My own life was worthless even to me, I knew, and I wanted nothing more than to rest in eternal peace with my friend Amrath, when the swords at my throat were suddenly removed. 'Leave this one alive!' someone had called, and the Huns obeyed the command. Little did I know then that it was the one called Osklath who had spared me. Aye, he kept breath in my lungs even as he ordered me dragged to the deepest palace dungeon."

Sharon's pity showed in her anguished face. "All this time?" she mumbled. "All this time in the dungeons?"

The once proud minister nodded. "It would serve no purpose to recount the tortures they put me through. Suffice it to say that never once did I betray my home or my friends. Again and again I was beaten, lashed within a hairbreadth of my life, to tell who the woman was who stole Kabul's eye." He shuddered at the memory of the torturers' skill. Then, strangely, he smiled, putting a finger beneath Sharon's chin and forcing her to look up at him. "Little did I dream that the woman might be you, or that the Panther of the Steppes might be the same child I loved."

Tariq looked at Ami; the Fuliwa sighed. "*I* told him," he admitted. "He had a right to know. In the name of Allah, he deserved at least that."

"You did well," said Tariq, overlooking that his friend had broken the code by telling an outsider. "You have no need to explain."

"In the loneliness of my cell," continued Hezekiah, "where my hands, legs, and neck had been chained as though I were a wild animal, I sought only release from this life. My lips refused the acrid water they brought, the stale bread. But the Huns are a cunning folk, my friends. They forced their sustenance down my throat, making me live day after day, sporting with me, placing on my head a crown of thistles and proclaiming me the last king of Samarkand."

Roskovitch gritted his teeth. "The swine," he growled. "One day payment shall be made for your suffering."

Hezekiah held up a hand, pained at the thought of further violence. "No," he said strongly, "my grief can never be repaid; my fate is to live with it until my last hour. But thank heaven I have come to warn you."

It was only then that Sharon recalled what Ami had said: Hezekiah alone knew the truth of Kabul's evil plan. "Tell us everything," she pleaded, "all you have learned these many months of your imprisonment."

The Hebrew minister sighed deeply and rubbed a hand above his brows, trying to reconstruct the foggy pieces as best he could. "The dungeons are always dark," he began. "A man has no way of ever knowing what is day and what is night. Time has no meaning. I was sleeping fitfully when the screams woke me—terrible screams of pain and torment. I leaped to my feet and peered between the small bars stitched across my doorway. It was then I saw him: a Kazir warrior, his desert robe smeared with his own blood and excrement.

To my shock, when he was stripped and tossed like a rag into the cell opposite, I realized that he was merely a lad, nothing more."

Sharon's hand flew to her mouth. "Asif!" she cried.

Hezekiah nodded darkly. "Yes," he said, "it was he— a frightened and badly beaten child, dragged to his prison like a common murderer. Little did I suspect that he was your friend, my princess, your valued comrade-in-arms." The Hebrew mopped his forehead, meeting Sharon's baleful gaze. "Day after day they tortured him. He was strapped to the rack, hot coals put to his feet, needles dug into his fingernails, punished well beyond any man's limits of endurance. Need I tell you how much I grieved for the lad, knowing that his tormentors plied their trade all too well upon him? An 'outlaw,' they called him, a 'renegade of the Steppes,' and they demanded to learn all that he knew. He was commanded to confess crimes both real and imagined as all the while they sought to learn the identity of the Panther and the location of her fortress. But Asif was a brave boy, the bravest I have ever known." Tears came to the old man's eyes, and his shoulders sagged heavily with his grief. "Never did he either admit to the crimes or give them the information they demanded, never—at least not until the very end."

"Go on," Sharon said breathlessly.

"Asif became wracked with fever; it happens to many down in the dungeons. His tormentors became wary of beating him again, but the one called Osklath grew angry and chided them; he threatened them with their own heads if Asif died before talking. So again the boy was tortured, more brutally than before, until, perhaps, blissfully, he fell into his delirium, not recognizing the grim world into which he had been thrown. The torturers themselves secretly displayed pity for him, but not Osklath. Daily he would return, examining Asif carefully before having them continue.

"I woke again from a restless sleep, fear in my heart,

and saw the brazen son of Kabul, his head swimming with wine, slip quietly into Asif's cell. The boy's wracked brain could not distinguish reality or recognize the face of his enemy. He cried out the name 'Tariq,' and Osklath cunningly responded." Hezekiah now turned his face toward the chieftain of the Stronghold, explaining how by deceit Osklath had tricked the lad into betraying his friends at last. "Asif died in his arms," Hezekiah went on, "and I saw Osklath rise and march triumphantly from the dungeon. I shall never forget the glint of menace in his eye when he'd finally learned the Kazir secret. Even a fool couldn't have failed to recognize the lust and hate written into his features. He now had the power to break Kazir strength, and he was ready and able to use it. Lucky for us all that the cursed son of Kabul did not suspect that I alone had heard everything that had transpired; otherwise none of us would be sitting here now."

The wind whistled eerily above their heads, gusting down from the heights of the Mound. "Then what happened?" asked Tariq, pulling his robe more tightly about him as he shivered.

"An old man was forced to learn new tricks," replied the Hebrew mysteriously. "As I've said, my own life was no longer important to me; but I knew that for the sake of all peoples everywhere the Huns must be stopped. 'Tis no lie that in all my years I have never been considered a friend to the Kazirs. Yet the menace of Kabul was greater. I knew that only by reaching word to you here could the terrible events already begun possibly be reversed.

"So, my plan was set. Hours later I rose from my straw mat, screaming like a madman when the guards came to question me. 'Bring me Osklath,' I said, cowering, pretending to fear the pain of their blows. The eldest son was sent for, and when he came, impatient with me after these many, many months of futile tortures, he was prepared to put me to the sword. 'Wait,' I pleaded, 'spare me! Let me live and I'll show you the way through the forest!' I groveled at his boots like a dog, whimpering and whining. Osklath lifted me harshly to my feet, saying, '*You* know the path through Grim Forest?' I nodded eagerly, like a schoolboy. 'I do, my lord. Years ago I learned of it from one of the emir's prisoners while yet I served Samarkand. Free me now, end my torture, and I shall guide you and your army.'

"He was most skeptical, as you might imagine, for why should I speak now, after so long a time? Still, the offer was hardly one he could refuse, as a man familiar with these lands was a rare commodity in the khan's court. My life was nothing to him; yet, if my word was good, I might still be put to use. 'Do you lie to me, old man?' he demanded, his fingers pressing at my larynx. I shook my head violently, gasping for breath. 'No, no! I cried. 'Let me prove it.'

"And so Osklath had me removed from the dungeons and brought into the light of day for the first time in more than a year. My wounds were tended, my shackles removed. Constantly guarded, I waited until the army was set to move and then, placed in the vanguard, close to the detachment of riders led by the youngest son, Frizul, I bided my time. Late the first night, while the camp slept, I found my horse and broke from the army. Arrows sailed past my head as I rode low in the saddle, drawing energy and courage only from the urgency of my task. Somehow I managed to elude them, but some leagues from their camp, my steed stumbled and fell, and I, weary and heartbroken, could only lie upon the sand, waiting for their patrols to finally catch me. It was not the Huns who came upon me that morning, though; no, it was the Kazirs, outriders of the Fuliwas. They brought me safely from the desert to their tents, fed me, cared for me, and sent for their chieftain. The rest you know."

Hezekiah had ended his tale on a harrowing note. Lost for words, the band of outlaws passed long moments reflecting upon their own thoughts. Then Roskovitch snarled, his barbarian's eyes flashing. "We must meet this army head on," he growled, "stop them before they press too deeply into the wood."

Tariq quickly agreed. "Word must be sent to every clan to gather our horsemen and cut them off before the forest is reached."

"Too late for that, cousin," said Ami with a sigh, looking glumly at his lifelong friend. "The Huns crossed the perimeter of the wood a day ago, razing the forest behind them with fire as they passed." The Fuliwa chieftain visibly shivered. "My own ride to reach the Mound here tonight was fraught with peril; Hun advance units have been fanning out along these very hills, seeking to encounter my men, while the main body presses on deeper into the bowels of the wood." His head shook ruefully. "By sunset tomorrow they will have passed the thickets, well on their way to finding the trail to the Stronghold."

Sharon and Tariq gaped in shock. "Then we are all in dire peril," Shoaib's son said at last.

"They must not be allowed free rein," hissed Roskovitch, darting his head from side to side, looking to each of his companions. "If we move quickly, word can be spread to the clans by midnight tomorrow."

Sullen and anxious, the handful of desert outlaws turned to Sharon, who sat silent and contemplative. The enemy was closing in too swiftly for debate, she realized. Action could not wait for all the clans to gather; something would have to be done and right now.

"Can the Fuliwas engage these advance units in the hills, pin them down?" she asked of Ami.

For the first time this night the chieftain smiled; she could see the glitter of his teeth as his lips parted in a bitter grin. "We can hold them" was all he said.

"Good." She sighed, then turned to Tariq. "Go back to the Stronghold," she told him. "Tell the saya what has happened; prepare our forces to ride. We must be at the side of the Fuliwas by darkness tomorrow. And send for Zadek; tell the mullah I have need of his wisdom and aid here at once." Next she looked at the troubled barbarian from Rus. "Bear, I need you tonight. Make all haste to the tents of Yasir; he must be convinced that the time is at hand."

"Yasir will not come," replied Roskovitch sourly. He still mistrusts you."

Sharon balled her fists. "There is no time to argue!" she flared, eyes smoldering as she stood and took command. *"Make* him come—one way or another. And get word to the other clans as well. Time is of the essence; we cannot afford to lose even a single moment."

Roskovitch stood, ready to go. "And what of you?" he asked.

The Panther bared her teeth. Her very soul cried with the quest of the moment. She alone knew what had to be done; she alone understood what might result should she fail.

Her companions looked on startled as she pulled the coiled cobra from her belt and held it fiercely in her right hand. Cloak swirling behind in the night wind, she lifted her arm toward the starry heavens. The eyes of the cobra glinted in silver light. "By the power of the Gift," she swore, "I am going to repay Osklath for what he has done. The witches have unleashed my power. Pray, good friends, that I may use it well, for the hour of decision is here at last."

Osklath ran a hand along his sweaty forehead, grimacing as the noon sun filtered through the branches of the twisted trees, golden light pouring over his horsemen and the trampled grass. Knotty pine, tall spruce, greeted his eye in thick clusters before him. He arched around, neck craned, and then glowed with satisfaction as he saw the distant smoke of the burning wood behind. Systematically his men had put the torch to this accursed place. When he was done, passed through the wood and once again on the rocky soil of the plain, there would be nothing left save smoldering heaps of charred brush and deadened stumps, a grisly reminder to all of the once great forest that had stood.

The horses, single file, followed the lead of his scouts, and while above the wind hissed, signaling the approach of a summer storm, his army trampled across the verdant terrain, bold invaders crushing the forest life underfoot. Moss and heather grew wild; thick vines twisted round the massive trunks of trees that became more dense the deeper they rode; huge gnarled roots shot up everywhere, deformed, causing the horsemen to grumble and curse this foul place as they were forced to slow down and hack and slash at the growth blocking their path.

"Damn this forest," hissed Osklath under his breath, watching his forces stumbling between thornbushes, lumbering around boulders and slimy turf. Again and again hooves stomped over sharpened rocks and pebbles, causing the animals to recoil with pain and rendering many of them lame and useless. If Osklath had been a superstitious man, he would have thought these petty hindrances placed purposely, set there by demons or goblins or god knows what to encumber him, force him to take twice as much time completing his journey than anticipated.

Bent, misshapen trees, unidentifiable, loomed ahead, blocking his careful route as if by design, branches writhing with the ever-increasing wind. Osklath peered up at the sky, still cloudless, wondering at what point the storm was going to strike. The rain would only compound matters, he knew, leave his army to push forward in a sea of mud, knee-deep in muck and the strange ooze that somehow seemed to seep from everywhere in this infernal place.

"Keep moving! Keep moving!" barked his commanders to the already weary men. And Osklath, sucking in air between clenched teeth, cajoled them on even more, forcing them to plow through the shoots and undergrowth and not slacken for an instant in this spongy mire.

The line faltered only briefly among the thick rows of scrub oak and hazel, armed men in the forefront again using swords and hatchets to slash wider paths through the densening foliage. Dulled weapons struggled against the creeping tide that stood before them, and again Osklath cursed mightily. Daylight was slipping by too fast; the angles of the shadows assured him that soon the sun would be gone and they would be forced to camp along the bogs, as they had the night before. And what a night it had been—clammy and cold, the incessant buzzings and chirpings of a thousand species of dreadful insects in their ears, stinging and biting with no end, and the wind, the terrible, weird wind that had frightened the picketed horses half out of their wits even as some of his best and fiercest men huddled like frightened children, making the sign of the horn and mumbling darkly among themselves about the strange tales of Grim Forest still whispered in Samarkand.

An army, though, needed rest, Osklath knew, and no matter how much valuable time might be lost, there was no way he could force his men to hack their way through this dizzying jungle without a few hours' sleep. His only hope was that nothing else would come along this night, nothing more to prevent his forces from making their way out of the forest entirely by dawn at the latest.

Osklath shook his head uneasily; the pervading silence was most unsettling, more so the deeper they marched. As the sun at last faded, the sky aflame in washes of brilliant azure and indigo hues, he doggedly pressed his army on, marching them until the very last glimmer of light had vanished. Then, as the eerie sounds of night in the wood replaced the silence of the day, he ordered his commanders to halt the line and set their camp as best they could along the rugged, boulder-studded terrain, hoping for his own tent to be set and secure before the first rain of the brewing storm fell.

There was a great chill this night, unusual for the time of year. Sharon sat motionless and cross-legged, the coiled cobra held in both palms, openly displayed. Opposite her, Zadek stared forlornly up at the starless night sky. The wind was blowing with a frenzy, clouds of dust roaring across the Steppes with untold ferocity. In the distance was the hazy outline of the forest, thick cumulonimbus clouds black and low hugging the line of giant oaks and hickories.

The hourglass lay between them, its sands no longer trickling but now rushing to the lower vial. The mad mullah turned his attention back to it, then reached out and touched Sharon lightly. " 'Tis almost midnight," he said.

As if woken from a trance, the Panther lifted her head just far enough to meet his eyes. She could feel the cobra beginning to stir in her hands, feel the cold steel bend of its own will as she called upon its power as the witches had told her to do. But what that power was, what form it would take, what havoc it might wreak, no one, not even they, could say.

Amazed, eyes slitted with intense focus, Zadek saw for himself the Gift come to life. The snake's forked tongue darted out as its head lifted, gazing about at the darkened terrain of the Mound.

"Strike," hissed Sharon, returning to the witches' incantation. "Strike down our enemies; rid the forest of its evil host."

The snake danced, curling up her arm, wrapping its scaly body around her neck. Sharon sat frozen, awed and terrified at what she alone had unleashed. Whether the cobra was a force of good or a demon from hell itself, she knew only that now the strange Gift bestowed upon her had been called to life, and there was no stopping it.

The cobra hissed, tongue lashing, venomous fangs glinting in the blackness. Sharon held her breath, not daring to move a muscle. The snake coiled, then slowly slithered to the ground, burrowing deeply into the earth.

"It's vanished!" cried Zadek.

Sharon shook her head. Her eyes saw that the last grain of sand from the hourglass had fallen. This was the precise moment of midnight. "It has not gone," she told the mullah, watching now the desert sand shifting below the surface, marking the path of the winding cobra. "It follows my command—and sets to strike at our enemies."

Zadek wrapped his arms about himself and shivered, and for a brief moment he felt both fear and pity for Osklath's army camped within the wood.

Forked lightning flashed above the forest, setting the world alight for an instant. The wind howled more strongly, and both he and the Panther sheltered themselves with their robes against its wrath. Then to the sky they gazed again, peering from the recesses of their hoods, watching while more lightning ribboned hither and yon, beading in zagged lines from one end of the horizon to the other. Swiftly followed the rumbles of thunder, but thunder neither of them had ever experienced before. So powerful was its shock that even here, leagues away from the storm, they could feel the ground beneath their feet shake.

Zadek quickly mumbled a prayer, sensing the unhallowed nature of the violence unleashed. A ball of flaming, white-cold luminosity leaped before their eyes; a miniature sun it seemed, blinding to gaze upon, shattering the shadows and replacing them with a full-colored spectrum of blinking hues. "In the name of the Prophet," cried the mullah, "what has happened to the world!"

Sharon fought against the wind, her eyes searching the sky. A giant bolt of lightning, channeling its way over the forest, made her recoil in fright. What indeed was happening to the world? she wondered. Where was Osklath now, at this very moment? And was he aware of the reasons for this?

Hair blowing wildly, Zadek fought his way to Sharon's side and pulled her away harshly. She was in a trance, he saw, transfixed by the powers of the Gift, unable to shift her gaze. But seeing all this could be dangerous, he realized; and while she dumbly stared, he threw her down upon the shaking earth, covering her with his own body. Above their heads, boulders were moving, ready to dislodge from the places in which they had rested for centuries. And while he sheltered her, certain the rocks would at any time come crashing down over them, he could only guess at the events that were transpiring inside the forest itself.

The wind was a beastly holocaust, a tempest blowing so cruelly that even the roots of the trees themselves were being torn from the soil, agonizingly uplifted. Amid the high-pitched wails of hysterical horses and anguished cries of his men, Osklath managed to push his way forward through the shattering tumult, now wrapping his arms tightly around the trunk of a spruce, clinging to it for dear life as a sudden powerful gust swept down from above. Before his startled eyes a giant oak was literally wrenched from the ground, branches whipping, breaking off and flying like missiles, and hurtled through the night across the bog and straight through the swirling mists, crashing unseen on the other side with a deafening roar.

Colder the air became, and the turf soggier with the worsening rain. Like tenpins the supply mules and picketed horses were sent bowling over, screaming, kicking, their lungs bursting while the pressure of the raging wind tore around them, scattering them about like toys. The entire camp had fallen into total disarray. Stout-shouldered Hun commanders fiercely held to their ground, bracing themselves to anything that didn't move, barking terse orders to panic-stricken soldiers who could barely hear above the din. Had there been safe shelter to reach, there would have been total bedlam among the superstitious ranks. But here, trapped as they were, there was no refuge, no haven in which to hide and wait out the storm. They were caught in it as sailors were upon the sea, hanging onto their possessions, fighting their battle against the ravages of nature unleashed upon them.

Left and right, loose weapons and camp utensils came flinging through the air, followed on occasion by some unfortunate fellow whisked up from his place by the furious wind and sent hurling high until his bones smashed against the trees or boulders. Men were lashing themselves as best they could to trees and rocks, to bushes, to anything secured; rain, with renewed fury, slanted down savagely from the highest branches, coarsely beating at them with relentless blows. And through it all the electric-charged bolts of lightning continued to strike again and again, flashing across the sky like the fingers of demons, tearing into wood, rendering ruthless blows upon everything helpless below. The rumbles of thunder were like low, wicked laughter, as if some unseen eyes were watching the carnage gleefully, enjoying the grisly scene.

As the lightning blazed, rippling from one side of the heavens to the other, stroking with barbarity from cloud to ground, the rising mist from the bogs grew thicker, obliterating from view the distant foliage and scarred terrain that had marked their route.

"Run! Run!" cried Frizul, bolting from his place and dashing like a wildman among the stricken ranks. "We are doomed . . . doomed!"

The shouts of the khan's youngest son sent those around him into a panic, for if Frizul himself so feared the wrath of this Grim Forest, how were they, mere soldiers conscripted to fight under Kabul's banner, to do any less? And so many untied their bonds and recklessly began to run, darting through the trees and haze, flinging off their mail and discarding their weapons as they ran off helter-skelter into the night.

Osklath ground his teeth and tackled his youngest brother, beating him to the ground. "Hold your places!" he commanded, hair hanging lank, beard dripping.

Frizul stared at him through frightened eyes. "No, no, we'll be killed, slaughtered! The devils are upon us!"

Osklath whipped out his curved sword and stuck its tip against the quivering Frizul's jugular. "Are we to retreat like cowards?" he shouted. "Panic from rain and wind and lightning?" He spat in his brother's face.

Frizul whimpered.

Osklath faced all those who could see and hear him and bellowed above the wind, "I shall kill the first man who runs!" He wiped the rainwater from his face and glared angrily about. "The storm shall pass, and we will move on!"

"We'll never find our way out of this quagmire!" cried Frizul. "You are leading us to our deaths!" And from everywhere, there came frightened shouts of agreement.

Osklath lifted his sword higher, holding the hilt with both hands; Frizul's eyes grew wide with horror as the blade slashed down, cutting through his gut, his bowels, pinning him to the earth. He moaned, then slumped. Osklath deftly pulled out the blade and held it out for all to see. His brother's blood dripped onto the earth, seeping into the soil. Osklath's men looked on in abject horror. Their commander had murdered his own flesh and blood; certainly he would do no less to them if they dared disobey.

"Who else would flee?" he demanded.

The soldiers of the khan lowered their eyes, apparently more willing to face the wrath of the gods than that of the fiery eldest son.

"Now, back to your posts," called Osklath, replacing his sword in the scabbard with a single stroke and stomping through the mud back toward the trees, boldly daring another bolt to strike him down in the open. None did, and his men watched in awe. Osklath's swagger and bravado had more than impressed them; they would do as he commanded, follow him into the depths of hell itself if that was where he led.

Osklath scornfully lifted his gaze toward the sky,

bitterly vowing a double revenge for the agonies of this day. Once the rain ceased, they would march again— oh, perhaps a bit more ragged for wear, but with an army still intact. Only this time there would be no more pausing within the wood. They would march straight through the day and all the next night if necessary, face all this again and more, if need be, for now that the deed was half accomplished, no power on earth would cause him to turn back.

The view was disquieting. Before them stood a valley, hills sloping sharply away on either side, so thick with trees the roots and branches seemed to join. The wind had shifted hours before, and that had been the first good sign that the storm was about to abate. Osklath had bullied his commanders into speedily readying the army even while the rain continued to sting their flesh. Browbeaten, in dire fear of his mighty anger, they had swiftly done all that he had commanded, and within an hour before the new dawn, tattered though they were, they were on the march again.

As the sky lightened, the rain subsided. Soon they could even see the sun, a pale, watery yellow ball, pushing its rays past the thin, pervasive haze, and while they sloshed in and out of the bogs and mires and soggy terrain, Osklath kept a steady gaze on the way ahead, determined to meet his goal and attack the Kazir Stronghold no later than tomorrow night.

For a time, all had seemed almost well; but now this strange valley lay before them, silent and deep, winding and twisting like a road through dense foliage for as far as they could see.

Osklath mopped his brow, turned, and grinned at his commanders. "We'll cross this valley by nightfall," he told them with a feeling of certainty. "And look"—his hand went out, pointing to the farthest images upon the horizon—"the Steppes! Can you see the hills?"

The dour soldiers peered into the distance. It was

true: From the heights on which they stood, they could clearly see past the end of the forest, right to the doorstep of the desert. Osklath had been a good leader, properly assessing the situation even when they had cowered. The journey was almost complete. Cross this hidden valley and they would be free, rid of the wood, able to set it ablaze once and for all.

Osklath made ready to remount; he glanced behind at his vast army fanning out along the narrow path, winding up and down across the wet, grassy hills. At his instruction the horns blasted, shrieking through the damp air and frightening the birds; he watched soaring flocks take from the trees to the sky, and grinned.

"Should we not camp tonight in the valley?" asked one of the generals at his side.

The son of Kabul scratched at his chin, staring down at the dense foliage. "No," he said with a shake of the head. "The sooner we cross, the better; I want to be rid of this place as quickly as we can."

And so the Hun's forces moved on, angling downward into the deepest, thickest of the forest yet encountered. Something, though, nagged at the back of Osklath's mind, something he could not quite put his finger on. The wood seemed the same, he thought, glancing about at the lumbering trees and glistening grasses, yet something was also different. Daring not to speak of it, he wondered if his commanders felt it also.

The sun had approached its zenith; overhead the clustered boughs had begun to filter out the light, leaving the forest dark and filled with ominous shadows. The way through the valley seemed to constantly narrow until no more than two horses side by side could negotiate the way. Hooves clomped over muck and thin layers of slime that covered the verdant topsoil. And, inexplicably, even though the hour was barely past noon, the mist from the ever-present bogs was rising again. The horses, nerves already frayed from the storm the night before, began to nervously whinny and refuse to go on. Angrily the riders whipped their steeds, tempers shortening as the trees grew even thicker and taller at every side and the wood seemed to be literally closing in.

Talk çeased. Osklath's vanguard dismounted, taking to their hatchets and cutting loose the tangle of vines and reeds that now blocked the trail entirely. They hacked and slashed, splitting reeds and casting them aside, yet for every one they rid themselves of another two sprang in front in quick replacement.

At the edge of his patience, the hefty eldest son dismounted again, holding the line up behind him and swaggering to the front. His boots sloshed ankle-deep in mud. Thistles from hanging branches tore at his vest; mosquitoes buzzed about his head. He flailed his arms to chase them away, hardly aware of the creeping mist closing in from both sides.

Exasperated, he cursed loudly at the shirtless men still chopping their way between the clinging vines, vines that suddenly had wrapped into a barrier of combined undergrowth and exotic brush.

"We can do nothing, my lord!" moaned the commander in charge of the detail. Osklath stared grimly ahead. It was like nothing he had ever seen before: The forest had turned into a jungle, a jungle of creepers and crawlers, slime and quagmires, all constantly pressing in on his army. And the trees themselves . . . He glanced about in utter confusion, realizing now that he could barely see the tops, so large they loomed.

"It's no use, Lord Osklath," panted the commander, wiping his sweaty hands over a hirsute chest.

The leader of the legions huffed, enraged at the slowdown. "Then bring more men!" he barked. "As many as you need! A hundred! A thousand! Only cut us out of this valley! Get us across to the other side!"

By the score they worked, vainly gaining inches instead of miles, pricked by barbs and thorns, attacked by swarms of dragonflies and hornets, while beetles and giant ants crawled over their flesh, burrowing and feeding in the men's sweaty pores. Hour after hour they struggled; the sun was on the wane again, and the air so close and dank that many could hardly breathe. The army had long since stopped moving entirely. Exhausted, frightened, both men and beasts waited tensely as fully five hundred men continued to hack and slash at the vines, blundering forward whenever they made the way forward at all.

Night was coming. Osklath berated them all, and only their fear of him kept them going. But it seemed that they were worse off now than before; the trees encompassing them swayed with a growing hot wind, almost moving from their places; roots, gnarled and contorted, seemed to grow before their eyes, taking on different and more terrifying shapes. In a beady sweat from head to foot, Osklath pushed a staggering soldier to the ground and swept up his fallen ax. The son of Kabul cut a wide swathe in the vines, cajoling those at his side to do the same. Many, though, were falling now from sheer exhaustion; they rolled into the mud, almost swallowed by it, gasping for a single breath of fresh air. And still the haze was deepening.

Someone screamed, and Osklath spun to see one of his ablest soldiers suddenly enwrapped in the very vines he had been chopping; they were squeezing him, tightening round his chest, tying his arms, twisting round his legs. The soldier fell, a purple tongue hanging from the side of his mouth as breath was sucked out of him. Osklath stared in disbelief. What was happening to him? Was he losing his mind? Could he really have seen what his eyes had told his brain?

The scream was repeated, this time from the other side. Another valuable soldier had fallen, this one tugging at the choking reed with all his might. But the reed would not give; it closed about his thick throat, and he staggered to his knees.

Knotted trees of all description joined together;

branches closed in from above, blotting out the sky completely. The ground beneath their feet was shaking, and from beneath the mossy and slimy rocks vipers had started to crawl, long, fork-tongued cobras, coiling and striking, causing the terrified horses to bolt and throw their riders. Osklath threw down his ax and dashed from the onslaught of encroaching vines. He could not see very far, as the bogs had settled everywhere, but the faraway cries of horses and men assured him that the same terror he faced here had spread along the entire length of his army.

A warrior beside him reeled as a bush pushed its way up from the soil, growing before his eyes at amazing speed, and impaled the soldier upon its long, needlelike thorns. Warped branches swept down like carrion from above, the boughs hideously bending askew, wrapping themselves over breathless horsemen who vainly fought to break free of the deadly grips.

The wails of his men became a nightmare. Osklath put his hands to his ears and started to scream himself. He was going mad, he knew, losing all control over reality. What was happening around him could not possibly be true; yet it was, as true as anything he'd ever encountered, as true as the Legend of Samarkand.

He threw off his helmet, drew his sword, and began to swing it wildly and savagely above his head; but the branches and vines paid no heed. Pitiful cries for mercy ringing in his ears, he sawed and hacked, trying desperately to run from this bedeviled valley. Stumbling, picking himself up, he watched comrades fall into the mud, looked on dumbly as their hands reached out for him to grab, their bodies swiftly sinking, sucked down into the deepening pool of foul muck.

In those moments an idiot he became, recognizing no one or anything, shrieking laughter at the top of his lungs, falling over corpses and rising up from sticky slime. He tore at the walls of weed with his bare hands, wrenching it aside, running berserkly forward, bit by

bit throwing off his armor, his belt, his scabbard, his
tunic. Nakedly he dodged the attacking foliage, his
flesh pricked in a thousand places, pinpoints of blood
dabbing his body from head to toe. The quagmire
gurgled, hungry for more humanity, and by the tens of
dozens foot soldiers were falling into it, even as the
lowering branches swept up others and crushed the life
out of them.

Nauseated, hammers pounding inside his feverish
brain, heart pumping at three times its normal rate,
Osklath covered himself with his arms, bending low,
squishing through muck and insanely growing grass,
laughing to himself maniacally while his entire army
slowly choked to death all around him, calling upon the
names of all his evil gods, as if to purge himself of the
disaster. His head was swimming; he no longer knew
even his own name. When the blackness of night overtook him, he stood stock-still, whimpering like an infant,
wiping his tears and sucking his thumb.

"We can only guess at the ordeal he must have endured," said the solemn-faced Chinese physician. He gestured to the sniveling heap on the floor, the man-infant cringing, biting his fingernails, clutching at the robe thrown over his shoulders. "Mad beyond saving," he went on. "Exactly like this when your patrol found him, shivering and laughing at the edge of the forest."

Kabul tightly clutched the armrests of his throne, sickened at the sight. He turned toward several of his other sons, wondering which of them would be the next to plot treachery against him now that Osklath was removed. "Can't any of you relate the tale?" he asked weakly.

The sons, bedecked in their furs and armor, shook their heads and hid their eyes from Kabul's wrath. "No, sire; as far as we know, he was the only one to come out of the forest alive. What fate really befell Frizul and the rest is a matter of little consequence, all we can be certain of is that they are dead."

The great khan of the Huns pounded a fist, his heart heavy and grieved not for his eldest idiot of a slobbering son—who now needed to be fed and changed like a newborn—but for the loss of his army, the bulk of the war machine that was to march against the kingdoms of the west. All his plans were shattered, his dreams and ambitions smashed like surf against a reef. What remained was merely a remnant of what had been before. And again other kings would laugh and scorn him. He rued the day he had taken this desert city of Samarkand, cursed the vanity that had led him to choose it for his capital. But it was too late for such misgivings, he knew; now he must try to pick up the pieces and begin again.

"Take him from my sight," he hissed.

Several burly guards put aside their weapons and dragged Osklath to his feet. The eldest son grinned and started to laugh, loudly, idiotically, his eyes ablaze with his madness. Down the ill-lighted corridor he was dragged, the sound of his laughter echoing off the stone walls, the shuffle of his feet harsh against the worn tile.

Kabul turned away in disgust and squinted his good eye: The bitch had won; the Kazirs ruled freely upon the Steppes. He rose from his throne and banished everyone from the court; then, as he sat down disconsolately in the shadow of the single brazier, he tensed, his eye averted as the Chinese physician took out his tray of needles and prepared to jab them through his pincushioned flesh.

Zadek and the saya dismounted slowly from their stallions, left their escorts waiting along the ridge of the hill, and slowly made their way down. The last rays of the setting golden sun filtered through the trees and over the deep-green grasses and soft-petaled wild flowers randomly scattered about. It was a lovely setting, a beautiful summer's setting, save for the remains of the carnage in the valley below.

Zadek stumbled over a rock, and Carolyn took his arm. Slowly they walked down the gentle slope, gazing about silently, even as the score of mountain Kazirs looked on from their vantage point along the crest. Black and gold banners dug deep into the ground, fluttered in the gentle breeze. The soil was still damp from the severe storm two nights before, but apart from that, there was no sign that it had ever taken place.

The trees had straightened, once again tall and proud, although here and there one remained grossly misshapen, a reminder of the balled lightning that had so viciously struck. And still clinging to those lifeless boughs were the corpses of Hun riders, faces twisted in death masks, eyes opened wide and disbelieving, staring sightlessly toward the sky.

Zadek and the saya picked a path between the bodies, stunned at the enormity of the devastation. While the Kazirs had gathered from across the Steppes and ridden like demons throughout the night, all this had taken place before they'd even had a chance to meet the Huns face to face. Now it seemed the fight was finished, without a single Kazir having had to shed blood. As to what had happened here, though, as to why and how the mighty army of the khan had been so totally overwhelmed, they could only guess.

"The witches played us no tricks," mumbled the mad mullah, peering dumbstruck at the endless field of strewn corpses and equipment.

Carolyn could only nod in response. She had never questioned the power of the Gift, or the horror it would wreak once unleashed. She felt a sudden chill as she thought upon this terrible and vengeful wrath, and she was glad at least she had not been the one entrusted to use it. She turned sharply toward Zadek. "Where is the Panther?" she asked. "Where has she gone?"

"Sharon is safe, saya, with Tariq, the Bear has assured me. Calling upon the cobra's power has left her drained and weakened, but soon she will be better. She needs rest, that's all. Give her time."

Without another word, sighing deeply, Carolyn turned away from the carnage and walked slowly to the ridge and her waiting companions. She had seen more than enough this morning—too much, perhaps. The Kazir Prophesy had been fulfilled: The Samarkand princess had without question earned not only her place among them but also the full right to claim leadership —exactly as had been foretold a century before at the beginning of the Hundred Year Solitude.

Tariq reached the obelisk tower of the Stronghold just as a blue-gray half-moon hid behind a rolling cloud. The sky above was bright and nearly flawless, the stars shining in full radiance while the world spun below. It was deeply shadowed along the curved stone wall, and he paused at the top of the steps, straining his eyes until at last he could see her. There she stood, a lonely silhouette forlornly watching the sky at the far end of the sturdy wall. Chin lifted high, eyes wetly aglow, she gazed wearily across the endless desert, in the distant direction of her beloved city of Samarkand.

He came toward her slowly, not wishing to disturb her private thoughts. She'd been troubled greatly since that night, he knew, since she'd been forced to use her power in self-defense against the khan's onslaught. No one needed to tell him how great the loss of life had been to keep the Steppes free. Moody and restless, Sharon had eaten little these past days, slept less, and spent most of her time in solitude, reflectively reminiscing upon a life she had lost and could never bring back again.

It was with this knowledge that Tariq, when he reached her side, whispered softly, *"Set your eyes upon Samarkand, and never forget you have seen her."*

Sharon snapped from her deep thoughts and turned to look at him, a half-smile, sad and wistful, on her lips. "How did you know what I was thinking?"

He shrugged slightly and sighed. "We are not as unalike as you believe. My father once said those words to me—long, long ago, before I was a man. He brought me as close to the walls of the city as a Kazir might go, forcing me to gaze at the sight. 'One day,' he said, 'one day soon we shall return.' "

The breeze was blowing stronger, and she tightened her desert shawl more closely about her. Lowering her head, she repeated in a whisper, "One day soon . . ."

Tariq smiled; he reached out and took her hand. It was cold. He enclosed it strongly within his own, and she drew closer, finding comfort in the strength of his arms.

"My own father loved Samarkand as much as any man," she told him after a moment's kiss, "and he wasn't a Kazir."

The young chieftain sheltered her again, his eyes lovingly staring into hers. "I know he did," he answered with a grin. "I've been speaking with Hezekiah; he's explained to me a lot of things I didn't realize before— about Amrath, about the people of the city we hated so much, about your life . . ."

Sharon could feel her face flush, wondering what girlish secrets the Hebrew might have recounted for him. She didn't mind, though; she returned his grin impishly, memories of that former life coming at her in a rush. It was her father, though, she thought of mostly, and how very wonderful it would be if he were alive, here now to share these victories with her.

"You know," said Tariq, "sometimes I think my own clans are even more bullheaded than your people. We spent the past hundred years believing that Samarkand could not belong to anyone except for us, the same way your emirs thought about themselves." He glanced up at the sky aglitter with tiny baubles. "Now both of us have lost it and learned a valuable lesson."

Sharon nodded and sighed. "A pity we didn't know it sooner. Perhaps together, my people and yours, we could have stopped all this from happening."

He kissed her lightly on the forehead. "Very wise for one so young." She laughed, dimples deep in her cheeks. Tariq shared her laughter, thinking what fools they all had been. "We need you, Little Panther," he said, smile vanishing, face becoming serious again, "all of the Kazirs."

Her eyes, filled with love for the handsome chieftain, were hopeful as she gazed at him. "And you?"

"And I? I need you most of all."

She threw her arms around him, crying, filled with happiness for their shared and secret love, yet still troubled and frightened by the role she was forced to play and the uncertain future that faced them all.

Hand in hand they stood watching the silent desert while the fires of the Kazir tents illuminated the sands below, bathing the huge compound in a soft glow.

"There need be no further bloodshed," Tariq said, mindful of the many battles. "The Steppes are free. The khan shall never invade our lands again; he knows the price he'll have to pay."

Sharon nodded thankfully for that much; but she

knew well that the struggle was far from over. True, no longer would the Kazirs be imperiled by the Huns. Kabul would be far too preoccupied with lifting himself from the shame of defeat. For all intents and purposes, the Kazirs had now gained the most sought-after goal of all—freedom—fought for and won fairly, so that it could never be taken away.

How many others were not as fortunate? How many still were forced to languish and suffer beneath the yoke of Hun slavery? Sharon thought of the peoples of Samarkand, all those of the former empire, who at this very minute were silently crying out in despair. How could she enjoy the fruits of freedom while they continued to suffer?

Tariq did not have to ask what she was thinking; these very thoughts had filled his own heart and mind as well. No longer could the Kazirs selfishly act only for themselves; the time for that was past, he knew, vanished forever the day the Samarkand princess came to the Stronghold and brought them all into a new light. The Kazirs would have to do their part.

Together the couple gazed from one end of the hazy horizon to the other, understanding now that the Kazir Prophesy entrusted to them had to be completed.

"It shall prove a long and difficult road," Tariq cautioned.

Sharon looked at him thoughtfully and nodded. "I knew it would be, my beloved. And it might mean that our love shall still have to wait."

Glumly Tariq agreed; the price for justice was never small.

"But a day *is* coming," Sharon went on proudly, her head thrown back, her hair shining in the glow, "a day when we *will* be together—openly, before the world, with no tears or shame."

Tariq squeezed her hand. "Until that time, no matter how distant, we won't lose hope."

"Promise it?"

"With all my devotion."

Their kiss was full and lingering, and when they parted, they did so with the knowledge that soon they would never be parted again.

"We're going home, Tariq," she said confidently, resuming her gaze toward the distant, unseen city, "taking back what is rightfully ours. And no one can stop us, no matter how long it takes." She shut her eyes, vowing to return. The deaths of all those she loved would not go unavenged. Until then, until the journey before her was truly complete and she was home in Samarkand again, other matters could wait.

They had set their eyes upon Samarkand, and would never forget.

PLAYBOY PRESS
PAPERBACKS
SCIENCE FICTION

A SUPERB SELECTION
OF THE BEST IN
SCIENCE FICTION
FOR YOUR READING PLEASURE